THE TERMITE QUEEN

VOLUME TWO

THE TERMITE QUEEN

Volume Two:
The Wound That Has No Healing

Lorinda J. Taylor

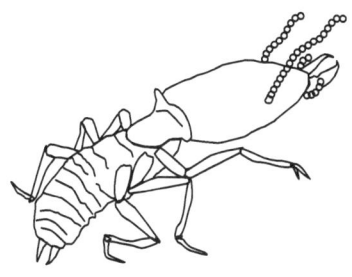

Acknowledgements of permission to quote copyrighted material in this novel appear on the following page.

Cover illustration by the author: The Champion and the Holy Seer receive the Speaking of the Dead.

ISBN-13: 978-1475283990
ISBN-10: 1475283997

ACKNOWLEDGMENTS

The author wishes to thank the following sources for permission to quote copyrighted materials in this novel:

Ten lines from "Especially When the October Wind," by Dylan Thomas, from *The Poems of Dylan Thomas*, copyright © 1939 by New Directions Publishing Corp. Reprinted by permission of New Directions Publishing Corp.

Five lines from "And Death Shall Have No Dominion," by Dylan Thomas, from *The Poems of Dylan Thomas*, copyright © 1943 by New Directions Publishing Corp. Reprinted by permission of New Directions Publishing Corp.

Thirty-three lines total from the following poems by Robert Graves: "Reproach," "She Tells Her Love While Half Asleep," "Intercession in Late October," "The Jackals' Address to Isis," and "In the Wilderness." From *Complete Poems in One Volume*, copyright © 2000 by the Trustees of the Robert Graves Copyright Trust, reprinted by permission of Carcanet Press Limited.

Five lines from *Beowulf*, translated by Seamus Heaney, copyright © 2000 by Seamus Heaney, used by permission of W. W. Norton & Company, Inc.

Twelve lines from "Nelly Trim," by Sylvia Townsend Warner, from *Selected Poems*, edited by Claire Harmon, copyright @ 1985 by Carcanet Press Limited. Reprinted by permission of Carcanet Press Limited.

Twelve lines from "April Mortality," by Léonie Adams, reprinted by permission of Judith Farr, Literary Executrix of the Estate of Léonie Adams.

Extracts from *The Mabinogion Tetralogy* by Evangeline Walton, used as an epigraph and quoted in the text, are copyright © renewed 1964 Evangeline Walton Ensley. Published in 2004 by The Overlook Press, Peter Mayer Publishers, Inc., New York, NY. www.overlookpress.com. All rights reserved.

The epigraphs on 27 chapters of this book are taken from public domain materials available at http://www.bartleby/com. The author wishes to thank Bartleby for the valuable scholarly service it provides.

Once more, I dedicate this book

to the memory of my mother,

Genevieve Kathryn Raitinger Taylor,

who left this life before I wrote it.

Synopsis of *The Termite Queen: Volume One: The Speaking of the Dead*

In the 30th century, an off-world expedition returns to Earth with a specimen of intelligent giant termite. The young linguistic anthropologist Kaitrin Oliva is able to find a way to access its unique form of communication; however, the creature dies and a second expedition is mounted with the purpose of making first contact. Griffen Gwidian, the entomologist heading the expedition, is a complex man with a dark personal secret. He and Kaitrin fall in love and form a union during the space flight. Afterward, Prf. Gwidian's mood and behavior change in some troubling ways.

Meanwhile, on the termite planet civil discord is brewing. Mo'gri'ta'tu, the Queen's Chamberlain, resents the power of the Holy Seer Kwi'ga'ga'tei and plots to assassinate her. She has engaged the services of an outland Champion, Ki'shto'ba Huge-Head, to fight this monster that has descended on them from the skies. The aging Commander Hi'ta'fu the Unconquered resents the intrusion of this outlander, and the word-crafty Chamberlain sees an opportunity to lure the Commander into his plot. At the very moment the murder is about to be committed, the second expedition arrives at the planet. Volume Two begins as the landing party descends to the surface …

CONTENTS

Weave a circle round him thrice,
And close your eyes with holy dread,
For he on honeydew hath fed,
And drunk the milk of Paradise.
        – *from* S. T. Coleridge, *Kubla Khan*

Part Three

2 Giotta 17A: Dissolution

Chapter 1

The Assyrian came down like the wolf on the fold,
And his cohorts were gleaming in purple and gold ...
   – from Lord Byron, *The Destruction of Sennacherib*

As the flyer approached the termitarium, Kaitrin peered through her VE. "They've come out again! But not nearly as many ... My goodness, the angle of the light is certainly different at midafternoon."

"Look there!" exclaimed Luku. "Those are pushing the little carts you saw."

"They've sensed us," said Gwidian.

"And they look even more panicked than the first time," said A'a'ma.

Julian was gawking with his mouth hanging open. "Look at those up on the side of the mound! They're in such a hurry to get down that they're almost falling off!"

"Oh, dear," said Kaitrin. "I wish they knew we aren't here to hurt them."

"Well, I suppose there's nothing for it but to commit ourselves," said Gwidian. "That area we agreed on still seems best. Captain, set the *Durga* down."

Will maneuvered the craft over the landing site and allowed it to settle onto the packed soil of the courtyard about 50 meters from the largest edifice, even as they had planned. The east-west orientation of the flyer placed the right wing, with the main hatch

1

beneath it, directly opposite the tower's entrance.

Will shut down the engines and the resulting silence seemed ominous. Everyone crowded around the northward-facing windows, peering through the settling dust. The perspective had changed; the termitarium towered above them, while the ground had turned into a flat viewscape with no sight of the mountains that stood in the distant west.

The largest structure rose well over twenty meters high, with the flanking edifices only a little shorter. The smoothly mortared walls lacked the ventilation ribs that buttressed terrestrial termite mounds, although they were randomly pierced by small apertures. The entrances were at the base, which sloped up slightly above the bare ground of the courtyard, probably to ensure drainage in the wet season. Large stones plugged most of those entrances from within.

There was no activity. All the Shshi had retreated into their stronghold, even the sentries. After the final soldier disappeared, a stone was maneuvered into the opening. The towers stood impregnable and blank, revealing nothing.

Gwidian said, "Well, my anthro colleagues, what's our next move?"

"I guess we wait awhile and observe from inside the flyer while they get used to our presence," said Kaitrin. "It's for sure we can't message them on the relay."

"We should set the external sensors," said A'a'ma a little nervously. "It will be dark in – what ? – about three hours? We need to fix our sleep schedule."

"Probably best to begin it about five hours into the dark period," said Gwidian. "That way we'll be asleep during the heart of the night, with five hours of darkness before and after."

"But that means we'll be sleeping again in the middle of the day," said Kaitrin.

"Best to be inactive during the hottest time," said Gwidian. "Let's at least have a go at this schedule. We can always make adjustments."

"Or it will adjust itself for us," said Kaitrin crossly. "What an aggravation that this planet had to have such a crazy rotation length!"

"We ought to be awake at the next sunrise," said Tió'otu. "If something is going to happen, that is a likely time."

"Come on, Kaitrin," said Luku. "Let's get equipment ready. It will not be long before we send Ti'shra's voice toward its siblings."

"Yes! I'm so excited! And you're right – they *are* its siblings! Every single individual in this colony has the same mother and father!"

"We don't know that yet," said Gwidian. "We know nothing about how they propagate. Even on Earth a termitarium sometimes has more than one queen."

The ship's external motion sensors noted no activity except for the occasional passage of a bird; not even the largest reptile was willing to dare the exposed ground of the courtyard. The only sign of habitation was a scattering of abandoned wheelbarrows. Arti and Julian kept visual watch from the flight deck windows while Will performed a maintenance check on the flyer and established the comlink with the *Featherlight*. The voice of a human communications officer emerged comfortingly from the speaker.

"Safe landfall duly noted and recorded – good work, *Durga*! We'll contact you again in five hours if we have not heard from you sooner. The *Featherlight* will always be here for you. ComControl out."

The rest of the team had gone below to settle in. Kaitrin and Luku worked on their equipment in the research bay, but Gwidian seemed restless. Finally Kaitrin said, "Griff, you've climbed up and down that ladder a dozen times. Come sit down here and let me show you what Luku and I are doing. You might have to help operate this apparatus sometime."

He complied, then withdrew to the laboratory to tinker with his own equipment.

The lander carried a supply of frozen meals for quick consumption, but everyone had agreed that they should have at least one real cooked meal a day, so fresh ingredients, as well as tinned, packaged, and dehydrated items, had been provided for food preparation. This task was to be rotated among the team members and the amicable Trea and her mate had offered to take the first shift. They concocted a stew from frozen chicken meat and Earth vegetables like fresh carrots, onions, and tinned water chestnuts, seasoned and thickened with a fragrant spice powder native to their own planet. During the whole operation, the only bread would be a packaged high-energy cracker made from wheat flour mixed with a meal ground from certain oily Krʃisí'i'aid seeds. Normally, all three mammalian species would eat the same thing, while Prf. A'a'ma would thaw himself a packet of his usual fish or reptilian flesh. However, today even the Big Bird shared in the contents of the pot; chicken was an Earth meat that he had learned to tolerate and even relish heat-damaged.

Frozen strawberries rounded out the repast. It was a satisfying meal, although Kaitrin was so excited that everything felt like sawdust in her mouth.

"It is good idea for all persons to carry emergency field rations whenever they leave flyer," said Trea. "Same for water flask."

"Always?" said Kaitrin dubiously.

"It cannot hurt," said Sev, "even if you cannot think of reason at this moment."

Kaitrin shrugged and dumped some packaged crackers, energy bars, and tubes of protein concentrate into her field pack.

At nightfall there was still no activity in the compound. They sat in the common area, feeling fatigued and a little let down, wondering if they should go to bed.

Then the sensor alarms went off. Everyone leaped to attention and scrambled up the ladder to the darkened flight deck, crowding around the windows with their VEs set on infrared.

The sensor readings showed perhaps half a dozen lifeforms at a distance of 50 meters. The team could discern a ghostly knot of Shshi milling around the entrance to the large structure.

Then a strange phenomenon occurred. A burst of shimmering light illuminated the entranceway.

"What the ... ?" said Gwidian, and flipped up his enhancer to gaze unassisted. Luku was also looking with naked nocturnal eyes.

"What is that?" said an amazed Kaitrin.

"It looks like bioluminescence," said Luku incredulously. "Like the glow torches we use on Quornam."

"My god!" said Gwidian, resetting his VE to day vision. "It's the wings of the alates! The wings seem to be emitting light!"

"You mean, like fireflies?" asked Julian. "Why would that

be?"

"In the firefly it's the abdomen that glows," replied Gwidian. "Of all the bioluminescent organisms on Earth, I know of none with photogenic wings."

"It's for light! Light in the termitarium!" cried Kaitrin. "If the alates can see, they need light! The Shshi not only grow their own tools, they grow their own interior lighting!"

"That sounds a bit far-fetched," said Gwidian.

"This whole species is far-fetched," Kaitrin retorted. "Remember, it was you who reminded us awhile ago that we know nothing about the true nature of these creatures. But at least now we can understand why the wings were glittering in the shade."

Trea was perched on a stepladder staring through her own VE and now she said, "On Pozúa many sea creatures use bioluminescence to make light in deep ocean."

"It's the same on Earth," replied Gwidian, but he shook his head incredulously.

They stared fascinated at the creatures across from them, whose wings pulsed not only with a white glow, but with subtle greens, reds, and golds.

"Let's turn on our lights," said Gwidian, "and see what kind of reaction we get."

They did so, and after a brief explosion of activity, all the small night-shrouded forms disappeared into the termitarium. The bright-winged alates were the last to vanish. "Phoo. We chased them away," said Kaitrin.

The sensors showed no further activity. After the humans had gaped awhile at the unfamiliar sight of two moons staring down among the towers, everyone began to think of sleep. Kaitrin and Gwidian sat in the research bay using their neural recorders to make a journal of impressions for future reports. Gwidian finished before Kaitrin. "I'm a bit bushed," he said. "Come to bed, Kait?"

"Go ahead," she said. "I'll be just a couple of minutes."

When she entered their compartment, Gwidian was standing before the small mirror, shaving. "I thought maybe you'd let your beard grow when you're in the field," she said.

He glanced at her in the mirror. "It's a bit hot here for that, what?"

"Too bad. I was wondering how you'd look with a beard.

5

Very distinguished, I'd guess, if you kept it trimmed properly and didn't let it get scraggly."

He shrugged and laughed. She quickly disrobed and hopped into bed, where he soon joined her.

She sighed, settling into the curve of his arm beneath the sheet. It was warm even in the flyer; they were trying to conserve power cells. "Wasn't it wonderful of them to give us this private sleeping arrangement?"

He kissed the top of her head in silence.

"Griffen, you don't seem very happy."

"Don't I? Well ... I suppose it's what we spoke of the other day. I worry too much about you."

"Oh, is that it? Now, you promised me ... "

"I know! I will! It's only ... I had been so anticipating our trip into space together and then the voyage turned out so exquisitely as I had hoped it might ... I rather lost track of the rest of it. This all seems a bit like an afterthought."

"Well, Griffen Gwidian, it's important to me! Come on, where's your sense of adventure? You're a xenologist – you know the lure of alien worlds gets to you!"

"Well, yes ... but if it comes to risking ... " He went silent. Then he said, "You know, I may not be the dauntless adventurer that you might like me to be. I may not even be – especially courageous."

"Griff. I wouldn't have you any different from the way you are."

"Kait, can you really mean that?"

"Haven't you been listening to me these past weeks? Now, let's try to get some sleep. Something could happen at any time!"

*　　*　　*

Kaitrin awoke about four hours later and lay wide-eyed in the dimly lighted room. The temperature had dropped, the enviros had shut off, and the ventilation fans were bringing in chilly outside air. Apparently, the long nights cooled considerably on this high plateau. She bundled the sheet around her neck.

She felt all at loose ends. The chronometer said it was 0100h. That was based on two twenty-hour time grids starting at midnight and at noon, planetary time. What time was it by ship's time?

6

And by her biological clock? The *Featherlight* was on a standard space day of 23.5 Earth hours. What time had it been when they left? And when had she last slept before now, reckoning as planetary time? She lay vainly struggling to figure it out, until the back of her neck felt as rigid as a splint. *G-r-r-r, this will never do ...*

Beside her Griffen was emitting his soft snore. She had never told him he snored, but he probably knew it already. It wasn't unpleasant, anyway – didn't bother her in the slightest. She lay as still as she could; his arm was resting across her waist and she didn't want to disturb him.

If it's 0130h here, then on the ship it's ...

In extreme annoyance, she booted that frustrating exercise out of her mind. *Think of something else. Think of the Shshi. Think of the recording ...*

That was worse than trying to reconcile the time. *¿bei'paho|? ♪↑ reisho| wei| Ɔ sho'a| d'il| ||* That impossible sentence, or rather, question. Almost undoubtedly a question ... *sho| Ɔ ti'shra'ze| || ¿bei'taio|? Ɔ loi'zi| || ...*

"Oh!" She jumped, then looked at Griffen. He only stirred a little and withdrew his arm. He stopped snoring but remained asleep.

That same pair of signals enclosed *bei'taio|* – she could see the waveforms in her mind. How could she have missed it? *¿bei'taio|? Ɔ loi'zi| ||* was also a question!

Taio|. If it meant "to have" as she had surmised in another instance ...

"I am Tish'ra. Do you have ... *loi'zi|*?"

"Do you have ... " something parallel to "Ti'shra," perhaps ...

She did not know the meaning of the two morphemes in *Ti'shra,* but by its nature it was ... a name! "Do you have ... a name?"

She sat bolt upright. *sho'laio| ♪↑ preivo| Ɔ loi'zi| ki'bei| ||*

"I want – to something – your name."

"I want to know your name."

"To know." "To know!" That was it! She had deduced how to say "to know"!

Now she could point to something and say, *sho'laio| ♪↑ preivo|* ... "I want to know ..." And when the time was right, she could ask her informants for their names.

Terrifically excited, she turned to Griffen, wanting to wake him up to share this latest epiphany. But he was sleeping so peacefully that she subdued the impulse; he would be appreciative, but it seemed kinder to let him rest. Perhaps Tió'otu or Luku ... but no. It could wait till everybody got up.

Carefully, she slid back down under the sheet and gave herself over to a rush of ecstasy. Nothing could be more wonderful than lying in bed on a planet thirty-two light years away from Earth, with the person she loved most in the universe sleeping at her side – and then realizing that the word she had most longed to learn had revealed itself to her!

She hugged the sheet against her breast, rolled over against Griffen's warmth, and at last fell back to sleep.

Three hours later the soft hum of a buzzer signaled that the sleep period was ending. Slightly grumpy individuals began emerging from their compartments. There was consensus among the humans that coffee with their oatmeal would be a great idea. Kaitrin began to babble about her latest revelation and she and Luku rushed to the research bay to record the new words.

Then an hour before dawn every external sensor on the ship began to emit an infernal clamor. Everybody grabbed their VEs and swarmed the ladder to the upper deck. The infrared setting showed a mass of Shshi pouring out from the west central edifice. They were not milling around, but coming in ranks, fanning out, forming compact units. And they were spreading all across the compound.

"I hate to say this," said Arti from the southward-facing windows, "but we're being surrounded."

"Damn," said Kaitrin, rushing to look, "they're everywhere! Is it soldiers?"

"Can't you see the mandibles glinting in this last bit of moonlight?" said Gwidian tightly.

"Now, no need to panic," said Will. "We can always jump out. No need to panic."

"Do you think maybe jumping out would be the wisest course?" croaked A'a'ma.

"They're keeping their distance from the ship," said Arti, continuing to scan. "But even if they swarmed us and sharpened their jaws on the hull, I don't think they could do any serious damage. I'd be for waiting to see what happens next."

"Me, too!" said Kaitrin. "We haven't come this far to be scared off so easily."

Will said, "The worst they might do is break a cam or a fan, but the essential systems have no elements exposed on the outside of the hull and all the com gear is on the top. I'll seal off all vents on the lower half of the ship as a precaution."

So they stayed put and waited. Dawn came, colorless, cloudless. And then they could see more clearly what confronted them.

Behind the flyer the line of Shshi was relatively thin, but between the *Durga* and the termitarium were perhaps five hundred soldiers in two companies, formed into phalanxes of fifteen creatures each. What appeared to be an officer stood at the head of each phalanx. A little space separated the two companies, and two large and imposing Warriors stood alone on either side of this space. Near the entrance to the principal edifice crouched a Warrior who was even larger, possibly the Commander of the operation.

"*‡He'etí <khe!dora]* They have deployed their whole army!" warbled A'a'ma.

"Does this make anybody else think we're in a bad holonovel?" asked Arti.

"Well," said Kaitrin, her voice quavering slightly, "nobody can say they don't take us seriously."

Gwidian was standing beside her, gripping her arm so that she thought the prints of his fingers would remain after he let go. "Perhaps we should reconsider jumping ... " he began, but Luku interrupted.

"*Hoi-a*! What are those?"

The light was increasing, and she was pointing to certain soldiers spread along each side of the dividing line.

"Hell's bells!" exclaimed Arti. "Those look like the pointy-headed ones that spray the chemicals!"

Gwidian focused his VEs. "Amazing! That's exactly what they look like."

The nasutes were smaller and more wasp-waisted that the others, and where the majority of the Shshi Warriors were a pallid buff with brownish heads, these were darker, reddish-purple in

9

color in color. They, too, were accompanied by one who appeared to be an officer.

Then the sun burst full upon the courtyard ... flashed from five hundred pairs of razor-sharp scythes ... glinted off the bulbous, hard-polished, purple crania of the nasute regiment. Five hundred pairs of antennae waved crazily on five hundred eyeless heads.

"God!" whispered Gwidian in a shaking voice.

Kaitrin said, "I want to go out there."

"What?" he shouted, snatching her around by the left hand with such force that she cried, "Ouch! You're hurting me, Griff!"

He let go of her. "Kaitrin, you're a bloody fool! Don't be a fool, for god's sake – or for mine!"

She nursed her hand where the grip of his fingers had forced the wedding ring into the flesh. "We're here to make contact!" she shouted back at him. "Just how do you expect us to do that if we don't ... ?"

"Look!" exclaimed Julian, who had kept his VE trained on the daunting scene.

The gap down the center had widened and activity was visible at the entrance of the main edifice, including a sparkle of alate wings.

"I'll bet anything the alates are the beefeaters of the society," Kaitrin said. "I think they are the ones we need to contact. We must go out and transmit the recording. Make those alates receive it."

"Too far. Signal is not strong enough to reach," said Luku.

"It ought to reach the closest soldiers. Maybe they'll pass the word up the line."

Trea said suddenly, "I agree. We should go out." Sev nodded assent.

"No!" said Gwidian. "Trea – Sev – you, of all people? Anyone who sets foot outside this flyer will be instantly killed!"

"You see, I really don't believe that," said Kaitrin. "And, anyway, we can just open the hatch and see what happens, and then if nothing does, we can step out on the ramp. If there is movement toward us, we can retreat quickly. They aren't all that close. I think it can be done safely. I think we must try it."

"I am willing," said Luku. "Arti? Julian? Will?"

"I can't swear the three of us will be able to protect you," said Arti a little worriedly, "but in the worst case a few blasts of a laser pistol fired at the ground ought to give them a good scare. They've certainly never encountered an energy weapon."

Gwidian had walked away and was standing with his back to them. After a glance at him, Kaitrin turned questioningly to Tió'otu.

He hopped distractedly. "I do not like taking risks," he said. "But if everybody else is set on going out, I suppose I will go along. But I am not fast on my feet. I think I will stay in the doorway behind you. Shove me through if you want me out of the way."

Kaitrin hugged him. "That's my doughty old grandbird," she whispered to his invisible ear.

Gwidian had turned around, making no attempt to mask his distress. "I think you've all lost your wits," he said.

"Griff ... "

"I'll join the rest of you if I must. But it will go into the record that I didn't approve this." He turned away, fumbling with the fastening of his pistol holster with unsteady fingers.

"Griffen," said Kaitrin sharply, "I don't want you to go all to pieces and fire that thing without a good reason."

He turned around again. "Oh, that's what you really think – that I will go all to pieces."

Trea laid both of her small hands on Kaitrin's arm. "Please, Kaitrin. What you should say ... 'If all of you show the restraint with firing pistol as Griffen will, we will be all right.'"

Kaitrin stared down at her, then guffawed. "Trea, you have me pegged perfectly! Doesn't she, Griff? I'm afraid I've committed my usual! I'm really sorry!"

There was a tense moment. Then Gwidian barked a little laugh and relaxed slightly. "Trea, I'm grateful you're here. It's only that this is not some kind of game. I do implore everyone, be careful. All right, Kait, if we must do this ... Get your equipment and let's get started."

Kaitrin hung the biopulse emitter on her belt while Luku carried the receiver-recorder. The team clustered together inside the hatch. As Will touched the control, the hatch door disengaged and slid up against the wing while the ramp folded down into place. At the thudding vibration, the nearest soldiers, about ten meters away, jumped violently and pressed backward against the ranks behind them.

"They're still scared to death," said Kaitrin from the hatch. "Now! Here I go!" And she stepped onto the ramp and descended to its foot.

A'a'ma twittered. Gwidian muttered an expletive. Everyone surged after Kaitrin, with Luku coming fearlessly alongside, activating the recorder as she did so. Arti and Julian flanked them, pistols drawn. Will and Gwidian were behind, also holding side arms. A'a'ma hovered at the top of the ramp, peering over the others' heads.

They were all in the shadow of the flyer wing, but the soldier termites could not see them in any case. They could smell them, however, and wriggling, side-scraping motions ran through the ranks like a wave. Antennae flailed, stiffening jerkily in various directions. The close-packed assemblage emitted an overpowering odor of its own in the morning sun – an earthy fungal smell mixed with sharp chemical accents that made the eyes water. A bizarre silence hung over the assemblage, a silence filled with the skitter of tarsal claws on hard ground, the dry grating of setae against integument – the snap and clatter of mandibles …

"Are you picking up anything?" Kaitrin asked Luku.

"A huge garble! Everybody seems to be talking! Complete chaos!"

"Keep recording," said Kaitrin. "Maybe we'll be able to filter out something."

There was a long pause, a standoff. Then the heads in the front lines turned toward the termitarium. The pathway through the center widened even further.

"Something is happening!" squawked A'a'ma from his perch atop the ramp. "I see at least three alates at the entrance, and some large workers, and the big soldier that we thought was the general. And … *hakhís↓~] ƆSetil vrai'u oví↑ ♫!i ♫psá·át♪ ai↑~]*"

Something had emerged from the entrance and was moving along the pathway toward them. It was certainly an isopteroid soldier, but it looked different from those of Ti'shra's lineage. Its oval head was nearly half its one-and-a-half-meter length. It had exceptionally long and powerful front legs, and a set of mandibles that were only slightly curved and wickedly pointed at the tips; they were perhaps ten centimeters broad at the base and thirty centimeters long. Its head was massive, like a stone, and as smooth and eyeless as a stone. Its antennae projected stiffly toward the position of the stunned observers.

"*¡Válgame Dios!*" exclaimed Kaitrin. "Goliath!"

Chapter 2

The heart is drained that, spelling in the scurry
Of chemic blood, warned of the coming fury.
By the sea's side hear the dark-vowelled birds.
— *from* Dylan Thomas, *Especially When the
October Wind*

[At the entrance to the fortress, Kwi'ga'ga'tei, Mo'gri'ta'tu, Di'fa'kro'mi, and others stand with No'kri and Hi'ta'fu, looking toward the closed flank of the crouching Sky-Monster. Ki'shto'ba waits behind them, just inside the entranceway]

[Kwi'ga'ga'tei]: I would not have had us send out such a force. The Highest Mother's words called for only the Champion to confront the Strange Ones – *to keep them humble*, she said. She did not advise making war against them.

[Hi'ta'fu]: It cannot hurt to make a show of force against so powerful an enemy.

[Di'fa'kro'mi]: If this Sky-Jumper is a creature that bears a name of the Nameless, it might be sacrilege to display such belligerence toward it.

[Ki'shto'ba, from behind]: The Warriors have passed word along the ranks that it does not move or emit pheromones. It only stinks vilely. It may be dead. To send out so much force against a dead thing is somewhat humorous.

14

[Mo'gri'ta'tu]: Perhaps it will speak to us. If it is dead and speaks, would that not satisfy a prophecy?

[Kwi'ga'ga'tei]: It was alive during the darktime when its eyes filled with light and stared at us. But now I cannot say ... Holy *ma'na'ta*|!

[Di'fa'kro'mi]: May the Highest Mother ward us! An orifice opens beneath its wing!

[No'kri]: Help, Alates! Tell us what is happening!

[Kwi'ga'ga'tei]: It is ... could it be? It is producing young! Smaller creatures are coming from the vent in its side, without the intermediary of eggs!

[Di'fa'kro'mi]: It is indeed a female creature, then!

[Hi'ta'fu, dances]: Do the hatchlings resemble nymphs? Must we fight so insignificant a thing – some outlandish creature's helpless little nymphs?

[Kwi'ga'ga'tei]: I cannot see clearly because the wing casts a shadow, but I see nothing that resembles the nymphs of the Shshi. But I think ... some of these creatures ... are like ones I saw once in a vision ...

[Mo'gri'ta'tu]: What? You have visions you do not reveal to the Holy One, dread Seer?

[Kwi'ga'ga'tei, ignores the Chamberlain]: And the Nameless One conveyed to me ... that those same creatures were ... speechless ... Huge-Head!

[Ki'shto'ba]: I am here!

[Kwi'ga'ga'tei]: Go forth! I think these emergent creatures are the Strange Ones that you were meant to humble. Go forth!

*   *   *

The monster Shi continued to advance a few steps at a time – a few disconcertingly quick steps with its head lowered, interspersed with pauses during which it reared up, elevating its head and swaying it from side to side defiantly. Its antennae continued to point stiffly toward the group of newcomers.

"Threat postures," said Gwidian hoarsely.

"It is sending transmissions!" exclaimed Luku.

"Zero in on them. Don't miss a blip," said Kaitrin tensely. Gwidian, directly behind her, had wrapped an arm around her waist and was pressing her back as if he would put her behind him. She looked sideways to see his right hand coming up with the pistol in it.

Before she could say anything, a small brown hand appeared and gently guided his arm downward. "Gwidian," said Trea's soft, husky voice, "please, put pistol in holster."

After a moment's hesitation, he did so.

Tió'otu said, "Here is what I think – you were right to call it 'Goliath,' Kaitrin! I think it is issuing a challenge. I think it wants somebody to come out and fight it one on one."

"*¡Caramba!* Who wants to be David?" queried Kaitrin, with a nervous grimace.

"You mean, single combat?" said Arti. She looked at Julian, who laughed and shook his head.

"Didn't train for that at the Academy," he said.

"Well, I know how to answer it," said Kaitrin. "Didn't the Mythmakers say, *Fight your wars with words, not weapons?*" And she pressed the switch on the biopulse emitter.

The display indicated that it was transmitting. The creature continued to advance as if nothing were happening. It had come about halfway along the path.

"Too far," said Luku. "I will enhance, focus ... " She bent over Kaitrin's equipment.

"I'll begin it again," whispered Kaitrin.

All at once the giant Shi stopped moving. It gathered its legs up against its body, its antennae quivering madly. Then it scrambled backward.

"Oh, god, it's working! It received the transmission!" cried Kaitrin ecstatically.

The giant turned to its left. Its antennae were pointing back toward the entrance of the termitarium.

*   *   *

[Mo'gri'ta'tu]: What is the matter with it? It is backing away like a nymph from a Nasute.

16

[Hi'ta'fu]: What?

[Ki'shto'ba's speech reaches them]: Holy Kwi'ga'ga'tei! The vision has found its answer! I have received words from the dead Shi Ti'shra!

[A great flurry of stamping, groveling, and exclaiming]

[Kwi'ga'ga'tei]: Preserve us ... preserve us ... [She staggers, steadies herself] I will go forth – alone! I will have no one with me!

[The Seer hastens down the pathway until she reaches the Huge-Head]

[Kwi'ga'ga'tei]: Tell me what happened.

[Ki'shto'ba]: I received ... But the same again ... Do you not receive it, too?

... beside the antennae ... There is no pain ... I know it will never hurt me ...

Why can you not understand me? I am Ti'shra ... Do you have a name? I want to know your name ... I want you to speak to me ...

Stay with me ... I do not want to die alone ... I want to touch you ...

I am a One Being, but One Beings are nothing ... when they are alone ...

Tell them in Lo'ro'ra that Ti'shra died in pain ... but it had a Comforter ... who was not evil ...

I am Ti'shra ... I am Shshi ... The Holy One is A'kha'ma'na'ta ...

I am the dead one speaking.

[The words strike like lightning bolts into the antennae of Kwi'ga'ga'tei. The sun sucks at the veins of the wings. The ground, the Cohorts of Shshi Warriors, the blue paleness of the sky, the blinding light ... all whirl ... until a merciful darkness comes ...]

*　　*　　*

"Look! One of the alates is coming out!" cried A'a'ma.

As it scurried forward, the visitors scrutinized the slender-bodied insectile form with the double pair of wings and the enormous compound eyes.

"What an amazing creature!" whispered Kaitrin. "Even in this light – all that shimmering iridescence on the wings!"

"And the eyes are jewels," said Trea.

"Once more for the recording ... " said Kaitrin, and she touched the key.

The alate reached the giant soldier just as the recording started. The pair of Shshi stood frozen. The recording concluded. Suddenly the alate began to shake. Its body twisted, writhed; the wings fanned unequally, and it fell twitching onto its side, crumpling a wing.

"It's dying!" exclaimed Gwidian. "God, Kait, we've killed it!"

"It seems like seizure," said Trea.

A'a'ma, his excitement overcoming his timidity, had emerged to stand with the group. "Kaitrin," he said, "you know what is happening? Think!"

She turned to look at him. "Oh!" The two of them exclaimed simultaneously, "Shaman!"

"What?" said Gwidian.

Kaitrin began, "A shaman is a kind of priest or ... "

"I know what a shaman is," he said.

"I don't," said Arti.

"In some pre-tech societies a shaman is a priest who bridges the gap between the world of spirit and the world of matter. They may go into trances – have seizures – and they might employ drugs to induce the proper mental state."

"Pozú have shaman," said Sev. "Not always just among pre-techs."

Everybody glanced at him, but this was not the time to pursue the subject. Out in the compound, the fearsome giant Shi was standing over the fallen alate, its head cocked, its mandibles resting on the alate's belly.

"*Hoi-a!* I think it is going to kill it!" exclaimed Luku.

"No," said Kaitrin. "Look! It's using its big head to shelter the other from the sun!"

They watched as two more alates and a couple of workers detached themselves from the group at the entrance to the termitarium and rushed out to surround the pair. For a few moments what was happening was hidden from view. Then the group opened enough so the team could see that the fallen alate was on its feet again, being licked on the face and under the wings by its attendants. They conducted it slowly back to the termitarium. The giant soldier supported its body gently with mandibles that could have severed the head from the thorax in a single snap.

The group disappeared into the edifice. Only one alate remained, along with the Shi who seemed to be the Commander. The pair lingered for a moment with their heads close together. Then this alate also withdrew. Certain soldiers ran to the Commander's side. There were more conferences. The soldiers dashed off to pass down the line of troops.

Apparently they were conveying orders, for the troops began to withdraw. While the team watched spellbound, those phalanxes in the rear began to melt into the structure from which they had emerged. In a gradual and orderly manner, no longer paying any attention to the scary newcomers, the entire army of the Shshi retreated, leaving only a few soldiers at the entrance to the edifice and a contingent of nasutes guarding the main building.

"No more to record," said Luku. "And memory is full, anyway."

"I think," said Kaitrin, "it's time for us to withdraw, too."

Chapter 3

Hamlet: Be thou a spirit of health or goblin damned,
    Be thy intents wicked or charitable,
    Thou comest in such a questionable shape
    That I will speak to thee ...
        – *from* William Shakespeare, *Hamlet*

Back inside the *Durga* Kaitrin jumped around the cabin like a crazy person. "I can't believe it! I just can't believe it!" she was shouting. "It surpasses my wildest dreams! Can anybody – anybody! – deny now that they're intelligent? They have an organized defense, they care for each other, they may have a priesthood – they have differentiated roles, filled by individuals! They sent out a champion against us, just like in ancient Earth-times! And they understood our transmission! – and they gave up the idea of fighting us after they understood it! What in the world will they do next? Come and knock on our door? Or should we go and knock on theirs?"

Sitting at the table, Gwidian seemed stunned. Now he gave a kind of groan. "Kait, that's just the sort of thing I was expecting you to say."

"Griff ... " Kaitrin bounced up, grabbed him around the shoulders, and hugged him. "That wasn't a serious remark! It's too soon for anything like that!"

"These creatures have received quite a shock," said A'a'ma. "We must be patient and let them recover from hearing – no,

20

'receiving' is a better word – the speech of someone they had believed to be dead. They may think that Ti'shra – yes, Kaitrin, I am prepared now to call our specimen by the name you gave it! – that Ti'shra is actually alive and present here, or that its ghost is here. They have no way of knowing that a machine could transmit this message."

"They do not know machine at all," said Trea. "They may have language and government and defense system and beliefs of the spirit, but their technology may be only wood and stone tools and wheel – probably not metal-knowledge or even fire."

"Tió'otu, how would you rank their technological development?" asked Kaitrin. "About a 5?"

He twitched his beak up affirmatively. "Somewhere near Neolithic. And yet … The tool situation is unique and they obviously have superb engineering capability. I wonder how far their math concepts have developed? We may have to insert a new TD subcategory – Shshi development, first contact level … "

"Kaitrin," said Luku, "when can we start analyzing new recordings?"

"Right now! Come on, let's see what we have!"

So the day sped by, with no further sign of activity from the termitarium except for an occasional changing of the skittish guard. Finally, a buzzer sounded to announce the ten-hour daytime interval was ending. Realizing they were all tired out, they ate a quick meal, set the external sensors, dimmed the lights, and prepared for bed.

In their chamber, Kaitrin rattled on to Gwidian about the new recordings. "We got nothing from the army. Too much talking all at once – it would take days just to extract one or two phrases. But we got the words of our Goliath very clearly! I'm calling it the Challenge Speech – it's so exciting to have another piece of text to work with! It includes some of the same words that Ti'shra used – *na'ta'zei|*, 'Queen,' and *kwi'il|* and *shkwi'sho'zei|*, which I still haven't figured out. And *shweio'zi|* must surely mean 'deaths' – that's a little ominous! And *shsho|* and *shbei'a|* must be 'we' and plural 'you' – makes perfect sense! It starts out with an unknown word that probably addresses us and then it says *sho'gano| ya| shbei'a| ||* – 'I speak to you.' What a thrill to be able to translate something! And Ti'shra's word *lo'ro'ra'mi|* appears four times,

21

three with a slight variant on the final syllable – say, you know what? That could be the name of this termitarium! Ti'shra probably said, 'Tell that Ti'shra died … ' somehow 'to them in Lo'ro'ra' – *i'i|* would be 'in.' I should have seen that before, but the word order was confusing me! *-mi* must be a place-name marker, the way *-ze* is a personal-name marker. I also got Goliath's real name and I've given it a syllabification: *ki'shto'ba'ze|.* 'I am Ki'shto'ba,' says our Goliath. What do you think, Griffen? Is there anything comparable to that monster among terrestrial termites?"

Gwidian was sitting on the bed in his bathrobe, waiting for the sonic shower to become available. "In fact, it reminds me of the Afriken species called *Macrotermes bellicosus* … "

Something in the way he spoke made her pause. It was very remote, as if he were hearing her and answering dutifully while not really listening. In the silence, he looked up.

"I'm sorry, Griff," she said. "I'm overexcited. I'm running on about nothing."

"Kait, I'm sorry I hurt your hand today – at the window."

"Oh, that!" Kait looked down at her fingers, noting a red mark on the middle one but not mentioning it. "Don't worry about it, love – no damage done at all."

There was a knock at the door and Will's voice said, "Professor, shower's empty."

Gwidian got up to go out.

"Just think, Griffen," she called after him. "Ti'shra said, 'Tell them in Lo'ro'ra that Ti'shra died.' And I have. I have told them. I've brought its words home."

He flashed her a rather grave smile and disappeared through the door.

Kaitrin hopped into bed and lay rolled up hugging herself. *I'll never go to sleep. Too much to think about. Too much to plan.*

And that was the last thing she remembered.

*   *   *

[The group escorting the weakened Seer pauses in the fortress entrance]

[Kwi'ga'ga'tei]: Commander, pull back the Cohorts. Withdraw them.

[Hi'ta'fu, quivering and making threat displays]: What is this? What is happening?

[Mo'gri'ta'tu]: To do that requires an order from the Holy One and King.

[Kwi'ga'ga'tei]: Bring your Warriors into the fortress. I have no strength ... to argue this. The dead one has in fact spoken even as the Champion's words indicated. That part of the prophecy is fulfilled.

[Much agitation. Even Mo'gri'ta'tu cringes]

[No'kri]: Commander, withdraw the Cohorts! The Seer has the prime authority here!

[Kwi'ga'ga'tei and her retinue vanish into the fortress]

[Hi'ta'fu]: What happens now? All has changed! The Holy Seer has been vindicated!

[Mo'gri'ta'tu, in fury]: Order the Chiefs to withdraw the troops, Hi'ta'fu! Obviously we cannot prevail at present against the windsweep of this new time, which is coming far too rapidly! But I do not concede defeat, Commander, and you cannot escape! I have not been alone in treasonable purpose! We each know things about the other that would destroy us both if they were spread about. Therefore, we can trust each other. We *can* trust each other, right? Do you not concur in that assertion?

*   *   *

[The outer chambers of the Seer's rooms are crowded with anxious and agitated Shshi. In the inner chamber, Kwi'ga'ga'tei rests on a bed of *tho'sei*| leaves. Her wings are dull and sag limply at either side of her body. Two Healer Alates minister to her. One places before her a container of water mixed with honeydew; another grooms and licks a wing that was creased during the fit. She raises her head, plunges her mouthparts into the bowl, and sucks in fluid]

[Healer]: The heat drew off the vital sap of your wing veins, Holy Seer. This will replenish you.

[Second Healer]: But I cannot understand – it was only an

23

early sun and it did not shine on you long enough for you to become so depleted.

[Kwi'ga'ga'tei]: It was not only the sun that weakened me. But I must, and will, recover.

[I'mei'o'nu enters, speaks]: I have imbibed the pure honeydew of the Alates' Flock, Kwi'ga'ga'tei. I bring it to you!

[The Seer's Steward abases, brings her mouthparts against Kwi'ga'ga'tei's, and infuses her gullet with the rich fluid.]

[Second Healer]: Ah, yes, this will work even better to invigorate you!

[Kwi'ga'ga'tei peers about]: Is Mo'gri'ta'tu present in the outer chamber?

[I'mei'o'nu]: No, he and Commander Hi'ta'fu went immediately to the Holy Chamber.

[Kwi'ga'ga'tei]: I feared as much. I should be there as well. No'kri ... If No'kri is without, ask it to come in and leave me alone with it.

[No'kri enters, the other Alates depart]

[No'kri]: We are all much alarmed, Holy Seer. Surely there is something that I can tell my Workers so they will not be so afraid!

[Kwi'ga'ga'tei]: I want you to call another Council meeting for five turnings of the water vessel. I will speak of these matters at that time. In the meantime, I ask a favor of you. I fear those who may exert unfavorable influence upon the Holy One and the King. You know of whom I speak. When you have the time, exercise your right as Chief of Workers and attend the Holy One as often as you can.

[No'kri, dances]: Chief I may be, but I am as eyeless as any other Worker, Holy Seer.

[Kwi'ga'ga'tei]: But with a perceptive mind, and an incorruptible one, I truly believe.

[No'kri]: Would you have me go to the Holy Chamber now?

[Kwi'ga'ga'tei]: I would, until I can come. Try to make A'kha'ma'na'ta and Sei'o'na'sha'ma understand that Lo'ro'ra must remain unified in purpose during these trials. And this you may tell your Workers: Do not be afraid! This mystery of Ti'shra's ghost surpasses any tale I have ever received for strangeness, but I sense nothing to fear in it. If we have something to fear, it comes from a different source.

[Presently Kwi'ga'ga'tei requests the company of the Nasute Chief and the Champion]

[Ki'shto'ba]: Holy Kwi'ga'ga'tei! I feared for your life!

[Kwi'ga'ga'tei]: I am recovering. I thank you for your concern and for your assistance. And I assure you, you are not done assisting me. I would ask you to roll the stone across the door. Thank you.

I will speak words to both of you in confidence, trusting that you will not betray me. In my last vision I endured a premonition of my own death, but I was prohibited from speaking about it. In fact, it was so obscure a premonition that I scarcely would be able to speak of it were it not forbidden. But, like the vision of Lo'ro'ra's destruction, this death does not have to be, I believe, if certain other admonitions are successfully carried out.

The Champion was to make the confrontation. This has been done. The Speaking of the Dead has occurred. Then two commands were put directly upon me, not upon the whole society; I know this because the Nameless used the word of one – *bei'sha|*, and not *bei'shsha|* – when she addressed me. First, I was charged to learn to know the Comforter.

[Ki'shto'ba]: The speaking of Ti'shra mentioned that word – *I had a Comforter*, it said. Who is that?

[Kwi'ga'ga'tei]: I do not know, but I must learn the answer. Then I was commanded to teach the Speechless One how to speak. But I believe that the Speechless Ones are these same ones that brought the Speaking of the Dead to us.

[Sa'ti'a'i'a]: But, Holy Seer, does that not contradict itself?

[Kwi'ga'ga'tei]: It was not these outland visitors who spoke Ti'shra's death words. It was some miracle of the Nameless One, or perhaps only something we have never experienced before – some new thing from this New Time of which we have no understanding. But I must learn to understand, and I can do that only if I myself approach these Strange Ones and explore their nature, as I was charged.

[Ki'shto'ba]: That could be quite dangerous, Holy Seer.

[Kwi'ga'ga'tei]: And so I would request that you attend me when I go out to them. They will not dare attack me if you are there. You will humble them, even as the Nameless Mother charged you to do. And, Nasute Chief, I have two services to ask of you. One is to provide a contingent of guards to accompany myself and the Champion when we go forth. This guard must remain alert but keep its distance. Only Ki'shto'ba will stand immediately at my side.

[Sa'ti'a'i'a]: That is not a difficult request. But would it not be better if Warriors native to Lo'ro'ra escort their Seer?

[Kwi'ga'ga'tei]: I say to my sorrow that I do not trust the Commander, or the Chief of the First Cohort, either. Hi'ta'fu consorts too much with Mo'gri'ta'tu, and Lo'lo'pai seems exceptionally agitated in its mind of late. No, I would ask you, Sa'ti'a'i'a of No'sta'pan'cha, to provide a Nasute guard for me whenever I approach the Strange Ones.

[Ki'shto'ba]: I think Chief A'gwa'ji can be trusted.

[Kwi'ga'ga'tei]: I agree. But if I draw on only the Second Cohort, I will be accused of favoritism, and rivalries will be intensified. I prefer to rely on outlanders and stand aloof.

[Sa'ti'a'i'a]: This can easily be done. But you spoke of two services, Holy Seer.

[Kwi'ga'ga'tei]: Nasute Chief, you have the right as Chief of the Liege Cohort to attend the Holy One and King. Would you do so frequently? Particularly when Hi'ta'fu and the Chamberlain are present? I have already requested that No'kri do this, but a reliable Warrior presence will have a steadying influence on our progenitors.

[Sa'ti'a'i'a]: Gladly. But I am somewhat uncomfortable

26

playing the spy.

[Kwi'ga'ga'tei]: I do not ask you to report to me what happens in the Holy Chamber. I simply ask you to represent me there and I trust you to perform this duty without oversight.

[Ki'shto'ba]: This appears to be a grave time for your fortress. You told me earlier that you saw the Shshi of Lo'ro'ra fighting one another.

[Kwi'ga'ga'tei]: That is true and the memory of that vision still appalls me. But again I say, I do not believe these things to be inevitable. Now go and ask I'mei'o'nu and the two Healers to return. I will determine the time of my going out to the Strange Ones and report to all of you at the Council meeting.

[The Warriors abase their heads and depart. As the Alates enter, Ta'rei'so'cha pushes in with them]

[Ta'rei'so'cha]: Holy Seer! Mo'gri'ta'tu is concerned! He dispatched me to inquire after your health and to offer assistance!

[Kwi'ga'ga'tei]: Return to Mo'gri'ta'tu and thank him for his concern. Tell him that I am much better and that he need not trouble himself that the present Seer of Lo'ro'ra will not be able to provide for our beloved fortress far into the future.

*   *   *

[The Council Chamber. Kwi'ga'ga'tei, crisp-winged now and strong of stance, addresses the assembled Counselors]

In answer to your question, Di'fa'kro'mi, I took no vision in the sun this day. I was merely stunned. And I do not know how the dead Ti'shra was able to speak to us. But I believe I know why, and I think we need not dread its ghost nor expect that it will pursue anyone through the corridors of the fortress.

At first I believed that this monster was expelling live young – it truly did appear so. Others have suggested that the monster itself is an egg that was in the process of hatching ...

[Mo'gri'ta'tu]: An egg! A flying egg? That is a conceit more humorous than the Champion's about fighting a dead thing!

[Kwi'ga'ga'tei]: I did not say that I believed this statement,

Chamberlain. After all, the hatchlings went back into the egg and sealed up the hole – is that how nymphs and eggs behave? And Warriors in the forward ranks insist that they smelled bird-stench among these hideous-appearing creatures. Others say they smelled musks that were unlike anything ever encountered on this ground. The shadow and the distance were such that I could not be sure of what I saw.

But I am sure of this: These creatures are visitors – guests at our fortress door. Perhaps they come from some far reaches of the world, for there is much of the world of which we citizens of Lo'ro'ra know nothing. Or perhaps the Nameless One brought them from some unknown place above the sky, for her power is beyond all conceiving. They visited us once before and took Ti'shra away with them, and it died in their possession.

But it did not die in the grip of evil ones! I do not know how they brought the spirit of Ti'shra here, but I am convinced that the sending of its speech was a message or greeting to us, to insure that we would welcome the Strange Ones who brought it! Ti'shra spoke of one whom it called *ru'zei|*. Ti'shra said, *Tell them in Lo'ro'ra that Ti'shra died in pain, but it had a* ru'zei| *who was not evil.* Tish'ra said, *I know that it will never hurt me.* Ti'shra addressed this Comforter, *Why can you not understand me? I want you to speak to me!*

But it seems that the Comforter could not speak. Perhaps that Comforter is one of those beings who emerged from the Sky-Jumper. We are called upon to teach it to speak. Perhaps it is eager to speak with us. Perhaps it wants us to teach it.

[No one responds except with much grooming and fidgeting]

[The Grower Chief Gwo'no, timidly]: But my Worker Ti'shra died in pain. They caused it to suffer.

[Kwi'ga'ga'tei]: Suffering is not always deliberately caused. Sometimes suffering comes about through a mistake, or a good intention gone awry.

[Di'fa'kro'mi]: Perhaps it only became ill. Perhaps their fungus is not the proper sort to nourish one of us. Perhaps the injury to its leg festered.

[Mo'gri'ta'tu]: Perhaps they killed it willfully and only

28

tricked it into believing they were kind.

[Kwi'ga'ga'tei, impatiently]: Indeed, that would be your sort of thinking, Mo'gri'ta'tu.

[A tense stillness]

[Hi'ta'fu, gloomily]: Gli'tha'mu was killed. Where is its word sending?

[Kwi'ga'ga'tei]: Gli'tha'mu undoubtedly attacked them; it was proper that it should have defended its friend and they undoubtedly defended themselves against it. It is likely that their Warriors have superior weapons, against which Gli'tha'mu could not prevail. I believe that they took its body away with them. In any case, they did not have its soul to bring back to speak to us.

[Hi'ta'fu]: What do we do, then? The Holy One is half-hysterical. Sei'o'na'sha'ma is worse than useless. I know only fighting, not these Alate subtleties.

[Lo'lo'pai]: The only course is to destroy these flying monsters immediately!

[Ki'shto'ba]: Has none of you paid any heed to Holy Kwi'ga'ga'tei's words? She has proclaimed that we should welcome these strange visitors! I am for that! I am a Warrior, invincible on the field of battle ...

[Hi'ta'fu emits imprecations and dances but is ignored]

[Ki'shto'ba]: ... but I do not believe in meaningless slaughter! I believe in trying the way of peace before the way of war. I challenged the Strange Ones and they had an answer – they answered like Alates, with words, not weapons. Attend to the counsel of your Seer!

[No'kri]: Then, Holy Kwi'ga'ga'tei, what course should we take?

[Kwi'ga'ga'tei]: We will observe and we will wait for an opportunity. And when it comes – and we will know it when it comes – I myself will go to them, with the Champion at my side to keep them humble, and I will seek to welcome them to the fortress of Lo'ro'ra.

[Mo'gri'ta'tu]: With those dangerous superior weapons, perhaps even the invincible Huge-Head will not be enough to preserve your life, great Seer.

[Kwi'ga'ga'tei]: Then you who remain will know that I was wrong, Chamberlain. I do not ask any other citizen of Lo'ro'ra to risk itself. I will take my death when it comes. I can think of some deaths that would appeal to me far less than one attended by this Comforter.

*   *   *

The buzzer went off and Kaitrin rolled over to find the bed empty beside her. "Griff," she said sleepily, "aren't you ever coming to bed?"

His soft laugh made her open her eyes. He was standing beside her, fully dressed.

"Such a little sleepy head," he said. "I was in bed and out of it whilst you slept. It's time to get up again."

"My heavens!" Kaitrin bounded up. "I can't believe it! I missed the whole night! Only it's not night! It's still day, isn't it? The same damn day! The gods certainly made a mistake when they set up this planet, Griffen! Do you suppose the shower's available?"

When she came back, he followed her into their compartment and she fired questions at him as she hastily dressed and braided her hair. No, there had been no activity in the termitarium except for the movements of the guard and an occasional alate's head peeping out to observe. Yes, sonic showers were not at all satisfying – they sanitized your skin but produced not the least feeling of refreshment. Yes, it was good she had deciphered a few more words of the Shshi language. No, Goliath had not been seen again – just as well, Griffen opined. And it was indeed hot as plasma in the flyer. The external temperature was about 33° C. They were exhausting energy cells faster than anticipated; Will was asking the *Featherlight* to send along a solar generator when the *Brozzae* came ...

Kaitrin watched him in the mirror as she stuck pins in her head. She thought he still seemed abstracted.

"Kait," he said, "I'm sorry about earlier."

"Again? I told you ... "

"No, I mean about doubting that your approach was correct. This anthropology thing – it's new to me, you know. I've never really given a lot of thought to the significance of first contacts."

"It's your expedition, Griff," she said. "After the way Towsen got attacked, you only want to keep your crew safe."

"You know it isn't only that."

Kaitrin went over to him and took his hand. "There's nothing to fret about – it all ended fine, better than anybody could have expected. And I'm sorry, too, that I sort of snapped at you about the pistol. Now! We've both apologized quite enough! Let's get something to eat!"

Over scrambled reconstituted eggs, cracker bread, and tinned apricots, Will looked from Kaitrin to Griffen and said, "So now what?"

"Well ... " Kaitrin hesitated, then plunged ahead. "We issue an invitation – set up a table under the wing of the flyer. You may have noted I'm wearing my field shorts and a sleeveless shirt – ready for the heat! Say, does this planet have mosquitoes?"

"We took some specimens of gnatlike blood-suckers," said Gwidian, "but perhaps they won't relish mammalian hosts. And it's the dry season."

"We will set up repellent barrier, just the same," said Trea. "Exotic parasites can be no fun. Might like bird blood, Professor," she added with a twinkle of mischief.

Tió'otu chirruped nervously.

Gwidian added, "We also took a specimen of a four-centimeter, aggressively carnivorous *Xenoapocrita* – a wasp – with a venomous stinger. It may be able to endure the dry season without estivating."

"But we made antitoxin for that," said Trea, "in case."

"Oh, dear," said Kaitrin. "Anyway, my idea was, set up the table in the shade of the wing – if the alates can't stand too much sun, that might seem more inviting – and go out there and sit and wait with our equipment at the ready. If they want to approach us, we'll be available – we won't venture into their territory on our own initiative. I really do agree with you, Griff – that would be highly unsafe."

"Yes," said A'a'ma, "an uninformed, physically powerful ILF can be very dangerous when it is frightened. But this plan is reasonable."

"I counsel that we should never bring them inside flyer," said Trea. "Make more likely we give them XTIS."

"We don't all need to go out," said Kaitrin. "I'll go, and Luku, of course. Griffen?"

"If you're going out," he said, "I will go as well."

"Julian and I will provide security," said Arti, "just in case."

"I'd like to go," said Will. "See these creatures close up."

"I will stay in," said A'a'ma. "There are enough odd smells and sights to frighten them without exposing them right off to a giant bird."

"Agree," said Trea. "Sev and I will also not go. Pozú have especially strange monotreme pheromones. Let them get used to humans and Luku first."

So they did that. Kaitrin and Luku sat in camp chairs at the folding table, studying the conundrum of the Challenge Speech and drinking water and sweating in the late afternoon heat. Will, Arti, and Julian played games on hand devices as they lounged on the ramp. The remote cams were ready to record everything that happened and convey it to those inside the *Durga*.

Then from the top of the ramp, A'a'ma gave a whistle. "Look! The main entrance!"

Gwidian emerged immediately and came down to stand behind Kaitrin. The security people rose and drew their weapons. They had all agreed that since the Shshi had no idea what pistols were, the sight of them would not frighten their guests.

"Oh, my god," whispered Kaitrin.

A small group had emerged from the mound and was moving hesitantly across the courtyard. It consisted of a contingent of five nasute isopteroids surrounding two other figures.

One was an alate, possibly the one who had suffered the seizure in the morning sunlight.

The other was the giant whom Kaitrin had named "Ki'shto'ba."

Chapter 4

Shut, too, in a tower of words, I mark
On the horizon walking like the trees
The wordy shapes of women ...
 – *from* Dylan Thomas, *Especially When the*
October Wind

"All of you, sit down," said Kaitrin. "Why am I whispering? – they can't hear us. But, Griff, you're twice as big as they are – you too, Will. Somehow in the enviro cube Ti'shra seemed larger. Sit down so we won't seem to be exhibiting threat postures."

"God," said Gwidian. "Their biomechanics – the way they move their legs – it's identical to that of an ordinary-sized insect."

The small group of Shshi had stopped about twenty paces away. Around the alate and the giant the nasutes had formed a circle, with their leader directly in front.

"Transmissions are coming," said Luku.

After a tense moment, the soldiers sidestepped and opened into a semicircle, still at twenty paces. The principals approached tentatively, the alate stopping only an arm's length away from the edge of the table. To everyone's relief, the giant remained slightly behind the alate. Its huge head was lowered like an insectile bull; its bald, eyeless cranium confronted them disconcertingly, the antennae twitching.

The alate's eyes were ten centimeters across, dominating the face between the antennae. Below them was an assemblage of

33

mouthparts, with clearly distinguishable mandibles and a pair of quivering segmented palps covered with soft bristles. The alate stood regarding them, tilting its head slightly from one side to the other as if puzzled.

"Those eyes," whispered Gwidian. "A dragonfly's may have as much as 30,000 facets, but this … There may be hundreds of thousands here, the size of pinpoints."

"Pinpoint gems," said Luku in awe.

"What are those pale bumps above the eyes?" asked Kaitrin.

"Undoubtedly ocelli – simple eyes," said Gwidian. "They seem vestigial."

The alate's antennae were pointed in different directions, one extended toward its companion's equally stiffened one, the other directed toward the strangers.

"They talk to each other," said Luku. "I cannot receive when they do not speak directly toward us."

"Apparently each antenna can send and receive individually," said Gwidian.

Groping for some gesture to initiate the dialogue, Kaitrin spread her arms wide in a sign of openness and welcome that most ILFs in the universe would likely understand. As she did so, the alate jumped back slightly. The giant named Ki'shto'ba sensed its alarm and bobbed its head up and down in warning. Gwidian's breath hissed and the security people brought up their pistols. But Kaitrin sat still, her arms stretched out.

The alate edged forward and brought its mouthparts close to her right hand, tickling the fingers with its hairy palps. Kaitrin wiggled her fingers gently. The alate flinched a little, then continued to investigate, probing and tasting.

"Just like Ti'shra," breathed Kaitrin. "Don't pull back on me, Griff. I'm in no danger."

The alate released her hand and she drew it away moist with the creature's saliva. Then Kaitrin raised her left hand slowly and touched the tip of the alate's right antenna with the tip of her finger. Simultaneously she keyed a word on the emitter.

The emitter projected three biopulses. *vei'ga'zi*|.

The alate and the giant both jumped. The alate lowered its head and directed its gaze at the emitter.

"Incredible. It seems it can focus its vision on near objects," said Gwidian.

Kaitrin pointed toward the Shi's antenna, which had twitched out of reach. Again she activated the emitter. *vei'ga'zi*|.

The alate continued to gaze at the box, communicating sidelong with its companion.

Kaitrin keyed in some words, gesturing at the Shi's antennae. *shvei'ga'zi*| *ki'bei*| || "Your antennae." Then she held up the emitter. *shvei'ga'zi*| *ki'sho*| || "My antennae."

In a moment the alate's head came up. It quivered, leaned forward, prodded the emitter case with its mandibles, turned it over, stared at the display screen. Kaitrin prayed that it would not fling it on the ground or crush it.

Instead, it spoke for a moment to its companion, then turned back to Kaitrin.

"It's saying one of Ti'shra's words!" cried Luku excitedly.

Kaitrin looked at the screen. The matrix was displaying, *¿bei'...? ru'zei*| ||

"Oh!" said Kaitrin. "That must be 'Are you?' Is the waveform similar to *sho*|? – yes, I see it is. Luku, enter *bei'sha*|. It's asking, 'Are you *ru'zei*|?' But we never figured out what *ru'zei*| meant. Ti'shra said, 'Tell them in Lo'ro'ra that Ti'shra died ... it had *ru'zei*| who was not un-something.' Oh, I hope I was wrong earlier! I hope *ru'zei*| isn't 'murderer'!"

The alate was regarding the box, obviously understanding that the answer would come out of it. Quickly Kaitrin keyed in, *sho'laio*| ⇃↾ *preivo*| ⥿ *ru'zei*| ||

The alate danced from side to side, seeming mightily perplexed. It communicated some more with the giant.

Kaitrin tried a different ploy. *i'i*| *gan'zi*| *ki*| *ti'shra'ze*| || "In Ti'shra's speaking." *sho'preivo*| ⥿ *shvei'ga'zi*| || *sho'preivo*| *wei*| ⥿ *ru'zei*| || "I know 'antennae.' I do not know *ru'zei*|."

Motionless, the alate regarded her. Then it gave a short leap, as if the light had dawned, and engaged Ki'shto'ba in a lengthy conversation. Finally it turned to Kaitrin, saying a number of things that she could not decipher. She in turn sat perplexed, then keyed in, *sho'preivo*| *wei*| || *sho'laio*| ⇃↾ *preivo*| || *¡galto*|*!* ⥿ *shgan'zi*| *ya*| *sho'a*| || "I do not know. I want to know. Tell me things that are spoken."

Again the alate and its companion fired words at each other.

And Kaitrin ventured to say, *sho'laio| ↲↑ preivo| Ϛ loi'zi| ki'bei| ||* "I want to know your name."

The answer appeared immediately on Luku's receiver. *>| sho| Ϛ na| kwi'ga'ga'... 'ze| ... 'zei| ...| ... 'zei| lo'ro'ra'mik ...| || ¡gano|! Ϛ loi'zi| ki'bei| ya| sho'a| ||* "Oh, no, that's impossible!" said Kaitrin.

"We do not have syllables for all of those words," said Luku.

"That's not the problem – we can assign them later," said Kaitrin. "What bothers me is, it asked for my name. And there is no way to render my name in biopulses."

Quickly, hoping she was not committing too many gaffes, she entered, *sho'taio| wei| Ϛ loi'zi| i'i| shgan'zi| ki| shshi'zei| ||* "I do not have a name in the spoken things of the Shshi."

This elicited a remarkable reaction. Both Shshi hopped and skittered about. On the periphery the nasutes came to attention and advanced a step.

But Ki'shto'ba waved them off and they retreated. The alate was quivering like a *toviz* string. It said something that ended with *tu| bei'sha| Ϛ ta'sho'zei| ||*

Kaitrin stared at the screen. "*ta'sho'zei|* – that's the female marker plus 'being.' Something, then 'that you are a female being.' Why would it care that I'm female? Good grief, I don't know how to say 'yes'!"

She pointed to herself and transmitted, *sho| Ϛ ta'sho'zei| || ¿bei'sha|?||* "I am female. Are you?"

Again, both Shshi seemed quite agitated. The alate said, ... *sho| Ϛ ta'sho'zei| ja| sho| wei| Ϛ wei'loi'zei| ||*

"What did it say?" said Luku excitedly.

"I think that first waveform must be *yes.* Key in *av|* for *yes,* Luku," said Kaitrin. "She is female and ... Oh! *ja* – we could never figure that one out – I believe it means 'but.' 'I am female, but I am not ... unnamed one? One without a name?' Why is that important?"

Then the alate repeated, *¿bei'sha|? Ϛ ru'zei| ||*

"*¡Ay de mí!*" sighed Kaitrin. *sho'preivo| wei| Ϛ gan'zi| ru'zei| ||* "I do not know the spoken thing *ru'zei|.*"

But the alate did not seem ready to give up. *ti'shra'ze| ⇄ fa'ganot| Ϛ tu| fa'tait| Ϛ ru'zei| ||* "Ti'shra said that it had *ru'zei|.*" Then came a string of words of which Kaitrin could decipher only pronouns, along with "We want to know," "it died," and two in-stances of the word for "spoken thing."

Gwidian, who had sat spellbound and ignored for some time, said suddenly, "Show it the vid of you and Ti'shra."

"Oh, I'm not sure we're ready for that, Griff," said Kaitrin.

"If it can connect the events on the vid with the words, maybe it will become clearer."

"Maybe, but she doesn't know what a vid is. We don't know whether these creatures have any kind of visual graphics. Besides, we didn't bring out the equipment for that today."

The alate was regarding both of them closely, observing the movements of their mouths. Then she stared at Gwidian and said, *bei'sha| wei| ϑ ta'sho'zei| ||*

Kaitrin gave a tiny giggle. "She said, 'You are not female.'"

Gwidian smiled tightly.

The alate said, *bei'sha| ϑ ma'sho'zei| || ¿bei'sha|? ϑ na'sha'ma| || ¿bei'sha|? ϑ na'sha'ma| ki'ta| ||*

Kaitrin's head was beginning to swim. She glared at Luku's monitor. "You are *ma'* ... From this context, that must mean 'male.' Then she said a word that was in the Challenge Speech – *na'sha'ma|* – but I didn't know what it meant. 'Are you *na'sha'ma|*?' And then *ki'ta|. ta* is the feminine sign – *ki'ta|* has to mean 'of her.' Oh, Griff, I think – *na'sha'ma|* must be ...   I think she's asking if you are my mate!"

"I didn't know it was so obvious," he said with forced light-ness. "These creatures must be more aware of sexual differences than I ... "

Av| replied Kaitrin.

Then an astonishing thing occurred. After displaying in-creased agitation, both the alate and the giant lowered their bodies and depressed their heads, rubbing their mouthparts in the dirt. A flick of the antennae apparently conveyed instructions to the nasute soldiers, for they began to exhibit similar submissive behavior.

Gwidian said, "I would swear that they're worshiping you, Kaitrin."

The alate said something of which Kaitrin could comprehend only, *na'ta'zei| bei'sha| ϑ ma'na'ta|>|| shsho'preivot| wei| ||*

"Damn!" said Kaitrin. "Ti'shra said, '*na'ta'zei|* – the Queen – is A'kha'ma'na'ta.' And now this creature is addressing me as

'Queen,' unless I've got the meaning wrong – and then she said, 'You are *ma'na'ta|*,' which is a portion of the Queen's name, and she added, 'We did not know.' What kind of impression have I given? This is all wrong! This is dreadful!'"

*   *   *

[Kwi'ga'ga'tei and Ki'shto'ba, surrounded by Sa'ti'a'i'a and its contingent, nervously approach the Strange Ones]

[Kwi'ga'ga'tei]: Chief, deploy your Warriors at single length intervals and remain at this distance.

[The Nasutes comply. Kwi'ga'ga'tei and the Huge-Head approach the place where the Strange Ones wait]

[Ki'shto'ba]: What disturbing odors! I have never taken anything like them! And I smell bird, moreover.

[Kwi'ga'ga'tei]: As do I – and I thought I glimpsed a large creature with feathers just as we were emerging from the fortress. The side of the flying egg is open, and I think I see other forms within it. They seem to use the egg as a shelter. The bird must lurk there.

[Ki'shto'ba]: Please, Seer, describe these creatures for me. I detect both male and female pheromones, but nothing sexless. That is strange, unless they are all Alates, and even if that were so, the smell is unsettlingly potent.

[Kwi'ga'ga'tei]: They certainly have no wings. Three of them crouch upon objects that I cannot see clearly, because they are behind a platform – a defensive barrier, perhaps. Three others are sitting on a ramp that leads into the egg's orifice. They are certainly the most grotesque creatures I have ever seen! And it is no wonder they cannot speak, for they are without antennae, even as birds and reptiles are. And like those same birds and reptiles, they have only four limbs. However, their bellies double forward in the middle, so they are actually sitting on their backs – it looks excruciatingly painful! Their rear legs grow from their posteriors. You do well to seem perplexed – I can make no sense of it! Their forelimbs end not in claws but in five jointed palps, and their bodies are covered over with a peculiar integument or perhaps

38

matted fibers of some kind. I wonder if that is a natural growth or if it is some disease.

[Ki'shto'ba]: What are their heads like?

[Kwi'ga'ga'tei]: Small for such large creatures, and covered partly with a growth like the fuzz mold that forms on diseased fungus, only coarser and in varying colors. Of those behind the platform, one has short, black fuzz, while another's is tan and tangled in a lump against its head. But the third creature – *da'pri'saia| ma'na'ta|>* – has that sort of growth all over its body, gray in color except for white around its head, and it has a long, flexible fifth limb with stripes on it that extends from its posterior. Perhaps that one has an antenna after all.

But to return to the heads – they are extraordinarily strange! They are like that globe fruit that grows upon the ground, and in the center of the side that is free of fuzz is a knob with two holes in it and above it two pits that hold colored balls. Those must be eyes – they do resemble the eyes of lizards and birds. They roll about constantly in the pits while a flap at the top flicks up and down. It is almost nauseating to watch! Then, below the knob is a small, fleshy orifice. That must be the mouth – it is somewhat similar to a lizard's mouth, except not so threatening because it does not project from the head and the teeth within it are blunt and square. The mouthparts of all of them move frequently, to no purpose that I can see – they are not eating anything – and there are no palps anywhere on the head, nor any mandibles. But the mold-covered one looks different – it has a somewhat reptilian snout with sharper teeth in it and two soft-looking projections on the upper sides of the head with tufts of fuzz attached to them. The function of those mystifies me – they are constantly turning to and fro, as one of your people might wag its cerci, Ki'shto'ba!

[Ki'shto'ba]: An antenna on its posterior and tails on the head! Amazing!

[Kwi'ga'ga'tei]: But that one's eyes! Bulbous and very large – actually more like ours, except that they are not faceted or colored but smooth and shiny black all over!

[Ki'shto'ba]: I am really glad I have no eyes, Kwi'ga'ga'tei! If I am to fight these bizarre creatures, it is better that I cannot see them!

[The Strange One with the lump of matted fuzz on its head spreads its forelimbs apart, and Kwi'ga'ga'tei jumps. Ki'shto'ba, sensing the Seer's alarm, makes a small threat gesture]

[Kwi'ga'ga'tei]: Be calm, Huge-Head! I sense no danger. I think it invites me to investigate it. I will answer so ...

[The Seer touches the Strange One's forelimb palps with her own mouth-palps. The taste is salty and disturbing. Then the Strange One touches the tip of the Seer's antenna with the tip of its palp. At the same time, a word-sending is received. *Antenna*]

[Both Shshi jump]

[Ki'shto'ba]: Who said that? Who is here? Is it Ti'shra?

[Kwi'ga'ga'tei]: I do not understand. This sending seems to have come from a box.

[Ki'shto'ba]: A box?

[Kwi'ga'ga'tei]: The creature points toward my antenna and ... there, again ... the box says, *antenna*.

[The Strange One indicates Kwi'ga'ga'tei's antenna. The box says, *Your antennae*. Then the Strange One holds up the box and the box says, *My antennae*]

[Kwi'ga'ga'tei]: Can it be ... ?

[She quivers, stretches toward the surface of the platform, prods the box, turning it about]

[Kwi'ga'ga'tei]: Somehow its antennae are in a magic box. It is not something that grows naturally upon a creature's body. It is something made, like a bucket or a bowl. It is hard and black, with wing-lights flashing in patterns on one side.

[Ki'shto'ba]: This grows strange beyond the point of being credible! Our associates inside the fortress will never believe it!

[Kwi'ga'ga'tei]: Perhaps it will understand. I will ask it something. I will ask: "Are you the Comforter?"

[The Magic Box]: *I want to know the Comforter.*

[Kwi'ga'ga'tei]: More puzzling yet. Are you receiving?

[Ki'shto'ba]: I am receiving.

[Kwi'ga'ga'tei]: Why would it ask to know the Comforter? I thought perhaps it *was* the Comforter. Does it, too, search for Tish'ra's Comforter?

[The Magic Box]: *Of the speaking of Ti'shra. I know antennae. I do not know Comforter.*

[Kwi'ga'ga'tei thinks deeply for a moment. Then she leaps in the air]

[Kwi'ga'ga'tei]: Ki'shto'ba, I believe I understand! It is not the Comforter itself this one wants to know, but the meaning of the word *ru'zei|*. This one has studied the words of Ti'shra, which they have magically imprisoned in this made thing as we would keep a memory in our minds. And they can make it repeat what it remembers even as we can speak words that are in our memories. This Strange One has puzzled out the meaning of some of the words but not of others. I think it is not true that these creatures have no speech. They have only a different language. It is like the Nasutes, who cannot speak to us until we teach them our words. Even you, Huge-Head, being of the race of Shshi from To'wak, do not form the word-sendings exactly the way the Shshi of Lo'ro'ra do. And these beings do not even have the organs of speech – they have to make magic antennae. But they may have some other way to talk among themselves. Perhaps the eyes or the mouthparts convey their speech; both move constantly.

[Ki'shto'ba]: This is a very great wonder. No one but you, Holy Seer, could have learned to understand it. I am glad it is you who were commanded to teach them, and not I.

[Kwi'ga'ga'tei]: I will speak to it of this and see if it can understand.

Strange One, this magic box that speaks to us is a wonder. We want to learn more of your speech and we would willingly teach you more of ours. In fact, I have been commanded to teach you how to speak.

[The Strange One does not reply instantly, then says]: *I do not know. I want to know. Tell me spoken things.*

41

[Ki'shto'ba]: It does not use the word *shgan'zi|* in a way familiar to me. There is no such thing as more than one of "speech." Should it not say, "Tell me words?"

[Kwi'ga'ga'tei]: Perhaps it uses *shgan'zi|* because it knows that word and does not know *vei'zi|*. In the speaking Ti'shra sent back to us, it did not use the word *vei'zi|*.

[The Strange One]: *I want to know your name.*

[Kwi'ga'ga'tei]: Ah! I am Holy Kwi'ga'ga'tei, Priest and Seer of Lo'ro'ra. Speak your name to me!

[After some agitation, the Strange One replies]: *I do not have a name in the spoken things of the Shshi.*

[Kwi'ga'ga'tei and the Huge-Head jump and skitter to and fro in alarm. The Nasutes come to attention. The Seer quivers]

[Kwi'ga'ga'tei]: No name! There is only one speaking being that I have ever learned of that has no name. [To the Strange One, anxiously] I sense that you are a female.

[The Strange One, bobbing the head]: *I am a female. Are you?*

[Kwi'ga'ga'tei]: Yes, I am a female, but I am not the Nameless One. [Then, after watching the seeming perplexity of the Strange One]: Are you the Comforter?

[The Strange One, repeating]: *I do not know the spoken thing "Comforter."*

[Kwi'ga'ga'tei]: This is most frustrating, Ki'shto'ba, but it is too important for me to concede defeat. If this one is somehow associated with, or was sent by, the Nameless One …

[Ki'shto'ba]: Was not the egg supposed to bear a name of the Nameless?

[Kwi'ga'ga'tei]: I do not even want to think about that Seeing at the moment! [To the Strange One]: Ti'shra said that it had a Comforter. I need to understand if you are that one. We want to know how it died … how it received comfort … what became of its body … how you preserved its speech and brought that speech back to us.

[The Strange One with the black mold on its head stirs, attracts attention to itself. The female Strange One turns to it. Kwi'ga'ga'tei observes their mouthparts' alternating movements]

[Kwi'ga'ga'tei, to the black-headed one]: You are not a female. You are a male. Are you a King? Are you her King?

[After more mouth movements, the female Strange One speaks]: *Yes.*

[Kwi'ga'ga'tei]: Highest-Mother-Who-Has-No-Name! They are progenitors! We have been speaking to the Holy One and King of these Strange Ones and did not know it!

[Both Shshi abase, rub their mouthparts in the dirt. Ki'shto'ba reverses its antennae and instructs the Nasutes to do likewise]

[Kwi'ga'ga'tei, to the Strange One]: Holy One, you are Mother. We did not know. Forgive us – tell us how we may serve you.

*   *   *

Desperately Kaitrin searched her minuscule vocabulary for some way to counter this false impression that she had managed to convey.

Gwidian was saying unsteadily, "I concede I've been quite wrong. They must have a single breeding pair and they must worship them. From discovering that you and I are a breeding pair, they've gotten the idea that we should be worshiped. What an irony!"

The Shshi had stopped rubbing their mouths in the dirt, but they remained with their heads abased. Kaitrin could say only, *wei| wei| ||*, hoping it meant "no" as well as "not."

Apparently it did, because the Shshi raised their heads.

"If I could only say," said Kaitrin, "'You're making a mistake. I'm not some kind of god. You must not worship me. I want to be your friend.'" Then she was struck by something. "'Tell them that Ti'shra died ... but it had a – friend? ... that was not – harmful?'"

"Perhaps 'was not evil,'" said Luku. "You Earthers make good and evil to be opposites."

"Oh! Then *thel|* would be 'good'! Luku, it pays to have everybody helping on this sort of thing! Do I dare think that *ru'zei|* is 'friend'?" To the waiting Shshi she said, *sho|* ↳ *ru'zei| ki'shbei| || sho'laio|* ↳ *tu| bei'shsha|* ↳ *shru'zei| ki'sho| || shsho|* ↳ *shru'zei| || fash|↪ thel| ||*

Kaitrin believed she was saying, "I am your friend. I want you to be my friends. We are friends. It is good."

*   *   *

[Kwi'ga'ga'tei and Ki'shto'ba receive the word-sending]

I am your Comforter. I want you to be my Comforters. We are Comforters. It is good.

[Kwi'ga'ga'tei]: Now she believes she has learned the meaning of the word *ru'zei|,* but she uses it in such an awkward way that I do not think she fully understands even yet. And she says *fash|↪ thel| ||* as if she were speaking of a person. Perhaps she speaks of Ti'shra ... But that would be nonsensical. I think she means to say *fa'she|↪ thel| ||,* speaking generally.

[Ki'shto'ba]: But she has learned that *ru'zei|* is a good thing. Perhaps she thinks it means 'friend.'

[Kwi'ga'ga'tei]: You may very well be right! If you are ... Ki'shto'ba, this is a *ma'na'ta|.* That may not mean the same thing for these Strange Ones as for us, but she is *ma'na'ta|,* nevertheless, and so a Holy One. And I believe that, in spite of her repellent form, she is quite intelligent. There is much here, much to learn and teach. But I think we have done all we can do for the moment. Holy One, I have grown tired. I must go away now, but I will come back. Show me the proper time and I will come back.

[The Shshi abase their heads once more, turn, and scuttle away across the courtyard with the Nasute Warriors closing ranks behind them]

Chapter 5

You've discovered so many bits, with your clever eyes,
And I'm a kaleidoscope
That you shake and shake, and yet it won't come to
     your mind.
Now stop carping at me ...
                    – *from* D. H. Lawrence, *A Spiritual Woman*

When Kaitrin and the others entered the flyer, they found Trea and Sev laughing their chattering little laugh at the expense of Prf. A'a'ma, who was hopping around in a state of extreme agitation.

"He goes out with you the next time," said Trea, "or he will pluck all his feathers, Kaitrin! He wanted so bad to go out."

"I am a xenoanthropologist," twittered Tió'otu. "I will take my chances that they will eat me or that I will scare them."

"But you observed it all, didn't you?" asked Kaitrin. "On the remote feed?"

"Yes, but it is not the same! I kept thinking of approaches you might take! *≠Khepsá·di nei'u]* Frustration!"

"I bungled it, Tió'otu. I unintentionally made them think I'm some kind of god!"

"Isn't she?" said Gwidian.

Kaitrin favored him with an exasperated grimace, but A'a'ma said, "Sometimes things like that happen. When I was young, my very first expedition was to a planet far on the other side of

45

Krisí'i'aid where we made first contact with a mammalian people called the Fó'o-at-zok. Now it so happened that the gods of those pre-tech ILFs were all feathered entities! You have never seen anyone feted and honored and fed and petted the way we were! It was embarrassing, but we could do nothing about it. We finally had to leave; it was impossible to establish a normal relationship. The Krisí'i'aidá never went back there again."

"¡*Dios mío!*" said Kaitrin. "I wonder what they thought afterward. Probably that their gods had abandoned them. You high-tech Birds probably wrecked their culture!"

As A'a'ma chirruped imprecations, Luku said, "Come on, Kaitrin! Let us start transcribing the conversation – finding new words!"

"Luku, we have got to finish that vocal interface so I can speak the phonemes and won't have to be fiddling with a touchpad all the time."

"What amazes me," said A'a'ma, "is that she understood about the emitter so quickly and accepted it as being your antennae."

"She's very intelligent for something that looks like a big, bristly bug," said Kaitrin with a snicker.

"I was also amazed," said A'a'ma, "at how much you could communicate with such a limited vocabulary. Do you really think *ru'zei*| is 'friend'?"

"I'm not sure, but my informant seemed to accept it. I wish I could have expressed concern about her health. She seemed in such bad shape earlier."

"We must work out her name," said Luku, "so you can address her in proper way."

"Kaitrin, there must be some way you can tell them your name," said Will Ayland.

"But there isn't," said Kaitrin. "Think about it – the correlation goes only one way. This language has no phonemes – no sound patterns – of its own; those exist only in the utilitarian fiction I've devised. Phonemes can be arbitrarily assigned to spectrographic patterns, but I can't reverse the process and transcribe Inj sounds into signals that would mean anything to them."

"Does 'Kaitrin' have meaning?" asked Trea. "Maybe after you learn more words, some will mean the same as your name."

"Well, it's a variant of the Inglish 'Katherine,' which comes from the name of an ancient religious martyr; according to her myth they tried to break her on some kind of torture wheel and the wheel flew apart, so they proceeded to behead her. The word itself derives from old Griek and means 'pure' or 'unsullied' – appropriate, since the girl was a redoubtable virgin." Kaitrin laughed. "I can't find much there to build on – certainly doesn't capture *my* essence! And even if I could learn a Shshi match for 'pure' or 'untouched,' that might just play into the god thing! And as for 'Oliva' – olives are a little scarce in these parts! I guess I could call myself 'Little Green Fruit'!"

"Just pick a word you like and tell them to call you that," said Gwidian.

"That seems awfully facile," said Kaitrin, "and a little dishonest."

"Let them give name to you," said Sev. "When you can, say to them, 'Since I have no name in your language, you give me name.'"

As Kaitrin pondered this possibility, Prf. A'a'ma said, "What bothers me most is the way they reacted when they learned you were nameless. It obviously implied something significant to them. Names can be a tricky business for the scientifically primitive mind."

"I know," said Kaitrin more soberly. "I must be sure to let them know that I do have a name in my own tongue. If I ever figure out how to say it. Let's see, 'I have words that are not your words.' *sho'taio| ᴦ shgan'zi| vi| shfash| wei| ᴦ shgan'zi| ki'bei| ||* I wonder if *gan'zi|* really is 'word' – I made it on analogy, but it doesn't feel right. And I don't like that verb form *shfash|*, either. The conjugation of 'to be' seems to be quite irregular, as in most languages … "

As she and Luku went off to the research bay to begin their analysis, Arti looked at the others and said, "You'd think she'd been speaking this language her whole life, but she's making it all up herself, out of nothing. That woman is remarkable."

"A goddess, I avow," said Gwidian with half-serious whimsy.

Kaitrin, Luku, and Tió'otu put their heads together over the name of the alate.   *>| sho| ᴦ na| kwi'ga'ga ...'ze| ...'zei| ...| ...'zei| lo'ro'ra'mik ...| ||*   "See that little blip at the beginning of

47

the sentence?" said Kaitrin. "It has the qualities of a link, but it's not a link. It occurs in the Challenge Speech, four times at the ends of sentences and once in the middle. And now here at the beginning, as well as at the end of that other sentence, *na'ta'zei| bei'sha| ⅁ ma'na'ta|>||* I think it's probably something like an exclamation point, but it could also serve as a word – maybe an interjection like 'ah!' or 'hey!' – especially in the initial position."

"It makes sense," said Luku, "that they want to express when they are excited."

"I want to skip ahead to the word *lo'ro'ra'mik|* … " said Kaitrin. "I think it means 'of Lo'ro'ra.' *-mik* may be a special genitive inflection used in place names. It appears two other times in the Challenge Speech; the most obvious is *shsho| ⅁ shshi'zei| lo'ro'ra'mik| ||* – 'We are the Shshi of Lo'ro'ra.' And our Goliath says, *sho| ⅁ ki'shto'ba'ze| no'no| um'zi| to'wak'mik| ||* – 'I am Ki'shto'ba' – something-something – 'of To'wak.'"

"Then that creature must come from a different termitarium," interjected Tió'otu. "That shouldn't surprise anyone, given its different appearance."

"The word *na|*," said Kaitrin, "is an element of *na'ta'zei|*, which I've taken to be 'Queen,' but it also turns up in that rather confusing word *ma'na'ta|* and in *na'sha'ma|* – the word for 'male mate.' You know, that could mean 'King'! In the Challenge Speech, there's the phrase *na'ta'zei| u| na'sha'ma| lo'ro'ra'mik| ||* If *u|* were 'and,' the phrase would then be 'Queen and King of Lo'ro'ra'!

"But back to *na|* … Our alate places that unit before her name as a discrete word; maybe it's a title or an honorific, like 'honorable' or 'distinguished.' That would fit with its inclusion in the words 'Queen' and 'King,' and also in *ma'na'ta|* … but what is *ma'na'ta|*? You know, maybe *ma'na'ta|* is 'Queen' and *na'ta'zei|* is some kind of title, like 'Her Majesty'! Then Ti'shra said, 'Her Majesty is A'kha-Queen' – or maybe it's inverted and we should say 'Queen A'kha.'" Kaitrin hooted. "This is getting screwier and screwier! Let's get back to the alate's name."

"It begins *kwi|*," said Luku, "same as that *kwi'il|* and *kwi'sho'zei|* that you have never figured out."

"I'll ask our alate in the next go-round: *sho'laio| ♫ preivo| ⅁ kwi|*," said Kaitrin. "Then *ga'ga|* – a reduplication of the base waveform of *gano|* and *galto|*. That's interesting. And I'm going to randomly assign *tei|* to the last syllable. 'Kwi'ga'ga'tei,' plus a personal noun, plus 'and,' plus another personal noun, plus 'of Lo'ro'ra.'

"Let's call the first noun *noi'zei|*. The second one is based on the *tei|* morpheme that appears in the alate's name. So we have *sho| ᘜ na| kwi'ga'ga'tei'ze| noi'zei| u| tei'zei| lo'ro'ra'mik| ||* 'I am the honorable Kwi'ga'ga'tei of Lo'ro'ra,' with her titles stuck in the middle there. I think our alate is quite an important person – *noi'zei|* and *tei'zei|* could mean 'priest,' 'shaman' ... maybe even 'ruler,' 'leader,' 'prime minister,' 'chief potentate' ... "

And so the study continued. It began to get dark outside, but the passionate linguists failed to notice. In the galley, Will stood looking at the cooking roster.

"It's Kaitrin's turn to make supper," he announced.

"You'll never pry her loose," said Gwidian. "I'll prepare it."

"That's not necessary, Professor," said Julian. "Arti and I can do it, or anyone."

"Nonsense," said Gwidian. "I often cook for myself. I think I can handle it."

After a while, Kaitrin looked up to see sitting at her elbow a tray of pasta with a sauce of tomatoes and rehydrated vegetables and a salad of chopped apples and *♪sf ^h·agu*, a large seed native to Krisí'i'aid. There was also a cup of soymilk and a packet of chocolate cookies.

"Is it time for supper?" she called out. "Who did this? – it looks pretty good. Mmm, tastes halfway decent, too."

Arti stuck her head into the research bay. "Prf. Gwidian did it. It was supposed to be your time to cook."

"It was? Oh ¡por piedad! It was! Griffen!" She got up and found him at the table in the common room with his own tray and a cup of tea brewed out of his precious store. She gave him a hug. "Thanks so much! You've got another talent I didn't know about!"

He returned her hug. "Actually, Luku provided a pinch of one of her hot spices for the tomato sauce and Arti suggested the Krisiad nuts, but I invented the salad dressing. It's dehydrated sour cream stirred up with a little sugar and nutmeg."

"It's scrumptious! And I promise, I'll do your shift next

time!"

"Don't make promises you don't plan to keep," he said with his light laugh.

"I'll expect you to cook dinner all the time when we get home to Earth."

"Home. Yes," he said. "I've found women tend to appreciate a man who's willing to tackle food preparation occasionally."

She laughed and tousled his hair, then ran to fetch her tray and sat down beside him. "I can use a little break. Isn't all this the most glorious thing that you've ever experienced?"

"Maybe not the most glorious, but it's definitely significant," he said.

"We've been working on Kwi'ga'ga'tei's final words. She addressed me as *na'ta'zei|* again. But I've about decided that doesn't mean 'Queen' but is a term of address for the Queen; the literal meaning is something like 'honorable female one.' But calling me by that word still equates me with the Queen – oh, dear! Then I can't get very much of what follows, except that the verb form of Ti'shra's *fa'u'isto|* appears at the end. That insertion of *'u'* in the middle of a verb also occurs in the Challenge Speech. It's got to be an inflection – could mark a different tense, maybe future. Kwi'ga'ga'tei said twice, *sho'u'timo|* – I'm guessing, *I will return.*"

Gwidian was listening with his usual grave attentiveness, but something in his face made Kaitrin pause. "Actually, you must find all this very boring, Griff."

"Don't think that," he said. "Nothing that gives you so much pleasure could bore me."

"You're my *na'sha'ma|*, Griffen – my King! Isn't that something?"

"Something," he said.

"What have you been doing with yourself while I've have been messing with all this – besides conjuring up this tasty meal?"

"Working on the first report back to Earth. Word came that the relay beacon is in place."

"Oh! That means that Mamá, and your sister, too, will soon know about the wedding."

He nodded. "I'd like to have initial reports ready by the end of tomorrow. Let's defer additional personal messages until we get replies to these that were just sent."

"And you want a report from me as well?"

"If you're ready to prepare one."

"Tió'otu has asked me to include something every time. I'm not quite sure why."

"Something to do with earning yourself that Professorship, I fancy."

Kaitrin stared at him. "Really? Well, I suppose, with this being such a unique situation, it can't hurt to bombard the beefeaters with stuff. But I'm going to keep it pretty informal. Nothing to be gained from putting everybody to sleep. I'll start working on it right away. We've probably done enough word-work for tonight."

"You can put off writing it until the next waking interval. There isn't such a rush."

"You know, I'm not used to going to bed every ten hours, Griff. If I get up at 0600h, I go to bed maybe at 2200 or 2300. That's being awake for seventeen or eighteen hours. Can't we arrange a schedule more like that?"

"Then we'll be completely irregular in relation to light and dark. I'm thinking we should be available to the Shshi at the same hours every day. I would think early morning and early evening, if the sun's heat distresses them. Wouldn't you agree?"

"Yes, I would!" said Kaitrin with a sigh. "All right, I'll suspend my work until we get up. It will still be dark then, for another four or five hours. How irritatingly odd!"

But Luku called to her. "Kaitrin, come and see. That place where the alate said, 'Ti'shra said that it had a friend … ' A moment later, she said, 'We want to know,' plus something, plus 'it died.' Prf. A'a'ma thinks it means 'how it died.' He says, 'We have another conjunction!'"

"Oh, I have to look at that!" said Kaitrin. "Griff, just a little longer. Let me work just a little longer."

He laughed, spreading his hands in capitulation. "I think I'm going to bed. Come in when you're ready. But don't be too long, Kait."

*　　*　　*

When Kaitrin finally tore herself away, she found Griffen sitting up in bed working with his neural recorder. "I thought you'd be sound asleep by now!"

He pulled off the transceptor and dropped it on the floor. "I was waiting for you."

Their lovemaking was some of the most passionate they had experienced to that point. When they lay satiated at last, Kaitrin felt warm, numb, a little overwhelmed. "Oh, Griff, what got into you tonight?" she breathed against his chest.

"Oh ... Maybe it was learning that the whole universe recognizes that we're mates ... Or maybe I'm still trying to compete with – the language thing ... "

She gave a tiny giggle, stroking his neck and the side of his face and smoothing the little frown creases in his forehead with her fingertips. She felt sleepy, giddy, a little out of control. He kissed the top of her head, his fingers tangling through her hair.

"Griff," she said, "when was the last time you had sex before us?"

He shifted his head in a slightly startled movement. "Oh ... it was – before the first expedition to this planet."

"That long!"

"There was a woman in Okloh ... She worked for Precinct Gov. Whilst I was away, she took a position with EarthGov and disappeared off to New Washinten."

"Were you sorry? Were the two of you close?"

"No. That is, I was a little sorry when I got back and found her – out of reach. We weren't that close, however."

"I thought maybe somebody on the expedition ... "

"I try to avoid liaisons with team members, unless it's someone I was involved with before the voyage."

Kaitrin giggled again. "Like me." Rashly, she added, "Or like Prf. Lindeman."

"That was several years ago! How did you know about that?"

"I, uh – I didn't know. I just ... well, you know the rumor mill. I've heard gossip that she was sometimes seen leaving your house."

Gwidian stirred impatiently. "God, what do they do, station spies outside the houses of people who've acquired a ... certain reputation? Yes, she would occasionally come for a drink – or something more ... But after she assumed the Chair, that mostly ceased."

I'm going way too far, Kaitrin thought. Gwidian was saying, "Kaitrin, I've always shunned casual sex – one-night affairs … I can't say I've never indulged myself in that fashion. But that sort of thing is neither safe nor satisfying."

A space of silence hung between them. Gwidian continued to plow her hair, a little roughly. The rise and fall of his chest was tense against Kaitrin's face.

But her frame of mind was not conducive to self-restraint.

"You've probably forgotten, but there was one evening right after we met. Luku and I were having supper in the XA dining hall, and you were across the way with this woman with a blue lion's-mane hairdo … "

"I remember," he said.

"You do? Amazing! Anyway, I realized you saw me looking … God, I was so embarrassed!"

At that, he gave a small, tight laugh. "I met that woman in the DB lab. I had recently learned of the departure of my Okloh friend and – I was … well, it had been awhile and – I was feeling at a rather low … " He cast about for a word. " … emotional ebb … It was obvious she was – available … "

After a moment, he said, "Nothing happened. I saw you looking at me and – suddenly I lost my taste for … I made some excuses and after finishing our meal we went our separate ways. I never had any contact with her again."

"Oh, Griff. Is that really how it happened?"

"Kait, believe what I tell you! Do you still doubt my honesty? Have I still not convinced you that I speak truthfully to you?"

"I didn't mean that."

"I've confessed to you that I've always enjoyed giving pleasure to women."

It went through her mind, *That could be interpreted as a very egotistical statement*, but fortunately she still retained a modicum of good sense and she left the thought unspoken.

"I remember you said that. I had always believed men want sex mostly for their own gratification. Maybe I made the tired old mistake of accepting a cliché as the truth."

"Well … But … Kait, I have no apologies to make for the life I've led. But it failed me. In the end, it failed to provide what I need."

"And I do?"

"Oh, Kait!" His voice trembled. "You can't know! You can't understand!"

"What is it you need, Griff? I need to understand if I'm going to provide it."

"I ... need ... real love ... "

In spite of herself, Kaitrin was drifting off. "I give you that ... you surely know it ... "

Through the fog of encroaching sleep, she was aware of his almost imperceptible whisper more as a breath against her hair than as a voice ... " ... and forgiveness."

Forgiveness – again? But she was too close to sleep to answer, and his words drifted into her dreams.

*   *   *

When Kaitrin awoke at the end of the night cycle, Griffen was already up, shaving before the mirror. She lay gazing at him, trying to remember what had happened the night before. There had been fantastic sex, then she had ... *Oh, hell ...*

She sat up, reaching for her robe. "Griff, good morning."

He glanced at her with a smile.

Before he could say anything, she said, "Griff, I seem to remember behaving really atrociously last night. I think your lovemaking intoxicated me."

"Oh." He gestured with the shaver, laughing.

"Everybody has the right to keep some things private, from their spouses, mistresses, friends, mothers – whoever. I didn't mean to seem to be putting you through an inquisition."

"No," he said, "you have the right to know anything you wish about me. It's just ... I haven't quite found the strength to speak everything I should, Kait."

And yet another enigmatic remark, thought Kaitrin, but she decided enough was enough and let it rest.

Chapter 6

... By the sea's side, hearing the noise of birds,
Hearing the raven cough in winter sticks,
My busy heart who shudders as she talks
Sheds the syllabic blood and drains her words.
– *from* Dylan Thomas, *Especially When the
October Wind*

[Mo'gri'ta'tu confronts Ki'shto'ba outside the entrance to the Holy Chamber]

[Mo'gri'ta'tu]: What is this? You and the Seer have expelled everyone from the Holy Chamber, even the Tenders and Light-Makers? And now you would keep me out as well? I, the chosen Chamberlain of many season-cycles? Move the stone, outlander!

[Ki'shto'ba]: I am sorry, Mo'gri'ta'tu. The Holy One and the King agreed to confer alone with the Holy Seer. If you had been in attendance, perhaps that would not have happened.

[Mo'gri'ta'tu, prances in fury]: Accursed Nasutes are crouching outside the rear entrances! What conspiracy is this? I will summon Commander Hi'ta'fu!

[There is a vibration in the stone]

[Ki'shto'ba, pushing it aside]: That will not be necessary, Chamberlain. Here is Holy Kwi'ga'ga'tei now.

[Kwi'ga'ga'tei, emerging]: I have finished my conversation with the Holy One and you may resume your duties, Keeper. All of the attendants may return as well. There will be a meeting of the Council in one turning of the vessel. I suggest that you be there.

[As Kwi'ga'ga'tei and Ki'shto'ba push past, Mo'gri'ta'tu speaks after them]: You had no right, Seer! You overstep your place! You cannot persist in this and expect to retain your authority in good repute!

[Kwi'ga'ga'tei, to Ki'shto'ba]: He grows frustrated, and hence more blatant.

[Ki'shto'ba]: I am not comfortable with this. I fear he will persuade A'kha'ma'na'ta to tell him everything you said to her.

[Kwi'ga'ga'tei]: Oh, he will, undoubtedly. But some of my influence will endure and it will all be made public in Council soon, in any event.

*   *   *

[The Council Chamber. Kwi'ga'ga'tei speaks to the assembled Shshi]

You may allay your fears! No death-dealing evil has come down upon us and Lo'ro'ra is in no danger from these Strange Ones. To the Worker Chiefs I say: it is safe to leave the fortress and resume normal activities.

[Gwo'no]: My Growers may return to the orchards without fear they will be attacked as Ti'shra was?

[Wi'tai]: The Builders may engage in their maintenance on the walls even in full view of the eyes of the monster?

[Kwi'ga'ga'tei]: They may all do so. But if it makes them feel more comfortable, let the Commander deploy its forces a little more generously than usual.

[Hi'ta'fu]: Be assured that I will do so! I do not trust these miscreant outlanders at all! What makes you think they are not dangerous? Where do they come from? How many of them are there?

[Kwi'ga'ga'tei]: I think their numbers are small. I saw six, but there were others in the egg, or rather, in their dwelling place. I think it is not an egg at all, but the place where they live.

[Mo'gri'ta'tu]: First, it is a Sky-Jumper, then a Sky-Monster, then a dead creature, then a creature producing young without the intermediary of eggs – finally a flying egg – and now it is a flying dwelling! All this makes me doubt the Seer's ability to see clearly into any truth!

[Di'fa'kro'mi]: Restrain your word-sending, Chamberlain! Let us learn more of Holy Kwi'ga'ga'tei's discoveries before we pronounce judgments.

[Kwi'ga'ga'tei]: I thank you, Remembrancer. As to the question of why I think they are not dangerous, I spent time with them and took no harm nor gathered any sense of threat beyond some easily resolved misunderstandings. I still do not know who they are or where they came from, but I know this: they only appear not to have speech. They captured the dying words of Ti'shra and placed them in a magic box ... Cease to stamp about so skeptically and with such alarm – not all things that can be called magic are dangerous! I saw this box with my own eyes – I touched it, I received words from it and answered them, and it returned answers to me. This box in fact serves as their antennae and their memory! And one of the beings especially wants to learn our language and to be our friend. Perhaps all of them want to be our friends.

[Mo'gri'ta'tu]: Does the Holy Seer not seem easily duped, my fellow Counselors? Which of you would so readily trust the pronouncements of unknown outlanders who have already killed two of the citizens of Lo'ro'ra and who work – you call it, *magic*? – using a mysterious box?

[Kwi'ga'ga'tei]: Believe me, Chamberlain, I would rather trust the words of this alien creature with whom I spoke than the harangues of some more familiar acquaintances.

[The Chamberlain stands in baleful stillness with his eyes fixed upon the Seer, while the other Shshi shift about uneasily and groom their claws]

[Kwi'ga'ga'tei]: There is something else ...

[Mo'gri'ta'tu]: The Holy One told me what it is. You have indeed charmed her with your talk of progenitors and alien Holy Ones. *tha'sask*|>||

[The agitation increases]

[Kwi'ga'ga'tei]: Their pheromones reveal that more than one of these beings is female. But the principal outlander is not only female – she also has a King! I saw him. They crouched side by side and she said to me, *Yes, this is my* na'sha'ma|.

[An outcry] What? Progenitors sitting above ground, beneath the sky? What sacrilege! Did she drop eggs? Where is their nursery? Who grooms her? Feeds her?

[Kwi'ga'ga'tei]: Please, attend me! I do not believe that the practices and the taboos of these outlanders are the same as ours – why would they be? This *ma'na'ta*| has no swollen belly – she seemed able to move about as easily as the others. Perhaps she can groom and feed herself. Her ovipositor is hidden under a fiber covering – it may be that for these beings the Nameless Mother decreed only that the progenitor must not allow the light to shine on her holy parts. And she does not seem to regard herself as more important than the others. She responded, *No, no*, when we abased to her. She wants to be our friend, to learn our language. Is this not a great tribute, to want to learn our language? My current thinking is that she and all of them are a gift to us from the Nameless One, but perhaps a test as well. Because – most telling of evidence! – this alien Holy One has *no name* in our speech!

[More outcries, amid much dancing and groveling]: No name! Everything created has a name, even *shma'na'ta*|! Is this not a Created One?

[Kwi'ga'ga'tei]: At first I was as stunned as you are. But her exact words were, *I do not have a name in the spoken things of Shshi.* These outlanders must have a way of speaking that is completely different from our own. So she may possess a name in her way of speaking that she cannot communicate in ours.

[Hi'ta'fu, impatiently]: We do not understand these things!

[Di'fa'kro'mi, excitedly]: I do, Kwi'ga'ga'tei! Language can come in many forms and patterns and is always a source of power.

Will you continue to study with her?

[Kwi'ga'ga'tei]: I will. I must.

[Di'fa'kro'mi]: I would like to go out with you. I would like to learn what it feels like to receive words from a magic box.

[Kwi'ga'ga'tei]: I cannot permit that immediately. But one ... day ...

[An oppressiveness fills the chamber. Kwi'ga'ga'tei's legs splay, her body is flattened]

You will bear the Wound if the Wounded One is not healed. Remember, but do not speak of this ...

[Kwi'ga'ga'tei]: I remember! I will remember! Pity us!

I do not abandon my Star-Children ...

[No'kri]: What is happening?

[Di'fa'kro'mi]: Highest-Mother-Who-Is-Nameless! She has entered the trance!

[Kwi'ga'ga'tei]: Where ... ? Ah, pain ... No! I am here! I receive you! It was only a passing vision ...

[Mo'gri'ta'tu]: How convenient to have passing visions! Will you share your blessing with us, Most Holy Seer?

[Kwi'ga'ga'tei]: No. No'kri, bring the meeting to an end. All will go forward. There is no danger coming from the Strange Ones, if we receive them with the proper spirit ... Let us accept this new time, Shshi, and make sure our beloved fortress flourishes in it.

*   *   *

In the dawn, Shshi could be seen dashing about nervously in the courtyard amid knots of soldiers, propelling carts before them toward the orchards, clambering up the walls of the edifices, dispersing in all directions. Among them, avoided by the larger Shshi, were some small, hump-bodied workers, purplish in color, with long legs and bulging clypei. Guarded by a few of the nasute soldiers, they huddled together as they scuttled quickly toward the boundary of the compound. All of the isopteroids stayed well away from the flyer, but they no longer seemed to regard it as a source of imminent peril.

Kwi'ga'ga'tei and the giant warrior Ki'shto'ba came again to where the aliens awaited them. This time they brought only two nasute guards, including the officer.

"It seems she got the message that we aren't as dangerous as they had thought," said Kaitrin, "and did a good job of passing it along."

"I wonder what really goes on inside that fortress," said A'a'ma, who was perching in Gwidian's place at Kaitrin's right side. Griffen had taken a seat on the ramp beside Julian, while Will and Arti remained inside the flyer with Trea and Sev.

"I like that word 'fortress' for their dwelling place," said Kaitrin. "'Termitarium' is really much too clinical. I don't consider these creatures to be termites, any more than I'm an ape, or Luku is a lemur, or you, Tió'otu, are an eagle."

As the alate and her companions approached, Kwi'ga'ga'tei said some words. *na'ta'zei*| *sho'* ...| ⤷ *bei'a*| ||

"Oh, I hope that's 'Hello,'" said Kaitrin. "Quick, Luku, put in *evo*| – *sho'evo*| ⤷ *bei'a*| || 'I – greet? – you.'" Toward the alate, she projected the same words in return.

But the alate was staring at Prf. A'a'ma, who chirped uneasily. Kwi'ga'ga'tei addressed some words to Ki'shto'ba, then cautiously approached Tió'otu, who gingerly put out his claw. Kwi'ga'ga'tei proceeded to taste him as she had tasted Kaitrin, then skittered around the end of the table and inspected him from top to tail, flaring her wings.

"Tió'otu, I don't think you taste as good as I do," said Kaitrin, giggling.

"Don't go off on us, now, Kaitrin," said Griffen. "They might mistakenly perceive that *you* were having a fit."

"I wish I could explain you to her, Tió'otu, and us, too," said Kaitrin. All she could think of to say was *ma'she*|↳ *thel*| || "He is good." She had constructed the verb form on analogy with *ta'she* and Kwi'ga'ga'tei seemed to accept it.

Then Kaitrin said, *sho'laio*| ↓↑ *preivo*| ⤷ *gan'zi*| …

vei'zi|, responded the alate.

Kaitrin regarded her, considering what this interruption meant. *wei*| *gan'zi*| ... *vei'zi*|, said Kwi'ga'ga'tei, dancing on her rear four legs. Then she uttered a whole string of disconnected words and said, *vei'zi| ... gan'zi| wei|>||*

"Oh, I get it," said Kaitrin. "I told you I didn't feel *gan'zi|* was right for 'word.' 'Word' is another wave pattern entirely – the one that appeared in the construction for 'antenna.' Say, that makes the literal meaning of *vei'ga'zi|* to be 'word-speak-thing'! Perfect!" To the alate, she said, *sho'laio| ↲ preivo| Ϛ vei'zi| ki| loi'zi| ki'bei\ – kwi| ||* "I want to know the word of your name – *kwi|.*" And she added, *ti'shra'ze ⇆ galtot| Ϛ vei'zi| kwi| i'i| shvei'zi| kwi'il| u| kwi'sho'zei| ||* "Ti'shra said the word *kwi|* in the words *kwi'il|* and *kwi'sho'zei|.*"

Kwi'ga'ga'tei made a remark to her companion, then turned to Kaitrin, bent her antenna downward, and touched the first of its beadlike knobs with her foreclaw. *kwi|*, she said. Then she touched the second knob, and uttered another word, then the third, and so on. When she reached the seventh, she spoke the word she had uttered on the second knob and added *kwi|* to it.

Gwidian stood up in excitement. "Kaitrin, she appears to be counting! They do have at least a rudimentary number sense!"

"I just caught on to that, too!" Kaitrin cried.

But Gwidian's abrupt movement had startled the alate; she stared up at him as he suddenly towered a meter above her. Ki'shto'ba sensed her alarm and whipped around toward Gwidian, its mandibles coming up.

"Oh, my god!" said Kaitrin. "Griff, they feel threatened! Sit down very slowly!"

He did so willingly. Julian had raised his pistol, a finger on the safety.

Kaitrin said in Shshi words, "*na|* Kwi'ga'ga'tei, my mate is not evil. Speak to Ki'shto'ba."

Kwi'ga'ga'tei did so and the huge soldier relaxed, dropping its mandibles into a resting position against the ground.

"Whew," said Gwidian a little shakily. "That may have been close, what?"

"And you accuse me of taking risks!" said Kaitrin.

The alate resumed the count on her antenna knobs, keeping an eye on Gwidian. "Kait, each antenna has eighteen segments," he said. "And they have six legs and six segments on the labial palps. Perhaps their numbering system is based on sixes."

"Definitely. The other numbers demonstrate it. 'Seven' is 'two' plus *kwi|* – it must mean 'second sequence – number one.'"

"What will they do after knobs run out?" asked Luku.

"Probably just say, 'many.' But let's work on that another time ... oh!"

Luku had picked that moment to pull off her goggles and rub an itching eye. Kwi'ga'ga'tei gave another jump and Ki'shto'ba backed up, swinging its head again. The shaman's antennae waved urgently toward it.

"Luku, to her it looks like you just ripped your eyes off!" said Kaitrin.

"*Jocha!* Did not think!"

"Lean over – show her your face. Let her see the goggles."

Luku cautiously complied. Kwi'ga'ga'tei approached with equal tentativeness, touching the muzzled face with her antennae, glancing between the blinking eyes and the goggles. She took the goggles in her claws and felt them with her palps, then held them before one eye and then the other, looking in different directions. She spent a long moment looking toward the sun, then she glanced back at Luku, then at the sun again.

"I think she understands the goggles' purpose," said Kaitrin in wonder. "Damn, I'd sell my soul for a bigger vocabulary!"

Kwi'ga'ga'tei gave the goggles back to Luku, who squinted at them. "I cannot put insect saliva in eyes."

Julian rose slowly. "Do you have another pair? I'll get them for you."

He did so. After a bit of dancing and fluster on everybody's part, the dialogue resumed. Kaitrin asked the alate for the meaning of her name. Kwi'ga'ga'tei seemed puzzled, but at length she came up with an explanation. "It is ... name of *tei'zei|* – one speaker-speaker who *fa'teio|.*"

"*gan'zei| gan'zei|*?" said Kaitrin. "Oh, I know! Reduplication must signify 'many.' If you want to say 'a lot of something,' you simply repeat the word. That's useful to know! So her name is, 'One of many speakers who ... ' To Kwi'ga'ga'tei she said, "Tell me words with *tei|.*"

This one turned out to be easy. Kwi'ga'ga'tei simply prodded her eyes with her claws.

"♫♪ 'Eye!' So the verb must mean 'to see'!" warbled

Tió'otu.

"Yes! 'One of many speakers who sees!' And *tei'zei|* must be 'one who sees' – a Seer! She probably said that her name is a traditional Seer's name, or a common Seer's name. She certainly is the Shshi's shaman or prophet!"

Now that the meaning of *kwi|* was known, *kwi'sho'zei|* and *kwi'il|* turned out to be no-brainers.

"'I am a One Being' – a person," said Tió'otu. "Their sense of individuality is strong enough that Ti'shra would use the word to describe itself when it was dying."

"'But individuals are nothing,'" continued Kaitrin, "' … they are … one,' plus adverb suffix. 'Only'? No, 'alone!' *kwi'il|* means 'alone,' Tió'otu! 'When or if they are alone!'"

"Then that other sentence – *sho'laio| wei| ɟʄ weio| kwi'il| ||* … "

"'I do not want to die – alone!' Oh, Griff – Tió'otu – Ti'shra was saying to me, 'I don't want to die alone.'"

Kaitrin turned to Kwi'ga'ga'tei, who stood unspeaking, carefully watching the mouth and hand movements of the Strange Ones, and said, *ti'shra'ze| fa'ganot| sho'laio| wei| ɟʄ weio| kwi'il| || fa'weiot| kwi'il| wei| || shot| …* Ti'shra said, 'I do not want to die alone.' It did not die alone. I was … "

She did not know how to say 'with' and Kwi'ga'ga'tei finished the sentence for her. *bei'shat| o| fa'a| || bei'sha| Ϛ ru'zei| ||*

"She said, 'You were with it. You are *ru'zei|*.' That word again," said Kaitrin. "'You are friend.' Somehow 'friend' doesn't seem quite on the mark."

"Not strong enough," said Griffen unsteadily. "It might mean – a helper or someone who cared … somebody who comforted it – made it feel better. Isn't that what you wanted to do, Kait – comfort that creature?"

"Oh. It's possible. I was its – comforter … "

Kwi'ga'ga'tei was speaking again. *bei'taio| Ϛ loi'zi| wei| i| shvei'zi| ki| shshi'zei| || wei| … 'il| bei'sha| Ϛ ru'zei| u| bei'sha| Ϛ ma'na'ta| || … sho'loio| Ϛ bei'a| o| ru'a'ma'na'ta| || ¿fa'she|?↵ thel| ||*

"Oh, my. I didn't have to ask her to give me a name – she just offered me one," said Kaitrin emotionally. "She said, 'You have no name in the – language? – of the Shshi.' Something … "

'You are – Comforter – and you are – *ma'na'ta|*. I name you with Ru'a'ma'na'ta. Is it good?'"

And Kaitrin replied to the Seer, *fa'she|↳ thel| na| kwi'ga'ga'tei'ze| ja| sho'preivo| wei| ↰ ma'na'ta|* || "It is good, *na|* Kwi'ga'ga'tei, but I do not know *ma'na'ta|*."

Then Kwi'ga'ga'tei responded, "*ma'na'ta|* is the Holy One – the progenitor – who together with the King renews us and gives us new life. Do you not do that for your people?" But Kaitrin could comprehend only scattered words of that reply, so she still fell short of understanding the full significance of the name that the Seer of Lo'ro'ra had given to her.

*   *   *

The sessions continued day after day. Luku perfected the vocal interface, which made communication equivalent to conversing with a speaker of a barely familiar Earth tongue. Soon Trea and Sev introduced themselves to the Shshi, to Kwi'ga'ga'tei's obvious discomfort; she surely had to be wondering how many more varieties of creatures were lurking inside the mysterious flying dwelling. Griffen finally conceded it was safe for Kaitrin to sally forth without him, and the normal support team dwindled to only Luku, Prf. A'a'ma, and one security person. The Seer of Lo'ro'ra continued to cooperate and even appeared to be enjoying the interaction.

Sometimes Kaitrin would lay out a group of objects and point to them, saying "I want to know … " The first presentation included a stone, a leaf, and a small piece of wood. Kwi'ga'ga'tei picked up the stone and said, *ku'a'zi| ↰ she| ↰ ka'zi|* ||

Kaitrin was not sure which of the words meant "stone." *loi'zi| ↰ she| ↰ ku'a'zi|* ||, she said, attempting to convey, "Its name is *ku'a'zi|*."

wei| wei|, responded the alate. That negative word was quickly becoming all too familiar. *ki'fa| loi'zi| ↰ she| ↰ ka'zi|* || "Its name is *ka'zi|*."

"Tell me *ku'a'zi|*."

It was Kwi'ga'ga'tei's turn to be puzzled. Then she pointed first at the stone. *ku'a'zi| ↰ she| ↰ ka'zi|* || "This is stone." Then, pointing at the leaf … *ku'o'zi| ↰ she| ↰ zhuf'zi|* || "That is leaf."

Thus as a bonus Kaitrin learned how to say "this" and "that."

Even through such impromptu exchanges, in which Kwi'ga'ga'tei displayed an amazing linguistic acuity, Kaitrin was able to learn abstract words like "what," "when," and "where"; "more" and "less"; "all," "some," "any"; "same," "different" – words that were part of the fabric of full communication.

Kaitrin played Ti'shra's dying words to use as a text, and their emergence from the magic box never ceased to fascinate the Shshi. In fact, Luku had to turn the gain down to a "whisper" to keep from attracting an audience from among the Shshi who were going about their business in the courtyard. They also used Ki'shto'ba's Challenge Speech, provoking yet more amazement. The big Warrior itself, who never missed one of these sessions, was obviously astounded that they could have "captured" its words.

¿bei'thomo|? ↢ shvei'zi| i| roi'za'zi| g'il| ru'a'ma'na'ta| || Kwi'ga'ga'tei asked.

And after this had been puzzled out and Kaitrin had learned more about questions and word order, she finally understood that that sentence meant, "How do you catch words in a box, Ru'a'ma'na'ta?" But she could find no way to explain, and when Kwi'ga'ga'tei said, *fa'she| ↢ a'tas'zi|*, Kaitrin could not construe a meaning for the final word.

What Kwi'ga'ga'tei had said was "It is magic."

Sometimes they played gesture-games, or, as Arti Robb put it, "Just imagine – we're playing charades with a termite!" In this way, they were able to illuminate words like *zifo|* – 'touch' – from Ti'shra's speech, as well as the other senses and concepts like directions, motions, and positions. Ki'shto'ba proved quite useful in these demonstrations, entering into the activity with childlike enthusiasm. Thus, when Kaitrin asked for the meaning of the root *ist*, which appeared in Ti'shra's words *ist'zi|, fa'u'isto|*, and *ist'il|*, Ki'shto'ba mimicked stabbing itself in the foot with a mandible, then staggered around on four legs, clutching the foot and tossing its head. Obviously the root meant "injury" or "pain." So finally Kaitrin understood the whole of Ti'shra's request – "Tell them in Lo'ro'ra that Ti'shra died in pain, but it had a Comforter who was not evil."

Kaitrin realized quickly that the Shshi language was much more than the rudimentary symbolization of a pre-technological intelligence – it was as rich in intellectual abstractions as any Earth tongue. When the day came at last that Kaitrin could translate the whole of the Challenge Speech, she felt like she had passed a milestone. "Strange Ones, I address you! I am Ki'shto'ba Huge-Head of To'wak, Champion of the fortress of Lo'ro'ra. We are the Shshi of Lo'ro'ra and if we must, we will fight you to keep our fortress safe. And yet I call the Challenge in the name of Lo'ro'ra's Holy One and King: Let there be honorable single combat so that the deaths of many can be avoided! Send out your Champion, Strange Ones, and alone I will fight it! If I prevail, then you must go away and leave Lo'ro'ra in peace!" From this, the anthropologists learned that, like some archaic cultures of Earth and indeed of Krisí'i'aid and also Quornam, the Shshi had a tradition of single combat as a surrogate for all-out war.

The word *da'fu|* in the sentence about single combat bothered Kaitrin. It clearly meant something like "honorable" in the chivalric sense, but in that case what did *na|* mean? There was a considerable difference in the contexts in which the two concepts were used. The answer came in a long session that began when Kaitrin first showed pictures to Kwi'ga'ga'tei.

The alate appeared greatly perplexed, eyeing the plasti-prints with one eye, then the other, then both together. "I don't think she's ever seen a picture of anything before," Kaitrin said to Tió'otu. "I'm convinced that they have never developed any kind of visual art."

"That makes sense," said A'a'ma. "Only alates would be able to experience it, and even with the wing-light, the fortress must be a dim place."

Kaitrin fetched an apple and put it on the table alongside a picture of the same apple. Suddenly Kwi'ga'ga'tei hopped in the air, body language that she often exhibited when understanding dawned. She said, *fa'she| ⌐ fi'zi|* || and then a long string of words ending with *fa'paho| ⌐ sho ⌐ na'zi|* || *ki| shyo'a'zei| shtuk'zi| ⌐ shshe| ⌐ shfi'zi| ki| shprai'mo'zi|* ||

Kaitrin sweated this out. "'It is *fi'zi|*' – I take that to be 'picture' or 'image.' 'We do not make – *i'ku|* ... ' Oh, I remember, that's 'such.' 'We do not make such images, but I know that image is ... of a thing ... outside ... it ... itself?' Could that be the way they make reflexives? By employing an emphasis indicator? Anyway, at the end she says, 'It can be – honor? A thing of honor?' Oh, that's so wrong – 'honor' ought to be something based on the *fu* root. 'Of – something … wings are images of … ' *¡Ay caramba!*" In mock despair, Kaitrin clutched her head, knocking her braid loose. "All right – let's start with *shyo'a'zei|* – a personal noun. Kwi'ga'ga'tei, what is *shyo'a'zei|*?"

sho|> ᔕ yo'a'zei| || said Kwi'ga'ga'tei, and fanned her wings with a sparkle of bioluminescence.

"Oh," said Kaitrin in awe. " 'I – myself? – am … ' I think that word must mean 'alate'!" In the Shshi language, she asked, "Worker, Warrior, Alate. Yes, Kwi'ga'ga'tei?"

av| came the reply. *om'zei| pai'zei| u| yo'a'zei| || son| shshai'zei| ||*

"*son|* is 'three' and *shai'zei|* must mean 'caste,'" said A'a'ma, "if we went to retain the entomological lingo."

Then Kaitrin returned to the Seer's original statement. "She said, 'Of alates, wings … ' No! In Inj it would be 'The wings of alates,' but in this language subjects are never separated from verbs. 'The wings of alates are images of … *shprai'mo'zi|*.' Kwi'ga'ga'tei, what is *prai'mo'zi|*?"

Kwi'ga'ga'tei pointed upward. *shfai'moro| i'i| prai'zi| zo| nof'i'wiv| ||*

"'They shine in the sky … ' I learned those words when we were discussing the sun a couple of days ago. What's *zo|*? Oh, I remember – it's 'during'! 'During the darktime – the night.' Oh, I've got it! Stars! She said, 'The wings of alates are images of the stars.'"

vi| ta'tai| wei| ᔕ loi'zi| da'pri'saia| ma'na'ta| ⇆ ta'fivot| ᔕ i'ku'zi| hu| ||

The highest ma'na'ta| *who has no name made it so.*

It did not take Kaitrin long to piece out this sentence, and so at last she understood why it mattered that she had no name. The Shshi worshiped a creator goddess who was also nameless.

As they continued to play with pictures, Kaitrin displayed stillvids of terrestrial termites. Kwi'ga'ga'tei stared and stared and finally said, *Those are images of Shshi, but the creatures are not Shshi.*

"They are very small like your insects," Kaitrin told her. "You can speak. They cannot."

I never saw such beings in the world. Where do you come

from, Ru'a'ma'na'ta?

It was the first time Kwi'ga'ga'tei had asked that question since Kaitrin had learned enough to understand, and impulsively she took a chance. *shsho'krovo| kei| shprai'mo'zi| ||* "We come from the stars."

At that, Kwi'ga'ga'tei and Ki'shto'ba again groveled and rubbed their mouthparts in the dirt. "I wish they wouldn't do that," said Kaitrin. "It looks so servile and none of us deserves to be worshiped."

na| wei'loi'zei| ↰ ta'choio| i'o| shprai'mo'zi| || bei'shsha| ↳ da'na| ik| || bei'shsha|↳ da'na'sai| oda| sho| ||

What she had said was "The *na|* Nameless One lives among the stars. You are *na|* also. You are more *na|* than I am." And it finally dawned on Kaitrin – *na|* meant, not "honorable" or "noble," but "holy" or "sacred."

"Oh, this is just great," she said over the team's next meal. "Not only do I not have a name, just like the Mother Goddess created them, but now Kwi'ga'ga'tei is even more convinced that we're holy – gods, if you will – because we come from the stars where their Creatrix lives. She's given me a name constructed like their own mother creature's name. Tió'otu, I'm making a fine hash of all this. Maybe you'd better take over."

"Not on your life!" he responded with genial colloquialness. "You have totally won over that isopteroid priest – much more completely than I ever could have."

"Not only she worships you, Kaitrin – she likes you," said Trea. "I can feel that. You told her truth. Now explain to her."

So Kaitrin tried to explain to Kwi'ga'ga'tei that they came from a world both similar to and different from the Shshi's, that that world "walked around" a star just as the Shshi's world did, that they had flown here in a flying fortress many times larger than the one the Shshi saw them entering and leaving, that at that very moment the big flyer was circling too high above them to be visible. They worked long and hard together to speak and to understand.

And finally Kwi'ga'ga'tei said, *I understand your words, but not how all this can be. But I accept. You say that the Nameless One did not send you, but if you come from a place among her stars, we will always believe that you belong to her and that she sent you to us for a reason, even if you yourselves do not know the reason.   So we have a special responsibility toward you.   We will treat you as guests and try to make you comfortable and welcome. We will guard you and treat you with honor, and try to do good to you.   That very onus has been set upon me.*

Even after Kaitrin had managed to work out most of what Kwi'ga'ga'tei was saying, she did not really grasp all the implications.   It seemed to her that the Seer was saying merely that the Shshi felt an obligation to be hospitable to visitors.

Chapter 7

Star-shadows shine, love,
How many stars in your bowl?
How many shadows in your soul,
Only mine, love, mine?
    – *from* D. H. Lawrence, *In a Boat*

[In his quarters, Mo'gri'ta'tu speaks to Hi'ta'fu, Lo'lo'pai, Ta'rei'so'cha]

[Mo'gri'ta'tu]: What kind of excrement is this that the Seer speaks? Beings flying down from the stars! Fortresses moving invisible through the sky! She has named this deformed imposter in the most sacred way of our people! *Ru'a'ma'na'ta*, indeed!

[Lo'lo'pai]: It has always been the Seer's privilege to name a new Mother.

[Mo'gri'ta'tu]: This is not a *ma'na'ta|* of the Shshi! This is an infertile, degenerate charlatan, who twists the Seer's reason with its feeble knowledge of our speech! Indeed, I would feel pity for it were it not so dangerous to our beloved citizens!

[Hi'ta'fu]: Kwi'ga'ga'tei's prophecies have come to pass. The dead, speaking …

[Mo'gri'ta'tu]: A trick! A talking box – what rubbish!

[Lo'lo'pai]: Some who have been in the compound when the

Seer is with the outlanders say they have seen the box and received its speaking.

[Mo'gri'ta'tu]: Trickery, I tell you! As ridiculous an idea as the creature with the removable eyes that protect its body-eyes from sunlight! *tha'sask*|>‖ And the pathetic Priest has not even considered asking what happened to the bodies of our esteemed Worker and our honorable Warrior! I tell you, the Seer grows old before her time. The living corruption is taking hold of her and she speaks madness. Even as a nymph, she was unstable. And now she has consumed the *bir'zha*| for too long.

[Ta'rei'so'cha]: It is true. Sometimes the *bir'zha*| eats away the power of thought. I have been told it happened to the last Seer. It could be happening to Kwi'ga'ga'tei.

[Mo'gri'ta'tu]: Why will she not allow anyone else to visit the outlanders? It is because she is afraid we will learn the truth – that this is all fool's play! I tell you, her time is past! She and those who support her – barbarous outlanders all! – must be … removed from influence, if we must so euphemize the deed – and then we must eliminate the so-called Star-Beings, before our mighty fortress of Lo'ro'ra takes irreparable harm.

[Hi'ta'fu]: I still shudder at what you propose, Mo'gri'ta'tu, but I can see truth in it. Things move too fast. Our center is compromised. The Holy One is confused. The King is timid and not overly strong of mind. And yet most of our citizens revere Kwi'ga'ga'tei for her peacemaking that ended the Nasute War. She feeds on that, bewitching all with her words and with her trances and visions of the Nameless One. How can we fight her without destroying ourselves and Lo'ro'ra as well, even while we strive to do it good?

[Ta'rei'so'cha]: The ploy of poisoned vision-fungus will not work now. My hastily made replacement was suspected. The Keeper of the *bir'zha*| told me so with much bewilderment. When the Seer seeks a vision of late, she makes the Keeper prepare the bolus in her presence and we dare not try to subvert the Keeper. So that course of action is closed to us.

[Mo'gri'ta'tu]: I counsel that we bide our time for a while, and speak privately and subtly with others to move them to our cause.

[Lo'lo'pai]: Should the Chief of the Second Cohort A'gwa'ji not be persuaded to join with us? If we are not united ...

[Mo'gri'ta'tu]: I would consider it imprudent to approach it; it has a stubborn and quite circumscribed view of honor, and a most limited perception. That is why you, Lo'lo'pai, whose grasp of realities is so much more generous, was named as Chief of the First Cohort and the chosen successor to Hi'ta'fu the Unconquered. Is that not so, Commander?

[Hi'ta'fu]: I have always relied on Lo'lo'pai. But I have no scorn for A'gwa'ji, or I would not have made it my third in command. Still, I agree – its mind is not overly subtle. But – I also have a Warrior's mind ... only a blind Warrior's mind ...

[Mo'gri'ta'tu]: I will make a large effort to learn more of these so-called Star-Beings. Kwi'ga'ga'tei cannot keep them isolated from the rest of us forever. I will try to determine their true motives and also their weaknesses, so that we may use those flaws to our advantage. So let us disband for now, avoid one another's company, and bide our time.

[The conspirators disperse. Hi'ta'fu and Lo'lo'pai traverse the corridors together]

[Hi'ta'fu]: Come, come, Lo'lo'pai, you emit too much stress pheromone.

[Lo'lo'pai]: I do not like our course, Commander. I entered into this because of my debt to you, and because I have faith in your honor and in the depth of your love for our great fortress. But it troubles me to skulk about and threaten one who has served our citizens so well. Kwi'ga'ga'tei is a Holy Star-Wing, after all, and all Star-Wings are blessed by the Highest-Mother-Who-Is-Nameless.

[Hi'ta'fu]: Mo'gri'ta'tu is also a Holy Star-Wing ... Lo'lo'pai, I cannot deny my own confusion and distress. But this path has been laid out and I think we must tread upon it. This new time is like a wet-season flood – we cannot stand against it.

[Mo'gri'ta'tu, alone in his quarters]: Well, they are all pathetic weaklings, susceptible to words. Kwi'ga'ga'tei is not the only one who can bend wills with speech. My hatred of her scares me at times. In the beginning, I only coveted her power. Now, because she has thwarted me so successfully, her destruction has become my personal cause. I think I see a way. These so-called creatures from the stars have bewitched her and are bewitching our citizenry through her. It may be that if I can accomplish their destruction, that act will take her down as well.

*   *   *

As the language lessons continued, Gwidian began to harp on his desire to make a physical examination of the isopteroids. Kaitrin discouraged him. "You'll never be able to dissect another one of these creatures. We don't know their customs regarding the dead."

He reacted testily. "I don't want to dissect them! I want to examine them alive, starting with the alate!"

"You can't go around sticking probes in the live body of a high-ranking member of their society!"

"I don't intend that, either, Kaitrin! But a brain and eye scan – some readings on that unique bioluminescence – those things would do her no harm."

"We have neural scanning equipment. We could rig power pack for use outside flyer," said Trea.

"Well, maybe," said Kaitrin, "but we must find a tactful way to ask Kwi'ga'ga'tei's permission first and I'm not sure she's ready. I mean, how would you like it if extraterrestrials swooped down on your doorstep and started poking sensors at you?"

"Krisí'i'aidá and Earthers had that very same problem when they first met each other," remarked Prf. A'a'ma.

So Gwidian agreed to wait longer, but he continued to chafe.

Over the three Earth weeks that had passed (twelve and a half days on 2 Giotta 17A), Kaitrin had fallen into a rhythm – work with the Shshi morning and evening, then spend the remainder of the waking time analyzing the day's data – assigning and recording syllabic equivalents, deciphering syntax, puzzling out idiomatic constructions, committing new vocabulary to memory (the easiest part for Kaitrin). If it was not the language, it was report-writing and filling her thought recorder with copious impressions. The routine consumed her; it was the most intellectually and emotionally taxing project she had ever undertaken and it indulged the first love of her life.

The team had set up an exercise block on the flight deck, but Kaitrin's sincere intention to use it rarely bore fruit. When it was her turn to prepare meals for the team, it usually slipped her mind, and someone else, frequently Griffen, filled in. When Zin !eye Taeva arrived in the *Brozzae* for the first resupply visit, she concerned herself only because she had to prepare her isopteroid friends for the arrival of a second sky-monster. Not even Luku's pleasure at seeing Zin or the fresh supply of meat and fruit could really engage her. The other team members humored her distraction because they knew that the work she was doing was intensely meaningful not only for her but also for the advancement of interstellar science.

Only the first TTR message from her mother, about two weeks into their sojourn, diverted her attention. *Oh, Kaiti,* Brigit wrote, *I'm so happy for you.* Niña tonta, *why were you so worried that I would laugh at you for having a marriage ceremony? It obviously meant a great deal to you and to Griffen. I may call him Griffen, mayn't I? I refuse to call him Prf. Gwidian! I know your work there means everything to you, but I can't wait till you come home! Bring him immediately to see me! If you put me off, I shall have to come and plant myself on your doorstep, and you know you won't want that while the honeymoon is still new! My wish for you – and please say this to Griffen, too – is that you will both be as happy as Jaq and I were, for many more years than he and I had.*

The messages came late in one of the ten-hour time units and Kaitrin went into the sleeping compartment as Griffen was getting ready for bed. "Let me tell you what my mother said, Griff! I'm quoting, roughly – 'Tell Griffen – what I wish for both of you is that you be as happy as Jaq and I were, for a lot more years than he and I had together.' And that would mean we'd be exquisitely, extraordinarily happy, Griff! And she didn't mind at all that we had a wedding, even if that did mean I betrayed my principles! She probably fainted at discovering her opinionated daughter could be flexible! She can't wait till we get home – she can't wait to meet you! And it's so funny! She asks – tongue in cheek, you know! – if she can call you 'Griffen' – says she refuses to call you 'Prf. Gwidian!' You know, all that flap we went through about what to call each other ... "

He smiled, glancing at her, but he seemed unresponsive. Kaitrin hesitated a moment and then said, "Did you get something from Rianna, Griff?"

"Oh, yes, of course. She is ... She also sends us every good wish."

Kaitrin wanted to say, *How formal*, but she held her tongue. *I've been so engrossed lately. The last three nights I've been too tired to enjoy sex much. Last night I fell asleep in the middle of things ...*

"Griff," she said, "I have just a little finishing up to do and then I'll be in."

He glanced at her again. "Good."

But one thing led to another, and more than an hour passed before she came to bed. When she did, he appeared to be already asleep, and she slipped in beside him without disturbing him. That night passed without any lovemaking.

*   *   *

Kaitrin introduced Kwi'ga'ga'tei to moving images on a reader screen. The alate was utterly mystified, mouthing the instrument all over, inspecting every side of it. Kaitrin hoped desperately that she would not shock herself on the power cell.

And then at last she showed Kwi'ga'ga'tei the vid of Ti'shra's death accompanied by the recording of its dying words. The Seer was dumbfounded; it took several viewings before the alate comprehended what she was seeing. *It is not only words but images, too, that you can catch in your magic boxes. It is beyond all understanding.*

"We do it with – with light. With little pieces of light. Holy Kwi'ga'ga'tei, believe me, it is not magic." Kaitrin had finally learned the meaning of *a'tas'zi|*.

If it is not magic, then it is a miracle of the Nameless One. And after perhaps the tenth viewing, the Seer said, *You are there in the image, too, Ru'a'ma'na'ta. Now I have seen with my own eyes that you were Ti'shra's Comforter.*

"Yes. And now I understand everything that Ti'shra said to

me. You have taught me well, Holy Kwi'ga'ga'tei, and I thank you deeply."

Why did you take Ti'shra away?

"At that time we did not know that the Shshi could speak and were intelligent. We did not know that you were any different from the Little Ones or from the tiny Shshi on our world. We only wanted to study Ti'shra and learn from it, but we never intended for Tish'ra to die. It became sick and we did not know how to save it. Now we are very sorry that we did this thing. I have wanted to tell you that for a long time."

Our Warrior's name was Gli'tha'mu. Did you kill it here or take it away with you?

"We killed it here. It attacked one of our people and we defended ourselves."

I thought it might have happened so. But you took its body away. What became of its body and of the body of Ti'shra?

"Again, we wanted to study them and learn from them. They are still on our world."

The whole fortress of Lo'ro'ra was angry when all this happened, Ru'a'ma'na'ta. We need the bodies of our dead for our sustenance.

"What is the meaning of the last word that you spoke?"

We eat our dead so that nothing is lost of the substance of the fortress – so that death does not weaken us but instead renews life. It is a sacred obligation. Even in war, no Shshi people would ever carry away an enemy's dead. It is unthinkable. That is why we believed you were barbarous.

As the meaning of all this was worked out, Kaitrin felt a chill go over her. "Julian," she said, "get Griffen out here."

Gwidian appeared promptly, looking a little alarmed.

"Griffen, are terrestrial termites ever necrophagous?"

He regarded her. "Sometimes. It conserves protein. And some have been known to kill living members of their society and eat them when the colony becomes overcrowded." He glanced at the waiting Kwi'ga'ga'tei. "I hesitate to ask why you want to know."

"She just told me they eat their dead, Griffen. That's why they were so upset when the bodies disappeared after the attack. Griff, you don't suppose that they … ?"

So with some trepidation she asked the Seer, and Kwi'ga'ga'tei replied, *Old tales tell that at one time fortresses killed their own citizens, especially unhatched eggs, when they became too crowded, but that was long before Lo'ro'ra was founded. Today we send our surplus citizens forth with a nymph-*ma'na'ta|. *They beg a nymph-King from another fortress and seek a place to make a fortress of their own. So Lo'ro'ra itself came to be many season-cycles ago.*

Then Kwi'ga'ga'tei asked, *Can it be that Star-Beings do not consume their dead?*

"We do not," said Kaitrin. "We bury their bodies or we ... I do not know the word – use on them the red thing that happens when lightning touches trees."

You mean, fire? You make to burn the bodies?

"Sometimes. When we bury them, we put stones over them to help us remember them, as you did over the place of Ti'shra's death. The bodies nourish the ground and nourish the plants, but we never nourish ourselves by eating those who die."

Then you are truly different, Ru'a'ma'na'ta. And yet I cannot find you unnatural or evil. Perhaps this is why my vision said, 'The time is new' – because we begin to learn new things.

Kaitrin felt another chill. "You have visions concerning us, Holy Seer?"

Many. Of some I can speak, but they are not all for you, or even for other Shshi, to know.

*   *   *

Over a hasty dinner, Kaitrin informed the fascinated team of what she had learned.

"That's spooky," said Arti with a shiver. "Do you think it's really possible to see across time and space like that? Can there be anything to it?"

"I don't know," said Kaitrin. "Prophets crop up on Earth from time to time, but I've never known any predictions to prove accurate. I think that if humans ever had that sort of gift, it's become lost in the realm of myth. Here it is, the year of the old calendar 2969 and already people are saying the world is going to end in the year 3000. And some people were convinced a catastrophe would occur in the year 200, even though the new calendar has no supernatural significance whatsoever – it only registers how long we've been flying in interstellar space."

"What things did Kwi'ga'ga'tei see?" asked Trea.

"She didn't tell me much, but she said she saw a flying monster with a ring of blank eyes and white steam coming out of its anus."

A nervous titter ran through the group. "That is a very accurate description of our *Durga*," said A'a'ma.

"My theory is that maybe somebody saw the flyer during the first expedition and told her about it, and then she dreamed that image but didn't remember being told."

"Does not sound plausible," said Sev, "or like what we know of this creature's mind."

Trea said, "Kaitrin, do you know if Kwi'ga'ga'tei has visions without help, or does she use psychotropic stimulant?"

"I don't know. You don't go around cavalierly demanding that Seers reveal their secrets. Maybe she'll tell me more as time goes on."

They ate in silence for a moment. Then Kaitrin said, "Griffen, you're awfully quiet."

"If you'd arrange for me to scan the alate's brain, I might be able to tell you something about her so-called visionary powers."

"Oh, Griff, that again? I wish you wouldn't be so impatient!"

"Impatient! I've been waiting for three weeks! – seems like forever with this bloody long planetary day! I need to accomplish some work of my own!"

This unusual outburst startled everyone and Kaitrin said, "Now, Griffen ... "

His face had reddened. "I'm sorry – I realize you can't push too hard. It's only ... " He rose to his feet. "This is not a field expedition. It's a bloody trap!" He turned abruptly and entered the sleeping compartment, slamming the door.

"*¡Ay de mí!*" said Kaitrin, feeling a flush on her own cheeks.

Tió'otu twittered in !Ka<tá. "It is a bit restrictive here, Kaitrin. We never get away from the flyer – never get any exercise. I am not so young and I have a lot of experience with this kind of expedition, and moreover I am a !Ka<tí, a species with quite sedentary preferences, so it does not bother me much. And I do not know whether exploring is safe in any event, but ... "

Trea was gazing thoughtfully at the closed door. Suddenly she said, "Kaitrin, go talk to Gwidian."

Kaitrin glanced at her, got up, and followed him into the compartment.

Griffen was doing his best to pace in the narrow space between the bed and the bulkhead. When Kaitrin entered, he came to a stop facing away from her and said, "What? Coming to give the rebuke?"

"Griffen, I'm sorry if you've felt trapped. I didn't realize. I'll see what can be done to get us out in the field. Maybe if you can work on your regular insects while we wait for ... "

Still turned away from her, he stood looking up at the joint between the ceiling and the bulkhead, his hands clasped tightly behind his back. "You know, of course – don't you, Kaitrin? – that this is your expedition. A'a'ma and I are both here simply to service you – drones in your hive, as it were."

Kaitrin was shocked. "Griffen! Have I made you ... ? You *can't* feel like a drone!"

He turned around then, his eyes filled more with dark desperation than anger.

"I concede that was an exceedingly inept analogy. It's more ... like I really am the termite king – useless for anything but insemination."

Doubly stunned, Kaitrin faltered, "Griffen, how can you ... ? I've thought I was the one – who wasn't giving as much to that as you wanted ... "

"Kaitrin, haven't you learned yet that it isn't just your body that I need?"

His face was again filled with that old unexplained vulnerability and it disturbed her greatly. "Griffen, I don't know what to say to you. I never do when you get like this."

He turned his back again and sat down on the bed. "The only way I've ever tried to hold a woman was by the flesh. But I've never wanted to hold one before, Kait – never desired to hold one longer than a few little months. The only time I considered trying to develop a bond stronger than the attraction of the flesh ... that was with the mother of my son ... I couldn't do it. It frightened me too much. I couldn't do it."

Kaitrin came around and sat beside him. His forehead was

bowed on the heels of his hands, his fingers thrust into the hair. "Griffen, why do you do this? Make everything so complicated and so hard? You don't have to keep trying to hold me – you have me. Even if you stopped wanting me, you would have me. I don't let go easily."

He shuddered. "In earlier days, when I would consider trying … to make a life with a woman … I would look down the years and I couldn't see any answers. The future never seemed … real … "

"What do you see now, Griffen, now that you have me for all time and you look down the years?" And then Kaitrin was not sure she should have asked that question.

He straightened up, his eyes hungrily searching her face. "I see you – I see you everywhere. But I'm not always certain – that I can see myself … "

That answer caused a terror of her own to ripple within her. She threw her arms around him and held him tightly. "Oh, Griffen, you'll be there. You have to be there! You're my answer, too – you fill my life, too."

He made no reply, clutching her as he had on their wedding night, his face against her shoulder. "You have me, Griffen," she whispered. "You have me for all eternity."

"I can't wait for eternity, Kait. I need you now."

Cut even more deeply, she said, "I'm sorry – I'm so sorry if I've neglected you. I never realized I was making you feel that way. I love this work I'm doing so much. But I love you more – I swear to you, Griff, that I do. I just get compulsive about what I'm doing. I have trouble letting go of it."

"Kait, sometimes I think you're too strong for me – I can't cope … "

"No, Griff, no! I tell you what … " She put him away from her, held him at arm's length so he had to look at her. "I'm not self-centered enough to believe that this is only an anthropology expedition. You're responsible for the scientific side of it. You have to produce reports the same as Tió'otu and I do and you have nothing yet to work with. I'll talk to Kwi'ga'ga'tei. I know her so much better now. She's such a wonderful creature, Griff – I'm sure she'll let you examine her. New things scare her a little, but she's very willing and interested. She's as eager to learn as I am.

"And maybe Ki'shto'ba will let you scan that thick head of his! I wonder how thick it really is? Did you know his name means 'Of the Invincible Mandibles'? Oh, bother, I can't get used to calling the soldiers 'it' instead of 'him'! Griff, did I tell you? – the words following Ki'shto'ba's name in the Challenge Speech – *no'no| um'zi|*, which means 'Big, Big Head' or better yet, 'Huge-Head' – that's an epithet like Charles the Bald or Pepin the Short or something! *It* really is like a medieval Champion – *it* came from another fortress to fight for Lo'ro'ra – to fight us, originally. But now its role seems to be to guard the Seer, although I'm not sure why she needs all that guarding in her own fortress. But I'm sure they'll both cooperate! I'll talk to them at the very next meeting."

She was getting Griffen's attention – freeing his mind from that cryptic mood of despair. "I would be very grateful if you could do that," he said. "And I absolutely swear that I will not harm them in any way – no tissue samples, no probes. Only sensor scans, exterior measurements – that sort of thing, don't you know?"

"I know you won't hurt them! And then – and I'm serious! – why don't you get out in the field? Collect some more of those little beetles you're so crazy about! Take Julian and Arti – you'll need somebody to watch out for reptiles and swarms of giant ants while you're busy. Will has more duties here, with the flyer and all, but he'd enjoy going sometimes. You really should have brought a trained field assistant with you."

"Go out in the field without you?"

Kaitrin cupped his cheek in her hand, slightly exasperated. "Griff, you sound ... " She stopped. She had started to say, *You sound like a little boy scared to go on his first school trip without his mother*, but she sensed that was inappropriate. Instead, she said, "We can't work together on everything, Griff."

"I know that," he responded quickly, as if he realized how childish his words had sounded. Then, with an attempt at levity, "You'd let me go out in the field with a woman?"

"Griff. Julian can chaperon the two of you! But I trust you so completely that I'd even let you go out alone with our Maj. Robb! Anyone who engineered the production of that incredibly bizarre wedding cake can't be too much of a threat! Of course, she was working with ornithoid bakers who think a cake is a hunk of bird-seed stuck together with fat! Whatever would we have done if they had served us something like that?"

He started to laugh then, and this moment of crisis slipped into the past along with the earlier ones.

Chapter 8

Iago: The Moor is of a free and open nature
That thinks men honest that but seem to be so,
And will as tenderly be led by the nose
As asses are.
I have 't. It is engendered. Hell and night
Must bring this monstrous birth to the world's light.
– from William Shakespeare, *Othello*

The tiny, enclosed galley was a good place for private conversation and Kaitrin cornered Prf. A'a'ma there a little while later. "Tió'otu, do you think I'm domineering? Does it seem like I've been trying to boss everybody around on this trip?"

His beak opened in one of his kookaburra cackles. "Is that what Prf. Gwidian said to his wife?"

"Well, something like that."

"Kaitrin, I have known you a long time. You have so much enthusiasm, so much energy – you always end by running things. You are not satisfied with anybody else's way of doing it. Do not look so horrified, *nei♪ bi'át♫♫*. It does not bother me in the least. I am used to you – I wave it off like a molted feather." He twirled his clawed fingers extravagantly.

"But I'm well aware that it's your expedition, and Griffen's! What kind of report will I get out of this, anyway?"

"From me? That you are a natural leader and show great

83

initiative and incentive – that you are self-motivating and are developing administrative skills – all that usual kind of thing. That before very long you will be ready to direct your own expeditions. Then you will not have to keep up the pretense of being a subordinate."

"*¡Válgame Dios!* Tió'otu, how did you develop such a wonderful command of Inj?"

"*Hei*, you should have heard me when I first came to Earth twenty-five years ago," he said. "Of course, I never learned the difference between 'burly' and 'burbly.'"

They laughed raucously together.

"But I wonder what Griffen will write about me," said Kaitrin.

A'a'ma hesitated. "I suppose I can say … He has excused himself from that obligation, Kaitrin, on grounds of conflict of interest."

"Hmm. Well … I can see how that might be the ethical thing to do."

*   *   *

At the next session Kaitrin spoke to Kwi'ga'ga'tei and Ki'shto'ba about the physical examinations. "My *na'sha'ma|*," she said, "studies the bodies of creatures and he wants to study yours."

Kwi'ga'ga'tei used a word unfamiliar to Kaitrin, explaining that it meant "one who helps the body to become well if it is sick or hurt."

"Healer. You have healers," said Kaitrin. "My *na'sha'ma|* is not a healer, but he studies similar things. The small female one … " This was the way she designated Trea; Luku was the large female one and Arti was the female warrior. " … is our healer. She will help. They will not hurt you. We will use small boxes like the boxes that you saw in the image – that I placed on the head of Ti'shra. Some will not even touch you."

Kwi'ga'ga'tei stamped and flared her wings, creating burst of light that never failed to inspire awe. *I will tell you this,* she said. *In my first Seeing after you took Ti'shra, I felt a death and I felt weights on my head, like these boxes. And now I will feel them in fact, but I will not feel death.*

This additional visionary revelation gave Kaitrin another *frisson.*

Gwidian's good spirits seemed restored as he and the Pozú prepared the equipment, and Kaitrin thought, *Whatever Tió'otu says now, that word he used earlier was right on. I really am heedless – and toward the person I care most for in the world. It's a fault I simply must weed out of myself.*

As Griffen and Trea scanned the crouching alate's wings and eyes and ran sensors over her body, she said to Kaitrin, *You make your* a'tas'zi| *upon me.*

"We do not call it 'magic,'" Kaitrin said. "We call it ... " For what was the root of the word "science," anyway? Knowledge. Systematic, demonstrable knowledge. The Shshi had two words that could apply: *preiv'zi|,* "something known"; and *parn'zi|,* "something learned." " ... a way of knowing, a way of learning. There is much that we do not know and these boxes help us to learn. So you should call them 'learning boxes,' not 'magic boxes.'"

There are things that you can learn from the Shshi?

"Oh, yes. A great deal."

The thing that we learn most from you is how much we do not know.

Ki'shto'ba was as willing as Kwi'ga'ga'tei to cooperate in the examinations. Kaitrin took much amusement, and A'a'ma considerable alarm, from watching Griffen and Sev measuring the Warrior's mandibles. The indisputably dangerous giant was exceedingly courteous and compliant, standing motionless while the two humans manipulated calipers and "learning boxes" over its awesome physical form. *Is this position acceptable?* it would ask helpfully. *Would you like for me to lift my head? Should I lean this way?* It did not even object to being hoisted off the ground in the sling of a field scale; even Kwi'ga'ga'tei submitted to the indignity of being so dangled. It put them both in a vulnerable position and clearly demonstrated how far Kaitrin had come in gaining her informants' trust.

*   *   *

Over a meal, which Kaitrin carefully remembered to prepare, Griffen discussed the preliminary results of the tests on the pair.

"Kwi'ga'ga'tei's body is slender and over a meter long," he said, "and her wings are 20 centimeters longer than that, but she weighs only 33.5 kilos; the alates are quite fragile creatures, or at least this one is. In contrast, the workers have plump little bodies; Ti'shra was under a meter and weighed 30 kilos when we first captured him.

"Now, Ki'shto'ba weighs 72 kilos and is more than a meter and a half long, with heavy musculature. The soldier we killed was about 115 centimeters in length and weighed approximately 40 kilos. I'm sure you've observed those bristle-covered cerci – tails – on our challenger's posterior. All the rest of our Shshi lack such appendages. And the differences in head and mandible shape are obvious. My guess is we're dealing with two distinct species. DNA testing should confirm that; we were able to get saliva samples."

Then Griffen asked Kaitrin if she knew that Ki'shto'ba was a vestigial female and she giggled skeptically.

"It's quite true, but it has no significance. The alates have distinct dormant genitalia and produce some sex pheromones – I was able to discern that without probing, Kaitrin! – but the workers and soldiers have only negligible vestigial structures and produce no sex hormones whatsoever. They are truly neuter. I'm certain none of them would be capable of transforming into secondary reproductives. The alates, I'm not so sure about ... "

"I think they're instinctively aware of all this, because they use neuter pronouns for the soldiers and the workers but not for the alates," said Kaitrin, then added with a hoot, "Does Ki'shto'ba's supersized cranium make it a genius or a bonehead?"

"Our scans show incredible head chitin – at least 15 centimeters thick," Gwidian replied. "It's so dense that our field equipment can't penetrate it except at the ducts of the antennae. But my guess is that its head is at least a third of its total mass and the brain within it is the same size as that of any Shi. The neck and foreleg muscles show unprecedented development for an insectoid, and the pronotal shield covering the neck joint is remarkably tough and flexible! And the belly, where the sclerites are thinner – have you noticed those marks on it? Scars, where a healed wound has roughened the texture of the chitin! This soldier has definitely seen battle. Truly a formidable creature – makes you shudder if you allow yourself to think about it!"

"Oh, I'm not intimidated," said Kaitrin. "Ki'shto'ba has never given me any reason to believe it's anything but the proverbial gentle giant."

Griffen continued expounding on the alates. "Of the three castes that we've examined, the alates differ the most from their terrestrial counterparts. The variations lie mainly in the alae and the eyes, and in the fact that, rather than having an ephemeral lifespan, they seem to mature into a dormantly but recognizably sexed, permanently winged imago whose reproductive function remains undetermined to this point.

"The bioluminescence comes from photophores distributed along the veins of the wings. These photophores are quite complex – they have lens bodies, reflectors, color filters, like some of those deep-sea aquatics that we talked about, Trea. Some are pigmented, some not. They utilize organic compounds that react in the presence of oxygen in a process similar to that found on Earth, but instead of being sequestered in the photocytes, those chemicals are produced by glands beneath the wing scales. They are dispersed to the photophores by a valved pumping mechanism that activates when the wings are fanned, thus controlling the intensity of the light. There is no flashing mechanism like that of fireflies.

"The wings are tougher than they look; they're firmly attached, lacking the suture where a terrestrial alate's wings are intended to break off. The membrane is like fine, tough, semitransparent parchment, but the veins are quite permeable; the alates would dehydrate quickly in full sun. This porosity probably serves to allow absorption of oxygen to help catalyze the photic reaction. These are creatures whose ancestors were adapted to life in a dark, humid underground, even though evolution has impelled them to walk in the light.

"Then, the eyes … The alate's vision is as unusual as I suspected. The eyes are located more frontally and placed closer together than in terrestrial termites and the antennae are located laterally and slightly to the rear. The pigmentation indicates that their vision encompasses the full spectral range, including red and probably rising into the ultraviolet. Do they have names for colors, Kaitrin? Yes?

"Each of the many thousands of ommatidia – the individual

facets – is strongly isolated from the others. This results in thousands of restricted individual images, a fact that theoretically should inhibit the ability to focus. But we ran some visual acuity tests and our subject could pick out individual stones in the side of the fortress from 50 meters. Our brain scan shows that the protocerebrum, stunted in our blind soldier and worker, is quite large and possesses a trio of specialized nodes. I'm hypothesizing that the central node reconciles the messages from the facets of each eye that are seeing the same image, producing binocular vision. It then fuses the whole into a panoramic sweep with extended peripheral sightlines. But with the eyes positionally fixed, it seems that our alate can conveniently turn the binocular function on and off – use each eye separately if she wishes. And the corneal lenses seem to be elastic, like the lenses of a human eye, allowing focus on near objects! I'm convinced that to this point such visual complexity in a compound eye has never been encountered anywhere in the explored universe!"

Trea said, "Is adapted to see well in low light, too – one might expect that thing. Fascinating to study."

"Isn't it just! Too bad we didn't know about these alates – we could have brought along a Specialist in arthropod vision. And Prf. Chandra would be in his element! Of course, he'd be frustrated that dissection is a no-no." Griffen grinned wickedly at Kaitrin, who made a face.

Then he continued, "Our scans discerned some axons leading to the vestigial ocelli, not from the protocerebrum but from deep in the deutocerebrum, which deals with language, communication, and reasoning and should have only a minimal relationship with vision. Those axons are producing a weak electrical signal, but I'm at a loss as to its function. The ocelli are covered by scales of opaque chitin and shouldn't be capable of even detecting light."

"Gwidian," said the doctor, "I have meant to say – I think ocelli contain inert process that may activate during the visionary episodes. The electrical signals you mention have characters of brain waves present in some mammals with electrocerebral disorders. Maybe needs some external stimulus to activate – some psychotropic or hallucinogen."

There was a pause while everyone chewed on this information. Then Kaitrin said, "That's interesting, but physiological activity of that sort doesn't explain what she sees – how she saw our flyer in such detail, or how she was aware of the weight of the transceptors on Ti'shra's head – or how she predicted they would receive the speaking of the dead. Did I tell you about that? She says that the Nameless One – their Great Goddess – instructed her to prepare for the 'speaking of the dead'! I'm predisposed to be highly skeptical about such things, but I can't help thinking that her visions may be more than an accident of brain chemistry."

"I did not say I believe vision power is only accident of brain chemistry," said Trea. "But a Seer needs certain kind of brain physiology to be Seer – is so among Pozú. Do I make clear?"

After pondering a moment, Kaitrin said, "Kwi'ga'ga'tei said fortresses usually have only one Seer at a time. She said the whole citizenry relies on her powers, so she bears a great responsibility. At least I think I understood her right. She also said that not everyone is always a friend of the Seer. I think she was implying that her authority is being challenged – maybe someone is trying to pull a coup. Could be why she needs the constant guard."

"♪♪♫," warbled A'a'ma. "Some things are the same throughout the universe. All ILF societies produce individuals who are self-serving and covet power – who resent and envy those who have it."

"Governing is definitely an alate function," said Kaitrin, "and I think we're dealing here with the *de facto* ruler of this society. Kwi'ga'ga'tei seems so unpretentious and deferent; she serves the *na'ta'zei|* – the Holy One, the Queen – and it makes sense that she should, given the analogy with termite society. But I'm sure the Queen is quite dependent on those who serve her. Kwi'ga'ga'tei has spoken of Chiefs of the different Castes. The soldiers – or Warriors, as I've started calling them – have a General Officer, whom I'm designating the Commander. I think we saw it on that morning when the army came out to greet us. The Chief of Workers is named No'kri – 'Big Leg.' And Kwi'ga'ga'tei has mentioned just in passing that the Queen has an Alate steward or majordomo called the *na'sta'mi'zei|*. That means literally 'holy room person,' but I'm calling *na'sta'mi|* – the place where the Queen and King dwell – the 'Holy Chamber,' so I'm translating *na'sta'mi'zei|* as 'Chamberlain.'

"But of all these officials Kwi'ga'ga'tei is surely the one who tells the rest what's what. I feel deeply honored that she would expend all this time and energy serving as our informant."

* * *

Griffen had collected some important data, but he was still fretting about getting into the field. "I need to compare the current status of the entomofauna with my records from last July," he said. "Eggs, pupae, dormancy, that sort of thing. And I want to search for other bioluminescent organisms and also for arachnids and amphibians; neither has been observed thus far on this planet. And the aquatic biota – that's virtually uninvestigated."

When Kaitrin informed Kwi'ga'ga'tei that they were about to start tramping through the nearby terrain, the Seer surprised her by seeming alarmed. *I can send guards with you,* she said.

"Holy Kwi'ga'ga'tei, I thank you, but that is not necessary. Our two warriors will go with the *na'sha'ma|.* They can protect him from the big reptiles."

The reptiles can be dangerous, yes, but they are not my main concern. The Seer was dancing about and flaring her wings in a rare manifestation of anxiety.

"What is it? Is there some danger that we do not know?"

But Kwi'ga'ga'tei seemed to take a resolution. *No. I will make sure that none exists.* Then she added, *Ru'a'ma'na'ta, I cannot see the weapons of your Warriors.*

Then Kaitrin thought she understood the hesitancy; Kwi'ga'ga'tei was more concerned about the safety of her own people than of the visitors. "We do not grow them from our bodies as the Shshi do. They are like the learning boxes – we make them. We carry them fixed to our bodies in separate little boxes."

How can such small and unseen things kill?

"They make a bright light and a loud vibration, like striking something with much strength. They are powerful weapons, Kwi'ga'ga'tei. They do not have to touch what they kill – they kill easily from a distance of many Shi-lengths. We used one against Gli'tha'mu. But you do not need to be afraid. We will never use them against the Shshi again, I promise."

Kwi'ga'ga'tei's jeweled eyes regarded her for a moment. Then she said, *A weapon is meant to be used when it is needed. Your King may go out and travel our marches without a guard*

90

of the Shshi.   But send your Warriors with him, with their magic weapons.

"He would also like to enter the *tho'sei|* orchard, to examine the trees and the creatures that he saw the first time he was here."

Your na'sha'ma| never speaks to us as you do.   Are your Kings unable to speak?

"They can speak to our own people, but mine has not learned how speak with the antenna-box. It is difficult to learn."

Many Workers will be in the orchards, and some Warriors, so it will be quite safe there.   I will make sure that the Worker Chiefs and the Cohort Chiefs know that he is coming so that no surprises will happen.

Kaitrin reported this strange exchange to Gwidian and the other team members. "I'm not sure what she meant when she said, *A weapon is meant to be used when it is needed.* It was almost as if she were giving you permission to use weapons on her fellow Shshi if you needed to. That makes me a bit uneasy."

"And I," Gwidian said. "But I believe I'll chance it, all the same. I'll work in the orchard first, and if I encounter too many of our isopteroid friends, I just might not go back. I'm not as comfortable in their presence as you are, Kait."

"If I went with you ... But, no, you go first and see how it goes."

"The Major and I will keep a good eye out," said Julian. "We won't let your Professor get into any scrapes."

Gwidian laughed and made a dismissive gesture, and so the plans were set.

*   *   *

Gwidian spent several four-hour shifts in the orchard. At first, the Growers scurried away timidly at the Strange Ones' approach and any Warrior guards that happened to be about put up brief threat displays. But soon they grew accustomed to the aliens' presence and would even creep up to touch them timidly and then scamper off, or stand with stiffened antennae, trying to talk to them.

"Kait, you really should come," Griffen said. "You could converse with them whilst I'm scuffing about in the leaf litter and turning over rocks. You know you'd love it."

"Well, yes – but actually I think Kwi'ga'ga'tei is reluctant to let us talk to anyone but her and Ki'shto'ba. I think it's coming, but I don't want to push it."

Gwidian discovered no eight-legged arthropods, but he did find some web-spinning hexapods, some estivating ten-centimeter beetles, and the bioluminescent larvae of an unknown insect. He brought back numerous pupa cases, as well as shells of hatched lizard and bird eggs discovered in nest cavities in hollow trees. He was also able to holograph a rotund, 15-centimeter saurian with a horned head, a ruffle of skin down its spine, and chameleon-like eyes. These discoveries whetted his appetite for a more lengthy excursion, and he hazarded a couple of jaunts several kilometers southward, outside the wall. The team recorded a variety of saurians and proto-ophidians but no true snakes and not a single amphibian. They identified a dozen species of birds of all sizes and degrees of strangeness, and that was only a beginning. Gwidian was now in his own element and tended to forget everything during these ventures. Arti and Julian trailed after him, keeping in touch with the flyer by MP.

In the outlying areas they did not encounter a single Shi.

Griffen seemed to have recovered his equanimity and Kaitrin was relieved; she found his repeated attacks of despondency disturbing. But she discovered that she missed his presence sorely when they were apart, and she began to seriously consider accompanying him on an excursion before much more time passed.

*   *   *

[The Charnel Hall. Workers are engaged in dismembering and masticating portions of five bodies in preparation for feeding the Warriors. Wooden bins and hollows in the floor are full of mandibles and pieces of inedible chitin. In the doorway Mo'gri'ta'tu converses with the Chief of the Charnel Workers]

[Mo'gri'ta'tu]: What I tell you is true, Ko'li, I swear.

[The Charnel Chief, aghast]: These outlanders do not consume their dead?

[Mo'gri'ta'tu]: I fear not. They are truly depraved.

[The Charnel Chief]: They leave them to rot away – to be lost

92

to the common good? Hideous! I shudder in horror!

[Mo'gri'ta'tu]: They even put fire to them, the Seer said. Destroy their substance utterly.

[The Charnel Chief]: They throw them into the volcanoes?

[Mo'gri'ta'tu]: I do not know about volcanoes. Perhaps they leave them in the dry grass and wait for the lightning to start fires.

[The Charnel Chief, increasingly horrified]: Reptiles or birds would consume them first! Even such speechless creatures know enough to conserve the substance of the dead!

[Mo'gri'ta'tu]: Such sacrilege is what we face in this new time, honored Chief. And what is really frightening is that Holy Kwi'ga'ga'tei seems to find no fault in this. Well, I go my way. Good day to you, Ko'li.

[Mo'gri'ta'tu scurries away down the corridor] Ko'li is a notorious gossip. I have ensured that this scurrilous bit of news will be all over the fortress by tomorrow.

[Later, in the corridor outside the Holy Chamber, Hi'ta'fu and Lo'lo'pai encounter Mo'gri'ta'tu]

[Hi'ta'fu]: Walk with us, Chamberlain. I have some horrifying information.

[Mo'gri'ta'tu]: What ... already?

[Hi'ta'fu]: Already, what? The Chief and I have just come from Kwi'ga'ga'tei. She tells us that the male Strange One she dares to call *na'sha'ma|*, together with the outland Warriors, will be spending time trampling about in the marches of Lo'ro'ra – for what purpose, who knows?

[Mo'gri'ta'tu]: Oh, that is old news. They have already gone forth twice, and among the *tho'sei|* trees as well. You knew it – you were told to instruct your Warriors not to attack them.

[Lo'lo'pai]: But the latest news is that they have magic weapons that can kill without touching. Kwi'ga'ga'tei favors us with obscure threats. *If anyone were to consider harming these visitors, their weapons would undoubtedly administer a fatal surprise.*

[Mo'gri'ta'tu]: So? I put no stock in such drivel. She continues to engage in word intimidation.

[Hi'ta'fu]: I cannot believe that weapons exist that can kill without touching. But I do not like ignorance of the enemy. It makes me uneasy.

[Lo'lo'pai]: A Warrior of Lo'ro'ra never flinches from any opponent, but it is ever useful to know the nature of the thing one fights.

[Mo'gri'ta'tu]: Ah ... You have given me an idea, noble Warriors. A confrontation ... A confrontation by well-planned chance. Has anyone observed the outlanders going out today?

[Lo'lo'pai]: My scouts detected the so-called King's departure several turns of the water vessel ago. The small and the large male Warriors went with him.

[Mo'gri'ta'tu]: Can you follow their trail?

[Hi'ta'fu, dancing]: I believe I understand where you are going with this.

[Lo'lo'pai]: They lay down an incredibly weak scent, but I think we could locate them.

[Mo'gri'ta'tu]: Then do so. Take a few trusted Lieutenants with you. Need I caution you that your purpose for the moment is not killing? Perhaps we can simply frighten them into flying away. I think it is always the best course to seek a peaceful resolution. Do you not agree?

[Hi'ta'fu]: At least we may discover what sort of weapon it is that we must go against.

[Mo'gri'ta'tu]: And of course, there is always a possibility that an accident might happen, if you take my meaning. If the Commander of Lo'ro'ra is threatened, who would not expect it and its companions to defend themselves?

*　　*　　*

[Lo'lo'pai]: We go round in circles seeking for this trail. One would think that the outlanders purposely avoid laying pheromones.

[Hi'ta'fu]: I am told that is exactly the case. They smother their scent glands by wrapping fibers around their bodies.

[Another Warrior]: And I was told that their shape and manner of walking is such that their bellies would not contact the ground even if they were unwrapped.

[Lo'lo'pai]: Surpassingly odd! How do they find each other?

[A second Warrior]: I have located the trail! It leads back toward the fortress!

[Hi'ta'fu]: Let us follow it.

[For a time they do so]

[The Warrior]: It turns suddenly toward the area of the lava hill. They may have realized we are following and seek to put a rock-wall at their backs.

[Lo'lo'pai]: Good. Let us approach!

[Hi'ta'fu]: But cautiously. When one is uncertain of the foe's strength, one does not gallop in headlong, Lo'lo'pai. There are five of us. Spread the semicircle – converge upon the outcropping from several points.

[The Shshi Warriors, heads raised in threat, mandibles agape and gnashing, fan out and move forward in short sprints. As they approach the rocks, the odor of the outlanders grows stronger; it is overlaid with potent pheromones of fear]

[Sa'ti'a'i'a appears unexpectedly behind the Shshi, with a contingent of four Nasute Warriors]: Commander! You are personally conducting patrols? But were you not instructed that what you are threatening is no enemy?

[The Shshi Warriors jump around, some lunging. The Nasutes discharge warning jets of acid that hit the ground in front of the Commander and the Chief. A few drops splash Lo'lo'pai's palps and it curses, raking at its mouthparts with its forelegs]

[Simultaneously, a powerful shock wave strikes the ground from the direction of the lava outcropping, then another to the right of the first. Two Shshi Warriors and one Nasute are knocked over, then scramble to their feet and retreat]

[Outcries]: It is the weapon! The weapon that kills without touching!

[The Shshi Lieutenants and the Nasute who were closest to the shock scamper off, but Hi'ta'fu, Lo'lo'pai, Sa'ti'a'i'a, and the remaining Nasutes stand their ground]

[Sa'ti'a'i'a]: Have you not learned to believe what Holy Kwi'ga'ga'tei tells you? Or would you like a closer acquaintance with this weapon?

[Lo'lo'pai, advances]: I am tired of these games! I say, attack!

[Another shock. Dirt and stones fly up against the face of the Chief of the First Cohort]

[Hi'ta'fu]: Retreat! It is enough! The purpose was only to gain information and we have done that!

[The Warriors hastily back off, then turn and scuttle away, with Lo'lo'pai last, sidling and threatening behind it as it goes]

[Sa'ti'a'i'a]: This was ill-considered, Hi'ta'fu! Not only did you disobey the express instruction of the Holy Seer, but you also almost got all of us killed! But maybe now you will treat her advice more seriously.

[Hi'ta'fu]: You speak insolently, Warrior of the Enemy. Do you know who your Commander is?

[Sa'ti'a'i'a]: I serve as Liegemate to Lo'ro'ra, Hi'ta'fu, and I take commands only from Lo'ro'ra's Holy One and King. And at the moment I do not believe that their commands come to me through you.

Chapter 9

"Saint Withold footed twice the 'old,
He met the nightmare and her ninefold ... "
– *from* William Shakespeare, *King Lear*

Gwidian's voice came over the comlink. "We're starting back now, but we're a bit farther afield than I intended, so it will take awhile. A lot of absorbing stuff today, Kait. Forgot the time – what? Sound familiar?" His laugh rumbled through the speaker.

Kaitrin grinned at his playful mood. "Well, shake a leg! It's not that long till the night cycle starts and I don't want to go to bed alone!"

"Ha! My Queen offers an incentive! We'll be there straight away, I promise!"

An hour later it was Will on the MP, sounding breathless. "Sensors show some Shshi out here, maybe following us. Intent unknown. That's pretty peculiar."

"Somebody is curious, I guess," answered Luku, who was monitoring the link.

"I don't know. The Professor thinks it's soldiers, from the mass on the readings."

This information alarmed Kaitrin briefly, but upon thinking about it, she said, "Kwi'ga'ga'tei must have decided to send a guard after all. I wonder why."

In the *Durga* they waited awhile. Finally Kaitrin said, "I'm going up and try to contact them again."

At first Luku could not rouse anyone, then widening the range brought a response from Julian. "What's going on?" said Kaitrin. "What are you doing so far south?"

"Evasive action," said Julian. "We got a glimpse of what's following us – five regular monsters. They keep wandering off course, but they always zero in and get closer."

"*¡Maldito!*" said Kaitrin. "But I can't believe they mean any harm! Let me talk to Griffen."

When he came on, he was no longer playful. "Can't talk, Kait. We're climbing toward some rocks – don't want to get caught in the open. Bloody hell! What's that? Let's get ... "

There was some clatter and some distant, unintelligible vocalizing, then static, then the link went dead. "Griffen!" cried Kaitrin, jabbing at the console.

She passed a very bad ten minutes, pacing around the flight deck and ranting. Every thirty seconds, she would pounce up to Luku at the com station to see if anything was coming through. Arti tried to reassure her. Trea finally took her arm and said, "Sit, Kaitrin. There will be word. Be calm."

"How do you know? My god! We've got to go find them! Or maybe I ought to go over to the fortress and find a guard and ask if ... "

At that moment the comlink came to life. It was Will. "Close call. They attacked us – well, sort of. Scary time. We're starting back."

"Griffen ... I want to talk ... "

"Nobody's hurt, Kaitrin! We need to save our breath for quick hiking. We'll see you as soon as we can and tell you everything." And they heard no more.

An hour later, Kaitrin's eyes were watering from peering out of the windows into the creeping darkness of the planet's long twilight. Arti Robb stood alongside her, comfortingly solid, while Luku sat futilely monitoring the silent comlink.

"Do you see them yet?" called A'a'ma from the bottom of the ladder.

"No! I'm getting awfully worried, Tió'otu! It's almost pitch dark!"

"Wait, I see a light!" cried Arti. "Coming in from the south!"

"I see it, too! *¡Gracias a Dios!* It's really them!"

They watched the bobbing of the field lights as the team trudged toward them. As they neared the flyer, Kaitrin catapulted down the ladder. "Tió'otu! Pop the hatch!"

In a moment Griffen was in her arms. After Julian and Will were inside, the Captain quickly turned and sealed the entrance.

"Griffen, love. Are you all right?"

"Yes, but … Oh, Kait … " Griffen was kissing her repeatedly, roughly.

"What in the world happened?"

"Those damned soldiers chased us for several hours," said Will. "Our sensors kept picking them up, then losing them, as if they were having trouble tracking us."

Julian said, "We circled south to try to evade them, but they started to close in, and then we saw them – five big soldiers … So we cut up toward those rocks to have something at our backs. They came fast at the end – formed a semicircle and pinned us down."

"The way they were waving their heads around and snapping their jaws, I thought we were goners for sure for a couple of minutes there," said Will shakily.

"¡Maldito! Why?" said Kaitrin, pulling away from Griffen so she could look at him. He was breathing hard, clearly stressed and exhausted. "I mean, why were they chasing you?"

"Who knows why these goddam freaks do anything!" he exploded, and he flung off his backpack and dropped into a seat at the table.

"Griffen." Kaitrin sat down next to him and seized his hand. With the other he snatched off his field hat and scrubbed his face, clawing back sweat-soaked hair. Luku had jumped to get water for everybody. Griffen took a long pull at the bottle and choked.

"Then to compound everything, a bunch of Nasutes appeared," said Will.

"They started shooting that stuff out of their snouts – that was the last straw," said Julian. "We felt it was necessary to fire on them."

Kaitrin cursed again and A'a'ma exclaimed, "He'etí <khe!dora] Did you hit anybody?"

"First we fired at the ground," said Will. "It scared them a lot."

"But one of the big ones – one of the leaders – it just kept coming," said Julian. "Prf. Gwidian fired at it … "

In Kaitrin's grasp, Griffen's hand contracted. "Kaitrin, I had to. Would you rather have one of them dead, or me?"

"Griffen, I hope you know the answer to that! But – did you kill it?" Kaitrin's mind was racing furiously. *What are we going to have to deal with here, anyway?*

"It ran off with the others," he said, "so I suppose I did not."

Will was shaking his head. "Your shot didn't hit it, Professor. It threw up a big spurt of gravel and some of that might have stung it a little, but that's all. That one was really defiant – it kept prancing sideways and shaking its mandibles at us all the time it was retreating."

Trea and Sev had been standing by quietly through all of this, but now Trea approached Julian. "It looks that same gravel nicked your face. Let me clean it for you." She began pulling supplies out of her omnipresent medical kit.

"I can't understand it," said Kaitrin. "Kwi'ga'ga'tei assured me it would be safe."

"I suppose you were sitting down here having tea with your friend as usual, whilst we were playing gazelle to their lions," said Gwidian in a harsh tone. He was beginning to react; the water bottle was shaking in his hand. Trea observed him as she cleansed Julian's scratches with a pad of antiseptic.

"Actually, Kwi'ga'ga'tei and Ki'shto'ba didn't show up this afternoon," said Kaitrin, capturing his hand and pressing it together with the other one. "That made me a little uneasy to begin with. They've come without fail ever since we started these sessions. But I can't understand about the Nasutes. They attacked you, too?"

"The whole thing didn't seem exactly like an attack," said Julian. "Will, what did you think?"

The pilot nodded agreement. "More like a threat or challenge, although it might have escalated in a hurry. I'd swear, when the Nasutes showed up, it was almost like they were weighing in on our side. One of them was that officer who comes sometimes with Kwi'ga'ga'tei. When they snorted, it seemed to be at the Shshi soldiers, not at us. Their discharge smells really unpleasant, like hot acid. It made my eyes smart."

"Well, now I think I understand something," said Kaitrin. "Kwi'ga'ga'tei said, *I can give you a guard.* The Nasute seem to be her guard. God, I wonder what this is all about!"

Griffen pushed himself up from the table, hunched over. "Sick," he mumbled, and retreated to the hygiene compartment. Kaitrin got up to follow him. Trea said, "Kaitrin, bring him into bedroom. I can help."

He had vomited in the toilet and was leaning with his hands against the bulkhead, his face white. "You see what I meant ... about courage?" he gasped.

"Griffen, something like this would scare anybody. When the comlink went dead, I was out of my mind! Do you know how awful it is not to know what's going on?"

"I dropped the MP. The brutes suddenly popped out of cover three meters away from us and we had to run for it. Then for a while we were a bit – tied up ... "

"Come on, Griff. Trea says she can give you something."

He let her lead him into their sleeping compartment, past the concerned gaze of the other team members. "Kait, I'm so glad – you weren't out there ... "

"Maybe if I had been there with my antenna box, I could have talked with them and found out what in the world was causing them act like that."

Trea had followed them in. "Sit, Gwidian. I will make what we call *zo-yevá*. In Inj 'touch-soul therapy' is some of meaning." She climbed up on the bed behind him and let her tiny, supple fingers wander over various points of his head, neck, shoulders, and spine. As she worked, she half-closed her eyes and chanted with a smooth, hypnotic rhythm some burring syllables of her own language. Kaitrin had never seen Pozú medicine in action and she watched in fascination.

"That's the trouble," Griffen was saying to Kaitrin. "It's difficult to confront something you can't communicate with – something that you know has intelligence but that looks like a living nightmare! I mean, I'm an entomologist – I'm used to insects. But on this scale ... " He shuddered. "A rhinoceros beetle is harmless, but if you met one that was two meters long ..."

"A reliable auto-translator that goes directly between Shshi biopulses and Inj is still some distance in the future," said Kaitrin.

"We haven't anything like a complete enough vocabulary or mastery of the syntax."

"Oh, I understand that," said Griffen. Under Trea's ministrations he was growing calmer. "And it's not like this is my first bad field experience, either. One time in the Pilenberg Preserve, I blundered right into an enormous lioness who was hiding new cubs in a thicket. She lunged at me, but it was mostly bluff and I got away. On another occasion I had to execute quite a sprint to escape some ill-tempered buffalos. Then I fell out of a tree and impaled myself on a stump in Ostrailia. But – excepting what happened the other time we were here – I've never experienced anything on any planet that was as frightening as this!" He took a deep breath. "I'm all right," he said. "Thanks, Trea. Do you know, I've never been sorry for one minute that I agreed to take you and Sev as this expedition's Medical Officers?"

"Good," she said with her grimacing smile. "I get you more water. All of you are dehydrated. Kaitrin, see he drinks it. And something to eat in an hour or so. I think it stays down then."

"You're not going to give him any medication?" asked Kaitrin.

Griffen had straightened up and was looking around in alarm. "I say, what's become of my hat?"

Trea shook her head, her chuckle chattering. "No need for medication. Just rest will work fine. We are safe in *Durga*. We can put off thinking until morning."

*   *   *

Griffen woke Kaitrin with a sharp cry. She rose on her elbow, hanging over him in the near darkness. "Griffen! Wake up! You're dreaming!"

He had already wakened himself. He retained his breath for a moment, then exhaled it with a rough vocalization. Kaitrin said, "Griff, it's all right. Just a nightmare. Was it – was it the drowning thing again?"

He struggled to sit up, pushing away the sheet. She reached to brighten the light. He was gasping, clutching the left side of his ribs. "Do you have a pain in your chest?" she said in concern.

"Yes ... no ... not in reality. It was – the drowning thing, but ... " He tried to swallow, but his throat was too dry. "I was just

... swimming normally ... and then this pair of – of pruning hooks
– came out of the water and seized me – right here ... " He indicated his ribs. "Pulled me under. God."

"Well, it's obvious where that came from!"

"Yes, we don't need Rianna to interpret that one, what?" He
fumbled on the shelf beside the bed, located a water bottle, and
took a long drink. Then he sank back on the pillow. "When these
creatures strike, they hit a human right about on the chest here.
Like Towsen. Only he was shorter, so they hit him – higher than
they would hit me."

"Oh, let's not even think about it!"

They lay in silence for a while. Kaitrin pressed herself
against Griffen, feeling his heart's heavy thump. At length heartbeat and breath quieted, but the will to sleep had abandoned both
of them.

Presently he said, "I used to dread having these nightmares
when I was alone. But it was even worse having one when I was –
with a woman ... Everything is so much better for me now, Kait.
Not being alone ... being with you."

Moved, Kaitrin hugged him hard. "Oh, Griff. I do so want to
make things better for you."

"I daresay you never have nightmares," he said, striving for a
lighter tone.

"Oh, everybody does, sometimes, but mine are never like
yours. I don't think I've ever dreamed I was dying. I have the old
scholar's nightmares – forgetting to study for a test or not being
able to remember the answers – things like that. One time I
dreamed I had to give a speech in Spainish, which I speak every bit
as well as Inj, and I couldn't remember a word. And – oh, yes! –
sometimes I get lost on campus! I actually did when I was fifteen
and I think the experience traumatized me for life! I got on the
underground going the wrong way and ended up way over in Soci-
etal Studies. I wandered around for what seemed like hours, too
embarrassed to ask for directions – or too stubborn! Finally, when
it started to get dark, I broke down in tears and messaged Tió'otu
and he came and rescued me."

Griffen laughed tenderly. "My poor Kait. You really were
very young to be thrown alone into that enormous place. I wish
you could have called me. Was I in Okloh then?"

"Eleven years ago?"

"Let's see – I was thirty-two … No, I was in Jonnsberg trying to figure out what in the world I could do to coax the Board into granting me a Professorship."

"You've never told me what your Professorial project was after you switched to xenology."

"I sampled beetles on eight different planets – I was off Earth almost constantly for two years – and correlated the findings with every jot and tittle of work that had been done up to that point. No stone unturned – literally! Then I reworked the existing cladistics system. I've managed to get myself recognized as a principal authority on Xenocoleoptera."

"Really? That's wonderful!"

"I've gotten rather sick of beetles, actually. Lately I've been dabbling in butterflies."

"Griffen, do you realize how little we know about each other? We really haven't been acquainted all that long. Like what you said earlier about impaling yourself on a stump. Is that scar on your back from that?"

"On the shoulder blade? Yes. I was climbing around in a tree searching for weaver ants and there was this snake … It was a brown tree snake, which is venomous but rear-fanged, so it isn't particularly dangerous to humans. But for a moment I was positive it was a fear snake, which is really lethal – dangerous even if you've been immunized. The two creatures don't look at all alike – besides, fear snakes aren't even found in that part of the continent – but somehow those Ossie elapids had me spooked. Rianna's partner Gerit is a snake man, you know, and he really dressed me down afterwards for making such a neophyte mistake." Griffen chuckled in chagrin. "Of course, I did know better, but it only took one moment of panic for me to lose hold of the branch and fall about three meters onto a sharp, broken stump. It struck the scapula and glanced off, cracking it in the process. Doctor said if it had entered a few centimeters to the southwest, it could have gone spot on between the ribs and stabbed me through the heart."

"¡Válgame Dios! Don't scare me like that!"

They rested quiet again for a few moments, comforted by their closeness. Then Kaitrin said, "I'm glad we're in different fields – it would be awful if we had to compete professionally.

I'm very competitive – you didn't realize that, did you? But I'm not that big on insects, although I do find all kinds of natural history fascinating – and you're not that much into anthropology, except maybe for folk art. But we both like the same recreational things – theater and poetry and music and art. I'll even make an effort to learn about hockey if you want to take the trouble to teach me. I never reject a new experience!"

Griff's fingers were moving incessantly in her hair and she turned her head into the touch, sighing blissfully. He said, "I noticed before we left Earth that Antiquarian Drama had announced the Shaksper productions for spring. *Lear* is one of them. There's an actor coming to Karlinius from Oxkam to play the lead. Then they're also doing *Taming of the Shrew*."

Kaitrin giggled. "We'll definitely want to attend both of them if we get back in time. But I don't know about seeing *Shrew* in your company! I'm afraid you'll tease me unmercifully!"

"Fancy your thinking that!" he responded, giving her a squeeze.

She snuggled even closer to him, nuzzling his neck. "Griffen, do you know this is what I love most about you and me? Quiet, intimate times like this, where we're just talking of this and that and aren't trying to solve problems or make momentous decisions."

"Oh, Kait ... " Then, in a moment, "You know, I really can't wait to get home – to start our life together, our everyday life. I'm looking forward to that so much, Kait! – so much that I can't begin to express it."

"Even if it means holographing tedious DB lectures on those ho-hum beetles, and sitting through endless committee meetings, and – horror of horrors! – tutoring bot-brained first-year postgrads?"

"Even that. I feel quite shaky about this planet, Kait. As I said, I've been chased by things – by animals – before, but they never projected anything so sinister. I concede it could have been merely my imagination, but I thought I could sense something more ominous than an instinct for self-preservation. It felt like – like willful malevolence."

A spontaneous little shiver went through Kaitrin. "But you don't feel that kind of threat from Kwi'ga'ga'tei, do you?"

"No, nor from our Goliath, who undoubtedly could take out any one of us in a heartbeat. But just the same, I'll feel relieved when we're both safely on our way home."

In a moment, Kaitrin said, "Are you going out in the field again?"

"I almost have to. Not immediately – I need a little recovery time! Besides, I've already gathered a good quantity of data and specimens and I need to follow up with some writing and lab work. But there is so much more out there – so many cryptic creatures … I got a glimpse of something with a reptilian tail and head, but I'd swear it had multiple legs, maybe eight or ten! That would have a certain uniqueness to it, to say the least! And I promised Asc. Keriya in xenobotany that I would bring back some seeds and plant specimens. I collected a few things in the orchard, but not enough."

In a moment he added, "I almost have to go out. But I shan't relish it as I did at first."

"I hope Kwi'ga'ga'tei shows up tomorrow," said Kaitrin. "I want to talk to her about all this. Maybe it was only a misunderstanding. And maybe we should take advantage of her offer of a guard. I really think she commands the Nasutes' loyalty – I think we can trust them not to be hostile. But I wonder why anyone in Lo'ro'ra would want to be hostile toward us. It's true, we did kill Ti'shra and Gli'tha'mu and we stole the bodies, as it were, but since we returned, we've done nothing to provoke anybody."

"Kait, you remember what A'a'ma said the other day? About all ILFs having their self-serving types? Maybe these creatures aren't so alien after all. Maybe they harbor a dark side that's only too much like Earth's humans."

106

Chapter 10

Along the river's level meads they stand,
Thick as in spring the flowers adorn the land,
Or leaves the trees; or thick as insects play,
The wandering nation of a summer's day: ...
So throng'd, so close, the Grecian squadrons stood
In radiant arms, and thirst for Trojan blood.
     – *from* Homer, *The Iliad*, tr. by Alexander Pope

In the morning Kaitrin, Griffen, and Luku ventured out to wait for Kwi'ga'ga'tei. Will and Julian, having a personal interest in what had taken place, took the guard detail.

"Here they come!" said Will from the top of the ramp.

Kaitrin shaded her eyes. "That's Ki'shto'ba, but that's not Kwi'ga'ga'tei. I think it's the Nasute Chief. I hope nothing has happened to Kwi'ga'ga'tei!"

The pair of Warriors approached the off-worlders at a purposeful pace. Griffen nervously fingered the fastenings on his holster.

"Greetings, Ki'shto'ba! Where is Holy Kwi'ga'ga'tei? She did not come yesterday, either."

She sent me to speak for her, Ru'a'ma'na'ta. I will do the best I can, Ki'shto'ba was bobbing and scraping its mandibles on the ground. *She told me to apologize to the* na'sha'ma| *– to the large and small male Warriors, also. And I do it from my own gut as well. It is impossible to justify what happened yesterday.*

107

Kaitrin quickly conveyed this to Griffen. "Huh. Well ... Tell it ... Tell it whatever you think best. I don't know what to tell it. I'm almost afraid to hear any explanation."

"no 'no| um 'zi| we do not understand why this happened. My *na 'sha 'ma|* was very frightened. Was there really danger?"

Yes, to our regret. But this is Sa 'ti 'a 'i 'a, Chief of the Nasutes, who was there. You have seen it before, but you have never spoken to it. The Holy Seer says you may speak to it now. It is your friend.

Kaitrin regarded the purplish, syringe-headed creature. It was the first time any of them had seen a Nasute close up. As Gwidian inspected it intently, Will holographed with enthusiasm.

"I am happy to greet you also, Sa'ti'a'i'a, Chief of the Nasutes. Were you trying to protect my *na 'sha 'ma|* yesterday? If you were, I thank you."

It sidled and waved its antennae, which had only fifteen segments. *Kwi 'ga 'ga 'tei sent me to protect those of you who were in the marches. We learned that certain ... meant to ... your* na'sha'ma|, *to frighten and perhaps harm him. But we should have discovered it sooner and prevented it.*

Kaitrin did not know two of the salient words and Ki'shto'ba, who was becoming adept at definitions, set about explaining. shwei'ai'zei| *are individuals who do not believe that the fortress is well governed.* zan'li'vimo| *means to follow prey while hiding yourself, the way certain reptiles do.*

Kaitrin quickly put this together ... *We learned that certain* dissidents *meant to* stalk *your mate ... Perhaps to harm him ... –* and she felt chilled. "Have we done something, honorable Warriors, to offend these Shshi?"

Nothing, said Ki'shto'ba. *These dissidents use your coming as an excuse to grow bolder. Kwi 'ga 'ga 'tei is very displeased.*

"Can Kwi'ga'ga'tei not come and speak to us about this?"

Yesterday Kwi 'ga 'ga 'tei was dealing with many things. Today she is recovering.

"She has been ill?"

She slept in the bir'zha| *chamber.*

"What is that?"

The place where the bir'zha| *fungus grows.*

"I understand *fungus,* but not the word *bir'zha|.* It seems to mean 'sour gut.'"

It seems to mean that, indeed, answered Ki'shto'ba in surprise. *I had never thought of it. I suppose it takes its name from its rank smell. But it is that fungus that helps to make the visions. She was seeking a vision.*

"Oh!" exclaimed Kaitrin in human speech. "Now we know, everybody. Kwi'ga'ga'tei does employ a hallucinogen."

To the Shshi she said, "I understand. Did she receive a vision?"

Always, said Ki'shto'ba, dancing ponderously. *But only she speaks of what she sees. You must ask her of that.*

"Oh, dear," said Kaitrin in Inj, then, to Ki'shto'ba, "Who were the Warriors that attacked my *na'sha'ma*|? They were large and strong and frightening."

Ki'shto'ba and Sa'ti'a'i'a pointed their antennae at each other, seeming to confer, then Ki'shto'ba said, *Commander Hi'ta'fu and the Chief of the First Cohort Lo'lo'pai and three Lieutenants of the First Cohort.*

"Those sound like strong enemies," said Kaitrin. "We do not want to be their enemies."

Ki'shto'ba said, *Hi'ta'fu is an honorable Warrior. It has served as Commander of Lo'ro'ra for twelve season-cycles. But that is a long time and it grows old. It was unhappy when Kwi'ga'ga'tei summoned me to be Lo'ro'ra's Champion. It saw itself as sufficient Champion. I cannot fault it for that, but I can fault it for the way it has responded. I have done nothing to take away from it its position in the fortress.*

Sa'ti'a'i'a spoke. *Hi'ta'fu has been a mighty Warrior – it has fought many battles for its fortress and earned its surname of "Unconquered." It defeated us, the Shrin'ok – the Long-Snouted Ones – when we ... Lo'ro'ra.*

"What is *ao'paio*|?" The verb incorporated the concepts of "unmoving" and "to fight."

It means to set Warriors all around a fortress to try to make it submit. To break its waterways and prevent anyone from going in or out to obtain food.

Kaitrin thought, *They 'besieged' Lo'ro'ra ...* To Sa'ti'a'i'a, she said, "I understand that now. So you are not of Lo'ro'ra."

Certainly, this fortress is not my hatching place. The Shshi of Lo'ro'ra – the Shum'za, that is, the Ones with Little Heads, as Ki'shto'ba's people call them – despise the Nasutes because we are small-bodied and our Warriors lack mandible weapons. Because our language is nothing like theirs. Because we ritually kill our surplus citizens when it is necessary. Because we come from forest regions and eat wood and rotted leaves and never this indigestible fungus of the Shshi. Because we re-ingest our dung and also chew it and use it in our mortar. Because we line our chambers with comfortable carton and make our tunnels on the surface of the ground and have different customs concerning our ma'na'ta| *and our* na'sha'ma|. *But we have weapons that they envy. For all these reasons they call us barbarians, and the Enemy. And we call them the same in return, although Kwi'ga'ga'tei has done much to change the thinking of both sides.*

Kaitrin's mind had gleefully reeled in Sa'ti'a'i'a's remark that the Nasutes had a different language, but she forced herself to file the information away for a later conversation. To Griffen she said, "The Nasute is giving us all kinds of facts about its people! You'll be fascinated."

But Gwidian made an impatient gesture and rose gingerly so as not to alarm the visitors. "You can tell me about it later," he said. "I'm getting nothing from this at the moment."

"Send out Tió'otu," said Kaitrin. "Tell him we're getting a lesson in culture."

Prf. A'a'ma emerged and settled himself beside Luku, twittering under his breath. "Every time I don't come out," he said, "something significant happens."

As Sa'ti'a'i'a continued, Kaitrin stopped interrupting for definitions and simply sat absorbing what she could, with the intent of analyzing the recording later. *Lo'ro'ra's Holy One is fruitful – more fruitful than a fortress needs. Therefore, it often sends out hordes to found new fortresses and they would come and build in lands that we Nasutes claim as our own. We became tired of this, because we need our forest space for food. So we sent a delegation to ask them to stop doing it, but Hi'ta'fu killed half the messengers and sent the others back alive to mock us. I was one of those sent back.*

We are a peaceful people, but this murderous insult was more than even we could tolerate. So several of our fortresses

joined together and formed a great army. We were willing to en-
dure the long and dangerous march from our homelands, which lie
far away in the fringes of the mountains, in order to rid ourselves
of Lo'ro'ra's insolence once and for all. This was three season-
cycles ago. Hi'ta'fu spoke for Lo'ro'ra then and it understood
only force. There was a strong King, Thei'ga'na'sha'ma, who was
fascinated by the idea of war. But he did not understand war –
what progenitor can understand anything that happens under the
sky? And at that time Lo'ro'ra's Seer was an old, feeble Alate who
had lost the ability to guide her people.

Ki'shto'ba took up the narrative. *Once they stop flinching*
from the Nasute acid and simply endure the pain, Shum'za are
mightier in battle than Shrin'ok. So the Nasutes sent emissaries to
To'wak, a fortress of my people, who are called the Da'no'no
Shshi because we are bigger than the Shum'za. We are also pro-
lific and seem especially to breed too many Warriors, so some-
times one of us will go and fight for another fortress. I came and
fought as Champion for the Nasutes against Lo'ro'ra.

"You both fought against Lo'ro'ra? But today ... "

With your permission, we will finish the story first, said
Ki'shto'ba, with the stubborn orderliness of one nurtured in an oral
tradition. *We besieged this place. There were many skirmishes.*
I fought Hi'ta'fu – it fought me well. Some of these scars on my
belly are from its jaws, while its thorax bears the mark of mine.
Fighting one-on-one against it, I defeated it, but I allowed it to live
because our fight was merely a chance encounter in the course of
battle and not a death-Challenge. For a while we seemed to be
prevailing, but in the end Lo'ro'ra launched a strong counter-
attack and broke the siege. The Nasutes were badly beaten.

Many, many were killed on both sides, said Sa'ti'a'i'a. *We*
Nasutes had so many dead bodies that most rotted before we could
consume them and we had to leave them for the reptiles and the
birds. We are not a people who enjoys fighting, but Hi'ta'fu's
murderous baiting had driven us to it. It was a most painful time.
And Hi'ta'fu would have slaughtered all of us if it had had its way.

The ma'na'ta| *of the Shshi can live a very long time,* said
Ki'shto'ba. *A'kha'ma'na'ta is the age of the count of two anten-*
nae and she is the only Holy One Lo'ro'ra has ever known. When
a Holy One of the Shum'za dies, a new Holy One is taken from

111

among the fertile nymphs of the same fortress. Then the old King is killed and a new one brought from another fortress to eat a piece of him and assume the role of inseminator. But the ma'na'ta| *usually outlives several Kings. When a King dies naturally before the Holy One, a new* na'sha'ma| *is fetched for her from another fortress.*

So it was that during the siege Thei'ga'na'sha'ma died, and the young and timid Sei'o'na'sha'ma was brought to climb the back of the Holy One. Then the old Seer also died and a stronger Seer immediately manifested – one who favored peace and wanted the killing to stop. That one was Holy Kwi'ga'ga'tei, who experienced visions even as a nymph, even without the bir'zha|.

So we negotiated, continued Sa'ti'a'i'a. *Lo'ro'ra's Council and its Holy One and King promised not to build new fortresses in Nasute lands unless we permitted it. As recompense for attacking Lo'ro'ra, we agreed to send a Cohort to fight in liege service to Lo'ro'ra and to defend its Holy One and King for six season-cycles. I am the current Chief of this Cohort. I am sworn to uphold the Holy One Akh'a'ma'na'ta and the King Sei'o'na'sha'ma. I have no love for the Warriors of Lo'ro'ra, but I value honesty and honorable dealing. Therefore, I value the Holy Seer because she stopped the killing and treated my people with honesty and honorable dealing.*

But, said Ki'shto'ba, *Mo'gri'ta'tu, who was Chamberlain to the Holy One and the King in the day of Thei'ga'na'sha'ma, retains his post even to this day. He is a subtle thinker, but not trustworthy. He relishes games and sometimes he ...*

Perhaps you talk too much, Champion, said Sa'ti'a'i'a.

Perhaps you are right, Nasute Chief. But when Ti'shra and Gli'tha'mu disappeared, the Highest-Mother-Who-Is-Nameless told Holy Kwi'ga'ga'tei to summon a Champion to fight for Lo'ro'ra's well-being, and now we may know why. It is not you the Nameless One wanted me to fight, Star-Beings. It is some trouble within the fortress. So I attend Kwi'ga'ga'tei and take my orders only from her.

Kaitrin finally spoke. "All of this interests me greatly, Warriors. But why should the Commanders of Lo'ro'ra want to do us harm? Is it because of the deaths we caused? We cannot give life back to those who have died, but we are very sorry that we killed

112

them and want only to be friends with all Shshi."

Sa'ti'a'i'a said, *Old Warriors and old Workers do not like to change. It is an adage both in the mountains and on the plains. And for Hi'ta'fu you are change. The Holy Seer prophesied that the time is new and the Commander finds that threatening. Its chosen successor is Chief Lo'lo'pai, who rashly pressed the threat yesterday and got its palps nipped by acid and its labrum chipped by the stones that your weapon threw at us. I find it a blunderer, and volatile – not a clear thinker. A'gwa'ji, Chief of the Second Cohort, is made of stronger chitin, I maintain.*

The foray yesterday was very suspicious, said Ki'shto'ba. *The Warriors had been ordered to allow your* na'sha'ma| *to go and come freely and without harassment. Mo'gri'ta'tu and Lo'lo'pai insist that it was a chance encounter that the Star-Beings misinterpreted. But there was no good reason for such high Chiefs to be patrolling so far afield.*

Sa'ti'a'i'a said, *After the encounter Hi'ta'fu spoke this:* The purpose was only to gain information, and now we have that. *I suppose, information about the weapon with which Kwi'ga'ga'tei threatened them. But if it could state a purpose, then the encounter was not by chance.*

Ki'shto'ba added, *So the Holy Seer is very disturbed and sought the counsel of the Nameless One last night. I do not know yet what vision came to her. But I know she means to come here in the late afternoon if she is strong enough. She sent me and the Nasute Chief to make apologies and to explain. I hope we have done that work to your satisfaction.*

"We accept your apology, Ki'shto'ba," said Kaitrin, "but we remain anxious. I wish your Commander could understand that we seek only knowledge from its fortress and will never do it harm. And I have one question – did Holy Kwi'ga'ga'tei really threaten it with our weapon? Because we had no intention of using it unless one of us was endangered, and when we were, our Warriors sent their weapons' force toward the ground and not toward any Shi."

Her threat was meant to deter. But it seems it had the opposite effect.

What is this weapon? asked Sa'ti'a'i'a. *It must be a shooting weapon like our nasi, which in fact is also a weapon that can do harm without the touch of two bodies to each other. Also, both our weapon and yours can be directed in given paths, it seems.*

"You are correct," said Kaitrin somewhat tensely, "but our weapon has much more power than yours and it can do damage over a greater distance."

It seemed to shoot stones. How can it do that?

"It does not shoot stones," Kaitrin said. "It shoots fire, which throws up the stones when it hits the ground."

Sa'ti'a'i'a was producing an effusion of words in its own language and Ki'shto'ba said, *You have fire in your bodies? How can that be?*

A'a'ma, who had been following the discussion on the receiver port, was making disapproving noises and Kaitrin thought, *Good grief, will I never learn to think before I speak?*

Then Ki'shto'ba turned toward Will, whom it perceived to be a Warrior, and said, *Would you demonstrate this weapon for me? I admit I am curious.*

"No," squawked A'a'ma.

"Is it trying to say something to me?" said Will.

"It wants a demonstration of your weapon," said Kaitrin.

"Hell, no," said Will. "Right here in the courtyard, with all these workers about?"

"I agree totally," said Kaitrin. "We must never discharge these laser pistols and certainly not the Presser rifles unless our lives are imminently threatened."

To the Huge-Head she said, "We cannot do what you ask. It would frighten everyone who is in the courtyard. And we carry this weapon only for defense. It is a – thing of which we should not speak. It is too powerful. I was wrong to speak as I did."

It is taboo? said the Nasute.

"I think I understand your meaning. Tell no one that our weapons emit ... *hum'zi|.*"

I will tell the Holy Seer, but no one else, said Ki'shto'ba. *Nasute Chief, you must also promise.*

I promise. But I do not understand how a creature can have an organ that ejects fire.

Kaitrin sighed and A'a'ma twittered. "I fear we may be putting too many notions in the heads of these technologically innocent creatures," he said.

"I'm definitely botching things again," said Kaitrin. To

114

change the subject, she asked Sa'ti'a'i'a, "Tell me this. You say you eat wood and not fungus. What do you eat here?"

We are given the prunings of the orchard. We also like old leaves and we can eat any dry plant – even the river grass and the leaves of the five-claw plant – if we have nothing else. We have our own Workers with us. They forage in the marches, but it is not easy.

"I believe we have seen them."

We dwell in a portion of the Warriors' Quarters set aside for us. It is a lonely life. The citizens of Lo'ro'ra shun us in our daily activities. Their Feeders are afraid to service us, so our small number of Workers must do everything. And yet our Warriors are as eyeless as theirs, and as valiant in their gut! Our Alates have Star-Wings and vision-powers no less than theirs! We speak our stories of the past even as they do!

Ki'shto'ba said, *It is difficult to trust those who are different from oneself, or to look upon them as being of equal value.*

Kaitrin puzzled a little over the final words, but she thought she understood. *"no'no| um'zi|,* you are right. Down through time, my people have had the same difficulty."

Then to Sa'ti'a'i'a she said, "There is a small fortress near here where the creatures called the Little Ones live. Was that a Nasute fortress?"

It was a supply post during the siege. There are several such structures in the vicinity.

"Well, at least we have an answer to Griffen's questions about why there was dung in the mortar," Kaitrin said to Tió'otu.

*　　*　　*

[Hi'ta'fu]: Chamberlain, your plotting invariably goes awry.

[Mo'gri'ta'tu]: It would not do so if you would speak as I instruct! How do you think to deceive an Alate as subtle as Kwi'ga'ga'tei if Lo'lo'pai and I tell her one thing and you tell her something else?

[Hi'ta'fu]: This was my plan – to learn of the weapon! I am accustomed to speaking honestly and following my own counsel!

[Mo'gri'ta'tu]: Your counsel is small and sightless, Commander! I am not pleased at all. Are the words *chance encounter* so hard to say? Is an excuse for patrolling the marches so hard to devise? You might have said that you went out to protect the alien so-called *na'sha'ma|* and that there was a misunderstanding. That would have served.

[Hi'ta'fu, displaying threat]: Do not lecture me, Mo'gri'ta'tu! I needed to know what it is that we might have to fight and I perceive no reason to equivocate about that end! My primary purpose is still to protect Lo'ro'ra. I doubt if even the Nameless One knows what your primary purpose is!

[Mo'gri'ta'tu, changes his approach]: Now, Commander, I tender my apologies to you. I am upset and rashly utter words that would be better left unspoken. Your motives are honorable – never doubt that I believe that! So what have you learned about this weapon that kills without touching? How do we fight it?

[Hi'ta'fu, somewhat mollified]: It makes a shock as if a great stone rolled off a cliff and shattered at the bottom. It even throws up stones as that would. It has no smell until after the shock is emitted and then it somewhat resembles the smell of Nasute acid, but still it is much different. Its odor is more like burning things, but not so much like that, either. I still do not understand it, and it may be that there is no defense against it.

[Mo'gri'ta'tu]: Well, if you – *we*, Commander, I mean *we* – do not continue to commit blunders, perhaps there will be no more confrontations. Let us guard our efforts closely and trust that some fresh opportunity will present itself to disrupt the work of the Seer and her Champion.

[Hi'ta'fu departs]

[Mo'gri'ta'tu]: Why is it always others who create the difficulties? If it were only I alone, everything would have been resolved long ago. So – the good Commander can find no way to defend against this weapon. Rumor says, although Hi'ta'fu does not seem to know it, that it is a magic-box kind of thing, not grown upon the body. I am taken with a fancy. If it is not grown upon the body, why could not a Shi use such a weapon as easily as an outlander? And any Shi, moreover – one would not have to be a Warrior to do so. I think I will seek a clandestine opportunity to talk with this *ma'na'ta|* imposter and see what I can learn for my-self.

*   *   *

Highest-Mother-Who-Has-No-Name, I feel you! You crush me, you press out the air! But you do not speak to me! Why? Have I offended you? Forgive me!

You do not offend me, my daughter.

Then I implore you, answer me! How can I overcome all these obscure forces of dissension in my beloved fortress? My directives are subverted on all sides. Subtle threats only incite these forces to grow bolder ...

I do not abandon my Star-Children, but I have already given them what they need. Therefore, I let the lesser things be ... Do you love the Strange Ones' ma'na'ta|?

Love her? I am drawn to her. She is my friend – I am sure of that. How, love her?

[There is no answer]

Should I love Ru'a'ma'na'ta?

Are you not all my Star-Children?

Who is the Wounded One, Nameless Mother? I do not under-stand.

You will understand, Kwi'ga'ga'tei, before the end ...

*   *   *

[Kwi'ga'ga'tei rests in her chamber. Ki'shto'ba and Sa'ti'a'i'a crouch before her]

[Ki'shto'ba]: She is anxious and wants us to know they meant us no harm with their weapons. I think she accepted our apology. I could sense stress pheromones in the *na'sha'ma|* – in-deed, in all of them.

[Kwi'ga'ga'tei]: If you did not, I would be astonished.

[Sa'ti'a'i'a]: She wanted to know who it was that attacked them. We told her who it was. And I told her a Remembrancer's

117

Tale of the Siege of Lo'ro'ra, or parts of it.

[Ki'shto'ba]: We told her of your role in ending it, Holy Seer. I hope that was all right. We told her that you favor peace. And she wants peace with us; of that I am sure.

[Sa'ti'a'i'a]: Huge-Head mentioned Mo'gri'ta'tu ...

[Kwi'ga'ga'tei]: I would just as soon his name were not uttered to them!

[Ki'shto'ba, squirms]: I know, Holy Kwi'ga'ga'tei. Sometimes I talk too much. I find I enjoy talking. Warriors hardly ever get to talk the way Alates do.

[Kwi'ga'ga'tei]: Well, I cannot fault you for that. What did you tell her?

[Ki'shto'ba]: Only that the Keeper of the Holy Chamber remained from the reign of the last King. And that he is subtle and not to be trusted.

[Kwi'ga'ga'tei]: How is it that circumstances can grow so twisted?

[Ki'shto'ba]: I asked if they could demonstrate the weapon for me, so that I as well as the Commander might understand it, but they refused. It would scare the Workers in the courtyard, they said.

[Sa'ti'a'i'a]: They said it was a taboo, not to be talked of.

[Kwi'ga'ga'tei]: That is quite to my liking. You should not have asked them to demonstrate it.

[Sa'ti'a'i'a]: Ru'a'ma'na'ta said something I can hardly believe – part of the taboo. She said that the weapon spits fire, or something like.

[Kwi'ga'ga'tei]: Fire!

[Ki'shto'ba]: How can a weapon spit fire? Fire destroys everything and would burn up any orifice of the body that enclosed it! They say that in volcanoes even the stones burn. It is a great perplexity to me.

[Sa'ti'a'i'a]: It is a fearful thing to contemplate! No creature can take hold of the wild thing called fire! I simply cannot understand.

[Kwi'ga'ga'tei]: If it is a taboo, we are not meant to understand. But this shakes me. I have not told you this before, but Ru'a'ma'na'ta said that the weapon is like the magic boxes – a thing-not-growing-upon-the-body.

[Ki'shto'ba]: More and more strange! A box would burn as easily as the body if fire were put into it!

[Kwi'ga'ga'tei]: I will ask Ru'a'ma'na'ta of this when I see her. I will go down this afternoon. Be ready, Ki'shto'ba.

[Ki'shto'ba]: I will be ready. But, Holy Seer, you were seeking a vision. Did you learn anything that can help us?

[Kwi'ga'ga'tei]: I fear, nothing. I do not get answers – I only get more riddles. I think this is a time when the Shshi of Lo'ro'ra must work out their own answers, and this disturbs me more than all else taken together.

Chapter 11

... And the flower children rush out
in dresses of pink and yellow and white.
Do you know, mother, their home is in the sky,
    where the stars are.
Haven't you seen how eager they are to get there?
Don't you know why they are in such a hurry?
Of course, I can guess to whom they raise their arms:
they have a mother as I have my own.
    – *from* Rabindranath Tagore, *The Flower-School*

Kwi'ga'ga'tei and Ki'shto'ba came as promised in the late afternoon. The Seer abased before Kaitrin, and Kaitrin rebuked her gently.

"We have accepted your apologies, Holy Kwi'ga'ga'tei, and there is no need for you to scratch the dirt before us. We are friends, and friends can forgive each other."

I am glad to receive these words, Ru'a'ma'na'ta. I promised you would be safe, but it is not always possible to control the intentions or the actions of others.

"That is very true. But, Holy Seer, no'no| um'zi| told me you were seeking a vision. Did you find one?" Kaitrin felt the shiver of trepidation that always came when she considered how this creature claimed the ability to communicate with a god.

Kwi'ga'ga'tei cocked her head at Kaitrin. *Not a satisfying*

120

one. I am having difficulty comprehending the Nameless One's pronouncements. But I think she would have us be caring of each other, even as you have just said.

"I hope we can be, Kwi'ga'ga'tei." Then, a little uncertainly, "So – you and the Nameless One talk about us?"

Often. She told me once that your flying dwelling has a name – a puzzling name. She said it had a name of the Nameless.

Kaitrin hesitated, then her scalp tingled. *Durga.* One of the names given on Earth to an aspect of the Great Goddess. And the Great Goddess of the Shshi was the Nameless One. ¡Maldito! *She couldn't possibly have known that.* And she also thought, *What a sacrilegious bunch we Earthers are! We casually name pieces of machinery after our moribund gods.*

Kwi'ga'ga'tei was saying, *I do not understand how the Nameless could have a name. The vessel cannot be full at the same time that it is empty.*

Kaitrin jacked herself up to try to give an answer that made sense. "The Nameless One is the Highest *ma'na'ta|* – the One Who Lays the Eggs That Make All Things. Is that not true?"

That is true.

"When we worship her on our world, we are allowed to give her names. It is not taboo. I cannot tell you the names for the same reason I cannot tell you my own. But in fact we do call our flying dwelling by one of the names of the Nameless. I am very surprised that you would know that. Oh, please, Holy Kwi'ga'ga'tei, do not do that ... "

The Seer had begun nuzzling the ground again. *To think speaking beings can be so different. And yet, in my latest vision, the Nameless One said to me,* Are you not all my Star-Children?

Then Kaitrin felt doubly unnerved. A'a'ma and Luku, who had been monitoring all this, were muttering together. Ki'shto'ba was scraping the dirt along with its Seer.

But then Kwi'ga'ga'tei elevated her head and composed herself. *Ru'a'ma'na'ta, we must speak of something else, something less ...* (Kaitrin did not know the word she used, but it may have meant 'mystical' or 'otherworldly.') *Ki'shto'ba tells me that there is a taboo on speaking of your weapon. I am sorry that I may have contributed to the breaking of it. But can you tell me this? What does it mean that the weapon spits fire?*

Kaitrin sighed. "Just that."

Sa'ti'a'i'a and I thought at first that it was your bodies that were spitting fire, said Ki'shto'ba, *but Holy Kwi'ga'ga'tei says the weapon is a box, not something growing on the body. But it seems no less incredible that you can keep fire in a box and then throw it forth.*

"Yet it can be done, just as images and speech can be put in a box. I cannot explain it in your words."

Kwi'ga'ga'tei said, *It is your magic, or what you call your knowledge. But what concerns me is that this fire-weapon is separate from the body. Tell me this: in the early days of our conversations, your Warriors always held an object in their foreleg-palps. Were those the weapons?*

"Yes, they were. We had been attacked before by one of your Warriors, so we were merely ready to defend ourselves."

I understand that. But I have seen that more than one of you can use the same antenna box. Could anyone use the same weapon box? Could one of us use it?

"What did I tell you?" warbled A'a'ma. "She is too smart to fool."

"Kwi'ga'ga'tei, this troubles me much," said Kaitrin.

Ki'shto'ba exclaimed, *I had not thought of that! This could be a great danger!*

There are certain citizens of Lo'ro'ra who will think of that, said Kwi'ga'ga'tei.

"Your Commander, Hi'ta'fu?"

I do not believe it knows yet that the weapon is not grown upon the body. Besides, it is only a blind Warrior, not subtle enough to understand this by itself. But rumors are circulating, and another exists who ...

"The one whom Ki'shto'ba called Mo'gri'ta'tu?"

The Huge-Head danced about clumsily, its mandibles throwing up the dirt. Kwi'ga'ga'tei eyed it sideways. *Even that one. Ru'a'ma'na'ta, I do not trust the Keeper of the Holy Chamber. He resents my authority and he stirs up discord; that is all I can tell you, for I hardly know more myself. I would simply warn you – if you meet him at any time, be cautious.*

Kaitrin thought, *Some kind of Byzantine power struggle is going on here, it seems,* but she said only, "We have nothing but good will toward all the Shshi."

It shames me to have to say that we of Lo'ro'ra are not all equal to you in depth of good will. Only be cautious.

"We will never allow these weapons to come into the possession of the Shshi. That would be a great misdeed. We have only a few of them and they are always guarded."

Ru'a'ma'na'ta, you are very wise, said Ki'shto'ba.

"Holy Kwi'ga'ga'tei, my *na'sha'ma|* would like to return to the marches after a few day-cycles pass. Will he be safe?"

We will make him safe. I will put Sa'ti'a'i'a and its Cohort at your disposal. Only inform me when he is going and we will send a Nasute guard with him.

"I thank you and I trust you. Has the time come when you trust me enough to let me speak with other citizens of Lo'ro'ra besides yourself and these two honorable Warriors?"

Kwi'ga'ga'tei considered for a moment. *I think it has. The Huge-Head and the Nasute Chief have played Remembrancer for you. I will send you the real one.*

"I do not know the word *thu'dal'zei|.* It seems to mean 'past thinker.'"

It is the one who speaks the tales of our past so that it will not be forgotten.

"Oh, a bard!" cried Kaitrin in Inj. "Tió'otu – Luku – she's going to let us speak with Lo'ro'ra's bard! What a thrill!"

A'a'ma let out a gleeful warble. "♫♪ Myths and legends! Nothing is more enlightening than learning a culture's myths and legends!"

"*thu'dal'zei|* – one who thinks about the past – remembers it … I'm going to translate it as 'Remembrancer.' That has a lovely archaic quality and really captures the feel!"

Unable to comprehend their obvious excitement, the Seer was saying, *I will also send No'kri, the Chief of the Workers. It can talk to you about the way we live in Lo'ro'ra, which may differ from the way you live among the stars. Have you any interest in such things?*

"Oh, much interest! And if I might speak again with Chief Sa'ti'a'i'a, perhaps it can teach me something about the Nasute language."

That can be arranged. And one day perhaps you can visit our fortress. But not yet.

"*Hakhís↓~]*" rasped Tió'otu.

"Oh, wouldn't I love that!" said Kaitrin in Inj. "But Griffen would be so upset! Don't either of you say anything to him, whatever you do! We'll face that hurdle when we have to."

To Kwi'ga'ga'tei she said, *I would be honored.*

Ru'a'ma'na'ta, said Ki'shto'ba, *will you return to your own world one day?*

"We will."

Kwi'ga'ga'tei asked, *If you and I look at the night sky together, can you show me where you come from?*

"No, you cannot see our star from this part of your world."

You have said that our sun is a star, too, but surely if we cannot see yours, you cannot see ours, either. How then did you know where to find us?

Kaitrin sat stumped. Then she said, "We have ways to make our natural eyes see what is difficult to see. But in fact, in our wanderings among the stars, we found you by chance."

It was not by chance, said Kwi'ga'ga'tei, and she danced and groomed her eyes with her forelegs as though disturbed. *When you have gone away, will you ever come back?*

"Holy Kwi'ga'ga'tei, I promise. I am learning to care deeply about your world and I promise that I will come back."

*   *   *

"I really don't care what anyone wants," declared Kaitrin at their next meal. "I'm not carrying my pistol any longer! The last thing we want to do is cause them to blow themselves up! So those of you who feel obligated to pack guns, for god's sake, be careful with them! And dammit all, keep those plasma rifles locked up!"

"All right, Kaitrin!" said Griffen. "I agree we must be cautious. We've probably already contaminated this pre-tech culture past all prudence."

"Personally, I am still obsessing about this vision business," said A'a'ma. "That shaman not only knew what the flyer looked like – she knew it was named for a goddess. How do they do it?"

"And she knew that the dead would speak to them," said Kaitrin.

"Some souls really can see," Trea said. "In some it is far-seeing – what you call, uh – 'clear voi-yanas,' I think. Others see the future, but twisted, incomplete. At least on my planet, is so. Perhaps it is like dreams – glimpses of alternate universes. That is one explanation. Perhaps it is truly god or spirit. We can never know for sure."

Griffen stirred uneasily. "You really think dreams are glimpses of alternate universes?"

Trea said, "Some believe it. Glimpses that are twisted and so make no sense usually."

Griffen stood up. "In that case, my alternate universes have little to recommend them over my native one. I'm off to do some work in the lab."

"Griff, you didn't finish your supper," said Kaitrin, but he had disappeared into the science bay.

"Gwidian has nightmare," said Trea, more as a statement of fact than a question.

"Occasionally," said Kaitrin, looking at the doctor, but Trea said no more and the conversation turned to other things.

After supper, Kaitrin went up to the flight deck and stood looking out into the declining day. Will was running his obligatory checks of flight systems. "The *Featherlight* is off to Starbase 30," he said. "*Stinger* is comfortingly in orbit, Capt. Van informs me. Everything's nominal." He joined her at the window. "Is there something interesting out there?"

"Oh, I was thinking what this compound must have looked like three years ago when the Nasutes were besieging Lo'ro'ra. Thick with bodies and gore, I suppose. The aqueduct broken, the orchards devastated. The Shshi Warriors slashing the Nasutes, and the Nasutes spraying the Shshi Warriors with their acid – horrible! Like something from Arti's holonovel or out of Earth's ancient history – Ejipt, the Romens, the First Dark Age ... Not like the Second – by that time the atrocities of war had become remote – radiant bombs – nanobotics – bioweapons ..."

"What's going on down there?"

Kaitrin peered where Will pointed. She saw three Workers sidling up close to the flyer, waving their antennae at it, darting away, approaching again, touching it, leaping back. But what caught her attention was the small formicidiform that was tethered to the foreleg of one of them.

"Oh!" She leaped for the ladder. "I have to go out! Luku, quick, the translator!"

The Tae Quornaz hastened to comply and Kaitrin said, "Luku, we need to miniaturize this thing, now that it's voice-activated and the emitter-receiver-recorder is all in one unit. Construct something I can hang on my belt, interfaced for earports."

"Can be done with a little work. I will get busy," said Luku.

Gwidian stuck his head out of the lab. "What are you doing?"

"Going out. Don't worry, it's only three Workers out there – and they've got an ant!"

When the ramp came down, the Workers leaped into the air in a panic, almost jerking the tethered creature in two. Kaitrin transmitted, "Don't be afraid! I saw you from the eye of our dwelling. Would you like to talk to me?" She squatted down to be on their level. They approached cautiously. *They look exactly like Ti'shra,* she thought. *Funny – this is the first time I've ever spoken with a Worker.*

Are you the flying ma'na'ta|*?* one asked. *The one who was the Comforter of Ti'shra?*

"Yes, I am that one."

There, I told you she would come out, the first one said to the others. *They say she is kind and good. The Holy Seer is fond of her and we know the Holy Seer is always right.*

But some say they commit sacrilege! They waste their dead! Their ma'na'ta| *walks about above ground and looks at the sky!*

They killed Ti'shra! said the third Worker. *They want to kill us!*

I do not believe that for an instant! said the first one stoutly.

Kaitrin ignored the business about sacrilege and said, "We do not want to harm you in any way. And we are sorry – we did not mean to kill Ti'shra. It became sick and we tried hard to save it, but we could not. But did you know Ti'shra? It was a very – good Shi." Kaitrin would have rather said 'nice' or 'gentle,' but she did not know the right words.

We were its hatchmates and its friends. We all worked in the Fungus Garden, said the bolder one. *This Little One was Ti'shra's pet – it named it "Zuf." It is ours now and we have brought it out for exercise. When the warnings came that no one should leave the fortress, Ti'shra did not receive them, so it took Zuf out to eat flowers and to play with it in the orchard. When Ti'shra disappeared, Zuf ran back into the fortress. I found it wandering loose in the sleeping hall. That is when we first realized something had happened to Ti'shra.*

"I am sorry," repeated Kaitrin, envisioning the pale little creature scampering around in the holoimage after the attack. "May I touch it?"

The Workers consulted excitedly. *All right. Rub here and it will like it. If you press there, it will put a drink of honeydew into your gullet.*

Kaitrin had no desire to apply her mouth to the backside of a thirty-centimeter ant, so she scratched it on the head. It stood and stretched up toward her. *It acts just like a dog,* she thought. *Ti'shra was out walking its dog when it was attacked.*

To the Workers she said, "I have learned the meaning of *shra|*. But what does *ti|* mean? It is present also in the word for this water that the Little Ones give – *ti'wa'zi|*."

da'ti| is the way that the honeydew tastes or the tho'sei| *flowers smell.* zuf| *means a single part of the* tho'sei| *flower, or any flower.*

And Kaitrin thought, *Aliens came and stole away and destroyed a gentle creature named "Sweet Flowers," who doted on a little pet named "Petal." That is the real sacrilege!*

And yet apparently some of these same creatures are violent and devious and quite capable of committing unscrupulous acts. Griff is right – they're far too much like us.

A movement caught her eye and she glanced up to see that Griffen had emerged onto the ramp. "Griff, come see! This is the same formicidiform that broke loose from Ti'shra when you captured it. It really was Ti'shra's pet. Move slowly and kneel down. Workers are very timid."

He did so. "Scratch it behind the antenna," she said. "It reacts just like your spaniel – Cookie, wasn't it?"

He laughed. "The mandibles are almost vestigial. And it's nearly colorless – almost transparent. Suited for life in the dark. I daresay it can't stay in the sun very long."

Under questioning, the Workers told Kaitrin that a big flock of Little Ones was kept inside the fortress and fed on both fresh and cured *tho'sei|* blossoms and leaves. Their honeydew was "milked" by the Feeders for distribution to the rest of the citizens. *We all love* ti'wa'zi| *– it is a treat and very nourishing!* they said.

"Domesticated dairy ants," said Gwidian. "It seems to have lost the wild ones' formic acid gland and stinger. And its eyes are significantly smaller than theirs were."

"They said, if you rub it here, it will give you honeydew," said Kaitrin.

Gwidian hesitated. Then he said, "I want to get something. Keep them occupied."

He returned presently with a beaker. "Do you think they'll object if I take a sample?"

"I'll ask them just so everybody knows what we intend."

The Workers seemed delighted that the Star-Beings were interested. Gwidian squeezed the gland on Zuf's posterior and it obliged by squirting liquid into the beaker. Gwidian brought it near his nose. "Actually smells like honey."

Kaitrin sniffed tentatively. "With sort of woodsy overtones. Really not unpleasant."

When the Workers were about to depart, Kaitrin said to them, "When you go in, tell everyone that the rumors are wrong. We do not want to kill you or hurt you, and we feel pain that Ti'shra died while we were caring for it."

We will tell that to everyone! And the Growers scampered off toward the westernmost edifice, where most of the Worker Caste dwelled. Gwidian and Kaitrin stood and watched them disappear through a stone-capped entranceway. The setting sun hung low, gilding the western flanks of the four towers and sending long, black shadows eastward. The crescent of one of the planet's moons hung in the sky between the Warrior's quarters and the main tower; the other moon was nearly full and just rising.

"I wish all the Shshi were as pacific as these," said Griffen.

"And as guileless."

"I'd like to investigate these Little Ones further, but I don't suppose there's any way to accomplish it. They're quite different from the wild formicidiforms. Like comparing wild Cape buffalo to Hemmias dairy cows. I wonder how they reproduce – do you suppose they have a queen? And I'd wager they have no soldier caste."

"Tió'otu told me you ran out through those wild soldiers to get specimens like a knight jousting with dragons. He doubted you'd come back alive!"

"Huh, did he say that?" said Griffen, with a rare flash of his boyish grin. "Actually, I was wearing enough protective gear to ward off twice the danger! But I must admit, when I reached the formicarium and looked back toward the flyer, it was a bit intimidating – all those jaws snapping, and the gasters cocked up to spray acid. But ... " The grin had faded. "I wasn't much concerned about risk-taking right then. Life was sitting rather lightly on me ... "

He turned away and started toward the hatch, and Kaitrin followed. *Now what did that ambiguous remark mean?* she thought a little uneasily. *I can think of at least two different ways to interpret it.* But other things intervened and for the moment she forgot it.

Chapter 12

The hall towered,
its gables wide and high and awaiting
a barbarous burning. That doom abided,
but in time it would come: the killer instinct
unleashed among in-laws, the blood-lust
rampant.
— *from Beowulf,* tr. by Seamus Heaney

Sev analyzed the honeydew and found it to be almost sixty per cent sugar, with a rather low pH from the acidic petals that the Little Ones consumed. The microbial load was surprisingly light. Trea pronounced it not a bad fluid for quick nourishment. "More water than Earth's bee honey, also contains some available proteins and minerals. I tasted a drop. Not harmful to mammals, and not unpleasant."

"That's nice," said Kaitrin, "but I doubt we'll ever have occasion to make a practical test."

On the following morning three unfamiliar Alates, accompanied by a unit of regular Shshi Warriors, issued from the fortress and crossed to face the strangers. One of the Alates, a creature larger and more sturdily built than Kwi'ga'ga'tei, addressed them. *I greet you, Star-Beings! I am Holy Di'fa'kro'mi, the Remembrancer of the fortress of Lo'ro'ra. I have been chafing to speak with you, and the Holy Seer has finally permitted it! I relish the power of words, Ru'a'ma'na'ta, and I want to learn anything you can teach. Kwi'ga'ga'tei has asked A'gwa'ji, Chief of the Second Cohort, to escort me, so that you may become acquainted with it. It is a mainstay of the Holy One and King.*

A'gwa'ji performed the usual bob-and-scrape. *I am honored that the Holy Seer has allowed me to meet you. I am at a loss to explain the behavior of my Commander Hi'ta'fu the Unconquered and of Lo'lo'pai, my peer of the First Cohort. I was not a member of the patrol that confronted your* na'sha'ma|, *for Hi'ta'fu did not order me to go. How they could have been so unaware of the identity of the beings they encountered is a mystery to me.*

"So that's the latest explanation?" said Gwidian when this was translated for him. "That they didn't know who we were?"

We believe strongly that the Holy Seer is a speaker of truth for the Holy One and King, A'gwa'ji continued. *Therefore, you can always rely upon me and the Warriors of my Cohort to honor her requests and treat you with respect.*

The Warriors then withdrew slightly and Di'fa'kro'mi introduced the pair of Alates who accompanied him as his *shparn'reig'zei|,* or "learning assistants," a term Kaitrin decided to translate as "apprentices." *One of our functions is to keep a record of the history of the Shshi and especially of the history of the great fortress of Lo'ro'ra. Whatever one of us learns is told to another so that, should the Remembrancer die, there is always another ready fill its place. We select certain Alate-nymphs who show promise and train them in the proper skills.*

"Fascinating," said Kaitrin to A'a'ma. "Pure oral transmission."

Is there is a special story you would like for me to tell, Ru'a'ma'na'ta?

Kaitrin asked how Lo'ro'ra came to be founded. With the Warriors and the other Alates attending as raptly as if they had not received the tale a thousand times before, Di'fa'kro'mi began the story. A band of many Shshi (too many for their number sense to reckon) – Workers and Warriors and Alate guides and mentors – had set out from far away (too far away for their distance sense to comprehend), and with them went three fertile female Alate-nymphs, of whom one would become the *ma'na'ta|* of the new fortress. The exact location of the place from which they had come had been forgotten, but it was in a land of many hills to the east or perhaps south. Only the name had been preserved: Zi'zos'mi, whose root words meant "Place of Bitter Time."

Their adventures were many and their troubles dire; they lost one *ma'na'ta*|-nymph to the attack of a giant reptile and another to a grass fire that nearly engulfed them all, so that finally only one named Mei'a'kha'bu still lived. At a fortress called Twi'mu'pai, they begged for a fertile male to become her King and were constrained to undergo trials in order to obtain him.

But at last they reached a place where beautiful trees with creamy, fragrant blossoms grew beside a flowing river and there they stopped. Mei'a'kha'bu named the site *lo'ro'ra'mi*|, which in element-by-element translation would mean "Strong Holding Flower Place" (more loosely, "Strong Land of Flowers") and the Holy Seer Za'pri'tei'tha gave Mei'a'kha'bu her progenitor-name, A'kha'ma'na'ta. She and her King, obeying the primeval imperative, danced together and broke off each other's wings as a sign of their commitment to the ground. Then they dug into the ground with the help of the Workers and made the Holy Chamber, where he copulated with her for the first time. So Lo'ro'ra was founded.

That was over twice the antennae-count ago. A'kha'ma'na'ta had lived into her fourth King, and still she laid and was prolific.

Kaitrin closed her eyes, trying to imagine what it would be like to be shut up underground for over thirty-six years, doing nothing but breeding and laying eggs while being worshiped as the ruler and progenitor of all the people. It probably was a good thing that the real power lay in the hands – or claws – of others. Yet how perilous it must be to exercise such regency. Her respect for Kwi'ga'ga'tei multiplied.

Then Di'fa'kro'mi said, *Tell us a tale from your world, Ru'a'ma'na'ta!*

Good grief! Kaitrin thought. *Whatever Earth story could I put into terms that these bugs could understand?* Quickly she searched her mind for short tales that would translate easily. *A fable*, she thought. *Esap. But those are too anecdotal – I need something with a little more plot ... Oh, I know! Androklis!*

So she made Androklis a Warrior who got lost in a great forest, and she replaced the lion with a ferocious reptile, and she described a fortress where the rulers took pleasure from witnessing life-and-death battles between captive Warriors and fierce beasts.

When she came to the end and the reptile had refused to kill the Warrior, leading to freedom for them both, Di'fa'kro'mi said, *Even so: compassion and gratitude are positive forces and peace should prevail over war. That is the lesson Kwi'ga'ga'tei teaches, and I hope those fortress leaders in your tale learned that and gave up that unpleasant custom of finding pain entertaining. We have stories like this, that have an instructional purpose. In some, animals are made to speak even as in yours. I will tell the story to the Holy One and King, and to Lo'ro'ra's citizens as well. They will relish it – they are always eager for something new.*

Over the next few days, Kwi'ga'ga'tei came sometimes, but when she did not, Di'fa'kro'mi came, accompanied by Second Co-hort Warriors or by Nasutes. Kaitrin got a chance to make recordings of the Nasutes' language and discuss it with its native speakers. It proved to be quite different from the speech of the Shshi of Lo'ro'ra, with a different word order, an extended system of indicators, and adjectives that were inflected for number. And yet, even in the limited vocabulary that Kaitrin was able to accrue, she could detect cognates and was convinced that the two languages shared a common root. Kaitrin was in paradise, having now a second spectrographic language to verbalize.

These new visitors willingly submitted to the learning-magic of Trea and Gwidian, who ran brain scans and obtained samples of Nasute acid. The scans showed a complete lack of neural activity in the ocelli of the Remembrancer or any of the other Alates, strengthening the hypothesis that this area was associated with a Seer's visionary powers.

At one point Kwi'ga'ga'tei told Kaitrin, *I sent Chief A'gwa'ji because I have concluded that I must make an ally of it. I have not wanted to divide the loyalties of the fortress, but I feel that they are dividing of themselves, so I seek to assure myself of support before it is subverted.*

"I hope our coming has not damaged Lo'ro'ra in some way, Holy Kwi'ga'ga'tei."

This disunity had begun to show itself before you arrived.

Then one day the Worker Chief No'kri came. It was large for a Worker, very courteous, and a staunch ally of the Holy Seer. It asked what they would like to know about life in Lo'ro'ra and

Kaitrin requested that it speak about the Shshi Caste system. Gwidian particularly wanted to learn whether the Shshi had genetically differentiated major and minor soldiers.

It seemed they did not; only personal merit was required to become an officer, although in practice the largest and strongest Warriors were more likely to attain the top commands. A ranking system also existed among the Alates, but again it was based on ability; those manifesting few talents ended up as Light-Makers or Nursery Supervisors.

Among the Workers, the Builders were the only genetic Subcaste, possessing a special gland on top of their heads. Asked to explain, No'kri, itself a Builder, pointed to its own *bak'zi|* and explained that it secreted *bak'gwai'zi|* – "mortar-gland water" – a fluid used as a moistening and binding agent in mortar (No'kri obligingly provided Griffen with a sample). *Dung is never used in our mortar! That is the way of the Enemy!* exclaimed No'kri, without regard for Sa'ti'a'i'a, who stood stoically nearby.

The ranks of the other two major Subcastes of Workers – the Growers and the Feeders – were filled according to size, talent, and inclination, and it was possible to change occupations if one were not happy with one's assigned role. Even the Builders were not locked in to their duties; there were always some Growers or Tenders who bore the *bak'zi|* on their heads.

The Growers were divided further into Outdoor Growers (the Orchard Workers) and Indoor Growers (the Fungus-Tenders and Herders). The Fungus Garden was located in the easternmost edifice, which also housed storage and processing of the *tho'sei|* petals and leaves, as well as the "stables" where Herders tended and "milked" the flocks of Little Ones.

The Feeders, and their Subcastes of Groomers and Tenders, consisted mainly of those Shshi too small for heavy labor. They were responsible for providing nourishment to the Warriors, who could not feed themselves because their enormous mandibles prevented them from getting the food into their mouths. So the Feeders consumed fungus and honeydew and petals and the carrion dead and then regurgitated into the crops of the Warriors, retaining enough to nourish themselves. Special Subcastes fed and tended the nymphs and the Holy One and King; Alates could feed themselves, although they were sometimes too lazy to do so.

Griffen was as delighted with all this new information as Kaitrin was with her new language. "These feeding practices have their parallels in the behavior of terrestrial termites, and we seem to have confirmation that this particular isopteroid species has lost its ability to metabolize wood and become dependent on cultivated fungus, supplemented with other vegetable and animal products and the protein derived from necrophagia. In this savanna ecosystem, the foraging of wood-eaters of such size would quickly deplete the supply of cellulose – it's no wonder they evolved a different survival strategy. Yet it appears that our forest-dwelling Nasutes took a different evolutionary path."

The Builders were the largest and strongest of the Workers. For the construction of Lo'ro'ra they had hauled stones from rocky outcroppings in the vicinity. Now this easily obtainable supply of building materials was dwindling; an inability to construct more living accommodations was one reason why Lo'ro'ra produced so many founding hordes. No'kri showed the fascinated visitors some of the Builders' tools – stone "hand" axes and wooden wedges for shaping and breaking rocks, chisels and hafted hammers of stone, wooden mallets.

Some subtle questioning on Kaitrin's part revealed that the Shshi had only the most rudimentary knowledge of mathematics, yet the Builders engineered edifices of great complexity and precision, giving them a maze of chambers and passageways, a ventilation system, underground tunnels connecting buildings, a water cistern fed by an aqueduct – all mapped in their brains by nothing more than an intuitive sense of reckoning and proportion, without aid of vision or writing. "These behaviors are totally the product of instinct," said Gwidian. "An ability to build was encoded in their genes millions of years ago when their ancestors were NILFs a couple of centimeters long and they have never lost it. Quite remarkable, actually."

The Builders had Subcastes of Crafters who fabricated wooden objects like wheels and cart frames, tool handles and containers. For woodworking they used their own jaws as well as mandible tools similar to those that the Star-Beings had seen in the orchard. They also chipped out stone pots and wove baskets and even coarse fabrics of river grass, making bags, curtains, and ropes. None of these was produced with any regard for visual aesthetics, although all Shshi had a sense of proportion, were sensitive to textures, and enjoyed tactile sensations; and the Alates were not without a visual awareness of natural beauty. Certainly the deaf Shshi had no concept of music, but they did have a sense of rhythm; Kaitrin allowed No'kri to touch the "magic box" while she played a recording of a song with a distinctive drumbeat. The Worker displayed astonishment and quickly began to jig in time with the thump that attacked its sensilla.

In spite of this paucity of aesthetic awareness, or perhaps because of it, they obviously had no lack of imagination. Kaitrin had concluded that the one artistic medium that came naturally to them was words. They poured all their creativity into the art of storytelling.

*   *   *

At the end of the second session with No'kri, the Worker Chief asked if they would like to walk around the compound for a firsthand inspection. *Holy Kwi'ga'ga'tei has given permission for it. Ru'a'ma'na'ta may come, and her* na'sha'ma|, *and the birdcreature, and the large female one, because those two understand some of our language. But no Warrior may come; Ki'shto'ba will accompany us and ensure your comfort. If you are willing, we will conduct the tour at the dawning of the next suntime.*

"Comfort" seemed to be a euphemism for "safety." Gwidian was not easy about the excursion and Arti was reluctant to cede the responsibility for security to their hosts. Tió'otu decided to decline. "!Ka<tí are not fast on their feet," he said. "If there is a need to move quickly, I will be an impediment. So, as much as I would like to see all this for myself, I will forgo this adventure."

Kaitrin tried to reassure Griffen. "I would trust my life to Ki'shto'ba, Griff. I would go anywhere under its protection. And we'll be out in the open the whole time. What can happen?"

"We'll be walking around under the guidance of blind and deaf creatures! That's hardly a comforting thought!"

"Oh, Griff, try to relax and enjoy this! Maybe you shouldn't come."

"And allow you and Luku to go out there alone? At the very least, I want you to carry your sidearm, Kait."

And to quiet his protests she gave in and agreed to do that.

The next morning they ventured forth, with Luku operating the holocam and Kaitrin employing her newly miniaturized voice-activated emitter-receiver, which had an earport to transmit an audible rendition of the biopulses.

No'kri and the Chiefs of the Subcastes were very thorough, even leading them among the stone storage cysts that were arrayed on both flanks of the compound.   Growers' tools and wheelbarrows were kept there, along with bins of plant materials used for bedding and weaving and fungus fertilization.   Still others were utilized as holding pens for the Little Ones when they were taken out in the flowering season to graze on fallen blossoms.   The tour group had no Star-Winged Alates with them to illuminate the interiors of these windowless cysts, but the Star-Beings' field lights allowed them to peer into the humped, musty structures.   Luku remarked that they reminded her of a type of ancient tomb from her home planet.

The main edifices of the fortress of Lo'ro'ra seemed even larger and more menacing when one stood near the cool bulk of their twenty-meter walls.   The entranceways, behind a double guard of fidgeting Warriors, seemed to suck in air, and No'kri said, *You who have eyes, if you look up, you may see Builders on the walls, mortaring loose stones and clearing away plants that take root in the crevices and cause cracks.   You may also see ventilation holes in the sides of the fortress.   They are occasionally used for entrances and also for exits, especially during times of war, although they are a tight fit.*

The ventilation shafts can be blocked up if the fortress is under siege, but not all of them – that would cause everyone to stop breathing, said Ki'shto'ba.   *They are mainly too small for the passage of Shshi Warriors, but Nasutes can fit through them.   A few raids were mounted in that manner during the siege.*

Kaitrin said, "I think it's time to talk to No'kri about the air samples.   No'kri, we have some little objects with us that can give us knowledge about the air inside your fortress.   We would like for one of them to be placed in each building, on the ground four or five Shi lengths inside the entrance.   They must remain there undisturbed until sunset.   Perhaps one of you can bring them back to us at that time."

The Shshi crowded around tasting and feeling.   *These are*

magic boxes? asked No'kri. Some of the Workers quivered and groomed apprehensively.

Not magic boxes! Learning boxes! declared Ki'shto'ba decisively.

Kaitrin sighed. "They will not harm any of you in any way. They will only sit there and seem to do nothing until you bring them back to us."

And then they will talk to you? How is that possible? said No'kri.

"They do not talk, but they can give us knowledge in other ways," said Kaitrin. "*no'no| um'zi|* is right – they are learning boxes."

Then Wi'tai the Builder Chief summoned up its courage and said, *I would be proud to take charge of this. I will place one in each of the locations that you specified and personally bring them back to you, if No'kri will permit it.* And it scampered off to perform its task like a schoolboy entrusted with the most important assignment of his life.

They moved toward the back of the fortress, where a disagreeable smell began to intrude. From a small rear entrance on each of the edifices, Workers were trundling carts toward the northeast perimeter of the compound. *Those are Dung Carriers,* explained No'kri. *That is one of the lowest Subcastes of Tenders, but still the function they perform is as necessary as any other. If the fortress is not kept clean, we will all sicken and die. They carry waste to the dung pit outside the wall, although some is used to fertilize the Fungus Garden and the orchards.*

The aqueduct proved to be a skillfully constructed stone-lined channel about two meters wide and one deep that diverted water from the river half a kilometer away. The channel had been excavated to a two-degree slope to allow the water to flow smoothly into an opening below ground level at the base of the main edifice. It fed into an underground cistern, Nok'ri told them, which held enough water to supply the fortress's needs for a year. A wooden baffle could be inserted at the ingress to stem the flow when the cistern was full.

In spite of his uneasiness, Gwidian was amazed. "This behavior has no parallels amongst these creatures' terrestrial kin," he said.

Kaitrin was looking westward, toward a wall that circled behind the Warriors' Quarters. "I hear a noise," she said to her human companions. "Ki'shto'ba, what's happening over there?"

That is the Warrior's exercise yard.   Would you like to observe?

Griffen emitted a quick expletive. No'kri was saying to the Huge-Head, *I do not know if the Holy Seer would approve of that.*

As Kaitrin began, "We do not wish to go where we ... " Ki'shto'ba interrupted.

Here is the Holy Seer now.

Kwi'ga'ga'tei was approaching them from behind, accompanied by Sa'ti'a'i'a and a pair of its own Warriors. *I am sorry I was prevented from joining you sooner. I hope No'kri has been caring for you.*

"Oh, very much so, Holy Kwi'ga'ga'tei." Noting that the Seer was looking at Luku's holocam, Kaitrin added, "That is the box that captures the moving images. It is not harmful. I will show you the images later, Kwi'ga'ga'tei. You will see yourself in them."

Is it not all too wondrous to be real? exclaimed Ki'shto'ba. *But we were speaking of the Warrior's exercise yard. Is it forbidden for the Star-Beings to go there?*

Kwi'ga'ga'tei danced. *Do you really wish to see the Warriors train?*

"Not really," said Griffen to Kaitrin after she translated.

But she said, "Oh, come on, Griff! This is amazing stuff and it may be the only opportunity we'll ever get! And think what a holoimage it will make! How can there be any danger with Kwi'ga'ga'tei and Ki'shto'ba and the Nasutes along?"

Griffen gave in and they crossed the aqueduct on an overlay of wooden planks and approached the wall of the enclosure, from whence came thumps and scrabbling and clattering sounds.

The ground was studded with small boulders, among which perhaps a dozen pairs of Warriors squared off at each other. Some feinted and sparred with their mandibles or seized each other by legs or necks, jumping and twisting, seeking to bear each other down by sheer weight. Others wrestled, clasping each other's head with the forelegs and swaying together, locked jaw to jaw, until one toppled.

"Isopteroid martial arts!" exclaimed Kaitrin in Inj, then, to Ki'shto'ba, "Do you ever hurt each other unintentionally?"

Sometimes. But we try to avoid that – it is a stupid outcome to good exercise. I have trouble finding sparring partners because I am so strong and so much bigger than the Shum'za. But there are a few bold ones who are willing to train with me in order to gain recognition. We also play a game where we run about among the rocks and seek to find another by vibration and scent. This sharpens the precision of our senses for the chaos of the battlefield. We lift heavy objects in our jaws in order to strengthen our necks and forelegs. And we practice jumping over the rocks and over each other. All Shshi are great leapers.

"Like that one on the left! Look how high it can jump! Isn't that Chief A'gwa'ji?"

It is, said Kwi'ga'ga'tei. *You grow skilled at recognizing our scents, Ru'a'ma'na'ta.*

Kaitrin giggled at that, then said, "Who is that Warrior over there who is lifting its opponent off the ground?"

That is Lo'lo'pai, Chief of the First Cohort, said the Seer.

Griffen muttered something, but Kaitrin watched in fascination as the big Warrior tossed its sparring partner, no small creature itself, onto its side and pounced on it, open mandibles raised for a potential death-slash, then sprang away with a great leap. Luku's holocam ticked away furiously.

Others are about to join us, said Kwi'ga'ga'tei, staring across the yard.

At that moment, a pause in the activity of the enclosure began at the left and rippled like a wave toward the right. All the Warriors, having apparently received a command, shifted to face the visitors, their mandibles raised in threat. Two Shshi had come out of an entranceway at the back of the Quarters – a big Warrior and an Alate.

"Now that's another one I've seen," said Griffen, his hands tightening atop the wall.

Kaitrin's equipment could not pick up the words that Kwi'ga'ga'tei sent across the yard. The Warrior was approaching them, while the Alate stayed where it was, its regard fixed on them. The Warriors stood down from their threat display, but remained at vigilant attention.

Kwi'ga'ga'tei said, *Commander Hi'ta'fu Wei'bao'zei, these are our friends from the stars – Ru'a'ma'na'ta, her* na'sha'ma|, *and their companion, the large female Star-Being.*

Hi'ta'fu, the largest Warrior of Lo'ro'ra that Kaitrin had seen, stopped about a Shi's length in front of them. Its integument bore many discolored blotches and grooves and she observed that it was missing a hind claw and the first two knobs from the left antenna. Its mandibles were especially torqued and fearsome, but their serrated cutting edges were chipped and battered. Kaitrin thought, *This one is old – close to being worn out.* She envisioned those mandibles reborn as pruning hooks and she doubted they would last long.

"Commander," she said, "please know that we do not threaten you or the wonderful fortress of Lo'ro'ra that you have protected so well for so long, nor do we threaten the Holy One and King that give it life. We have come only in peace and friendship. Can we not be friends?"

This was apparently not what the Commander had expected. It danced ponderously. *I am a plain, blunt Warrior*, it said. *I want to know what I am facing. This is a confusing time. I cannot accept that you have flown here from the Nameless One, or in the Nameless One, or whatever bizarre tale it is that the Seer tells.*

"We did indeed fly here from the stars and we are your friends. Those are the simple things that I want you to believe."

Beside Kaitrin Kwi'ga'ga'tei twitched. The Alate who had emerged with the Commander had slipped up beside it unnoticed.

Kwi'ga'ga'tei said, *Ru'a'ma'na'ta*, na'sha'ma|, *female one, this one is the Keeper of the Holy Chamber, Mo'gri'ta'tu.*

The different word order and the curtness of the introduction clearly suggested disrespect, a circumstance that was not lost on Kaitrin

The Chamberlain stood quite still and stared with his head cocked. *Ru'a'ma'na'ta, I am honored. It is not every day that we are visited by beings sacred to the Nameless One. I have been reproving the Holy Seer for not permitting me to pay my homage to you. I would hope that grievous oversight could soon be rectified.*

There is, however, said Kwi'ga'ga'tei, *a good chance that Mo'gri'ta'tu's duties in the Holy Chamber will not allow time for such a visit.*

Come now, Holy Seer, my work is always in good order and I have excellent assistants. But we who lack the vision power must abide by the decrees of the Holy Seer, who is always right. At least let me take this present opportunity to assure you that the perceived attack on the na'sha'ma| *here* ... He had fixed his glittering gaze on Gwidian, who had stood rigid and uncomprehending throughout this encounter. ... *was a mistake – only a mistake of communication. The honored Commander will bear me out on that. Commander?*

It was certainly a mistake, said Hi'ta'fu stolidly.

Kaitrin was thinking, *They're right. This is where the real threat lies. Even with the unfamiliar body language and no vocal expression to read, I can sense this one is dangerous.*

To Mo'gri'ta'tu, Kaitrin said, "We have accepted the apology of the Shshi for this mistake. We are friends to all of you, Holy Chamberlain, and seek only good will and knowledge."

Admirable goals, ma'na'ta| *from the Stars – ones all of us should pursue.*

The Chamberlain's eyes were scrutinizing the gear that was strapped around the visitors, lingering on the emitter box, the provision kits, the lights – the sidearm holsters. *First time I've ever felt undressed by the eyes of an insect*, thought Kaitrin.

Kwi'ga'ga'tei flared her wings. *I think the time has come to pass on to other activities*, she said. *Good day to you, Commander – Chamberlain. Warriors, you may resume your training. Mo'gri'ta'tu, you may resume whatever ... Indeed, what were you doing here? But no matter. Come, my friends, the Champion and I will walk you partway back to your dwelling.*

Kaitrin was impressed; she had never before witnessed Kwi'ga'ga'tei in her imperial mode. As they moved toward the south side of the fortress, Luku said, "*Jocha!* I am a little glad that is over."

"Right on," said Gwidian.

"I thought it was fascinating," said Kaitrin. "Kwi'ga'ga'tei, I agree with you. I sense much hidden intention in Mo'gri'ta'tu's words."

Yes. Perhaps it is good that you encountered him. Be careful, Ru'a'ma'na'ta. Ki'shto'ba and the Nasute Chief and I can protect you from the Commander, but from one like Mo'gri'ta'tu, you must be able to protect yourself.

*   *   *

[Mo'gri'ta'tu and Hi'ta'fu reenter the Warriors' Quarters]

[Hi'ta'fu]: You, even you, could be wrong, Mo'gri'ta'tu. I sense no deception in her assertions of peace and friendship!

[Mo'gri'ta'tu]: When did you become expert at sensing hidden intentions, Commander? It is difficult enough for us seeing ones to detect such things! I tell you, the one with the smoothest seeming is the one to be trusted least. So it is with Kwi'ga'ga'tei! And with her, moreover, there is the further corruption of the growing *bir'zha|* madness.

[Hi'ta'fu]: Yes, you should understand about smooth seeming, Chamberlain.

[Mo'gri'ta'tu, annoyed]: You appear to be one who can learn only from hard lessons, Hi'ta'fu. There is not the least doubt that these false ones would like to destroy our Holy One and King and they must be brought down along with their supporters, the Seer and her Champion, before their nefarious plans bear fruit. Have you become a proponent of the new way? Where softness rules the fortress until only brains and guts are left for wild vermin to pick over?

[Hi'ta'fu, postures]: Never! Never will I yield Lo'ro'ra and my Holy A'kha'ma'na'ta to destruction, as long as my spiracles suck breath!

[Mo'gri'ta'tu]: Now you begin to resemble the Commander I knew of old! The Champion of Kwai'kwai'za! The mainstay of the Nasute Siege! You and I will keep the glory of Lo'ro'ra alive, mighty Hi'ta'fu the Unconquered, until the last Remembrancer fades into the stars! Only hearken to the counsel of Mo'gri'ta'tu, and all will end as you know it should!

[Later, Mo'gri'ta'tu alone]

Well, all does not go as I would like, however. It is difficult keeping this shambling old Warrior on the course. *tha'sask|>||* It turns my gut to have to flatter it like that, but I have no means to control it by physical threat. And Lo'lo'pai is unpredictable. The

143

Seer has seized hold of A'gwa'ji and no hope remains of deflecting it to our cause, or any of the Warriors in its Cohort.

If we had the distance weapon … If we could kill Ki'shto'ba with it, we could make it look like the work of the outlanders … Or better yet, kill Kwi'ga'ga'tei at the same time and make it seem the outlanders murdered both! These are stimulating thoughts! But how to get the weapon? I wonder if their false *ma'na'ta|* is vulnerable to manipulation. Something tells me she will not be as easy as the Commander and the Chief. But I think I see my opportunity to try. Some Growers, friends of Ti'shra, enticed her out at an unappointed time the other day. I will build upon that – see what I can do. I would rather not have all this spill into open revolt. Civil war is a nasty business and I want something left to rule when I take power. Well, I will see what I can achieve.

Chapter 13

2d Witch: By the pricking of my thumbs,
Something wicked this way comes.
Open, locks,
Whoever knocks!
– *from* William Shakespeare, *Macbeth*

"This place," said Kaitrin, over the last meal of the day-cycle, "reminds me of one of Earth's ancient city states, where whoever could seize power did, and the more he had to scheme and plot to do so, the more fun it was."

Gwidian said, "So this Mo – Moki – whatever … Why do you give them such peculiar names, Kaitrin?"

"If I've already assigned syllables to the wave forms, then I'm stuck with them, but if the individual elements of the name are new, then I just assign sounds that I like. I want to find out more about their naming system. *mo'gri'ta'tu'ze|* seems to mean something like 'The shining sun is her wing' – yes, 'her, even though our Chamberlain is male. Maybe 'her' refers to the Big Mamá in the sky. Have you noticed that all the Alates' names have four syllables; and all the Warriors', three; and the Workers', two? See, I thought you hadn't noticed!"

"I noticed," said Tió'otu grumpily. He was beginning to regret not taking the tour.

"Well, so what is it we have to fear from this Chamberlain?" persisted Griffen.

145

"I don't think we ourselves have anything to fear, but if you could have monitored his words ... A real Makiavel – all oily flattery and ambiguity ... I don't believe there's a sincere bone in that creature's body! I know, Griff, I know! Insects have no bones! A sincere sclerite, maybe?"

Everybody laughed and Kaitrin continued, "To get serious, he seems to be trying to undermine Kwi'ga'ga'tei's position – appropriate the power of the city state to himself. That's what really worries me. I don't see how he can do us any damage, but someday we'll have to leave. And when I come back – and I'm sure I'll come back, Griffen, no matter how much you grimace over there! – will Lo'ro'ra still be the same place? Will Kwi'ga'ga'tei even be alive? I'm getting really fond of that mysterious little creature."

*   *   *

Amid an escort of Second Cohort guards, Wi'tai marched up proudly in the late afternoon with the air monitors swinging in a bag from its mandibles. Kaitrin went into the laboratory awhile later and found Griffen chuckling. "It seems every creature in the fortress had to taste the magic boxes. One is cracked, one crusted with mud – at least, I hope it's mud! – and all four are mucked up with saliva. At least I got some composite biological samples."

"These gauges are pretty indestructible, though," said Will, who was helping Griffen with the decoding. "We got readings. Oxygen and nitrogen levels are close to average for this planet. Carbon dioxide is a little higher than in the outer atmosphere."

"No dangerous levels of naphthalene, methane, or acetate," said Gwidian. "We found traces of some of those in the ant mound, but we've learned it was originally occupied by wood-eaters, who produce greater quantities of those gases."

"So the air inside would be safe for a human to breathe," said Kaitrin injudiciously.

"I certainly wouldn't want to chance it without further tests," said Gwidian, frowning at his microanalyzer's portscreen, where microorganisms from a saliva sample were displayed. "Fortunately, there's no reason for any of us ... " He stopped and abruptly shifted his gaze to Kaitrin. "Kaitrin! You're not thinking ... ?"

"Oh, no, no!" she said too quickly.

"Kaitrin. My god. You're a very bad liar."

"Well, Griffen, Kwi'ga'ga'tei did sort of issue an invitation ... Now, don't look at me like that! Probably nothing will ever come of it! The corridors are undoubtedly too small, anyway! *¡Ay caramba!* My big mouth! And here I told everybody not to say anything to you!"

At that, Gwidian slammed down the cover of the annie and stalked out of the laboratory. Kaitrin heard their compartment door bang. She looked at Will in despair.

He grinned back. "It's hard on a man when he's in love, Kaitrin Oliva," he said, "and the woman won't take his worries seriously."

She went out into the common area. Trea was regarding the closed door. "You upset Gwidian, Kaitrin."

"I know. I'll go in and see if I can fix things."

"No," said the Pozúu. "This time let him be. It is anger he is feeling – he needs to work through that by himself."

"Trea, you have such insight into people. Did you study psychology as a subspecialty?"

Trea grimaced and started to answer, but Arti called down from the flight deck. "Communications coming in, people! TTR messages! Everybody come!"

It was only the third receipt of messages in the six weeks since the *Durga* had landed. Kaitrin opened their compartment door and said, "Griffen! We've got TTR messages coming in! Please come out. I'm sorry."

He appeared, pushing past her with a sidelong look. "If you come to some harm, Kait, 'sorry' won't be enough," he said a little hoarsely.

"I know. Don't be angry with me. I can't stand it."

He hesitated, then came back, grasped her shoulders, and kissed her hard on the lips. "Come on, let's get our messages. Just don't hide things from me to spare my feelings, Kait. It never works, you know. We're such a small group."

"And I'm my own worst enemy!" said Kaitrin, relieved to be forgiven. But she was thinking, *But, Griffen, I know you're still hiding things from me.*

The message from Kaitrin's mother contained only one item of special consequence. Kaitrin relayed it to her associates.

"My mother says a big interest has developed in the reports

our team is sending back. I mean, outside of academic circles. A pop link had got hold of them and is publishing them and it's generating lots of public excitement! Can you imagine?"

"Prf. Lindeman tells me the same thing," said Griffen. "It seems the idea of giant talking bugs with an archaic civilization has seized the public imagination. I can't imagination why that should happen. Most of what we're sending back is raw preliminary data."

"But Kaitrin's reports are very lively and entertaining," said Luku. "They would give me interest if I was back on Earth."

"Well, the haphazard regulation of Earth's information dissemination system encourages this sort of thing," said A'a'ma. "Now, take the way it works on Krisí'i'aid – very creaky, very fragmented, very suspicious. After more than two thousand years of continuous electronic communication, we still never believe anything unless half a dozen live experts verify it."

"Look at it like this: Maybe popular fame will help us to get private funding for some future … " began Kaitrin, but at that moment one of the proximity sensors began going off.

"Now what?" said Griffen, rising and heading for the ladder. He and Kaitrin and the security people mounted to the flight deck and peered out of the windows into the twilight.

At first they saw nothing; then a glimmer of light caught their attention. A lone Alate was scuttling along the flanks of the *Durga*, peering up at the windows, standing with its front and middle legs against the side in order to get a better look. It displayed absolutely no fear.

"Is that the Seer?" asked Arti.

"Can't be," said Kaitrin. "Kwi'ga'ga'tei wouldn't be out running around by herself. If she wanted to get our attention, she would send Ki'shto'ba or Sa'ti'a'i'a."

They observed for a few minutes. The Alate made a complete circuit of the flyer and reappeared in the same spot. Then it disappeared under the wing. In a moment Tió'otu called, "What is going on? Something is scratching on the hatch."

"Let's open it – it can't do any harm! I'm not afraid of one Alate, for goodness sake! Quick, Luku, the translator!" Kaitrin slid down the ladder and headed for the control panel.

"Careful!" said Luku. "Door will hit it when it pops up."

"It's all right!" called Arti. "I see it below the windows again."

"Persistent, what?" said Gwidian a little nervously.

As Kaitrin emerged onto the ramp, the Alate was already approaching. Kaitrin stopped halfway down, with Griffen filling the doorway behind her. The Alate was forced to look up at them.

Kaitrin knew it was Mo'gri'ta'tu, even though she could not have named specific identifying characteristics. It was the arrogance, even an amused arrogance, in the stance of the creature, the little twist of his head, the slight list to the left in his balance. Kaitrin understood instinctively that it was better to maintain her position of dominance on the ramp rather than to come down to the Chamberlain's eye level.

He made a little obeisance, just enough to reinforce the impression of impudence. na'ta'zei|. *I told you I would find the opportunity to pay a visit of homage to you. The Keeper of the Holy Chamber always keeps his word.*

"I am happy to converse with any Shi, Chamberlain. But I do not want you to call me 'Holy One.' That name is only for your A'kha'ma'na'ta."

But you have accepted our title of ma'na'ta|. *Should I not honor the* ma'na'ta| *of the Star-Beings?* Mo'gri'ta'tu had sidled around to the foot of the ramp and come about a third of the way up it, something no other Shi had yet dared to do. The audacity of this creature was beginning to make Kaitrin uneasy. She backed a step or two up the ramp. She could feel Griffen still behind her, see Mo'gri'ta'tu peering around her at him, eyeing him up and down.

"I have a name of my own that cannot be uttered in the language of the Shshi. Holy Kwi'ga'ga'tei gave me the name *ru'a'ma'na'ta|* in order to have a way to address me."

That is not the reason she gave us for naming you in so sacred a manner. If she only wanted a means of common address, she would have called you bu| *or* kri| *or* ka| *as we name new-hatched nymphs or little pets.*

Kaitrin thought, *A one-syllable name. The lowest order. Ti'shra named its pet "Zuf." But a Queen's name has five syllables.*

"She honored me with the word *ru|* because I was *ru'zei|* to

Ti'shra, something that was both an honor and a sorrow for me," said Kaitrin.

But ma'na'ta|*? I must admit I have been skeptical. You lack a swollen belly. Where are your Tenders? Your eggs? Your nymphs? Do you keep them inside this flying dwelling? How is it that you can dwell above ground without incurring the wrath of the Nameless One? Enlighten me, Ru'a'ma'na'ta, because I also come seeking knowledge, even as you profess to do. Is it not distressing to be ignorant of strangers' ways?*

¡Maldito! thought Kaitrin, *I wish Kwi'ga'ga'tei were here. How far should I go with this slippery creature? He's giving me the creeps.*

She decided to play it close. "Our *shma'na'ta|* do not produce many, many offspring as yours do. Instead, our people have many females who each produce a few offspring. That is all you may know. There are mysteries in the universe that have not been revealed to the Shshi, nor should they be."

Mo'gri'ta'tu made a perfunctory groveling motion. *Such a dictum is only too true. Indeed, the Holy Seer convinces herself that she comprehends more mysteries than I believe she possibly could, or ought to.*

Kaitrin simply waited without responding, wondering where all this was leading.

I have taken a rumor – and you know how far one should trust rumors, Ru'a'ma'na'ta – that Kwi'ga'ga'tei considers inviting you into our dwelling. But I am not aware that you have ever invited the Shshi into yours. Why is that? But perhaps you have invited us and the Seer is too timid to accept the invitation. I would be delighted and honored to be the first Shi to enter the dwelling of a Star-Being.

"Griff," said Kaitrin, "he's actually inviting himself in. Apparently he wants to see the inside of the flyer."

"Never!" said Griffen.

From behind him came Trea's voice. "Too much danger for them of infection."

Kaitrin decided to be honest. "Although it would honor us, I cannot ask any Shi to enter our dwelling. Ti'shra died on our world partly because there were things there that made him sick. Such things might exist also inside our dwelling, and we do not want to make any of you sick. So you must not come in."

Mo'gri'ta'tu considered this explanation, his head cocked. *Indeed, what a caring reason you give. Are these dangerous things anything like the weapons that kill without touching?*

"Oh, Griffen, now he's brought up the weapons."

Gwidian made an impatient movement and Kaitrin heard Arti's and A'a'ma's expletives.

Mo'gri'ta'tu was saying, *We are all curious about these weapons. If Commander Hi'ta'fu and Chief Lo'lo'pai and their Lieutenants had not experienced them, no one would believe such things exist. Indeed, many of us believe that these blind Warriors' senses may have deceived them. Certainly one of us Seeing Ones ought to know what they can do. Now, the Holy Seer is undoubtedly too timid to ask for a demonstration of them, but not all Shshi are so fearful, even among the weak-bodied Alates. Would you not let me see how they work? Indeed, the Holy One has instructed me to ask this favor of you.*

How odd this is becoming, thought Kaitrin. *I'm sure he thinks that invoking the command of the Holy One will compel me to do as he asks. Well, dream on, Chamberlain!*

"We will not show our weapons to any of you," she said to Mo'gri'ta'tu. "It is not in Lo'ro'ra's best interests."

And you know what those are? Well, perhaps you do. If you really come from the Nameless One, you certainly must know what is best for this fortress, more so than those who have spent their lives working to make Lo'ro'ra great.

Kaitrin thought, *A hit – a palpable hit*, and waited to see what the Chamberlain would do next. In a way, she was enjoying this repartee; it was entirely different from anything she had encountered among the Shshi. And yet she wondered what twisted motives underlay Mo'gri'ta'tu's mocking sarcasm.

Am I looking at the weapon? persisted Mo'gri'ta'tu, regarding the translator at Kaitrin's waist.

"No, this is the antenna box that allows me to speak to you."

Oh, the renowned magic box! Rather like the magic boxes that Wi'tai carried away so self-importantly this afternoon! Do all your magic-making fabrications look alike?

Before Kaitrin realized what he was doing, he had darted up the ramp, the brilliant tissue of his wings brushing against her, and half collided with Griffen, sticking his palps against the objects on his belt, including the latched sidearm holster.

Gwidian gave a yawp and shoved at the Shi's head. From inside, Arti lunged up beside Griffen, but Kaitrin cried, "Everybody stand still, but don't let him pass! Just let him investigate! He won't hurt anybody! He knows we could easily take him down!" *Good grief, the audacity of this creature!*

But the push on the face had told Mo'gri'ta'tu that he had gone too far, and he backed off, abasing and scraping. *Many pardons, friends from the stars. I overstep myself, I see that. Madness grows on all of us in this new time. Indeed, it is no longer the province of our unfortunate Seer alone.*

"What do you mean?" Kaitrin asked.

Oh, the Seer – the pitiable Seer! Everyone knows that the Seer is no longer the same excellent governor who so brilliantly ended the Nasute Siege. I feared you might not be aware of this. Those who eat the bir'zha| *fungus – you know of that – for too long a time begin to have disturbances of the mind in their waking times. I feel much pity for Holy Kwi'ga'ga'tei! She is certainly in decline – sees much that does not exist and cannot fully understand much of what does exist. She definitely can no longer be relied upon to behave rationally.*

Kaitrin stared open-mouthed at the Chamberlain. *He can't be serious ...*

I am the Keeper of A'kha'ma'na'ta's Holy Chamber and I have known the Holy One much longer than the Seer has, so I feel that it is my responsibility to protect the Holy One and the King from any misguided counsel – even from the counsel of the Holy Seer when that One Being is no longer competent. And so I tell you these things, in greatest confidence, na'ta'zei|, *because, as you are* ma'na'ta| *also, I believe I should seek to protect you as well.*

Kaitrin wished it were possible to make spectrographic words convey coldness. "I will consider what you say, Mo'gri'ta'tu, and give it the weight that it deserves."

Mo'gri'ta'tu hesitated, then said, *Only watch yourself, I beg you,* na'ta'zei|. *Do not let one who seems sane entrap you who are an innocent one. Beware the Holy Seer's delusions, that is all I ask. And if you need advice as to how to proceed, you are welcome to consult me at any time. Any Warrior of the First Cohort will be happy to carry a message to me.*

He backed down the ramp, turned, and scuttled off into the nearly complete darkness, his wings fanning and flashing.

Griffen grabbed Kaitrin and hauled her into the flyer, closing the hatch. "What was that all about?"

"Kaitrin, you look grim," said A'a'ma.

"I'm speechless!" she cried. "I'm appalled! This creature had the audacity to inform me that Kwi'ga'ga'tei is mentally incompetent – that the hallucinogen she uses is destroying her reason!"

"Can happen," said Trea.

"I know that, but Kwi'ga'ga'tei? Never! I'd say this is the one who's unbalanced!"

"You're sure of that?" Gwidian said. "How much do we really understand about these creatures' minds? Why should you believe one of them over any other?"

"There, you see?" cried Kaitrin. "You didn't even understand what Mo'gri'ta'tu said and already he's twisting your thinking! This creature really is perfidious! I may have been wrong when I said he can't do anything to harm us."

"His interest in these weapons of ours is truly disturbing," said A'a'ma. "I shudder to think why he wants to know about them. I am sure it is not intellectual curiosity."

"I can't believe that the Queen really told him to ask us to fire one for him," said Kaitrin.

"He said that?" exclaimed Gwidian.

"My next quandary is, do I tell Kwi'ga'ga'tei about what Mo'gri'ta'tu did tonight?" said Kaitrin. "We ought to stay neutral if a conflict is brewing here."

"That would certainly be best," A'a'ma agreed.

"But Kwi'ga'ga'tei is my friend," said Kaitrin. "I'd be devastated if something happened to her that I could have maybe prevented."

Luku said, "Kaitrin, they can't get weapons. They would not know how to fire them if they did."

"Or they would dislodge the safety and fire the thing by accident and kill themselves or an innocent bystander," said Julian.

Trea said, "I believe Kwi'ga'ga'tei knows her own situation, Kaitrin. Did she not warn you about Mo'gri'ta'tu? My counsel is

– say nothing."

"Let sleeping dogs lie, in the old adage," said Will Ayland.

So with considerable reluctance Kaitrin agreed to stay out of the dispute and not even mention this encounter to Kwi'ga'ga'tei. "But I'm not going to let this get in the way of our friendship, or my research, either," she said. "And if that includes going ... " She stopped and did not finish the sentence, but she had no doubt that Griffen knew what she had started to say.

*   *   *

[Mo'gri'ta'tu scurries through the darkness]

That one is not such an easy mark and perhaps I overplayed it. If she scampers to the Seer with tales of this ... But what harm could that do? Perhaps I have sown a few seeds of distrust. A'kha'ma'na'ta favors me in spite of all the Seer's blandishments. I am one of the few people she has left who was alive in the time of Thei'ga'na'sha'ma, and no matter how her whims shift, she always comes back to me for support. If I cannot get hold of these weapons, I will find another way. My name should be "Resourceful." I cannot fail to prevail. I hate Kwi'ga'ga'tei too much to be denied her destruction.

Chapter 14

Darkling I listen; and, for many a time
I have been half in love with easeful Death,
Called him soft names in many a musèd rhyme,
To take into the air my quiet breath …
— *from* John Keats, *Ode to a Nightingale*

When Kwi'ga'ga'tei and Ki'shto'ba came the next morning, however, it was the Seer herself who introduced the topic of Mo'gri'ta'tu's visit.

There were Shshi in the courtyard who observed the Chamberlain speaking with you under the wing of your dwelling, she said. *Surely Mo'gri'ta'tu did not think he could keep his visit secret. I wonder what thing he is scheming now.*

Kaitrin hesitated, then decided as usual to be forthright. "I have talked of these matters with the other Star-Beings, and we all feel it is not a good thing to – stay on one side more than another – or try to change the lives of those we visit. So I decided not to speak of the things Mo'gri'ta'tu said to me."

The static brilliance of Kwi'ga'ga'tei's eyes pierced Kaitrin. *That decision does not surprise me. You seek the peaceful way always, as do I. But I hope whatever he has said to you will not turn you against me, because I value your friendship.*

"I will not let anything do that, because I value yours, also."

Ki'shto'ba was less circumspect. *The Chamberlain deserves a foul end! He dishonors his fortress and he dishonors the Commander by drawing it into unworthy actions. Do not allow him to*

155

poison you as well with his dissembling speech.

Kaitrin was unfamiliar with the epithet that the Huge-Head applied to Mo'gri'ta'tu's speech, but its implication was not difficult to guess.

Later in that day's discussion Kaitrin turned the talk to the Shshi naming system.

What you perceive about the speech units of names is correct, said the Seer. *All new-hatched nymphs look the same; their Caste is revealed only at the third molt. So the Namers give the hatchlings a little name like* lo| *or* shra| *or* gwaf|*; when its Caste becomes known, its name is amended. Thus* lo| *can become* lo'lo'pai'ze| – *"Warrior of Many Strengths."* shra| *can become* ti'shra'ze| – *a Worker called "Sweet Flowers." And* gwaf| *can become* a'gwa'ji'ze| – *a Warrior's name meaning "Belly Slash." In that name* a'| *has no meaning; it is used simply to fill the required number of speech units.*

The Huge-Head polished the flat surfaces of its fearsome mandibles with its claws and said, *My nymph-name was* shto|. *When it became clear I would grow into a Warrior of much power, I was named as I am. I received my surname of* no'no| um'zi| *after my first battle. The Holy One of To'wak – my own much beloved* ma'na'ta| – *granted it to me as a field honor.*

Said Kwi'ga'ga'tei, *Some names are traditional and have lost real meaning, thus my own, which has often been assumed by Seers in this fortress.*

"And it was known you would be a Seer because you had visions even as a nymph. Ki'shto'ba mentioned that."

That is true. In my case I was given that name at third instar, but some Seers take a new name later in their lives after their gift has manifested. But you can learn more of these matters when you visit the nurseries and meet the Namer Alates. I hope you will visit our dwellings, Ru'a'ma'na'ta. It will make you even more a part of our lives.

Kaitrin took a deep breath. "I am not sure that I can do that. There is the question of the air in the fortress. It may differ from the air that is healthful for my kind. And the tunnels – will I fit within them, Holy Kwi'ga'ga'tei?"

The Seer regarded Kaitrin critically. *Not standing in the posture that you use when you move about – on the rear legs.*

So unnatural, remarked Ki'shto'ba.

Kaitrin quelled her urge to giggle. "But we are most comfortable in that posture. It truly is natural for us, Huge-Head."

Some of the chambers are high enough for you to stand like that, but you would have to walk properly on your four legs in most of the corridors. We would of course provide Alates at all times to light your way.

Oh, dear, thought Kaitrin, *if I do this thing, I'll have to forget about claustrophobia. Too bad Mamá would never let Jaq take me spelunking.*

Kwi'ga'ga'tei was saying, *I have spoken of this with the Holy One. She is willing for you to enter because you are* ma'na'ta|. *But she is afraid of the others who are with you. Only you may come in. She does not even want your* na'sha'ma| *to enter. I hope that is not sacrilege.*

Me, alone, Kaitrin thought. *But I can't see Griff wanting to go, anyway. Besides, he really is too big. But this is going to upset him so much. I'll have to stall – figure out some way to get him accustomed to the idea ...*

Fortunately, Kwi'ga'ga'tei was saying, *You do not have to agree immediately to do this. I realize there are things that I do not understand. We will speak further of it at another time.*

So Kaitrin was able to defer her decision and she decided to say nothing yet to Griffen.

*   *   *

Griffen worked all day in the laboratory. For a while Kaitrin worked with him; he was teaching her how to identify beetles. She was beginning to get really interested in the process, but at length she felt obligated to return to her own work. Later, she stuck her head into the lab.

"Griffen, I've been writing my message to my mother."

He glanced at her with a smile. "I've completed mine to Rianna. Only just sent it off."

"I was wondering if you'd like to add a few words to my mother. You can have part of my space."

He straightened up from the slide he was preparing, seeming startled. "Oh ... No, I don't think so. No, definitely not."

Kaitrin regarded him quizzically. "Don't act so alarmed. I'm sure Mamá would love to get a note from her law-son. Does that designation sound peculiar to you? I certainly haven't gotten used to 'wife' yet!"

"Oh, well ... No. No, I'd rather not. I wouldn't know what to write." Griffen laughed, but he seemed genuinely unsettled by the thought of communicating with the mother of his bride.

"You, at a loss for words? You told me once you wanted to meet her – you remember, on the trip home from the North Star. You could break the ice with a letter."

He made a quick, vague gesture. "Those were entirely different circumstances ... But I don't mean that I don't want to meet her. Of course I do. I only ... "

"You must have met the mothers of lots of the women you've been involved with. What would you have written to them?"

Surprisingly, he said, "Actually, I can't recall ever meeting the mother of anyone I've been with."

"Never? None?"

Griffen glanced furtively at her. "I've always avoided that sort of commitment, you know. I told you that."

"It's not much of a commitment – meeting somebody's mother!"

"Well, whatever," he said, turning back to his work with a slight frown. "I've never done it. And I think I will not write anything to – Brigit."

"All right. That's perfectly all right," she said, still puzzled, and she turned to leave.

"Kait."

She turned back. He was looking at her again.

"Thanks for thinking of asking me. I do appreciate it."

She smiled, waved a hand at him, and went out.

At supper, Griffen was in one of his preoccupied moods, and even while they were preparing for bed, he responded to Kaitrin's usual ramblings with monosyllables. As she brushed her hair, she could see him in the mirror, sitting idle on the edge of the bed inspecting a fingernail and chewing his lower lip. Occasionally he would glance up at her.

She gestured with the hairbrush. "Is there something you want to say to me? I can read you a lot better than I could in the beginning – I always know when you're waiting for me to shut up so you can get a word in."

He released a small laugh. "I, uh ... I was only wondering ... I realize I didn't want to write to your ... mother ... today, but ... Once, you said something ... You said your ... she ... wanted to think of me as a ... as a son ... Do you think she still would ... I mean, feel that she could ... ?"

His stammering articulation alarmed Kaitrin and she went over and sat down beside him. "Accept you as part of her family? Of course she will, Griffen! It makes me really happy to hear you ask that!"

He glanced diffidently at her. "Does it? You think she could ... accept me ... ?"

"Why ever would you think not?" she chided him, with a mild exasperation.

He looked down at his hands. "Mothers usually want the best for their daughters."

She gave his arm a little shake. "And you think you're not the best for me? Griff!"

"There is no one in the world who could be worthy of you, Kait."

Kaitrin said quietly, "Griffen, don't do that. As I said, I've learned to read you a little better. I used to think that you were only trying to dazzle and seduce me when you would say those flattering and extravagant things, but I know better now."

"And, uh ... what do you think now?"

"I think you do it to divert attention from yourself – to conceal yourself, your real self. There's no reason for you to hide like that from me, love."

He continued to avoid her eyes. "I must confess – there's truth in what you say. My whole persona is a ruse, a pose – one I've cultivated for so long that I myself can't always tell the difference between the false and the genuine."

Kaitrin took his face between her hands and forced him to look at her. His eyes held that troubling look of exposed vulnerability, and she realized that she would have to see that expression many times more before she would really be able to fathom whatever secrets that cultivated persona was protecting. "How is it, Griffen," she said, striving for a tone of gentle humor, "that when we first met, you seemed so cocksure, so confident – so arrogant, even?"

He pulled down her hands and held them together between his own so that he could avert his gaze again. The inarticulateness had returned. "When I first met you, Kait ... I told you ... I was at a low point ... I was quite at the end of the plank ... and that posture of ... of arrogance, if you will ... it was like the last bit of flotsam ... all a drowning man has to hold onto ... "

"Griffen," she said, shaken.

"It was the biggest pose of all," he said.

"Griffen, what are you trying to say to me?"

"What was uppermost in my mind ... at that time was ... suicide ... "

"Griffen!" Her shock rang through her voice.

But he sat back from her. "That's all changed! Don't get alarmed! I really hadn't meant to say that, to tell you that ... because it's all past, and I'm fine! Don't get upset – I'm fine, I'm fine! I only wondered ... whether your mother truly could regard me as ... a son ... I feel I might be ready for that now."

With a surge of fear, Kaitrin embraced him and held him close to her. "Oh, yes, love! Believe it! Why do you need all this reassurance, Griff? Why are you like this?"

"You've joined yourself to a man who is ... really ... " He groped desperately for the right word. " ... really inadequate, Kait. One who can always find something to be afraid of."

"Oh, dear god, *mi querido*, don't be afraid! I tell you what – I don't really want you to stop paying me all those extravagant compliments. They do dazzle and seduce, you know – they make me feel like I'm something special and I'd miss them terribly if you stopped. Don't stop, Griffen. And I'll tell you this again: I love you just the way you are, all of you, outside and inside, the parts I know and the parts I don't know. That will be true forever! You understand?"

He took a long, unsteady breath and laughed shakily. "I remember when you said that. And I'll remember about the compliments. I love to tell you how wonderful you are, because ... oh, Kait, it's true – that was never a pretense." He returned her embrace ardently, murmuring against her ear, "I went from the lowest point to the highest so quickly that sometimes none of this seems real to me. But right now I believe that of all men in the universe, not one has a greater hunger for life than I do … "

*   *   *

In bed their union was brief but impassioned and Griffen went to sleep quickly, with a hand nestled between Kaitrin's breasts. Their conversation seemed to have given him release, like the exhalation of a long-held breath. But she lay awake, more shaken than she wanted to admit by what he had confessed. She thought back over other things he had said: *God, my life is empty. Fill it for me, Kait … I was at a low emotional ebb … Life was sitting lightly on me.* He had made that last remark just a few days ago when they talked about his sortie among the ants. *Why have I been so obtuse? And so self-absorbed! I didn't pick up on these hints at all. He asked me never to take him lightly, but I have. I've always taken a shallow view, maybe just regarded his needs as a mere play for attention. That has to stop.*

Maybe this is what he's been hiding – guilt about wanting to kill himself. Maybe this is why he's always asking for forgiveness.

But that seemed far too simplistic. If a man saw death as the only escape, there was a reason for it. It was the thing that had made him want to die, not the desire itself, that he needed to expose. And so the quest into his soul was not complete. Possibly it was only beginning.

Again she wondered, *Am I strong enough for the quest this man has set me on?* Uneasy, she rolled over on her back. His hand slipped away from her breast; he, too, stirred a little, sighed, murmured an unintelligible word, and continued to sleep.

*   *   *

A couple of time units later, Kwi'ga'ga'tei said to Kaitrin, *I regret that I must ask you this: A rumor is spreading that inside their dwelling the Star-Beings carry a poison – the same thing they used to kill Ti'shra – and that they mean to spread it through Lo'ro'ra and kill us all. Did you say something to Mo'gri'ta'tu that could be so interpreted?*

An appalled Kaitrin now felt obligated to tell the Seer more of Mo'gri'ta'tu's visit – how he had wanted to enter the flyer, why they had prevented it. "There is no poison, Holy Kwi'ga'ga'tei! It is simply something that might make you ill. You have illnesses, I

161

am sure, that spread through your people in a mysterious way."

Kwi'ga'ga'tei named several diseases that they all dreaded.

"We have such illnesses, too, but because the causes are dif-ferent, ours can spread very fast and be extremely deadly on a world where the people are not used to them. That is why Ti'shra died so quickly – because the illness was new to it. We wish to prevent that from happening here, so that is why we cannot invite any of you to enter our dwelling, where such influences would be strong."

Kwi'ga'ga'tei considered this. *I believe I understand. But you see why I sought to keep Mo'gri'ta'tu from speaking with you. He is unmatched at twisting words to his own ends.*

"Why is he like this, Kwi'ga'ga'tei? What does he have against you?"

Kwi'ga'ga'tei fanned her wings and postured in a distress display. *At first I thought he merely wished to unseat me and take my power. Yet he has no gift of Seeing – none at all – so he sought other paths of influence. And now I fear he has passed beyond mere ambition. I no longer understand his motives. I only know that he seems to hate me and I fear he will be the cause of Lo'ro'ra's destruction. I have seen the threat of such destruction. A ... is coming, Ru'a'ma'na'ta, but its nature is not clear to me and I am truly afraid. I think I may have to ... if certain events come to pass or do not come to pass. But I do not know what whose events are and I do not know if I am strong enough to make the right things happen or to ... if they do not.*

Some of these words were new to Kaitrin, but she could un-derstand enough to be alarmed. *It seems*, she thought, *that this big termite and I both have a quest and we both doubt our strength. It's surpassingly odd – odd enough to be really disturbing.*

Chapter 15

They shall have stars at elbow and foot;
Though they go mad they shall be sane,
Though they sink through the sea they
shall rise again;
Though lovers be lost, love shall not;
And death shall have no dominion.
– from Dylan Thomas, *And Death Shall
Have No Dominion*

After a few more lab sessions, Griffen announced that he was
ready for the field again. Kaitrin made the arrangements for a
Nasute escort, which Griffen accepted willingly, saying, "At least
there'll be something out there that I can view as an ally."

Kaitrin teased Griffen about the disreputable old hat he wore
in the field and he retorted good-naturedly, "That's my lucky hat –
it's genuine Ostrailien camel felt! It has been on every planet
where I've done fieldwork, including Earth – and you shan't get it
away from me!" And off he went at dawn, accompanied by Arti
and Julian, Sa'ti'a'i'a and four of his Warriors. When he first
reported in, he had just found some unusual double-lobed pupa
cases and was excited about bringing them back and trying to in-
cubate them.

Tió'otu remarked, "Is it my imagination, or does Gwidian
seem more relaxed than he did for a while there?"

"Not your imagination," said Luku. "I noticed, too."

163

Kaitrin, working in the research bay on the ballooning lexicon of Shshi words, smiled and said nothing. Griffen's revelation might not have resolved everything, but it did seem to have helped revive his enthusiasm for their work on this planet, so she was content.

The team made some excursions along the river, where Griffen observed many aquatic reptiles but not a sign of amphibians. He was also puzzled at discovering no true vertebrate fishes; instead macro-invertebrates were the dominant lifeform – six-legged crab-like arthropods, snail-like mollusks that swam by jetting water through a hyponome like a nautilus, and even small cephalopods quite similar to squid. The closest things to fish were whiskery vermiforms with scaly integuments and primitive notochords. This presented an evolutionary dilemma; how had this planet's land vertebrates managed to evolve without the intermediate steps of fish and amphibians? Or if such had existed at one time, what had happened to them?

Griffen postulated some kind of extinction event like that which had occurred at the end of Earth's Devonian, when most of the fishes disappeared for a gap of 15 million years, allowing the marginal species now called sharks to evolve to dominance. In the case of 2 Giotta 17A, such an extinction might have happened after land vertebrates were already established; it would have had to be something that devastated all aquatic habitats while leaving remnants of the land biota extant. Certainly a more extensive investigation was called for. Marine biologists would need to probe the planet's unexplored seas, geneticists would have to study DNA samples from the several planetary missions in an attempt to piece out the evolutionary record, and paleontologists would have to search for fossil evidence of protovertebrates.

These absorbing field excursions tended to disrupt the ten-hour cycles that the team had been able to maintain quite consistently to that point. A couple of times Griffen returned so late that Kaitrin was already asleep. On one such occasion, she woke up and mumbled to him, "I miss you, Griff … Try to get back on time … "

He laughed and kissed her. "Next time I'm nipping off to the orchard. Come with me!"

"I can't – I haven't got a hat. I forgot to bring one."

"That's a poor excuse! I have an extra one you can use."

"Too big ... "

"Oh, it will only protect you all the better – fit over the braids!"

So Kaitrin donned the oversize hat even though it pushed her ears out like jug handles, and accompanied Griffen. While he scrabbled around among tree roots and pried up bits of loose bark, she talked to the Orchard Workers, doing her best to counter the incessant proliferation of false rumors. Griffen laid down a tarp under a tree, which they then shook, collecting all the insectoids that dropped out of it – "Can't fog them out," he said; "mustn't contaminate the alien ecosystem." Kaitrin ended by climbing into the branches, picking egg-encrusted leaves for him and slicing off bark-galls with a field knife. Together with Arti and Will, they lunched in the shade, but the shade was hardly necessary. The temperature had been dropping and the humidity rising. As they emerged into the courtyard on the way back to *Durga*, they heard a distant rumble of thunder. For the first time since they had arrived on the planet seven weeks before, a bank of clouds could be discerned moving out from the invisible western mountains.

They walked back through gusting wind, with a troop of Workers swarming adoringly around them like adolescents around a pop star. Kaitrin asked them about the changing weather and they told her that the cold season – *chi'nol|* – was beginning. There would be rain but not as much as in *gwai'nol|*, the true time of flood.

"This must be a secondary, or winter, wet season," said Gwidian. "I'd best be bringing my fieldwork to a conclusion. Not too pleasant slogging about in mud, what?"

That evening Kaitrin entered the sleeping compartment to find Griffen cutting his own hair. A human barber had been part of the *Featherlight*'s crew, but here the only recourse was to do the task oneself. Griffen's usual tonsorial elegance had become a mere memory.

She stood watching him. He caught her glance in the mirror, thought he read what she was thinking, and laughed apologetically. "Sorry to look so unkempt. I'm no adept at barbering, I fear."

"You could just let it grow. That's what Julian and Arti are doing."

"Oh, good gracious me. Too annoying and too hot."

She went to him, ran her fingers into the thick thatch of hair on the uncut side, and said impishly, "Will is threatening to shave his head. How about doing that?"

He glared ferociously at her.

"When we left Earth, men's hairstyles were changing – I guess it's the influence of that holostar Echiro Sharifee. Some of the incoming male students were wearing their hair really full and I actually saw a news vid of a GC Councilor who had a regular bob – not a bit of ear visible! Even Prf. Jerardo was looking shaggy in the neck and he's hardly a trendsetter! So if you did let it grow, you'd be right in style when we get back."

He emitted a skeptical grunt.

"You surely keep up with the styles, Griff. In everything except hats, that is."

He chuckled at that. "Well ... In the past I have. But the fact of it is, whilst I can't abide a shaved pate, if I don't keep my hair short, it gets a bit unruly ... like my father's ... "

"Your father had unruly hair?"

"Well, you know, the sea ... all that wind ... " His voice faded into remoteness.

She continued to muss his hair. "I'd like it full enough so that the wave would show. It has beautiful waves down the back, but you wear it so short, no one would ever know. It would make you even more handsome if it showed. And did you know that most women would die to have your eyelashes? You really are a disgustingly handsome man, Griffen Gwidian!"

He looked at her with a surprised lift of the eyebrow. "I thought you weren't going to tell me that. I already had a quite sufficient sense of my own good looks, you said."

Kaitrin regarded him thoughtfully. "I think I was wrong. I think you need to be reminded about all your positive qualities. You project this assertive image, Griff, but I think that inside you have the smallest, most fragile ego that could ever be. Don't take that wrong."

He stood silent a moment, looking down at the clippers in his hand. Then he said lightly, "But I fancy that could be an asset. You know, all the clichés about the overbearing male ego, that sort of thing."

"Well ... But I'm not so sure. But I suppose if you had a different inner image of yourself, you wouldn't be Griffen Gwidian any longer."

"Oh, Kait. I rather wish that Griffen Gwidian could be a little different inside. Or a great deal different." He rushed ahead, forestalling Kaitrin's query. "Rianna spent half her life trying to give me a different self-image – to give me a stronger sense of my own worth."

"Why? I mean, why was that necessary? I still don't understand. Were you ... ? Did you have a learning disability or a stutter or something tangible like that, that might make a child feel inferior?"

"Oh, no, nothing of the sort. I never had any difficulties with academics, as long as I didn't have to work closely with other people or perform in front of groups ... This was when I was quite young, you understand. I was ... Well, I've always hated the word, but I suppose it's as good as any. As a child I was just excessively shy ... didn't relate very well – socially, you know. I was always afraid ... someone would discover ... " Griffen fell silent, his finger tracing the edge of the clippers.

"Discover what?" asked Kait, sensing the imminence of a revelation.

But he said, "Oh, nothing, really. That they would discover I wasn't as good a student as I was reputed to be. That I would disappoint people."

That isn't it at all, Kaitrin thought. *Or it may be a part of it, but there's something deeper.*

"But you're not shy now," she said, and she couldn't resist adding, "Nothing bothers you except wedding ceremonies!"

"Well, I grew up. I learned ways to compensate – to implement that artificial persona we talked about before ... "

He was beginning to look stressed and Kaitrin was afraid she was botching things, so she said, "Why don't you let me try to cut the other side?"

"You know how to cut hair?"

"Never cut any in my life! But when did a lack of experience keep me from trying something new? Here, give me the clippers!"

He yielded them with a laugh that was definitely apprehensive, although it may have incorporated a hint of relief at the conversation's altered tack.

"You're too tall for me," she said, "or else my arms are too short."

"I can sit on the bed."

"Ugh, no. These clippers are supposed to suck up the hair, but look at how much is on the floor! I don't want it in the bed!"

"Oh, definitely not! I'll fetch the servobot in here straight-away to sweep up."

"I tell you what. You sit on the floor and I'll kneel up behind you. That will make it just right."

He started to comply, then suddenly stopped as if paralyzed, standing a little sideways, his eyes fixed on something not present with them in the room.

It scared her. "Griffen?"

He jerked around with a frown and reached to take the clippers from her. "I'll finish it myself," he said. "Weren't you in the middle of something ... out there ... ?" He gestured vaguely at the door.

Kaitrin stood staring at him. "Oh! Of course. I didn't mean to ... " *Suddenly he wants me to go. I've pushed something too far. But what?* She turned to the door.

"Kait."

She turned back.

"Forgive me," Griffen said, regarding her with a carefully controlled focus. "It's only ... I suddenly recollected something I hadn't thought about in years. When I was a very small boy, I used to sit on the floor and ... my mother ... would kneel behind me, the way you suggested ... and cut my hair. I hadn't remem-bered – hadn't thought of that in years. It just came to me. It was a little painful. That's all. I didn't mean to be dismissive."

"Oh, Griffen, I understand. It's all right. You see, if you tell me these things, how much better it is. I need to understand the things that trouble you, Griffen."

He took a deep breath, turning back to the mirror. "I know. I'm trying, Kait, I really am. Forgive me."

Again, that, she thought.

"If you don't mind too much, I'll go ahead and finish my hair myself," he was saying.

"That's fine," she said. "You probably do a better job than I would, anyway."

He smiled at her in the mirror and she went out and left him to himself.

Later, they lay in bed in the darkness and Kaitrin started to trace the folds and hollows of Griffen's ear with her finger.

"Kait, that tickles! What are you doing?" he said sleepily, reaching for her hand.

"I'm trying to learn every inch of your body," she said, "so I can know it all even in the darkest night. I thought I'd about mastered it, but I suddenly realized your ear had escaped my attention. So I was studying it."

His laugh rumbled against her face. He captured her hand, touching for a fleeting moment the ring encircling the third finger, then laid the palm against his throat. She fell asleep with the warm pulse of his life's blood beating against her fingers.

*   *   *

When she awoke in the morning and rolled over, she found him lying wide awake, looking at her with a big, open smile on his face. "Well, good morning!" she said. "Good gracious, Griff, you look like the Cheeser cat – but you don't know what that is, do you? Griff, what in the world … ?"

He had risen up and scooped her in his arms, kissing her with such passionate tenderness that she was overwhelmed. "Oh, Kait, I had a wonderful dream! I so rarely experience good dreams, but this was wonderful … "

He sank back again, and she hitched herself up on her elbow, fingering her tingling lips. "¡Maravillosa!" she gasped. "Can you share it with me?"

"It was … First I have to tell you this. You remember when I said we kept horses at the Bock compound when I was growing up? One was a chestnut stallion – a racehorse who had injured his leg and been put out to stud. He had gotten old and wasn't being bred any longer, and Gerit had given him a home out of charity when he was about to be put down. Nobody paid much attention to him and to me he seemed lonely – maybe because I was lonely … Anyway, I used to ride him – just throw an old saddle and a pair of reins on him and pelt off across the veldt. His injury wasn't so bad that he couldn't run and he did like to run. I never pushed him, just gave him his head and let him go as he liked. This was when I was twelve, thirteen years old – really a bit young for such a big horse, and a rider so inexperienced. I remember Rianna was pretty upset when she first found out what I was doing. It *was* dangerous, I'll admit. But it gave me a sense of freedom – of escape ... "

He fell silent, lost in the past. Kaitrin held her breath, waiting.

He made a little movement, returning to the present. "Well, anyway, in this dream, I was riding like that, on Glider – that was his name. But I wasn't on the veldt – I was in the sky, amongst the stars, as we were in *Featherlight*, only open, with the whole brilliant panorama of stars, galaxies, nebulae ... And there was another horse running alongside – you were riding it, Kait! It was a beautiful mare, golden, with a silver mane and tail streaming back, the colors of your wedding veil ... And we rode together – you and I rode through the stars together – and that was all ... except I knew that it would never end – that this was eternity and we would go on forever like that and it would never end! Oh, Kait ... " He pulled her down to him again and held her close to his breast with a deep sigh. "Oh, Kait, it will never end – I know that now. Maybe my nightmares are finished – they'll fade and leave me in peace at last. Maybe at last I'll have nothing but good dreams. Oh, Kait, it's all from you, *'ngariad* – you are my miracle! You changed my life. You have made me so happy."

Chapter 16

Ay, in the very temple of Delight
Veil'd Melancholy has her Sovran shrine ...
– *from* John Keats, *Ode on Melancholy*

In the days that followed, Gwidian seemed to have lost all sense of foreboding about their situation. He took Kaitrin out in the open field with him without any protest; in fact, he proposed it. While she was scrambling around recklessly in a brushy gully with Griffen hovering behind her, she flushed one of the elusive multilegged creatures that he had glimpsed earlier. They netted it and found it to be in truth a saurian about twenty-five centimeters long, with skin blotched with rust-red scales and ten skinny legs, unlike anything from any planet that they could find in Griffen's database. They scanned it, took samples of skin and blood and saliva and some scat that it graciously deposited on their clothing, weighed and measured it, holographed it from every angle – and released it to scamper back to its insectivorous life in the underbrush.

Kaitrin was caught up in the excitement of discovering a potentially new order of fauna and was having a glorious time until late in the day when it began to rain. It was the first rain they had experienced since they had come to 2 Giotta 17A and initially it felt good. Then it became a little drenching and cold even though they were wearing ponchos heated by solar disks. But they laughed as they and Will and the stoic Nasute Warriors slogged back through puddles, stopping to make holograms of some little

171

hexapod "crabs" that popped belligerently out of the mud, their estivation terminated by the moisture.

Back at the flyer, they tracked in mud and laughter, cleaned up, ate ravenously. Afterward, they worked together in the lab until it got late, then retired to a blissful bed. The next day the rain had stopped, although clouds still brooded. Griffen went out again anyway, with Arti and Julian, while Kaitrin stayed behind to catch up on her own work. She and A'a'ma were writing the next set of reports to be transmitted to Earth.

"This man," said Tió'otu, referring to Gwidian, "is more unpredictable than any Earther I have ever known. On the first expedition, he was unsociable and even cranky, then he fell in love and got married and became likable – well, I can understand that. Then during the first part of this planetside venture, he was gloomy and fearful about everything. Now nothing is too free for him! Confusing."

Kaitrin did not answer immediately, because she found it impossible to explain Griffen to anyone else when she could not completely explain him to herself – and somehow it felt like treachery even to try.

But Trea was nearby. Looking at Kaitrin, she said, "Dreams influence souls, for good, for bad."

A little tremor went through Kaitrin. "How did you know?"

"Know what?" said A'a'ma, sensing that he was missing something.

But Kaitrin turned the question away, reluctant to speak about this most emotional and private of subjects.

Later, however, Kaitrin found herself alone with Trea in the galley as they worked together to prepare a meal. "How did you know Griffen had had a good dream?"

"You once asked if I study psychology," said the Pozú doctor. "I have done that, of course, but more – I am empath. I can sense feelings – moods – even through walls. It is useful – sometimes curse. Mostly useful, in my profession. Mind and body are close acquaintances."

"I see. I think I understand," said Kaitrin slowly. "Trea, then you can sense that Griff – that he isn't always very happy. But this dream seemed like a turning point – it seemed to change his whole mindset. Can such things happen?"

172

"Dreams can have great influence on attitude of waking person. Or they can reflect real change. Which this is, can't say."

"You don't think it will last?"

"Can't say. It takes more than a dream usually to heal for good the pain of soul."

"Pain of soul ... Trea, is that what is in him? Why does he have this – pain of soul?"

"Don't know, Kaitrin." And she added, "Does knowing this change your feeling for him? Make you wish you had not committed?"

"Oh, no! I really love him, Trea. But – maybe we love each other too much. What you said once – about immoderate love ... "

Trea grimaced. " ... can bring pain. I remember. But the cause of this pain is not too much love for you – I sensed it in him even from my early meetings of him. And the positive of love is often stronger than the negative. Just remember that you love him, Kaitrin, and in the end both of you will be all right."

*   *   *

The damp, chilly weather had made hot food seem like a necessity and Trea and Kaitrin had prepared a pot of soup energized with some of Luku's eye-watering Quornat peppers. While the team members ate their meal, Kaitrin listened closely as Trea and Sev occasionally exchanged comments in their own tongue, calling each other "Ama" and "Par." Kaitrin decided to inquire about their naming system.

"'Trea' and 'Sev' are clan names," the doctor said. "'Ama' is given name. The end part of 'Amarezka' indicates that I am female."

"In same way," said Sev, "'Parozka' is male name. When we mate, we put 'Dol' between names to show we are ... " He lacked a word.

"To show we are not looking for mate – in your tongue, you might say we are 'taken.'" Trea chuckled. "So 'Trea Dol Amarezka' and 'Sev Dol Parozka.'"

Hoping to draw out their Pozú companions further, Kaitrin said, "May I ask you another question? If it's out of order, please say so and we'll talk of something else. Trea, do you have family on Pozúa?"

"Is not out of order. I have what you call sister. My mother was fortunate. She produced two normal offspring."

Sev said, "My mother and father are alive, but I have no hatchmates."

"Have the two of you ever had any offspring?" asked Kaitrin softly.

Trea hesitated momentarily, then said, "Pozú do not speak of such things much, because we do not like to make gloom." She smiled her peculiar, drawn smile. "I have laid nine eggs – many more than that would be impossible. Seven were infertile. Two hatched, but hatchlings were deformed – lacked parts of brain. They died soon. Sev and I have contributed nothing to stop decline of our people."

"But we try," said Sev stoutly. "Some have stopped trying. If that more widely happens, we surely are doomed."

"We are doomed anyway," said Trea, gazing at her soup bowl contemplatively. "Sev cannot accept that. I have."

Everyone at the table sat silent, gazing at the face of this tragedy.

"I am past the age to lay more eggs," said Trea. "But Sev and I have mated so long, stayed together so long, we cannot part now, even though the purpose has lost meaning."

"So we continue to mate," said Sev, "even though it is by judgment of time fruitless."

"Isn't there anything anybody can do?" said Kaitrin in deep distress. "All the advances in genetic engineering – all the resources of all these planets – Krisí'i'aid, Quornam, Earth … Isn't there anything that can be done to correct the defects in your reproductive DNA?"

"Nothing has been found," said Trea. "Anomalies always reappear."

"We Krisí'i'aidá have worked on the problem for hundreds of years without success," said A'a'ma gruffly.

"In a year or two, I think Sev and I will end Confederation fieldwork and go home," said Trea. "In our late days we would like to work in Pozúa's bioresearch facility. We still hope. Even after the failing of nine offspring and acknowledging our doom – even I still hope that Trant will make a miracle." Then she looked up and grinned. "But this is not time for gloom! Everyone here is happy! By now we all are family – do you feel? This is a good place to be! Eat soup! Luku says peppers taste bitter when they get cold!"

Kaitrin's eyes were watering from more than hot peppers as she ate her soup. She felt that she had never met a braver creature in her life than this little egg-laying alien doctor.

*   *   *

Since the weather seemed unlikely to improve over the next few days, Griffen stayed out for almost the entire twenty-hour daylight cycle. When Kaitrin awoke from the daylight sleep period, he was still not back and the weather had worsened; the temperature had dropped to about 5° and the wind had come up. Griffen checked in to say they were on their way back.

Just as it was beginning to sleet, the three of them blew in chilled and exhausted. Kaitrin spoke briefly with Sa'ti'a'i'a, who told her that the weather was too cold for the Nasutes to go out again. *This is the time of waiting – closing up portals and sitting inside the fortress*, said the Chief. *The bodies of Nasutes function better than the bodies of Shum'za when water freezes, but even we prefer to stay indoors.*

"How long will this cold last?" asked Kaitrin. "I suppose neither Kwi'ga'ga'tei nor anyone else will be able to come here."

I believe Kwi'ga'ga'tei means to come tomorrow unless the weather makes it impossible. She is sleeping in the bir'zha| *chamber today. She may have visions to speak about.*

¡Ay de mí! Kaitrin thought.

Trea fussed over the returnees, plying them with the remaining soup, tending some scratches. Griffen cleaned up, drank two cups of hot tea, and went straight to bed without bothering to shave. It was too early for Kaitrin to join him, so she sat chattering away, meaning to return to her language work presently. He fell asleep in the middle of one of her questions.

She bent over him, gently stroking the hair out of his eyes, letting her thoughts wash over him. *Love, you can't know how much I missed you last night ... That beard stubble looks so strange – so unlike you ... I think I see a little silver in it ... You look really tired – the little lines – the eyes – the mouth corners ... I love you, Griffen. You're seventeen years older than I am, so when I'm forty, you'll be – fifty-seven! Older than my mother is now! When I'm sixty, you'll be seventy-seven! Now that's scary! Maybe we'll die at the same moment – true lovers ought to do that. I wouldn't mind dying young if it meant I could avoid having to live without you. What an incorrigible romantic I've become! What will my mother think?*

If we died together, we could ride off together to the stars on those magic horses you dreamed about. Dreams are alternate universes, Trea said ... Was that very thing happening in an alternate universe when you dreamed it? Our other selves were really doing that? How fanciful! But quite lovely ...

She straightened up, continuing to look down on him. *Why do I love this man so much? I can't find any good reason for it. Life probably won't be easy with him. I don't mean I think he'll be unfaithful. After that wonderful, passionate wedding vow – no man would dare be unfaithful after speaking something like that! ... We've never watched our wedding vid together – we were going to do that ... He said I was the first woman he ever loved. And I believe it. Isn't that amazing – that I believe it?*

She bent over him again, kissed his temple. "Good night, Griffen," she murmured.

He stirred, mumbled, "Good night, Kait," and threw out an arm into the empty place in the bed, groping about and frowning at finding nothing.

Phoo, I'm going to bed, she thought. She quickly undressed and slipped under the covers. His arm found her, clasped her waist, pulled her body against his. She felt the unwonted roughness of his cheek against her forehead. *His feet are still cold. Good thing I came to bed.* She reached to pull up an extra cover that lay across the end of the bed, then settled down to lie sleepless and blissfully content in his arms.

*   *   *

After outsleeping everyone in the morning, Griffen announced that he had enough of fieldwork for a while. "In the cold weather, everything goes to ground," he said, "so there isn't a lot to observe, anyway."

The sleet had stopped, however, and the temperature had risen slightly. Shshi were stirring in the courtyard, including Nasute foragers setting off on their perpetual quest for appropriate food. Kaitrin put Julian to watch through the windows for signs of Kwi'ga'ga'tei while Will and Luku set up a portable field heater on each side of the table under the flyer wing.

And Kwi'ga'ga'tei did appear, accompanied by Ki'shto'ba. Kaitrin, Luku, and A'a'ma received them. They explained the heaters to the Shshi so they would not burn themselves, and they, who did not have even hearth fires to warm their well-insulated fortresses, were awed by yet another miracle of the Star-Beings' magic.

I have brought myself out here today because the Nameless One has put demands on me, said Kwi'ga'ga'tei, who seemed particularly fragile, trembling as she crouched before Kaitrin.

Kaitrin's reason kept insisting that the visions of this giant bug had no validity, but ancient instincts kept interfering. With a stirring of foreboding, she asked, "What have you seen?"

Kwi'ga'ga'tei peered up at Kaitrin. *Earlier, the Highest-Mother-Who-Has-No-Name commanded me to teach the Speechless One how to speak. Have I fulfilled that command, Ru'a'ma'na'ta?*

"Yes, Holy Kwi'ga'ga'tei. You have indeed taught me how to speak and understand the language of the Shshi." And Kaitrin thought, *She really was commanded to do that? Her Goddess wanted me to be able to communicate with them?*

Kwi'ga'ga'tei moved her legs weakly, as if in relief. *I really believe your coming is* uks'zi| – uks'zi| *of the fidelity of the Shshi of Lo'ro'ra to the Way of the Nameless One.* thel'il| shsho'ei'liso| wei| ↳ uks'zi| fei'zi| ↹ fai'u'zoso| ||

Kwi'ga'ga'tei was using some of the same words that Kaitrin had failed to understand earlier; she had now assigned syllables to them, but the meaning remained unclear. The present context implied that *uks'zi|* meant "test"; if so, then earlier the Seer had said, *A test is coming,* and now she said, *A test of the* tav'zi| – that is, "loyalty" or "fidelity" – *of the Shshi* ... But Kaitrin remained shaky about the final sentence, which was syntactically complex, and also about the ambiguities of the word *fei'zi|.* The sentence meant literally *Well we complete not the test,* fei'zi| *will happen.* In other words, *If we do not pass the test* ... Kwi'ga'ga'tei had previously used the verb *feio|*; Kaitrin had learned that it carried a primary meaning of "to return" or "to give back." So *fei'zi|* would mean "a return," a "giving back" – "compensation" or "recompense," maybe. "Compensation will happen"? That did not make much sense.

In the earlier conversation the Seer had said, *I may have to give back* – that is, make compensation – *if certain events do or do not happen ...*

And then it dawned on Kaitrin. "Price!" That was the meaning! Kwi'ga'ga'tei was saying, *If we do not pass the test, a price will happen* – in other words, *there will be a price to pay.* Earlier she had said, *I may have to pay a price and I do not know if I am strong enough ...*

So now Kaitrin took a deep breath. "You mentioned that before, but I cannot understand. What kind of test? What kind of price?"

Of those things I am forbidden to speak. But the principal thing that I would beg of you today, Ru'a'ma'na'ta, is that you enter into our fortress so that all our citizens will know that you are honored in Lo'ro'ra.

"Oh! I want to, Kwi'ga'ga'tei, but there are still difficulties ... "

Work out the difficulties! I implore you, work out the difficulties! It is no longer only that the Holy One is willing. It is a command from the Highest-Mother-Who-Is-Nameless! She called on you by name! She called you kai'tri'ze| – kai'zi vi| fai'trio| kei| shprai'mo'zi|. *Those were her words. Do they mean anything to you?*

"The wind that goes out of the stars." Kaitrin was really shaken. Beside her, A'a'ma's crest was standing on end and he was twittering. "How did she know that you assigned those syllables in that way – *kai|* to signify 'wind' and *trio|* to signify' to go'?" he said.

"It is a god! No other explanation!" exclaimed Luku.

"Damn," said Kaitrin. "That really gets to me! I never intended for those syllables to reflect my name. I just assign syllables randomly or else give similar ones to similar wave patterns, like *gan and galt*. It didn't even occur to me that *kai* and *tri* could be taken as elements of my name. And like you say, how would she know?"

She looked up at the cloud-laden sky, half expecting some monstrous, pallid, oppressive force to descend out of it.

Kwi'ga'ga'tei was saying, *It seems that it does mean something to you. Is this your real name, Ru'a'ma'na'ta?* kai'tri'ze|?

"How can I explain it to her?" Kaitrin asked A'a'ma. "It makes no sense to me."

"Simply acknowledge it," he said. "Do not try to explain it."

So Kaitrin said to Kwi'ga'ga'tei, "*kai'tri'ze|* is indeed something like my name among my own people."

But you said your name could not be spoken in the language of the Shshi.

"When I first came, it could not. Now it seems we have grown in understanding and it can be expressed. It is an amazing happening, Kwi'ga'ga'tei."

What should we call you? Are you still our Ru'a'ma'na'ta? asked Kwi'ga'ga'tei humbly.

Ru'a'ma'na'ta. The Comforting Mother. I've kind of come to like that, Kaitrin thought. To Kwi'ga'ga'tei, she said, "I am both, Holy Seer, but it especially honors me when you call me *ru'a'ma'na'ta|*. Please continue to do so."

Kwi'ga'ga'tei said, *You have said that you call the Highest Mother by many names, so it is not improper that you have two names. Will you come into the fortress, Ru'a'ma'na'ta? The Highest Mother has ordered that you should do so and I fear greatly what will happen if you do not. You will be safe within our walls. We will keep you safe and make you welcome.*

Kaitrin took a deep breath. "I will come in, Holy Kwi'ga'ga'tei. Give me a little time to prepare and I will come in."

*   *   *

When the Shshi had gone, Kaitrin took a deep breath and said, "What am I going to do? I have to tell Griffen about this. Right away. Right now. And I hate it. I really hate it. He's in this wonderful, confident, optimistic frame of mind. I really hate to dump this on him."

"You spoke of it before to him," said Luku. "So it is not completely new idea."

"But look how he reacted! And this time it isn't just a

possibility – I definitely mean to do it. Oh, hell. Tió'otu, advise me. What should I do?"

"I cannot," he said, nictitating in distress. "I call you *nei♪ bi'át♪♪*, but you are not really my nestling any longer. You must weigh your professional curiosity and your feelings for this Seer against your marital needs."

"Unfortunately, they really conflict here," she said. "Maybe in the future Griffen and I shouldn't go on joint expeditions."

"That might be a wise course," said Tió'otu. "Gwidian is a worrier. I likely would be, too, if it were my wife wanting to throw herself headlong into such a perilous adventure."

Kaitrin shook her head, looked over her shoulder at the open hatch. "Well, there is no way around it. Let's go in."

Inside, she called out, "Can we all come to the table? We need to have a team conference. Griffen! Would you come out?"

He emerged looking slightly apprehensive, delicately holding a beetle specimen that he was in the process of mounting. "What is it?"

"Come and sit down," said Kaitrin, waving a hand.

He disposed of the specimen and complied, frowning a little. Trea glanced thoughtfully between them. Kaitrin wondered what her empathic sense was telling her.

First she told them about Kwi'ga'ga'tei's vision of her name and they chewed on that for a while. While this was inexplicable and even uncanny, it was not threatening and Kaitrin could sense Griffen had begun to relax. Then she was forced to say, "In Kwi'ga'ga'tei's vision, the Nameless One commanded her to bring me inside the fortress. And I think I'm obliged to go."

To a person, everyone looked at Gwidian. He sat still for a moment. Then he leaned back in the chair, letting his chin sink. "I knew it would come to this," he said. "It's not a surprise to me."

A little relieved, Kaitrin said, "Oh, Griff, I did so hope you would understand. There won't be any danger ... "

"Bloody hell, there won't be!" he responded roughly.

She began to speak quickly, trying to forestall an outburst, to compel him to a rational acceptance. "We'll run some more at-mospheric tests. Will, can you make up about five air monitors? Kwi'ga'ga'tei will send someone for them around midday. I'll stay up to give them to the messenger. She'll put them in locations deep in the fortress and make sure nobody contaminates them this time. They'll bring them back late in the evening. Otherwise, there's nothing to do. If a corridor is too small, I simply won't try to go through it. The emitter needs some work, though. I'll need a fresh power pack and that one earport has a buzz in it ... "

She had been watching Griffen, watching his mouth tighten, watching a little muscle twitch in his jaw. He interrupted her, saying in a low, barely controlled voice, "You can't do this. Kaitrin, I can't let you do this."

"Griffen, I have to!"

He stood up, throwing out his arms. "Why? A'a'ma, is there some kind of imperative amongst anthros that they must imperil their lives in order to satisfy their intellectual curiosity?"

"Of course not," squawked Tió'otu.

"It isn't only curiosity!" said Kaitrin. "I feel like I'm putting Kwi'ga'ga'tei and maybe the whole fortress in some kind of danger if I don't ... "

"So you put yourself in danger?" The volume of Griffen's voice swelled. "Because an alien lifeform tells you a god spoke to her? I thought you didn't believe in gods! What is it that you really do believe?" He jerked around, almost knocking over the chair, and paced across the room and back.

"Griffen, for goodness sake! Sit down and consider this rationally."

"Rationally! Is it rational to want to enter that hellhole because a god told a so-called Seer ... "

"It's a goddess!"

"Whatever! Dammit, A'a'ma, do something! I can see I have no influence! I'm only her – mate – King – whatever you want to call me. Trea! Trea, surely you can see the folly of this! Can't you bring her to her senses?"

Several people started to talk at once. Kaitrin put her head in her hands in misery. This was exactly what she had dreaded. *Oh, Griffen, Griffen, let me be myself! I love you so much, but I just don't have as many fears as you do. Why do you have so many fears?*

Trea took charge. "Quiet, quiet!" she said. "Prf. Gwidian, come sit. Prf. A'a'ma, sit, too! Let us look at danger. Let us not react with just emotion. Gwidian ... " She went and grasped his arm. "Come sit. Come."

As in earlier moments, he responded positively to her influence and let her lead him back to his chair.

"Gwidian," Trea said, "what kind of danger do you fear for her? She will be with friends, have good protection from the one called Huge-Head and from others. She goes only to look and talk. It will be an increase of knowledge. The inside of the termite people's mound. Does that not interest you?"

"It might if someone else were the one going in, on someone else's expedition," he said.

"I'll only stay a couple of hours," Kaitrin said, and when he made a hopeless sound, she said, "Maybe not even that long. The only hurt I might take is sore muscles and scraped knees from crawling around on the ... "

"Must use knee protectors," said Sev, "and gloves for hands, also."

"Don't you feel the least twinge of claustrophobia?" said Griffen.

"Well, I'll simply have to fight it! Keep my eyes set ahead. I'd better have a light, though, in case the batteries in the Alates' wings burn out." She laughed shakily, watching Griffen clench his teeth. "Kwi'ga'ga'tei says I'll be able to stand or sit upright in some of the chambers. Personally, I'm absolutely fascinated by all this! Griffen, I really want to go! Please, please, don't take it like this. I'll come back to you just fine. Please believe me."

He made no response and Trea said, "Kaitrin, could someone go with you? I think most are too big, but Sev and I are small and would fit nicely ... "

Kaitrin shook her head. "The Holy One will allow only me to come in – the one who speaks for these strange Star-People who dropped on them out of the sky."

"You see? She won't have even one of us to help her," said Gwidian hoarsely.

Then Will said very unwisely, "Don't some alien races practice human sacrifice, or living sacrifice, or whatever?"

Kaitrin could have strangled him. There was another outburst of voices. Griffen lost color and caught a hard breath. The look he turned on Kaitrin told her that all that dream-inspired joy had drained out of him and her heart was torn. She reached toward him, but he flinched away, clenching his arms against his chest.

Will realized his mistake and his look of despair was almost comical. A'a'ma said, "Certainly some alien ILFs practice living sacrifice, but we don't have … Actually, what do we know about the Shshi's religious rituals?"

"All of you, stop it!" said Kaitrin. "I thought of that! I asked Kwi'ga'ga'tei point-blank about the sacrifice thing. She tells me that the only time anyone is ritually sacrificed is when the Queen dies. Then they kill the King and the new King eats part of him. I know, Griff – I know that sounds terrible! But they're insectoids to the core and it's their way, and anyway I'm not their King – how could that mean any danger for me? The only other thing is that an individual can make an altruistic sacrifice of itself if the fortress has a need. But I'm certainly not going to do that! I firmly believe I'm in no peril whatsoever."

Arti Robb spoke up. "As Security Chief on this team, I have to say I don't like for you to go in there alone. I doubt Maj. Bidba would approve of my letting you do that."

"There, you see?" said Griffen. "Really rational heads can't possibly sanction this."

"Will you take a sidearm?" said Julian.

"Absolutely not!" said Kaitrin. "We're trying to keep the malcontents from getting their claws on one of these weapons! It would be very easy to take it away from me when I'm in there! And anyway, what good would one pistol be against the whole … ?"

That only made it worse. Griffen hunched over the table, rubbing his fingers incessantly to and fro across his mouth.

"Griffen, stop looking like that – like the world is ending! I'll be back here before you know it!"

"And then you'll want to go in again."

"Well, there's a good chance I might go in more than once, yes. Especially if I don't get to stay very long."

Griffen buried his face in his hands, then dragged his hands down, looking at Kaitrin over the fingertips. "It's obvious that nobody will be able to talk you out of this."

"No," said Kaitrin, setting her jaw. "Nobody."

Tió'otu said, "Gwidian, when you meet Brigit Oliva – that is Kaitrin's mother, for those of you who might not know – ask her about Kaitrin's stubborn streak."

"Kaitrin has already told me about it herself," said Griffen.

Trea stirred. "I think there is not much chance she take a disease in there. I am as sure as can be that immunizations were effective. But don't eat anything, Kaitrin. You might get poison or parasites. I will give you some preventive injections. Perhaps right now would be good time – have a little time to spread agents through body. But one other thing is troublesome. Kaitrin, have you thought about bringing XTIS diseases into fortress?"

Gwidian looked up, discerning a new cause for hope. "Yes, Kait," he said, "you wouldn't want to damage your friends in that way, would you?"

Kaitrin took a gulp of breath. "I did think of that awhile back, but it had skipped my mind for the moment. And Mo'gri'ta'tu has been spreading rumors that we mean to poison everybody! But if the Nameless Goddess ordered me to come in, it should be safe, and somehow I feel like I belong in that place ... Now, don't all of you look cockeyed at me! I'm not as crazy as what I just said makes me seem! Trea, what can we do to minimize the possibility of XTIS? What pathogens am I carrying?"

"Nothing dangerous to humans," said Trea, "but even normal, beneficial bacteria of human gut and mouth could be trouble for this world. We will set detox unit for human flora and put you through right before you enter. We can reinfect you later, if need ..."

"Trea!" said Griffen despairingly, seeing this final hope evaporate.

"Try to avoid close touching and contact," the doctor was saying to Kaitrin. "Probably will be safe but can't guarantee." Then she grinned half playfully, half seriously. "You may be right about goddess protecting Shshi at this time. Gwidian, she will protect Kaitrin, too."

"Trea," whispered Griffen, sinking his forehead against his clasped hands.

"I'll get the monitors ready," said Will, getting up. "Kaitrin, I'm really sorry about that remark I made."

"I will prepare translating equipment," said Luku. "I will make a little strap to put around the neck. That way unit will hang down when you are crawling and the Shshi can receive better, and it can lay against your upper chest when you are sitting upright. You should also wear miniature holocam on belt ... "

They scattered. Griffen continued to sit slumped at the table. Kaitrin went to him, gripping his shoulders urgently, laying her cheek against the top of his head. "Griffen, love, it will be all right. I promise. I swear it."

He touched her right hand. "So, my termite queen, you've become a prophet of the future now, too?"

She knew the note of levity was false. She bent and whispered in his ear, "It will be all right. Trust me, my own dear love."

He got up, kissed her, and withdrew into the laboratory. But when Kaitrin looked in on him awhile later, he was not working, only sitting before the microanalyzer gazing at something no one else could see.

*   *   *

Kaitrin stayed up in order to deliver the atmospheric monitors to the Shi messenger and Griffen stayed up with her. She sat trying to review knotty Shshi verbal constructions, but Griffen was making her nervous; he roamed the flyer restlessly, going up and down the ladder to the flight deck and staring out at the fortress towers that brooded dimensionless under a thick, gray sky. Finally No'kri itself came and took away the monitors and Kaitrin went to bed, half afraid that Griffen would not come.

He did, however, and tried to make love to her, but for the first time in their relationship he was unable to produce an erection and they lay unsated and unfulfilled.

"I'm sorry, Kait," he said. "I'm sorry. I'm just – very upset ... "

"Don't be sorry, Griffen. I love you for much more than your body, too."

That seemed to ease him a little, but in a few moments he said, "The nightmare has come back, you know."

"Oh, Griff. Don't. That hurts me so." But she wondered if he were thinking, *But you don't mind hurting* me ...

"It couldn't last. Nothing good lasts for me. But for a few moments I truly believed this time it could."

"Griffen ... "

"But it's you I want to keep, Kait. That's what frightens me –

what I'm so afraid of – losing you … I love you so much."

"You won't lose me, Griff! Hold on to that! You won't lose me! My dearest love, my darling, everything will turn out all right!"

But in her heart Kaitrin was whispering, *I did this to him. I took away this joy that had come to him. How can he continue to love me in this – immoderate – way?*

Chapter 17

"Far hence be souls profane!"
The Sibyl cried, "and from the grove abstain!
Now, Trojan, take the way thy fates afford;
Assume thy courage, and unsheathe thy sword."
She said, and pass'd along the gloomy space;
The prince pursued her steps with equal pace.
          – *from* Virgil, *Aeneid,* tr. by John Dryden

[Mo'gri'ta'tu scurries erratically out of the corridor leading from the Holy Chamber, collides with Hi'ta'fu]

[Mo'gri'ta'tu]: Watch where you throw your jaws, Commander!

[Hi'ta'fu]: I was coming to find you. The rumor has it …

[Mo'gri'ta'tu]: Rumors! Rumors! The Seer has gone completely mad!

[Hi'ta'fu]: I understand the Seer has had a vision that she will not share with the Council.

[Mo'gri'ta'tu]: But she shares it with the Holy One, and the Holy One shares it with me. If the fool wants to keep it secret, why does she tell the Holy One and the King?

[Hi'ta'fu]: I understand she has invited the female Star-Being to enter the fortress.

[Mo'gri'ta'tu]: Yes, and the Holy One approved it. I was on my way to question Kwi'ga'ga'tei about these things.

[Hi'ta'fu]: I will come with you.

[Mo'gri'ta'tu]: That is not wise ... But what if we are seen together? By now, the whole fortress knows who among us is dissatisfied with the governance of Lo'ro'ra. We will see what we can learn.

[Mo'gri'ta'tu and the Commander enter Kwi'ga'ga'tei's chambers]

[I'mei'o'nu, blocks their path]: You may not enter! The Holy Seer is resting.

[Mo'gri'ta'tu]: What, still? Her vision was many turnings of the vessel ago.

[I'mei'o'nu]: From going out in the cold to speak with the Star-Beings.

[Kwi'ga'ga'tei emerges halfway from the inner chamber]

[Kwi'ga'ga'tei]: I will receive them. I have been expecting them, although not at the same time, perhaps. Say what you would say.

[Mo'gri'ta'tu]: What a curt greeting, Most Holy Seer! To those who come only to express concern for your well-being!

[Kwi'ga'ga'tei]: You do not cozen me as easily as you do others, Chamberlain. What is your purpose here? I am tired and have no wish to spar.

[Mo'gri'ta'tu]: The Holy One tells me that the creature known blasphemously as Ru'a'ma'na'ta is to be allowed entry into the fortress.

[Kwi'ga'ga'tei]: So?

[Mo'gri'ta'tu]: So a weaponed one, the confessed perpetrator of poisonings, is to be conducted around the nurseries and the gardens more freely than a legitimate delegation of our fellow Shshi pleading for a King-nymph?

[Kwi'ga'ga'tei]: The Highest-Mother-Who-Is-Nameless

commanded me to bring her into the fortress.

[Hi'ta'fu]: What? In a vision?

[Kwi'ga'ga'tei]: How else, Commander?

[Mo'gri'ta'tu]: Why?

[Kwi'ga'ga'tei]: The Nameless One does not always reveal her reasons.

[Mo'gri'ta'tu]: Has it not ever entered the thoughts of the Most Holy Seer that some of the phantasms she perceives in the *bir'zha|* chamber may be meaningless, or false?

[Kwi'ga'ga'tei]: Is that it? I am falling victim to the *bir'zha|* sickness? I should have known that was coming, or had come! I tell you, if I never ate *bir'zha|* again, I would still see more honestly than you do, Mo'gri'ta'tu!

[Hi'ta'fu, grooms its head miserably]: I humbly beg, why must the Strange Ones enter our fortress, Holy Seer? If we could but know what is to come ...

[Mo'gri'ta'tu]: *tha'sask|>||*

[Kwi'ga'ga'tei]: There is a test upon the fortress of Lo'ro'ra in the beginning of this new time. Her coming is a part of it. That is all I know.

[Mo'gri'ta'tu]: And what roles do the Holy Chamberlain and the Commander of Lo'ro'ra's mighty Cohorts play in this test?

[Kwi'ga'ga'tei]: I cannot see that. I think you determine your own roles. But I believe this: if Ru'a'ma'na'ta is not treated as a welcome guest and accorded every honor and courtesy, it will not bode well for the future of our fortress. Now go; you only weary me.

[Mo'gri'ta'tu]: But one more question, Most Holy Seer. Will this Strange One enter the fortress more than once?

[Kwi'ga'ga'tei]: If she wishes. She may be able to remain in our world for only short periods. Why would you ask this?

[Mo'gri'ta'tu]: Only so that we may know for how long we must be prepared to pay homage on the moment. [He scrapes the floor] Now we leave you, Holy Kwi'ga'ga'tei. We leave you with every show of respect, which is more than the Holy Seer has given us this day.

[Mo'gri'ta'tu and Hi'ta'fu go out]

[Kwi'ga'ga'tei]: How did they get in here so easily? Where is my guard?

[I'mei'o'nu]: Forgive me, esteemed Kwi'ga'ga'tei. The Huge-Head went to be fed and Sa'ti'a'i'a has not arrived yet. I believed there was no danger.

[Kwi'ga'ga'tei]: Do not believe that, my innocent friend! I feared their rebellion had at last broken open and they were going to make Charnel meat of me! Although what that would accomplish for them, I cannot imagine.

[I'mei'o'nu]: Here are Sa'ti'a'i'a and its contingent now.

[Kwi'ga'ga'tei]: Good! Then I can rest secure again! [Withdraws]

*   *   *

[Mo'gri'ta'tu in his chambers, with Hi'ta'fu]

[Mo'gri'ta'tu]: So. I see a new path, Commander! Perhaps more than one. You have not forgotten, have you? – what I told you the other day? That the weapon of the Star-Beings is a magic box not grown upon the body? The outlander from the stars may bring such a weapon into the fortress with her. If she does, we might find a way to purloin it, in which case that plan of killing Ki'shto'ba and Kwi'ga'ga'tei and blaming it on the Star-Beings is still viable. But if she does not bring the weapon, or if we cannot steal it, then we must kill her ourselves.

[Hi'ta'fu, dances and postures in distress]: *tha'sask|>||* You received the Seer's words!

[Mo'gri'ta'tu]: Commander, can you still be under the spell of this failing prophet, after all I have told you? No, we must kill this false *ma'na'ta|* and make it appear that Ki'shto'ba did it. Then Kwi'ga'ga'tei will be discredited both for having brought such a villain as the Huge-Head into the fortress and for having failed to

190

protect an honored guest. She will be forced to step down, perhaps even to sacrifice herself for the good of Lo'ro'ra. And I will be exalted for having predicted rightly that both were flawed.

[Hi'ta'fu]: And I? What benefit will I get from this?

[Mo'gri'ta'tu]: Why, Commander, the right to reclaim your rightful status as the only Champion Lo'ro'ra needs!

[Hi'ta'fu, nervously]: I would like the assurance that I will keep my status until my natural death. This is all I ask.

[Mo'gri'ta'tu]: You have it, Commander Hi'ta'fu the Unconquered, Hero of the Nasute Siege! You can be assured that when I rule in the Alates' Assembly as well as in the Holy Chamber, you will never be supplanted!

[Hi'ta'fu, still dancing in agitation]: So how do we kill the female and make it seem the work of Ki'shto'ba? I am not very eager to undertake that task myself.

[Mo'gri'ta'tu]: Lo'lo'pai.

[Hi'ta'fu]: What?

[Mo'gri'ta'tu]: Lo'lo'pai owes you a debt – make him discharge it! If we can distract the false *ma'na'ta|* away from her guard – and Ta'rei'so'cha might be of use here, for the outlander is unacquainted with her – then Lo'lo'pai can kill her with certain blows of the head and straight thrusts of the mandible that will mimic the fighting style of the Da'no'no Shshi. Then it can make the announcement that it has found her dead – after it has cleaned itself of body fluids, of course ... What is it now?

[Hi'ta'fu]: I still do not like murder and I do not like this corrupting of Lo'lo'pai. Murder is dishonorable, no matter how it is done. And this – this is heinous ... I cannot really discern any evil in this female – anything that would make this a righteous act.

[Mo'gri'ta'tu]: Commander, remember the end! Is not the end the thing, not the means to it? It is Lo'ro'ra and the safety of its citizens – and the honor of its defenders – on which our existence must focus. Do you want to live the rest of your life as a faded, barely tolerated old Warrior, eating the dregs left in the Feeders' maws? I thought not. Besides, these so-called Star-Beings are really only inferior creatures from no one knows where, of no consequence in our world. Do those words not sound familiar to you? Did not you yourself express a quite similar sentiment when you ordered the slaying of the Nasute emissaries? You were not so delicate at that time as to what constituted murder!

I see from your posturings that you do remember that circumstance. So let us return to the plan. We should do nothing during the first visit of the creature – allow her to build up a false sense of security, then attack her during the second or third visit. Therefore, let us not recruit Lo'lo'pai until after the first visit. It can be skittish and the fewer who are privy to our plans, the better it will be.

*   *   *

In the early morning darkness Kaitrin readied herself for her adventure. The air samples from inside the fortress had revealed no gases or particulates that would seriously harm a human being. The temperature maintained an amazingly constant 26° C, achieved without the benefit of artificial heat. Kaitrin rejected an injection to numb the olfactory nerve, wanting nothing to falsify the impact of her experience. However, recollecting the nauseating stench emitted by the ranks of soldiers baking in the sun during their initial encounter, she accepted Trea's offer of a nasal filtration ointment in case she felt overpowered. She donned a long-sleeved shirt and long pants sewn with knee pads and accoutered herself with her communications equipment, holocam, and basic gear – a field light and a pack with water flask, food rations, and a medkit that included an emergency oxygen generator.

As dawn began to break, Kaitrin stood on the ramp waiting for her guide, Holy Kwi'ga'ga'tei the Seer of the Strong Flower Fortress, to come and conduct her ...

... *down the Rabbit Hole*, she thought. *Here goes Alice!*

Griffen stood with her, gripping her arm. He appeared to be bearing up, perhaps even to have become reconciled to her obstinacy, but she suspected much of that was a retreat behind the old carefully orchestrated mask.

When she saw the small delegation of Shshi leave the main fortress tower, she turned and gave him a quick kiss. "I'm not saying goodbye because I'm not really going anywhere. Just look at it as my fieldwork, no more dangerous than your own."

But he said in an unsteady voice, "Goodbye, Kait."

She stepped down the ramp and went to meet her guides.

*   *   *

Di'fa'kro'mi and I'mei'o'nu accompanied Kwi'ga'ga'tei, along with No'kri, Ki'shto'ba Huge-Head, and a contingent of regular Warriors under Chief A'gwa'ji's command. *All partisans of the Seer,* thought Kaitrin. At the entranceway, the Shshi turned and groveled to her in a ritual of welcome as No'kri said, *In the name of A'kha'ma'na'ta our Holy One and Sei'o'na'sha'ma our King, I No'kri Chief of Workers for the Fortress of Lo'ro'ra, welcome you, Ru'a'ma'na'ta, to our dwelling place. May you find comfort and peace within, in the company of Shshi!*

"I am honored to enter here," Kaitrin replied, "and I accept your welcome with a grateful spirit." *That sounds good,* she thought. *I hope it's satisfactory.*

Their body language of dancing and antenna grooming seemed to indicate that it was. The Shshi entered single-file, with Kaitrin between Ki'shto'ba and Kwi'ga'ga'tei.

Darkness engulfed them within three meters of the entranceway. The wavering light of the Alates' wings tended to deceive the senses as to distance and the nature of objects revealed within it. The corridor, narrow at the entrance, soon broadened out so that three Shshi could walk abreast and Kwi'ga'ga'tei slipped up to crawl beside Kaitrin. The height remained near a meter, however, and Kaitrin had to be careful not to raise up suddenly and whack her head on the ceiling. She could not move rapidly on hands and knees, so the company proceeded at a sedate pace toward an unknown destination.

She glanced over her shoulder in spite of herself. There was nothing to see behind the light of Di'fa'kro'mi, nothing ahead except Ki'shto'ba's wagging cerci as the giant Warrior scuttled blindly in front of her. The earthy, fungal smell, sharply accented with chemical odors, was growing more intense. Generations of hurrying Shshi had eroded a slight depression down the center of the stone floor; it contained a cushioning of humus-like particles the origin of which Kaitrin preferred not to contemplate. Insectile claws produced a disquieting skittering tick in the cave-silence.

She contemplated letting out a yell to see if there was an echo, then feared that her cry would be swallowed up in this place that had never known a voice and she herself would not even hear it.

The corridor was ascending slightly; it turned and branched to the left and again upward and downward, and Kaitrin knew if they made one more turn, passed one more side passage, she would be hopelessly lost. She fought a swelling panic. ¡Válgame! – *what am I doing in here? Maybe Griffen was right. What if they abandon me? I'd never find my way out. I'm completely at their mercy, and what* do *we really know about them? I must be crazy! Thesus and the Minotaur, not Alice ... Frodo and Sam in the mines of Moria ... I should have brought a ball of thread ...*

Somehow the recollection that she was not the first hero to descend into an underworld fortified her. Then they passed through a wider opening capped with a heavy lintel stone and entered a spacious chamber with an elevated stage at the opposite end. The chamber was packed with Shshi of all Castes, with Alates ranged around the side so the wing-light was evenly distributed. Her earports began receiving an indecipherable buzz of antenna signals.

Kwi'ga'ga'tei's sending took precedence. *Ru'a'ma'na'ta, come and be introduced to our citizens.*

The ceiling was high enough to allow Kaitrin to walk on two legs with only a slight stoop. As A'gwa'ji forced a corridor for them through the crush, the Holy Seer conducted her toward the dais. Mo'gri'ta'tu was crouching at its foot. *Holy Ru'a'ma'na'ta,* he said as she passed by. *We are indeed honored to receive you into our fortress. If I may serve you in any way, speak, I implore you.*

She acknowledged his words, noticing that his eyes were again raking her up and down. Commander Hi'ta'fu and Chief Lo'lo'pai were on the dais. The Commander stood like a stone, but Lo'lo'pai was prancing and twitching its antennae hectically. A'gwa'ji took a place next to Lo'lo'pai, while Ki'shto'ba remained below, calmly settling down beside Sa'ti'a'i'a the Nasute Chief.

Kwi'ga'ga'tei led Kaitrin onto the dais, where the elevation forced her to kneel. As she hastily checked her holocam to make sure it was working, Kwi'ga'ga'tei began to speak, ratcheting up the gain of her signal transmission so much that Kaitrin had to adjust the volume in her earports.

Shshi of Lo'ro'ra, this is the Star-Being of whom everyone in the fortress has been speaking. She is Ru'a'ma'na'ta, who was called in my vision kai'tri'ze|, *a wind that goes forth from the stars. The Highest-Mother-Who-Is-Nameless commands that we honor her within our fortress!*

At the title of the goddess, every Shi groveled. *Even without the Highest Mother's command, our code of hospitality dictates that we honor all visitors who come in peace,* Kwi'ga'ga'tei was continuing. *She must be given all the respect that we would accord the representatives of a friendly neighboring fortress – that we would pay to a delegation begging for a King! If we fail in this, our peace will be shattered – this I have seen! Receive my words, Shshi of Lo'ro'ra, and hearken to them!*

Someone in the crowd sent forth the words, *We know that you comforted our sibling Ti'shra, Ru'a'ma'na'ta, when it was dying and we acclaim you for that!* A fresh outburst of signals followed, accompanied by the waving of heads and foreclaws, an action perhaps comparable to applause.

Certain words prevailed above the babble, uttered by the Remembrancer Di'fa'kro'mi. *Hail to the Holy Seer Kwi'ga'ga'tei, for showing us that there is no evil in the Star-People! Our Seer is great and good! May she be long in life and strong in power!*

Kaitrin was thrilled to hear her friend so exalted. But her attention was attracted by Mo'gri'ta'tu as he squatted motionless at the base of the dais, denied a place of honor. To a human, the insectile Shi visage was expressionless, but Kaitrin sensed an exhalation of a force so powerful that she shuddered away from it. It was an emotion of hatred, of malevolence, of pure evil. Then it was gone, controlled, absorbed in the general ferment of excitement. *What is this creature, anyway? If I can sense this, what would Trea sense from him?*

*   *   *

I know you cannot stay long within our walls, Kwi'ga'ga'tei said to Kaitrin after the assembly disbanded. *What would you like to see, Ru'a'ma'na'ta?*

Kaitrin asked to visit the nurseries and she and the Seer set off, with Ki'shto'ba lumbering along behind, its big head filling nearly all the space in the narrowing passages. They proceeded downward into an area where the stone-lined tunnels and chambers were hollowed out of the ground. The air was more stagnant here, warm and heavy with earthy humidity. They passed a major side passage from which a line of Workers was issuing, carrying buckets sloshing with the sweet fluid that Gwidian had milked from Tish'ra's pet.

As they squeezed to the side to allow the column to pass, Kwi'ga'ga'tei explained that the Workers were conveying the *ti'wa'zi|* to the Alates' refectory. *They have come through the tunnel that leads from the building that contains the Fungus Gardens, the dwelling of the Little Ones, and the* weio'so'mi|.

Kaitrin asked about the meaning of that last word. "It seems to mean 'place of the dead body.'"

So it is. It is the chamber where our dead are taken to be prepared for consumption.

Good grief, she thought, *how should I translate that? Perhaps – Charnel Hall! I'm not sure I want to see that! But I suppose in the interests of science I should see everything I can ...*

Kwi'ga'ga'tei was saying, *In this other direction lies the water cistern. Air that draws inward across the cistern cools the fortress in the hot time, and in the cold times the vents are closed up. But Builders could explain such matters to you better than I can.*

"What is in the higher part of this structure, Holy Kwi'ga'ga'tei?"

The Council Chambers are there, and the Alates' quarters and refectory. The is'mi| *is there – the place where the Healers care for the sick and injured – as well as the group of chambers that we call the Alates' Holies. My own quarters are there, as well as the stables of the Alates' Flock, which produces the sacred honeydew of ritual, and the* bir'zha| *chamber, where the vision-fungus is grown.*

"Is it permitted to ask where the Holy One and the King dwell?"

Kwi'ga'ga'tei paused and pointed with an antenna. *The corridor that you see ahead leads to the Holy Chamber. It is the oldest part of Lo'ro'ra.*

Kaitrin saw a low entrance topped by another thick capstone

and flanked by two big Warriors. As the Seer and her company passed by, the guards abased, then followed them vigilantly with their antennae.

At the entrance to the nursery complex, Ki'shto'ba withdrew to wait in a nearby guardroom while Kaitrin and the Seer entered the incubation chamber, where the eggs laid by the Holy One were cared for prior to hatching. It was very warm and moist there, and the smell was sweetly fetid. Sweat started to accumulate on Kaitrin's forehead and trickle under her clothes as she sat cross-legged inside the door of the low-ceilinged hall, straining her eyes to peer into the darkness. Kwi'ga'ga'tei fanned her wings to pump up light, but she was the only Alate present. Kaitrin was forced to activate her field lamp, providing yet another source of amazement for the Seer.

The beam pricked out neat rows of perhaps a hundred yellowish ovals arrayed according to their age on beds of leaf mulch. Tenders – Workers smaller than the ones who labored in the orchards or repaired the walls – were licking and turning the eggs; others were bringing in the day's laying, carrying the grapefruit-sized ovoids in their mandibles. Some bustled about cleaning dirt and fungal growths from the walls, scraping up old bedding material with mandible tools and little fiber brushes, spreading fresh leaves from wheeled bins.

"How many eggs a day does the Holy One make?"

As many as two antennae count are possible. But in this cold season she lays only a few or may go for several day-cycles and produce nothing.

Kaitrin was thinking, *Griffen was right – the output is nothing like the thousands a terrestrial termite queen can lay in a day! ... I'm feeling a bit strange – light-headed ... It's so humid ... and this smell ... even with the ointment ... Buck up, Kaitrin. You may never have this sort of adventure again in your whole lifetime! Don't botch things up by fainting.* She took some deep breaths, uncapped her water bottle and took a long pull, then wiped her forehead with her sleeve.

"And do they all hatch?"

No. There – the Tender is removing one that is far past its hatching time and shows no signs of life.

"What is done with those that do not hatch?"

They go to the Charnel Hall to be prepared for consumption.
The same is true for the molted skins of the nymphs.
Kaitrin thought, *I might have known. Termites are the uni-*
verse's premier recyclers!
The Holy Seer directed her guest's attention toward the far
end of the chamber, where eggs were hatching. Kaitrin watched
the white, squirming nymphs – first instars, in the terminology of
terrestrial entomology – being pulled from the wrinkling, splitting
cases of their portable wombs. The Tenders licked and groomed
them – uncurled their bodies, pulled and flexed their legs, stroked
the miniature antennae. They looked quite similar to adult Workers, except their legs and antennae were short and spindly and they
were tiny, about twenty-five centimeters long. They splayed out
their legs, trying to stand up, falling down, their antennae wobbling.

Kaitrin thought they were adorable. *I must be a little addled*
in the head! A newly hatched insectoid, slimy and squirmy and
stinking, and I think it's cute? The fact is, these things make
Tió'otu's grandnestlings look like little dolls!

Three Alates entered through a side entrance, displaying
alarm at the unfamiliar brilliance of Kaitrin's light. *The Namers*,
said Kwi'ga'ga'tei. *Come – I will introduce you.*

So Kaitrin met the Namer Alates, who kept a memory list of
all the names in use within the fortress, and witnessed a naming.
One new-hatched nymph they called "Dit," which meant "Happy,"
and another, "Gri" – "Sun" – and still another, "Kwai," or "Mountain."

So, the Chief Namer explained, *when Dit reaches fourth in-*
star and we find it is a Worker, it could be called "Dit'ra" –
"Happy Flower." If Kwai is seen to be a Warrior, it could become
"Kwai'um'pai," that is, "Mountain Headed Warrior," or perhaps
"Lo'kwai'to" – "Strong Mountain Mandible." And Gri – should
Gri become an Alate, he or she could be called "Mo'gri'ta'tu," if
the Holy Chamberlain is not with us at the time when these ma-
ture! We never duplicate imago names among the living.

As they were leaving the incubation chamber, the Seer said
confidentially to Kaitrin, *I will discourage naming anyone*
"Mo'gri'ta'tu" for a while, should I ever be so fortunate as to be
rid of the present one.

They continued touring the rest of the nursery chambers, where all four of the instar stages resided. The first set of chambers housed the new hatchlings. Kaitrin was fascinated to see the devotion with which the Tenders cared for them, fondling and grooming, chasing after them, playing with them, scolding them when they misbehaved.

Kaitrin thought, *So we have additional evidence that these are more than big insects acting instinctively. They have a transmitted culture, a sense of caring, a sense of individuality that begins at the first moment of hatching.*

"Holy Kwi'ga'ga'tei, if one of these should die, do the Tenders mourn?"

Of course. The whole fortress mourns the loss of any of our siblings. There are sh…'wei'dit'zi| *of different types for different Castes and ages, that spread through the whole fortress by patterns of touch after a death.*

"I understand what *wei'dito*| means – to have sorrow that someone has died – but what does the first part of that word mean?" *I'll call it* ying, Kaitrin thought.

Kwi'ga'ga'tei made a swaying, jigging motion. *It is a movement of the body in which we touch others, to share our sorrow at the death.*

Ah, "dance!" thought Kaitrin.   shying'wei'dit'zi| *means "mourning dances."   They grieve by sharing their emotions through vibration and touch!*

"You mourn, and then you eat the corpse."

Of course. It is the final demonstration of respect – to take back into the common good the substance that the Nameless One has emptied of life.

"Do none of the offspring have eyes when they are hatched?"

No, we all start our lives blind. It serves to keep us humble, although not every Alate remembers the lesson of its early days …

"Can the nymphs speak as soon as they are hatched?"

No. They must be taught. Come this way.

They entered the second set of chambers.   Here Teacher Alates were instructing the second-stage instars, who were about half-a-year old and twice as big as when they were hatched. Kaitrin sat down on a block of stone just inside the entrance and, even though she remembered Trea's admonition not to get too close to her hosts, there was nothing she could do to keep the curious nymphs from approaching. A few timid ones hung back, but most swarmed around her, tickling her with their soft setae and palps and small, prickly claws. Their immature antennae babbled at her, like human baby talk – word emissions malformed or used incorrectly, tenses and numbers confused. Kaitrin recorded and vidded furiously; she could have stayed all day monitoring the infantile word patterns and observing the activities of the Teachers.

She asked what was in an adjacent room, and Kwi'ga'ga'tei said, *That is the molting chamber for the second instars. I will not take you there. Molting is a somewhat painful process and I do not believe that the nymphs, or their Tenders, would enjoy being observed.*

Kaitrin was disappointed, but she could understand. *If I had to shed my skin,* she thought, *I certainly wouldn't enjoy having a stranger watch me.* "After you become imagines, do you ever molt again?"

No. We continue to grow larger very slowly for a while, and if we are injured, the wounds heal, but we do not molt. And Kaitrin thought that this statement supported Griffen's theory about the role of the fibrous understructure of the chitin.

In the third instar stage, Teacher Alates instructed the nymphs in the culture and history of the Shshi and taught them appropriate behavior. On this day they were having a lesson on the proper ways and times to abase and who was deserving of that honor. When Kaitrin asked questions, the Teachers reminded their charges that it was rude to wave their antennae around when they were talking – they should point them courteously at the interlocutor so the words could be easily received. Kaitrin's fascination continued to grow.

By the fourth stage, the Caste of each new Shi had been revealed. These nymphs were only slightly smaller than the imagines they would become after a fourth molt at two years of age, and their mandibles, heads, and bodies were assuming adult forms. Some were developing eyes and lengthened bodies, and all of these had wings with pronounced sutures. In this stage, nascent Workers and Warriors were conducted about the fortress and taught the roles that they were predestined to fill, while the Alates remained mewed up in the nurseries, studying with specialized Teachers.

Those, said Kwi'ga'ga'tei, indicating a certain group of Alate nymphs, *those are potential* shma'na'ta| *and* shna'sha'ma|.

Kaitrin could see no difference between this group and the other Alate nymphs. "How can you tell?"

Ru'a'ma'na'ta, your sense of smell is indeed poorly developed! It is a matter not of form but of strength of pheromones. If the Holy One should die – may the Nameless One forbid! – a replacement would be chosen from this group. Certain rituals involving the consumption of the old King would ensure that she remains fertile after the last molt and the Seer would have the privilege of naming her. If another fortress should come to us seeking a new King, a male fertile nymph would be selected for them if we deemed them worthy. If a certain time passes and new progenitors are not needed, the rest transmute at the final molt into ordinary Alates.

"I had thought, Kwi'ga'ga'tei, that you might become the new *ma'na'ta|* if such unfortunate need arose."

Me! No, no! Once we pass fourth molt, we cannot return to a fecund state. Once I was indeed one of these fertile nymphs, but from the beginning I was endowed with the power of Seeing. I would never have been chosen – there has never been a Seeing ma'na'ta|. *I was destined for a much more difficult role.*

Kaitrin chewed on this for a moment, thinking, *At least that helps to answer Griffen's and Lindeman's question about secondary reproductives.* Then her attention was caught by a Tender turning a wooden container upside down on a ledge. "I have seen that being done in other chambers, Kwi'ga'ga'tei. What is it?"

Why, have you nothing like that? It is the water vessel that marks the time. It has two compartments with a small hole in the partition and when the top is filled with water, it flows down into the bottom at a known rate. An official vessel carved from stone is maintained in the Alates' Holies, and a courier runs through the fortress six times in a suntime and six in a darktime, so that the divisions of the day-cycle are marked for all. But many Shshi maintain their own vessels in order to keep a tally of time for themselves.

Kaitrin was delighted. She started to show Kwi'ga'ga'tei her watch and realized with a shock that she had been in the fortress for four hours. *Oh, god! Griffen! I told him two at the very most!*

"Kwi'ga'ga'tei, I have to leave! I have been here much longer than I intended! My friends will worry about me. My *na'sha'ma|* will be especially worried. He cannot believe that I am safe here. I must go!"

Will you come back, Ru'a'ma'na'ta?

"Oh, yes! I want to see everything. I want to see the Fungus Gardens, the flocks – everything."

Soon a ... Ritual will be held. I will permit you to witness it if you wish.

"I do not know that word – it seems to mean 'new-grow ritual.'"

ziv'lat'nak'zi| means to make long lines throughout the fortress where we touch, feed, lick, and groom one another, ending with the ma'na'ta|*. This scent-speaks to her and keeps her laying eggs and it tells her what Castes are most in need of more members. If we have had a war, the Holy One will then produce more Warriors, and if we have had a sickness that has killed many Alates or if many Workers have died in a flood, she will lay more Alates or more Workers. If we do not conduct this ritual regularly, the fortress will not thrive. We call this the* na'wei'theik'zi| ki| ziv'lat'zi|*.

Kaitrin was even more excited; Prf. Lindeman had mentioned how pheromones and hormones passed from individuals to the queen within a termitarium, to send the queen a message as to which castes were lacking in the colony and cause the ratio of her production to shift. *This is wonderful! That natural process has evolved into a ritual among members of this advanced species! They call it the "holy unexplained thing" – the "miracle" – "of new growth." "Regeneration" is maybe the best translation! So* ziv'lat'nak'zi| *means "Regeneration Ritual."*

"I believe I understand, holy Kwi'ga'ga'tei!" said Kaitrin. "And yes! I very much wish to see such a ritual – it would be a great honor for me! And if it is satisfactory, I will come back in the next suntime. But now it is most necessary for me to leave."

*   *   *

Ki'shto'ba alone escorted Kaitrin back across the courtyard. The sun was blinding after the blackness of the fortress and she shaded her eyes, squinting toward the flyer. "Something looks different," she said. "What's the matter?"

I was told that the sibling of your dwelling arrived today, said the Huge-Head.

"Oh, yes, that's what is sticking out on the right side. I thought it was coming tomorrow. It seems I lost track of that time, too."

Ru'a'ma'na'ta, are your dwellings male or female?

Amused, Kaitrin said, "I think a better name for them is 'Workers,' Ki'shto'ba."

Amazing! Workers that can fly! The Star-Beings become stranger all the time!

Curiouser and curiouser, thought Kaitrin, then she spotted activity in front of the *Durga*. With real affection, she ruffled the sensory hairs that grew around the juncture of Ki'shto'ba's foreleg and thorax – its thick head had few such sensilla and practically no feeling – and said, "I see my friends, *no'no| um'zi|*. You can leave me. I will be fine by myself now."

Griffen had come down the ramp to meet her. When she reached him, he said nothing, only took her in his arms and hunched over her, pressing his face into her shoulder. "Griff, I'm back – I'm fine! I had the most incredible experience of my life! Griffen, come on – let's go in. Griffen, can you even hear me?'

He gave a gasp, released her, and let her lead him up the ramp. Inside, there was chaos; the flight deck's utility hatch had been opened and supplies were being transferred from the *Lifeline* to the *Durga*. Julian and Arti were on the upper deck handing crates down the ladder to Will and Luku. Zin's husky voice could be heard issuing orders. Storage areas in the floor and ceiling had been opened and clutter was everywhere.

A'a'ma was hopping about and chirping and Sev was in the Medical Bay inventorying supplies, but Trea was standing near the table. "Was it good?" she said to Kaitrin.

"It was more marvelous than I can express! I can't wait to tell you everything!"

"I worried," said Tió'otu, "but I was not surprised. I knew you would forget the time. I know you, Kaitrin. It is too bad Prf. Gwidian does not know you as well as I do."

Griffen made an incoherent noise and embraced Kaitrin again, breathing her name against her neck.

"Griff, you're squeezing me to death! I'm sorry, love, but I was learning so much – having such a wonderful time … Trea, is he all right?"

"Oh, Gwidian is fine," said the Pozúu, but, facing Kaitrin from behind Griffen's back, she grimaced in a way that surely conveyed a negative.

"*Jocha*, Kaitrin!" exclaimed Luku, passing near them with a carton to be stowed. "You smell bad! Like termite!"

"Do I? I suppose I do! Here, Griffen, get away from me! You'll smell just like me!"

"I don't care," he said, but he did pull back and she took him by the arms and gazed into his face. He looked haggard and haunted.

"Kaitrin, you're going in again, aren't you? There's nothing I can do to stop you, is there?"

"But now you can see there's no danger," she said to him. "Here I am obviously in one piece and kicking, just a little smelly! Griffen, I saw the nurseries, the incubating chamber! I saw eggs hatching! I saw nymphs being named and being cared for with every bit as much love as humans have! I have recordings of them learning to talk! Oh, I have so much to tell you – I know you'll be interested in all of it! Tió'otu, they use a primitive water clock to keep time – something like an hourglass. And Kwi'ga'ga'tei is going to let me witness a Regeneration Ritual – that's where they pass along pheromones that tell the Queen what kind of eggs to lay! I have enough material already to write half a dozen reports – maybe even a monograph – if you'll help me work out all the insect parallels, Griff, so it'll sound like I know what I'm talking about! But I'd better go change and shower and get these clothes washed! I'll want them again before long. Here, Luku, take the recorder and the holocam – everything was running the whole time …"

Griffen followed her into their compartment while she changed. "Kaitrin, can't you do what you say you'll do? If you say two hours, can't you mean two hours? Do you have to put me through this?"

She paused, tying her robe. "I truly am sorry, Griffen. I looked at my watch and four hours had gone by – it seemed like one! I instantly realized how much you must be worrying. But you know one can't always predict how these situations will work out. You've gotten carried away in the field once or twice yourself."

"And you worried about me then, too – and missed me – or you said you did."

"Of course I did, but that's different … well, maybe it isn't so very different … Anyway," she continued, at once disgruntled and anxious, "I tried the MP, but I got nothing but messages saying transmissions were blocked. That masonry is just too thick. I don't suppose you received … Griffen, for goodness sake, don't look at me like that with those eyes of yours all hopeless! Everything is all right and it will always be all right. Now, I've got to go shower and wash my hair. Why don't you try to get some rest? You look dreadful."

Later, with the supplies unloaded and cleared away, Zin !eye Taeva sat down to a meal with the lander team. The *Brozzae* would remain overnight and Luku was going to spend it with him in the flyer. "You two seem to be getting pretty serious!" Arti remarked. "Can we expect another wedding on the way home?"

Luku and Zin eyed each other and laughed. "No," he said, "but we may make trip back to Quornam together after this voyage is over. Meet families. Talk to priests. Who knows?"

"If we marry," said Luku, "and we talk about it – yes, Zin? – we will do that on Quornam. But is hard – Zin is career pilot with Confederation and I am ComTech on Earth. I am thinking about joining Space Force and becoming Com Officer, but no guarantee that we are assigned to same ship. So there is much to think about before we decide if our fates really join."

"So we enjoy the moment," said Zin. "We will play music and sing for you later if you like. I brought the *klu-e*."

"I'd love it," said Kaitrin, "but I'm pretty tired and sore from crawling through what seemed like kilometers of corridors. Thank goodness I could at least sit up straight in most of the chambers." She glanced at Griffen, who had hardly said a word during the meal and eaten next to nothing. "I think we'll both have to turn in early. Phew!" She had left her hair loose after washing it and now she pulled a strand over her nose. "Smells ghastly! Termite stench is awful – really pervasive!"

Everybody laughed except Gwidian, who only shifted in his

chair, looking like a man who has been stunned by a nightmare.

Later, as Trea examined Kaitrin in the MedBay, she said, "So you go back into the fortress, Kaitrin?"

"I do intend to."

"This is very difficult for Gwidian."

"I know that. And it makes me ... It really hurts me. But I can't give up my work, Trea! He must get over this – this ... Well, I don't know how to describe it!"

"What means more to you, Kaitrin?"

Kaitrin gazed at her, perplexed. "But surely, Trea, surely he can come to accept that we can't do everything together – that I have to live my own life and make my own career! I mean, I want him to live his own life and have his own career! It never occurred to me there could be any question about that."

"It is more than that," said Trea. "But I only sense things – no data."

"I guess I've had other loves, too, Trea – I never thought about it that way. I never swore to give them up, the way Griffen did. Should I have?"

Trea chuckled softly. "Is a little different. Better to make your loves flow in harmony, like big and small waves following one and other."

Kaitrin only looked at her, not fully comprehending.

Trea said, "Just be kind to him tonight, Kaitrin, and try to get back when you say next time. Maybe he gets used to you taking these risks. And we will probably go away from here in another three or four weeks, at longest. *Featherlight* will make run to Starbase 30 after Zin returns. Will be last one. Funding is running out, you know."

"Well, you're quite right about that, unfortunately! I'd better think about what I really need to accomplish. The end is a lot closer than I realized."

Just be kind to him tonight, Trea had said. But when they went to bed, Griffen had little to say; he only lay and held her almost too tightly, incessantly caressing her hair that smelled of the fortress. In her fatigue she fell asleep quickly, and so the night passed away.

Chapter 18

These six things doth the Lord hate:
    Yea, seven are an abomination unto him:
A proud look, a lying tongue,
    and hands that shed innocent blood,
An heart that deviseth wicked imaginations,
    feet that be swift in running to mischief,
A false witness that speaketh lies,
    and he that soweth discord among brethren.
               – *Proverbs* 6:16-19

[All the conspirators except Lo'lo'pai huddle together in the Warrior's Quarters]

[Mo'gri'ta'tu]: She had no weapon. When I sampled the pouches of the so-called King, I could tell which was the weapon – it smells like nothing else. She had none of that smell on her. So the plan involving the weapon is unworkable.

[Hi'ta'fu, grooms jerkily]: So that means – murder ...

[Mo'gri'ta'tu]: It all meant murder, Commander, in your sense of the word. It is only the method that differs now. But I tell you, the word to use is not "murder," it is "cleansing"! The Holy One is excited about this visit. This vermin of a Seer constantly leads her astray. Such corruption of our *ma'na'ta|* is execrable – sacrilegious! [Mo'gri'ta'tu stamps, casts about, bobbing his head and fanning his wings] The degenerate makes her believe that

207

only this blasphemously named outlander can save our fortress from – what? Kwi'ga'ga'tei will never say! She has no notion! She is an abomination on the great tradition of prophecy! She tramples on my rights – demeans me! She deserves to be de-winged – to be torn to shreds – to be …

[Ta'rei'so'cha]: Holy Chamberlain! Your rage is frightening the Commander!

[Mo'gri'ta'tu convulses, draws the wings tightly together, and crouches immobile]: Yes. Your pardon, esteemed Hi'ta'fu. My indignation at the abominations committed by this miscreant overwhelms me. Let us comport ourselves like the rational creatures that we are.

[Hi'ta'fu]: If you have a proposal, Mo'gri'ta'tu, state it. I have no wish to spend more time in your company than I must.

[Mo'gri'ta'tu]: Take care what you say, Commander, if you want the end to be as you desire. But here is the plan: I have learned from rumor that the Seer proposes to bring the female to the Fungus Gardens at the beginning of this next suntime. That bodes well for the springing of our trap. The Apothecary is adjacent to the Gardens. It is not at all extraordinary for Ta'rei'so'cha the Healer to frequent that place. And I have hinted to the Holy One that Kwi'ga'ga'tei lately spends too little time in her presence, so she has ordered the Seer to attend her at the time that the female is to be visiting. Therefore, Kwi'ga'ga'tei will send the female to the Gardens with I'mei'o'nu and Di'fa'kro'mi and perhaps No'kri, who are likely to be more trusting than the Seer is. Ki'shto'ba will be there as well, of course, but that fits into our plan.

[Ta'rei'so'cha]: The Fungus Gardens are always awash in Workers. In the confusion I will approach the female, who does not know me, and offer to show her the Apothecary Garden. She has a great curiosity about our way of life, so I am sure she will follow me. A'dei'no'no, who is an overseer in the Fungus Gardens and is not known to be an associate of the Holy Chamberlain, will watch outside the Apothecary Chamber. When he sees Ki'shto'ba searching for the female one, as it certainly will when it discovers she has disappeared, he will attempt to direct it to some place where it cannot be observed. He will let me know when this

208

is accomplished and I will signal Lo'lo'pai, who will be concealed within the Apothecary Garden.   It will kill the female using the Huge-Head's weapon style.   In a few moments, A'dei'no'no will come in, "discover" the corpse, and raise the alarm.   It will look as if Ki'shto'ba did the deed, for it will not be able to prove its whereabouts.   Lo'lo'pai and I will escape by a back way.   The odors in that place are so aromatic and confusing to the senses that it will be impossible to detect that Lo'lo'pai was ever there.

[Mo'gri'ta'tu]: You have the plan exactly, Ta'rei'so'cha.   I commend you.

[Ta'rei'so'cha, scrapes]: I thank you, Holy Chamberlain.

[A'dei'no'no]: I also understand my role and should have no difficulty performing it.

[Hi'ta'fu]: And you, Chamberlain, where will you be while this is going on?

[Mo'gri'ta'tu]:   I will also be with A'kha'ma'na'ta in the Holy Chamber, making myself obvious.   I would counsel you to do the same.

[Hi'ta'fu]: This is very complicated.   All manner of things could go wrong with it.

[Mo'gri'ta'tu]: So give us your plan, Commander.

[Hi'ta'fu]: I have none.   A Warrior has no skill or experience with such odious and devious dealings.

[Mo'gri'ta'tu]: The only alternative to such a plan as this – you realize, Commander, do you not? – is open rebellion. Do you want that?

[Hi'ta'fu]: No! Never! Never will I allow Lo'ro'ra's protectors to rip at Lo'ro'ra's gut! We will try this plan.

[Mo'gri'ta'tu]: Good! Now only one thing is wanting – to recruit Lo'lo'pai to the cause.

[Hi'ta'fu]: I summoned it to meet us here. It should be arriving presently.

[Mo'gri'ta'tu]: Good! Then let us repose ourselves to wait and meanwhile talk of more pleasant things. I was examining the new crop of fourth-stage instars yesterday and I noticed two or three who seem timid and compliant. Any of the three might be promising to groom as our new Seer, to replace our late and not at all lamented Holy Kwi'ga'ga'tei ...

*   *   *

[Later in the day. Alone, Lo'lo'pai scuttles back and forth in its quarters]

I am being importuned to commit murder! The face put upon it is that the creature I must kill is a profane imposter and a murderer herself, and a dire danger to our beloved fortress. Are these things true? Is there really a justification for this act that I have agreed to perform? I respect Commander Hi'ta'fu more than any One Being in the world, but I cannot read its signals. It insists that I do this – it calls on my debt to it – so I feel I must comply. But I am not easy with this, or satisfied that Hi'ta'fu is easy, either.

Is Kwi'ga'ga'tei the villain they make her out to be? I was only a Lieutenant during the Nasute War, and I was as disappointed as anyone that we were not allowed to finish off the Enemy but must instead make soft peace with them. But it has indeed led to the prosperity of Lo'ro'ra. Perhaps there is something to be said for diplomacy – even Hi'ta'fu prefers not to kill without good cause.

But it thinks this cause is good, or so it says. What am I to believe? After all, this creature is not a Shi, but only some deformed thing more akin to the vermin of the plain than to one of the Nameless One's First Created. Can there be more harm in killing it than would be in killing a poisonous reptile? But still I am disturbed, because it is a speaking creature ...

Warriors are good at taking orders and passing them along. We have no skill for fine reasoning as the Alates do and are not taught such; we are taught to believe that the Eyed Ones speak truth, because they can see and we cannot.

Yet both Kwi'ga'ga'tei and Mo'gri'ta'tu are Alates ...

I am confused. I do not understand.

I will do as Hi'ta'fu and Mo'gri'ta'tu ask me. I can do this deed – I am not afraid. But whether it is right, I cannot say. I wish I had someone I could trust – someone neutral who could counsel me. But there is no one.

Well, a Warrior must not think too much but only do as its Commander orders. I will do this deed and take the consequences.

*   *   *

[The corridor leading to the Fungus Gardens]

[I'mei'o'nu]: Again, Ru'a'ma'na'ta, I make the apology of the Holy Seer. The Holy One demanded her attendance and when that happens, one has to comply. I assure you, she was looking forward to visiting the Gardens with you today.

[Ru'a'ma'na'ta]: I understand. I also am disappointed. Perhaps for my next visit she will be free.

[No'kri] I am sure she will arrange it.

[Di'fa'kro'mi]: Here we are at the entranceway.

[Ki'shto'ba]: I will follow you in, Holy Alates.

[The Gardens, shadowy in the light of only a few Star-Wings and the spectral gleams of luminescent growths around a lofty ceiling. Steeply terraced walls are lined with woody combs embedded with the fibrous mycelia of fungi and adorned with their plate-like fruiting bodies. Workers scurry up and down the terraces, excising foreign growths, harvesting the fruiting bodies, spreading spores, working dung into the combs. The air is heavy with spicy fragrances and odors of excrement; the atmosphere is oppressive, with water dripping in places from ceiling intakes. Workers with wheelbarrows scuttle between bins of harvested fungus and several exits, transporting the material to the refectories]

[Ru'a'ma'na'ta, peering into the dusk]: What a remarkable place! I wish my *na'sha'ma|* could come see this!

[No'kri, being jostled by curious Workers]: He would be welcome.

[Ru'a'ma'na'ta]: I think he is too big to fit comfortably in the corridors, Worker Chief.

[A Worker]: It is the one we talked to! I told you she would come!

211

[Another Worker]: It is the Comforter of Ti'shra!

[Workers surround Ru'a'ma'na'ta and hustle her a short distance away from her escort]

[Ru'a'ma'na'ta]: Did you all know Ti'shra? Are you all its friends?

[Workers]: Oh, yes! We all knew it! We all grieved! But we understand you meant it no harm! The Holy Seer has assured us it is so! It sickened because it had no proper food. Because your world was too strange for it.

[A Worker]: So you came here to visit us and tell us you are sorry, because we cannot go to visit you. We could not live in your world.

[Ru'a'ma'na'ta]: In fact, all that is so, my friends.

[A Worker]: It is good to share friendship! Come and see our bountiful crop, Ru'a'ma'na'ta. We are very proud of it!

[Gwo'no, Chief Grower, approaches No'kri]: While you are here, may I talk to you about a problem with a water duct that I cannot convince the stubborn Builders to fix?

[As No'kri allows itself to be drawn away, a Worker recognizes Di'fa'kro'mi]: Oh, do you know who that one is? It is the Remembrancer! Are we to have a tale? Give us a tale!

[Di'fa'kro'mi]: I cannot, I fear. It is not part of the day's plan.

[Workers begin to bombard the Remembrancer with questions and praise regarding his last Tale-Telling. I'mei'o'nu is shoved to one side. Ki'shto'ba is recognized, mobbed with word-sendings]: It is the Champion! Visiting our Gardens! What an honor! Great Warriors never visit Gardens! Tell us about the fortress of To'wak, Huge-Head! Are its Gardens even half as wonderful as ours?

[A'dei'no'no, at a side exit, gives a signal. Ta'rei'so'cha enters the Gardens, approaches Ru'a'ma'na'ta]

[Ta'rei'so'cha]: Forgive my interruption, Holy One. I am Ta'rei'so'cha, a Healer Alate.

212

[Ru'a'ma'na'ta]: Oh! I have never met a Healer of the Shshi before!

[Ta'rei'so'cha]: I was wondering if you would like to visit the Apothecary Garden. It is right through this entranceway.

[Ru'a'ma'na'ta, following the Alate]: I do not know the word that you use to describe this garden.

[Ta'rei'so'cha]: It is the place where we grow the fungi and herbs that we use in healing.

[She draws Ru'a'ma'na'ta toward the door, past A'dei'no'no, who converses with several Workers with his rear to the passersby. The Star-Being must crouch down to pass through the door. They enter a medium-sized chamber lighted only by the wings of the Healer Alate. Many types of fungus and colorless subterranean plants grow on combs and in earth-filled niches around the walls. Some gleam with eerily colored bioluminescence]

[Ta'rei'so'cha, moving toward an obscure alcove]: Come see the plants in this area.

[Ru'a'ma'na'ta]: Wait! What is this spectacular glowing thing here by the door? Could I take samples of some of these with me? Is it forbidden?

[In the alcove, Lo'lo'pai crouches, bunched and tense, antennae quivering, mandibles open, waiting for the Star-Being to come around the corner]

[In the main Gardens, Ki'shto'ba lifts its head, rises on claw tips and hoists its belly to test the scents in the air]

[Ki'shto'ba]: No'kri! Di'fa'kro'mi! Where are you? Where is Ru'a'ma'na'ta?

[No'kri does not receive the sending. From a distance, Di'fa'kro'mi answers]: I do not see her. Holy Nameless! Where did she go?

[Ki'shto'ba, plows a few steps through the crush]: I will find her!

[A'dei'no'no, approaches hastily]: Great Champion, I saw her wander with some Workers into the Sorting Chamber.

[Ki'shto'ba turns, casting about]: Where is that? I do not know this place. Would you be so kind as to conduct me there?

[A small Worker rushes up, patting Ki'shto'ba fearlessly on the palps to get its attention]: That is not where Ru'a'ma'na'ta went! I know where she is, magnificent Huge-Head!

[At these words, A'dei'no'no prances in desperation, his antennae bouncing]

[Ki'shto'ba, swaying impatiently, trying to be courteous]: May I ask that you tell me where she is, little Worker?

[The Worker]: I was cutting fungus portions over there when one of the Healer Alates took her into the Apothecary Garden. The entrance lies behind me at six Shshi lengths.

[Without waiting to offer thanks, Ki'shto'ba leaps across several Workers, knocks others over, locates the exit. The little Worker scuttles off and disappears into the press before A'dei'no'no can lay his claws on it. The conspirator clutches his antennae. He is too far from the entrance to send any warning to Ta'rei'so'cha]

[Ki'shto'ba, jamming its head through the small door]: Oh, there you are, Ru'a'ma'na'ta! I lost you for a moment.

[Ru'a'ma'na'ta, turns back from approaching the alcove]: I just met Ta'rei'so'cha – I had never met a Healer before. She – is it *she*? – offered to show me some of the medicinal plants. It is all very interesting to me!

[Ki'shto'ba, wriggling through the door, samples the air]: Ta'rei'so'cha, is it?

[Ta'rei'so'cha, crouching against the rear wall]: Indeed. Would you also like to learn about our simples, Champion? Over here are the herbs that can be used both to poison and to heal. A real paradox.

[Ki'shto'ba, still sampling the air, approaches the alcove]: Show them to Ru'a'ma'na'ta, Alate, while I determine what is in this alcove.

[The Huge-Head squeezes into the alcove, but it is empty.

There is an open exit in its far wall. Ki'shto'ba backs through the exit in order to contact the air and floor of the corridor with the scent receptors on its belly, then returns to the chamber and stands vigilant during the remainder of the conversation between Ru'a'ma'na'ta and the Healer Alate.]

* * *

[In the quarters of the Holy Seer are gathered the Champion, I'mei'o'nu, Di'fa'kro'mi, No'kri, and Kwi'ga'ga'tei]

[Ki'shto'ba]: I tell you, there was a scent of Warrior, but that place so overwhelms the senses that I could not make a proper identification.

[Kwi'ga'ga'tei, agitated]: Ta'rei'so'cha is an associate of Mo'gri'ta'tu – that is well known. I know her duty is to work with the medicaments. But to draw off Ru'a'ma'na'ta alone … I have not the strength nor time to be present everywhere! Can I trust no one not to fail me? Even you, Ki'shto'ba?

[No'kri and the Alates grovel in misery at the Seer's rebuke and the Huge-Head bangs its mandibles on the floor with a ringing sound no one can hear]

[Kwi'ga'ga'tei]: Are you sure it was Warrior scent?

[Ki'shto'ba]: I am sure, Most Holy Seer.

[Kwi'ga'ga'tei]: Hi'ta'fu?

[Ki'shto'ba]: I do not think so. That one has the peculiar fusty odor of the older Shi. This was a younger smell. But I cannot say whose smell it was. Perhaps it was someone whom I do not know.

[Kwi'ga'ga'tei]: There would be no reason for a Warrior to be in any of those Gardens.

[Di'fa'kro'mi]: Might a Warrior have come with a message or to get help for an injury?

[No'kri]: A Warrior would seek help for an injury in the infirmary, not the Apothecary Garden, and generally it is Workers who run errands and carry messages. Why would anyone send a Warrior?

[An uneasy pause]

[I'mei'o'nu, timidly]: Perhaps the Star-Being should not come again into the fortress. Perhaps this is a sign that we should be prudent and not test ourselves too far.

[Kwi'ga'ga'tei]: She must come again. A'kha'ma'na'ta has taken it into her head that she must meet Ru'a'ma'na'ta and I cannot dissuade her. Mo'gri'ta'tu sits balefully at her side and encourages her. He effuses his endless flatteries. He insinuates that only he knows what is good for the Holy One and the King. *tha'sask|>||* How can I be rid of this villain, short of falling to his level and slaying him?

[The other Shshi quail, unaccustomed to witnessing their Seer so openly incensed]

[Ki'shto'ba]: Holy Kwi'ga'ga'tei, I promise I will be more vigilant.

[Di'fa'kro'mi]: We are all at fault. But – a threat in so pacific a place as the Fungus Gardens? Even I whose task is to compose tales could not envision such a thing.

[Kwi'ga'ga'tei, collapses onto her belly, her head sinking]: I really cannot blame any of you. It is difficult to contend with one as subtle as the Chamberlain. And nothing really happened. If it were not for the scent of Warrior, I would not be overly concerned. But I tell you all, no harm must come to Ru'a'ma'na'ta in our fortress or Lo'ro'ra will fall – of that I am as sure as if the Nameless One spoke the words to all of us at this very moment!

*   *   *

[Mo'gri'ta'tu, raging]: Must I do everything myself? You were too slow! Why did not A'dei'no'no distract the Huge-Head more subtly? Why did you wait for her to enter the alcove? Why did you not … ?

[Hi'ta'fu]: If Lo'lo'pai had jumped instantly into the Apothecary Garden's main chamber, Ki'shto'ba would have come upon it in the act! Would you have had it end that way?

[Mo'gri'ta'tu]: Then at least there would have been someone to lay the blame upon!

[Lo'lo'pai, scrabbling about, threatening]: I, take the blame? Is that the word of one of good intent? I would have fought the Huge-Head if it had come upon me – maybe I would have killed it! Then two of your enemies would have been done away with.

[Mo'gri'ta'tu]: Small chance of that! And Kwi'ga'ga'tei would still have kept her lofty reputation and her power!

[Ta'rei'so'cha]: A'dei'no'no and I did the best we could. The Commander was right – there were too many variables that had to come together at the exact moment. Ki'shto'ba was too quick in realizing that its charge was missing. And who knew that a little Grower would be paying attention to the comings and go-ings and would have the courage to approach the Champion and contradict an Alate? The Huge-Head is dedicated to its duty of keeping the false female safe. I do not see how we can kill her unless it is done openly and then we gain nothing but our own downfall.

[Mo'gri'ta'tu crouches quivering in silence for a time, then speaks]: Did the Huge-Head detect the scent of Lo'lo'pai?

[Ta'rei'so'cha]: It went into the alcove and checked the scents in the corridor outside. It sensed something. But I doubt if it could identify anyone in that odorous atmosphere.

[Lo'lo'pai, prances]: Never did I think I would be in such a situation!

[Mo'gri'ta'tu, gloomily]: I am out of ideas. This may yet be forced to open rebellion.

[Hi'ta'fu]: Never! Never! I have engaged in behavior that would have made me destroy myself a few season-cycles ago, but never will I countenance the division and destruction of Lo'ro'ra!

[Mo'gri'ta'tu]: Division, yes, but it should not be destruction – only the ultimate cleansing. Excise the weak and fraudulent elements that threaten our Holy One and King. Well, we will make no decision now. The Holy One is demanding that the false female attend her. I have encouraged her in that whim. We'll see what comes of it. Some new ploy may yet suggest itself to me.

Chapter 19

All's vast that vastness means. Nay, I affirm
Nature is whole in her least things exprest,
Nor know we with what scope God builds the worm.
  – from Francis Thompson, *All's Vast*

This time Griffen did not emerge from the flyer to meet
Kaitrin. She rushed in and flung her arms around him. "Now,
how was that? I'm only five minutes – five minutes! – over the
three hours I allotted myself! Surely you can forgive five
minutes!"

He put her away from him, then took her face between his
hands and kissed her, seeming more in control than upon her first
return. "All right, Kait! I believe perhaps I shall learn to endure
all these chancy undertakings! Although – it would be a comfort if
the comlink could be made to work."

She looked at his eyes, his tight smile. *How much of this positive display is real, Griff? What's going on inside of you?* Her
glance sought out Trea's, but the Pozúu gave no particular response. *Maybe that's a good sign.*

Kaitrin said, "I kept the MP activated the whole time, but I
never got anything but static.

"We adjusted the gain as high as it could go," said Will. "I
don't think there's anything else we can do with this technology."

"What is in the bag?" asked A'a'ma.

"Yes – and sticking out of all your pockets!" added Luku.

"Oh, I've got fungus samples! Their edible fungus is shaped
like plates, Griffen – they don't grow those white balls like the

218

Afriken termites. And I have plants, too – I visited the garden where they grow medicinal stuff! I met a Healer Alate and she gave me the grand tour – how lucky is that? She let me take as many samples as I wanted! Look at these, Griffen! I can't believe there's anything on Earth like them. They all grow in total darkness! Your botanist – Asc. Keriya, wasn't it? – will be ecstatic! This one is a succulent that has bioluminescent flowers pollinated by little translucent insectoid things that sort of look like fleas! Apparently the bioluminescence attracts them! I've got some of the flowers, with bugs included, sealed up in this sample pouch. Why don't you take everything into the lab while I clean up? This time I smell like a putrid, overripe mushroom!"

The specimens had indeed piqued Griffen's interest; later he and Kaitrin worked together in the lab where he examined the insectoids and she made entries in the science database, recording the Healer Alate's information about the plants and the kind of ailments they were used to treat. After they had worked awhile, he straightened up from the DNA extractor, staring abstractedly across the room.

"Kaitrin, are you going back over there?"

"I don't know yet. Kwi'ga'ga'tei had other duties and didn't go to the Fungus Garden with us. She'll come late this afternoon, I imagine. But I really hope I can go back, Griff. I haven't seen the Little Ones yet – surely you want me to do that! And then there's the Regeneration Ritual – I don't know when that will take place …"

He bent over the display again. "It's all right. I'm only trying to – to determine how much longer I must keep up this – this … " He gestured helplessly as the word for what he was trying to express eluded him.

"Griff, why is this so difficult for you?"

"I've told you," he said with a shade of impatience. "I'm terrified of losing you. Why is that so hard for you to understand?"

Kaitrin regarded him. Trea had said, *Which means more to you?*

Try to make your loves flow in harmony …

This is a man who was contemplating suicide not so long ago and I don't know why …

"Griffen, two more times. Once to see the flocks and once for

– well, once as a reserve. Then I'll tell Kwi'ga'ga'tei that I can't come again, even if I have to miss the Ritual. I realize we're nearing the end of our stay here. It's just – somehow I feel funny about all of this. Like something isn't going to be finished before we leave. Like – if we leave too soon, this place will somehow vanish like something out of a fairy story and not be here when I come back."

He had turned to her. "Two more times?" he said eagerly, as if he had not even heard the last part of her remark. "Will you promise me that, Kait? Will you promise that an end to this is really in sight?"

"I promise, Griffen," she said in some perplexity. "We'll leave and go back to Earth and start that life together that we've kept on hold for too long."

He laughed like a man who has just received a reprieve and turned back to the extractor. "You know, Kait, I really never have seen anything like these 'fleas,' as you called them. I think we have a new order of xenoarthropods here. It's a great bonus that you were able to bring them back. Come take a look at this one in the analyzer and I'll explain what's different about it."

*   *   *

They were just going to bed when the proximity alarm sounded. It was set to pick up creatures only within three meters, since Shshi were always present in the courtyard these days.

Kaitrin stuck her head out of their compartment and Julian called down from the flight deck, "I see Kwi'ga'ga'tei and Ki'shto'ba going under the wing."

"Oh, dear," said Kaitrin, "I'll have to get dressed." She grinned over her shoulder at Griffen. "But I guess a bathrobe will serve. I could go out naked and the Shshi wouldn't know the difference."

She went out and sat on the side of the ramp. "I did not know you were coming, Holy Kwi'ga'ga'tei," she said. "I was ready to take rest. I'm glad to see you. I missed you in the Fungus Garden."

Her hair was hanging loose and Kwi'ga'ga'tei was eyeing it with great curiosity. *Is it permitted for me to touch this part of you?*

"Go ahead." Kaitrin bent her head and underwent the extraordinary sensation of having her hair nibbled by an enormous, inquisitive, and very gentle insectoid. But then Kwi'ga'ga'tei took a grip – and pulled.

"Ouch!" Through the emitter she said, "Please do not do that! This substance grows from my body, Kwi'ga'ga'tei. It hurts me when you pull on it."

Kwi'ga'ga'tei desisted at once, abased, and scrabbled in the dirt. *Forgive me, Ru'a'ma'na'ta. I thought it was like the material that covers your body – something you put upon yourself for protection.*

Kaitrin sighed, rubbing her head. Delicately, she extracted some long hairs from among the Holy Seer's mouthparts. "No. It is more like your sensilla, but not exactly, because ours give us no sensory information." *That isn't exactly true,* she thought, thinking of how sensual it felt when Griffen played with her hair, *but I'm not about to try to explain that to these sexless creatures!*

You endlessly mystify us, Ru'a'ma'na'ta, said Ki'shto'ba, shaking its mandibles.

Kwi'ga'ga'tei abruptly changed the subject. *Ru'a'ma'na'ta, I have come for a reason. The Holy One and the King have commanded that you come into their presence.*

It took a minute for this to register. Then Kaitrin's stomach did a flip-flop. "The Holy One ... I'm to be permitted to visit the *ma'na'ta|*?"

Yes. A'kha'ma'na'ta and Sei'o'na'sha'ma are both very curious about you. Nothing will serve but that I bring you into the Holy Chamber.

Oh, my goodness, thought Kaitrin. *I've never dared hope for that. I'm to enter the presence of something that lays eggs the size of grapefruit! What will it be like?* A vision of the monstrous, pulsing queen in Prf. Lindeman's vid weighted down her mind.

But the phrasing of the Holy Seer's statement made her pause. "Kwi'ga'ga'tei, you speak as if you would perhaps rather not take me there."

Kwi'ga'ga'tei danced. *I do not mean to seem reluctant. It is perfectly proper that such a visitor as you should come there. Ru'a'ma'na'ta, could you come this day, halfway between high sun and nightfall?*

Kaitrin squinted up at the sky, where the star Giotta 17A had not quite reached its zenith. "So soon? I was just beginning to take rest, as I said. But perhaps ... "

The Holy One has a poor understanding of time. Suntime and darktime mean nothing to her, nor the proper times of rest and activity. When she wants a thing, it must be done at once. I managed to persuade her to wait this long, but to try to make her wait until the next darktime has passed will be incomprehensible to her.

Kaitrin thought, *It's not prudent to oppose the wishes of an absolute monarch.* "All right, Kwi'ga'ga'tei. I am quite willing. I will rest briefly, then be ready at the time you said. But tell me how to behave! I do not want to break any taboos or appear discourteous. Should I make any particular kind of gesture when I meet them?"

Kwi'ga'ga'tei considered this. *We try to keep the head abased lower than the Holy One's, but I do not see how you can do this, since you walk vertically. How do the Star-People bow or greet each other?*

Kaitrin thought quickly. One rarely bowed to anyone on 30th century Earth. And shaking hands was hardly appropriate, or kissing the cheeks, as was still done in some parts of the planet. *This is like a First Dark Age culture. Maybe I should ... hell, I can't curtsy!* She emitted an irrepressible guffaw, fortunately imperceptible to the Seer. Then she thought of something she had read once – that two hundred years ago during the first contact with the Krisí'i'aidá the crew of the expeditionary ship had employed the Inden gesture called "namaste." "Kwi'ga'ga'tei, this gesture is a show of respect. I will abase like this." She stood up, laid her palms together at her breast and inclined her head.

It is good. I will tell the Holy One and the King that you make obeisance in that fashion.

"What do I call them?"

Call A'kha'ma'na'ta 'na'ta'zei|.' *Call Sei'o'na'sha'ma by his name. If you speak to both at once, say,'* na'ta'zei| u| na'sha'ma|.'

"I will do so. Is there anything in particular they want me to speak about to them?"

That we cannot plan. I can never predict where the Holy One's fancies will take her. I will come for you at midafternoon, Ru'a'ma'na'ta.

"It will be a great honor for me, Holy Seer."

*   *   *

Back in the flyer, Kaitrin announced, "You'll never guess what's happening! I'm to be taken to see the Queen! She has personally requested my attendance upon her! Yes, Tió'otu – even A'kha'ma'na'ta herself! In all her splendid physogastric majesty! At least, I suppose she looks like that – I'll find out soon! Isn't this exciting?"

"When?" said Griffen.

"It has to be today at midafternoon. The Queen doesn't … "

"Midafternoon?" said Griffen. "That will give you no time to sleep. We've been up for fourteen or fifteen hours as it is."

"Well, one can't always get enough sleep," said Kaitrin. "Didn't you ever pull any all-nighters when you were a student, Prf. Gwidian?"

"Of course, but that was a long time ago."

"Well, it hasn't been nearly as many years for me!"

He turned away with a kind of snort and Kaitrin realized her propensity for tactlessness had bubbled up again. "Griffen, I'm sorry. I wish I could stop putting my foot in it like that."

"Oh, you're right," he said. "I've had a good deal more experience than you – enough to know how easy it is to muck things up when one is tired. I'm going to bed." He retreated into their compartment.

Kaitrin looked at A'a'ma, who flapped and nictitated fatalistically. Luku grinned and Trea cocked her head expressionlessly at Kaitrin. "I'm going to bed, too," Kaitrin said. "I'll set the alarm for a couple of hours. The rest of you needn't even get up."

Griffen was already between the sheets when she went in and she crawled in beside him. "Don't be angry with me, Griff. This will count as the first of my last two visits."

"I'm not angry with you. I love you too much to ever be more than – just a trifle vexed." He laughed unsteadily.

Kaitrin hugged him. "You make me ashamed."

"Oh, no, I don't want to do that."

She groaned a little. "My knees hurt – and the thigh muscles and all down the calves."

He sat up, reached beneath the covers, and began to massage

her legs. "Oh, Griff ... That feels so good. You have wonderful hands – strong and gentle at the same time. But you don't have to do that. You're tired, too."

"I'd do anything for you, Kait – anything."

Again, she said, "You make me ashamed. Lie down. Hold me. I'll have to get up soon enough. Just hold me and let's sleep."

*   *   *

In spite of her admonition, most of the team got up to see her off. Kaitrin hunched over the table in the common area, washing down oatmeal with gulps of strong coffee. "They'll be here any minute. I think that little tidbit of sleep made it worse. Caffeine, work your magic!"

Will called down from the flight deck. "The *Featherlight* has left orbit for Starbase 30. The *Stinger* is in place – full crew. Capt. Van says all's well. Luku, Zin sends his love."

Luku emitted a purring trill.

Gwidian sat at the table with Kaitrin. "Slower – you'll choke," he said with a grave smile.

She stuffed a last dried apricot and bite of cracker bread in her mouth. "Do I look all right? One doesn't meet royalty every day!" She hastily checked the pins holding her braids.

"You should let it hang loose – let the Queen nibble it, too," said Griffen.

She grimaced, scanning his face. *He seems to be taking all this in stride.* Ay de mí, *I hope so.* "Griff, I can't say how long I'll be. But surely before dark. Try not to worry."

"I know. I won't."

For a man who admits to hiding under a facade for years, he's a pretty bad liar!

Luku was reattaching the miniaturized cam to Kaitrin's belt; it was the size of a large button, with a small hollow projection in the center "Try to face Queen. This will focus of itself on major objects."

"Kaitrin, I see them coming," called Julian from above.

"Oh, good grief. I have to go. Wish me luck." She hastily kissed Griffen, pecked Tió'otu on his beak, and descended from the flyer.

*   *   *

Outside, the wind was gusting. The cloud cover had been rent into rags and tatters, with bits of the planet's pallid blue sky showing through. In the west thunderheads were gathering, absorbing a billow of steam from a distant volcano. As Kwi'ga'ga'tei and Ki'shto'ba escorted Kaitrin across the compound, the wind caught the Holy Seer's wings and turned them inside out. Ki'shto'ba sheltered her with his big head.

"Holy Kwi'ga'ga'tei, is there anything more that I need to know?"

No. Simply speak to A'kha'ma'na'ta as you would any of us. You do not need to be afraid of her, Ru'a'ma'na'ta.

"Oh, I assure you I am not afraid, Holy Seer. But I must tell you something. Our visit to Lo'ro'ra is coming close to its conclusion. I can come into the fortress only one more time after this and then we must leave."

Ki'shto'ba pranced and Kwi'ga'ga'tei looked up at her. *So suddenly? Have we offended you in some way, Ru'a'ma'na'ta?*

"Oh, no! It is only that the time we planned for the visit to your world is drawing to its end. We must return to the lives that we live on our own world. But I will come back. I have promised you that."

Kwi'ga'ga'tei said nothing for several moments, then, *If this must be, I will make the Holy One accept it. I would ask you to say nothing of your leaving to any other Shi just yet.*

"I promise you, if that is your wish." A little perplexed, Kaitrin looked down on the expressionless head of the Holy Seer as they proceeded across the courtyard.

A moment later they reached the entrance to the fortress and passed within.

Chapter 20

Her lips were red, her looks were free,
Her locks were yellow as gold:
Her skin was white as leprosy,
The Nightmare *Life-in-Death* was she,
Who thicks man's blood with cold.
     – from S. T. Coleridge, *Rime of the Ancient
Mariner*

Kaitrin and her escort passed between the vigilant guards and entered the short corridor that led downward to the Holy Chamber. There, a pair of Nasute Warriors flanked the entrance; beyond it, they were within Lo'ro'ra's womb. Kaitrin pressed the activation tab on her holocam.

The hall was oval, eight or nine meters in diameter, with a shallow dome lofty enough for Kaitrin to stand upright with plenty of headroom. Three side exits were visible in the glimmering wing-light of Alates who were stationed at regular intervals around the walls. Many Shshi were present, mostly tiny Workers, all focusing their attention on the thing that rested in a leaf-filled hollow in the chamber's center.

It looked in the wavering light like a yellowish sail filled from below by a fitful wind. It billowed in irregular pulses that began at the near end and proceeded along its segmented length to its extremity, sending the segment stripes surging up and down like a sea wave. It was three meters long and a meter in diameter, and it stank – of life and of death, of ovulation and of darkness – of endless, moldering entombment on a birthing bed.

But there was more to it than that. At the anterior end projected the foreparts of a gigantic termite. Six legs splayed out, the third pair useless, weighted by proximity to the enormous belly, the second pair capable only of lifting the torso a short distance from the floor, the first pair able to twist from side to side the segmented thorax with its desiccated wing stubs. The head was huge, with folded mandibles, writhing palps, and the glittering eyes of an Alate. In contrast to the belly, the head and thorax together were less than one meter long, but this portion in itself was larger than the Workers who tended it.

Next to this creature stood the King, his one-and-a-half meter body pressed against his consort's, his labium resting on her thorax. He, too, had wing stubs and an Alate's eyes; with his fat belly and prominent stripes, he somewhat resembled a less hirsute bumblebee.

The Tenders of the Holy One clustered tenaciously around her, ignoring anything else that was happening in the Chamber. At her caudal end, Workers like those Kaitrin had seen in the incubation chamber waited motionless, as they would wait eternally whether she laid or not, to receive the precious gift of the ova of life into their waiting jaws should any be extruded. At the Holy One's flanks other Tenders were licking her and anointing her with honeydew and herbs, moistening and massaging the ancient cuticle to keep it elastic and nourished. Others similarly groomed the King, but not with the same ardor. Sei'o'na'sha'ma could be more easily replaced than A'kha'ma'na'ta, the only Mother that Lo'ro'ra had ever known, and his function was less fully comprehended.

Around the Holy Chamber were ranged the court and council of the *ma'na'ta*| – Di'fa'kro'mi the Remembrancer was there, and No'kri the Worker Chief; and on A'kha'ma'na'ta's left, the Commander of her Warriors, Hi'ta'fu the Unconquered, and the Keeper of her Holy Chamber, Mo'gri'ta'tu. The Chamberlain crouched motionless, his legs tense and flexed as if primed to spring.

Kwi'ga'ga'tei said, na'ta'zei|, *I have brought the honorable female of the Star-Beings. This is Ru'a'ma'na'ta.*

Kaitrin stood staring, feeling a little dizzy and overwhelmed. She realized that she had never actually believed that such a thing could exist. *Prf. Lindeman was right – proportionally, she's smaller than a terrestrial Queen, but even so ...*

The Holy One was forced to bend back her head to see Kaitrin, and Kaitrin thought, *This will never do.* So she knelt down, laid her palms together, and made her namaste. *"na'ta'zei|,* I am deeply honored that you desired speech with me."

The Holy One moved her legs in as close an imitation of prancing as she could achieve and said, *This is so delightful! I will call you "Ru." I call all my children by their nymph-names. Is "Ru" your nymph-name?*

"It will do nicely, Holy One," said Kaitrin, looking into the strange, enormous face in some perplexity.

I call my Seer "Tei" and my Chamberlain "Gri" and my Commander "Fum." They are all my offspring – did you know that?

"Yes, I know that, Holy One."

Let me see you put yourself in that other position, as you were when you first came in.

Kaitrin rose to her feet, towering above all the Shshi, even the Champion Ki'shto'ba, who had taken a place at the Holy One's left, separated by a little distance from the Commander and the Chamberlain. Kwi'ga'ga'tei remained beside Kaitrin.

Wonderful, exclaimed A'kha'ma'na'ta, scraping her front claws together as if she were clapping. *Tei said you stood on two legs like the birds and I did not believe her. But you do! How do you keep from falling over? Gri – Fum – can you stand like that, on your third set of legs?*

Never, said the Chamberlain. *It is a totally aberrant and absurd posture.*

Ru, let me see you move about.

Dutifully, Kaitrin paraded back and forth.

Stranger and stranger! Is that the way the birds go, Tei?

Somewhat like that, na'ta'zei|, said the Seer.

But where are her feathers? I know what feathers are – they brought me some once. Gri, where are my feathers? I want to show them to Ru!

Mo'gri'ta'tu stirred restlessly. *They were put away when you tired of them,* na'ta'zei|. *It would take some time to find them.*

In wonderment, Kaitrin was thinking, *This creature is completely childlike – an ancient, fecund child!*

228

No matter. This is much more interesting! But I thought you had feathers, Ru. Tei, you told me the Star-Beings had feathers.

"We are of different kinds, Holy One," said Kaitrin. "One of us does have feathers, but I do not."

I want to see the one who has feathers!

Kwi'ga'ga'tei said, *Holy One, you insisted earlier that only Ru'a'ma'na'ta should be admitted to the fortress.*

"The one with feathers cannot crawl easily," said Kaitrin. "I am afraid that he could not move through the corridors."

Oh, that is all right then. But I am disappointed. I have to learn everything, you know, Ru. They all depend on me. I have to make all the decisions. It is very important for me to understand everything.

Mo'gri'ta'tu kept shifting his weight, but Kwi'ga'ga'tei remained motionless, head abased, eyes vigilant.

Kaitrin said, "I know you are supremely important to your children, *na'ta'zei|*. When my friend Ti'shra was dying, it spoke your name."

Did it? Oh, that pleases me! Did you know that, Tei? Gri? Kri, your Workers know my name! That pleases me!

All your offspring know your name, ma'na'ta|, said No'kri. Everyone in the Chamber wagged their heads in acknowledgement.

Come down to the floor again, Ru, and get close to me. I want to touch you.

They were Ti'shra's words – *sho'laio| ʃʔ zifo| ϛ bei'a| ||.* Kaitrin obliged. A'kha'ma'na'ta mouthed her up and down with her long, moist palps. *How many times now have I been snuffled all over by termites?* Kaitrin thought in amusement.

The Holy One said, *What are these hard things sticking to your body?*

"This one is the antenna box that lets me speak to you."

Oh, the magic box! I did want to see the magic box! The Holy One tried to close her mandibles around it, and Kaitrin gently pushed her mouthparts away.

"You must not bite or lick it, or it will not work, and then I will not be able to speak to you," said Kaitrin.

It is taboo, Holy One, said Kwi'ga'ga'tei.

You told me that, Tei, but I forgot. But what is this, Ru?

A'kha'ma'na'ta had placed the tip of an antenna squarely on the end of Kaitrin's nose.

Please, you universal gods, keep me from laughing, thought Kaitrin. "Holy One, that is the organ through which I breathe. I also smell with it. It is the only organ that I have that allows me to smell."

This caused quite a stir in the room, of wonder and skepticism.

A'kha'ma'na'ta said, *That is a spiracle? On your head? And you have only one? How can you get enough air through one spiracle to be able to live?*

"Our bodies are very different from yours, Holy One."

But you know, Holy One, said Kwi'ga'ga'tei, *that the reptiles and the birds also respire in that peculiar manner.*

Oh, yes, I had forgotten. But you smell with it, too? With only that one little knob?

"That is correct," said Kaitrin, extremely thankful that no human had to understand her vocalizations. "Our sense of smell is much inferior to that of the Shshi."

Do you receive that? We are better than they are in something, even if they do come from the stars! Do you receive that, Gri?

I receive, said Mo'gri'ta'tu. *Indeed, have I ever told you otherwise, Holy One?*

Perhaps not. Perhaps it is Tei who tells me they are superior to us. But the truth is that the Shshi are superior to all other beings because we were made first by the Nameless One. Everybody knows that. Everything else is secondary, and secondary can only be inferior. Isn't that right, Tei?

Kwi'ga'ga'tei stepped from one claw to the other. *We did not know these Star-Beings existed, Holy One. We do not know when the Nameless One made them, or how.*

But quite patently, said Mo'gri'ta'tu, *the Holy One cannot be wrong. Secondary assuredly can never be of equal consequence with primary.*

Somehow Mo'gri'ta'tu's utterances always seemed fraught with double meanings. Kaitrin said, "We are not superior to anyone, Holy One – only different. The Star-Beings and the Shshi each have abilities that the other lacks." To turn the subject, she said, "But I wonder if Sei'o'na'sha'ma wants to speak to me or to touch me."

Obviously accustomed to being ignored, the King came around the side of A'kha'ma'na'ta and touched Kaitrin delicately with his antennae. *You are* ma'na'ta|, he said. *That is what the Holy Seer says. She says you have a King.*

"I do."

But he is not with you.

"Like the feathered one, he could not move comfortably in the corridors."

I do not understand, said A'kha'ma'na'ta, *how you can be* ma'na'ta| *and yet walk about above ground, and go where you want without your King, and have no belly. And your King is bigger than you are, they say! Gri says all this makes it unlikely that you really are what Tei says you are.*

"Again, we are different. Star-Beings do not have only one *ma'na'ta|*. About half our people are female and can be *ma'na'ta|* and the other half are male and every one of those can be *na'sha'ma|*."

This caused a real sensation.

It is so with the reptiles and the birds, said Kwi'ga'ga'tei. *They have no neuters – they all are either Kings or Mothers. The Healers have told you that,* na'ta'zei|.

It is the secondary order, said Mo'gri'ta'tu, *lower even than the Enemy. No speaking being is of this order, and it is sacrilege to maintain that it is so.*

Then by your own reasoning these visitors must be of the primary order, said Kwi'ga'ga'tei, *because they do speak.*

There was a wordless moment as the Chamberlain mulled over the recognition that he had bested himself with his own logic. Kaitrin felt things were getting out of hand. "Holy One," she said, "you spoke of being created first by the Nameless One. Do you have a tale telling of your creation? I would like to receive it."

Yes! We have many such tales! Dit told me he had related for you the tale of the founding of our fortress. In those days I went about above ground as you do. I believe I did see birds then, but I have forgotten what they look like. I was very young and frightened on that journey. But the Highest-Mother-Who-Is-Nameless forbade the progenitors to come above ground once they had shed their wings and copulated. Dit, give us the tale of why that is so.

Kwi'ga'ga'tei said, *Perhaps Ru'a'ma'na'ta does not have the time.*

Kaitrin sneaked a look at her watch, thinking, *This is silly. I can look at my watch openly – they have no idea what I'm doing. But I've been here under an hour. And what anthro can resist a creation myth?*

"I have the time," she said, rechecking her recorder to make sure it was working properly. "It would give me great pleasure to receive the tale of your creation."

The Shshi settled down with a kind of collective heave that seemed expressive of resignation. Undoubtedly, Kaitrin thought, they had all been subjected to this tale a thousand times before. Di'fa'kro'mi mounted a little dais at the end of the chamber opposite the Holy One and began to speak.

In the most ancient of times the Highest-Mother-Who-Has-No-Name filled all the sky and she hungered for the Nameless King and devoured him so that she was impregnated with his egg-maker ...

When he had finished, Kaitrin was both impressed and moved. Here was a myth as classic as any discovered on any planet, with as many universal themes. *I'm ecstatic I came today,* she thought. *This is worth any amount of sore knees. I wish we didn't have to leave so soon. Oh, Griff, if you could only overcome these fears of yours!*

It is a good tale, but so often told, said the King a little wearily.

I am glad I do not have to eat you, Sei, to take your egg-maker, A'kha'ma'na'ta said to him. Then she looked at Kaitrin. *Now you tell a tale, Ru! Dit told us that you are also a Remembrancer. Imagine, a* ma'na'ta| *who is a Remembrancer! He told us your tale about the Shi who helped the beast, who saved him in gratitude. It was a fine tale! Tell us another one! Something new! Something exciting!*

Oh, my word! thought Kaitrin. *I wasn't expecting this!* "Oh, I am not a real Remembrancer!" she said. "I am not prepared!"

Oh, come, said Mo'gri'ta'tu, eyeing her sideways. *You, the superior Star-Being, so beloved of the Nameless One – you must*

232

know some trifle suitable for the amusement of this secondary race.

Kaitrin thought, *You invidious, wormy little creature! I'll show you!* "Give me a moment, Holy One, to order my thoughts."

She buried her face in her hands, aware of all the attention on her, of the peculiar voiceless shufflings and skeletal rattling sounds that always pricked insectoid silence. *What can I tell them this time? It should be something a little more substantial than Androklis. But our cultures are so utterly different. Nothing with any love interest. Try explaining* Romeo and Juliet *to these unsexed creatures! Chivalry – no! They're closer to Iron Age, Bronze Age. Heroic battles. Single combat. That sort of thing. An adventure tale, but something simple.* Baowolf – *too dependent on poetic form ... The* Iliyad – *too complicated ... The* Odysy. *The* Odysy! *Yes! I know what I can do!*

She sat for a moment longer, searching and ordering the pockets of her mind. At last she said, "Holy One, I have something." She got up and went and sat on the edge of the little dais, stretching out her sore legs in agonized bliss. Kwi'ga'ga'tei turned herself about to almost face Kaitrin. Ki'shto'ba did a little dance of anticipation. Even Commander Hi'ta'fu, who had stood gloomy and unresponsive through this whole session, rotated toward her. Mo'gri'ta'tu continued to crouch motionless, sardonic and baleful.

Then Kaitrin began.

Chapter 21

Tell me, Muse, of that man, so ready at need,
who wandered far and wide, after he had
sacked the sacred citadel of Troy.
– from Homer, *The Odyssey*, tr. by S. H. Butcher
and A. Lang.

"This is an old, old tale and my world is very different now, but it still speaks meaning to all of us. It is the story of a male Warrior of my kind whose name was – Ul'i'seit, because he was a wanderer." *That's clever,* she thought. Ul| *is "always"* – i| *is "in"* – seito| *is "to travel"* – *ergo, "always traveling," ergo, "wanderer!" It even has the right number of syllables!*

"Ul'i'seit had fought in a great war. His people had been victorious. And now he ... But I must explain something. A large part of my world is covered with water – water that goes on as far as you can see, even as the plains do here ... "

no'no'gwai'zi|, said Kwi'ga'ga'tei. *We have tales that tell of such a thing.*

"Huge water," Kaitrin thought.

But we never believed it really existed, said Di'fa'kro'mi, seeming greatly excited.

Is it real? asked A'kha'ma'na'ta, almost bouncing with delight. *Is there really such a thing as the* no'no'gwai'zi|?

"Yes, it is real. Even here on your world. When we fly above your world, from very high up we can see that *no'no'gwai'zi|,* far

234

to the south of here."

There were stirrings of wonder. Only Mo'gri'ta'tu remained secret and unmoved.

"So," Kaitrin continued, "Ul'i'seit had to cross this ocean in order to get home, because he lived in a fortress that was built on a very small piece of land in the middle of the ocean. There were many such small pieces of land scattered about in that ocean, just as there are in the ocean on your world. In order to cross the *no'no'gwai'zi|*, Ul'i'seit and his Warriors made containers – wooden containers that float. These were so big that Ul'i'seit and all his Warriors could sit inside them. They put poles in the middle and hung – *bu're|* mats – on them so the wind would push the box along … "

Magic, magic! cried A'kha'ma'na'ta gleefully.

"And when the wind did not blow, they used long pieces of wood to push themselves across the water. So that is how the Warriors intended to get home. But they needed to bring their boxes to rest on land occasionally in order to find food, so they stopped at a small piece of land where a much less civilized race of beings lived, called the … " Kaitrin stopped and thought a minute, while many in her audience squirmed impatiently. *Cyclops. One-eyed.* kwi'tei'zei|. *Too much like Kwi'ga'ga'tei's name. Actually, the Griek means "Ring Eye." I've got it. Round Eye!"*

"They were called the *shzin'tei'zei|* – the People of the Round Eye. You see, today all the beings on my world have two eyes, even as the Alates do, and as you do, Holy One and King, but the Shzin'tei had only one eye, right in the middle of their clypei – and what is more, they were giants, like mountains, as big as the towers of Lo'ro'ra. You do right to tremble – they were ferocious and dangerous creatures!

"These Shzin'tei had never learned to tend orchards or gardens, or even how to build fortresses. They lived in natural caves in the mountains and they raised flocks of … well, like your Little Ones, only these creatures had hairs all over them, like this … " Immersed in the spirit of her tale, Kaitrin yanked the pins out of her hair, quickly disentangled part of the braid, and shook her hair at the audience fiercely. Some of the Alates who had crept closer jumped back in alarm, but Ki'shto'ba exclaimed, *Like what? Like what?*

235

Oh, hell, I'm forgetting that part of my audience is blind. Before she could answer, A'kha'ma'na'ta cried, *I know! I know! Tei told me! It is like those other Star-Beings, with the fuzzy growths all over their bodies! Oh, I would so like to see them, too!*

"The Holy One is right. And, Huge-Head – Commander – No'kri – what I was doing was shaking the fuzzy growth that grows on my head in order to demonstrate."

I thank you for explaining, said Ki'shto'ba, courteously scraping its mandibles.

Kaitrin thought, *I can see this is going to be a very protracted session.* "The fuzzy growth was very thick and long – longer and thicker than mine – and the Little Ones were much bigger than your Little Ones, but they also made a substance like your honeydew. And that is what the Shzin'tei ate. But they also killed some of the Little Ones and ate their bodies."

Oh, no, one never does that, exclaimed the Holy One. *One never kills a Little One and turns it into food! That is forbidden!*

"Then you can see how uncivilized they really were," said Kaitrin. "So it happened that Ul'i'seit and his Warriors came into the land of the Shzin'tei. They approached one of the caves of these people and went in and found no one there. Only a single Zin'tei lived there and he was out with his Little Ones, although some of them were penned in the cave."

What do you mean, 'out with his Little Ones?' asked Di'fa'kro'mi. Kaitrin was sure he was committing this tale to memory.

"These Little Ones are different from yours. They live out-of-doors mostly and must eat fresh grass and leaves outside daily in order to stay strong."

Like the wild Little Ones, said Sei'o'na'sha'ma, eager to show off his knowledge.

And like the Little Ones of my people, the Da'no'no Shshi, said Ki'shto'ba. *They must be taken out frequently to forage, or they languish.*

Nok'ri said, *If the Zin'tei went out with his Little Ones to take care of them, perhaps he was not so terrible a creature after all.*

Struck by this remark, Kaitrin regarded the Worker Chief thoughtfully. "I will let you decide that. Some of Ul'i'seit's Warriors wanted to steal the Little Ones that were in the cave and take them back to their vessels, but Ul'i'seit would not let them. He wanted to wait for the cave's inhabitant to return, hoping that, by the laws of hospitality, he would give them food as a gift.

"But when the giant came in, he made such a horrible racket that he frightened Ul'i'seit and his Warriors, and they ran and hid in the back of the cave. Then the Zin'tei rolled a great rock across the entrance to his cave to keep the Little Ones from escaping while he slept. But that meant that Ul'i'seit and his Warriors also could not escape."

There were general twitches and hops of apprehension. Kaitrin thought with amusement, *Termites do make a very fidgety and restless audience, but I doubt you could find a more responsive one.*

But she was very much aware of Mo'gri'ta'tu, who stood stone-still, only shifting his gaze from herself to the Holy One to Kwi'ga'ga'tei and back again.

Could the Warriors not simply have moved the rock aside? asked a perplexed Ki'shto'ba.

"You are forgetting that the Zin'tei was a giant," said Kaitrin. "He was many, many times larger than you, Huge-Head, and the stone was as big as the top half of this fortress!"

Additional stampings of amazement and fear.

"Then the Zin'tei saw Ul'i'seit and his Warriors! He made a great ruckus and when they spoke to him and asked for hospitality, the Zin'tei seized two of the Warriors in his – claws – and he ate them, bones and all!"

Oh, what a frightening story! cried A'kha'ma'na'ta. *But such an exciting one! Sit closer to me, Sei! Put your head on my neck!*

Touched, Kaitrin watched the King comply with his consort's wishes, even though he probably needed reassurance more than she did. Kaitrin glanced at Kwi'ga'ga'tei. "Is this too frightening a story for me to tell, Holy Seer?"

Oh, do not stop! cried the Holy One. *We all want to know what happens!*

It is satisfactory, said Kwi'ga'ga'tei, but Mo'gri'ta'tu said, *Then you will stay with our Holy One and comfort her when she has unpleasant dreams, Holy Seer?*

I think things exist that might give her worse, said the Seer.

Kaitrin thought, *Huh. More insinuations.* "I will continue," she said. "So, after the Zin'tei ate the two Warriors, he went to sleep, and Ul'i'seit considered killing him with his – with his very large, sharp weapon … "

I was wondering why such a great Warrior would not simply use his mandibles to slay the monster, said Ki'shto'ba.

But he could not! cried Sei'o'na'sha'ma in triumph, *because if they killed him, they would never have been able to roll the stone away from the door!*

"That is exactly right!" said Kaitrin.

How smart you are, Sei! said A'kha'ma'na'ta, nuzzling her King's mouthparts.

"So they hid in the back of the cave and waited. When the giant woke up, he seized two more Warriors and ate them for his first meal, then rolled back the stone, drove the flocks out, and re-placed the stone. He had captured several days' worth of tasty nourishment.

"Then Ul'i'seit came up with a scheme. There was a long tree trunk lying in the cave that the giant used for a – tool. The Warriors cut a sharp point on the end, very weaponlike … " *Shall I have them harden it in fire? I don't think so. They have no concept of controlling fire and I have to get out of here sometime. Besides, if I tell them that fire can be tamed, that could interfere with the natural evolution of their culture.* So Kaitrin continued, "Then they hid this huge weapon under a pile of dung, for, you see, this giant was so uncivilized that he did not even clean his cave.

Exclamations of *Outrageous! Like the Enemy! He truly was a secondary being!*

"When the Zin'tei came back, he again sealed the door of the cave, ate two more Warriors – half of the Warriors that Ul'i'seit had brought with him were now, alas, dead – and then the tricky Chief began to work his scheme." It seemed to Kaitrin that Mo'gri'ta'tu was beginning to pay closer attention. "Now I have to explain something else. The people of my world take fruit and press out the juice and keep it until certain changes happen in this juice, so that if a person drinks it, it makes him feel very pleasant and happy. But if he drinks too much of it, it makes him feel dull and sleepy, and finally it makes him fall sound asleep."

That happens sometimes to the honeydew, said No'kri, *when it is kept too long. It goes bad and addles the senses of those who drink it. We throw it into the dung pit.*

I'll bet that can happen, thought Kaitrin, *what with the high sugar content of that stuff and all the fungus spores floating around here.*

"Well," she said, "the people on my world enjoy drinking this juice and it is not harmful if you do not drink too much. Ul'i'seit had some of this juice with him and he flattered the Zin'tei and offered to give him some to drink. The Zin'tei drank it readily, for it was of an excellent quality. So Ul'i'seit gave him more and more, until the giant said, 'Tell me your name. I would like to give you a gift in return for providing me with such an excellent drink.'

"So crafty Ul'i'seit told him his name was Wei'zei." She paused for effect.

The Holy One said in perplexity, *Wei'zei? But his name is Ul'i'seit, you said. And why would any person be named "Nobody?"*

"Well, you see, that was not really his name. He was tricking the giant. You will find out why soon enough.

"The Zin'tei answered, 'Then I will eat Nobody last, and the rest of you before him! Wei'zei, that is my promised gift to you!' And with that the unnatural creature fell down asleep."

There was an outcry, *Oh, what a trickster! What a dreadful creature! He deserves anything he gets!* But Kaitrin noticed Mo'gri'ta'tu's taunting gaze was fixed on her and she felt more than slightly uncomfortable.

"Then while the Zin'tei was asleep, Ul'i'seit and the remaining Warriors took the sharpened tree trunk and drove it into his eye – his only eye, remember – and made him blind!"

This really caused a sensation. The Holy One groomed her eyes agitatedly. Kwi'ga'ga'tei lost her usual composure and shifted and danced. And Ki'shto'ba said, *Many of us were fated to be blind and we think nothing about it. But if an Alate loses its sight, it is disturbing indeed, so I think Ul'i'seit exacted a severe punishment, even for something as heinous as eating one's guests.*

Oh, dear, thought Kaitrin, *I hadn't thought about how this plot-turn might affect these creatures. But I might as well finish it.*
"The Zin'tei woke up and commenced making such a commotion

that it could be sensed all the way through the stone over the door. Friends who lived in other caves nearby came running to see what was happening. They asked him, 'What is the matter in there? Is somebody harming you? Who is it?'

"But, of course, here is what the Zin'tei answered: 'It is Nobody's work that is doing this to me! Nobody is doing me harm!'"

As this sank in, Kaitrin experienced a very strange phenomenon. The Shshi commenced to bounce themselves up and down with little springs of their forelegs, spinning their antennae in wild circles so that any words they were transmitting were broadcast unintelligibly in all directions. They swung their heads in U-shaped motions. Even Kwi'ga'ga'tei participated in this exercise, and the Commander Hi'ta'fu was somewhat ponderously caught up. Mo'gri'ta'tu, however, only gave a couple of tiny hops and held his antennae motionless.

Clever! said Di'fa'kro'mi. *Most entertaining!*

"Nobody" did it to me – *That is quite humorous!* said Ki'shto'ba, using a word Kaitrin had never encountered before, but whose meaning seemed clear from the context.

It was a revelation. *This must be how they laugh! The Shshi have a sense of humor! I never would have thought it! What a gift to discover this!*

Gleefully, she continued. "When his neighbors took the Zin'tei's words, they said, 'If nobody is harming you, then you must be calling out because you are sick and we cannot help you, so we will go away and pray to the spirit beings, for they are the only ones who can help you.' And they went away.

"Then the Zin'tei pushed back the stone so he could get some air, but he sat with his forelegs outstretched – he had four limbs just as I do – ready to grab any Warrior who tried to escape from the cave. So the always clever Ul'i'seit bound the Little Ones together three abreast – remember, they are much larger than your Little Ones and they stand up off the ground on longer legs – and he slung one of his Warriors under the middle one of each group of three, and bound himself under the belly of the largest one. With the cave entrance open, all the Little Ones began to run out.

"As they did so, the blind Zin'tei felt each one to be sure nothing else was there. But he could feel nothing because he could not reach the bellies of the middle Little Ones, and the really long

240

hairs of the big one that carried Ul'i'seit hung down like curtains and hid the Warrior Chief completely. So they all escaped, captured the Little Ones, and drove them to their ocean boxes.

"But wait – the story is not quite over yet. Ul'i'seit could not take his victory quietly. He taunted the Zin'tei from his ocean box, saying, 'That is the punishment you must have for violating the law of hospitality and eating your guests!' And the Zin'tei picked up a piece of rock the size of one of your storage cysts and flung it at the box, barely missing it and causing a huge motion of the water that almost turned the box upside down.

"And still Ul'i'seit was not satisfied. He spoke out his real name. 'I want you to know who did this to you! I am Ul'i'seit the Champion of the Great War that my people have just won! It is Ul'i'seit who has punished you for your evil deeds!'

"Then the Zin'tei said, 'So! A prophecy has been fulfilled! A great Seer once told me that a person named Ul'i'seit would one day make me blind!' It so happens that the, uh … " *Good grief, how to say 'Neptune, the god of the ocean'?* " … the King of this Zin'tei's Highest Mother was in charge of the ocean that Ul'i'seit was about to cross. And so the Zin'tei said, 'But the *na'sha'ma|* can heal my eye. If you will come here to me, I will give you a gift and ask the *na'sha'ma|* to allow you to cross the ocean safely.'

"But Ul'i'seit answered, 'I would rather see you die, because you are not to be trusted and the *na'sha'ma|* will never be willing to heal you.'

"So then the Zin'tei called upon the Ocean King to put a curse on Ul'i'seit. He said, 'Make it so that he will never reach his home, or, if he does, let him come alone, with all his friends dead, and find nothing but trouble in his home after he gets there.'

"But Ul'i'seit in his pride would not believe that curse, either, and, still taunting the Zin'tei, returned to his travels on the ocean. But there was truth in it, as it turned out. Ul'i'seit did in fact get home, but only after much loss and many more hard adventures, and his homecoming was not a happy one."

Kaitrin stopped. She was getting really fatigued; the caffeine had worn off and lack of sleep was taking its toll. She had created the language, but this was the longest she had ever tried to keep her brain attuned to it and her mind was feeling numb and sluggish.

Is that the end of it? said A'kha'ma'na'ta.

"That is the end of it."

You said Ul'i'seit had more adventures. Tell another one, Ru!

"Oh ... not now, Holy One."

I want another story! It is new! Di'fa'kro'mi, you never have any new stories. I want another new one!

Kwi'ga'ga'tei took charge. *Holy One, Ru'a'ma'na'ta must be tired. She needs to return to her friends. Perhaps she will come again, tomorrow when the suntime starts. Ru'a'ma'na'ta, will that be possible?*

She had told Griffen, one more time. "Yes, I will come then." *Oh, dear, I'll have to figure out another story to tell! How did I get myself into this?*

Mo'gri'ta'tu was saying, *Besides, it is time for you to eat, Holy One.*

Oh, eat, eat! It is all I do! Ru, do you have to eat all the time in order to lay proper eggs? I am tired of it!

Kaitrin giggled into her hand. "No, Holy One, I do not have to eat all the time."

Your people are so lucky! You must tell me more of your people – how they produce their eggs and how they care for them. I do not think I understand all of this yet. Tenders had gathered around the head of the Holy One, regurgitating gobbets of food into her mouth, infusing her with big sloshes of honeydew that dribbled off her palps.

When you're a Shi, thought Kaitrin giddily, watching the quiver of A'kha'ma'na'ta's antennae, *you don't have to worry about talking with your mouth full.*

But Kwi'ga'ga'tei was still thinking about Kaitrin's tale. *The Zin'tei offered a gift but Ul'i'seit would not trust him, preferring rather to wish him evil. It is then that the Zin'tei curses him. Perhaps if Ul'i'seit had chosen to trust him, he would have avoided being cursed.*

Kaitrin regarded the Seer stupidly, too woolly-brained to embark on a discussion that ordinarily she would have relished.

But Mo'gri'ta'tu said, *It is far more likely that the giant would have killed him. Better to wish evil now and take what you can than to trust anyone to do good for you.*

Both Kaitrin and Kwi'ga'ga'tei looked at the Chamberlain, and the Seer said, *I believe that has ever been a principle of yours, Mo'gri'ta'tu.*

Perhaps one day you will wish you had made it one of yours, Most Holy Seer.

Sparks of animosity could almost be seen crackling between the Seer and the Chamberlain.

Then Kwi'ga'ga'tei turned away. *Come, Ru'a'ma'na'ta, I have asked Ki'shto'ba to conduct you back to your dwelling.*

As Kaitrin was leaving, the Holy One called after her, *You will come back, Ru? I think that Tei is right and Gri and Fum are wrong! Beings who tell such fine tales cannot have evil in them! Gri, you and the Commander, go away! You are too gloomy. Tei, you stay, and Dit. I want to talk about this tale. I want both of you to help me understand its larger meanings.*

Chapter 22

Macbeth: They have tied me to a stake, I cannot fly
But bearlike I must fight the course ...
– *from* William Shakespeare, *Macbeth*

[Mo'gri'ta'tu and Hi'ta'fu hurry along the corridor]

[Mo'gri'ta'tu]: She dismisses us like insubordinate nymphs! For five season-cycles I have been her Chamberlain, since before the Nasute Siege, since the time of Thei'ga'na'sha'ma, and she dismisses me like some novice Tender who licks her dung hole!

[Hi'ta'fu]: Restrain your sending, Chamberlain! Do you want your rage broadcast to the whole fortress? What has become of your subtlety?

[Mo'gri'ta'tu]: I have no subtlety left! The dastardly Seer will move against me soon – I can feel it! Mocking me with my own words! Spouting pious platitudes about trust when obviously she plots my downfall! I tell you, I will not stomach it! This is running toward open rebellion! I can see it now!

[Hi'ta'fu, in misery]: Chamberlain, not that kind of treachery, I implore you ...

[Mo'gri'ta'tu]: Treachery is treachery, Commander, no matter how you gloss it!

[Hi'ta'fu]: That is not how you recruited me to this!

[They reach Mo'gri'ta'tu's quarters and enter. Hi'ta'fu is

244

much relieved to be behind stone because the Chamberlain is still raging]

[Mo'gri'ta'tu]: *I think Tei is right. Go away, Gri, you are too gloomy! People who tell such fine tales cannot be evil!* It is all the work of this insidious female stranger! She is even subtler than I thought – too good at word games! Did it never strike you, old Warrior, that victories are won with words, not force? You cannot understand that, can you? Kwi'ga'ga'tei understands it! I understand it! And this female meddler in the affairs of our noble fortress – this worm of a secondary creation – understands it! Who would have thought it? Well, I am ready to try your way! Open force! I want this female killed and I want Kwi'ga'ga'tei dead! No poison! No subterfuge! I want them torn apart!

[Hi'ta'fu, dances, emits terror and distress pheromones]: Mo'gri'ta'tu! Do not speak like this! I cannot have a part in open murder!

[Mo'gri'ta'tu]: Why do you find it so much worse than hidden murder? Are you so eager to save your own life? I thought it was Lo'ro'ra you cared about, not the aching body of a worn-out Warrior who cannot even fight its own battles any longer!

[Hi'ta'fu postures, tossing its head, agonizing]

[Mo'gri'ta'tu]: You and I will both be finished unless we take action. The only way to keep our power is to cut down the spirit of the opposition and seize control. If Kwi'ga'ga'tei is dead and the female stranger as well, the Holy One and the King will have no one to turn to except us. The Seer has no friends who are not timid weaklings.

[Hi'ta'fu]: What of Ki'shto'ba? And Sa'ti'a'i'a?

[Mo'gri'ta'tu]: Do we not still have Lo'lo'pai and the First Cohort on our side? Why do you think I recruited the Chief? I admit, it is not fully dependable, but its Lieutenants follow it like pet Little Ones, as it does you. And the Warriors follow the Lieutenants the same way. Strange how Shshi are constituted, but you would never think it strange, so no matter.

[Hi'ta'fu]: You mean, you plan for a contingent of us to fight Ki'shto'ba? And the Nasutes? Because every member of the

Nasute Cohort will back up its Chief.

[Mo'gri'ta'tu]: What else does open rebellion mean? Excise the rotten parts! Send the body of the so-called Champion to the Charnel Hall, and its stone-head to the dung pit! Even Ki'shto'ba cannot defeat eighteen Warriors, including you and Lo'lo'pai, attacking it all at once. If some die, they have given their lives for the good of Lo'ro'ra and will be remembered forever as heroes!

[Hi'ta'fu]: But if the Nasutes are there as well …

[Mo'gri'ta'tu]: They will not be. Kwi'ga'ga'tei is using Sa'ti'a'i'a and its Cohort to guard the Alates' Holies, her own quarters, the entrances to the Holy Chamber, that kind of thing. So here is my plan. The female Star-Being said she would return tomorrow morning. Order A'gwa'ji to be occupied elsewhere – in the exercise yard, perhaps, reviewing the training of its troops. You should yourself beg off attending the Holy One. It will not be difficult since A'kha'ma'na'ta thinks you are gloomy and has for the moment become indifferent to you. I myself must attend to defer suspicion. Station yourself and Lo'lo'pai and your strongest Warriors in those little storage rooms off the corridor outside the entrance to the Holy Chamber.

[Hi'ta'fu, grooming and scraping in absolute misery]: What of the outer guard?

[Mo'gri'ta'tu]: Is your brain even weaker than I suspected? Are you not the Commander? Make sure trusted members of the First Cohort are stationed there at the proper time. The female one and Ki'shto'ba will leave the Holy Chamber together; if we are lucky, Kwi'ga'ga'tei will come out with them. If she remains in the chamber – well, we can deal with that. When the female and Ki'shto'ba enter the corridor, have your Warriors leap upon them and take down the Huge-Head at once. Set Lo'lo'pai the task of killing the female with one swift slash. If Kwi'ga'ga'tei comes with them, I want her dead, too. If she does not emerge with them, she may run out to see what the disturbance is, in which case, you can kill her then; or she may escape out one of the back entrances of the Holy Chamber. In that last case, we will hunt her down …

[Hi'ta'fu, twisting its head, snapping its mandibles open and shut]: We are to make this kind of battle within the fortress, outside the Holy Chamber? *Ai-i,* Nameless Mother – *ai-i,* Nameless Mother ... What if I say I will not do it?

[Mo'gri'ta'tu]: Have you really grown so feeble? More feeble even than gossip reputes? If you cannot carry out this simple act of cleansing for the good of your fortress and of your beloved Holy One and King, perhaps you really do not deserve that place in my governing council when I take the power! Perhaps I should go to the Holy One and the King and tell them the truth about you and Chief Lo'lo'pai – that it was a plot of your own devising to assassinate the female's *na'sha'ma*| that day in the marches, against the express orders of the Holy One! In the tale told this very day, a One Being was blinded for violating the code of hospitality. What do you think would happen to you? Death, perhaps – but worse yet – dishonor!

[Hi'ta'fu, standing stone still, head twisted downward, mandibles wedged underneath the thorax.]: I know it now. It is you who are evil, Mo'gri'ta'tu. I should have understood that your words were hollow and self-serving – never should I have attended to them! I should have accepted my fate of being supplanted by those who are younger and stronger – does it not come to all Champions? But I am a plain, blunt Warrior who knows only force, not words, even as you say. You have caught me. I could go to Kwi'ga'ga'tei and tell her about your intents, but you would still find some other way to twist things to your will. You have caught me. I will do as you ask. But I will never let harm come to the Holy One, as long as there is a twitch of life left in my body!

[Mo'gri'ta'tu]: Nor I! My purpose – and however disingenuous you think my words, this much is true – my purpose would never be to harm the Holy One! Such a thing smells of unthinkable horror. It proclaims the death decree for the Shshi Way of Life.

[Hi'ta'fu]: It would not surprise me if you promoted such a death decree. But no matter. I have been defeated. I will engage in this enterprise of desperation. I will go speak to Lo'lo'pai and condemn it yet again to serve your unholy cause.

*　　　*　　　*

[The Commander, in its black chamber, waits for Lo'lo'pai]

We are all set upon the path to doom. That eruption of the fortress that Kwi'ga'ga'tei saw – who was to think that I, who love this home of mine and its Holy One and King more than my life, would be an agent of the destruction! For it is I as much as that depraved, self-serving Alate. I could have stopped this at any time – I could stop it now. But I am tainted. Confusion taints me. Warriors were not created to fight this kind of word-magic. Am I to go to A'kha'ma'na'ta and say, *I betrayed you. I, who have guarded and protected you for twelve years, have betrayed you*? I am too ashamed! Better to make the treachery palpable – let all see it and then take my punishment and die, as I know I will.

One of my foulest crimes is to have ensnared Lo'lo'pai in this. Lo'lo'pai is an honorable Warrior and I am fond of it, yet I have used its debt to me to corrupt it. I cannot expect it to act against orders – it is not the nature of our Caste to think independently. In that, Mo'gri'ta'tu is right. And if I do not engage it, Mo'gri'ta'tu will accuse it to the Holy One of purposefully attacking the outland *na'sha'ma|* and it will be outcast or its life will be forfeit.

I have only one comfort – the Chamberlain may not win. He may be defeated. His schemes have continually been foiled; this one may be no different. Kwi'ga'ga'tei is not a fool; neither is Ki'shto'ba nor the Nasute Chief. The female Star-Being – I do not understand her role in this or even what she is. Her death would not trouble me greatly, except that the Seer seems to attach great importance to her.

But if Kwi'ga'ga'tei should prevail and kill us all – if Mo'gri'ta'tu should perish – then Lo'ro'ra will be cleansed indeed. Then the evil Chamberlain will get the wish he spouts so facilely! If I can live to see this unnatural Alate's downfall, then even if I die dishonored, I will die happy, because I will have saved Lo'ro'ra after all.

In that case, why do I not simply spring upon the creature and tear him apart myself?

Kill a Star-Winged Alate! My gut shudders at such sacrilege! It transgresses all that Shshi are taught from the egg's hatching!

And yet I have agreed to kill Kwi'ga'ga'tei …

[Guard, outside the entrance]: Commander Hi'ta'fu, here is Chief Lo'lo'pai.

[Hi'ta'fu]: Nameless One, take pity! Do I dare even invoke you? Let the Chief come in.

[The guards roll back the stone and Lo'lo'pai enters the darkness of the chamber]

[Lo'lo'pai]: Commander, I sense much emotion from you – fear, distress, confusion. What is happening now?

[Hi'ta'fu]: Lo'lo'pai, the Holy One dismissed both me and Mo'gri'ta'tu from her presence. We fail to please her, at least at the moment.

[Lo'lo'pai]: Commander! What can have provoked such a reprimand?

[Hi'ta'fu]: As always, the Seer and this one whom you failed to kill in the Gardens.

[Lo'lo'pai]: The female Star-Being? It is said that she pleased Akh'a'ma'na'ta with a fine tale. Perhaps that has only distracted the Holy One. She suffers grievously from boredom.

[Hi'ta'fu]: Lo'lo'pai, you promised to discharge your debt to me in the Fungus Gardens and you failed ...

[Lo'lo'pai, grovels]: I know. I know. And I am half afraid to ask what new charge you would put upon me.

[Hi'ta'fu]: The Chamberlain's schemes have been unsuccessful. He wants to take more direct means.

[Lo'lo'pai]: Direct means? I do not understand.

[Hi'ta'fu]: The Chamberlain would initiate a battle within the fortress – open rebellion, Lo'lo'pai. I will not sweeten it.

[Lo'lo'pai]: Open rebellion!

[Hi'ta'fu]: We are to attack the female Star-Being and Ki'shto'ba as they issue from the Holy Chamber tomorrow and we are to kill the Seer as well if she is with them. If not ...

[Lo'lo'pai, with growing horror]: What? Kill the Seer? A

Star-Winged Alate? The Holy Seer?

[Hi'ta'fu]: You knew the plan all along was to rid Lo'ro'ra …

[Lo'lo'pai, grooms distractedly]: Mo'gri'ta'tu promised that Warriors would not have to kill Holy Alates with their own weapons! I have no objection to killing Ki'shto'ba, even by less than honorable means; it should never have been brought here. And the outland female – I do not know what I should think about her – but to kill a Star-Winged Alate? The Holy Seer? *tha'sask|>||* Highest Mother! Commander, do you really support that course?

[Hi'ta'fu, also grooms and grovels]: The Seer may not emerge from the Chamber with the others. Today she did not. If she does not, she will be destroyed some other way. But if she does, perhaps we can make it appear that she was caught in the midst of the fighting and killed by accident. However that may be, your role is to kill the female Strange One promptly, then turn and help us take out Ki'shto'ba. It will require at least ten of our Warriors to insure success. I need you to adjust the scheduling – make sure the outer portal of the Holy Chamber is protected by guards from the First Cohort. Give them orders that if they witness a skirmish beginning in the corridor, they are to join us, not try to prevent us. And for our attack unit find me your most obedient Lieutenants and any young, powerful Warrior eager to make a name for itself, for if this succeeds, they will surely take honor. It will be better if you do not tell them that the Seer might be killed in the altercation. Only you and I must …

[Lo'lo'pai]: Honor! There cannot be much honor to be had in this enterprise!

[Hi'ta'fu]: Lo'lo'pai, the Highest Mother knows I wish you only good. But again I call upon your debt to me. I do not consider that you have ever failed me willfully. I put great faith and trust in you! Can you find enough faith and trust in me, your Commander and mentor, to follow me one more time?

[Lo'lo'pai]: Commander, you know I am loyal to you, as my Warriors are to me. I will follow wherever you lead – prove once and for all that my loyalty to you is beyond question!

[Hi'ta'fu, to himself thinks, *You are a fool, my good friend Lo'lo'pai. But so am I a fool and I desperately need a friend, and so I will accept the loyalty of a fool and drag both of us down to our doom.*]

Chapter 23

Your grieving moonlight face looks down
Through the forest of my fears,
Crowned with a spiny bramble-crown,
Bedewed with evening tears. ...

The black trees shudder, dropping snow,
The stars tumble and spin.
Speak, speak, or how may a child know
His ancestral sin?

       – from Robert Graves, *Reproach*

Kaitrin burst into the flyer, stamping her feet to shake off the mud left by a thunderstorm. "I have just had the most remarkable experience of my entire lifetime! I'll never forget it as long as I live! Griff, are you all right? How long was I? Almost four hours? That's not bad, considering everything I ... But let me get cleaned up! God, I'm tired! My brain's in a fog! Have you got anything to eat? We'll get to that later! I've got to clean up – the stench in the Holy Chamber is the most appalling of anywhere! I certainly am glad my sense of smell isn't as acute as yours, Luku! Here, take the cam – I got some fabulous pictures of the Queen ..."

She disappeared into the sleeping compartment. Her companions looked at one another, laughing. With a squawk, A'a'ma remarked, "Something tells me we are going to hear quite a lot about this!"

252

"Cannot wait to hear!" said Luku, rushing out to offload the contents of the cam.

But Griffen followed Kaitrin into their compartment. She was shedding her clothes, dropping them on the floor and yanking on her robe. "This robe is getting washed to death. Every time I put it on for the shower, it smells awful afterward."

Griffen was collecting her garments from the floor to take to the laundry and she paused momentarily to look at him. "Griff, are you all right?" she repeated

"Oh, quite," he said lightly. "I told you I was getting accustomed to this. Was this ... ? Are you going back?"

"I promised them one more time. Tomorrow morning. I told Kwi'ga'ga'tei it will be the last. She accepted it. So, you see, sometimes I keep my word."

He came and stopped her frenetic dashing about, and hugged her. "Oh, Kait. You always do."

"Well, I try. I guess that's about all we can do sometimes, isn't it?"

He kissed her below the ear, his breath trembling warm on her neck. "I think ... Yes, that's about – all we can do ... " Then, "Why is your hair down? Did you let them nibble it after all?"

"Oh, that! I used it as a visual aid! The Queen – wait till you hear about the Queen! – she's so incredible! Di'fa'kro'mi narrated the Shshi Creation Story and then the Queen asked me to tell a tale. Guess what I told them! Odysus and the Cyclops! Do you know that story?"

"Indeed!" Griffen laughed, his hands plowing her hair, holding her face against his shoulder. "Did you really tell them that? That must have been – incredibly remarkable!"

"I was trying to make them understand what sheep were, so I shook my hair at them to illustrate what a woolly animal is like. Scared some of them!" She laughed immoderately, then kissed him swiftly on the mouth and pulled out of his embrace. "Let me get cleaned up, and then I hope there'll be something to eat. While we're eating, I mean to tell all of you the whole amazing story. And then I'm crazy to go to bed! Did you get any more sleep?"

"Not really. I was ... I did rest for a while. Tried to do some report work. Didn't make much progress."

She glanced at him, but she was still under the spell of her experience. "I'm off to take one of those frustrating showers," she said. "At least I can wash my hair with water!" And she skipped out.

*   *   *

The nine members of the team gathered around the table for a meal Julian and Arti had concocted – a stew of soy nuggets, tinned string beans, and frozen squash thickened with tomato-spice flour. It was accompanied by *gusota* plums, a hard-husked Quornat fruit that contained sweet, juicy flesh and would keep almost indefinitely. Sitting between Gwidian and Luku, cleaned up and somewhat refreshed, Kaitrin talked about her adventure. "The vids I brought back actually don't do justice to the reality – they mostly show the Queen head-on. She's three meters long and the belly is a meter in diameter – truly an immobilized physogastric Queen – unbelievable! Exactly like Prf. Lindeman's vid, only smaller in proportion to the Workers. She really is hideous – the belly is a kind of a deathly yellowish color with brownish segment stripes and a slimy shine. And it surges and ripples all the time – enough to make you seasick. And she stinks! They've got her on a nest of leaves – I wonder if they ever change them … I suspect they do. They're really very clean in their own way. The Tenders were grooming her the whole time I was there."

"How would they move her to change the bedding?" asked A'a'ma.

"I don't know. There's a lot I don't know that I would like to find out. Now, Griffen, I know – we're going to leave any moment! Some of this will have to wait for the next expedition. My guess is, they roll her over. Do you know, it's a lot like taking care of an invalid, a bedfast invalid. I wonder if she gets pressure sores. She's been shut up in that cavern – a tomb, really – for over thirty-six years. Can you imagine?"

"I shudder!" said Luku.

"Kind of pathetic, isn't it?" said Will, staring at his fruit.

"You know, it really is," said Kaitrin. "A'kha'ma'na'ta, the Mother of Lo'ro'ra, the Holy One. And do you know what? She's a child! A complete child!"

"How could she be not?" said Trea. "She does not know the world at all."

Kaitrin said, "She's so hungry for new experiences and so eager to be entertained. She has playthings. Somebody had once brought her some feathers – she wanted to show them to me, but they had been put away. She was confused and thought I was supposed to be feathered. She wanted to see the new creature who has feathers, Tió'otu."

"I would go in if I could," said A'a'ma. "I feel I am missing a lot on this expedition. I think I am getting a little old for this kind of primary encounter."

"Hardly, my old grand-bird! But here is this – this ghastly, puerile breeding machine – this weary, bored child – sitting there convinced she rules the fortress; and here are all these vigilant courtiers around her, who are fully aware of how important she is to their fortress's survival but who take advantage of her to carry out their intrigues – and I'm sure there are intrigues. In some ways this place reminds me of a Talian city-state of the First Renaissance. It's a very unusual culture – primitive technologically, but quite sophisticated on a behavioral level – unique in Confederation experience, I think … " Kaitrin stuffed a bite of cracker bread and a couple of spoonfuls of stew into her mouth and chewed for a moment, then gulped water.

Griffen, who had been listening in silence as he so often did, said, "What of the King?"

"Oh, yes, the King. Sei'o'na'sha'ma. He's about a meter and a half long, with dark stripes – much less repulsive. He seems devoted to his mate – they nuzzled a lot. He reminds me of an adolescent. He is her fourth King, I think. I believe he's maybe only five years old. The Nasute War was three years ago, and this King came into the picture after that. It takes about two years for the nymphs to mature. I think Kwi'ga'ga'tei must be about seven. She became Seer near the end of the Nasute War. Mo'gri'ta'tu – that creepy character! – is older – maybe ten or eleven. He was the Queen's Chamberlain during the War. Hi'ta'fu is pretty old – it has been Commander for twelve years, so it must have had several years of subordinate command before that. It may be as old as twenty years. I'd say, except for the Queen, twenty years is about the limit of the Shshi's lifespan. It's sad, really."

As they all pondered her words, Griffen said, "Tell them about your storytelling, Kait."

"Oh, yes! There was some talk of how the Shshi were created, so Di'fa'kro'mi related their Creation Myth for me!"

Tió'otu chirped ecstatically and Kaitrin continued, "Isn't it exciting? For everyone's information, there is nothing that cultural anthros relish more than recording the Creation Myths of newly discovered ILFs! But then the Queen said she was tired of the old stories, and wouldn't I tell one? So I told them the tale of Odysus and the Cyclops. Do you all know that one?"

The tale was familiar to the Earthers and A'a'ma was well versed in the lore of his adopted planet, but neither Luku nor the Pozú were acquainted with it, so Kaitrin gave them a quick summary, emphasizing the amusing parts. "Guess what? These creatures have a sense of humor! They got the 'Nobody' pun without any trouble at all and they exhibited a certain body language that can only be equivalent to laughter – whirling their antennae in a circle and bouncing. That was the biggest revelation of the whole session!"

"Well, I'll be," said Arti. "I had them pegged as really earnest, gloomy, humorless little beasties!"

"They do give that impression sometimes," said Kaitrin.

"I didn't see anything of that on your holoimage," said A'a'ma.

"I know! The minicam only picked up what was in front of me. By the time I thought to twist around, the episode was over. The next time we come here, we've got to get more than one person into that fortress. What's the matter, Griffen?"

He had shifted uneasily in his chair. "Nothing. This talk of another expedition – it makes me a bit nervous, that's all."

Kaitrin eyed him in concerned perplexity. "Well, you know there will be one sometime. Eat, Griff. Your stew is getting cold."

He hunched over the table and dutifully took a bite.

"Are you feeling all right?" she said.

"Just – fatigued … The short sleep and all. I thought you were tired."

"Well, I've passed tired. I'm so keyed up, I'm not quite ready to go to bed yet – I don't think I could sleep. You go ahead if you want to."

"No, no, I'll wait for you. I wouldn't want to miss anything."

Kaitrin continued to regard him. He had seemed in control

ever since she got back, but something indefinable about him disturbed her. She glanced at Trea, but the doctor was biting into a chunk of *gusota* fruit.

"Anyway," said Kaitrin, "I've been conned into going back in the morning and giving the Queen another story. I'll have to get up in time to figure out what to tell – I want to be better prepared than I was today. She wants another Ul'i'seit tale. Maybe I could do Silla and Karybdis, or … I don't know. I'll have to think.

"But I told Kwi'ga'ga'tei that I would come back only one more time. I'm well aware we're going to have to leave soon. In fact, I think maybe we should leave as soon as the *Featherlight* gets back. Is that satisfactory with everybody?"

Griffen had looked up eagerly and A'a'ma said, "Gwidian talked to me about the possibility and I have no objection. We've collected so much data that I think it will take a year just to process and publish everything."

"I'm really sad about it," said Kaitrin. "I still have this feeling that something isn't finished. Maybe it's because the Shshi are so short-lived and I've become so fond of Kwi'ga'ga'tei. I have this fear that I'll never see her again. But I know we have to go. Griffen, I want to go."

He had been regarding her with an intensity that was almost pathetic; now he turned his gaze back to his nearly full bowl. Kaitrin watched him with continuing perplexity. The adrenaline was beginning to dissipate and she sighed and commenced eating her fruit rapidly.

"You have not told the Creation Myth," said A'a'ma.

"Oh, I do want to do that before we finish up here. It's a sort of variant on the Cosmic Egg plus the Divine Female as Creator …"

Tió'otu interrupted. "The !Ka<tí are birds, but we do not have a Cosmic Egg myth. Instead, we have Creation by Song! When He'etí and Chu'umí♫♫ sang their first love duet together, the universe came into existence! ♫♪♫ "

"Beautiful!" said Kaitrin. "I've always loved that!"

"Then they made a nest - our planet – and Chu'umí♫♫ proceeded to lay two eggs, but He'etí was hungry so he tried to eat one of them. Desperate to save her progeny, Chu'umí♫♫ attacked her mate and in the ensuing scuffle the egg was thrown out into the sky where it immediately hatched into a star – Krisí'i'aid's sun. Then the other egg hatched and out came the first of us !Ka<tí. That is why in myth our sun is sometimes called 'Tigáchichet' – that is, 'Sibling.' But the everyday name for our sun came later out of a different myth – 'Chuzaw<,' which means 'Mother Fire.'"

Kaitrin grinned. "You Bird people have excellent myths, Tió'otu! Anyway, the myth of the Shshi starts with a Creatrix – the Highest-Mother-Who-Has-No-Name – filling up the sky and eating her impregnator. So it seems even among insects we find the motif of the sacrificed king. It's reflected in contemporary Shshi culture when the King is killed and eaten by his successor. Actually, that act is a genetic imperative – it seems to play a role in ensuring fertility. But back to the myth … After insemination, the pregnant Creatrix gave birth to the stars, so you can see why our coming from the stars made such an impact. But soon there were too many stars, so she cast some of them down to the ground, where they became the first Alates – the Star-Winged Alates. Isn't that a charming etiology for the luminescent wings?

"Then two of the Alates copulated and started the first fortress. But a taboo was put on them; nobody – and I should say that all Castes had eyes at first – nobody was ever allowed to look at the stars except the Alates. Of course, an Unnatural Worker and an Unnatural Warrior – that is, ones that don't conform to the requisite code of behavior – as well as the Queen and King themselves, violated that taboo. So the Nameless Mother punished them – one of those divine punishments for transgression against an arbitrary and even meaningless stricture. She made the Queen's belly swell so that she was rendered physically incapable of coming above ground, and she ripped out the eyes of the Workers and the Warriors so it became impossible for either of those Castes to ever disobey that command again. That, of course, only augments the Alates' power. They were the only ones who never transgressed. I think it's likely that it was Alates who invented the myth. They are definitely the most canny of the Castes."

A'a'ma said, "That business of the god who punishes because a meaningless taboo is broken – the Wéwana have a tale like that. Their chief gods are water gods – swamp gods, to be specific. When these gods made feathered creatures, they all drowned because their feathers became waterlogged. So the gods commanded that they should nest on high platforms in trees – much like terrestrial storks! – from which they could easily take flight above the swamps. But later some of these birds made their way to drier land and began nesting on the ground, so to punish them the god Tak'korúkh took away their power of flight. To this day the Wéwana nest on platforms two meters high and consider an egg to be violated if it touches the ground. So superstitious." A'a'ma shook his head in resignation at the follies of his fellow ornithoids.

"That kind of taboo violation was central to the old religion of the god Yawa," said Kaitrin, "and also to the cult of Jesu that had so much influence, both positive and negative, in the First and Second Millennia."

"I'm a little familiar with that," said Will. "My grandmother used to tell me some of the Romish stories – that one about the Tree of Knowledge and the serpent."

"Yes, that's what I was thinking of," said Kaitrin. "It's in the ancient mythohistorical compilation commonly known as the Bibel. After we had that discussion of religion on the ship, I reviewed some of those myths – my knowledge had gotten sadly rusty! But this was it: The First Man and the First Woman – Adem and Eva – were forbidden to eat the fruit, usually called an apple, of that Tree of Knowledge that you mentioned, Will. But the serpent, who embodied the Devil – that is, the force of evil – tempted them to do it, or rather tempted Eva, and after she transgressed, she wheedled Adem into eating it, too. I've never thought that was quite fair, to put the blame for the male's sin onto the female."

"Well," said Tió'otu, "the myth originated in a patriarchal culture. Earth's culture has long had a patriarchal bias. Even today plenty of remnants of that exist."

"How were they punished?" asked Gwidian in such a strange, tight tone that everyone looked at him.

"They immediately realized they were naked," said Kaitrin. "The phenomenon of sexual prudery entered the human psyche at that moment! And they were cast out of the beautiful garden land that Yawa had created for them and made to work for a living. That's probably the worst punishment! No more free food and loafing about in paradise!"

There was general laughter. Kaitrin continued, "But actually the truly serious result, at least according to some branches of the Kristen culture, was that every human soul was left tainted by that one disobedience – the 'Original Sin,' the Romish Church called it – and it left Earthers with a need to be redeemed. So when that son of Maria came along, the one supposedly fathered by Yawa, he was seen as the Redeemer of humankind. He took their sins – not just Original Sin but all sins – upon his own head, willingly suffered a painful death to atone for them, and was resurrected after three days and taken in bodily form into Yawa's heavenly kingdom. That's where I mixed up the idea of Mery and Eva – it was Maria who ultimately crushed the serpent that had deceived humankind. The god allowed her to be born without the taint of Original Sin, so she would be a perfect vessel to give birth to his son, the Redeemer. And that's part of how the religion of Jesu-worship came about.

"Actually, of course, it's the same old concept of the seasonal god-king who is sacrificed and reborn in order to keep the wheel of life turning, only deepened and abstracted, with a lot of the goddess/fertility-role stuff blotted out. It introduced the concept of forgiveness of sins – atonement, absolution … If you repent your misdeeds with the right spirit, your soul will be saved from further punishment. There is something quite appealing about that, although the whole dogmatic system became so corrupted over time that we're undoubtedly better off today without that religion."

Kaitrin saw Trea make a little movement. The Pozú was looking at Gwidian, and Kaitrin followed her gaze. Griffen had sat back, pressing against his chair as if a force were leaning into him. There was a hollow, unnerved look in his eyes.

He said, "Do you think that kind of forgiveness exists? Unqualified? Do you think a man can be forgiven in that way?"

Kaitrin ran a hand over her face, pushed distractedly at her hair. *There that is again – forgiveness …* "Actually, it's all metaphorical," she said. "I've told you, Griffen, my own beliefs lie firmly in the camp of the Mythmakers – the concept of personal responsibility … "

"But it speaks to needs," said Trea softly.

"Actually, a patriarchal god like that," said Arti Robb, "it seems to me a hell of a lot more forgiveness would come from a Mother Goddess than from a male god. Personally, I've always believed that mothers will forgive their children anything. I know mine would."

Trea leaned forward sharply. Griffen had gotten up, stumbling against his chair. Then he turned and entered the sleeping compartment, closing the door hard behind him.

"What in the world … ?" said Kaitrin stupidly. Her fatigue was overwhelming her and everything seemed difficult and incomprehensible.

Trea said urgently, "Kaitrin, go in to him."

Kaitrin looked at her.

"Go in to him, Kaitrin. He needs you."

"Oh! What in the world … ? All right." Under the concerned eyes of the rest of the team, Kaitrin got up and followed Griffen into their compartment.

There, the light was dim, set on night-level. Griffen was sitting on the bed. Peering uncertainly at him, she said, "Griff, what's the matter? Did Arti's remark about male gods insult your … ?"

Then she detected a sound and certain movements going through him. "Griff, are you sick at your stomach? You hardly ate … "

She brightened the lights. He was bent over, his head locked between his arms, his body shuddering.

"Griffen!" She realized then that he was crying, not a mere trickle of tears, but desperate, wrenching sobs. She went to sit beside him, clutching his shoulder. "Griffen, what in the world? What's the matter? Griff, don't do this! You're scaring me! Stop!"

He only sobbed more uncontrollably. She shook him a little. "Griffen, I don't know how to cope with this. I don't know what to do." She tried to put her arms around him, pull him to her, but he resisted, keeping his head down almost between his knees.

"What set this off? We were talking about forgiveness – that same old thing – and Arti made that remark about mothers being more forgiving than fathers … Griffen!"

This precipitated a long-drawn breath that Kaitrin would have sworn was the breath of one who was dying. "Stop, Griff! Can't you talk to me? Can't you tell me what it is that sets you off like this? Only never this bad before … I just can't understand."

He gasped her name, clutching her left hand and holding it against his forehead so that she could feel the wedding ring pressing into his skull.

"Does it have something to do with your parents' death? Your mother? Griff, stop shaking like that! It does, doesn't it? Something you need forgiveness for. What happened, Griffen? Have you told me the truth? Did your parents really die the way you said, or is there something else?"

"No," he said, so brokenly that she could barely understand him. "No, I swear ... they died ... the way I told you ... I don't lie to you, Kait ... I swear ... "

"Well, then, why would you feel guilty about anything related to that? So what is it?" She was tired, and getting more tired and stressed, and she was getting exasperated. "You just beat around the edge of things – you never tell me the things I most likely need to know. You said you wanted breathing room, but haven't you had enough? It must be something terrible – some kind of crime – for you to be hung up on forgiveness like this. What in the name of all these gods and goddesses is hiding inside of you?"

He twisted away from her, then back, his hands coming up imploringly. She got her first glimpse of his face, and it was the face of a man in a terminal agony. He choked out words ... "Kait, I'm ... trying ... I'm trying ... so hard ... "

There was a tap at the door. Griffen swung away again, gouging his face with his knuckles, striving futilely to gain control. The tap was repeated, more insistently. Irritated, Kaitrin went and cracked the retractable door.

It was Trea. "I come in," she said, pushing through. "I can sense – not going well."

Kaitrin was desperately relieved to see her. "Trea, I'm at the end of my wits."

"I know. I sense need. Maybe I can help."

She went to Griffen and laid a hand on each side of his neck. "Gwidian, I am empath, you know. I will try to help you."

"Trea," he whispered, "can you ... ? Are you ... able ... to read my mind?"

"No, I am not telepath. Only empath. I cannot see thoughts, but I sense much of soul – the inward feeling. I know you suffer. I do not ask to know why. Lie down now – yes, on side, like that, will do. I will work a little *zo-yevá*. Yes." She commenced her hypnotic alien murmur, touching him almost delicately, eyes only half-closed but unseeing, or rather seeing something other than the space in which she worked.

Under that touch Griffen began to grow calmer. Kaitrin stood at the door, watching miserably. *Oh, if only I were an empath and could influence him like that. Dear god, he talks sometimes as if I were his savior, but I'm making a rotten job of it. What am I going to do?*

Trea looked over at her. "Come here, Kaitrin," she said. "Sit here beside him. Touch. Put your hand here. See, he will be all right. Just don't demand, Kaitrin. Not right now."

Griffen lay facing away from her and she huddled over him. His eyes were closed, his breathing ragged, and an occasional shiver still ran through him, but he was no longer crying. She stroked the tear-moisture away with her fingers and he took her hand and held it against his lips.

"I will get medication," said the Pozú doctor, and went out.

In a few moments, she was back. "Something for both of you," she said. "Sometimes *zo-yevá* alone not enough. A simple sleep herb from my planet. No worry – very mild, and safe for any warm-blooded mammal species! Both of you are overstressed, too fatigued – need sleep. Here, Gwidian, sit up a minute."

He complied, and she gave both of them a dose of liquid and a cup of water. "Oral is slower but lasts longer than transdermal," she said. "Go to bed. Will seem better after sleep."

When Trea went out, Kaitrin followed her. The rest of the team had dispersed, except Tió'otu and Arti, who still sat at the table.

Arti said, "Is Prf. Gwidian all right? It seems like I said something wrong there, but for the life of me I can't figure out what it was."

"I don't know, either," said Kaitrin.

"I think Gwidian is right," said A'a'ma gloomily. "It is time to go home."

Kaitrin followed the doctor into the MedBay and shut the door. "Please, Trea, I need to talk to you a minute."

Trea turned to her and Kaitrin said, "I really need help. I don't know what to do with Griff. He seems to be getting worse.

How can I help him?"

Trea thought a moment. "Not worse. The layers are coming off."

Kaitrin stared befuddled at the small face below her.

Trea said, "I told you that for long I have sensed something in him. A darkness. A torment. But it grows stronger. Not the torment – it is the same. Just my sense of it. Kaitrin, he will find light soon."

"I saw something of a troubled side in him from early on, too, but for some strange reason it seemed to start getting worse after the wedding."

"Again, not worse. Just – rising. Like something drowned coming up to light."

Kaitrin shivered at the analogy, which carried an appropriateness that Trea could not possibly be aware of.

Trea said, "Gwidian has a wound in the soul, Kaitrin. It needs to be healed."

"Can it be healed?"

"Yes. I do believe it."

"I'm not sure I can do it. Can you read my soul, Trea?"

"You have strong soul. I can help him, soothe him, but I cannot heal him. But you can. He chose you well, or fate chose you for him, as Luku says."

"Really? But I don't know what to do for him! Sometimes I think I only make him more miserable."

Trea repeated, "You have strong soul. But you expect others to be as strong. You get impatient when they are not. You expect those who look like you – who share genes with you – to be like you. Off-worlders who do not look like you – you accept that they are different."

"Griffen said something like that to me once."

"Time, patience – those are his needs. Do not demand too much of him. Let him bring to you whatever it is that eats in his soul. He will come to it in time. Time is the friend in this. I believe that such as happened just now is really good thing – shows progress. One day, the thing will come out, the infection will cleanse itself, and your Griffen will heal. Now go in – go to bed! Sleep while medication works itself."

*   *   *

264

Kaitrin turned down the lights, undressed quickly, and slipped between the covers. While she was gone, Griffen had risen, taken off his clothes, and gotten into bed. He lay with his eyes closed; she thought he was asleep, but when she bent over him, his eyes opened and his brows drew together. She kissed him on the place between the brows.

"I'm sorry," he said. "I'm sorry for making such a scene. I'm sorry I'm such a fool – that I showed myself for such a fool. I'm just ... sorry for everything."

"Even that you married me?" she said, and could have flayed herself the moment the words were out of her mouth.

His eyes twisted shut. "Don't torture me, Kait."

"Oh, Griff! Dear god! – I don't mean to! What is the matter with me? I must have my quips and little brittle words – why? You and Trea are both right about me! I can show more compassion for those aliens over there in that fortress than I can for the person I love most in the world!"

"Oh, Kait ... *'ngariad* ... it's all right ... don't berate yourself. It's only ... I'm in so much pain ... "

She wanted to say, *For every god's sake, Griffen, why are you in so much pain?* But she had learned better ... Time and patience ... Don't demand ... They would go home and with time everything would be all right ...

With the Pozú drug working its gentle magic in their souls, they drifted off to sleep in each other's arms.

Chapter 24

She tells her love while half asleep,
   In the dark hours,
     With half words whispered low:
As Earth stirs in her winter sleep
  And puts out grass and flowers
    Despite the snow,
    Despite the falling snow.
       – Robert Graves, *She Tells Her Love ...*

Near the end of the sleep time, Kaitrin woke first and everything came back to her. She lay on her right side; Griffen slept facing her, his left arm thrust down under the cover, his right hand lying on the pillow between them. She delicately inserted her left hand into his right and his fingers tightened on it, although he did not wake.

She lay trying to distinguish his face in the shadowy nightlight. What had really happened before they slept? Trea had said it was a good thing. The layers are coming away, she had said. The pain is rising to the surface. *When it reaches the surface, will it simply evaporate into nothing like steam and blow away? Oh, Griffen, my own love, I hope so. I hope so, for your sake – for both our sakes. I love you. Why in the world do I love you so much?*

They were going home. In her thoughts the word rang with a mysterious timbre. Home had always been an apartment in Pikes Precinct, with a vivacious woman and a big grumpy cat greeting her at the door. Soon home would be a townhouse of seven rooms near the Karlinius campus in the Northwest Quad Consortium, Okloh Precinct, Planet Earth.

What will it be like when we get there?   We'll come into Herinen, all of us together, on the Lunar shuttle, and there will be a lot of confusion while we confirm our baggage, and then we'll all board the mag together, and finally we'll reach Okloh and then the campus. Everything will look strange – familiar yet unfamiliar, the way a place always does when one has been away for a while. And we'll all say goodbye and go our separate ways.

And we won't go to my apartment – that can wait for the next day. We'll go straight to Griff's house – our house. He'll unlock the door because it's not keyed to my thumb yet, and I'll run around looking at everything and laughing and acting like my usual idiotic self. The house will smell a little closed, but it will be very neat and tidy, I'm sure, because that's the way Griffen is. That won't last! But I must make an effort to be a bit more tidy and maybe he'll make an effort to tolerate a bit more confusion, because that's what it means to be committed – both people have to make the effort to change a little for the sake of the other.

I'll say, "Is there anything to eat in this house?" And he'll say, "Nothing perishable, I fear," while I rummage about and complain that I'm hungry and wonder how quickly we can get a delivery. Then he'll say "We can nip off to the dining room" in that British way of his. But I won't want to – I want to eat our first meal back on Earth in my new home. So we'll sit down and eat protein biscuits and tinned chicken and fruit, and mix up powdered soy milk as if we were still in the field, and Griffen will brew up some old stale tea that was left in the cupboard, and it will be the best meal we ever had because we'll be together – together, Griff, for all eternity, just like in your dream ...

Greatly moved, she rose up on her elbow and waved the light higher. The motion woke Griffen and he rolled over on his back. His eyes opened, holding the bleared look of one who cannot yet remember what he must face in the day ahead. Then they cleared; he turned his head to the right as his face gathered into the pain of recollection. "Is it morning?"

"Yes. I'm sorry I woke you. Are you ... ? Do you feel better? It was a good sleep."

He sighed heavily, rubbing the back of his hand across his

face.

"I'm going to have to get up. I have to figure out what tale I'm going to give the Queen on this last visit. But you don't have to get up yet."

"I have to go out there, Kait, and face all those people."

"Only Trea knows what happened in here. And they're all concerned about you, Griff. We've become such a close group. There really is a lot of love among all the members of this team."

"Yes. I'm aware of that. It's a bloody shame they've had such a poor excuse for a leader."

"Oh, Griff, that isn't true."

"At least they've had Prf. A'a'ma – somebody to bring some balance to this affair."

"Oh, Griff. Do you know what I was doing just now? Lying here fantasizing about what it will be like on our first day at home. I can't wait to get home!"

His eyes turned to her. "Really, Kait?"

"Really!"

"You won't mind living a pedestrian life for a while?"

"Not in the slightest! Because it will be with you!"

He pulled her down and held her close against him.

"Griffen, I want to say … Will you let me say this? I don't need to know what it is that you're so desperate to be forgiven for. Let me finish, love. I don't need to know. I forgive you for everything – anything and everything that you might ever have done. You said once that you didn't think I was the kind of woman who judged on hearsay rather than on what she observed. I hope that's true. And I observe nothing but good in you, Griffen Gwidian. It doesn't matter what you need to be forgiven for. I forgive you for everything, without conditions. I love you, Griff."

She rose on her elbow again to look at him. He had shut his eyes hard and a tear was trickling silently from beneath each closed lid. She wiped them away with a finger and kissed the spaces under each eye. "I love you, Griffen. I do love you." She sank down against his breast again.

In a few moments she said, "I suppose I'd better get up."

"I might stay in bed till you're dressed." Then he whispered against her hair, "I love you, Kait, more than you'll ever be able to understand."

"I'll see you outside in a little while." She kissed him once more, on the lips quickly, and slipped out from between the covers.

*   *   *

[Lo'lo'pai scuttles distractedly around the walls of its quarters]

In two more turnings of the water vessel, the Star-Being will come – in another turn or two she will emerge from the Chamber. What am I doing? I have organized the support – I have called upon my best Lieutenants and my strongest Warriors, and the Commander has addressed them, rallied them to commit this sacrilege ... Or is it sacrilege? Is it really for the good of the fortress and the Holy One? My thoughts are so disordered – I wish there was someone who could help me understand why I am doing this thing.

[A Lieutenant, one Ni'shto'pri, arrives to speak with its Chief]

[Ni'shto'pri]: I come seeking reassurance, Chief Lo'lo'pai. This thing you and the Commander have ordered us to do – is it really for the best? It goes against everything I have been taught – to initiate warfare against our own fellow citizens in our own halls!

[Lo'lo'pai, grooms miserably]: Have you not been taught to obey your superior officers?

[Ni'shto'pri]: But I sense that you yourself are not sure of the course. How can we who are lesser be expected to understand if you, our Chief, be not sure?

[Lo'lo'pai]: Ni'shto'pri, it is true that I am troubled. But do you see me openly doubting and questioning my Commander? Sometimes one must simply obey orders, assuming that those above know best.

[Ni'shto'pri]: With much respect, Chief, I have sometimes wondered if that is the wisest course in every circumstance. Are we not all One Beings, with the minds of One Beings?

[Lo'lo'pai]: Warriors less than others! If we did not obey our superiors' commands, the fortress would fall into chaos! I am scandalized! What kind of Lieutenant have you become?

[Ni'shto'pri, abases]: Honored Chief, I will prove to you that my loyalty is above reproach! But what will happen if the Holy Seer or the Remembrancer comes out of the Chamber along with the outland female and the Huge-Head? It is possible that they might be caught in the battle and harmed.

[Lo'lo'pai]: The Remembrancer ... I had not thought of that! It would be a terrible deed if he were killed!

[Ni'shto'pri]: And how much worse if the Holy Seer died!

[Lo'lo'pai, thoughtlessly]: The Chamberlain has already picked a replacement for Kwi'ga'ga'tei after she is ... [It catches itself, writhes in misery]

[Ni'shto'pri]: 'After she is' – what? May the Highest-Mother-Who-Is-Nameless forfend! Is that the plan? To 'accidentally' kill the Holy Kwi'ga'ga'tei? The Chamberlain – the Chamberlain has a part in such a thing? Surely not!

[Lo'lo'pai]: I misspoke! I had no intention of implying that the Holy Seer was to be deliberately killed! *tha'sask|>||* I was not constituted to speak deception! [Grovels]

[Ni'shto'pri]: I am shaken! And horrified!

[Lo'lo'pai]: You are my best Lieutenant, Ni'shto'pri, whom I mean to elevate to Chief when I am Commander. Will you prove unreliable? Must I remove you from duty?

[Ni'shto'pri, again abases]: Chief, I am loyal to Lo'ro'ra and to the Holy One and the King, and to those who protect them. You can certainly count on me to perform my duty!

[Lo'lo'pai]: Say nothing of this, I command you. Go and ready yourself for the attack.

[Ni'shto'pri leaves. Lo'lo'pai resumes its agitated circuit of the sightless chamber]

I make a botch of things! If this were only over! Too many people are involved. I cannot see any good outcome. I sense that Lo'ro'ra is about to split asunder and I will be the cause!

[Ni'shto'pri scuttles through the corridors in great distress]

Again I wonder, is a Warrior always obligated to carry out its officer's commands, even when those commands seem to go against a greater good? I realize that if it were not so, no fortress could stand, and that we lesser Warriors are not always meant to understand everything. But are there exceptions? Moments when loyalty and thoughtless obedience are not the same? Why is it that I seem to be the only one ever to concern itself with such questions? Assuming that there could be exceptions, what is the greater good here? Is it not always to protect the interests of the Holy One? But how am I to know how those interests are best served?

I could consult Chief A'gwa'ji, but I do not know where it stands in this, and to abandon one's own Cohort … Or I could go to Sa'ti'a'i'a – everyone knows that its loyalties lie firmly with the Holy Seer. But it is a barbarian – an individual of the inferior Enemy – and I find confiding in it distasteful. But Mo'gri'ta'tu is implicated? That, too, puts a different slant on this. His hatred of the Seer and his desire to increase his own power – those things are common gossip. Can he have sunk so low as to plot this dastardly act?

I must return to quarters and ponder this dilemma. Such thinking is difficult for a Warrior – it requires some lengthy breaking down of parts. And it may well be I will decide that to go against Chief Lo'lo'pai and the Commander is a greater treachery than what they have plotted. Well, I will think on it and come to a decision as quickly as I can …

*   *   *

Griffen emerged while Kaitrin was eating breakfast. No one said anything to him beyond the usual morning greetings; eyes were friendly, smiles warm. She said to him, "Come and sit with me. Have something to eat. We've got scrambled reconstituted eggs – halfway decent if you eat jam with it. Some real toast would be nice, though."

He sat down and Trea brought him his breakfast and poured his tea. "Eat," she said. "I saw the supper plate." She clucked at him and he meekly complied.

Kaitrin watched him for a moment. "It really is time to go home. You're almost out of tea."

He smiled wanly. "I left a supply on the *Featherlight* for the voyage back." Then he added, "So what story have you decided to tell?"

"I believe I'll start with the winds in the bag and then move to Silla and Karybdis, where Odysus loses the last of his men. I'm going to omit the Sirens – how do you explain stuffing ears with wax to creatures who can't hear? I definitely can't do Circy or Kalypso – too much sex. I'm trying to avoid explaining the birds and the bees to the termites! Of course, this will mean the Shshi will be left never knowing what happens when Odysus gets home."

"Maybe the next time you come," said Griffen.

Kaitrin nodded, still watching him. "Next time, Griff. But can you imagine what these ancient Earth stories are going to be like after they've been retold in an alien oral tradition for ten or fifteen years? It's hilarious to think about!"

"Maybe you can come back then as well, and find out," he said.

"Thanks, love." She reached to squeeze his hand. "Well, I guess I'd better go and study the text and work out the names so I won't have to do it extempore this time."

She sat in the research bay mulling over her tale while Griffen worked on his own data in the lab. Outside, the slow sun started to rise. The temperature had moderated from the freezing weather of a couple of weeks previously, but the sky was streaked with high cirrus and a bank of heavier gray rain clouds was gathering in the west, in what seemed to be a typical pattern for this time of year. Three hours remained before Kaitrin's escort would arrive.

On the flight deck, Will Ayland was making a routine check of flight readiness when the comlink came to life. "*Durga*, this is *Stinger*. Do you copy? Over."

Will activated the link. "Copy, *Stinger*. Do I have Capt. !eye Taeva?"

"Correct. All nominal planetside?"

"No complaints! Spaceside?"

"Nominal. *Featherlight* is safely on way to Starbase 30. Will bring back special frozen meat for Prf. A'a'ma."

"Excellent! When *Featherlight* returns, the plans are to end the expedition and prepare for the flight home."

"Copy! Will pass that along. Is anybody on deck with you?"

"If you mean someone with a long tail, no. Shall I fetch her?"

"Please! Capt. Van gives me two minutes!"

Will chuckled and went to summon Luku. She bounded up the ladder and spent a few moments purring in Glin Quornaz with Zin. At length, a chirpy voice was heard in the background and Zin switched to Inj. "Have to sign out. Captain is complaining. See you soon, Luku! *Peroi mae!*"

"*Peroi mae*, Zin! *Voi tupta!* Take back, Will!"

"Capt. Ayland, we make next contact in ten hours! *Stinger* out!"

"Copy, Capt. !eye Taeva! *Durga* out." Will terminated the link and, still grinning, returned to his systems check.

*   *   *

On board the *Stinger*, Zin shut down the link and went to eat lunch. The *Stinger* carried a crew of seven – the !K♪a<tí Captain He<it Van, Zin serving as First Officer, a human navigator, a galliform Engineer, a Wéwan maintenance crewman, and two security people. An hour passed. Zin returned to the flight deck and the navigator and the Engineer headed for the Mess. Capt. Van was at the controls.

Suddenly the navigational readings fluctuated wildly and the gravity matrix cascaded so that the craft felt like a rapidly falling lift. Capt. Van bounced in her perch harness and Zin's head bumped the ceiling as his feet left the deck. A malfunction warning began to shriek. Quickly compensating, Van swore in !Ka<tá. "ꝭ<*Kheda<e gi psa·]*"

"*Hoi-a!* Magnetic storm!" exclaimed Zin, futilely punching commands into the navigator's console.

"Call Maj. Tar·aga up here!"

"Com down. I go get." Zin leaped to fetch the Engineer.

They tinkered. "Huge stellar flare. Emissions are off scale. Where did that come from? Last scan showed nothing," said Tar·aga.

"Comlink is completely *quink!a*," said Zin in concern.

"What does that mean?" asked Capt. Van impatiently.

"Sorry. Broken. Fried up."

"*Hei*, fix it!" coughed Capt. Van.

"Completely fried up – needs whole new unit. Do we have backup?"

"We have backup," said Tar·aga. "But we look at maybe twelve, fifteen hours' work."

"To install unit?" queried the Captain skeptically.

"Is not only unit," said Zin. "I think internal power transfers are *quink!e*, too."

"For sure," said the Engineer. "If we do not rewire internal com, it keeps aborting the planetary link."

"Can't we sever the connection to the intercom?" asked the navigator, who was working on stabilizing the orbit.

"Stupid design flaw in ships built by !Ka<tí," barked Tar·aga. "Two com systems must be connected for each to operate."

The !KƧa<tí Captain muttered ill-naturedly at this disparagement of her people's technology.

"And the emissions keep coming," said the navigator. "Have to enter different orbit while the bombardment persists, or the new link will be as quinkie as the old one."

"Massive coronal ejection. Where did this thing come from?" repeated Tar·aga.

Van was running a diagnostic on her flight systems. "Get to work! I hate to miss check-in with *Durga* – only eight hours away."

"It will scare them," said Zin.

"I am changing orbit," said Van. "Will hold on planet's night side while you fix systems. By then maybe we can at least transect *Durga* coordinates long enough for contact."

"Will still take lots more than eight hours," said Tar·aga.

"Cannot help it. These things happen. We will hope planet team continues not to need us. Never has yet."

"Where did this storm come from?" said Tar·aga.

Chapter 25

'So they spake, and the evil counsel of my
company prevailed. They loosed the wallet,
and all the winds brake forth. And the violent
blast seized my men, and bare them towards
the high seas weeping, away from their own
country ... '
> – *from* Homer, *The Odyssey*, tr. by S. H. Butcher
> and A. Lang.

"I see the Shshi coming!" called Julian from the flight deck.

"All right! Bye, Griff!" Kaitrin gave him a peck on the cheek. "Trea, look after everybody! Here goes Alice's last adventure!" She pulled out of Griffen's grasp and ran down the ramp to join Kwi'ga'ga'tei and Ki'shto'ba. They headed across the compound.

"I was so pleased to meet the Holy One and the King, Kwi'ga'ga'tei! It was much what I expected, but I never thought she would be so – friendly."

Kwi'ga'ga'tei looked up at Kaitrin. *Ru'a'ma'na'ta, the Holy One is the thing that gives us life. But she is not a thing of spirit or of power. Some equate the* ma'na'ta| *with the Nameless One and do not understand that she is a real Shi and she gets lonely and angry and sad like all One Beings.*

"I can understand that, Kwi'ga'ga'tei. The Star-Beings are not so different."

Ki'shto'ba said, *Do you have to leave so soon?*

I feel much sorrow, said Kwi'ga'ga'tei, *that we have not suc-ceeded in making you feel welcome among us.*

"It is not that," said Kaitrin. "I feel very welcome and I would like to stay longer, but I must leave for the sake of my *na'sha'ma|*. This sojourn has not been good for him. We must go home for a while."

He is sick? said Kwi'ga'ga'tei.

"You could say that he is."

Kwi'ga'ga'tei hesitated a moment. *It could not be – surely it could not be – that he has – a wound?*

Kaitrin found this a surpassingly strange question. The word *ist'zi|* denoted both "pain" and "wound." The Shshi Seer seemed to be echoing Trea's words.

"Well, yes – you could say that he has a wound."

Kwi'ga'ga'tei's quick insectile legs seemed to falter. *It is not visible.*

"Not all wounds can be seen. This is a wound – in the inner part of him, the part that is not the body."

The inner part ... yes – i'kei'zei| ... I take your meaning. But I had ... failed to understand. Your King has never spoken words to me. But this wound will heal if you go home?

"I hope so. Yes. I am sure it will." Kaitrin looked down on the top of the Seer's head, perplexed.

Then you must go home. I see I have been wrong. You must go home. I will make our Holy One understand.

Kaitrin was so mystified that she said nothing.

But yet it is strange, Kwi'ga'ga'tei said. *I feel something is incomplete. Unfinished.*

Now, this really is uncanny, Kaitrin thought. "It is strange, indeed. I have felt the same thing. What is at work here, Holy Seer?"

I do not know. It is difficult being Seer, Ru'a'ma'na'ta. Oth-ers expect me to know everything, but I am shown only glimpses – riddles. It is very difficult. Also very lonely. It drains the spirit – what you called, the inner part.

"I understand, Kwi'ga'ga'tei. Prophecy has always been like that."

Everywhere among the stars?

"Everywhere among the stars."

They entered the fortress and crawled down into the depths where the Holy Chamber brooded. At the entrance, the blind guards stood like stones. They passed between them and came into the presence of the Mother of Lo'ro'ra.

*　　*　　*

[At the wall surrounding the exercise yard, Ni'shto'pri monitors the commands of Chief A'gwa'ji as it reviews its troops]

It is engaging in a meaningless exercise because the Commander ordered it to do so. It never thinks, *Why did it order this?* That is the ideal Warrior. But when such a Warrior becomes Commander, it is incapable of thinking, *Why does this Alate order me to do such a deed?* even when that order is most certainly dishonorable.

I am due even now outside the Holy Chamber to hide in storage rooms and jump out to commit murder like nymphs playing an innocent game, because my Chief has so ordered me.

I am unnatural – a deviant. I cannot obey this order. I will go to the Nasute Chief even though it is the Enemy, and I will tell it what I know. If it bring me dishonor, I will take it. If my life be forfeit, I will sacrifice my life. But I believe that my duty to the Holy One and King comes before my own honor and before my duty to confused superiors. I will go to the Nasute.

[Ni'shto'pri turns and scurries toward a rear entrance of the main edifice]

*　　*　　*

[The corridor intersecting the entrance to the Holy Chamber. At the inner end, Hi'ta'fu, Lo'lo'pai, and nine large Warriors appear. The guards stiffen their legs, then abase]

[Hi'ta'fu]: Have they entered?

[Guard]: Even now, Commander.

[Lo'lo'pai, nervously]: I call for the names!

[Hi'ta'fu]: No time! We must enter the closets. If so many of us are noticed …

[A Lieutenant]: Where is Ni'shto'pri? I find no scent of Ni'shto'pri!

[They all cast about, rubbing their bellies together, touching antennae]

[Lo'lo'pai]: It is not here! A'zim'gwa, you are in its phalanx.

[A'zim'gwa, scraping]: Chief, I do not know where it is. It did not come with me. I did not encounter it. Perhaps it forgot to turn the water vessel or missed the courier's announcement.

[Lo'lo'pai]: Ni'shto'pri never neglects the time! It disobeys my direct orders! What have I done?

[Hi'ta'fu, flustered, paying no heed to the Chief's words]: Never mind! We have enough! Into the closets!

[The Warriors push under the *bu're|* mats and enter the storage chambers, readjusting the coverings. All appears as it was before they arrived]

*   *   *

Again, Kaitrin sat on the stone dais, surveying her eager audience. The Holy One was fairly bouncing with anticipation and Sei'o'na'sha'ma was crawling around in excited circles. The Remembrancer and Nok'ri were in attendance, along with a couple of the Chiefs of Worker Subcastes, the Holy Seer's Steward I'mei'o'nu, the Chief Healer, the Keeper of the *bir'zha|* cyst – indeed, the Holy Chamber was quite crammed with dignitaries and bright with Alate wings. Kwi'ga'ga'tei crouched at the right side of the hall. Mo'gri'ta'tu had stationed himself at the left, near one of the side exits.

Where is Commander Hi'ta'fu? asked Kwi'ga'ga'tei. *And I had thought Chief A'gwa'ji would attend today.*

A'kha'ma'na'ta said, *Fum sent word that it was otherwise occupied. It is of no matter. It has forgotten how to be amused! And I do not know where Gwaf is. Do you know, Gri?*

Mo'gri'ta'tu stirred. *I understand it chose to review troop exercises today.*

Odd, said Kwi'ga'ga'tei. *I personally invited it to attend. I thought it would relish a tale.*

Perhaps the Commander ordered it to review the troops, said

Sei'o'na'sha'ma. *Warriors. Who can understand how they think? Who, indeed?* said Kwi'ga'ga'tei.

Kaitrin looked around and grasped why Kwi'ga'ga'tei was concerned. Except for Ki'shto'ba, there was no Warrior presence at all in the Holy Chamber. *Is something afoot?* thought Kaitrin a little uneasily. *I don't want to get caught in some kind of inter-necine intrigue.*

A'kha'ma'na'ta had begun bouncing again, impatiently. *I want to know the story!* she said. *Ru, tell your story!*

"I can give you another tale of Ul'i'seit, *na'ta'zei|*," said Kaitrin, grinning in spite of herself. "Will that be satisfactory?"

Yes! Yes!

"Then here it is! After he encountered the Zin'tei, Ul'i'seit traveled a long distance over the ocean in the wooden box. There were many storms. Storms can make the boxes turn upside down so that everyone – and I must ask a word here – dies by being covered with water so that no air can come into the spiracles."

weio| o| gwai'zi| ||, said Kwi'ga'ga'tei.

"To die with water," thought Kaitrin. *Makes sense that these dryland creatures would have no discrete word for "drown."* "So, if a box turns over, everyone can be killed in that way. But finally Ul'i'seit was able to obtain a gift from the wind-spirit. It was a container that would hold all the big winds inside so the ocean-King could not create any storms. And then the wind spirit made a smaller wind for the wanderers that blew them in the right direction, so they actually came close enough to their homeland to see it. But Ul'i'seit had been managing the floating box himself for many days and he was tired, and when they came in sight of his homeland, he at last let himself go to sleep.

"Unfortunately, his companions were neither very dependable nor very honest. Some of them believed the container did not hold the winds at all but instead held things of value and they wanted those things for themselves, and so they opened the container to steal them. What do you think happened then?"

Sei'o'na'sha'ma cried, *All the big winds escaped and a storm arose – a terrible storm!*

"Exactly right!" said Kaitrin, chuckling inside. This was like reading a story to a bunch of human five-year-olds. "The winds were released and Ul'i'seit and his Warriors barely escaped with their lives. They were driven all the way back to the land of the wind-spirit, who would not help them again, since it seemed that all the powers of the world had placed a curse on Ul'i'seit."

The curse of the Zin'tei! said A'kha'ma'na'ta in triumph.

"Exactly! So then ... "

There was a sudden commotion at the side entrance behind Kwi'ga'ga'tei. She jumped around to face it, wings fanning. The Nasute guard who had been outside the entrance backed into the Holy Chamber, abasing. Sa'ti'a'i'a burst through the door herding ahead of it a Shshi Warrior who appeared very frightened.

Mo'gri'ta'tu bristled. *What is the meaning of this interruption, Nasute?*

You surely know, traitor! said Sa'ti'a'i'a.

What word is that? cried the King, jumping on the Holy One's thorax with his forelegs.

Kwi'ga'ga'tei had moved closer to Kaitrin, while Ki'shto'ba stepped in front of them both. Alarmed, Kaitrin stood up so she could see over the Huge-Head.

Sa'ti'a'i'a was prodding the Warrior with its snout. *This is Ni'shto'pri, a Lieutenant of the First Cohort. It is an honorable Warrior who understands what real loyalty means and it is astute enough to see through the deceptions of traitors. It has informed me that Chief Lo'lo'pai has set ten Warriors in ambush in the corridor to kill the Champion and the female Star-Being when they leave the Holy Chamber, and perhaps – most sacrilegious intent! – the Holy Seer herself! Would you have the Huge-Head and my Cohort investigate,* na'ta'zei|?

Kaitrin yelped an imprecation as specters of all of Griffen's fears rose in her mind. A ruckus had broken out. The Queen cried, *How can that be? Gri, that cannot be! Where is Fum? I want my Commander!*

Sa'ti'a'i'a said, *Poor Holy One, your Commander is in the thick of it. It is by its order that the unnatural Lo'lo'pai, who had not even the wits to keep all the plottings to itself, has arranged this deed. It is likely that you will find Hi'ta'fu at the forefront of the attack and your Chamberlain standing by approving it, for Lo'lo'pai implicated him in Ni'shto'pri's presence. Surely it was Mo'gri'ta'tu who concocted the plot – the mind of a Warrior could never have devised something so dastardly!*

My Chamberlain? Gri? A traitor? A murderer? I want this Enemy out of my sight! It is the traitor! Ki'shto'ba was exclaiming, *They have not even the consideration to challenge me properly but must seek to ambush me and overwhelm me by numbers? Vile vermin!* It was swinging its mandibles right and left in indignation and banging its head on the stones.

Kaitrin was getting really frightened. Kwi'ga'ga'tei had edged her back against the wall in great alarm, but now the Seer herself stepped forward. *Ki'shto'ba, restrain yourself – you will wound someone! Nasute Chief, block the exits! Send someone to the exercise yard to alert A'gwa'ji that the Second Cohort may have to fight its siblings! Where is Mo'gri'ta'tu?*

But it was too late. The exits had not been closed quickly enough and the Keeper of the Holy Chamber was nowhere to be found.

281

Chapter 26

Alone, alone, all, all alone,
Alone on a wide, wide sea!
And never a saint took pity on
My soul in agony.
　　　　　– *from* S. T. Coleridge, *Rime of the Ancient*
Mariner

[Mo'gri'ta'tu scuttles into the corridor outside the entrance of the Holy Chamber and darts into the nearest storage room, almost impaling himself on Hi'ta'fu's mandibles]

[Hi'ta'fu]: Chamberlain! I sense the alarm! Why are you here? What is the matter?

[Mo'gri'ta'tu]: Chaos! Your weak-brained Second has prattled loose words to a disaffected Lieutenant who has betrayed us to Sa'ti'a'i'a. Where is Lo'lo'pai?

[Hi'ta'fu, dancing in horror]: This cannot be!

[Mo'gri'ta'tu]: The Nasute drags the turncoat into the Holy Chamber and accuses all of us! I barely escaped! You must …

[Lo'lo'pai, sensing the disturbance, thrusts its head into the closet]: Chamberlain! You, here? What catastrophe has happened?

[Mo'gri'ta'tu]: You are the catastrophe! Your Lieutenant Ni'shto'pri has betrayed us! Kwi'ga'ga'tei has summoned the

Second Cohort – *Tell A'gwa'ji they may have to fight their siblings*, she says! The open war is upon us!

[Lo'lo'pai, scrapes and grovels in anguish]: *A-i-i*, Nameless One ... *A-i-i*, Nameless One ... pity ... pity ...

[Mo'gri'ta'tu]: Stop behaving like halfwits and get yourselves out of here! Redeem yourselves by rallying the First Cohort! Form ranks in the courtyard, in front of the Warriors' Quarters. Try to prevent the Second Cohort from organizing!

[Hi'ta'fu]: The Holy One – did she ask for me?

[Mo'gri'ta'tu]: Naturally she blathers for you – she knows nothing else! But it is too late for that! You are condemned as a traitor! It is too late. Now get yourselves out of here and rally your phalanxes before the Nasutes arrive! They and Ki'shto'ba will be headed this way!

[Hi'ta'fu]: Mo'gri'ta'tu, you intend now to abandon us?

[Mo'gri'ta'tu]: How humorous you are for a Warrior, Commander! I am as discredited as you are – I cannot – *abandon* you, as you call it. Form up your Cohort and I will join you! I have my own plan of escape!

*   *   *

[Mo'gri'ta'tu runs upward through the corridors. The vibration of the alarm beats palpably in the stone]

The Commander can fight its way out but I cannot, and I do not trust it to protect me. They will be searching for me in the lower levels. This is the best plan. Hold – I sense a Nasute ahead. I will take this turning ... Now who is that?

[Ta'rei'so'cha and A'dei'no'no approach from above]

[Ta'rei'so'cha]: Mo'gri'ta'tu! I see Nasutes everywhere – has the plan failed? One asked me if I had seen you and spoke the word *traitor*.

[Mo'gri'ta'tu]: The plan has failed, and more than failed. This is civil war. I was not going to bother about ... But since you are here, you can come with me. Into the shaft!

[A'dei'no'no]: The shaft!

[Mo'gri'ta'tu]: The ventilation shaft! Do you not know they are used for boltholes during sieges?

[The Alates enter the shaft, which is only big enough to accommodate them snugly in single file.]

[Ta'rei'so'cha]: This seems airless! How can a ventilation shaft be airless?

[A'dei'no'no]: Some of these shafts have been sealed at the outer ends! What if this is one of those?

[Mo'gri'ta'tu]: I am the only person left in the world who is not a dimwit, it seems. Do you think I would pick a sealed shaft for my escape? But if it is, perhaps you can back up, my friend. If you cannot, then someday when time brings down the stones, there will be found shreds of a few nameless Star-Wings in the debris. Would you prefer to be withered by Nasute acid? I thought not! Now, climb!

*   *   *

In the Holy Chamber, A'kha'ma'na'ta had called to Kaitrin. *Come and sit by me, Ru'a'ma'na'ta. I am scared. What do they mean, Fum and Gri are traitors? Tei, where are you? Sei, I am scared!*

Kaitrin thought, *You aren't the only one!* She sank down next to the huge form of the Holy One and rubbed the top of her great, bristled head. "Kwi'ga'ga'tei is very busy, *na'ta'zei|*. Be calm and let her work. She loves you and she is loyal to you and will not let anything hurt you." *And myself, I hope.*

I think I am going to lay. All the excitement. But the eggs will be tainted.

A'kha'ma'na'ta produced three eggs, small and immature in appearance. The Tenders, going about their duties as if nothing were happening, licked them, cleaned the ovipositor, carried them away to be incubated, as they would do even if this were the Last Day of Time.

Kaitrin scrubbed her head, thinking, W*hat a nightmare this has turned into! What's going on out there?* She could feel vibrations through the fiber of the fortress and momentarily she thought it was an earthquake. Then she realized she was sensing head-drumming – alarm behavior exactly like that of terrestrial soldier termites.

Ki'shto'ba and two Nasutes rushed in through the front entrance. *They are gone, Holy Seer! Sa'ti'a'i'a and I found nothing. The outer guards were also gone. It seems they were from the First Cohort – likely in league with the traitors. The Nasute Chief went on to pursue them, but I felt I should come back to protect you and Ru'a'ma'na'ta.*

Kwi'ga'ga'tei stood stiffly in the forefront of the Holy Chamber, with No'kri and the other Alates around her. *Could you detect who had been in the corridor?*

I could definitely take the scent of the Commander and of Lo'lo'pai, and of other Warriors. It seems they had hidden in the storage rooms along the hall. And Mo'gri'ta'tu's smell was there as well, very fresh.

He went to warn them, said Kwi'ga'ga'tei. *You Nasutes – scour the fortress. It is time to put an end to his villainy. Take him prisoner if you find him. I want to make an example of him. All you Warriors – do not let him talk overmuch to you! He corrupts everything that receives his words.*

A'gwa'ji burst in, banging its head on the doorposts. *Holy Seer! I was deceived! I did wonder why the Commander required me to review ... I should have been here! We encountered Hi'ta'fu and Lo'lo'pai issuing from the fortress – fighting Nasutes! We tried to intervene, thinking the Nasutes had betrayed us, but then our own Warriors attacked us! And we were overwhelmed! My troops did not understand that Hi'ta'fu could be the enemy. Now they do! The Commander and Lo'lo'pai each killed one of my Warriors and wounded others!*

Kaitrin was taking all this in with growing terror. *My god!* she thought, hugging the laboring Queen's neck. *This is civil war! And here I am stuck in the middle of it!*

How much of this was visible from the *Durga*? *Griffen ... what can Griffen see?*

Kwi'ga'ga'tei was saying, *A'gwa'ji, Lo'ro'ra no longer has a Commander. As of this moment, by decree of the Holy One and the King, you are the Commander of the Cohorts of Strong Flower fortress.*

Holy Seer! I am honored! But I am also devastated and confused! I do not ...

I do not want Gwaf! Where is Fum? cried A'kha'ma'na'ta. *I want to talk to it! It has always loved me! I will not believe it is a traitor!*

But the King said, *I think it is, Kha. I think we have only one friend that we can trust and that is the Holy Seer Kwi'ga'ga'tei. Attend to her words.*

Ru, you are my friend, are you not? said the Holy One pathetically.

"I am very much your friend, but I am afraid, too," said Kaitrin tensely. "Kwi'ga'ga'tei, what is happening out there? I need to get back to the other Star-Beings. They are going to be very worried about me if they see fighting."

I will take her, said Ki'shto'ba.

But A'gwa'ji said, *Not yet. With respect, Champion, even you could not bring her through safely. The Cohorts are emerging from everywhere, milling together. The Lieutenants are running around searching for their troops and the Warriors are desperate to find their phalanxes. Rumor holds sway. Nobody knows whom it is supposed to fight. You would both be set upon instantly.*

Kwi'ga'ga'tei said, *Commander of Lo'ro'ra, go out and lead the rally. Do you know your own troops?*

I know my own Lieutenants and they know their phalanxes. But it will take some time.

Ni'shto'pri had been cowering at the side throughout all this exchange, but now Kwi'ga'ga'tei addressed it. *Ni'shto'pri, come forward! Because you understood the true meaning of loyalty, the Holy One honors you with promotion to Second to the new Commander – in effect, Chief of the only Cohort that Lo'ro'ra now possesses!*

Ni'shto'pri abased and groveled. *Holy Seer! You do not condemn me as unnatural for disobeying my superiors?*

I am not one to assert that rules should ever be inviolable, Lieutenant. In this new time, I would rather have our Warriors led by those who know when to use their reason. Now both of you go and draw up Lo'ro'ra's loyal troops around the main fortress. Force Hi'ta'fu and the rebels to assume a position around the Warriors' Quarters and contain them there. Then perhaps we can negotiate some kind of surrender.

In spite of her circumstances, Kaitrin found her admiration for Kwi'ga'ga'tei's leadership abilities increasing. At that moment, a Nasute entered. *Huge-Head! Holy Seer! There has been a crazed attempt to assault the Star-Beings' dwelling! Rumors are spreading that they are responsible for this catastrophe.*

Oh, no. Oh, no, thought Kaitrin, standing up.

But the Nasute was saying, *Chief Sa'ti'a'i'a has taken it upon itself to protect the dwelling and has driven back the attackers. There is a standoff now, but several were killed on both sides. Assuming you would wish it, the Chief has thrown up a defensive perimeter around the dwelling and will set the entire Nasute Cohort to guard the Star-Beings.*

Thank goodness, Kaitrin thought, but inside she was moaning, *Griffen ... Griffen ...*

"Kwi'ga'ga'tei, I have to get back over there. My *na'sha'ma|* will be terrified for me. I must get back."

Kwi'ga'ga'tei turned to her. *I believe it is not wise to try it yet. You are safe here in the Holy Chamber. They will never attack us here – even Mo'gri'ta'tu would not commit such sacrilege. Is it not better for your* na'sha'ma| *to be worried for a while and then have you back safe at the end, than for you to venture out too soon and be killed?*

Kaitrin shivered. "Yes. Yes, of course." But in her heart she kept on crying, *Griffen ... Griffen!*

*   *   *

On the flight deck Julian did a double take as he passed the window. He leaned against the glazing, scowling. "Will, come over here a minute. Bring your VE – let me have it ..."

Julian applied the vision enhancer to his eyes, stared. Will looked out unassisted.

"Looks like a bunch of Shshi running out of the main entrance. What's going on?"

Julian said, "It's more than just ... I think those blasted bugs are fighting each other!"

"No way!" Will took the VE and peered. "Hellfire! That's what it looks like! That's the one they call the Commander, I'd swear. And they're fighting Nasutes – one of them is down and not moving! Holy lasers! Look at them leap!"

"I see a bunch of Warriors running from behind the barracks building, where the exercise yard is … Hey!"

Julian was shoved aside roughly. Through the open trapdoor, Gwidian had overheard.

"Kaitrin is in there." It was not his voice. He seized the VE from Will and swept the courtyard.

A'a'ma, who disliked climbing the ladder, screeched up from below, "What is happening?" Luku and Arti appeared, jostling each other in the hatch.

A group of Warriors from the exercise yard had advanced on the skirmish and were attacking somewhat skittishly. After a brief engagement the Commander and its party broke away, leaving two more bodies behind, and ran for the Warriors' Quarters. The Nasutes were regrouping, milling around with the newly arrived Shshi Warriors, then the two groups separated, the Shshi entering the fortress, the Nasutes fanning out across the courtyard.

Luku and Arti and the others were observing all of this through their own VEs, exclaiming with astonishment. On the lower deck, A'a'ma was chirping agitatedly to Trea and Sev. But Gwidian had jerked off the device and let the hand that held it fall to his side. His face was ash white. "Kait," he whispered.

Will took hold of his arm. "Prf. Gwidian, she's got to be all right. This is probably just some kind of misunderstanding. She was to be in the Queen's Chamber, right? I can't believe there would be any fighting in the … "

Gwidian pulled loose. "We have to get her out," he said.

"Wait, Griff," said Arti. "There's no way we can … "

"What are you security people here for?" he said in that unrecognizable voice. "We have to get her out. Are you coming or not?" He lunged toward the trapdoor.

"Professor!" Will started after him.

Arti and Julian looked at each other as they followed. Luku remained above, continuing to observe the courtyard.

Griffen almost fell down the ladder. Below, A'a'ma gave a squawk. "What is all this? Gwidian!"

Griffen had his sidearm out of the holster and was heading for the outer hatch. He turned around, waving the weapon precariously. "What are you security people for?" he shouted at Julian and Arti. "We have to get her out of there! Are you going to back me or not? What kind of incompetents did I engage?"

"Professor, calm down!" said Arti.

A'a'ma was hopping up and down distractedly and Will said to him, "There's fighting in the courtyard. Who knows what's happening inside?"

"*He'eti <khe!dora] <chuklí|chuklí]" shrilled Prf. A'a'ma, fanning his crest madly.

But Trea simply said, "Ah," in her soft voice.

Gwidian emitted a strangling sound. "The rifles ... We need the rifles ... "

"Prf. Gwidian!" said Arti. "Get yourself under control! We can't just go out there blasting away! We don't even know how extensive this is or what it means! It may not be ... "

Luku called down. "More Warriors are coming! Keep pouring out! Big confusion! Fighting – running around – no order!"

Gwidian turned to the hatch, fumbling at the control panel. Julian and Arti leaped to prevent him from opening it. "Gwidian, what are you planning to do? Go out shooting into chaos?" said Arti. "Calm down! Even if we got into the fortress, we couldn't get through the corridors, and even if we could, we don't know where she is in there! There's no light! We aren't prepared for an invasion!"

"Blast out the side," he said.

Julian shook his arm. "Griffen, think. What would that accomplish? We don't know Kaitrin's location. The blast just might kill her."

Gwidian shuddered.

Will said, "Let's go back up top and monitor the situation. I'll message *Stinger*. Maybe they can fly down and detonate a couple of atmospheric charges. That would certainly put a scare into those bugs – maybe stun them a little bit! Come on, Griff, put away the pistol. Let's go up and see what's going on."

Gwidian submitted then and let himself be led back to the flight deck. As they emerged from the trapdoor, Luku was saying, "That was strange! Three Alates came out of one of those holes high up on side of the fortress!"

"I thought those were air ducts," said Will, heading for the communications console.

"When we toured compound," said Luku, "they told us, used sometimes as escape holes. But what is strange – after Alates came out, they opened their wings and sort of glided down the side – very steep, too. I did not know Alates could do such a thing. When they reached ground, they ran off toward back of Warrior's building."

"Looks like there's some organizing going on, like a muster," said Arti, scanning the area through her VE. "Some are grouping together over there in front of the Warriors' Quarters and others around the main fortress."

Will was activating the comlink. "This is *Durga* calling *Stinger*. Do you copy?"

"Look at that!" exclaimed Arti. "Are they suicidal? Beating their heads on … Hell, what's this? A bunch of Warriors are rushing toward our flyer!" Instantly all the proximity sensors started clamoring.

Below them, about twenty Shshi Warriors began to scrabble around the *Durga*, standing up against the hull, hacking at it with their mandibles.

Will was saying, "Let me douse these blasted alarms – I can't hear myself think … *Stinger*, come in, please! Capt. Van – Capt. !eye Taeva, come in! This is *Durga*. Urgent. Do you copy?"

The scratching and clattering of jaws and claws could be heard on the outer hatch, like bones rattling against the outside of a coffin, eager to get in.

"*Chi taru Eyekz*! Maybe we ought to jump out!" said Luku, beginning to get unnerved.

"No!" said Gwidian, who had been glaring out with his fists clenched on the window grips. "She's in there! I'll never leave her!"

"I agree with you on that," said Arti. "I think we're safe in here, as long as we don't open the hatch."

"Of course," said Luku in chagrin. "I do not want to leave Kaitrin. I do not think well."

"Confound it, *Stinger*! Where are you? I can't raise them!"

Luku went over to help. They ran a frantic check of the systems. Gwidian stood like a man turned to stone, staring at the towers of Lo'ro'ra, waiting for someone to emerge.

"Hey! The cavalry!" Arti cried.

"The Nasutes!" said Julian. "They're fighting off the ones attacking us! Goddam! I've never seen them in full-blown battle mode before! Look at that spray! Look at the soldiers roll to try to get it off them! Didn't you say that stuff is stronger than stomach acid, Griff?"

Gwidian made no answer. He had pressed his forehead against the window, staring at the fortress, paying no attention to anything happening on the ground below.

"The Nasutes are driving back the Shshi Warriors," Arti called to A'a'ma and the Pozú on the lower deck. "There are several of each down, motionless. One Nasute is still twitching. I can see a big gash in its belly."

"My god. Oh, god," whispered Gwidian.

"Nothing wrong with our end of comlink," said Luku. "Where is *Stinger*?"

"I don't know, but we can't make contact," said Will. "It's like they're not there any longer. Where did they go? *Stinger*, this is *Durga*. Urgent. We need assistance. Dammit! You promised to be there when we needed you!" He banged his fist on the console in frustration.

"Do not break!" said Luku. "That will not help!"

"I guess we're on our own," said Arti uncertainly.

With a choked sound, Gwidian broke away from the window and plunged down the ladder, emerging before the startled eyes of Prf. A'a'ma and the steady gaze of the Pozú.

"I'm going to get her out," he said. "I don't care whether anyone helps me or not." He headed for the weapons locker.

A'a'ma squawked. "Get away from there, Gwidian! What do you think you are doing?"

The others had rushed down the ladder after him. Arti and Gwidian both had the code to the weapons locker, but he was having trouble keying it in. The security pair approached him. "Come on, Professor," said Julian, reaching for Gwidian's arm. "You can't just … "

Gwidian turned on him with a vicious jukara move. Fortunately, Julian's own expert training had given him superb reflexes and he dodged in time to take only a glancing blow on the shoulder instead of full impact on the side of the neck. He let out a yelp of pain, grabbing his shoulder and staggering back. Trea and Sev jumped toward him.

Gwidian turned again to the locker. Will made a move; he outweighed the Professor by eighteen kilograms, but he was no martial arts adept and he hesitated. But Gwidian had caught the motion out of the corner of his eye and he swung around. His pistol was out again and he waved it menacingly at Will.

"Get away from me!" Gwidian said. "You can't stop me from doing what I must."

A'a'ma twittered. "Prf. Gwidian, you are crazy! I am worried about Kaitrin, too, but this kind of behavior does not help. Put up the gun!"

"Stay away from me!" Gwidian leveled the pistol at A'a'ma, who squealed.

"Damn!" said Arti. "He's got the safety off!"

They all backed away. Gwidian's eyes looked abnormally bright; he was holding the ready weapon in his right hand and steadying it with his left, but both hands were shaking.

Trea said, "He is *surál*. I will get gun."

"Trea, you'd better stay away," said Arti tensely.

"I will get gun," the Pozú repeated softly. "You will not hurt Trea, will you, Gwidian?"

Slowly she moved toward Griffen, who watched her approach. Trea reached up with both hands, took hold of his forearms, and gently pulled his hands down so the gun pointed at the floor. She ran her hands up and down his arms. "You do not want to hurt anybody, Gwidian. Look inside. You know that. Let Will come and take weapon."

Gingerly Will approached and took the pistol from Gwidian's relaxing fingers before he dropped it. Turning away, he quickly reengaged the safety and handed the weapon to Arti.

Gwidian's legs buckled. He sank to his knees, his hands clutching his thighs, his head bowed. He rocked back and forth. "Trea ... I ... have to ... save her ... I have to ... "

"I know. But this is wrong way, Gwidian. There are a hundred Warriors out there – two or three hundred, maybe more. One man with one weapon, or three or four people with weapons – not enough. You will be killed. And maybe Kaitrin is all right. Ki'shto'ba and the Seer – they care about her, too – I can feel. They will not let her take harm. And if you run out and get killed yourself, and then Kaitrin come safe out of fortress and find you are dead for no reason, what will that do to her, Gwidian? She loves you."

Everyone could hear his heavy breathing. Trea said, "Come. I go with you into sleeping room and we talk more. Come, Gwidian. It will be all right. Will, help here."

Griffen allowed Will to help him to his feet and into the bedroom. Trea went in after him, then Will came out, and Trea shut the door. Standing before the closed door, Will said, "I feel very bad about all this. I like Prf. Gwidian. I enjoyed the earlier expeditions I flew with him and I've enjoyed the fieldwork on this one. I don't know what's happening to him."

Tió'otu had sunk down beside the table, much shaken. "I really thought he was going to shoot me," he quavered. "I had visions of never seeing my own wife again."

Sev was palpating the shoulder of a wincing Julian. "I think, no break. Come into MedBay – a scan will tell."

"Sev, were you not scared for Trea?" asked Luku.

Sev glanced at her. "No. Ama knows what she can do. Never do anything she is not sure with."

"I forgot about his black belt," said Julian, going out with Sev.

Arti was looking at Gwidian's gun. "Are we all agreed that, no matter what happens, Prf. Gwidian should no longer have access to weapons?"

"Definitely agreed!" said A'a'ma. "He is too unstable just now to handle something as dangerous as a laser pistol or to have access to that locker."

"I'll stash this in the locker and change the code. Two people ought to have access to it. I'll give it to Julian, if everyone agrees."

"Suits me!" said Will. "I'm going up and try to raise the *Stinger* again."

But there was no raising the *Stinger* and soon he came back down and sat discouraged at the table. Some of the team stayed upstairs to monitor activities in the courtyard. The Warriors continued to mill, but they were clearly organizing into two contingents facing each other across a buffer zone of about nine meters. The contingent in front of the Warriors' Quarters was ragged and agitated, straggling closer to the flyer than the other. Sa'ti'a'i'a's troops continued to crouch around the *Durga*; occasionally, a Shi Warrior would dart at the Nasutes, who would spit at it and drive it off. Brief skirmishes broke out occasionally between the lines. Sometimes, a flurry of internal fighting would erupt within the forces on the left; twice several Warriors exploded from the nearer ranks and rushed to the other side, where they abased and scrabbled abjectly in front of a large Warrior whom Luku identified as A'gwa'ji.

"It is civil war, for sure," she said, scanning through her VE. "Remember how they had neat units when we first came? All disorder now. I see the Commander Hi'ta'fu over on the left, about halfway down, and that other one who attacked Prf. Gwidian – Lo'lo'pai. Three Alates are with them, right out in middle of soldiers. I think it is that one who does not like Kwi'ga'ga'tei. Mo'gri'ta'tu. Yes, I am sure."

"They would pick a time to fall apart when Kaitrin was inside," said Arti.

In a moment, Luku said, "Sa'ti'a'i'a is out here. Prf. A'a'ma and I could try to talk to it – get information on Kaitrin. I can use original emitter and receiver."

"We don't dare open the hatch," said Arti.

"I suppose you are right. And biopulse transmissions will not penetrate hull."

At length, Trea came out of the bedroom. "Gwidian will be all right," she said. "Quite sane now. But I am a little worried. His soul has become so twined in Kaitrin's soul. I think if she die, his soul will cease to be."

They all looked at her in some bewilderment, except Sev, who seemed to understand exactly what she meant.

"I want him to rest," Trea was continuing, "but I will not give sedative because I do not know what crisis we might have happen, so I do not want him unconscious. Please treat him in normal way when he comes out. Prf. A'a'ma, can you do that?"

"♪♫ I will try."

After a while Griffen did come out. He stood in the doorway of the sleeping compartment, his shoulders sagging, his hollow eyes shifting around the faces.

"Julian," he said, "did that blow do you any damage? I've

never lost control like that before ... only – once perhaps ... "

Julian flexed his arm, grinning ruefully. "I'll have a pretty deep bruise – nothing serious. It's the old element of surprise, Professor. Gets you every time."

A fleeting smile crossed Gwidian's face, followed by a shadow of pain. He turned to Tió'otu. "Prf. A'a'ma," he said in a tautly modulated voice, "I want to offer my abject apologies to you. I ... have no excuses. I hope you will accept my apologies."

A'a'ma quivered. "I accept, Gwidian. We may not have always gotten on perfectly, but on this trip, I think I have learned to know you well enough to understand that it was only the stress of this crisis."

"I want to formally resign from co-leadership of this expedition. I don't seem to be fit at the moment to do a rational job."

A'a'ma nictitated in surprise. "Oh, it is all a formality, anyway, Prf. Gwidian. And right now things are not very formal, are they? I would prefer to let things stand as they are."

Gwidian stood silent, seeming too spent to engage in any contention. Then he said, "Have we heard from the *Stinger*?"

"Nothing," said Will. "It's as if it weren't there. There must have been a massive comlink failure. Or it could be ... "

Nobody encouraged him to finish his conjecture, especially Luku.

"What's happening out there?" asked Gwidian.

Trea said, "Go up and look. I will go with you, Gwidian."

"Trea," he said pathetically, "can I bear it?"

"You need to know what is outside," she said, taking his arm. "You must face it and find strength to wait. I feel sure it will have good outcome. Will, give me boost up ladder."

Gwidian stood looking out at the opposing armies, breathing tightly. "It's a civil rebellion, isn't it?" he said. "It looks – halfway under control. Why don't they send her out, if she's all right? Why would she not make them bring her out, if she's all right?"

His voice was swelling and Trea put a warning hand on his arm. He turned away from the window. "You're wrong, you know," he said harshly. "I can't bear it." And he went back down the ladder and reentered the sleeping compartment, shutting the door behind him.

Chapter 27

... Names in my ears
Of all the lost adventurers my peers ...
... in a sheet of flame
I saw them and I knew them all. And yet
Dauntless the slug-horn to my lips I set,
And blew. *"Childe Roland to the Dark Tower came."*
  – *from* Robert Browning, *Childe Roland* ...

[In the midst of the former First Cohort, Mo'gri'ta'tu and his fellow Alates crouch with Hi'ta'fu]

[Mo'gri'ta'tu]: How can you say everything is lost? We have nearly as many Warriors as they do. The First Cohort is better trained. Get yourself among the troops – stop these defections! Make them see the rectitude of what is happening here!

[Hi'ta'fu, scrabbles over the top of its head with its claws]: Rectitude!

[Mo'gri'ta'tu]: Do not spew such odors of despair – you demoralize your own Warriors! Rally yourself! Rally your troops! Form an attack plan! I personally will never concede defeat! If a weak-bodied Alate can so sternly persevere in battle, what should the renowned Commander Hi'ta'fu the Unconquered do?

[Hi'ta'fu]: Are you insane? Have your eyes dropped off your head? Can you not comprehend what is happening? I am no longer the Commander! This is no longer the First Cohort! I have been supplanted by my Third in command! I am accursed! I will be cast out! All to feed your hatred and promote your petty lust for power! Why did I let myself become ensnared in your heinous scheming?

[Mo'gri'ta'tu]: You are old and weak, Hi'ta'fu, and too ready to forget our glorious goal. We can retake the fortress, reclaim our rightful places – emerge stronger than before! Plan an attack! Do not wait for your enemy to make the first move. Does a weak-bodied Alate have to lay strategy for you?

[Hi'ta'fu]: I have no strategy and I make no plans.

[Mo'gri'ta'tu, growing more and more incensed]: Your ineptness is evident in your choice of a Second. This is all Lo'lo'pai's fault. Look at it over there – it can do nothing but grovel in the dirt. It knows its guilt. I hope it meets its end dishonorably on this field! That is a fit end for traitors!

[Hi'ta'fu, snaps mandibles]: Be careful what you wish for, Alate.

[Mo'gri'ta'tu, ignoring Hi'ta'fu's threat, worms his way through the swarm and reaches Lo'lo'pai's side. The Chief cringes away from him]

[Mo'gri'ta'tu]: You faithless coward! No, 'weakling' is a better word! You must have spewed our intentions to that Lieutenant like a bit of putrid fungus!

[Lo'lo'pai]: I trusted Ni'shto'pri. It was only an inconsequential slip. It swore to be true to its duty.

[Mo'gri'ta'tu]: But it construed its duty differently from you! And now there it is, opposite you in the field, commanding a unit of defectors, its former comrades from the First Cohort! Does that not gall you? It should!

[Lo'lo'pai, writhing]: It does, Chamberlain, it does!

[Mo'gri'ta'tu]: What if I told you there was a way you could atone for this transgression – regain your status in the new order that is coming to Lo'ro'ra when your Commander reclaims its rightful place?

[Lo'lo'pai]: I will do anything – anything – to restore my honor and my Commander's trust!

[Mo'gri'ta'tu, regarding the Warrior with blatant malevolency and secretly calculating thoughts]: I will remember that, Chief Lo'lo'pai, and help you to find your way.

*   *   *

In the Holy Chamber, Kaitrin waited, trying to check the swell of panic, telling herself that she was fine, that Griffen would understand, that he would be all right once she got back to him. She was getting thirsty and she drank off half the contents of her water bottle and chewed a chunk of energy bar. *... must keep up my strength ... be ready for ... whatever ...*

Kwi'ga'ga'tei was involved in everything. Messengers that came and went, distraught Workers, panicky Alates – she dealt with them all. Her Steward I'mei'o'nu, her personal Healers, all fussed over her, bringing her honeydew, grooming her, afraid she would be unable to bear up to the strain. But as the waiting continued, she alone appeared to confront the crisis with steadfast courage and a clear head.

Kwi'ga'ga'tei explained her intentions to Kaitrin. *I will offer amnesty to the rebels. They will be permitted to leave Lo'ro'ra, taking whatever Workers and Alates wish to go with them – there will be some, but I think not many! They can found another fortress, if they have the will – it is not an easy task, especially for outcasts. But they will not be permitted to take a fertile Alate-nymph with them. They will have to beg both* ma'na'ta| *and* na'sha'ma| *from other fortresses if they wish to be successful. That will be their punishment.*

And one other thing – before I release them, they must surrender Mo'gri'ta'tu and leave him behind. His corrupting influence must not be allowed to endure.

"What do you mean to do with him, Kwi'ga'ga'tei?" asked Kaitrin in some trepidation.

We will allow him a chance to sacrifice himself willingly for the good of Lo'ro'ra and thus redeem himself. But if he will not, we will kill him, Star-Wing or no, and leave his corpse in the marches to suffer the fate of all who have willfully broken faith with the Way of the Shshi.

I will undertake the execution if Kwi'ga'ga'tei requests it, said Ki'shto'ba. *Since I am not of Lo'ro'ra, I will take less stain from this act.*

Death is a rare penalty even for the greatest crimes, said Kwi'ga'ga'tei, *and if there were any other way, I would take it, but such a deviant as Mo'gri'ta'tu cannot be allowed to live and continue to spew poison.*

*   *   *

Most of the time, Kaitrin huddled against A'kha'ma'na'ta, with the King on his Holy One's opposite flank. All three of them needed the comfort of a touch, although it did cross Kaitrin's mind that she might be contaminating the progenitor of Lo'ro'ra with alien pathogens.

After laying, A'kha'ma'na'ta drowsed for a while, then all at once began to talk again. *Ru, after you return to the other Star-Beings, will you come back to see me again?*

Kaitrin was too stressed for pretense. "I do not believe so, Holy One. We mean to leave your world as soon as I get back to our dwelling."

You are going to leave? I did not know that. Nobody tells me anything! Tei, did you know that?

But Kwi'ga'ga'tei was embroiled with No'kri about the problems of feeding the Warriors. No'kri was scandalized that the Holy Seer refused to allow Workers to cross the lines and feed the rebels. *They have rebel Workers with them and they have access to the Warrior's refectory,* said Kwi'ga'ga'tei. *Let them do what they can. One does not coddle traitors, no matter what one's instinct counsels.*

A'kha'ma'na'ta was saying to Kaitrin, *Do you leave because we have not been properly hospitable? Do you curse us for it?*

"I would never curse the Shshi, *na'ta'zei|*!"

Call me Kha, said the Holy One of Lo'ro'ra.

Kaitrin smiled in spite of the echo of Griffen's pain in her soul. "You honor me. And I must say this: I told Kwi'ga'ga'tei that I would come back one day and I will do that. Times will be happier then, Kha."

The worst thing, said A'kha'ma'na'ta, *is that I will never know the end of the story of Ul'i'seit. You said before that it – he*

– finally reached his home.

"Yes. All his Warriors were killed, but he reached home and was reunited with his *ma'na'ta|*."

Sei'o'na'sha'ma, who was receiving all this with his head resting on his Queen's back only thirty centimeters from Kaitrin's face, said, *Ul'i'seit had a* ma'na'ta|*? He was a King?*

"Yes. That is why he was so eager to return to his home. But when he finally did, he had been gone so long that everyone believed he had died and his *ma'na'ta|* was about to take a new King. He had to fight to keep her."

Your shna'sha'ma| *can fight?*

"Yes. We do not have Castes as you do, you see. We all have eyes, no one has wings, and we do not grow our weapons upon the body. So all are equal and anyone can do anything."

I would be afraid to fight, said Sei'o'na'sha'ma.

Workers came to feed the Holy One and the King, and A'kha'ma'na'ta said, *They can feed you, too, Ru. Open your mouth.*

"Kha, we cannot eat your food. I am sorry. Ti'shra could not eat ours and that is part of the reason that it died. It would be the same if I tried to eat yours."

It is all so very strange, is it not, Sei? Then after a moment A'kha'ma'na'ta added, *Did you ever have an adventure, Ru?*

"This is my adventure – visiting you. Becoming friends with the Shshi."

Really? But we are only ordinary One Beings, even if we are the primary creation. How can that be an adventure?

"Would it be an adventure for you to come to my world?"

Oh, yes!

"So – you see?"

I did have an adventure once, said the Shi Queen. *The journey from Zi'zos'mi – the place where I was hatched. At that time I was Mei'a'kha'bu – my Alate name. I could dance then – I danced with my first King all the way from Twi'mu'pai where he joined us. I saw the stars – the little lights in the black sky. I saw the two moons glowing – the eyes of the Highest Mother. I will never see those things again. The Seer says my spirit will one day dance among the stars beside the Nameless One, but I do not understand such magic things. I am getting old, Ru. When I die, they will cut up my belly, and the new* ma'na'ta| *and all the others in Lo'ro'ra will eat a tiny portion of me. So I will live on in my children. I can understand that.*

But, Ru, do you know what? I would rather wander under the stars as you do and have adventures. I would rather be Ul'i'seit.

On the other side of her, her King was nuzzling the side of her head. Close to tears, Kaitrin stroked the area around the base of her antennae. She was covered with their saliva and with the exudations of the Holy One's integument – she had long since grown impervious to the stench – and she did not care. She loved this grotesque atom of creation. But at the same time her soul was crying only one thing: *Griffen. Griffen! Will you be all right when I get out of here? Oh, love, you have to be all right – you've become the whole heart of my life!*

*　　*　　*

Kaitrin could see Kwi'ga'ga'tei consulting with two Warrior messengers, then with Ki'shto'ba. Finally the Seer came over to her. *I am told that the situation has grown as stable as it will get for a while. I will go with the Champion to assess things. We may be able to take you out.*

Oh, god, thought Kaitrin, scrambling to her feet.

Oh, are you going to go? Do not go! said A'kha'ma'na'ta. *Tei, do not let her go!*

"I must, Kha. My *na'sha'ma*| will be frightened. He needs me."

I would be frightened if I were separated from you, Kha, said Sei'o'na'sha'ma. *I understand why she must go.*

Kaitrin bent and laid her hands tenderly on the heads of each of them, then straightened up to stand and wait for Kwi'ga'ga'tei's return. She consulted her watch, made some calculations. She had entered shortly after the beginning of the twenty-hour daylight cycle. She had been in here about six hours. *Griffen ...* It was two hours before midday. She had been out of bed eleven hours and had nothing but those miserable field rations since the scrambled egg substitute. *Griffen ...* She drained the last two swallows from her water bottle and distractedly ran her hand over her face and head. *Griffen ...* Her hair was falling down; impatiently she yanked out the pins and stuck them in a pocket. *Let it go loose –*

who cares?

Ki'shto'ba and the Seer returned. *We have blocked the main entrance,* said Kwi'ga'ga'tei, *but the stone does not go all the way to the top, so I was able to look out. The lines are separated by a reasonable distance, with the rebels' command closer to the flying dwelling than to the fortress. I could see Hi'ta'fu and Lo'lo'pai, and I glimpsed Alate wings – I have no doubt it is Mo'gri'ta'tu. I could see that Sa'ti'a'i'a and its Cohort are still guarding your dwelling. I believe we can take you through safely, Ru'a'ma'na'ta.*

At last, at last, thought Kaitrin.

I have chosen six stout Warriors to surround you, said Ki'shto'ba. *I will go in front. No one will dare attack. Let us go.*

It is time for a display of authority, said Kwi'ga'ga'tei. *I will go with you to the entrance and show myself, so that all will know I am still alive and have charge of things. Then we will make them wait awhile longer. It is important to wear down the will.*

They left the Holy Chamber. Behind Kaitrin, A'kha'ma'na'ta cried, *You said you would come back, Ru! Promise me that you will come back and visit us again one day!*

Kaitrin turned around and said, "Kha – Sei – I promise. I will come back."

The Holy Seer and Kaitrin traversed the corridor abreast. *Ru'a'ma'na'ta, I value that you befriended the Holy One and King today. It made my task a little easier, that I did not have to use my strength keeping them reassured.*

"It was not difficult. I have come to care about them and all of you, Kwi'ga'ga'tei."

What you said at the end – did you mean it?

"Of course I meant it! I have every intention of coming back. And I will see you again, Kwi'ga'ga'tei, before we leave."

They approached the entranceway. Kaitrin hunkered inside, firmly inserting the earports of her "antenna" so she would not lose them. Her legs ached and felt both stiff and wobbly. *I hope I can run if I have to.*

The Warriors rolled aside the stone. Kaitrin could see A'gwa'ji and the Lieutenant Ni'shto'pri a short distance down the line to the left. Swaying and stamping went through the lines on both sides as word spread of activity at the fortress's entrance. The flyer hulked in the distance, tightly closed. It seemed a very great distance. *It's never seemed that far before.*

She stood up. A'gwa'ji's Warriors formed up, two on each side of her, two behind. In front of her went the Huge-Head, filling the space of two Warriors. *How does Ki'shto'ba know which direction to go? I suppose it can sense the distance to the lines on each side. Their awareness of their surroundings is so uncanny ...*

They left the safety of the fortress and started through the gauntlet.

*   *   *

[Lo'lo'pai and Mo'gri'ta'tu at the front of the line, two-thirds of the distance from the entrance to the fortress]

[Lo'lo'pai]: What is happening? What is this disturbance?

[Mo'gri'ta'tu, standing at full stretch to see over the troops]: A party of Warriors has issued from the fortress. Ki'shto'ba leads them. They escort the false female *ma'na'ta|*. Ah, Lo'lo'pai ...

[Lo'lo'pai]: What? What is it?

[Mo'gri'ta'tu, brings his antennae close to Lo'lo'pai's]: Here is your chance! Have you not been twice ordered to kill the female, and twice you have failed? Here is your chance to redeem yourself – to discharge your debt to the Commander. Are you still eager to redeem your honor?

[Lo'lo'pai, swaying]: What would you have me do now?

[Mo'gri'ta'tu]: I want you to attack them. Kill the female. You can leap over the Warriors. There are two on this side. You can leap behind the Huge-Head, kill her instantly with one slash, then leap over the two Warriors behind and escape.

[Lo'lo'pai, squirms, twists its head, scrapes]: I will likely take my death.

[Mo'gri'ta'tu]: Are you really so craven? Would you die in total disgrace, without making the slightest effort to redeem yourself? Show me if you are worthy of a place in this new time! Earlier, you said you would do anything to recover your honor!

[Lo'lo'pai]: I will! I will do it! I will show you, Mo'gri'ta'tu – show my Commander that I am still worthy of its trust!

[Mo'gri'ta'tu]: Make ready then. They approach. Do you sense them?

[Lo'lo'pai, moving forward a few paces]: I sense them. I am ready.

[Mo'gri'ta'tu, to himself]: *Then goodbye, dimwitted fool. Soon I will not have to coddle you any longer. And perhaps I will have a modicum of revenge as well.*

*   *   *

In the *Durga*, the team tried to eat a meal but found throats a bit dry. Now they sat around the table, or paced about, or climbed to and from the flight deck to observe. Gwidian had emerged from the sleeping compartment again, only to vanish into the lab, leaving the door open a few centimeters. No one knew what he was doing inside. There had still been no contact with the *Stinger*.

On the flight deck Arti suddenly gave a whoop. "Somebody's coming out! Oh, great gods! It is! It's Ki'shto'ba with some Warriors, and there's Kaitrin in the middle of them! Griffen, Kaitrin is coming out! She looks like she's all right!"

Gwidian appeared in the lab entrance, hanging onto the doorframe. The look on his face was indescribable – an agonized mix of relief, fear, and disbelief. A lot of excited talking and warbling erupted. Luku seized A'a'ma and they hopped around the room. Trea and Sev hugged each other. Arti came sliding down the ladder from the upper deck.

"Hey!" cried Will, lunging forward.

Nobody had noticed that Gwidian had made a dash for the hatch. Before anyone understood what was happening, he had released it. The door sprang up and the ramp came down, but Gwidian was jumping off the side of the ramp before it hit the ground.

"Hey, Professor!" cried Arti. "Come back here! Wait till they get closer!"

Arti and Julian, with Will right behind, jumped onto the ramp after him. The startled Nasutes scrabbled around to face them, posturing and spurting a little acid on the ground.

"*Hoi-a!*" cried Luku. "Trea, try harder to teach this man patience!" With A'a'ma, she and the Pozú crowded into the hatch opening.

Gwidian had stopped, peering toward the fortress, shading his eyes against the glare of a hazy sun.

"Is that a pistol?" cried Arti incredulously.

"How did he get that?" said Julian. "I saw you lock the ... "

Will slapped his head. "Kaitrin's! Nobody thought of Kaitrin's gun! It was probably in their sleeping compartment!"

"This is getting out of hand," said Arti, drawing her own sidearm. "Julian! Will! Be ready for anything!"

Those two also drew their weapons. A'a'ma and Luku coughed imprecations. Trea and Sev poised in front of them.

Motionless, Gwidian waited. Kaitrin had come almost two-thirds of the way and they saw her yank out her ear ports and stuff them in her pocket so she could hear human speech. She began waving both arms energetically. "Griffen! What are you doing out here? Go inside! Love, it's all right! I'm all right!"

There was a sudden commotion. From the front of the rebel line, something erupted, bounding toward the passing group with blind purpose.

Emitting a howl, Gwidian leaped forward, firing his pistol at the hurtling form.

Kaitrin screamed, "*Griffen!*"

The laser blast gashed Lo'lo'pai's right flank, shattering a leg and tearing into its belly. The big Warrior somersaulted backwards, then scrambled up and around to face this unexpected attacker.

Gwidian's momentum carried him onward, his aimless firing narrowly missing Ki'shto'ba, who had sensed Lo'lo'pai's approach and leaped to meet it. However, the counterattack from the direction of the flying dwelling had taken the Huge-Head by surprise and Lo'lo'pai's suddenly arrested course caused the Champion to land short of its intended target.

Near the flyer several rebel Warriors took advantage of the distraction to attack the Nasutes. Will and Julian fired at them, taking down two. Arti struggled to aim at Lo'lo'pai, but Gwidian was in her sights. Tossing its head in agony, Lo'lo'pai had bunched its five remaining legs and now it sprang in the direction of this unknown foe.

Gwidian fired a third time, but the close-range blast deflected harmlessly into the air as Lo'lo'pai took him down. The Shi had attacked in the instinctive way of its kind, hooked jaws open, head swinging. The slash caught the human on an angle, one torqued hook beneath the left rib cage, the other higher, between the ribs. The jaws snapped shut. Lo'lo'pai had never encountered such chitin as this; it jerked its head and ripped out the mandibles along with a large chunk of flesh and splintered bone.

Gwidian's cry of agony was audible to the horrified spectators on the ramp, but more audible, echoing over the whole chattering silence of the battlefield, were Kaitrin's persistent screams. *"Griffen! No! God, no!"* And she burst away from her shocked guard and ran helter-skelter toward the place where her love lay rolling on the ground.

But Ki'shto'ba's second leap had brought it down on top of Lo'lo'pai even before its jaws had torn free of Gwidian's chest. The Champion's straighter mandibles plunged with all the power of its massive head deep into the neck area of the doomed Chief. Gwidian's blood spattered from the dying Warrior's mandibles as it thrashed on the ground, its head half severed from its body. Trampling on Lo'lo'pai's corpse, Ki'shto'ba cried, *Craven traitor! You have attacked a King! May the World Beyond reward you with everlasting dishonor!*

But in the entrance to the fortress of Lo'ro'ra, a weight that was heavier than horror oppressed the Holy Seer Kwi'ga'ga'tei.

Now you can see – the wound has been made visible. I am not pleased. This one is not dead yet. If this one dies, you will pay the guilt-price for Lo'ro'ra.

Nameless One, have pity! I have tried! I have tried so hard to tread the right path!

You will take the Wound-That-Has-No-Healing if this one dies.

Nameless One, pity me! I learned too late – how was I to know this was the Wounded One? I implore you, let this pain pass elsewhere ...

You will take the Wound-That-Has-No-Healing if this one dies!

Kwi'ga'ga'tei turned from the implacable Speaking in her head and, dragging her belly painfully after her, withdrew into the fortress.

Chapter 28

Four he hurt, an' five he slew,
On the dowie houms o' Yarrow,
Till that stubborn knight came him behind,
An' ran his body thorrow. ...

She kiss'd his cheek, she kamed his hair,
As oft she did before, O;
She drank the red blood frae him ran,
On the dowie houms o' Yarrow.
— *from* Anon., 17th c., *The Dowie Houms*
of Yarrow

Chaos had been loosed upon the field. The skittish rebels had
taken the vibrations of battle and the scent of body fluids as a signal to attack. Phalanxes were charging across the buffer zone and
plowing into A'gwa'ji's forces, which responded with a mixture of
confusion and ferocity. The new Commander was issuing frantic
commands, trying to bring order to its loyalist Cohort. Ki'shto'ba
and the guards that had emerged with it were fighting for their
lives. Vainly the Huge-Head swung its body about, trying to find
the scent of Ru'a'ma'na'ta, but there was too much sensory clutter
and too many slashing jaws distracting it. It and the guards began
to retreat toward the fortress.

As soon as Gwidian had fallen, Trea and Sev had jumped off

the ramp, dropped to all fours, and run toward him, heedless of flailing mandibles and Nasute acid. "Holy hell!" cried Arti. "Look at them!" She ran after them, firing randomly to open a path through the turmoil. Julian and Will were not far behind.

Luku and A'a'ma were left huddled in the open hatch. The panicked !Ka<tí, warbling madly, started to retreat into the flyer, but Luku grabbed onto him. "Professor! They are running over the Nasutes!"

Indeed, the line of snouted Warriors had been split in two by a focused assault. Sa'ti'a'i'a scuttled past the ramp, its antennae stiffly extended toward the pair in the hatch, but without a receiver they had no idea what it was trying to tell them.

"We cannot stay here, Professor!" Frenzied Shshi Warriors were jumping at the ramp. Luku had pulled her pistol, but A'a'ma was not packing his weapon and he was scared witless. Luku fired at the group and they tumbled backward, but others instantly filled the gap. One Warrior was leaping at the side of the ramp, close enough to snag a few of A'a'ma's tail feathers in its tossing jaws. Squawking in terror, A'a'ma let Luku yank him off the opposite edge and propel him out into the field, where Arti, Julian, and Will had formed a perimeter around certain huddled forms. Tió'otu had not realized how fast he could run when it was necessary.

"What are you doing out here?" cried Julian as they approached.

"That!" cried Luku, waving over her shoulder as she dragged A'a'ma into the circle.

"The bastards!" cried Julian. "They've gotten into the *Durga!*"

Warriors were scampering up the ramp, disappearing through the hatch. Sa'ti'a'i'a and the remains of its Cohort had dashed toward the Star-Beings and encircled them, spraying acid indiscriminately to discourage approach. But the Nasute Chief was dancing madly and waving its antennae at them. It proceeded to dart through a small gap between fighting units and head toward the stone storage cysts at the east side of the compound.

"I think it wants us to follow," said Arti. "Will, can you and Julian manage Gwidian?"

"I can get him by myself," said Will.

In the eye of this chaos Kaitrin had no idea what was

happening around her. She hunched over Griffen, her hands trying to dam the blood that welled from his side. Trea and Sev were ripping back his shirt. Will hovered above them. "We've got to move him – find some shelter. They've taken over the flyer."

From the sky came a sudden burst of thunder. One of those quick storms was moving across the plain. Lightning flashed against the fast advancing clouds.

Trea pulled back. "Move him! Need a refuge place."

Julian took Kaitrin under the arms, lifting her to her feet. "I can't leave him. I can't leave him!" she moaned.

"We aren't going to leave him. But we have to make a run for it. The Shshi have taken over the *Durga*. Come on, Kaitrin."

With the strength of desperation, Will had single-handedly picked up the unconscious Gwidian in his arms. As his blood spread over the former wrestler's shirt, they all dashed for the storage cysts with the Nasutes protecting their rear.

*   *   *

[Mo'gri'ta'tu]: Commander! You stand like one who has been struck on the head! Exert your authority! Rally your troops! We can win this battle! [Mo'gri'ta'tu is jostled into Ta'rei'so'cha and A'dei'no'no, who huddle together in dazed terror, realizing at last the full implication of their treachery] Stand away from me! You are useless! You are all useless to me!

[Hi'ta'fu]: What did you say to it? What did you do to make it attack like that?

[Mo'gri'ta'tu]: Lo'lo'pai? Why, did it not redeem itself, Commander? Or at least bungle another attempt to do so?

[Hi'ta'fu]: I might as well have killed it myself with my own jaws.

{Mo'gri'ta'tu]: Are you going to take charge or not? Must a weak-bodied Alate take command of the troops of Hi'ta'fu the Unconquered? For shame! Show that something of your power endures, for the sake of your Warriors, if not of yourself!

[Hi'ta'fu, bestirs itself painfully]: This becomes quite humorous. I will pursue this jest, even though I believe I can perceive its climax. A'dai'dos! Po'ar'ka! Command the Lieutenants to marshal their phalanxes! At least there will be some order on the field at the end of this disaster!

*   *   *

The cyst was a place of perpetual night, with a mere smudge of light seeping through the low entranceway. The air was close and earth-chilled, redolent of the decayed sweetness of the *tho'sei* blossoms often stored there. At the moment the cyst was empty, containing only some bundles of tree limbs in a pile at one side, along with some tools and buckets.

Outside, thunder rumbled and a brief, intense rain pattered down. If the battle still raged, the sound did not penetrate the stonework. The Nasutes crouched before the entrance, like protective spirits.

Within the chamber, A'a'ma and Luku huddled together against the wall; he was half beside himself and she was talking him back to sanity. Julian and Arti stood guard inside the entrance, craning their necks over their shoulders to watch what was going on in the center of the enclosure, where Will had activated a field light.

A dazed Kaitrin sat holding Griffen's shoulders and head in her lap, trying to assimilate the enormity of what had happened. Trea and Sev were working feverishly to control the bleeding, conferring together in the quick, gruff tones of Poz-até.

"Trea," said Kaitrin in a quavering voice, "he isn't in that much danger, is he? You can fix him, can't you?"

Trea looked up, her lips drawn back over her teeth. "I will try," she said.

'I will try.' Oh, Griffen. Oh, Griffen. "You're supposed to be such a wonderful healer, Trea. You can save anybody. They said Pozú doctors can save anybody."

From where he held the light, Will said softly, "Kaitrin, she'll try. It's a bad wound."

"How bad? Don't hide things from me!"

Trea's hands continued to work as she spoke. "You are right – you must know. Much blood loss – organ damage. We have only field surgical kits – only a little clean water ... No hemosynthesizer ... If we could get back into flyer ... Kaitrin, you look here! This is pieces of broken ribs sticking out. Lung is torn – this is it, pushing through sucking wound. The diaphragm was punctured, torn. Maybe spleen, not sure."

"It's a bad wound," repeated Will, his voice cracking.

A wave of nausea swept Kaitrin, but she fought it off. She bent over Griffen's unconscious face, kissing his bloody mouth, rocking him. He was so colorless that she could not tell his lips from his skin. His breathing was very labored.

Sev was monitoring Gwidian's vital signs with a sensor. Now he growled a few words in Poz-até, then, in response to a command from Trea, scrabbled in his kit and came up with a transdermal injector. He applied it to Gwidian's neck, then began to administer oxygen from a portable extractor. Trea said, "Blood pressure drops. This drug will help stabilize. ... Arti, run check – who has water?"

"I drank all of mine," said Kaitrin despairingly. "But – Trea, I have my medkit! It has an emergency oxygen unit just like that one!"

"Ah, I remember. Will help. These have small power cell – are not meant to last long. Anybody else have that?"

But no one did and only Trea and Sev, Arti and Julian were carrying water bottles; Will, Luku, and Prf. A'a'ma had not been wearing their field packs. "Ration out two bottles among you," said Trea. "Save two for Gwidian." But everyone agreed not to drink, if it could make a difference for the expedition chief's survival.

Then almost miraculously Gwidian began to regain conscious, turning his head, moving a hand, gurgling in his throat. "Talk to him, Kaitrin," said Trea. "In flyer, he was desperate for you."

Kaitrin glanced up fearfully at her, then down at Gwidian. "Griffen, it's Kaitrin. I'm here – I'm all right. Griffen, can you hear me? Love, *mi querido*, my own dear love ... "

He blinked his eyes, tried to focus them on her face. "Kait ... Kait ... "

Kaitrin laughed hysterically. "You kind of scared me there, Griff. Promise me you'll never scare me like that again." She was massaging his hands and his grip responded.

"Kait ... Are you ... " He stopped for a moment, gasped, then whispered, "You're here? Really all right?"

"Oh, Griff, yes, I'm fine, love – I'm just fine."

He gasped again, more stridently. Then he said, "Kait ... you ready ... another alien ... die in your lap?"

"Griffen!" Terror swept her. "Don't say ... " Then reaction set in. "Griffen, why did you have to run out shooting like that? Ki'shto'ba was protecting me! It certainly would have stopped Lo'lo'pai before ... " Her bravado deserted her and she clutched him helplessly.

"I love you, Kait," he whispered. "You know ... men in love ... not rational ... "

"Griffen, Griffen." She swayed above him in agony.

"I couldn't let you die," he said.

As she bent lower, his body convulsed, the words bubbling in his throat. "Hold me ... anchor me ... drowning ... afraid to drown ... " A fresh gush of blood issued from his mouth and his breathing ceased.

"Trea!" shrieked Kaitrin.

The doctor barked at Sev, who pulled some archaic-looking tubing from his kit, then applied another injection. Trea was cutting the tube, starting an oral intubation. "Two problems," she said tautly. "Good lung collapsing. Torn lung still receives blood from arteries, fills chest, backs up into trachea." She applied her mouth to the end of the tube, sucked, spat Gwidian's blood onto the ground. Above them Will made a strangling sound. Kaitrin squeezed her eyes shut.

Trea glanced up, breathing hard. "Sorry," she said. "Quickest way for suction."

She repeated the action several times, then worked the tube deeper. "We have small respirator pump – but again, only minimal power ... " Sev was using the pump to re-inflate the collapsed lung. Griffen caught air, began to breathe again, with the pump assisting when he faltered. He clung to Kaitrin's hand, his eyes twisted shut. With the tube in his trachea, he could not speak. His chest labored heavily, up and down, up and down. Kaitrin thought she would go mad.

"Is not good fix for long," said Trea. "I must do surgery."

"Here?" rasped Kaitrin.

"Cannot get to flyer. Cannot wait." She was reaching under Griffen's neck, feeling his spine. "Have drugs that would serve for anesthetic, but better this." She spoke some words in Poz-até and applied some quick pressure, and he suddenly relaxed. His eyes opened and he looked at her. She, too, seemed to relax, as her empathic awareness of his pain lessened. "Gwidian, you should not hurt now. All numb below neck. If true, blink eyes, please."

He blinked, then looked up at Kaitrin. His hands had gone limp in hers, but obviously his agony had eased. She rocked, whispering to him.

"Gwidian, I will tell you what I do," Trea was saying. "I have to go into chest, ligate blood vessels, then excise damaged lung. Then suture up diaphragm, insert tubes to draw off air and fluids, and close outer wound. This will stop bleeding and ease breathing. Is all right?"

He barely responded. Kaitrin said, "They can grow a new lung for you later, Griff. It's not so bad to lose a lung."

"Yes, labs can bioengineer," said Trea. "If you feel pain, Gwidian, blink eyelids fast to tell me. Julian or Arti, one of you please come scan vital signs. You know how?"

With Will holding two lights above them, Julian monitoring the sensors, and Sev assisting, she began the surgery. Tió'otu had pulled himself together and Luku crawled over to Kaitrin and put her long arms around her. "Lean on me," she said. "You will wear down sitting like this. Lean into me."

Kaitrin settled into the warm, furry embrace. Physically, she was indeed flagging badly. Her mouth was so dry that she could hardly swallow. *... really thirsty ... but must save water for Griffen. Griffen ...* She was sticky with his blood and with the secretions of the Shshi Queen.

"Trea, infection – what about infection? I sat right against the Queen for hours. I have termite all over me."

"Least worry at moment," said Trea as she lasered away rib fragments. "This environment – procedure – all septic. Only limited antisepsis agents in these kits. These drugs, this equipment – never meant for this kind of surgery. Meant only for temporary fix in field, then treatment in proper facility afterwards. But maybe vaccines we gave will hold ... If we get back to flyer soon ... "

Tió'otu's voice came sepulchrally out of the perimeter of darkness. "If we can get back at all ... "

"Luku," said Kaitrin hoarsely, "what about communications? If the *Stinger* ... "

"Something happen to *Stinger*," said Luku, her own voice wobbling. "When the armies came out, we tried to message *Stinger*. Could not raise them. I am worried about that, too."

"Oh, god." It seemed to Kaitrin that some mythical hell had erected its misery into the universe. "The MPs – who has MPs? Can't you link with the *Durga* through one of them?"

"I try just now and got something odd – malfunction message, then static, then – nothing."

"Malfunction!" said Will. "We both checked that unit not two hours ago. Maybe we missed something and *Stinger's* silence was our fault after all."

"More likely those blasted bugs wrecked it," said Arti, who had left the entrance where nothing seemed to threaten and come to sit beside A'a'ma in the darkness.

"On the flight deck?" said Will.

"Well, the trapdoor was open and they can certainly climb," Julian replied.

"Luku," said Kaitrin, "can't you rig something strong enough to reach space directly?"

"Would need big power source. Let me see – what do we have besides three MPs?"

"The holocam!" said Kaitrin. "Oh, god, I forgot to turn it off – do you suppose it recorded the attack? Here, Luku, look at it!"

"Dead," said the Tae Quornaz. "Stopped working hours ago."

Increasingly desperate, Kaitrin said, "The pistols! One or two of the lights – we've got five of them! And the translator – what about the translator?"

"I wouldn't recommend dismantling the pistols," said Arti, "and the translator – we can't communicate with the Shshi without that."

As she worked over Gwidian, Trea said in her quiet way, "Little power sources like MPs and lights or even pistol will not make space com function. And we ought to save those cells, anyway – maybe can use in respirator and oxygen extractors."

"Oh, yes, of course," said Kaitrin, "we have to ... But it's hopeless then – we really are alone ... Damn! My earports! Where are they?"

Will said, "We saw you jerk them out and put them in your pocket right after you came out."

"Did I? I don't even remember … " Kaitrin rubbed her eyes. *I'm so tired. I'm missing something. What am I missing?*

"This is the last unexplored planet I will ever visit," quavered Prf. A'a'ma. "The next trip I make will be to Krisí'i'aid. If I live to make another trip."

Trea continued the surgery, her small, deft, four-fingered hands working blind inside her patient's thorax. Griffen was unconscious again. Kaitrin bent over him, ceaselessly caressing his face, not knowing how to pray.

*   *   *

[Kwi'ga'ga'tei lies splayed on her belly in a corner of the Holy Chamber as her Healers fuss around her. Di'fa'kro'mi sits by the Holy One and the King, trying to keep them calm. In front of the Seer, Ki'shto'ba sways distractedly from side to side]

[Ki'shto'ba]: Holy Kwi'ga'ga'tei, what would you have us do? Advise us!

[Kwi'ga'ga'tei]: Do as you think fit.

[Ki'shto'ba]: What happened? Why have you stopped advising us?

[Kwi'ga'ga'tei]: I had a vision. It is not one I can endure.

[There is dismay throughout the chamber at those words]

[A'kha'ma'na'ta]: Tei! Do not give up! There is no one else to tell me what to do!

[Kwi'ga'ga'tei]: I am afraid. How can I suffer this?

[Ki'shto'ba]: If you are afraid, Mo'gri'ta'tu will win! Will you have him come in here and rule your Holy One again?

[Kwi'ga'ga'tei shivers]

[I'mei'o'nu]: I have taken the sacred honeydew. I have it for you, Holy Seer. Let me sustain you.

[A'kha'ma'na'ta]: What has happened to Ru? Why will no one tell me?

[Kwi'ga'ga'tei]: Huge-Head, what did happen to her? To them all? To her *na'sha'ma|*?

[Ki'shto'ba]: Sa'ti'a'i'a sent a messenger to say that they took refuge in a storage cyst. The Nasutes are guarding them there. The flying dwelling is full of rebel Warriors – they chased the Star-Beings away from it. The messenger says they seem safe. There have been no words with them.

[Kwi'ga'ga'tei]: Her *na'sha'ma|* took a wound. Lo'lo'pai leaped upon him. I saw it.

[Ki'shto'ba]: He could be dead.

[Kwi'ga'ga'tei]: He is not dead. I will know if he dies.

[Shudders around the room]

[A'kha'ma'na'ta]: If he is wounded, we should help! Send Healers!

[Kwi'ga'ga'tei, raises her head]: Help. Yes … I'mei'o'nu, you have the honeydew? Give it to me.

[Ki'shto'ba, relieved that the Holy Seer is regaining will]: The battling has been fierce. It has reached another stalemate. Both sides are retrieving the dead. Still, nothing has been decided. What should be done?

[Kwi'ga'ga'tei]: Wait. Something will happen. Send word to A'gwa'ji that it should not initiate attack, but neither should it allow the rebels to get the upper hand. Give me another drink. Ki'shto'ba, scout safe ways to reach this storage cyst. I will go out to the Star-Beings myself as soon as I regain some strength.

[A Healer Alate]: Huge-Head, take a vessel of water to them. There is no water near those cysts. If they have wounds, they will want water.

*   *   *

Sev steadied Trea as she sealed the last suture and sat back exhausted. The amorphous mass of Gwidian's lung had been deposited in Will's bloodied shirt and Will had taken it to a corner and placed it in one of the Shshi's buckets.

"Blood pressure is dropping – 85 on 35 right now," said Julian.

"Too low," said Trea. She spoke to Sev, who retrieved the

second of two bags of sterile water from their medical kits and re-inforced it with some additives. The first had already been dripped into Gwidian's veins. "Have only two of these infusions. Not enough."

Kaitrin said, "He's sweating, shivering. He's cold. Trea ... "

"He needs blood," said Trea. "Do any of you humans know blood class? We tested you before the mission start, but data is on flyer – no access! Do not know Gwidian's, either." She slapped herself on the chest in frustration.

Will was saying regretfully, "I have Class 2B and Julian and Arti both have Class 3A. I'm sorry, Trea." And then Kaitrin realized what she had been missing.

"Oh, Trea, I have Class 1A – the one that can be donated safely to anybody! Why didn't I think of that sooner?" Then she swayed dizzily against Luku.

Trea looked at her. "Could use. But look at you. You are dehydrated yourself, famished. Save him, kill you, maybe ... "

"I don't care! If he needs my blood to live, take it! I beg you to take it!"

Trea ran her hand agitatedly over her ears.

"He's so cold, Trea. It's shock, isn't it? Take my blood! He was willing to give everything to save me. I couldn't live if I did less."

"All right! Sev, we have more tubing?"

Luku shed her tunic and trousers and they used them warm from her body to bundle around the chill of Gwidian's unresponsive form. Trea set a needle into a vein on Kaitrin's arm and attached the tubing. From one life's stream to the other, from heartbeat to heartbeat, Kaitrin's blood flowed to Griffen Gwidian.

Kaitrin sat against Luku's soft-furred breast, her eyes closed, feeling woozy and light-headed. The cyst slowly revolved around her. *Griffen ... is that you, love? I think I see stars – I see horses ... I see something coming against the stars ... hurrying ...*

Then she rallied herself. *Stop it, Kaitrin Oliva! He isn't dead! He's going to be all right! Don't ever, ever let yourself expect anything else!*

"I stop now," said Trea gruffly. "Dangerous to take any more."

"Is it enough for him? Will he be all right now?" whispered

Kaitrin through a throat so parched that her voice would only croak.

"He could use more." Trea raised a hand. "But I will not kill you! You think he would want that? He is nothing without you, Kaitrin. I understand that now."

Befuddled, Kaitrin stared at the visage of the small, brown, furry empath from a distant world. Then there was a scrabbling outside the cyst. Arti and Julian ran to the entrance. "Sa'ti'a'i'a is out here – and Ki'shto'ba! Kaitrin, I'm sure they want to talk to you."

Kaitrin felt like she was about to faint, but she said, "Let me put in the earports and turn on ... I don't feel much up to going out – maybe they can come in ... "

Sa'ti'a'i'a entered but Ki'shto'ba was too big; it crouched with its head jammed into the opening, waving its antennae. *Ru'a'ma'na'ta,* it said. *We worry – Kwi'ga'ga'tei worries. Do you need water?*

"Water! Oh, Ki'shto'ba! Could you bring us water?"

I have brought it. Its head withdrew, then its mandibles appeared with a covered bucket swinging from them. *The Healers thought you would want water.*

"Oh, paradise! Water!" Kaitrin leaned, strained toward it as Arti set it in their midst.

Trea pulled off the lid, peered, sniffed the contents. She shook her head. "Seems clean enough, but appearances sometimes deceive. But we must have it – must use. This will help." She swished a chemical into the bucket and produced a cup from one of their kits. "Here, Kaitrin. Then everyone else. We save the water bottles from flyer for Gwidian."

Kaitrin did not care what organisms the water might contain; it tasted better than anything she had ever drunk in her life. As she and the others slaked their thirst, she talked to Sa'ti'a'i'a and the Huge-Head.

I ask for your forgiveness, Ru'a'ma'na'ta, said Ki'shto'ba. *I would have taken out the traitor if your* na'sha'ma| *had not hit it with the weapon-not-grown-upon-the-body. That caused it to roll away from me and so my leap missed its target. By the time I sprang again, it was too late.*

"It was not your fault, Ki'shto'ba. Everything just – came

together wrong."

In turn the Nasute Chief apologized for allowing the Shshi to take the flyer. *Everything got crazy after your* na'sha'ma| *ran out. The Shshi occupied your dwelling and are still inside it.*

"We very much need to get back there," said Kaitrin.

Sa'ti'a'i'a danced in distress. *I lost many Warriors – I do not have enough left for a major assault. We would all be killed and nothing would be gained.*

Ki'shto'ba said, *Kwi'ga'ga'tei saw Lo'lo'pai attack your* na'sha'ma|. *She is very concerned. Is he all right?*

"He is alive, but he has a bad wound and is not doing well," said Kaitrin. "That is why we want to get to the flyer. There are things inside it that would help heal him."

We can send Healer Alates to you.

Kaitrin glanced at Trea. "It asks if we want them to send Healer Alates to us."

Trea grimaced. "In normal time, I would want to meet Shshi Healers. But not now."

"Ki'shto'ba, we have a wonderful Healer of our own. The small female one is our Healer. But we thank you."

I will talk to the Holy Seer about retaking the flyer. She is resting now – she is not well herself. But she means to come to you. Is there more that you would need when she comes?"

"Certainly more water. I cannot think of anything else."

Food?

They had a limited quantity of field rations. "No food, Ki'shto'ba. I do not believe we can eat what you eat."

The flying dwelling that brings you supplies. Does it know you are in trouble?

"Something has happened to it or to its magic box. We cannot talk to it any longer."

Worse and worse, said Ki'shto'ba. *I will go and report to Holy Kwi'ga'ga'tei. It will be a while before she comes. In the meantime, I will have some Warriors of the Second Cohort bring more water to you.*

Chapter 29

How hard the year dies: no frost yet.
On drifts of yellow sand Midas reclines,
Fearless of moaning reed or sullen wave.
Firm and fragrant still the brambleberries.
On ivy bloom butterflies wag.

Spare him a little longer, Crone,
For his clean hands and love-submissive heart.
   – Robert Graves, *Intercession in Late October*

Rehydrated and again in touch with someone outside the confines of their avernal refuge, Kaitrin felt relieved and a good deal more optimistic.

"I will try to wake Gwidian," said Trea. "His GI tract is undamaged. Maybe we get water into him in natural way. First I will remove intubation. I think he can breathe now by himself, with oxygen supplement. Would be good if he and you can talk, Kaitrin."

She did as she said, waiting to be sure Griffen was safely breathing on his own. His respiration, at first ragged, soon settled into a regular, shallow rhythm. Trea manipulated the nerve centers and gave him a mild stimulant out of the dwindling store of medications. Sev had rigged a nasal cannula so that he could take oxygen without a mask.

He opened his eyes. Kaitrin bent over him, chafing his hands, caressing his face. "Griffen, can you hear me? It's Kait. Talk to me, love."

He tried, choked. "Cough a little, Gwidian," said Trea. "There. Not too hard. Just need to clear trachea."

Finally he could whisper. "Kait, you're here ... Are you all right?" He seemed to have forgotten what happened during his earlier period of consciousness.

"Yes! Remember, Griff? Trea did the surgery – fixed the bleeding."

"Oh ... yes ... remember." He flinched and rolled his head, gasping.

Trea performed some more manipulations. "Help pain without paralyzing everything. Have opiates, but will try this first."

Griffen said, "I suppose ... successful ... I'm still alive ... Am I alive?"

"Oh, yes, love, you're alive. We're both alive."

He seemed to grasp their surroundings for the first time. "This isn't ... What ... ? Where are we?"

"The rebel Warriors drove everybody out of the *Durga*," Kaitrin said. "We've gotten ourselves pinned down in one of the little storage buildings. But it's all right. I've talked to Ki'shto'ba. It brought us water, Griffen. It and Kwi'ga'ga'tei will find a way to get us back into the flyer soon. Don't worry – everything will be all right."

She was not sure whether all that registered with him. A transient smile crossed his face and he gripped her hands tighter. "Oh, I'm so thankful you're alive, so thankful. I don't deserve to be alive. I behaved ... quite badly ... whilst you were gone ... "

"You did?"

"Yes ... I ... They took my gun away ... I almost killed A'a'ma."

"What?"

Tió'otu warbled. "Kaitrin, he got a little distraught."

Gwidian was saying, "I had to save you, Kait. I was sure you were going to die."

Luku said softly in Kaitrin's ear, "He was going to get rifles and blast into fortress. Julian tried to stop him ... "

"I almost broke ... Julian's shoulder," Gwidian was saying. "Jukara ... element of surprise ... you remember, Kait?" He tried to laugh.

Kaitrin rocked above him. *Griffen ... oh, Griff ...*

"I pointed the pistol at A'a'ma. Trea ... stopped me. Oh, god ... god ... If it had fired ... I'm sorry, Kait. I'm so sorry ... "

"I already forgave him," said Prf. A'a'ma roughly.

Kaitrin whispered, "I've forgiven him for everything."

Gwidian did not seem to hear them. "They locked up my gun. But I knew all along ... if I had to ... yours was in the drawer."

Arti made a regretful noise. "We forgot all about yours."

"That was my gun you were firing? Oh, Griff! I should have taken it with me after all!"

"I've made a ... hash of everything, Kait. I've done that ... my whole life ... "

"No, Griffen. I understand why you did what you did. Actually, it was incredibly heroic – rushing out like that to save me! Just like some knight from the days of chivalry, you know?"

He seemed vaguely surprised. "You think so? I daresay you're right ... It does make me seem ... a bit of a ... hero ... doesn't it?" Again he tried to laugh, but this time his whole body contorted and he writhed in pain.

"Trea," said Kaitrin in agony.

"Kait," he whispered, "I couldn't let you die."

He was slipping back into a half-conscious state. Trea did some work on him. "I think," she said, "he will go in and out. Just let him rest – take the conscious times as gifts."

Kaitrin glanced fearfully at Trea, but she had turned away, busying herself with her equipment.

*   *   *

In his next lucid interval, they managed to get some water into Griffen. Kaitrin tried to drip it into his mouth with a syringe, but she was so tired herself that she was not having much success so Trea, who seemed to run on inexhaustible batteries, took over. Luku went to rest for a while and Tió'otu replaced her as Kaitrin's support. She exchanged a furry for a feathery embrace and fell asleep within it.

Griffen's overwrought breathing woke her. Trea was injecting him with some medication. "That is last of it," she was saying. "Dehydrated – blood sugar, electrolytes, all low ... Oxygen extractors running low on power. Not good. If lose brain function, have no stimulator – no neural boosters … "

"Trea … " began Kaitrin in horror.

"Oh, awake. But best to know. Staying here much longer not safe."

At that moment Kwi'ga'ga'tei arrived outside the cyst. She entered and stood in their midst, with Ki'shto'ba's antennae projecting through the doorway. In the small cyst the Seer's Star-Wings shone with an awesome radiance.

Kwi'ga'ga'tei abased and groveled before Kaitrin and her wounded King. *I have failed you, Ru'a'ma'na'ta. I have failed to keep safe you and the ones you care for. Can your* na'sha'ma| *be healed?*

"Oh, yes! But he is very weak. He needs so much that we do not have here. Is there any way that you can help us to get … ?"

Kwi'ga'ga'tei interrupted her, misinterpreting what she was about to say. *Ru'a'ma'na'ta, I have gone and taken the honeydew directly from the Little Ones of the Alates' Flock. It is the purest and richest of the honeydew, the most nourishing of fluids. We use it for holy purposes – sealing of oaths, healing the sick, strengthening the weak. I have it stored cleanly in my crop – let me nourish you and your* na'sha'ma| *with it. I have enough for the two of you. Allow me to do this for you. Let me heal you both with our* na'ti'wa'zi|.

"Oh!" Kaitrin knew how the Shshi fed each other and she knew what the Seer intended. "Kwi'ga'ga'tei, let me consult our Healer."

To Trea she said, "She wants to feed Griffen and me the honeydew – the sacred honeydew of the Alates' Flock. I've been with the Shshi so closely – I don't mind taking it their way. It's a great honor. And perhaps this substance does have some healing power, Trea."

"I tested that fluid," Trea said. "It is very nutritious – rich in sugars, a little acidic but not enough to harm … " She thought a moment. "And perhaps it has other, spiritual influence – who knows? Pozú never take any practice of other peoples lightly. If you want to do this, Kaitrin, I think, will not harm. But it have to go into cup for Gwidian. A direct feeding in that insect way will make him aspirate."

Kaitrin tried to explain to Kwi'ga'ga'tei about the interconnection of the Star-Being's breathing and swallowing tubes. The Alate remained mystified but nevertheless obligingly regurgitated some of the honeydew into a container while Kaitrin related to the others what was about to happen so they would not be shocked.

Kwi'ga'ga'tei approached Kaitrin, who lifted her head and opened her mouth. The Shshi Priest pronounced her invocation.

Receive, Ru'a'ma'na'ta, the honeydew – the gift of the Highest-Mother-Who-Is-Nameless – from the mouth of her Priest and Seer, that she may bless, protect, and heal the Star-Beings who have come to the most distressed fortress of Lo'ro'ra. Nameless, spare the Wounded One, so that the Seeing of your Priest need not be fulfilled. But according to your will, Highest-Mother-Who-Has-No-Name, your Priest accepts the burden of your strictures, for good, for ill. And always, we beg your aid and mercy for all of your creation!

Kwi'ga'ga'tei brought the grotesquerie of her mouthparts close to Kaitrin's face. The palps, the mandibles, spread to each side; the maxillae, the labium, covered Kaitrin's mouth, the labrum pressing on her nose so she was almost suffocated. The bubble of honeydew gushed forth. Kaitrin tasted the warm, sweet, slightly acrid fluid on her tongue, in her throat. There was a surprising quantity of it; she had to swallow rapidly, then gasp for air. But it was not unpleasant and Kaitrin felt no revulsion, no horror at this insectile intimacy; in fact, she experienced a strangely comforting, sacramental exhilaration.

Trea, Sev, and Luku watched with grave reverence, while Tió'otu averted his head and twittered. Arti and Julian stared open-mouthed and Will looked as if he might be sick. But Griffen was barely conscious, not fully aware of what was happening.

And Kaitrin thought, *I've never before seen Kwi'ga'ga'tei acting in her role of Priest. What did she mean, 'Spare the Wounded One so that the Seeing need not be fulfilled'? What did she see? What does she know of what is to come?*

She swiped her fingers across her sticky mouth and said to Kwi'ga'ga'tei, "I thank you, Priest of the Holy One of Lo'ro'ra. I am honored that you would share this with me and with my *na'sha'ma|*."

Kwi'ga'ga'tei said, *Will you feed him now? I would like to see him take the honeydew.*

So Trea and Kaitrin tried to feed Gwidian with a syringe but could not get very much into him. "He cannot swallow now. We will try later," said Kaitrin, and Kwi'ga'ga'tei seemed distressed but almost fatalistically acquiescent.

Then Kaitrin asked her about how they could retake the flyer. After paying sober attention to their needs, Kwi'ga'ga'tei said, *If we attack, we will lose many Warriors. The rebels seem to have made possession of the flying dwelling a symbol of their dominance. Hi'ta'fu has been seen going in and out, and Mo'gri'ta'tu also. They will fight hard to remain there.*

Desperate, Kaitrin said, "I do not want to cause more destruction to the Shshi, Kwi'ga'ga'tei, but if we cannot get back to our dwelling where our healing things are and to the box that talks to our friends in the sky, I fear for the life of my *na'sha'ma*|."

Kwi'ga'ga'tei shuddered as if in pain. *Let me go back and think – consult with A'gwa'ji and the Huge-Head. I will send word, or I will come myself. It will not take long. Be assured – I will do something.*

And she hastened away.

So they waited. After several attempts Gwidian managed to ingest some of the honeydew and it actually seemed to give him strength. He was still drifting, but at intervals he was able to speak.

"Kait, bring your face down … Let me touch your hair."

It had been hanging around her shoulders for some time. She bent down and took his hand, guiding it into her hair. "Oh, Griff, it's so dirty from the Queen."

"I don't care … I want to feel it … one last time … "

A chill went through her. "Griffen, don't talk like that! There will be many more times!"

Sometimes he would murmur things that she could not understand and she would hunch over him in agony, loath to lose the slightest word. Once she caught a repeated phrase – "*'Nghariad … dwi'n dy garu … dwi'n dy garu, 'ngariad … *" And another time, at the end of a long, incoherent murmur, with brilliant clarity, "'I shall but love thee better after death … '"

She swayed to and fro over him, terror paralyzing her soul. They were down to the third oxygen extractor. Arti agreed to sacrifice a pistol to gain a fresh power cell and Luku and Sev worked frantically to install it, but the extractors had been constructed as sealed disposable units and it proved impossible to repair them. In the twilight aura of the weakening field lights, Trea crouched next to Gwidian, her hands relentlessly pressing his chest or throat or brow, willing his life to stay within his body.

At one point he had been lying still a long time staring at nothing, kneading Kaitrin's hands between both of his. Suddenly he spoke quite lucidly. "All I ever wanted ... was to wake up each day seeing your face ... to come home in the evening and find you waiting for me ... or for you to come home and I would be there ... waiting to kiss you when you came in ... That's all I ever wanted, Kait."

"Griffen," she moaned.

" ... and maybe have a child with you ... that we could love together ... with the kind of love a child ought to have ... Is that too much? Was that too much to ask? I knew I ... didn't deserve anything, but I had begun to think ... perhaps ... that was not ... too much ... "

Then at last Kaitrin wept. The tears started running down her face, falling on his forehead, on his eyes. "Oh, Griffen, Griffen *mi querido,* don't talk like that. You'll have those things – those simple things. You must never, never stop believing that you will."

He was beginning to drift again. "'... if it be now, 'tis not to come ... if it be not to come, it will be now ... ' Tell Rianna ... I've always cherished her ... " His whisper faded into a twitching of the lips.

Farther away, A'a'ma sat with his claw-fingers folded around his beak. He was twittering words that included *He'etí He'etí,* and he was not speaking the name of the Sky-God as an imprecation. As she again supported Kaitrin in her arms, Luku was whispering some pleading words in Glin Quornaz. Trea, flagging at last, laid her head against Sev's shoulder, murmuring something. The word *Trant* could be discerned over and over.

But Will, who was monitoring Gwidian's vital signs, said, "His temperature's rising."

"Oh, god," whispered Kait. "Oh, dear god." *Why can't I pray? Why do I use the word* god – Dios – *as a careless expletive that means nothing?* "Trea, I don't know how to pray. Will it do any good? Give me a god. I don't know what god to pray to."

Trea, attending to Gwidian again, glanced distractedly at her. "It does not matter. All are one. Look into your strong soul. Speak silently to what you see there."

So Kaitrin looked, but she found only words, and her love and her fear, and so many things that she could not understand. *All the gods and the goddesses are one ... nameless ... Nameless One, does he have to die? Can't you see how good a man he is? How can you let yourself be called Mother and still let him die?*

Trea was saying, "I have given every antipathogen we have. Is not much. We must get to flyer. *Featherlight* better yet but is not here."

They could do nothing but wait. Griffen was semi-conscious, responding only sporadically to words and touches, his mumbling incoherent. They waited through the long decline of the endless daylight hours of the planet called 2 Giotta 17A, while the infection continued its consuming advance.

*　　*　　*

On board the *Stinger*, Maj. Tar·aga the Engineer called out, "Installation complete, Captain. Ready to test."

"*Hoi-a!*" said Zin. "Short here. Not serious. Give me another transfer circuit ... "

They worked in silence, urgently. "Now, Captain, activate, please!"

Capt. Van manipulated controls. Lights oscillated, numbers scrolled. "Running diagnostic," she said.

After a while the screen flashed in !Ka<tá, *All com units functional. Powering link. Stand by.*

Van said to her navigator, "Plot course for planetside coordinates. It should finally be out of the direct path of CME. Damn slow rotation on this planet."

Zin came and sat down at his console. "Make quick," he said.

They finally came within range and Zin started to transmit. "*Durga*, this is *Stinger*. This is Capt. !eye Taeva. Do you copy? Come in, please!"

Silence. "Planetside team, this is *Stinger*! Come in, please!"

Silence. "*Durga* – Capt. Ayland – do not play games! Respond! Sorry for earlier silence – we will explain. Come in!"

"I will run acute level diagnostic," said Tar·aga, and proceeded to do so.

"*ǂKhepsá·di nei'uʃ*" growled Capt. Van. "Our system works fine now."

"*Durga*, this is *Stinger*," said Zin, beginning to sound desperate. "Where are you? Respond!"

"Could the storm have knocked out their end of the comlink?" asked the navigator.

"Possible," said Tar·aga, "but probably not quinkied whole unit. Capt. Ayland and Luku would have reset it by now."

"Unless they did not discover it," said Van. "Maybe nobody is on the flight deck. Keep trying."

They tried for fifteen minutes. Zin was beginning to gibber.

"Out of touch too long," said Capt. Van. "I am going down and find out what happens."

"But it will take another four hours to get there," said the navigator.

*   *   *

After what seemed like an endless wait in the toils of a nightmare, Kwi'ga'ga'tei returned. She stood amidst them, once again brightening their darkness with her wings, stamping and fidgeting in agitation.

He is worse, she said. *I knew he was. The honeydew was not the answer. Ru'a'ma'na'ta, there is a way to end this. Ki'shto'ba is willing. I know now that this is why it was called to Lo'ro'ra. We can challenge Hi'ta'fu to single combat. The opposing armies must agree to abide by the outcome of their Champions' battle.*

Kaitrin stared at her, trying to focus her mind, to wrench her concentration away from the tortured breathing of the one lying in her lap.

But there is a ritual that must be followed, Kwi'ga'ga'tei was saying. *The Holy One and the King must call for the Challenge. And A'kha'ma'na'ta and Sei'o'na'sha'ma are very distressed – too distressed to speak decisively. The Holy One has always loved her Fum, her Gri. She cannot bear to call the Challenge on them. She knows it means willing their deaths. She understands that they must die so that many more of her children can be saved, but she cannot bring herself to give the command. Can you understand this, Ru'a'ma'na'ta?*

"Yes," said Kaitrin, "I can understand. So is there no hope then?"

There is hope! The Holy One has asked that you call the Challenge.

Kaitrin looked stupidly at Kwi'ga'ga'tei. "I do not understand that."

You are ma'na'ta|. *Lo'ro'ra has taken you as its own – fed and succored you – and you have comforted the Shshi. You can stand in the place of our Holy One. You can issue the Challenge to the Unnatural Commander and its confederates.*

Kaitrin shoved distractedly at her hair. "How do I do that?"

You must come out. You must stand with me and Ki'shto'ba and face the Warriors and speak the words of Challenge. I will tell you what to say.

On her lap, Griffen's breath rattled in his throat. She cupped his cheek, felt the sweat on it through the stubble of beard. "I can't go out," she said in agony. "I can't leave him."

If you do not, said Kwi'ga'ga'tei, swaying, *I do not know how to end this except by long fighting. If you want to return soon to your dwelling, Ru'a'ma'na'ta, you must do this.*

To the others, Kaitrin said, "She wants me to go out with her and issue a challenge of single combat between Ki'shto'ba and Hi'ta'fu. The Holy One can't bear to issue it and has deputized me to do it. It can be ended this way. But I can't – I can't go out! I can't leave him! The last time I left him, such a terrible thing happened."

But on her lap Griffen stirred. "Kait ... best go out. I can't ... hold on ... much longer ... "

"Griffen ... "

"Go out, Kait. End it. I can't ... wait much ... " His voice faded off.

"Griff ... All right!" To Kwi'ga'ga'tei she said, "All right. I'll go. Here, Luku, hold him ... "

With a whimper, Luku took Griffen's head into her lap. Kaitrin bent over him. "You'll be here when I get back," she quavered, somewhere between an order and an entreaty.

"I'm trying ... so hard ... " he whispered.

His hand slipped from hers as Kaitrin staggered to her feet.

Will supported her. "Hey, get your legs back before you go out there," he said.

In a dream state she found herself moving between Kwi'ga'ga'tei and Ki'shto'ba, surrounded by an escort of Nasutes and Shshi Warriors. As they went, Kwi'ga'ga'tei gave her the words to say, and mechanically she entered them into the transmitter.

From among the storage cysts, they emerged onto the perimeter of the battlefield. Kaitrin could see the *Durga* with the hatch open and a gaggle of Warriors swarming around the ramp. Hi'ta'fu and Mo'gri'ta'tu stood not far away in front of the restless rebel forces. Two other Alates huddled near the flyer. On the other side of the compound, ranged around the main fortress tower, A'gwa'ji's army was drawn up, carefully organized into proper phalanxes. Here and there across the field were scattered body parts – leg joints, mandibles – that the Charnel Workers had missed in their hasty scavenging. There was a smell of death – sour body fluids mingled with the stifle of wet earth from a second shower that had just passed over. A gusty wind and distant thunder portended a third storm.

A swaying passed through both armies as word of the new arrivals spread along the ranks. Hi'ta'fu took a few steps forward, stopped. But a little to its right, Mo'gri'ta'tu spoke tauntingly. *Why have you come out, false Seer, with your minions at your sides? Are you ready to surrender?*

Kwi'ga'ga'tei answered him. *We have come to issue the Challenge, Mo'gri'ta'tu.*

The Challenge! Mo'gri'ta'tu pranced, swung his antennae in a derisive circle. *A'kha'ma'na'ta will never call for our deaths. It is a most humorous thing to contemplate, and a most pitiable ruse and lie on your part, deceitful Seer!*

She has appointed Ru'a'ma'na'ta her surrogate to speak the words.

There was fresh agitation in the rebel ranks as this information circulated.

Ru'a'ma'na'ta! said Mo'gri'ta'tu. *Truly, a jest! No one will honor that sort of fakery!*

She has the right! Kwi'ga'ga'tei said. *She is* ma'na'ta|. *The rule has ever been that the Challenge has to come from* ma'na'ta|

vi| ta'she| ki| cha| – *the* ma'na'ta| *who is of the fortress. And Ru'a'ma'na'ta belongs to Lo'ro'ra as much as A'kha'ma'na'ta herself does! Is that not true, Warriors?*

In a spreading wave, an acclamation went up through the mass of the loyalist ranks. *Ru'a'ma'na'ta belongs to us! She is* ma'na'ta| *of Lo'ro'ra! Let her issue the Challenge! All must abide by the outcome, whatever it may be!*

Kwi'ga'ga'tei said to Kaitrin, *Speak now, as I taught you.*

Caught up, distracted by the thrill of the primeval scene that was playing out before her, Kaitrin took a step forward. The emitter was set on full power as she broadcast the words. "I call the Challenge to single combat! In the name of the Fortress called the Strong Land of Flowers and its Holy One A'kha'ma'na'ta and its King Sei'o'na'sha'ma – and by the advisement of Lo'ro'ra's Holy Seer Kwi'ga'ga'tei and the witnessing of the Remembrancer Holy Di'fa'kro'mi – I summon the former Commander Hi'ta'fu, Champion of the unnatural rebels, to fight to the death in single combat with the Champion of Lo'ro'ra's loyal citizens, Ki'shto'ba No'no Um'zi of the fortress of To'wak. Whoever prevails, its side shall be declared the victor in this conflict."

Ki'shto'ba stands here! cried the Huge-Head. *I acknowledge the Challenge and join my will to it! Let Commander Hi'ta'fu respond and fight me!*

Kaitrin continued to transmit. "There is one condition. If the Champion of Lo'ro'ra prevails – and the righteousness of the cause says that it will – then the Unnatural Alate Mo'gri'ta'tu, on whose head all this needless slaughter can be laid, must surrender himself to the judgment of the Holy One and her chosen Council. If that surrender does not happen, then the determination is not final and the slaughter will be renewed!"

Surrender! Never! began Mo'gri'ta'tu, but a powerful sending from the former Commander Hi'ta'fu cut him off.

I will speak for myself! I will no longer permit this dastardly betrayer to speak for me! I accept the Challenge gladly and I give my oath that my Warriors will abide by the outcome. The final cleansing begins at last – it has been too long coming! If I am defeated, seize the accursed deviant Alate and do as you will with him! Hi'ta'fu twisted around suddenly, swinging its open mandibles at Mo'gri'ta'tu. The Alate jumped back, wings fanning. *Get behind me, evil one! You dare accuse me of betraying you? Cease your invidious word sendings before I sever your antennae!* Hi'ta'fu advanced a few steps. *Where are you, Huge-Head? I have wanted to fight you for a long time! I think you are in need of some exercise!* And Hi'ta'fu lunged as Ki'shto'ba sprang toward it.

Kaitrin stood pressing her fingers over her mouth. *I'm witnessing something straight out of the most primitive ...* But even as the words were passing through her mind, a voice – a human voice – penetrated her consciousness.

"Kaitrin!" shouted Will somewhere behind her. "Kaitrin! Where are you? Come quick! Kaitrin!"

Kaitrin's eyes opened wide and she gasped, swinging around to see Will waving his arms furiously. Next to her, Kwi'ga'ga'tei, sensing her panic, stepped sideways and looked up at her face with her expressionless insectile gaze.

Griffen ... Kaitrin started to run, away from the start of the battle, toward what she dreaded most in the world.

She reached Will, who seized her arm and propelled her along. "Will, what is it? What's happening?"

"Turn for the worse. Hurry."

Kaitrin could hear the stertorous breathing even before she entered the cyst. Luku surrendered her burden to Kaitrin, who bent over Griffen, feeling more pain than she had ever thought could exist. Next to her Trea knelt, her hands pressing down on him, fighting to deny the parting of the body and the soul.

The fever had given way to a terrifying chill. The last vestige of his strength was being channeled into breath. The tube in his chest was expelling reddish fluid, and with each breath, a little blood trickled from the corner of his mouth – his blood, Kaitrin's blood.

"Griffen, I'm here. Griffen! Trea, do something – anything ..."

Trea bowed over his chest, speaking in Poz-até, desperate words. Sev clenched his mate around the shoulders and said, "Bleeding inside again. Something is bleeding again."

Griffen ... Kaitrin hunched over him. "Don't leave me, Griff! Damn it, don't leave me! I love you, Griff. I love you. You can't leave me!"

He whispered almost imperceptibly, "Forgive me ... I couldn't let you die."

She bent so that her ear was near his lips. "Griff. Get better, Griff. We have to go home. I want to take you home."

"I love you, Kait ... "

"Oh, Griffen ... Oh, Griffen ... "

The breath rasped inward, long-drawn. The words were so faint that they were barely a stirring of the air against her ear. " ... time's winged chariot ... too soon ... "

His eyes lost focus. The hand that was clenched in hers went slack. The cyst was silent. The urgent entreaty of his breath had ceased.

Then Trea cried out, "Gwidian! I command! Come back!" She hit his chest with her fists.

But Sev seized her hands, pinioned them. "Ama, stop. His soul has gone. You cannot do more."

"*No!*" The cyst echoed with Kaitrin's anguish. "Trea, save him! I thought you could save him! Oh, god, oh, Griffen, oh, Griffen ... " She dragged his body up against her body and huddled protectively around it. Her breast against his face closed his eyes.

She commenced to wail – his name, but mostly wordless moans. Then Trea and Sev set up a keening – a universal, primordial reproach against whatever gods refuse to allow life to endure for its allotted time. Against the wall, A'a'ma and Luku prayed to their own gods. At the exit of the cyst Arti Robb and Julian Way crouched – guardians at some archaic portal, vainly trying to prevent the spirit from passing from this life.

In the middle of the cyst knelt Will Ayland, his big hands folded together beneath his sunken chin. He also prayed – the prayer his grandmother had taught him – the Woman's Prayer ...

Ave Maria ... gratia plena ... benedicta tu in mulieribus ...
Sancta Maria, Mater Dei, ora pro nobis peccatoribus ...
Ora pro nobis, nunc et in hora mortis nostrae ...

In hora mortis nostrae. Amen.

Amen.

333

Chapter 30

Othello: Will you, I pray, demand that demidevil
    Why he hath thus ensnared my soul and body?
Iago: Demand me nothing. What you know, you know.
    From this time forth I never will speak word.
                   – *from* William Shakespeare, *Othello*

[The battlefield. Wind and distant thunder. Kwi'ga'ga'tei and those near her are the only Shshi who are aware that Ru'a'ma'na'ta has left the perimeter. Kwi'ga'ga'tei twists to watch her go, turns back, hunching her body down between her legs.

[In the area between the lines of Warriors, Hi'ta'fu and the Huge-Head circle each other]

[Hi'ta'fu]: Coward, stand and front me!

[Ki'shto'ba]: It is not cowardice that makes me cautious, Hi'ta'fu. I carry the scars of your mandibles and I respect your battle skill. I have never had anything but respect for you, Commander. Never have I spoken otherwise. I wish your opinion of me had been as generous.

[Hi'ta'fu]: I am weary of words, Huge-Head. I am weary of life. I would have this ended so that Lo'ro'ra may be cleansed. But in spite of all, I will leave a mark or two before I go!

[Hi'ta'fu springs. Ki'shto'ba dodges, throws up its head, and

334

catches Hi'ta'fu under the thorax. The old Commander is flung sideways, narrowly missing impalement on Ki'shto'ba's mandibles. Hi'ta'fu scrambles up, circles around disoriented, seeking its opponent, then springs again. The Huge-Head rears to meet it and the opponents lock mandibles and writhe against each other, forelegs clutching.

[The wrestling is brief. Ki'shto'ba's superior strength breaks the hold, flinging Hi'ta'fu the length of two Shshi. It lands on its side, hemolymph dribbling from the seat of its left mandible.

[Quickly it is on its feet, but before it can get its bearings, the Huge-Head attacks from the side and butts Hi'ta'fu with its lowered cranium, swinging away to avoid the slashing scimitars. The blow rolls Hi'ta'fu over twice, but again it is up, belly heaving, mud caking the spiracles]

[Hi'ta'fu]: I would finish this! [It springs a third time, comes down full on Ki'shto'ba's massive head and seeks to slash behind it, between the second and third thoracic segments. It succeeds in slicing the surface, but a rearing Ki'shto'ba flings up its head and with all the great muscles of its neck and forelegs throws Hi'ta'fu into the air. The old Commander descends upon the Huge-Head's upthrust jaws, which penetrate its belly]

[Ki'shto'ba]: That was an unwise move, Hi'ta'fu – but I wager, a deliberate one.

[Hi'ta'fu, rolling in agony, hemolymph spurting from its wound]: Champion, you read me well.

[It strives to regain its feet, its clawlesss rear leg finding no purchase in the churned muck of the battlefield. Ki'shto'ba leaps, lands with its body astride the old Commander, its head oppressing the Commander's head, driving the mandibles into the ground]

[Hi'ta'fu]: Finish, then! Let us make an end of this!

[Ki'shto'ba]: I will finish, Hi'ta'fu. It is my duty. But I am regretful. I will repeat – I never felt any ill will toward you. I will make sure that the Remembrancer speaks tales about this battle.

[Hi'ta'fu]: That is the unkindest blow. I would not be remembered for these acts of my later days. I would rather not be remembered at all than for betraying my Holy One, my King, and my Lo'ro'ra. Finish this!

[Ki'shto'ba]: Do not fear ignominy! I will see to it that Hi'ta'fu the Unconquered takes honor in the Remembrancing, Commander of the Cohorts of Lo'ro'ra! And so I make the end!

[Ki'shto'ba hoists its head, backs up a little, and brings its mandibles down to pierce the neck, severing the neural channels between head and body. Then it jumps away to escape the spasmed thrashing of the dying Commander]

[Ki'shto'ba, casts about, locates Kwi'ga'ga'tei]: It is done, Holy Seer! The Champion of the rebels has been slain!

[Kwi'ga'ga'tei]: I see it, and Di'fa'kro'mi the Remembrancer witnesses it! Now, you Lieutenants and you Warriors of the former First Cohort of Lo'ro'ra, understand that your Commander is dead! Heed what can happen when you follow those who choose to set their private, evil purposes above the common good! Abase your heads, display your submission to the Holy One and King, and deliver over to me the Unnatural Alate named Mo'gri'ta'tu, who bears the responsibility for your Commander's death and indeed for all your suffering and loss!

[Great scuffling and disorder among the rebel forces. Some run about in panic, some run seeking escape, some abase and scrabble their jaws in the dirt in miserable submission. But others turn upon the former Keeper of the Holy Chamber and his two confederates in treachery. Ta'rei'so'cha and A'dei'no'no wheel and try to flee, and all expect Mo'gri'ta'tu to do the same.

[Instead, Mo'gri'ta'tu whips about and confronts the Champion and the Seer]

[Mo'gri'ta'tu]: It was a weak and vacillating leader in any case. I am the one that you must deal with. Come, we will make a bargain!

[Kwi'ga'ga'tei]: We will bargain with those you have misled, Mo'gri'ta'tu. For you there are no bargains, except the one of sacrificing yourself for the good of the fortress.

[Mo'gri'ta'tu]: Oh, I assure you, that is the path I mean to take! [Unexpectedly, in a manner most unlike an Alate, he rushes forward, fanning his wings. As he leaps, the wind catches the wings and lifts him. He clears the tossing jaws of Ki'shto'ba and lands atop Kwi'ga'ga'tei]

[Mo'gri'ta'tu]: And I will take you with me, contemptible, false Seer!

[Mo'gri'ta'tu's sharp mandibles pierce the wing, clamp into the flank of the Seer's belly just below the thorax. Locked together, they tumble over and over. Word-sendings and pheromones of horror flash around the whole compound, among rebels and loyalists alike, at this Warrior-like act committed by a weak-bodied Alate.

[But Ki'shto'ba has twisted, sprung, seized Mo'gri'ta'tu in its jaws, and plucked him away from the crumpled form of the Holy Seer Kwi'ga'ga'tei]

[Ki'shto'ba, flailing the Alate's body against the ground]: So end, unmitigated traitor! May the Nameless Mother curse you! May only shame be heaped upon you in the words of the Remembrancers!

[Mo'gri'ta'tu]: Oh, I will have the last jest, Champion! They will speak of my exploits long after yours are forgotten! Do you not know that villainy always makes a better tale than the maunderings of virtue?

[Ki'shto'ba, ripping off Mo'gri'ta'tu's antennae]: End your lying words! Die at last! [It shears away the Star-Wings, tosses them into the air, slashes the thorax] Die at last! If you have killed our Holy Seer, no torment you could ever receive would be great enough to ease the sorrow of the world!

[Among the rebel forces, frenzy has prevailed. Some are fleeing toward the periphery of the compound, some are fighting each other, some are groveling before the loyalists, begging to surrender. In the midst of the turmoil, other Alate wings are tossed into the air, along with legs and pieces of bodies. A'gwa'ji and its troops are dashing about, seeking to gain control.

[At the place where the Unnatural Alate attacked the Holy Seer, Healers and attendants have gathered around, relieved to discover that Kwi'ga'ga'tei is not dead. They turn her onto her belly, lick the wound in her side, prepare to help her into the fortress to receive aid.

[But the Nameless One speaks to Kwi'ga'ga'tei even during the torturous progression to her chambers]

My daughter, Lo'ro'ra has failed. The healing is flawed.

I know – I understand. The Wounded One is dead and I have taken the Wound-That-Will-Not-Heal. I understand, and I accept. But it is bitter, Greatest Mother, and I still do not know why it had to happen in this way.

But you have been true throughout the struggle and you ease the way. Your suffering need not endure forever. Another has been wounded today. When she is healed and returns to you, your travail will be finished.

Ru'a'ma'na'ta? I do not think she will return, Nameless One. Am I to suffer forever, then?

I will not burden you again, my daughter, with any Seeing ...

You take my Seeing from me? Do not do that! It is a dire gift, but it is what I am, have always been! Come back, Highest-Mother-Who-Is-Nameless! Do not abandon me! I implore, come back to me!

[But as Kwi'ga'ga'tei lies calling amid the throbbing of her pain, she is alone. The Vision Power has already passed away from her, soon to expand the inner Seeing of another.]

Part Four

Earth: Absolution

Chapter 1

Pain has an element of blank;
It cannot recollect
When it began, or if there were
A day when it was not.

It has no future but itself,
Its infinite realms contain
Its past, enlightened to perceive
New periods of pain.
                    – Emily Dickinson

It rained. It rained while A'gwa'ji's troops were expelling the remnants of the rebel forces from the *Durga* and when it stopped, Sa'ti'a'i'a came to tell the fugitives in the storage cyst that the flying dwelling was theirs again. Through mud and thickening fog, across an empty courtyard, Will Ayland and Julian Way moved in a slow dream-state to fetch a stretcher from the *Durga's* MedBay. The need to re-enter the flyer no longer carried any urgency.

They returned with the news that the flyer had been trashed. The common room, the hygiene compartment, Gwidian's laboratory – all had been tossed and pounded by the frenzied thrashing of Warriors who could not understand where they were or why their Commander had given them the orders that it had. As Arti had suspected, the flight deck above the open trapdoor had not been spared; the Shshi had clambered up the ladder and smashed port screens and consoles, scarred and punctured cabinets and decking. Fortunately, the sleeping compartments, galley, and MedBay were intact; their doors had been shut tight and the Shshi did not know how to open them.

They pulled Gwidian's body from Kaitrin's arms and placed it on the stretcher. Julian and Will carried it back, across the courtyard where some signs of painful life were stirring; some of the scattered rebel Warriors and Worker sympathizers were creeping back toward the fortress and Charnel Workers and Dung Carriers had come out to clear the battlefield of its remaining detritus. The bodies of Commander Hi'ta'fu, of Mo'gri'ta'tu, of the other Alates – all had disappeared. It seemed no company of outcasts would be setting off to found a fortress.

But the eight remaining Star-Beings no longer cared what happened in Lo'ro'ra. Behind the stretcher, through the slow dusk of the alien planet, Arti Robb shepherded Trea and Sev while Luku and Prf. A'a'ma led Kaitrin, holding her by the arms. She had finally stopped moaning but had spoken no word since.

In the flyer she did speak. "Put him on the bed," she said, gesturing toward the sleeping compartment.

"Kaitrin," Sev said, "to take him home, we must use cryounit – if it function."

"Put him in there," Kaitrin said, and they did. She knelt on the floor by the bed and laid her forehead against Griffen's hand and continued to grieve in silence.

But soon Trea came in and crouched beside her. "I ask you to forgive, Kaitrin," she said. "I could not hold him. It needed miracle that was not to be."

Kaitrin said nothing. Trea said, "I help you clean up yourself, Kaitrin, and then we will wash and shroud him. Together we will make his body ready. And then it must go to cryo. Unit works. Must go to cryo, Kaitrin, so he can go home to Earth."

Then Kaitrin said, "Yes, of course. I must take him home."

While the sad rituals of the dead were being performed, Will and Luku numbly set about making the comlink operational. Control panels had been damaged and some connections severed, but the essential components of all the flyer's systems had been beyond the Shshi's ability to penetrate. Luku thought they could have a functional com in an hour or two.

Fortunately, the door to the shower stall had been closed, so that necessity remained operable, but the termites had seemed to sense the intended purpose of the hygiene compartment and had used it as a place to deposit their frass, including in the toilet itself, the sink, and the inside of the laundry unit, the doors of which they had pried off. They had also broken the water valves in the sink, causing a small flood that had turned the termite dung to a foul mud. Fortunately, a sensor had detected the excessive discharge and shut down the flow before the main water reservoir had lost more than a few liters.

The servobot had been smashed, so it fell to the team itself to clean up this horrific mess – to muck out and sterilize everything, repair the water valves and the laundry unit, and then submit to a detox treatment, for whatever good it might do after such profound contamination. Then at long last they were able to rest and take nourishment.

Prf. A'a'ma refused the detox, saying the last thing he needed was another abnormal molt. He squatted at the table muttering to himself, trying to work up the will to take charge of the situation. He had never before been so scared and overwhelmed during the course of an expedition; furthermore his heart was broken. He could think of only one thing – what was he bringing home to Brigit Oliva?

Then, before the repairs to the comlink were finished, a whining sound was heard, and the starless darkness of the befogged sky was filled with ghostly light. Luku's voice, in great relief and joy, cried, "It is *Stinger*! It is *Stinger*, coming in to land!"

It was indeed *Stinger*, come too late to save the life of Griffen Gwidian.

*   *   *

There were six more Earth days to wait before the *Feather-light* would return from Starbase 30 to the shock of unanticipated news. Zin !eye Taeva and the *Stinger's* Engineer Tar·aga came over to help Will and Luku check out and repair the systems on the *Durga* so it would not have to be left behind. If the *Featherlight* had not been absent, no one would have even considered waiting to repair the flyer. Nobody wanted to remain on the ill-fated planet

2 Giotta 17A any longer than necessary.

Everyone, that is, except Kaitrin; no one could tell what she wanted, beyond the unspoken thing that all of them longed to have undone. She did not talk, except in the most basic way, to express elemental needs. With finality, she announced that she would not sleep in the compartment that she and Griffen had shared, so they arranged one of the five bunks in the women's unit for her. She slept a great deal, more than seemed natural even in her exhausted state. Or she seemed to sleep; the only evidence was that she lay in the bunk with her eyes closed for much of the time.

At the same time, she was unfailingly polite and generally co-operative. If Luku brought her water and told her to drink it, she thanked her and drank it; if Trea brought her food, it was the same. If someone told her that the ventilation system was working again, she smiled formally and said, "Good work."

Only Sev knew if Trea was having a difficult time coping with her failure; she went about her duties as positively as ever, but she seemed spent and she and Sev frequently lingered in their cur-tained bed niche, murmuring in their own language. The Pozú also undertook the task of bringing some order into Gwidian's smashed laboratory; all the specimens except what was in a small cryounit had been ruined, but his notes and holography were recoverable and his thought recorder had been shut in a cabinet that the Shshi had not penetrated. They offloaded the notes to portscarps and brought them and the holography and the encrypted recorder to Prf. A'a'ma, who had finally been able to undergo detox in the *Stinger's* Kr♪isí'i'aid unit and was now engaged in the harrowing task of trying to compose messages to Earth.

At one point, Will came into the lab and sat down to talk to the Pozú. "Trea, she's giving me the creeps. I've had deaths in my family – who hasn't? My father died a couple of years ago, and my grandmother died when I was twenty, and I helped some good friends of mine through the loss of a baby – that was pretty distressing ... But the way she's acting – is it normal? Where has Kaitrin Oliva gone?"

Trea sighed. "Gone to ground. She is in there, Will. But her soul is wounded now."

"I hope it will heal," said Will wistfully. "I'm a kind of a sen-timental man, Trea. Maybe you've figured that out. I've really gotten to like everybody on this team, and I'd hate to see this tragic thing destroy Kaitrin's life."

"Not sentimental – true feelings," said Trea with her grimacing smile. "I think she will heal, not ever all, but enough so life will not be destroyed. The layers she hides beneath – they are not thick. Not long standing, like Gwidian's. Yes, he had layers, layers over pain. Never knew what his pain was. Never will know now. That is one problem for Kaitrin. But her layers will come away. Just need a little time, the right people. Just need to get her home."

*　　*　　*

In the afternoon of the second day, Luku glanced out of the window of the flight deck and cried, "*Hoi-a!* I see Ki'shto'ba coming and – I think it is Kwi'ga'ga'tei and some other Alates! They are coming very slow. What is Kaitrin doing?"

Kaitrin was sitting on the edge of her bunk, washing down oatmeal with painful gulps of water. "I don't want to see them," she said.

Luku and A'a'ma stood before her. A'a'ma said, "Please, Kaitrin. It is not Kwi'ga'ga'tei's fault that this thing happened. You know that."

Kaitrin bent her head over her bowl. "You go out. You know how to talk to them."

Tió'otu warbled in despair. "Kaitrin ... "

"I won't go out."

Tió'otu thought, *At least I see a flash of the old Kaitrin there. Stubborn.* "All right. Luku, come with me. Help me with the vocabulary. I have not made a big effort to become proficient."

They went out with their equipment and were shocked. Kwi'ga'ga'tei crouched under the wing, leaning to her right against Ki'shto'ba's mighty head. The edges of her left wings were in tatters and in the left side of her belly was a purplish, oozing wound – flesh ripped toward the center in double gashes. Her body torqued into a lateral curve in an effort to relieve pain-inducing tension on her integument. Her aides clustered around her, powerless to help.

"Holy Kwi'ga'ga'tei, you are hurt," said A'a'ma. "We did not know. How did this happen?"

Where is Ru'a'ma'na'ta?

"Our Healer. Perhaps our Healer can help you … "

No. This wound has no healing. Where is Ru'a'ma'na'ta?

"She hurts also. She does not want to come."

You will leave soon. I must talk to her.

A'a'ma conveyed this to Luku. "What should we do?"

"I will speak to her again," said Luku.

Inside, Kaitrin had lain down. Luku said to her, "Kaitrin, Kwi'ga'ga'tei has a big wound in her side. I do not know how it happened. In the battle somehow, I suppose. We do not even know how that battle ended."

Kaitrin frowned. Her mouth opened, but she said nothing.

"Please, Kaitrin, go out and talk to her. There may never be another chance."

Kaitrin's frown deepened, then faded. "Of course there won't," she said. But she sat up, hesitated another moment, then said, "All right. I'll go out."

"Oh, good, good. Here is the translator."

Kaitrin went out and stood on the ramp looking down on Kwi'ga'ga'tei. The Alate looked up awkwardly from the torsion of her pain. *Ru'a'ma'na'ta, will you not speak to me?*

"You were hurt in the battle. How is that possible?"

How it happened does not matter. Ru'a'ma'na'ta, I am sorry. I am sorry that I failed.

Kaitrin made no reply, only sucked in a gulp of air as if she were suffocating.

You are hurt also. Will you ever heal, Ru'a'ma'na'ta?

"No. It is not possible."

Kwi'ga'ga'tei writhed, her head coming around toward her wound. *If you do not heal, then ...* But she did not finish the sentence. *You will come back? You promised me, and you promised the Holy One, that you would come back.*

A short, mirthless laugh issued from Kaitrin, imperceptible to the Shshi. "Oh, no. That has changed. I will never come back. I could never come back to this place again."

There was a moment without words. Then Kaitrin said, "I hope you feel better soon, Holy Seer. Goodbye." And she turned around and went back into the flyer.

*   *   *

346

[At the foot of the ramp, Kwi'ga'ga'tei puts her head down and slowly scrapes her mouthparts back and forth hard in the dirt, twisting her head from side to side as she speaks]

When she is healed, the Nameless One said. *When she is healed.* Not *If she be healed.* I thought perhaps there would be a way ...

[Ki'shto'ba]: Perhaps there is a way. Perhaps Ru'a'ma'na'ta cannot see it yet. I beg you, do not cease to hope, beloved Holy Seer.

[Kwi'ga'ga'tei turns slowly and begins the agonizing return across the compound]: Do not call me Holy Seer, Ki'shto'ba. My day is past. There is only the enduring. The New Time may be for others, but it is not for me.

*   *   *

With Will and Zin piloting, the *Durga* limped back to the *Featherlight*, escorted by the *Stinger* bearing Gwidian's body and the remainder of the team. Kaitrin was given lodgings on a different deck from the one where she had learned how to love, and Luku gathered up the possessions Kaitrin had left in her former quarters and brought them to her. All of Gwidian's things, both from the *Durga* and from his quarters on the *Featherlight*, were packed up in his travel bags and also conveyed to Kaitrin. At first she hardly reacted, but later when Luku came to check on her, she found her sitting motionless, clutching his old field hat against her midriff, with his comb and razor and a shirt and his canister of tea in her lap. Luku went out, found Zin, and keened to him awhile.

Upon boarding, Prf. A'a'ma went immediately to advise Capt. Skrei and to make sure that the messages that he had been struggling to write for the last six days were dispatched by transtemporal link before they left orbit. The catastrophe had left the staunch Captain of the *Featherlight* much shaken.

"I've never lost a team member on one of my ships before," he said in his own tongue to his fellow Krisí'i'aidá. "I once had an old Pozúu fall sick with a heart problem and the mission had to be aborted, but I've never had anybody killed."

A'a'ma's tongue quivered in his open beak. "I will never head up this kind of expedition again, Af'fork. Getting too old.

How quick can we get back to Earth?"

"Last time we pushed too hard and that may have precipitated the gravity failure. We'll run at 2.16 TQU – that's within tolerances. We're well supplied and won't need to stop at any base. We should be back in fifteen or sixteen days."

A'a'ma sighed, pecking at his breast feathers. "That seems like forever, but I realize it's best to be safe. We don't have a fragile specimen this time."

"Just a sad thing in cryo," said the Captain, "and fragile people. You know, I never officiated at a wedding before, either. Maybe it's bad luck." He rose and resettled, fanning crest and breast plumes restively. "Well, where are your scarps, Tió'otu?"

"Here. But I have a special request. Do you still have the recording of the wedding?"

"It's in the base. Why?"

"I want to relay it to Kaitrin's mother. I want her to have some idea of the enormity of what Kaitrin has lost."

"*Tak'korúkh* u*dabúr*! Send vid by TTR? Will your university pay for that?"

"I'll pay for it myself if they won't. I want Brigit to understand what's facing her."

"Tió'otu, that's really more than duty requires!"

"It's not duty, you old peck-rump!" said A'a'ma testily. "It's friendship. Guilt. Pain."

"Well, whatever. We'll pull it out and let you view it to make sure it's what you want, and then send it at the same time as the other messages. It will take twice as long to get there."

"That's all right," said A'a'ma. "It will still get there quite awhile before we do."

The *Featherlight* left orbit on 12 February 215 (2970 old cal.), with plans to arrive at Earth on the 27th or 28th. The days, passed so quickly and joyfully on the voyage out, dragged miserably. The whole crew, who had witnessed the burgeoning love of Kaitrin Oliva and Griffen Gwidian and adopted them as their own, were stunned and depressed. Arti Robb and Julian Way occupied themselves with physical training and by taking regular security shifts. Will Ayland worked with the *Featherlight*'s Engineers to complete repairs on the *Durga*. Luku spent a lot of time watching over Kaitrin; when she was not so occupied, she and Zin could usually be found together. Trea and Sev returned to work in the Medical Bay, putting themselves and the other team members through rigorous evaluations and detox therapy. No one seemed to have taken any serious ill effects from the long exposure to exotic microbes or from the ingestion of honeydew or contaminated water.

When A'a'ma wasn't wandering the ship like a lost soul, he could often be found with Skrei; despite his habit of making fun of the Captain's species, they were long-time friends. They would perch in the Captain's quarters with bowls of diluted *trilowa*↑~ and commiserate with each other.

"When is she going to come back to us, Af'fork?" said A'a'ma on one occasion. "I can't bear to look at her. You don't know humans like I do – they normally express their emotions in their faces with smiles and frowns and what are called *grimaces* in Inj. But now Kaitrin never smiles, or if she does, it's someone else's smile. She never laughs. What I wouldn't give to hear that irresistible laugh get the better of her again! I've often been the object of her jests over the years, but I would gladly be that object eight times a day for the rest of my life if that's what it took to make her laugh again."

"Grief is an odd thing," said Skrei. "Some of us keep it all inside and go on as if nothing had happened. Some only make a show of grieving because it's expected, and then others put everything they have into it. Are Earthers any different in that?"

"No different. And that last is Kaitrin," said A'a'ma gloomily. "She puts everything she has into everything she does. She put everything she had into her love for that strange *aidifá*↓, so why wouldn't she put everything she has into her grief over losing him? But the peculiar thing is, she doesn't cry, either."

"I don't understand this tear-shedding thing. Why would sorrow make the eyes water?"

"That's also a human thing, Af'fork. Kaitrin has always prided herself on not being sentimental or getting emotional. But some humans say crying is good for the soul ... She just cried once, and that was before he died. After he died, she keened and moaned but produced no tears. If she has shed any since then, it's been when she was alone."

"I saw her the other day in the Mess Hall. Is that a good sign?"

"I don't know. If you tell her to go to the Mess Hall, she goes. She does just about anything you ask her to do. That isn't like Kaitrin, either." Moodily, A'a'ma poured *trilowa*↑~ into his lower beak, tipping his head back to swallow bird-fashion.

"When I saw her, she seemed to have trouble breathing," said Skrei. "She would give a gasp every so often, like her throat wouldn't work. Maybe the doctor should check that out."

"Trea has examined all of us so thoroughly, there can't be anything left to check. But do you know what Kaitrin did – oh, day before yesterday?"

"What?"

"She cut off her hair."

Skrei nictitated quizzically at his companion.

"Luku came in and she was sitting there with those clippers that Gwidian used to cut his own hair ... *psa·* – I am so glad Krisí'i'aidá have feathers and not fur! ... and she had just hacked it off. She was holding the clippings in her hands in her lap and staring at them and every once in a while feeling her head. Luku was horrified and asked her why she had done it, and she just kept saying, 'It smelled of termite. I've washed it and washed it and I couldn't get the smell out. I didn't know what else to do.' So Luku told her that it would look fine if she would go to the barber and have it properly trimmed, but she refused, so Luku took the clippers and tried to even it up and make it presentable. Luku says she thinks Gwidian had a special fondness for her long hair, so this is incomprehensible to me."

"*Ú↔kha*! How can a male be attracted by something as gross as head hair?"

"That's not the point, Af'fork," said Tió'otu.

"I don't believe I've seen her since that happened."

"You may not notice the difference – she always wore it twisted up in that braid. But I notice. As I said, I'm used to humans and how they look."

On another occasion, a few days before the voyage was to end, A'a'ma said to the Captain, "You know, Af'fork, this whole affair still mystifies me. I've been on several planets where the cultural development and intellectual evolution of the ILFs were at pre-tech level and I've observed my share of occult practices and shamanic rituals. But I've never seen anything so bizarre and incomprehensible as these Shshi, and it isn't only that externally they look and act exactly like big insects. It's as if that shaman that Kaitrin named Kwi'ga'ga'tei truly did have a mystic link to an omniscient power. She predicted they would receive the speaking of a dead Shi, she knew what the flyer looked like, and she knew it was named for a manifestation of the Great Goddess. Her spirit told her to teach the visitors how to speak – instruct them in her language – which was one of our purposes in going to 2 Giotta 17A. And she came up with syllables that corresponded to Kaitrin's real name. How could she know all that?"

Skrei rustled and whooped, causing A'a'ma to shake his head and stick a claw in his ear. "That's uncanny!" said the Captain. "So you think she really has supernatural sight? *S'sa*, I don't believe such powers exist!"

"The most scientifically oriented of us all – Trea Dol Amarezka – probably would tell you they do. But there is something else, Af'fork. What caused that CME? There had been no sign of threatening stellar activity – no flares or significant storms – and after it abated, which it did promptly as soon as the *Stinger* landed, no more activity occurred. It was as if it had never happened."

"Are you trying to tell me that it wasn't a normal astrophysical phenomenon? That some supernatural force … ? Really, Professor!"

Tió'otu nictitated, ruffling his crest. "It flusters me, too. But it's as if something didn't want the *Stinger* to contact us. Was something protecting the Shshi? After all, one blast of the *Stinger*'s armament could have obliterated the fortress. Kwi'ga'ga'tei said something about a threat of destruction on their fortress – that the Shshi of Lo'ro'ra were being tested. Did something want Gwidian dead? Or were we all supposed to be left on our own to solve some kind of problem, and we failed, and Gwidian took the punishment?"

"*Tak'korúkh skrat!* And you call the Wéwana *wᒐei'i↑wei'i↑*? Tió'otu, you need a rest!" The Captain shook his feathers so that the preening powder flew about.

A'a'ma hunched up his shoulders, his beak sinking against his chest. "You're probably right, my friend. I need a big noisemaker like you around to keep me sane these days." He drank off the last drops of his *trilowa↑~* and they sat silent for a time.

Then Tió'otu said, "Our team members are all going to scatter as soon as we reach Luna Base."

Skrei waved his beak, relieved to come back to something he could comprehend. "Yes. Maj. Bidba has recommended extended Earth-leave for Maj. Robb and Sgt. Way; afterward the CDF will reassign them. Capt. Ayland also has time off, but he wants to remain in the Interplanetary Space Force. I'm pleased at that – for a human, he's a very good flyer Captain."

"An excellent one among any species. We were lucky to have him." Then A'a'ma added, "Luku !eya Kash – you know about her and Capt. !eye Taeva?"

Skrei twitched his beak in assent. "Capt. !eye Taeva is taking leave, too. It's understandable that the two of them would want to spend some time on their home planet."

"I wish Luku would stay awhile on Earth. She and Kaitrin are good friends. And I could use some support myself."

"The little doctor has informed me of her intention to return to her home planet. She and Sev have not made a firm decision yet, but I know they are considering resigning from the ISF."

"I think losing Gwidian under such stressful circumstances impacted Trea a good deal more than she lets us see," said A'a'ma somberly.

"I agree." Capt. Skrei touched the rumpled feathers of the scar on his throat. "Pozú medical people are very dedicated to life."

After another silence, Skrei said, "What about you, Tió'otu?"

A'a'ma twittered. "I'm the only one available to tie up the loose ends of this ill-fated expedition, but once that's done, I'm heading back to Krisí'i'aid for an extended stay. I realized while I was looking death in the face that I haven't been home in almost two years. I need to spend some time with Hwi<ve↑, my wife. I think I've forgotten what she looks like."

"We Wéwana are fortunate that we don't mate for life," said Skrei. "People who spend much time in space shouldn't make long-term bonds. But what about Kaitrin Oliva, Tió'otu?"

"She doesn't know it yet," said A'a'ma, "but she is going home to her mother."

Chapter 2

We make ourselves a place apart
Behind light words that tease and flout,
But oh, the agitated heart
Till someone find us really out. ...

But so with all, from babes that play
At hide-and-seek to God afar,
So all who hide too well away
Must speak and tell us where they are.
– *from* Robert Frost, *Revelation*

The *Featherlight* birthed into real time 20,000 kilometers from Luna Base and activated its plasma propulsion engines, the vibrations intrusive after the deep silence of the transtemporal pod. Presently the intercom in A'a'ma's quarters came to life and Skrei's long beak loomed on the screen. "Earth message – sad," said the Captain. "Com will patch it to your port."

The source was the legal firm of P. Vedders Associates in Jonnsberg, Southern Afrik. *To Capt. Skray A. Fork of the Confederation research vessel* Feather of Light ...

A'a'ma muttered testily, "Ignoramuses!"

... It is our understanding that the Feather of Light, *which will be arriving today at Luna Base, is conveying to Earth the body of the deceased Prf. Griffen Gwidian. At this time, at the request of*

353

the said Prf. Gwidian's sister Rianna Gwidian-Bock, who is the sole guardian of the said late Prf. Gwidian's estate, we wish to lay title and claim to the body of the said Prf. Gwidian and we request that said body be conveyed at once by express shuttle of the Mortuary Courier Service, in cryo, to Mendala Space Port in Jonnsberg Precinct, Afrik, Southern Section, from which disposition is to be made according to the intent and pleasure of the said Rianna Gwidian-Bock, sister of the late ...

"Lawyers speak the same language on all planets," said A'a'ma. He sat staring at the screen. *I knew this would happen. Kaitrin* – nei♪ bi'át♫♫↓ ...

Needing moral support, A'a'ma went to find Luku, who was in Zin's quarters.

"I have decided something anyway," said Luku. "I think Kaitrin needs to have female with her on trip to mountains. Please, I do not mean to offend, Professor. But she is my friend and I would like to go with you and her. Can help maybe – do you think?"

In fact, A'a'ma was relieved; he had been dreading the long flight alone with this Kaitrin whom he did not know. "What about Zin?"

The pilot said, "I will take shuttle with other crewmembers to Herinen and wait there for Luku. She will come right back with you. I have friends in space port – I can visit. No trouble."

Luku went with A'a'ma to Kaitrin's quarters. They found her sitting stolidly in front of the port wall, dressed for the end of the journey. Her shorn hair with its ragged fringe of bangs and nape hair made her look strangely young and vulnerable. However, when A'a'ma managed to force his distressing news into words, she surprised them.

With a single nod, she said, "I knew it would be like that."

Luku and Tió'otu looked at her. "You had thought of this?" said Luku.

Kaitrin took a little gasp of air. "I had no claim. I've known that from the start. There wasn't time to make it otherwise." In a moment she added, "He belonged to his sister first. She has a prior claim."

A'a'ma did not know whether to be grieved or relieved at her passive acceptance. He and Luku glanced at each other in despair and did not pursue the conversation. In the corridor, however, Luku said to Tió'otu, "You did not tell her we are going to Pikes, Professor."

"It does not matter to her."

"Can she really be like that – so calm and indifferent?"

"I hope not. I am counting on Brigit to make her cough up her misery."

*   *   *

Kaitrin and her companions disembarked from the *Featherlight* and approached the interrail that would take them through the tunnels to Earth Base where they would board the shuttle for home. A few events people with their earpieces and ticking holocams appeared, jostling to get close to them. "Asc. Oliva! Prf. A'a'ma! Do you have anything to say to the people of Earth?" "Asc. Oliva, did you know that your story has captivated the whole world?" "How are you feeling, Asc. Oliva? How soon can we expect a statement?"

Kaitrin's eyes turned in bewilderment toward the barrage of questions, then she ducked her head. As the door of the rail car closed behind them, A'a'ma muttered, "What was that all about?"

The events people had expected the entire company to take the Herinen flight and so Prf. A'a'ma and Luku were able to whisk Kaitrin unnoticed into the transport vehicle headed for the smaller Pikes Precinct shuttle. This process did draw a quizzical frown from Kaitrin, and Tió'otu responded, "Kaitrin, we are not going to Herinen. We are going to Castle Bluff."

She turned her head and looked at him then, her brows gathering tighter. "I have to get back to the Consortium. I have things to do."

"Not yet," said A'a'ma gruffly. "You are going to stay with your mother for a while. I do believe I am quite capable of tying up the Expedition's loose ends without your help."

Kaitrin took a breath as if to protest, then shut her mouth. Apparently making a fuss was far too much trouble. Once aboard the shuttle, the three of them settled into their seats and made the journey largely in silence. For most of the flight, Kaitrin sat with her hands folded in her lap, staring out of the window at the expanding Earth.

*   *   *

Glancing uneasily at a couple of pop link reporters who were attempting to holograph over the shoulders of security officers, Brigit Oliva watched the crawler tube move into position against the side of the shuttle. Then, after what seemed like an interminable wait, A'a'ma and Luku emerged from the tube mouth with Kaitrin between them, and then they were through the gate and onto the concourse.

"Brigit," said A'a'ma in great relief. "Thanks to He'etí that you are here."

But Brigit was paying no attention. "Kaiti! What did you do? Your hair ... " She took Kaitrin by the shoulders, looking her over anxiously.

Kaitrin ran her fingers tentatively over her head. "It smelled like Shshi," she said. "I had to cut it off. I couldn't get the smell out." She seemed to run out of air and sucked a little gasp.

Brigit's eyes consulted A'a'ma, who was thinking miserably, *I forgot she didn't know about the hair.* "Brigit, have you met Luku !eya Kash? I know you have heard of her."

Brigit turned to Luku. "I knew who you were," she said with a tremulous smile.

"Come on, Kaitrin," said Luku, eyeing through her goggles the reporters' antics behind the security line. "We will get into the transport. Your mother and the Professor will take care about the baggage."

Alone with Brigit, A'a'ma said, "I am so relieved you were able to come here today. So you received my communication?"

"What a shock that was, Tió'otu! It was so like when I got the news about Jaq ... All I could think was – how ironic that a mother and a daughter should both lose their loves in a sudden catastrophe in a space of three years! At least I have some idea what Kaitrin's going through."

"You can't believe how miserable writing that news made me," said A'a'ma. "But what is this publicity? There were events people on Luna, too. We dodged them at Earth Port, but it seems word arrived here ... "

"Kaitrin's reports are making for quite a story and the news of Griffen Gwidian's death has only wrought things up to a higher pitch. There's even an awful animated vidnovel about the termites

running on the pop links, and the team's pictures and bios are post-
ed, too."

A'a'ma cursed copiously in !Ka<tá. "Can you keep all that
away from her for a while?"

Brigit took a deep breath. "I'll try. Tió'otu, the wedding vid
– it was so wonderful of you to send that."

"I thought it would give you some understanding of what
Kaitrin has lost. So it was viewable?"

"Typical TTR quality – color was horrible – but still ... It's
the most candid thing I'll ever see of my law-son and it simply tore
me up. Tió'otu, are you going right back to Okloh?"

"Both of us. We plan to catch the next flyer out. So you
think you can handle things?"

"Mothers can handle about anything."

"Some bravado you have, Brigit."

"Tió'otu, what about Griffen Gwidian's body? You said you
thought his sister ... "

"She did claim it. It went to Jonnsberg."

"¡Ay de mí! And what really did happen to my daughter's
beautiful hair?"

"Just what she said – she has never given any other reason.
But I would say that Kaitrin is – what is the Inj? – in shock, that is
it. I cannot begin to say what she is really thinking because she
still hardly ever talks."

"That's hard for me to imagine! Will you be at the Consortium if I need to contact you?"

"For as long as it takes to finish things up. I am hoping that
Kaitrin will be herself again before long and will be able to return
to campus before I leave. I am going back home to Krisí'i'aid for
a good long visit. But I am not abandoning my profession quite
yet; I am scheduled to chair the department in the spring of 216
and mean to be back by that time. Still, I may never undertake
another off-world expedition."

Brigit entered the transport, Luku gave Kaitrin and her mother
each a fervent hug, and then A'a'ma and the Tae Quornaz hastened
off to await their return flight. Without further incident, Brigit and
Kaitrin boarded the Intertrain and settled down in a private compartment for the ride to the south side of Pikes Precinct.

The trip began in silence. Brigit watched Kaitrin gazing at the

Rampart Mountains with their mantle of fresh snow, watched her daughter absently turning an antique ring of plain yellow gold around and around on her finger. The sight nearly unraveled Brigit's composure again. *So that's what it looks like – so simple – so significant* ... She glanced at the small square-cut emerald in the ring on her own left hand.

Then she thought, *I'm not going to ride all the way down to the Hollow Mountain with my daughter and not say anything.*

"Hug me, Kaiti. I don't think we ever before met up after being separated and you didn't hug me."

"Oh, didn't I, Mamá? I didn't even realize ... "

They hugged. *Well, that's a start* ...

"You know, Harly knew something was up this morning when I didn't go to work."

Kaitrin said, "I'm sorry you had to take off. I won't stay long. I can't think why Tió'otu brought me here, anyway."

"Can't you, *querida?*"

Kaitrin glanced at her guardedly.

Brigit put her arm around Kaitrin and held both her hands. Kaitrin laid her head on her mother's shoulder. They continued to ride in silence.

Brigit's IQDB-sponsored apartment was in a gated, well-secured neighborhood. Everything was quiet; apparently nobody had yet discovered Kaitrin's destination. *I'm happy to be anonymous*, thought Brigit as a robotransport whisked them discreetly to the door of her unit.

Inside the apartment, Harly lifted his head in the chair where he was sleeping and uttered a chirp, then stood up and stretched. Kaitrin stood looking at him as her mother and a servobot brought in the luggage. When this task was done and the transport had departed to deliver its remaining passengers, Brigit turned to see Kaitrin sitting in the chair hugging and stroking Harly; he was rubbing her chin with the top of his head and purring vociferously.

"He certainly didn't forget you, did he?" said Brigit.

"Do you know, Mamá, Griffen never had a cat?"

"Is that right?" said Brigit, trying to keep her voice steady.

Again the air seemed to stick in Kaitrin's throat. "I was going to bring him home. I mean, home here. Just as soon as we settled into his house ... I mean, our house ... " Kaitrin kneaded Harly's flanks. "I wanted to see if he got along with cats. I thought I might get one. But I wanted to be sure he got along with them first. Not everyone does, you know. But most good people ... do ... "

¡Válgame Dios! *How am I ever going to get through this?* thought Brigit. *Maybe what I said to Tió'otu about mothers handling anything wasn't so true after all ...*

Aloud, she said, "Come on, Kaiti, help me with all these bags. Your room is ready for you. Let's go put things away."

*   *   *

Brigit had supper ready, but when she went to bring her daughter to the table, Kaitrin had fallen asleep on her bed still dressed in her travel clothes. Tenderly, Brigit laid a quilt over her and let her be. It was Brigit who did not sleep that night.

In the morning a quick check of Kaitrin's room showed Brigit that her daughter was out of bed and in the shower. Brigit went to prepare breakfast, and soon Kaitrin came into the kitchen toweling her short hair, wearing an old bathrobe from her adolescent years. "I'm really at home, aren't I?" Kaitrin said. "When I woke up, I couldn't remember where I was for a minute."

This looks promising, thought Brigit. "Happens to everybody," she said.

"I smell something. Smells like – waffles?"

"Your nose is working all right! You went to sleep on me and didn't eat any supper. And I had homemade vegetable soup and that Talian bread from Donatelo's that you like – and ice cream!"

"Ice cream?" said Kaitrin, sitting down at the table. "Chocolate?"

"Unfortunately, delivery mixed up the orders and sent caramel chip."

"That's good, too." She went silent.

Brigit glanced at her, bringing a hot-plate of waffles to the table. Kaitrin sat staring at the tablecloth.

Then she gave one of her gasps and looked up. "I never found out if Griffen liked ice cream," she said.

"Oh ... "

"I know he liked chocolate. I mean, he gave me chocolate, so I suppose he liked it. But that doesn't prove anything, does it? I never ate chocolate with him – we never ate it together, so I guess I don't really know … " Again her voice trailed off.

"Didn't you write that he had hot chocolate made for breakfast after your wedding night?"

"Oh, you're right … But that doesn't count really … Didn't taste much like chocolate. The cooks were Birds … "

"Kaiti," said Brigit gently, "eat your waffles while they're hot."

Kaitrin ate a bite, then another, and then ravenously. After a while, she said, "I seem to be hungrier than I thought I was. Could I have a couple more of those sausages? Is this soy? Tastes too good to be soy."

There was another silence. Brigit felt it was best to simply allow Kaitrin to work her own way through, but she thought, *Oh, Kaiti, if there were only some way I could speed up this process and spare us both.*

At length Kaitrin said, "There are so many things I don't know. I don't know if he could whistle. He knew I couldn't – it came up once, not long after we first met. But I don't know if he could. He never just whistled while he was doing something else, like shaving. Remember how Jaq used to whistle while he was shaving?"

"Yes," said Brigit.

"Griffen never did. I don't believe he was relaxed enough to do that. Or hum. He never hummed or sang, spontaneously, the way you and I do sometimes. I wonder what his singing voice sounded like. I'll bet it was good. He had such a thrilling speaking voice … Mamá, I wish you could have heard it."

"Kaiti, Tió'otu sent me the vid of your wedding. So I have heard it."

Kaitrin looked up quickly at that. "He sent … By TTR?"

"Yes. Kaiti, Tió'otu wanted me to understand … " *What you had lost*, she wanted to say, but it seemed a little soon for that.

Kaitrin bent her head, then suddenly got up. "I'd better go dress," she said, and fled the room.

Brigit sat for a moment pushing a final bite of sausage around in the syrup on the plate, then got up to clear the table.

*   *   *

360

Later Kaitrin came out and sat in the living room staring out at the terrace. It was snowing lightly, large flakes swirling in the air. "They say we're going to have an early spring this year," Brigit said tentatively.

"Mamá, about the wedding vid. I have a copy of it. But I've never watched it."

"Really?"

"Right after the wedding, Griffen didn't want to look at it. That ceremony – he was the one who wanted it, but ... it was so difficult for him. He said he wanted to wait awhile to look at the vid. So I didn't look at it, either. I wanted to look at it with him. And so neither of us ever saw it ... " She sat twisting the ring on her finger.

"That was his mother's ring, you told me."

"Yes. I was going to buy one for him when we got home. He didn't have his father's. His father drowned – did I tell you that? – when Griffen was a little boy and the ring was lost in the ocean."

"How did he happen to have his mother's ring with him? Was he planning ... ?"

"He said he always kept it with him. As a reminder ... "

"A reminder?"

"He didn't say of what, only that maybe now he wouldn't need to be reminded. It was one of those odd little things – intimations, you might call them – that he would come out with some- times ... " Kaitrin sucked a breath, rocking herself.

"May I see the ring, Kaiti?"

"What? Oh, of course." She slipped it off and handed it to Brigit, who turned it over, then peered inside. Nothing was en- graved there, but she could see what looked like a shiny scar.

"This looks like something was once engraved here but has been removed."

"It does? Do you know, I've never looked inside? I've hard- ly had it off my finger since the wedding. It does look that way. Another mystery. Another mystery I'll never be able to solve." Kaitrin started rocking herself again, clenching the ring in her fist.

"Kaitrin, *mi hija* ... "

Kaitrin stopped rocking and sat bent over, holding herself hard. "Do you know the worst?" she whispered. "You know the kind of memory I have. I remember all the words he ever said to me, all neatly pocketed up. I lie there or I sit, and I go over them as if they were a foreign language to be learned – I try to make sense out of everything he said to me – to make sense out of him. But there's one thing I can't remember – the most important thing …"

"What is it, *querida*?"

With a big gasp, Kaitrin said, "I can't remember what he said to me when he was dying. I can't remember his last words."

"Oh, Kaiti."

"He said, 'Forgive me, I couldn't let you die.' He said, 'I love you, Kait.' And he said something else – very faint, but I understood it at the time. But now I can't remember what it was. Mamá, it's driving me crazy!"

Brigit went to where Kaitrin was rocking herself violently in the chair and put her arms around her. "Oh, Kaiti, let it rest! It will come. It's just the shock. Let it rest. It will come."

"Do you think so, Mamacita?"

"I'm sure of it. Now, why don't we go into your bedroom? There are two traveling cases in there that I've never seen before, and I'm guessing they were Griffen's and have his things in them. Would you show me some of the things that were his, Kaiti? So I can treasure them with you?"

Kaitrin nodded and let her mother draw her toward the bedroom. "Mamá, I made a mistake. I'm beginning to think bringing me here wasn't such a bad idea. Maybe Tió'otu wasn't so crazy after all."

Chapter 3

Ophelia: I hope all will be well. We must be
patient. But I cannot choose but weep to
think they should lay him i' the cold ground.
— *from* William Shakespeare, *Hamlet*

Over the next few days they talked sometimes, but often they did not. Brigit would cook Mehiken food while Kaitrin helped by preparing the fruit. They gobbled avocados and salads of strawberries, papaya, lime juice, and the fruit of a genetically engineered spineless cactus. Once they consumed a pork and tomato concoction containing Brigit's famous blend of five chilies, baked in a corn flour crust. They washed it down with Mehiken beer and copious drafts of water, swore a lot in Spainish, and actually laughed a little. On another day they made cherry chocolate tarts, one of Kaitrin's childhood favorites. They cleaned house, doing the things too delicate to entrust to a servobot, like washing light covers and dusting bric-a-brac and the backs of pictures. They listened to music and viewed episodes of a currently popular, laughably melodramatic vidnovel. During those sessions Kaitrin usually fell asleep on the couch with Harly draped across her thighs. Brigit was content to wait, hoping that a return to the familiar, homely things of her early life might help Kaitrin to heal. But she set a filter on the DB, to prevent the shock of a surprise encounter with those crass pop links.

One evening Kaitrin emerged from her room holding a

teal-green garment. "This is what I was wearing in the wedding vid," she said.

"Oh! Is that the dress you bought for your party? On the vid it looked so yellow."

"I had nothing else that would even halfway serve. It was all very makeshift. Griffen – Griffen wore a new, kind of formalized field outfit. The color actually clashed with my dress, but it was the best we could do."

"I couldn't tell what color his suit was."

"It was dark blue. I have it in there."

"I recognized the scarf."

Making no reply to that, Kaitrin held out the dress to her mother. "What shall I do with this?"

"What do you mean? You want to keep it, don't you?"

"Do I?"

"Well, of course!"

"I finally threw away Griffen's toothbrush. I put it in the recycler this morning."

"Your wedding outfit is a totally different thing from a toothbrush, Kaiti!"

Kaitrin flopped in a chair, draping the dress across her lap. "Sometimes I think I ought to get rid of everything that reminds me ... Make a clean break – forget it like it never happened ... Other times I want to wrap myself up in these few things that I have and never come out."

Brigit waited. *Her voice is a little shaky. Is she going to cry? I wonder if she ever has. She needs to cry.*

"I don't have much that was his, you know," Kaitrin said. "We hadn't made a contract yet. I've changed my mind, Mamá. A contract *is* important if you really love somebody. I had no right even to claim his body. His possessions should have gone back to his sister, too. But I'm not about to give up these few little things that I have of him, even if she drags me into legals!" A little fire flashed up in Kaitrin's eyes, then faded.

"Oh, I doubt she would begrudge them to you, Kaiti," said Brigit. "Have you thought about getting in touch with her?"

"With Rianna? Oh, god, no. At least not yet. And maybe never ... "

Brigit thought about Jaq's memorial service in Nouvelle

Victoire; it had been held there because that was where his brother and the rest of his birth family lived. But his body was buried here in the shadow of Pikes Mountain. "Kaitrin, his funeral, or memorial service, or … "

"It doesn't matter to me. Let Rianna have that. Let her bury him, bury him … I've said a funeral inside myself already. His dying was his funeral – my funeral. I don't need someone else's words to eulogize him for me."

She was rocking herself again. "Mamá, he died on my lap. I held him all day, except for those few moments when … His blood was all over me, on my face, in my hair … I didn't want to get rid of my clothes because they had his blood on them, but Trea said I couldn't keep them. Wasn't that crazy, that I wanted to keep those awful, bloody clothes?"

"Oh, Kaiti." *Querida mía, you love and grieve as immoderately as you do everything else.*

"I have Class 1A blood – you remember? – so Trea used my blood to transfuse him, vein to vein, right there in that stone hut."

"I didn't know that."

"But it wasn't enough. Why couldn't I save him? I promised him on our wedding night that I would keep him from harm."

Now that's a strange thing to bring away from your wedding night, thought Brigit.

"But I didn't – I couldn't. My love wasn't strong enough." Abruptly Kaitrin flung the dress on the floor and retreated into her bedroom. A little while later, when Brigit looked in at her, she was lying on her bed with her eyes closed, but her face still bore no trace of tears.

*   *   *

The next morning Kaitrin stood scrambling eggs – fresh eggs, not reconstituted fieldfare – while Brigit heated rolls in the wave cooker. Out of the blue Kaitrin said, "Griffen was a pretty fair cook, Mamá. At least I learned that much. He would fill in for me when I was too busy to take my turn cooking for the team."

"Or when you forgot," Brigit dared to say.

Kaitrin gave her a pallid smile. "You know me too well. He wanted to meet you, Mamá. For a while he didn't seem too keen on it. He had – a thing about mothers. He said he'd never met the mother of any woman he … But I think it was really because he was – shy … "

"Shy?" repeated Brigit, wondering if she had heard right.

"Underneath, he really was. He told me he had difficulties with shyness as a child, but he had one of those personalities that overcompensated. I suppose that was it … I told him about what you had said, about welcoming him as your son, and it seemed to alarm him – scare him. But later on he asked if you really would accept him as part of the family. He was – coming around, the way Trea said … Mamá, you would have accepted him, wouldn't you?"

"Kaiti. How can you doubt it?"

"I don't, Mamá."

"Whoa! The eggs are burning!"

"*¡Maldito!* I'll bet Griffen would have done a better job scrambling eggs. I wish he was here. Oh, god, how I wish he was here – right here in this kitchen with us, making scrambled eggs. You would have liked him, Mamá, I know you would have. And he would have been happy – happy … Oh, god, I wanted so much for him to be happy and I botched it so badly!"

She rocked against the cooktop, but still there were no tears. *How bad does it have to get before she can cry?* thought Brigit Oliva.

*   *   *

A few days into Kaitrin's visit, Brigit had a message from Tió'otu marked *Eyes-only encryption.* It was brief: *Check those links I know you are familiar with. And encrypt your relay. Pronkers have found out where K. is and I think you are about to get bricked. I would like to have a word from you as to how things are going. T. A.*

While Kaitrin was asleep, Brigit checked her messages and did indeed find some twenty-five communications from total strangers addressed to her daughter. They were mostly expressions of condolence, some half hysterical or laughably maudlin, but there were also some crank items, including a rant about how anybody who went roaming through space consorting with alien demons deserved whatever bad fortune came to them. There was also an offer to console Asc. Oliva with sex. Disgusted, Brigit scoured the whole lot, then wondered if she should have saved the more compassionate ones.

She coded her port to receive only messages from IDs in her personal address bank, then scrambled the news links, which were displaying vids of Kaitrin and the team arriving at Luna Base, along with a distant and twitchy glimpse of the arrival at Castle Bluff. But on the pop links Brigit found a lengthy, bathetic piece of poetry elegizing Gwidian, accompanied by an offer to sell – sell! – a relay number where the bereft widow might be contacted. Incredibly, there was also a copy of the order to convey Gwidian's body to Jonnsberg, accompanied by invectives against his sister's hardness of heart. *If these pronkers can break through an attorney's encryption, they can break through anything,* she thought. *We live in a really scary world.*

I wonder how Rianna Gwidian is handling all this ...

She wrote a note to A'a'ma. *I see what you mean. I've taken care of my personal communication problem – I hope. Now, if I could only strangle the people who create pop links ... K. has made a little progress, but there is a long way to go. More another time. B.*

*   *   *

A couple of days later, Brigit found Kaitrin sitting at the port wall with some scarps scattered in front of her. "I took these with me for entertainment on the voyage," she said. "Some of them aren't labeled – you know how I am. I thought maybe I'd mark them, but the feeder is out of labels. Do you have any?"

Brigit loaded the feeder and sat down beside Kaitrin, who said, "This is that *Startrek* serial – I was going to do some cultural history research on that. Oh, this one is already marked ... " As she quickly laid that scarp aside, Brigit saw the title: "Shaksper Sonnets." "This one ... " Kaitrin inserted a scarp in the port to identify it. "Oh, '16th-18th Century Poetry.' I'll label it ... " She did so. Brigit noted that her hand was not too steady.

Brigit picked up an unmarked one with a peculiar red loop on one end. "This is a Bird scarp. What in the world is on it?"

"Oh!" Kaitrin took it out of her hand. "Yes, aren't KrJisí'i'aid portscarps funny? They're compatible with Confederation regulations, but the Birds add that red handle so they can pull it out of the port by hooking a claw ... " Her voice died. "Mamá, this is the wedding."

"Ah ... " Then Brigit heard herself say, "Kaiti, let's look at it."

Kaitrin's brow gathered. "You've seen it."

"Only on that sick TTR version. I could hardly see the ring in Griffen's hand."

"The ring ... " Kaitrin fingered it, staring at the scarp indecisively.

Then she said, "All right!" And she stuck the scarp into the port.

She watched, pressing her fingers to her mouth somewhere halfway through. Brigit mostly watched Kaitrin. When they came to the spot where Kaitrin hugged Gwidian before the introduction of the ring, Kaitrin made a small, strangled sound. "I hadn't seen ... I couldn't see his face right then. Oh, Griffen – my love, my darling ... Why was the act of marrying me so painful for you?"

She grabbed her head in her hands and started to moan, pulling on her ragged hair. "Oh, Griffen ... Oh, Griffen ... "

"Kaiti, stop!" Brigit imprisoned her hands, smoothed her hair. "Kaitrin, why did you cut off your long hair?"

"I told you. I couldn't get the termite smell out of it."

"Is that the real reason?"

Kaitrin pushed her mother away, banged on the keypad to stop the image, then got up and paced the room. "Of course it is! Of course it is. Oh, Mamá ... No, it's not! It did smell like that, but lots of washing was making it go away ... just like his blood ... it was going away ... It was just that I – I couldn't stand it all of a sudden – because I realized he would never touch it again. He loved my hair – he had the most sensuous hands ... " She plowed her fingers into what was left of her locks and clenched her head between her palms. "He loved my hair. On the first night we had sex, he unbraided it and said he'd been longing to touch it for so long – and when he would run his fingers through it and gather it up in his hands, it sent electricity through me – like lightning through me. When he was dying and he knew it but I hadn't accepted it yet, he asked to touch it – one last time ... And now to know I will never feel that – that ecstasy again ... It's unbearable! And I thought maybe it would give me some relief if ... so I took the clippers he used to cut his own hair ... and I just – I just ... "

"Kaiti, *querida mía* ... " Peculiar spasms were running through Kaitrin as she stood hunched over. Brigit went to her and drew her to the couch.

"It's all right, my little one. Cry. Cry. It's all right."

"Oh, Mamá, it hurts so bad ... the pain is so bad ... I thought I could keep it locked ... but I can't ... Will it ever get so I can stand it? Will it ever go away? Does it ever go away?"

"Not all of it, *niñita mía*. But it does ease to where you can bear it. I promise you."

"Oh, Mamá, I'm so sorry. I grieved for Jaq, too, but I never truly realized what you were going through – I never really understood ... I'm so sorry – that I neglected you ... "

"You didn't neglect me, Kaiti," said Brigit, her own tears trickling silently down her face as she rocked her daughter in her arms. "You had your own life. I never wanted more from you than what you gave me. I understood."

Kaitrin sobbed until she had exhausted herself, then huddled against her mother in a stillness punctuated only by an occasional shudder and hard-drawn breath. Then Brigit gently straightened her up, reaching for a handkerchief box on the side table. "Here, blow your nose."

Kaitrin did so, scrubbing at her swollen eyes. She gasped again. "Mamá, when it hits me – what I've lost ... it suffocates me – so I can't breathe. Maybe it's because of the way he died – the lung thing ... or those drowning dreams he had ... Have you noticed how I ... ?"

"I've noticed."

"Was it like that for you?"

"No, it was more as if something heavy was pressing on top of my head."

"Really? You know, I remember! For the longest time you would keep your head bent down and when you wanted to look up, it was as if you were pushing up a weight. I wondered if you had something weird wrong with your neck. Wasn't I – heedless? But you don't do that now."

"No, it went away."

"Then maybe there's hope for me. Maybe I'll be able to get my breath again someday." Kaitrin sat slumped on the couch, pulling at the skin on her throat. Next to her, Brigit felt almost equally drained.

Kaitrin said, "I first met Griffen – it was over the relay – on the 12th of August. He died on … well, the Earth standard date is 5 February, I think. It was six months – less than six months. That's as long as I knew him. We first made love on the 10th of November and we were married on the 22nd. That's all. That's all the time we had together. Oh, god, it makes me want to scream inside. It isn't right. It isn't fair! To have so little time together! What is the universe made of, anyway? – to give us so little time together!" Her voice had gone up in pitch, but she restrained it. "Oh, Mamá, at least you got to have Jaq for twenty-two years. Just think if you had had him only a little half-year."

"At least you got to be with Griffen when he died. What if you had just gotten an impersonal message on the relay?"

"At least Jaq died instantly. What if you had had to watch him suffer for eight hours and not be able to help him, and know, no matter how your soul rejected it, that you were surely going to lose … " Kaitrin's voice broke and she sobbed again.

After a few moments, Kaitrin said, "There's no good way for things like this to happen, is there?"

"No, there's no good way."

In a moment, Kaitrin reached over and wiped her mother's cheek with a tissue. "Come on, let's go in the bathroom and wash our faces," she said.

As they went, Brigit smiled through the tears. Here was the old Kaitrin, taking charge. She had not come all the way, but surely she was going to be all right.

Chapter 4

A wanton, you say –
Yet where's the spouse,
However true
To her marriage-vows,
To whom the lot
Of the earth-born allows

More than this? –
To comfort the care
Of a stranger, bound
She knows not where,
And afraid of the dark,
As his fathers were.
      – *from* Sylvia Townsend Warner,
                  Nelly Trim

After a night of recovery, Brigit sat down by Kaitrin on the couch and said, "Kaiti, tell me about your date with Griffen in Okloh. Is there any reason why you can't talk about that now? I've been so curious, *hija*."

"Oh, that." Momentarily, Kaitrin's grin flickered. "I gave him my word that I wouldn't talk about what happened."

"What in the world was so bad that you couldn't even tell me about it?"

371

"Well, I'm sure at the time you would have been the last person Griffen would have wanted to know, but now … I suppose it's all right."

So Kaitrin told the tale. "I behaved so dreadfully that night. I was in the most awful mood. I wouldn't even let him pin his corsage – a gardenia – on me himself. I made a scene in the restaurant … "

"Kaitrin, you didn't!"

"Honestly, I did! Actually, we both did. We started quarreling – one of those quarrels where you can't even remember afterwards how it got started. I said something that insulted him, in my usual blunt way, and one of his old loves showed up, only … "

"I thought that happened over in the Arts Studio."

"This was another one! Only it wasn't, really. I jumped to conclusions. This was only a former student who had never been more than a friend. But I got so irate that I stomped out of the restaurant and started walking to the Intertrain alone – through SW15, Mamá – in the dark!"

"*¡Válgame! ¡Qué muchacha temeraria!*"

"*¡Es verdad!* – it was very foolish. A man started following me and I'll admit, I was pretty scared! Then this other man ran at me out of an alley and that was the last straw! I turned around and let loose with the wickedest Ostrich kick I've ever executed or ever will. And it was … it was – Griffen … " An odd little squeak came out of Kaitrin.

"No! *¡Ay caramba!* Did you hurt him?"

"I got him right where a woman wants to get a man in that situation. Yes, I hurt him – he ended up on the ground. The other man … ran off … after I shouted … "

"Kaiti, is that a laugh? It sounds so peculiar. Are you crying again?"

"I don't know what I'm doing, Mamá. You see, at the time, I got one of my laughing fits and I couldn't stop, and he – he was so funny himself, making all these painful little jokes while he was trying to recover – like … this was the last time he was going to worry about me …" Suddenly Kaitrin reached out helplessly, then clutched her midriff and rocked to and fro. "But it wasn't, was it? He was trying to protect me then and he died trying to protect me."

"Oh, Kaiti, I'm so sorry."

She gasped. "It's all right. It's only, I hadn't thought of that. At the time it was incredibly funny. He took to laughing, too, and then a patrol came by, and – and that was the first time I ever called him by his given name. On the Intertrain coming back, we had such a good talk. He asked me why I had agreed to have dinner with him since it was obvious I hadn't forgiven him for the Arts Campus fiasco. I told him I agreed because my mother said I ought to, and that really made him laugh! He said no one had ever given that reason for dating him before, and – how did he put it? – you were obviously a woman of impeccable discernment!"

Brigit chuckled. "And this is the man you said was too shy to meet me?"

"You know, he was so contradictory. What he was showing me then was an aspect of his personality, but it was a – a public aspect. It was his armor – his protective shell. It was so attractive – so charming ... But no matter what he said – it wasn't the real Griffen Gwidian ... " Kaitrin fell silent.

"I can see why he wouldn't want you to go blabbing all over campus about what you did to him," Brigit said.

"You know, Griffen himself had a black belt in jukara."

"He did! Oh, you got away with something, then!"

"I certainly did. We agreed after that to have a sparring match in the gym. We were doing Cheetah and I got caught up in one of my bull-headed spasms of competitiveness. I honestly thought I could best him in a few matches, and when I came out on top in only one, I accused him of purposely allowing me win. Then he came at me unexpectedly and threw me really hard – knocked the wind out of me and I had bruises on my shoulders the next day. I've tried to figure out why he did that. It was so unlike him."

"When you wound a man's pride, he doesn't always take it gracefully, you know."

"Yes, but ... He regretted it afterward, I'm sure, although we didn't talk about it much. After it happened, he asked me never to take him lightly. And he never would spar with me again. He said we shouldn't put ourselves in a position to hurt each other."

There was a lull while both women pondered. Then Kaitrin said, "I like talking about these things with you, Mamacita. A few days ago I thought I would never want to talk about Griffen with

373

anybody."

"I like sharing it all with you, Kaiti," said Brigit softly.

"After that, I got in touch with Griffen myself because I realized I wanted to keep the relationship going. I wonder what he would have done if I hadn't. I suggested that we just do some ordinary sociable things together and it worked really well. We ate lunch and went to the art show and attended a couple of plays. We started getting comfortable with each other, sharing some insights. And then came my party – I told you about that already."

"The poem you recited at the wedding ... "

"It was exactly the way he kissed me that night. When I found that sonnet, I couldn't believe how right it was. And his to me – we didn't arrange that. Neither of us knew what the other was going say. I have to wonder why he felt it was so necessary to make that passionate public affirmation of his love, particularly when he had such stage fright. Or that's what he called it ... I'm missing something, you know. And it's all closed to me forever." Kaitrin stood up suddenly. "I'm a little tired. I think I'll go lie down."

"That's fine, little one. We'll talk again."

"Oh, yes, Mamá, we definitely will."

*   *   *

And they did, the next day, about the courtship on the *Featherlight*. "It was an exquisite experience, but excruciating, too. I couldn't make up my mind. I was feeling more and more drawn to him, but I was having trouble trusting a man who had candidly confessed that he had never kept faith with any woman in his life. I mean, on the one hand, he seemed so caring and so honorable, and on the other – why had he never cared enough to stay with any woman? It was a great puzzle. Actually, it still is a great puzzle.

"So I really put him through a lot. We had one silly quarrel that had a rather alarming conclusion. It was the first time I ever saw his ... terror ... "

"Terror?" repeated Brigit.

"That's all you can call it. There was something inside him ... Even then, before I had agreed to anything, he was afraid of losing me. But I still kept testing – probing ... And then I arranged for Luku to play music for us so we could dance. It was –

very sensual – and I know Griffen expected that I would come around after that, but I didn't. He was almost painfully patient with me. Oh, god, why didn't I come around sooner? Then I would have a few more days to remember." She gasped.

"Then what?" asked Brigit, almost holding her breath.

"I felt really mean about the way I'd been behaving and I tried to sort through my feelings, and I decided I couldn't imagine life without him. So I asked him to read love poetry to me. That was the main reason I took all those portscarps – I had been wanting him to read poetry to me in that expressive voice of his even before we left Earth. I told him to pick and the first thing he picked was Marvell's 'To His Coy Mistress.' He was trying to keep things light."

"Oh, yes, I know that one – 'Had we but world enough and time … ' And that wonderful conceit about our 'vegetable love.'"

"But in the middle there is a more serious part that he had forgotten about … "

"I remember! 'But at my back I always hear / Time's wingèd chariot hurrying near … ' Kaiti? Kaiti, what's the matter?"

Kaitrin had frozen, her hands over her mouth. Her face had gone white.

"Kaiti?"

"That's what he said," Kaitrin whispered. "His last words. ' … time's winged chariot … too soon … ' That's what he said. 'Too soon' – oh, too soon … "

"*Ay, querida.*" Brigit slid over, put her arms around her daughter, and held her hard.

Brigit's shoulder was wet with silent tears. After a few moments, Kaitrin whispered, "That hurts so much. But I don't have to go crazy with it any longer. I know now and I won't forget again. I feel – relieved, actually. Sort of cleansed … "

For a long time, they rested together in silence. But finally Brigit whispered, "What happened after the poetry?"

Kaitrin pulled away, wiping her eyes. "I asked him how many other women he had read poetry to like that, and how could I be sure he wouldn't leave me as he had left so many others, and he … That's when he told me that I was the first woman he had ever loved."

"The first woman he … ? *No comprendo,*" said Brigit.

"It's like what he said in his vows – all those other loves were not really loves. He didn't mean sex or physical attraction, or just being fond of somebody. Real, deep love that is unique and abiding and – in some mysterious way, forgiving. He got very impassioned. He told me that his life was empty and he begged me to fill it. And I gave in. That's when I gave in." Kaitrin got up and paced the room. "You know how indifferent I've always been to the carnal side of love. Sex always seemed so trivial to me, and even repellent. After all, these days you don't need it to have children. But with him … " She shivered. " … with him … He told me, 'I can love you any way you could ever wish to be.' And he could – he did. Oh, it was so beautiful with him – so exquisite – and I miss that part of him so much. It took such a short time to get accustomed to him, and now I can hardly stand the bed without him in it next to me. I tried to learn all of his body and now when I can't sleep, I lie there and try to reconstruct it, but it doesn't work – fantasy can't be the same as the real, warm flesh. Oh, Mamá, was it that way with you, after Jaq died?"

Brigit ran her hand distractedly through her hair. "We had twenty-two years. The passion had mellowed a bit – turned more into – comfort, familiarity … But we still had our moments ... And I do still miss that part of our relationship, Kaiti. I wouldn't want not to miss him that way."

"No. No. I wouldn't, either. But if only I could have had him just a little longer."

*　　*　　*

The intensity of the effort to rehabilitate her daughter was taking a lot out of Brigit and the next morning she overslept. When she went into the kitchen, she found that Kaitrin had prepared oatmeal and already eaten. As Brigit ate, her daughter sat and glared at her.

"What's the matter?" Brigit asked.

"I was bobbing on the DB for something to amuse myself with and found you've got a filter on the pop links. I really think I'm old enough to view anything that's in there."

"Oh!"

"Goodness! Don't choke! What is it you don't want me to see?"

There was no way around it. "Oh, Kaitrin. You remember

when I wrote you that your preliminary reports were showing up on the links without authorization?"

"Oh, yes, I'd forgotten. So ... " Kaitrin's mental processes were sharpening. "Ah. There's something ... Those events people at the port ... What's going on?"

Brigit sighed. "After I finish eating, I'll show you."

Before long, Kaitrin sat staring at her words on the screen. "This is nothing," she said. "I admit I didn't intend these for publication, but I don't think there's any real harm ... "

"But then there is this." Brigit called up the bios.

"Oh!" Kaitrin flinched a little when Gwidian's face came up, but then she leaned to gaze hungrily. "Well, if people want to know when and where I was born, and who my father wasn't, and what a prodigy I was when I first went to university, I don't care. And Griffen – there's nothing here that isn't available in public Consortium records to any prospective student. Damn, there we are arriving on Luna! Good grief, didn't I look awful? Right there – that's Will Ayland, our pilot, Mamá, and that's ... but what's this?"

She stared at the legal order for the delivery of Gwidian's body to Jonnsberg and the denunciation of Rianna that followed it. "God! What is the matter with people? And how in the world did they manage to pronk legal encryption?" Then she discovered the sentimental elegy and blanched. "They're selling my relay code? What in the world is going on?"

"Your story has become a popular sensation. It's incredibly romantic, you know, if you can view it objectively. You can see why I didn't want you to stumble across this unprepared."

"Oh, puke! 'You shall never more taste her winey breath / Because on a termite battlefield you went to your death.' That makes me want to throw up! What kind of illiterate nincompoop writes this stuff? It doesn't even scan properly! An NDR could write better verse!" Kaitrin started to slap off the feed, but Brigit stopped her.

"One more thing. Might as well see it all." And Brigit pulled up the animated novel.

Kaitrin stared open-mouthed at the fictionalized isopteroids. "Good grief! Is this what I made them sound like? The Shshi aren't anything like this! They actually gave them lips that move when they talk! And alates flying in swarms above the tops of volcanoes! This makes me want to get back to work! Put a stopper on some of this rot!"

That made Brigit smile. "It's all because you do write well, you know. Your accounts are immensely entertaining."

"Well, I never meant them to be distributed outside Shiras-Peders! Or to be fictionalized! This is dataright infringement! Why hasn't the Consortium protested?"

"Publicity," said Brigit succinctly.

"Oh, well ... I thought of that myself when you first wrote about this. But this is going a little far."

"That's my ID the other link was peddling. I had to encode my relay. The public has been sending you condolence notes, offers of sex, derogatory rants – the usual disgusting smut. You're famous, Kaitrin, whether you want to be or not."

Kaitrin made a nasty noise, then said, "Condolence notes? Can I see those?"

"I'm afraid I scoured the whole lot when I saw the sex proposition. And since then everything has been locked out."

"Well, that's all right. I just ... well, I'm getting to the point where a little commiseration ... As long as it's not ghastly drivel like that poem!"

Brigit was relieved that Kaitrin was taking the intrusion with so much spirit, but she hoped nothing more disturbing would crop up.

* * *

That evening Kaitrin said suddenly, "I want to message Tió'otu."

"You do? Oh, Kaiti, he'd be delighted! I think he was afraid you were never going to talk to him again."

Kaitrin entered the codes for A'a'ma's apartment and in a moment his fierce gold-rimmed eyes were glaring from the screen. His crest shot straight up at the sight of Kaitrin and his beak opened to show his quivering tongue.

"Hello, Tió'otu," said Kaitrin a little sheepishly. "I'm sort of back."

"♫♪ <Khelora↑ He'etí ♪] Nei mong'i da^i to↑↓ 'ike go'ol nei♪ bi'át♫♫ b♪elá↑~] "

Brigit was laughing in the background and Kaitrin said, "Stop, Tió'otu, you're scaring my mother! I think she's afraid the frequencies of those warbles will blow the circuits!"

"You are feeling better, Kaitrin? Do you know how worried we have been?"

"Oh, I expect you have been. I apologize. But you don't look so good yourself."

In fact, the avian's feathers were a bit disorderly. "I am starting to molt a little early – partly stress and partly the continuing effects of all that human detox last fall, but I will be all right. But you ... "

"Thanks for having enough sense to bring me here, Tió'otu."

"Mothers are good for many things on all planets, Kaitrin."

"Right!" Kaitrin turned to grab Brigit's arm and give it a vigorous shake.

"Are you already in a shape to come back to campus?"

"Uh, not quite yet. I seem to get really fatigued – I think I still have some issues to work through. But I'm coming back. I want to try to squelch this pop link thing."

"Oh, you saw that?"

Brigit stuck her face in cam range. "I couldn't help it. She got peeved when she discovered I had locked her out."

A'a'ma said, "I already filed protests with the Ethics Committee and the Datarights Committee, and with IQDB Link Security. I don't know what more we can do."

"The IQDB has no legal control over how a chartered pop link set can be used," said Brigit.

"But it has influence, does it not? Everybody on this strange planet has influence over everything else, it seems – except when it is not in someone's self-interest."

"Well," said Kaitrin, "I only wish the stuff was in better taste and better written. That elegy ... " She shuddered exaggeratedly.

"I know. Not even worthy of the word 'doggerel.' Pathetic," said A'a'ma.

"Tió'otu, what is the rest of the team doing? I feel guilty because I never even said goodbye. At least I don't remember doing it."

"Luku is helping me put the final reports together for the Committee. It will take some time. Zin is staying with her. I think Arti is at home in Okloh and Julian went to Shan-hy. Will is visiting his family in Niu Nederlend, but he plans to return to the *Featherlight* and serve on its next assignment. It is still docked on Luna, being refitted. Trea ... "

"I feel the most guilty for not saying something to her at the end."

"She and Sev are still aboard the *Featherlight*. They mean to return to Krisí'i'aid with it and get a flight to Pozúa from there. I think Trea understands, Kaitrin."

"She understands so much," said Kaitrin. "I wish I did. Tió'otu, have you talked to entomology – to Prf. Lindeman? Are they planning any kind of memorial service, or ...?"

"Not yet. Everybody is still pretty much in a state of shock. I think they are all waiting to see what you do."

"Really? But it's going to be a while. I mean, just sitting here trying to talk rationally to you like this, Tió'otu – I feel like I'm going to have to go to bed. I'm sort of frazzled out."

"*<Khedazi go'ol Kaitrin]* We all understand. Take your time. I am merely happy that you are willing to talk to me again."

*   *   *

Brigit could see that Kaitrin was growing restless. She roamed the apartment, tormenting Harly until he was driven to seek safe harbor under the bed. She worked out on Brigit's exercise block. She delved into her storage closet and pulled out all her old clothes and keepsakes. She went through the contents of her thought recorder and began to transcribe them in preparation for writing reports later. But at other times she would simply sit and stare out at the warming spring sunshine, at the wind-tossed limbs of the spruce tree, at the daffodil leaves spiking out of the earth in Brigit's planters. At these brooding moments, Brigit stayed quietly available in case Kaitrin felt an urge to share her thoughts.

One day she said, "How do you cope with the guilt?"

"What do you feel guilty about, Kaiti?" asked Brigit gently.

Kaitrin got up, paced the room, sat down again. "I'll think of something that I said at one time or another that made Griffen feel bad and then I get to thinking of all the things I said and did ... Even on that last night, after ... Why did I do that? Why was I so obtuse – so indifferent to his feelings? It seems like I always have to have that clever little last word."

"I know."

Kaitrin looked at her mother. "You do?"

"Everybody who knows you knows how good you are with a killer quip."

"Really? Oh, dear … Why did you let me be that way? You're my mother – why didn't you teach me to behave better? And now why are you laughing?"

"Mothers would be in real trouble if they couldn't cope with guilt, because they get blamed for everything! Kaitrin, how many times have I said to you in your life, 'You should be more considerate of others' feelings'?"

"Well, yes. I do remember. But why didn't you force me to pay attention?"

Then they both laughed, but Kaitrin shook her head. "Griffen never did that. I mean, in the beginning he was – annoyed about the way Tió'otu foisted me on him … But usually, even if he chided me for something, it was always deserved and done so courteously, or with so much – well, 'diffidence' is the only word I can think of – that you couldn't be angry with him. One time he advised me to take some lessons in diplomacy from Tió'otu … "

"Did he, really? You know what? I think that's a brilliant idea!"

"Oh, Mother!" said Kaitrin, giving Brigit a light swat on the arm before quickly turning serious again. "Mostly, lovely things came out of Griffen's mouth. He was so adroit at turning a compliment. He could be so sophisticated, but sometimes he could be so childlike."

"Well … They say all men are children."

"I know that's the cliché, but … it wasn't like that. Griffen's parents died when he was so young and it was as if that caused him to lose his childhood and he was always trying to recapture it or complete it. But that still doesn't feel like a satisfactory explanation. You see, the trouble is, I never really understood him. We were getting closer to it – Trea said we were. But now I'll never know what was in his soul that made him the way he was. Trea said he had a wound in his soul …"

"She did? What did she mean?"

"I don't know, you see. I don't think she knew, either. She's an empath and she could feel pain in him, but she couldn't identify the cause any more than I could. He was so fearful, so afraid of loss. He was always telling me how he lacked courage, but I think what he lacked was belief in himself. He was always asking me to forgive him for something, but he never could express what it was. It worried me a lot. The only consolation I have is that on the night before he was killed, after he had ... I told him I forgave him for anything he needed to be forgiven for, unconditionally."

"You said that? Isn't that a little dangerous?"

"Oh, I don't think so. I think it eased him ... like the ancient concept of absolution ... "

Not really understanding, Brigit watched Kaitrin sitting with her head bowed, twisting her wedding ring ceaselessly on her finger.

"And now I need somebody to absolve me," she said.

Chapter 5

Rebellion shook an ancient dust,
   And bones bleached dry of rottenness
Said: Heart, be bitter still, nor trust
   The earth, the sky, in their bright dress. …

With all the drifting race of men
   Thou also art begot to mourn
That she is crucified again,
   The lonely Beauty yet unborn. …

Be bitter still, remember how
   Four petals, when a little breath
Of wind made stir the pear-tree bough,
   Blew delicately down to death.
      – *from* Léonie Adams, *April Mortality*

On another occasion, in the evening, Brigit sat embroidering a quilt and Kaitrin was reading, or seemed to be reading, lying on the couch. All at once she dropped the reader on the floor and sat up.

"Mamá."

Brigit looked up a little apprehensively. "What?"

"You aren't religious. You brought me up to be a skeptic."

"Actually, what I tried to do was bring you up to think for

383

yourself."

"Did you pray when Jaq was dying?"

"Oh, Kaitrin. You know I didn't know that he was dying."

"But would you have prayed if you had known?"

Brigit stirred uneasily, searching for an answer. "I've never been a diehard atheist and I never intended to raise you to be that, either. I suppose I might have prayed if I had been in a situation like the one you were in."

"What would you have prayed to? Because I tried; everyone else was praying – Luku – Trea – even Tió'otu ... "

"Even him? Our rationalistic old bird?"

"Yes, even him. But I didn't know how. I didn't know what god to pray to. So I asked Trea what to do and she said that all gods were one and to look within my soul. So I tried, but I couldn't see any gods there, Mamá, only words. Only questions."

"Oh, Kaiti ... " murmured Brigit, drawing a long breath.

"So I tried to pray to the Nameless One – to the Shshi goddess – because it seemed to be the closest thing I could get to, shut up in their damned, blind, foul-smelling storage hut. But I got no answer, no solace – only more questions ... And Griffen died. So I'm still left with nothing but questions."

Kaitrin got up and paced the room, speaking as she did so. "The fact is, I'm so angry. I'm so angry, Mamá! At all these gods that I've researched and analyzed so clinically and so detachedly – all those gods that Trea's prayer invoked at the wedding. I've always had such pat answers, but now I find that all I've learned is there are no answers at all. So what would you have prayed to?"

"I don't know. How could I know? I would have to be in that situation before I could tell you. I think it's different for everybody."

"¡Maldito! Mothers are supposed to know everything!"

"But we don't! You're old enough to have shed that illusion long ago." Brigit laid aside the quilt and rose. "Come and sit on the couch with me, querida. Try to relax a little and let me hug you. Come on."

Kaitrin settled into her mother's arms. "I'm sorry," she whispered. "I'm just looking for somebody to take things out on, and you're here, so you're the goat."

"Mothers are especially good for that."

In a moment Kaitrin said, "Maybe that's what was wrong with Griffen. He lost his mother so young, before he learned she didn't have all the answers. He had Rianna, but somehow a sister is quite different from a mother."

"Quite."

"I never have told you everything that went on right before the end. Let me see – what had happened in that last message I sent?"

"You said the attack of those Warriors gave Griffen nightmares – that's not surprising! – and that you thought he would be glad to get home. And you said later that he had a positive dream that seemed to give him a whole different mindset – almost miraculous. But you never had enough units to give the details."

"That was before I made up my mind to go into the fortress. Let me start with the nightmare. It gives me cold chills to think about it, because it prefigured his death. He had always had nightmares about drowning because of the way his father died, but this time he dreamed he was swimming and these hooks – a lot like the jaws of Shshi soldiers – came up out of the water and seized him and pulled him under. And when he woke up, he was clutching his ribs, right here, right where the wound was going to be."

"Now that *is* uncanny!"

"Was it really a premonition? So many inexplicable things happened on this expedition ... But then he had the other dream – the good one. He said he hardly ever had good dreams. He dreamed that he and I were riding through space on horses ... "

"Horses?"

"He used to ride horseback when he was a boy in Southern Afrik. He dreamed we were riding together forever through eternity. And it changed his whole perspective – for about a week, he was the happiest I ever saw him. He seemed to lose all his fears – took me out in the field with him ... It was like on the *Featherlight* after we first had sex and before the wedding. Isn't it odd? – after the wedding, he didn't seem as happy. He seemed anxious – fearful. Why was that?"

Kaitrin pulled free of her mother and began to pace again, gesturing extravagantly. "But the effect of the good dream didn't last. Maybe it would have, if I hadn't been my usual self-absorbed ... When I told him I was going into the fortress, it devastated him. That was the only time, when we tried to have sex, that he couldn't do it. He told me, 'The nightmare has come back,' and it broke my heart. But it didn't break it enough! I should be scourged! Why couldn't I have paid attention to the signs? Right after the first attack in the field, why couldn't I have had some sense and said, 'We'll have to end this expedition – it's getting too dangerous. Maybe we can come back again later.' But no, I had to squeeze every bit of experience I could out of it. It was all I cared about. I let my love of learning new things rule me and blast everything in my life that was so much more important!"

Kaitrin's voice had risen to a shriek and she began hitting the sides of her head.

Horrified, Brigit jumped up and pinned her daughter's hands. "Kaitrin, stop! Stop! It won't bring him back if you hurt yourself! Stop!"

Kaitrin drew a long, strident breath and allowed her mother to pull her down again on the couch. After a while she said against Brigit's shoulder, "You know, he told me – the evening before the good dream, that's when it was – he told me that when we first met, he had been thinking of killing himself."

"*Dios mío*! Really?"

"His life had become meaningless, he said. But that I had given it meaning, and now – now he wanted to live more than any man in the universe ... He wanted to live, Mamá, he wanted to live! And I let him die ... "

Then Kaitrin cried again, for the third time.

"Kaiti, Kaiti, it's enough for now – it's enough ... "

But Kaitrin struggled up. "No, I have to take this to the end! On the night before he died, he had a real breakdown. I had visited the Shshi Queen that day and heard the Shshi's creation myth, and I told everybody the story. Then something was said about atonement and forgiveness ... "

"Ah."

"Yes, always that. And Griffen asked if we thought there was such a thing as – I think his word was 'unqualified' – as unqualified forgiveness, and then somebody remarked that mothers were more forgiving than fathers. He just got up and went into our sleeping chamber and shut the door. Trea knew something was wrong and she sent me in after him – and he was crying – crying so hard … Mamá, it was so pitiful. But he couldn't tell me even then – he couldn't tell me what was wrong or why forgiveness was so important to him, and I didn't know how to comfort him, and I … That's why I said that to him the next morning – about forgiving him for everything, without reservation."

Kaitrin had risen and was pacing again while Brigit watched her tensely. "You see, I failed him. At that moment, the very latest I could have done it, I should have said, this is it, I won't go into the fortress again and we'll leave as soon as the *Featherlight* gets back. But I didn't – I had to go one more time because I had promised the Queen I would come. Better to break a promise to some alien that I'll probably never see again – to leave things unfinished – than to destroy … So it's my fault – my fault – and it's all right for me to have to bear the pain. But why did *he* have to suffer? I loved him, Mamá – I loved him, I loved him, I … " She was beating her head again.

"Stop, Kaiti, stop! You can't keep going on like this! Am I going to have to get you some professional help?"

"No!" Kaitrin flung her head up, her eyes wide and wet, her hands fisted against her mother's restraining arms. "No! Just let me go through this – this one time! But … " She whispered then. "Sometimes I wish I'd never met him, Mamá. If Tió'otu hadn't signed on to Griffen's expedition, and Ti'shra had never been captured, and I had gone to Aleska and watched moose in the Denaly Preserve – I would have come back and taught my new class and worked on my !Ka<tá project, and then one morning I would have caught an item on the Consortium news link – *Noted Xenocoleopterist found dead, an apparent suicide* – how? Hanging? A drug overdose? Drowning? Drowning in the bathtub, maybe. And I would have looked at the picture, and given a little skeptical snort as I recalled rumors I'd heard about this man, and thought, *He was a good-looking bastard – I wonder what could have gone so wrong in his life?* – and gone on my heedless way and never thought one more thing about it."

Kaitrin stared at Brigit, who stood transfixed with misery at the bitterness of this speech. "You know what I think? I think it's far preferable to die by your own hand at a moment when you don't want to live than to die by another's when life has everything to offer you." She swung around and disappeared into the bedroom, slamming the door.

Brigit stood a moment, then a fear seized her. "Kaiti!" She ran and opened the door, but Kaitrin was only lying on the bed face down. Brigit went and knelt beside her. "Kaitrin, you can't be thinking ... "

Kaitrin rolled over, looked at her mother. "What? Oh! Hell, no. I have to suffer in this life for this. And wouldn't it be the final insult to Griffen, though? – if I killed myself after he died to save me? I would never take that way out. It's not my style."

Brigit laughed shakily. Kaitrin sat up and hugged her. "I'm sorry, Mamacita. I didn't mean to scare you. I had to get that out of my system because it's been eating at me. But I suppose the anguish will dim out in time. I think I can keep it properly bottled up now and get on with things. Thanks for being so patient with me."

"Oh, Kaiti, it's all right. It's only ... well, this has been hard. I had had no idea, really, of how hard it would be."

Chapter 6

Yet we would say, this was no man at all,
But a dream we dreamed, and vividly recall;
And we are mad to walk in wind and rain
Hoping to find somewhere, that dream again.
– *from* Conrad Aiken, *The Divine Pilgrim, IV,*
Senlin: A Biography

Brigit bunked up with Kaitrin that night, and they slept hugging each other like babies. Over the next few days, Kaitrin seemed to have finally achieved enough stability to begin considering what the next step in her life ought to be. One day she called her mother into the bedroom. Brigit found her staring disgustedly into the mirror.

"Look at this!" she said, yanking on wisps of hair. "It's longer on this side than that and shorter on the crown than in the neck! And the bangs are all scraggly! It's hopeless!"

"You need a professional haircut," said Brigit. "Wasn't there a barber on the ship?"

"Yes, but I wouldn't have anything to do with her. Luku tried to even it up, but what does a nice, short-pelted lemur know about cutting human head-hair? Who's that person who cuts yours when you go through one of your periodic 'I'm tired of messing around with this long stuff' phases?"

"You remember – Merci Blatt. She's at the Yellow Canary now. It's a walkable distance, or we can ride our two-wheelers.

389

Why don't I make an appointment for you?"

"'Yellow Canary?' Isn't that kind of redundant? But do make me an appointment – soon!" Kaitrin continued to tug on her hair. "I told Griffen once that I might like to cut it short sometime and he sort of humbly requested that I keep it long, but he said he would love me even if I shaved it to the scalp." Her voice quivered a little. "Maybe I should do that."

"Let's not get carried away!"

"I'll have to find a hair artist – that's what they like to be called now – when I get back to campus. The women in the office will know somebody." Then in a moment she added, "Mamá, I think I'm going to have to do some shopping."

"¡Maravilloso! You're definitely getting better, Kaiti!"

Kaitrin giggled. "Or weaker! But to be serious, there's this problem of the events people. I took a walk around the complex yesterday and I saw some suspicious people loitering outside the gate. One had something that might have been a holocam and another was talking into an MP. I believe I'll get some dark glasses for camouflage and maybe a couple of hats – drab, anonymous things with big brims. Oh, god, that reminds me ... Why does everything have to hurt? I could wear the hat Griffen leant me, but it's too big ... "

She went on in a rush. "And I need some new suits, maybe a little more feminine than I usually get ... Isn't that ironic? Griffen fell in love with plain old Kaitrin who was too stubborn to change for anybody, and now she wants to be more feminine."

She trailed Brigit into the kitchen. "You know how I always wear pajamas? Well, Griff and I didn't wear anything in bed ... " She tittered as her mother gave her a look. "I had planned to surprise him by getting some really sexy, un-Kaitrin-like nightgowns when we got back. Now it doesn't matter, does it? I think I'll order some more of those comfortable, oversized pajamas."

In a minute, she said, "I'm sorry you'll never have grandchildren – los nietos, Mamá."

"Oh, I have you, mi hija. That's what I care about. Besides, you don't know."

"Yes, I do," said Kaitrin a bit sharply. "Haven't you been listening over these last god-awful weeks? I loved Griffen Gwidian and I love Griffen Gwidian and I swore myself to him and I will never, never have sex with any other man for all the remainder of my life."

As Brigit regarded her daughter, she knew that it could be no other way.

"Kaitrin, is there any chance at all that you could be pregnant?"

"Oh, I thought of that. I thought of that a lot. I took the contraceptive subdermal that's part of the off-world medical package. When you're on an alien planet, the last thing anybody wants to bother with is a pregnant team member. But I thought, maybe I'll get a little bit lucky. Maybe I'll be the one-in-a-million case where it doesn't work. But Trea gave me the most thorough physical exam I've ever had in my life during the return trip and I'm sure it included a pregnancy test. I didn't ask her about it because I wasn't talking about anything at the time and she didn't volunteer any comment, but she would have if the results had been positive."

Both women sat in wistful silence for a moment; then Kaitrin said, "Did I tell you that Griff has a daughter and a son, by two different women?"

"No! He told you that?"

"He knew I was likely to find out, but in any event he was always candid with me about that sort of thing, even when it made him uncomfortable. The daughter was by a woman in Ostrailia when he was in his early twenties and he never stayed in touch with her. The boy happened later, in Jonnsberg right before he came to Shiras-Peders. I think he cared quite a bit about that last woman. He was still sending her money to support his son."

"But he didn't stay with her."

"No. I suppose he didn't really love her. It's odd when you think about it. Why is it he never found any woman who could give him what he needed – whatever that was – until he met me?"

*   *   *

Kaitrin and Brigit thwarted the events people by visiting the Yellow Canary early in the day, and Kaitrin got a close, boyish haircut that would grow out into an easily maintained natural style. Then they took the Interurban Transport into the heart of Pikes and invaded the private specialty shops. Kaitrin held up gamely and came back sporting dark eyewear and a plain, wide-brimmed straw hat. When she got home, she decided the hat was too plain, so she decorated the band with some of the feathers that had been wedding presents from the *Featherlight*'s crew.

Then Brigit returned to work. "You might as well," said Kaitrin. "I still haven't worked through the entire contents of my thought recorder and all the language data is total chaos. I need to condition my mind for when I get back to campus. I think I'll leave around the end of March. I will have been here a month." Then she said, "I wonder what became of Griff's recorder."

"There are a lot of rules regarding those things."

"I know. There should be a lot of rules."

"It probably was sent to his sister, since she's the guardian of his estate."

"Huh. That means I'll never see it again."

Brigit glanced at Kaitrin, who had spoken lightly but looked gloomy. Brigit wanted to say again, *Why don't you get in touch with Rianna?* But if Kaitrin was not ready for that, there was no use pressing it.

On Brigit's second day back on the job, Prf. A'a'ma messaged her, twittering in great agitation. "Brigit, <*khelora↑ He'eti♪* that I can talk with you away from home. There has been a catastrophe – a serious breach of trust!"

"What's happened?" cried Brigit in real alarm.

"Somebody pronked Kaitrin's wedding vid and has sold it – sold it! – to the same link that is running the revolting poetry!"

"What? From your transmission?"

"Capt. Skrei does not think so. But he does think that, when I asked to have it transmitted, somebody on the crew got an idea. Everybody knew that our expedition was stimulating interest back on Earth and some scoundrel decided to exploit that. You Earthers, Brigit! Sometimes I do not know why I stay on this planet!"

"¡*Maldito!*"

"Skrei has postponed the *Featherlight*'s departure. He is absolutely furious – you have never heard such trumpeting! He has canceled all leave and has Maj. Bidba, the Chief of Security – what is that expression? – frying everybody … "

"'Grilling,'" interpolated Brigit, emitting a Kaitrin-like chirp of laughter in spite of her dismay.

"Yes, grilling, grilling! He is concentrating on the human

crewmembers, especially the com people. It should not take him long to ferret out the culprit. You can be sure that person will never fly in a Confederation vessel again!"

"But even so ... "

"Even so, the damage is done. Do you know that the link is selling copies of the vid? It is a CET – for 10 regs you can view it once or by paying 18 right off, you can both view it and get one offload to a non-reproducible scarp."

"And it will be only a matter of time before somebody breaks the encryption on the scarp and sets up a pirate link at 15 ... This is horrible!"

"There is no way you can keep Kaitrin from finding out."

"No. Better for it to come from me."

"How is she doing, really?"

"She's planning to return to campus in about a week."

"Oh, splendid! But this latest thing may ... "

"I know. She's made a lot of progress – talks a lot – as much as she used to, in fact. She's got herself under control, but she's still pretty brittle beneath the surface."

"Is she coming back too soon?"

"I don't think so. I don't believe she can improve any more here. She has to start dealing with the idea that she has a future."

So after supper that evening, Brigit said, "Kaitrin, I have to talk to you about something."

Kaitrin regarded her askance as she loaded the dishes in the sterilizer. "I thought you weren't acting normal. Preoccupied. _¡Maldito!_ They didn't fire you for taking so much vacation time, did they?"

"No, no, of course not." She told Kaitrin what had happened and listened to her daughter spout profanity that would made Brigit's earthy Eirish mother proud.

They went and scrambled the offending link and there it was, following the elegy – a few teasing cuts to whet the curiosity – Kaitrin speaking the words "I love you, dearest. Can I make a stronger vow than that?" and Griffen's trembling voice, "There can never be another love for me but you, Kaitrin ... " And then, in ornate crimson letters trumpeting from the screen – _Exclusive! Available Now! The Wedding of Kaitrin Oliva and Griffen Gwidian! All Original – No Dramatizations! A Genuine Heart_

Wrencher! Not Three Months of Bliss Before She Lost Him! View for 10 Regs! Or for Only 18 Regs View and Offload Simultaneously and Experience the Ecstasy Again and Again! Where Else Can You Get Such Enduring Passion and Heartbreak for 18 Regs? (Warning – Commercially Encrypted Transmission. Invalidated offloads will be prosecuted. Biometric verification required. Scroll here for detailed instructions).

Kaitrin sat clenching her gritted jaw in her hand. "God, Mamá, what an indignity! Griffen was such a private man! To have this … The other stuff was bad enough! I agree with Tió'otu – I think I'll move to Krisí'i'aid."

"Shall we view it?"

"I'm not going to pay 10 regs to look at my own wedding!"

"Don't you want to know if they edited it – or how?"

"Oh. Well, I suppose you're right. And I suppose it wouldn't hurt for me to own a copy, as evidence in case I want to prosecute somebody. Pay them the 18 regs right off!"

So Brigit inserted her regscarp into the contact slot, followed the instructions, and the vid opened. The color had been enhanced – Kaitrin's dress was grass green and Griffen's suit was definitely black, while Tió'otu's feathers looked purplish – but nothing foreign had been added and everything was there, flaunted before the world's eyes – the joy, the emotion, Trea's prayer, the anguish on Griffen's face as he and Kaitrin embraced.

"There's absolutely nothing we can do about this," said Brigit. "I'll file a complaint with Link Security, but it won't help. It's an invasion of privacy, but there's nothing libelous here. Nobody has control over these gray areas – it's one of those sensitive individual freedom issues."

"I realize that. I'll just have to take my lumps. Maybe I can buy a mask as well as a hat. I'll never want to go off-campus. Even on campus it will be bad enough."

Surprisingly, however, at breakfast the next morning Kaitrin said, "I did a lot of thinking last night and I've decided the publication of this vid may not be as heinous as it appears at first."

"How can you say that?"

"It will depend on how the world takes it. If it arouses only prurient interest – but there isn't much of that in there to feed on. The emotion is beautiful and genuine and a little cryptic and the poetry is lovely, and only the most bigoted atheists could really object to Trea's prayer since it came from off-worlders. And I remember what Griffen said when he asked me to go through a marriage ceremony with him – something like 'I want to make a public affirmation so the world will know that Griffen Gwidian belongs only to Kaitrin Oliva.' 'I want the world to know,' he said. So now the world will know. If only they'll take it the right way."

"Kaiti, it's generous of you to look at it like that."

"Well, as you said, I can't do anything about it, anyway. I'll simply have to wait and see what develops."

And the reaction to the publication of the vid was immediate and overwhelming. The link crowed that in two days, a hundred thousand people had viewed the wedding and 20,000 copies of the vid had been sold. "That sounds like a huge exaggeration, but still … " said Brigit.

They spoke with A'a'ma. "Kaitrin, when you get back, do not be surprised to find your relay link bricked solid."

"I'm a little interested to see what kinds of messages I get," said Kaitrin. "I may open a second ID number encrypted for private communications only."

*　　*　　*

Kaitrin worked on her field data, but at dinner one evening she said to Brigit, "My research isn't going well. Trouble concentrating."

"I'm not surprised."

"I keep looking for anything to do besides work. I've annoyed Harly so much that he's begun to run away when he sees me. I've swept the terrace. I've even been poking around in the kitchen for something to cook!"

"Cook! *Ay*! That's got to be some state of distraction!"

They hooted, and Kaitrin said, "It's really the subject matter that's a problem. I'm uncomfortable with my memories of the Shshi. I still feel that something was unfinished when I left. Kwi'ga'ga'tei told me she felt the same way. Of course that was before Griffen … But you'd think I would feel everything was finished, if he was fated to die there … "

"You think he was fated to die there?"

"I don't know. Kwi'ga'ga'tei had mystical powers, I'm sure

of that. But I don't really know if she – foresaw ... And now ...
You know, she was wounded when we left at the end and I should
have felt something because I got very fond of her. But I couldn't
feel anything – I couldn't care. I don't even know how she was
wounded, or how the fight between Ki'shto'ba and Hi'ta'fu turned
out. And I still can't feel anything. That bothers me. Why don't I
care?"

"Those creatures killed Griffen. How could you care?"

"But it really wasn't their fault. It was only that a lot of
things happened at the same time and a lot of wrong decisions
were made on both sides about a lot of things that nobody really
understood. It certainly wasn't Kwi'ga'ga'tei's fault – she did everything she could ... She said it was some kind of test for the
Shshi. Her prayer when she gave me the honeydew – something
about asking the Nameless One to protect Griffen so some kind of
prophecy wouldn't have to be fulfilled. And she was wounded at
the end. Why? What does that mean? What was the prophecy?
That's why I can't get any work done. It causes me to think too
much about things that really disturb me. I can't get a handle on
any of it. It slips away."

"Well, go back to campus, *niñita*. Getting back into that environment may help."

But Kaitrin continued to say in great perplexity, "I ought to
care about Kwi'ga'ga'tei. Something tells me I ought to. I had
promised to return someday. Then, at the end, I think I told her,
oh, no, I'm never coming back. And I don't think I will. The very
thought of seeing the image of that damned planet on the viewports
nauseates me."

*   *   *

A major turning point in Kaitrin's life occurred three days before she was to return to campus. She and her mother were getting
ready to go to bed when the relay signaled.

"Who's that at this hour?" said Brigit, popping out of her bedroom.

Prf. A'a'ma's beaky face appeared on the viewport. His molting feathers were much disarrayed and he was warbling in his own
language and hopping from one foot to the other with his raggy
crest standing on end.

"Tió'otu! *¡Ay caramba!*" said Brigit. "What's the matter now?"

He managed to discipline his throat to the monotone of Inj. "Where is Kaitrin? I have to talk to her."

"I'm right here," said Kaitrin from behind her mother. "What in the world?"

"Kaitrin, you have it! You have it! I worked it through – conferred with the Board members in Oxkam and in Moska – and it came through!"

Kaitrin said, "Whatever are you blathering about? What came through?"

A'a'ma bounced and chirped impatiently. "Your Professorship, Prf. Oliva! Awarded as a field promotion. Double Specialties – Linguistics and Xenoanthro … "

Brigit shrieked and Kaitrin said, "What?"

"You have set your record, Kaitrin," said Tió'otu. "Double specialties, at twenty-six years of age – unheard of! Nobody will ever … "

"What?" repeated Kaitrin.

"Kaitrin," said Brigit, "he's telling you that you're now a Professor – Prf. Kaitrin Oliva – no more 'Associate!'"

"But I haven't done anything to earn it," said Kaitrin. Then she bristled. "Look here, I don't want this! I don't want this just because everybody feels sorry for me! That's not the way I want it at all! I'll turn it down!"

"Kaitrin!" cried both Brigit and A'a'ma, and Tió'otu said, "Those old wheezers, or tweezers, or whatever the word is, are tough as titanium, Kaitrin! They never award anything because they feel sorry for the recipient! I ought to know – I have served on that Board!"

"But I haven't done anything yet!"

"You have only constructed an entire language from nothing! Made first contact and successfully communicated with a unique alien ILF! Certainly you have more to do – consolidating all this material into – well, I would say, three or four monographs at least. But your work has been unprecedented, Kaitrin, and so significant that they could not ignore it. In fact, communications from the Board were waiting for me when I got back to campus. So all this happened not merely at my instigation. You will have some clout now, Prf. Oliva. You will be able to request funding – mount your own expeditions – employ the staff of your own choosing … Say, Kaitrin … Brigit?"

Brigit turned to her daughter. Kaitrin was crying. "I've wanted this so long," she sobbed. "And now – and now – I would gladly trade it for one thing – the one thing I can never have … "

"Oh, Kaiti … " Brigit embraced her daughter, while A'a'ma twittered in distress.

"Kaitrin," he said, "do not take it like this. I thought I could make you happy, *nei♪ bi'át♫♫*. It was earned – do not doubt that. You deserve it – you would have gotten it whether your Gwidian had lived or died. Do you think he would not want you to be happy? Take your promotion and let it help to make you happy again."

*   *   *

So Asc. Oliva accepted the promotion and set her biometry on the documents from the World Board on Academic Promotions, instantly receiving the right to call herself "Professor" and to be addressed as such. It had been her goal since she was ten years old, but now that it had finally come, it was so bittersweet that she could hardly bear the taste in her soul. *I'll never hear his voice say the words – 'Professor Kaitrin Oliva.' And I'd give ten thousand Professorships just to hear him call me 'Associate Oliva' again.*

On the 28th of March, in a cold spring drizzle that threatened to turn to ice and crush the newly blooming daffodils, Kaitrin stood in the living room of her mother's apartment trying to say goodbye. She squeezed Harly inordinately hard. "Take care of Mamá," she whispered against the squirming feline's ear. "Don't let her be lonely when I'm gone."

"Cats really are so much company," said Brigit. "After you find a bigger apartment, you should get a kitten."

"So I'll have something to cuddle with on cold winter nights instead of having sex?"

Brigit winced a little. Superficially Kaitrin seemed healed, but occasionally a bitter remark like that betrayed her continuing spiritual rawness.

Kaitrin put Harly back in his chair and came to her mother. "I'm sorry, Mamacita. I haven't learned my lesson very well, have

I? I'm not as good as Griffen was – at building up the layers over the pain." She stared blankly over her mother's shoulder for a moment. "If I could only know what his pain was … " Then she shook herself. "Come on, the transport is waiting. It's time to get back to real life."

Chapter 7

"No human being, if irreplaceable, can ever
be wholly lost, for the desire to touch and
handle seeks the flesh and not the individual.
And a thing truly precious must be drawn
into the lover's heart and spirit to abide there
an image forever."
– The words of Gwydion, *from* Evangeline
Walton, *The Island of the Mighty*

From the flyer, Kaitrin watched Herinen enlarging in the distance. She had worn her summery hat and dark glasses when she boarded even though the day was gloomy, but nonetheless she was aware of surreptitious glances from the flight crew. *This celebrity business is not for me,* she thought. *It's going to get pretty old pretty quick.*

She had thought she was ready for the return, but during the flight she could feel only a dreamlike sense of unreality growing upon her. She spoke to people, said and did all the proper things, but it was as if she were watching herself from afar going through puppet-like motions. It was the same as she boarded the maglev, and again the Intertrain. She dodged events people or simply smiled, gestured at them, and fled; she inserted her finger in scanners or applied her eye, argued with baggage attendants. *I'm functioning very well,* she thought. *Why do I feel like I'm not really*

here? Maybe Mamá was right. Maybe I need professional help.
In Okloh Prefecture the warm midday sun felt pleasant as she
was arriving at her residential building. She hesitated on the walk-
way. *I'm not supposed to be coming here today. It was supposed
to be tomorrow, after we spent our first night in Griffen's – in our
... No! Don't do this! It only makes things worse!*
The door to the building stood open while the Maintenance
Tech serviced the lockdown hardware. "Hello, Jere," she said.
"Looks like we have a doorman today."
He glanced up without recognition. Kaitrin pulled off her
glasses and pushed back her hat. "Oh, Asc. ... I mean, *Prf.
Oliva!*" he said.
"Goodness, has word of that spread already?"
"Oh, yes! You're pretty famous!"
"So I've found out," she said ruefully.
Jere followed her into the vestibule. "I want to say – every-
body who knows you is really torn up by what you went through –
and a lot of people who don't know you, too. Everybody's seen
that vid. It was such a tragedy."
"Well, thank you, I ... I'd better be getting upstairs. My
baggage – my baggage should be here within a couple of hours –
campus delivery ... "
"If I'm still out here, I'll see you're notified. Otherwise
they'll page you."
"I know they will. Thanks ... " She fled into the elevator.
This is going to be a lot harder than I thought.
Upstairs, Kaitrin opened the apartment, went inside, turned on
the lights, closed the door. The atmosphere was tepid and stuffy
and she felt the enviros activate as the sensors picked up her body
heat. Everything was as she had left it, but it looked unfamiliar.
*That's because I've been gone so long – or because there isn't
much clutter ...   Or because the person that left and the person
coming back are not the same ...*
She advanced a few steps, looking around the room – the port
wall, the table, her contour chair, the kitchen alcove ...
She looked down at her feet. *It was here – I was standing
right here – when he kissed me ... Oh, dear god ...*
Her gaze came up, fastened on the wall where her illuminations were displayed. She went over to it. The miniature of the

griffin was still pinned in its prominent central spot. She put out her hand, touched it with a fingertip. *Griffen, Griffen ...*

Her eyes dropped to the books. He had stood here and held the Keats chapbook in his hands, paging through it. She picked it up, let it fall open.

"Heard melodies are sweet, but those unheard
Are sweeter; therefore, ye soft pipes, play on;
Not to the sensual ear, but, more endeared,
Pipe to the spirit ditties of no tone ... "

That's a lot of bullshit, Kaitrin thought, snapping the volume shut. She laid it on the shelf, plucked the image of the griffin off the wall, and placed it face down on top of the book. A large blank space gaped at her from the center of the collection. She turned away.

Sitting down at the port wall, she activated her relay link. *Port memory full. 200 messages.*

Good grief, Tió'otu was right. I'm not ready to tackle this yet. I hope there isn't anything important mixed up in there. She bypassed the messages, entered her mother's ID.

Almost instantly Brigit appeared. They talked about the trip, the weather. No, she hadn't messaged Tió'otu yet, or Luku. Yes, the apartment was all right.

"Kaiti, are *you* all right?"

"Why wouldn't I be?"

Brigit eyed her critically. "Kaiti, if you need help – if everything gets to be too much – you know where you can come. Always."

"I know, Mamacita. But I have to work through this by myself. Mamá, thanks again for everything – you're the best mother in the world."

When they had closed off, Kaitrin entered A'a'ma's ID and waited till his frazzled head appeared.

"Kaitrin! You made it!"

"Of course. *Ay,* you look worse than ever."

He pecked at his neck and a couple of feathers fell out. "Oh, I think it has passed its climax. Are you all right? I could have met you."

"No need. No offense, but it's easier to dodge cam operators without a moth-eaten !Ka<tí on my arm."

"Never any offense, Kaitrin! Have you had lunch?"

"No, but I have to wait for my baggage. Tió'otu, I think I'll put off seeing you until tomorrow. I'm a little tired and ... How about 0830h, in your office?"

"Whatever is best for you, *nei♪ bi'át♫♫*. Oh, I wanted to tell you – Capt. Skrei identified the miscreant who stole the vid. It was an Earther, a ComTech."

"What else?"

"Skrei has inserted a Level 1 censure in her ... "

"*¡Maldito!* It was a woman?"

"I fear so. Skrei inserted a Level 1 censure in her permanent file and referred the case to the Confederation Forces' Disciplinary Council. She will probably get a stiff fine, maybe even some prison time. Skrei would have liked to pluck her bald, except it is impossible to inflict that punishment on you featherless humans! He feels that his reputation – his integrity in the eyes of the Expeditionary Assignment Wing – was compromised."

Kaitrin shrugged futilely. "This matter of blame, of censure – what does it really accomplish? Tell Skrei I don't hold it against him. Or maybe I'll tell him myself. Is the *Featherlight* still on Luna?"

"Yes. Maintenance and refitting are still ongoing."

"Are Trea and Sev still on board?"

"They are. It would be good if you contacted them, *Prf.* Oliva."

"Can't resist that, can you?" said Kaitrin with a thin smile.

"Now at last you can get a larger apartment!"

"I plan to, when I work up the energy."

"There are three empty office suites over here for you to choose from."

"Hell. So much to do. I need to talk to Luku."

"She means to contact you this evening. She has returned to her native nocturnal lifestyle."

"How long does she mean to stay?"

"Not long, I'm afraid."

"Oh, dear ... " Kaitrin felt dull in the head. She gave a gasp. *Damn it, I thought I had stopped doing that.*

I don't want to revert. I don't want to revert to that deadness

– that defense mechanism …

"I'll see you tomorrow then, Tió'otu."

"Very good. Are you sure you are all right?"

"Oh, yes, I'm just fine. Bye."

She sat at the port wall and put her head down on her arms. *I'm tired, that's all. I never used to get so tired.*

Have I got anything to eat? Ugh. Something old and storable. Just like I thought we'd eat on our first night … But now it sounds revolting.

I can't go to the dining room. I have to wait for the baggage. Besides, I'd be sitting there expecting to look up and see somebody standing … and hear, Asc. Oliva! May I join you?

Desperate, Kaitrin got up, went to the kitchen alcove, and opened a storage unit.

The bottle of wine that Griffen had brought to her party leaped out at her. She picked it up. *Oh, god, oh, god,* she thought. *Wherever I look … We could have opened this when we came over here to get my things on the second day – and sat and laughed and remembered …*

How am I going to stand all this? I hadn't realized how much was here to remind me.

The door chime sounded. *There's the baggage – that was quick … Jere must have sent them right up …*

Still holding the bottle, she went to open the door. But it was not the baggage; it was her neighbor Salli from across the hall. She was carrying a tray of savory-smelling triangular pastries, hot from the oven.

"Kaitrin, welcome back! I heard you come in. I thought you wouldn't have anything to eat, so I brought you some of these chicken pies."

Kaitrin stared at the tray and Salli stared at the bottle. "Oh!" said Kaitrin. "That was really wonderful of you. Come in."

"I can't stay. Cinthie is over there by herself."

"Cinthie … She must be about nine months old now. Here, let me … " Kaitrin tried to take the tray with the bottle in her hand, Salli tried to take the bottle, and they juggled everything for a moment and ended up laughing.

"Where did you learn to make these things? They smell terrific," said Kaitrin, managing to get the tray deposited on the table.

"When Cinthie was four months, I started taking home design classes on a cert program – they have a nice nursery over there – and in order to learn about kitchen design, I had to know more about cooking, so I took a cooking class. And do you know, I got so interested that I'm switching my field to culinary arts and planning to go for grads! Maybe I can manage a dining room someday!"

Kaitrin smiled at her neighbor's youthful enthusiasm. *Actually, though, she's only three or four years younger that I am ...*

Salli was looking at the bottle again. "Oh," said Kaitrin, "you remember the little party I gave? This was a gift." In a rush she said, "Griffen – Prf. Gwidian – brought it. I – saved it."

"Kaitrin – or maybe I'm supposed to say 'Prf. Oliva' now!"

"Heavens, no. But you've heard about that, too?"

"Oh, it's all the talk! But what I was going to say – it was Prf. Gwidian who sent you those roses, wasn't it?"

Kaitrin took a breath, but no words came out.

"If I'd known about all this then, I would have dried or plastiformed them or something and given them back to you."

Touched, Kaitrin said, "So you know how to do craft stuff like that, too?"

Salli giggled. "Well, to be honest, no, but I think it would be fun to learn. But I wish I could have done it. Kaitrin, everybody feels so bad about what happened. It's just terrible. And stealing your wedding vid like that ... but it was such a beautiful ceremony – it was almost too beautiful not to be shared. It's ... well, I try to imagine what I would feel like if I lost my Diego." Salli impulsively threw her arms around Kaitrin, who responded to the hug, her eyes closed.

"Salli," she said, pulling away, "I tell you what – why don't you bring Cinthie over here, and we'll open this wine and eat the pastries, and ... What do you say?"

"Open the wine? That's a terrific vintage! Don't you want to save it?"

"It's been saved long enough. Some things are better used – shared."

"Well, all right!" Again Salli giggled. "Wait till I tell Diego that I had fancy wine for lunch! He'll never believe me!"

So Salli fetched her baby and let her play on a pallet on the floor while they ate the tasty chicken pastries and a dish of straw-berries and bananas and sipped Griffen's wine out of water glasses. Kaitrin watched the baby and tried to explain what it felt like to travel through another dimension and gave Salli the official reason for why she had cut her hair. She showed Salli her wedding ring and managed to keep her composure while she did it. When Salli was ready to leave, the two women hugged again.

"Why didn't I get to know you better before?" said Kaitrin.

"Oh, you were always busy doing important faculty things, and I was busy having a baby. And now I suppose you'll be moving out soon. Nobody on a Professor's pay would stay in one of these postgrad flats. We're stuck here for a while, I'm afraid. Diego is in line for an Assistantship, but you know what that pays."

"Even if I move, we could still be friends," said Kaitrin.

After Salli had left, Kaitrin changed into some old clothes, ordered a delivery of groceries, and began to empty her bags, which had arrived during lunch. She cleared a drawer and put her memories into it – Griffen's clothes, the suit he had worn at the wedding, his personal grooming items, watch, and VE. She stood holding his old field hat for several minutes before she put it in the drawer. She added her wedding dress and the scarf he had given her that had served as her veil, and the feathers and other little gifts that the ship's crew had devised for them. She poured the remains of the wine into a different container, rinsed the bottle, and put it at the end of the drawer next to Griffen's tea canister. Into a corner she tucked the box that had held the chocolates from the North Star. Inside it she had placed the wedding vid and the scarps of the poetry he had read to her, with the miniature of the griffin and the handwritten letter inviting her to dinner on the top.

These things were all that she had left of her love, and one drawer held everything.

Then she messaged Luku, who came to the port looking sleepy and tousled. She woke up quickly, however, when she saw Kaitrin. "I was coming to see you this evening," she said.

"Would you mind coming about 1900h and bringing up some supper? I don't really want to go to the dining hall – I'm not quite ready to face all those eyes and well-meaning sympathy."

After Luku arrived, they sat down over containers of chickpea and romaine salad and crusty rolls spread with garlic cheese. "Kaitrin, your hair looks so good!" said Luku. "I am sorry I could not do better job with trimming. Te Quornaz do not need to cut hair."

"You did a fine job," said Kaitrin. "I'm sorry I put everybody through so much anxiety."

"We did worry, and we did grieve, too, Kaitrin."

"I know. I realize I wasn't as alone as I felt."

"You are all right, now, though. Aren't you?"

Kaitrin took a long breath. "I suppose so. Luku, are you going home?"

"As soon as there is ship going to Quornam. May be two weeks – maybe four, not sure."

"Oh ... I was hoping you'd stay."

"Zin and I want to talk to families about marriage, but I have decided I am going to come back for a while. I want to work longer with you, if you will have me now that you are Prf. Oliva."

"Oh, Luku, that doesn't make any difference at all as to how I feel about you. There's still a lot of work to do and you understand this technology better than anybody else."

"Are you eager to get back to it?"

Kaitrin hesitated, stirring her dessert custard. "No," she said. "I can hardly stand to think of it."

"Well ... Not enough time, Kaitrin."

"Luku, fate didn't ward our paths."

Luku looked up quickly, fixing her large, liquid eyes on Kaitrin. "It twisted your paths together for a while. Beauty came from that, but tragedy, too. Then the paths came apart again. It is the way with Fate. You never know."

"And you just have to accept."

"That is part of it."

"What if you don't want to accept?"

Luku thought for a moment. "I do not know. That is not Quornat way. We may fight and we may grieve, but we always have the sense of when we must accept. It makes serenity."

*   *   *

After Luku left, Kaitrin's plan was to attack the two hundred messages, but she lay down and fell asleep. Two hours later, she

407

staggered up, put on pajamas, and went back to bed. About 0400h she dreamed she was with Griffen and woke up and cried in the empty bed. *I'm so sick of crying. I never used to cry. But how can I stand it? I'd rather not dream about him. It makes it so much worse when I come back to reality.*

So she got up and tackled the messages. These included a sprinkling of crank communications, including a couple of fulminations against the public invocation of gods in the wedding ceremony, deemed a shocking violation of the Global Charter. Most of the messages, however, were filled with sincere compassion and good will. She scoured the cranks, transferred the most appealing of the others to storage, and left that relay ID active. Then, according to her earlier intention, she opened a new, encrypted link coded only for her frequent contacts and campus colleagues.

After spending a couple of hours with Tió'otu, Kaitrin reported in to Chairperson Prf. Ranovich and toured the available research suites. At lunchtime she took a deep breath and headed for the dining room, alone. She had to get used to it. She did not remain alone for long, however; the most remote acquaintances had to stop at the table, to offer condolences on her loss and congratulate her on her Professorship. Then events people from the campus news link spotted her and started pestering her for an interview; dining hall security showed up and escorted them out, but she finally abandoned the remains of her lunch and fled.

Back in the flat, Kaitrin checked out her finances. She could not believe what good shape things were in. Her salary had quadrupled overnight, and all the expeditionary bonuses had been credited. She set about paying off some old debts.

Then her new link ID activated and a vaguely familiar face appeared on the screen.

"Paul Missions here," said a pleasant voice.

Kaitrin frowned at him.

"Supervisor in the Archaic Crafts Studio."

"Oh, of course. How rude of me."

"Not at all. You've had other things to think about. Let me congratulate you on your promotion, Prf. Oliva."

"Thank you. I haven't gotten used to the title yet. Uh ... did I go off owing a bill?"

Paul laughed. "No, no! But I have something over here for

you."

"Something for me? I don't recall ordering anything."

"You didn't. Would you be able to come by soon?"

What in the world ... ? "Can't you put it in delivery?"

"I think you ought to come personally. I'd like to talk to you about it."

A little annoyed, Kaitrin said again, "I don't recall ordering anything."

"You didn't. This was ordered by Prf. Gwidian."

"What?"

"Right before you left on the expedition."

Kaitrin's heart had jumped into her throat. "All right. I can get there in about an hour."

*   *   *

Kaitrin entered the Studio in its Old Elizabethen building, her eyes searching for Paul Missions. *Funny, I never knew his last name.* She saw him in the back; he spotted her at the same moment and beckoned her to his office. *What is this, anyway?*

"Prf. Oliva, Prf. Gwidian came into the Studio – I believe it was two or three days before you shipped out – and commissioned a book for you. It's a 20th-century work entitled *Island of the Mighty*, by a woman named ... I see you know it."

"He ... he commissioned it? How?"

"It was to be set in type and printed on our hand press on our finest handmade paper, illustrated with six illuminations and a frontispiece, and bound in tree calf with hand-printed marbled endpapers. He saw some examples of those things here that he liked. Prf. Oliva? Are you all right?"

Kaitrin felt dizzy. She could see an octavo volume lying on Paul's desk, encased in rich leather. "I think I'll just sit down."

"Of course. I'm sorry. Would you like some water? Tea?"

"No. I'm all right, really. Is that it there?"

"Yes." He picked the book up gently, running his fingers over the whorled pattern of the cover. Then he placed it in Kaitrin's hands. "He wrote an inscription to be bound in before the half-title." Considerately, Paul turned his back, busying himself at a table behind his desk.

With unsteady fingers, Kaitrin opened the cover, turned the

flyleaf, and gazed at Griffen's handwriting.

Dearest Kait,

This is for Jaq Mokiba, who rescued this tale from oblivion – and because I love you.

With deathless devotion,
Griffen Gwidian

Kaitrin sat bent over the book, tracing the words with her finger, rocking a little. *Griffen. Griffen. Oh, my dearest love, what a gift ... what a gift ...*

She looked up. "Paul ... " Her voice cracked and she had to clear her throat. He turned with a smile and took a seat at his desk, wordlessly pushing a box of handkerchiefs toward her. She took one and blew her nose. "He ordered this – before the expedition left? Not by TTR?"

"He ordered it before. He wanted it finished by the time the expedition returned – the end of February, he said. He was very particular – wanted everything to be top quality. I hope he would have approved of the results. He knew exactly which plot-points he wanted illustrated. He wanted the color for the illuminations to be rich but not garish, and the gilt accents to be subtle. Our designers and craftspeople really got into this. I fear it would not have been completed if you had returned to campus as soon as you got back to Earth."

Kaitrin was leafing through the exquisitely printed volume. The frontispiece depicted Mâth ap Mathonwy, his feet in the lap of the footholder Goewyn, with Gilvaethwy moping in the corner – and here was Mâth with his wand, changing Gilvaethwy and Gwydion into deer, and here was Gwydion and Arianrhod standing on the strand with the necklace of stars ... And Gwydion and his small son with Arianrhod in the naming scene ... and Llew Llaw Gyffes as the eagle in the tree, sloughing his flesh, while Gwydion stood below, coaxing him down with the Englyns ... and here was the flower woman Blodeuwedd at her creation, and here was the owl woman flying into the night after Gwydion had cursed the thing he had created ...

Kaitrin looked up again. "This is so – so ... This must have cost him a fortune. Is there anything owing on it?"

"Oh, no. Prf. Gwidian paid handsomely and left an order to cover any overruns. There was one small overrun; I believe we underestimated the amount of ink that would be required – also some labor time. We aren't used to tackling pieces of such length." Paul smiled as Kaitrin clasped the volume against her heart.

"It's so beautiful," she said. "How can your people bear to part with it?"

"We can see it's in good hands." Paul rose. "You can understand why I didn't want to have it delivered."

Kaitrin rose also. "And he ordered it *before* ... You see, I have trouble with that because at that time I didn't even know if I was in love with him or not."

Paul continued to smile. "Apparently, Prf. Gwidian knew that he was in love with you."

"Yes."

"Here, let me give you the case for that, and a bag ... "

Kaitrin rode the Slorail all the way back, sitting in a daze with the bag on her lap. When she got home, she carefully cleaned the table, then laid the magnificent artifact in the middle and bent over it, turning the pages, keening over the inscription. *Dearest Kait ... With deathless devotion ... for Jaq Mokiba ... because I love you ...*

The only example she had had of Griffen's handwriting had been the studied formality of the dinner invitation. Now she had another example – one in which he opened the narrowest glimpse into his soul. And he had ordered it before they left ... What if their love had not flowered? He would probably have given it to her anyway. He had already loved her then. For him, there had been no going back, as there was no going back for her now.

Kaitrin opened the volume to the very end and read the epilogue, a part of the book that she had forgotten, where the author invoked Gwydion as *the writers' particular and personal god.* She read the last two lines: *Accept this offering, Gwydion the Golden-tongued, whose speech was stronger than the arms of men.*

Gwydion the Golden-tongued.

My Gwidian. My Griffen.

Kaitrin sat hugging the book, rocking it. Except for the leaf with the inscription, he had never touched it, but somehow his spirit seemed to abide within it. She sat rocking the volume and something began to pull together within herself. Gwidian's spirit seemed to be there with her as she had never felt it before.

It was the first moment since his death that Kaitrin had felt anything like joy.

She got up at last and went to the memory drawer. She took out the miniature of the griffin and restored it to its proper place in the gaping hole in the center of the square of miniatures. Reopening the Keats volume, she again read the lines from "Grecian Urn" and could not understand why she had reacted so bitterly to their sentiment before. She took the Walton book into the bedroom with her and slept hugging it to her heart that night.

When Kaitrin awoke, she saw the book lying against the pillow next to her. She picked it up carefully and placed it on the bedside table. Then she lay pondering, with a clarity of purpose that she had not been able to achieve since her life had been blackened by that day spent in death's underworld. She got up and dressed, then took out Griffen's canister of tea and made herself a cup. She sat drinking Griffen's tea, with the germ of a plan forming in her mind.

Chapter 8

Ah, when to the heart of man
Was it ever less than a treason
To go with the drift of things
To yield with a grace to reason,
To bow and accept the end
Of a love or a season?

– from Robert Frost, *Reluctance*

"Tió'otu, I think I've settled on a suite," said Kaitrin, sitting with the Professor in his office. "The one two doors up the hall. It's close to your office, so when we're working ... "

"I have to tell you, Kaitrin – I have been dreading it, but ... I am planning on returning home. Since the refitting of the *Feather-light* is taking longer than they expected, I have decided to take a different ship – a fast freighter. It will be leaving for Krisí'i'aid in three days."

"Oh, so soon? But I only just got back, Tió'otu!"

"I know, I know. ♫♪ I feel very bad. But I am missing my wife – my family, Kaitrin. I want to get to know Tió'otu *st♪a< 'u*, my new grandnestling, before he fledges."

Kaitrin gazed somberly at her old mentor. "Well, I certainly can understand that."

"I really thought I was going to die out there, Kaitrin. I need to do a little regrouping of my own. I am no longer – how do you Earthers put it? – a chicken of the spring."

"I understand," repeated Kaitrin, her lips twitching. Then she added, "But you *are* coming back, aren't you?"

"*Hei*, yes, but it will not be until the beginning of spring term. I'm scheduled to chair xenoanthropology then. Ranovich will have made her departure. I need you to keep the department in line till I come back. Keep Prf. Jerardo from running amuck."

Kaitrin smiled, shifting in her chair. "I'll do my best. Say, maybe I could sublet your apartment."

"*Tsit tsit* – you could not live there; it is designed for my kind. Messy nest – no bed. A big whirly tub and a fluff dryer instead of a shower. Toilet in the floor, usable only by Birds. Besides, I have already sublet it, to a compatriot of mine who is coming to study Earth's social engineering and political structure. He thinks our people might have something to learn from Earthers! He is a Gro'á'a – what can one expect?" A'a'ma cackled wickedly.

"Well, then, I guess I'll have to look for a place. But in fact I may not be here myself for a while. Prf. Ranovich has granted me extended leave time."

"Where are you going? Back to your mother's?" asked A'a'ma in some alarm.

"No, not that. I think I'm going to play Ulisses for a bit and do some traveling."

"I had no idea you wanted to do that."

"I only decided, Tió'otu, after this gift came to me yesterday. There are things I must try to learn and I can't do that by staying in Okloh."

*   *   *

Back in her apartment, Kaitrin went through the rigmarole necessary to contact the *Featherlight* at Luna Base. After a short delay, Skrei's fierce beak loomed on the screen and he whooped at her. "Prf. Oliva! Professor, now! I makes deep aplopogy – deepers! Speak still at me?"

"Of course, Captain! This whole business with the wedding vid isn't your fault – it's the fault of our crass Earther mentality! There are always humans looking to make a profit from somebody else's misfortune! And, anyway, I think less harm was done than you might have thought. Reactions have been mainly positive. Maybe some genuine compassion has been generated on this planet for a change."

Skrei was not sporting his auto-translator and Kaitrin was not sure how much of that understood. He continued to cough and shake his head. "You say to that not muches too angry me?"

She struggled with what he meant. "No, Captain – or yes, I am not angry. Please know that."

"You need again ship, you ask have me. But you not again want *Featherlight*, or maybe Capt. Skrei Af'fork, also. Too muches rememory – bad. I ask other ship for to command – maybe you likes me if that make."

"Capt. Skrei, I would have you as my ship's Captain any time! I'll remember what you just said. But that could be years into the future."

After a bit more chatter, Kaitrin asked to be patched through to Trea and presently the doctor's familiar small, brown, wizened visage appeared on the screen.

"Trea! I'm back in Okloh. I couldn't let you leave without saying goodbye and thanking you."

Trea looked down, then up. "Kaitrin, good to see you. You do not have much for to thank me."

"Yes, I do. You never failed to make me see more clearly. You helped Griffen more than anyone else could have and I don't mean only when he was dying. Prf. A'a'ma told me everything about what happened while I was in the fortress that last day. You prevented what might have been an even more terrible disaster. Trea, he said that when Griffen was pointing the pistol at him, you called Griffen by a word in Poz-até – could you tell me what it was?"

"*Surál.* I looked for Inj word when I was back on *Featherlight*. I think, 'fey' ... "

"Oh," said Kaitrin, "'death-seeking' ... Did you really think ... ?"

"Not death-seeking so much as – death-ready. *Surál* is soul-eagerness to find answer – make the end. I was some time with Gwidian in sleeping room afterward. We did not speak about his soul-pain, but I could feel answer in him – or part of answer, not all ... His soul was too much yours, Kaitrin."

"'Too much ... ' I don't understand, Trea."

"Is not easy to understand." Trea huffed a small sigh,

displaying her strange, alien smile.

"Trea, when he was dying – what was in his soul then?"

"Ah, that is difficult time for empath doctors. Must try to shut out the death-feelings or own soul can take damage. I am sorry, Kaitrin, I cannot … "

"It's all right. I understand."

"But in the hours before, I felt some peace – regret, longing, pain still – but maybe more peace than one expects. And another thing that you should know – I felt so much love – love for you, Kaitrin."

"Oh, Trea … If only my own love had been … "

"And one more – what is word? I think – gratitude … "

"Gratitude? Why? For what?"

"Maybe is wrong word. *Igantz* … No, 'gratitude' is closest in Inj. I cannot say why his feeling of that was so strong. Maybe he loved you so much, he was grateful he had chance to know that love."

Troubled, Kaitrin sat rubbing her fingers up and down across her mouth, then forced herself to pocket away this conundrum with all the rest and continued in a rush. "After he died, it seemed like I was blaming you for his death, but I was in so much pain myself, I just … I realize that no one could have made the outcome different. I never blamed you in my heart."

"I knew. And I can see you are becoming yourself again, Kaitrin."

"Yes, the key word is 'becoming,' isn't it? Most people think either you're a candidate for the IPD or else you're completely recovered and back to exactly the way you were before."

"You speak wisely on that."

"Trea, I have to tell you about something that happened that has helped me so much. When I got back to the Consortium, I discovered that Griffen had left me a gift – a book he was having made for me, with an inscription in his own writing. Receiving that unexpected blessing made something wonderful happen. It was like a piece of him opened up to me – something that had been there all along, but I was pushing it away."

Trea nodded. "You will heal, Kaitrin. I learned you well."

"But I still don't understand why he suffered the way he did. You said once that time was the friend in learning to understand his soul, but – time ran out – too soon … So now I'm thinking of trying to see what I can learn about that by other means. Do you think that's wise?"

Trea hesitated. "Maybe. Depend on what you learn and how you feel about it. You could learn a thing that changes the way you feel about Gwidian."

"You mean, I might learn something that would damage my love for him? Oh, Trea … I suppose that could happen, but – I just don't think it's possible with my kind of love. Anyway, I'm willing to take that risk in order to understand. I don't want to spend the rest of my life wondering."

Trea continued to nod. "I think, Kaitrin, that for you this is right course." And then she added, "Maybe you will think also of other things you need to do." But again Kaitrin did not know what she meant.

"Trea, you're going back to Pozúa with the *Featherlight*, aren't you? Are you ever going to come back to Earth? I wish you would."

"Do not know yet. Sev and I will make soul quest on Pozúa, at Trant's temple in our home city. Then we will decide what is best for our future."

"I'll probably talk to you again before the ship leaves. Give Sev my love. Once more, thank you for everything. You made all our lives so much better."

Trea smiled, making her warding gesture, and the small face vanished.

*   *   *

Kaitrin frantically edited reports and reviewed the expedition status with A'a'ma. She established herself in her new office. She attended a party for Luku and Zin at Ich Oquaz, saw Tió'otu off at Herinen, talked to Brigit every evening. And she spent a lot of time looking at the book and a lot of time thinking.

Two days after Luku left, Kaitrin sat at the port station in her intimidatingly large and empty office and procrastinated. Her palms were sweating. The time had come for action.

She searched the campus address bank, found an ID, spoke it. The smooth, bland, slightly smiling face of a young man appeared. "Department of Xenoentomology," he said. "How may I be of service to you?"

Typical office assistant, Kaitrin thought. "This is Assoc ... Prf. Kaitrin Oliva over in XA. I was a member of Prf. Gwidian's expedition to 2 Giotta 17A. I was wondering if Prf. Gwidian left any unencrypted files over there ... "

When she spoke her name, the young man's eyes rounded and his eyebrows went up slightly. "Oh, Prf. Oliva," he said. "Would you hold the link open a moment, please?"

His face vanished. An interim picture appeared, meant to entertain while one waited. Tiny and very noisy cricket-like insects flitted about in a bush. Then the picture shifted, became a huge, red-whiskered beetle industriously rolling a ball of purple and green dung that emitted a bizarre glitter. A discomfiting ticking sound accompanied the image. Kaitrin stared in fascination. It had to be one of Griffen's vids, brought back from his earlier explorations of distant worlds.

Then the screen flashed and Prf. Jana Lindeman's face was before her. *Damn!* Kaitrin thought.

"Kaitrin!" she said. "I apologize for not contacting you myself, but I thought it would be better to give you time to settle in."

"Oh, Prf. Lindeman, I didn't intend to bother ... "

"No bother. And please call me Jana. Vick tells me you're inquiring about Griff's files. I need to talk to you about that sort of thing, and a couple of other matters. Why don't we meet for lunch?"

Am I ready for this? I guess I have to be ... "Well, all right. Where?"

"Why don't we meet somewhere halfway between our departments? Say, the dining room in the Lara Institute?"

The Institute of Applied TQ Physics ... She wants to meet me on neutral territory. "All right. I know where that is."

"About 1145h then? See you there!"

At the proper time Kaitrin stood in the food line, nervously picking out something that would be easy to swallow. Glancing back, she saw Jana Lindeman a short distance behind her in the queue. Together, they found a table for two in an out-of-the-way corner.

"Temporal quantum physicists are strange birds, aren't they? And I don't mean Prf. A'a'ma's sort," said Prf. Lindeman, eyeing an oldish woman with white hair swept back on each side of her head like the eyebrows of a crested auk.

"That rarefied subject requires a special kind of mind," said Kaitrin, examining Lindeman as unobtrusively as she could. The entomologist had changed her own coiffure; it was now short, strawberry-blond, and puffed high on the head.

"Looks like we both cut our hair," said Lindeman, peppering her salad.

"So it does," said Kaitrin a little uncomfortably.

Lindeman paused and regarded her, pepper mill in hand. "Kaitrin, we've all been in a state of shock. Griff was very well liked. He could be a bit moody at times, but he was really popular with the students and the younger faculty – very fair and accessible – courteous – considerate of people's feelings ... He never had the rough edges that so many field scientists have, myself included. Kaitrin ... " She paused, then went on abruptly. "Could you tell me what really happened out there? Prf. A'a'ma's written reports were so dry and formal and he seemed to be avoiding personal contact with me before he left."

Kaitrin stared into her soup. "A civil insurrection broke out in the society we were observing. I happened to be inside the Shshi fortress at the time. As my hosts were escorting me out, one of the rebels attacked in my direction. I was well guarded and probably in no real danger, but Griffen didn't realize that and he ran out shooting. The wounded attacker turned on him and – and inflicted a very severe injury. We were driven out of the research flyer and had to take refuge in a stone hut, with no recourse but primitive field medicine. He died about eight hours later. That's really all ... " She stopped.

"Did the flyer cams holograph any of the attack?"

"No, they had been turned off because we were running short of power cells. The expedition was almost at an end, you know."

What a ghoul, Kaitrin thought.

Jana Lindeman sighed. "I can see I'll probably never know everything I'd like to know. Did Prf. A'a'ma talk to you about the possible investigation by the Committee on the Ethics of Off-World Contacts?"

"Yes. One would expect something like that whenever someone is killed in a first-contact situation. He thought it would be possible to keep everything within the purview of Shiras-Peders, since there was obviously no foul play involved – at least, where humans are concerned. But he also thought it might be possible to scotch the whole thing."

"How do you feel about all that?"

"Of course I'd like to avoid a hearing. I'm not sure I can take ... But I feel compelled to say – the standards for off-world behavior are quite contradictory. There really is no single, unified code to guide conduct. If you plow through the archival material from the last two centuries, you can find examples to justify everything from restricting observation to long-distance, no-contact monitoring all the way through total paternalistic interference in a culture." Then she added, "I'm willing to acknowledge – we didn't conduct ourselves as well as we should have. We didn't preserve an appropriate anthropological or scientific detachment, whatever standards one employs. I especially didn't. If there had been formal codified ethical directives, then maybe ..." Kaitrin fell silent, her spoon idling in her soup.

"I agree with A'a'ma," said Lindeman. "I think we can talk the Committee out of holding open hearings if we simply submit a report candidly acknowledging the expedition's perhaps overly informal and enthusiastic behavior – taking our lumps, as it were. It wouldn't hurt to include a bit of a dissertation expanding on what you just said about contradictory ethical standards. But I don't think anything will happen until next fall or until you come off leave, whenever that is. We all need some time to recover – it's not every day Shiras-Peders loses a major faculty member on an off-world jaunt. Kaitrin ... "

Prf. Lindeman pushed away her plate as if food carried little appeal at the moment. "Kaitrin, I've seen that vid of your wedding ... blasted pronkers! I suppose everybody on the campus has. And ... well, that is a Griffen Gwidian I never knew existed."

Good, thought Kaitrin vindictively. Then she thought, *No, Kaitrin, don't be like that. She obviously feels really bad about all this.*

"You know, Kaitrin, Griffen and I were intimate at one time."

"I knew that."

"You did?" Jana looked up in some surprise. "I didn't think it was that obvious!"

"There were rumors. And then – we talked about it. He was very honest with me about his past life."

"Anything serious between us was long over. But I had been a bit worried about him lately. He'd been quite unresponsive – preoccupied. I was really heartened when I saw that vid. It looked as if he had finally found someone who could – well, meet his needs. I never understood him all that well, really. But he ... " She tittered a little self-consciously. " ... he was the most thrilling lover I've ever had, bar none!"

Kaitrin was not sure whether she wanted to cry, scream, or laugh.

Lindeman apparently knew when enough was enough. "About his files," she said.

"Yes, is there anything that's legally accessible?"

"Plenty. But ... " The Professor dropped her voice mysteriously. "There are also some things that are not legally accessible."

"What do you mean?"

"Prf. A'a'ma asked me in his initial communication to get in touch with Griffen's sister in Afrik. The department had all the information for just this kind of tragic contingency. But I also knew that as soon as she found out about his death, she would have his private files encrypted – financial stuff, address bank, that sort of thing. He didn't keep any of that in the departmental ports. So – I pronked it!" She emitted a high-pitched laugh, half-shamefaced, half-triumphant.

Kaitrin stared at her. "You pronked it?"

"Well, not personally. I enlisted a ComTech in our lab who got his hands slapped a few times for his pronking exploits when he was younger. He didn't have much trouble breaking Griff's encryptions, I'm afraid. I'm sure he thought his private ports were a lot more secure than that, although he had scoured his relay files. Probably scarped whatever he wanted to keep."

Kaitrin sighed. "I'm not sure I feel that it's appropriate for me to receive information gathered in that manner."

"Humbug. I knew the two of you were married – everybody knew it by then. I knew you couldn't make a legal contract till you got back to Earth, but I think you have every bit as much right to that information as his sister does. Wouldn't he have shared it with you if he had been alive?"

"Yes, but … " Kaitrin stirred her cold soup, troubled. "All I want is his address bank."

"Huh. I can give you his sister's address myself. Is there someone else?"

"Maybe."

"Do you know if Griff took a neural recorder with him on the expedition?"

"He did. Prf. A'a'ma told me he sent it to Rianna Gwidian-Bock's lawyers at their request. The law mandates it."

"I'd really like to get hold of the information in it. I'll be the one working over Griff's research notes for publication – myself and one of his assistants who is familiar with his writing style. I'd appreciate your input, Kaitrin. Prf. A'a'ma won't be here. Besides, he never went out in the field with Griff the way you did. So if you think you could … "

"Of course, I'd be happy to help. Prf. Lin – I mean, Jana – I have another question. What is being done with his – his house? We were – looking forward to living there together."

"It's been locked down on legal order. It's just sitting there – with everything still in it, as far as I know."

"It hasn't been cleaned out and sold or anything?"

"Not as far as I know. I know it hasn't been sold. It's just sitting there, locked down."

Kaitrin puzzled over this for a moment. Then she said, "I'll take the financial bank as well as the address bank. You can have the portscarps delivered – no, on second thought I'd rather come get them. I don't like the idea of them chasing around campus."

"I don't blame you. After what you went through with the vid, you must feel pretty burned."

And you pronking his files isn't particularly reassuring, either, thought Kaitrin. *But I'm glad you did, in spite of my misgivings.*

As if she could read Kaitrin's mind, Jana added, "I assure you, I haven't looked at any of that stuff. It'll be a relief to get rid of it, actually. You want to come back to the office with me now?"

Kaitrin did not want to spend that much time making small talk with this woman who had been "intimate" with Griffen. "No, I have to be somewhere. I'll come late this afternoon."

"I'll leave the packet with Vick at the reception desk."
Kaitrin thought Prf. Lindeman seemed equally relieved. As
they were leaving the dining hall, Jana said, "There had been absolutely no relations between Griff and myself for months – well,
since I became chairperson – and before that, only rarely for a
couple of years. I don't begrudge you anything, Kaitrin. I have
only the highest regard for you, as I did for Griff."
"You don't have to justify anything to me," Kaitrin said.
"I don't think I could ever have committed to a man like him,
even if he had wanted to. There was always a barrier in him that
you could never penetrate – so much beneath the surface that he
would never show. I consider you a courageous woman."
Kaitrin only laughed a little.
As they were parting, Jana Lindeman said, "But he was a hell
of a good lover, Kaitrin, and I'm going to miss him, damn it! I'm
going to miss that part of our relationship a lot!"

*   *   *

That evening Kaitrin sat at her port wall, turning the scarp
over in her fingers. Griffen's private address bank ... Would she
find what she was looking for?
Then, with a fatalistic shrug, she inserted the scarp and
opened its contents. It was fairly extensive and as meticulous as
she would have expected his files to be, carefully indexed by professional and personal – on-world and off-world – by geographical
area – by alphabet.
She flicked open the files under "Personal" and requested
"Gwidian-Bock."
Three entries came up. *Rianna Gwidian-Bock and Prf. Gerit
Bock. Bock Holdings, Far Point Rd. Sta., Rusberg Precinct,
Jonnsberg Prefecture, Afrik, Southern Section.* And a second ad-
dress, *Department of Herpetology, Vitsrant Environmental Univer-
sity, Southern Afrik Consortium, Jonnsberg Precinct ...* Obviously
Gerit's professional address ...
A couple of relay ID codes followed, one marked *Rianna*, one
Gerit. Then a couple of other names were listed: Gwinneth Bock,
plus a government address and a home address, both in New
Pretor; and Charles Griffen Gwidian-Bock, with the same address
as his parents.

Kaitrin offloaded all of this information into her own bank and sat staring at the screen. All of a sudden, these people became real for her. She had been talking and thinking about Rianna for months and now she realized that Griffen's sister had never seemed real.

She gave her son "Griffen" for a middle name – he never told me that ... Maybe that was what made them come to life ...

With even more trepidation, Kaitrin requested everything with an Ostrailien address. Quite a few professional contacts came up, but there was only one in the list designated "Personal."

Felisha Elswerth, Sidny? Address unknown. Last communication, 10.6.195. No relay ID was given.

Twenty years ago. Griffen would have been twenty-three – no, twenty-four because his birthday was in May. This had to be what Kaitrin was looking for.

There was a pathos about this little entry that Griffen had preserved all those years. He had said she had been living in Sidny when he last heard from her. Felisha Elswerth. Her name had been Felisha. Griffen had never told Kaitrin the name of the woman who had born his first child.

Or of the one who had born his second. Quickly Kaitrin offloaded the scant information on Felisha Elswerth and returned to the Afriken entries.

There were not as many under "Personal" as one might have thought. Some were obviously former teachers or colleagues or perhaps friends from younger days; some were names of women that Kaitrin had no wish to speculate about. But one with two addresses caught her attention.

Emmi Shermayne, 3002D Cape Court, Jonnsberg Precinct ... Dept. of Music, Southern Afrik Consortium Preparatory School ... And there was an ID code.

Emmi. Her name had been Emmi. She played the flute and taught prep, Griffen had said.

Having gone this far, Kaitrin plowed ahead. She scrambled the World Relay Information Exchange and entered "Elswerth, Felisha." And, with amazing ease, after a bit of chattering and flashing, the screen spit a dozen entries at her. Of these, two lived in Ostrailia, one in Adelade and one in Sidny. Kaitrin bobbed for bios and uncovered loan information on the one in Adelade. That

Felisha Elswerth was seventy-four years old and had four children, all boys, and had been cosigning for a loan to buy robotic manure collectors for her youngest son's nascent livestock business.

Kaitrin couldn't help grinning at that. Additional searching located the employment resume of the Felisha who lived in Sidny. Her full address was *Building 20, Apt. C2, Parmata Interrail, Blue Mountain Sector, Sidny Precinct/Prefecture* ... She was a Resources Manager for a firm that manufactured diving equipment. She was uncontracted. She was forty-eight. And she had one daughter, who was nineteen and was named "JoiLene."

Kaitrin wrinkled her nose. *Horrible name!* Then she thought, *Griffen could have looked up this information as easily as I did. Why didn't he? Was he really that scrupulous about keeping the bargain he made with this woman? Perhaps he did look it up and chose in this one instance to lie. With a name like JoiLene I wouldn't blame him! But I can't believe that. There was a lot he didn't tell me, but he didn't lie deliberately. And he specifically said that he didn't even know the baby's name ...*

He didn't tell me the name of his son, either. And I could probably find it in school or birth records. But I don't think I will ...

Kaitrin finished offloading the pertinent information and went to bed. She had stopped sleeping with Griffen's book on the pillow for fear she would damage it, but it rested, a comforting presence, on the nightstand beside her. A little bit amazed at her own audacity, she lay for a while contemplating what she intended to do and then fell asleep.

In the morning she did not go to her office. About 1000h, when it was evening in Jonnsberg, Kaitrin moistened her dry mouth with a sip of water, sat down at the port, and entered the relay code of Rianna Gwidian-Bock.

After a bit, the screen came to life. She saw the face of a youth with tightly curled, sandy-brown hair; light eyelashes surrounding brown eyes; and a pleasant, round, freckled face. "Charles Bock," he said in an unexpectedly deep voice with the predictable Afriken intonation.

Kaitrin smiled in spite of herself. "My name is Prf. Kaitrin Oliva. I wonder if I might speak to Rianna Gwidian-Bock, please."

The young man's eyes popped. "Hopping crackers!" he exclaimed. "Just a minute!" He bolted, leaving the port open. Kaitrin could see a large, shadowy room with some pieces of heavy furniture – a table, a couch – and she could hear Charles yelling, "Mum! It's that woman Uncle Griff married!"

Kaitrin almost cut the link, then steeled herself. In a moment, a woman appeared on the screen. She was large-framed, with a strongly boned face and a quantity of red hair. She had creamy, slightly freckled skin and blue eyes several shades paler than Griffen's, and she had not been gifted with the thick eyelashes or any trace of dimples. Her face exhibited thoughtful intelligence. Apart from a few lines at the corners of eyes and mouth, she did not look twelve years older than Griffen.

"Prf. Oliva," she said, her voice quavering a little. "I'm so glad you rang. I've wanted to get in touch with you, but I've been so broken up over this, and even more so after that vid … Not to imply that I think you haven't."

"Please, call me Kaitrin," said Kaitrin, her voice none too steady either. "Griffen talked a lot about you. I feel – I feel we ought to get to know each other."

"I'm Rianna. Griff called me 'Ree' mostly."

"Oh, did he? He never told me that."

"I daresay there was a lot he never told you."

Kaitrin regarded Rianna for a moment, digesting those words. Then Rianna said, "That was part of the problem, wasn't it?"

"Problem?" said Kaitrin, with a little edge. "Why would you think there was a problem?"

Rianna laughed with a seeming lightness. "I know he loved you more than any man ought to love a woman. That creates problems in itself, doesn't it?"

Remember, she's a psychologist, thought Kaitrin. Aloud, she said, "Actually, you're right. There are things I need to know."

"And things you ought to know. Why don't you come visit me? Can you get away from your work? I believe talking to you would help me to heal, too."

Kaitrin took a long breath. "I'm on indefinite leave. I was hoping you'd invite me. I gladly accept. But I've set a kind of quest for myself and there's somewhere else I want to go first."

"Where's that?"

"There's someone in Ostrailia that I want to look up before I come to Afrik."

Rianna hesitated, regarding Kaitrin speculatively. Then she said, "Ostrailia, is it. Well. When you're ready to come to Jonnsberg, just give me a couple of days' notice – that's plenty. You're welcome to stay with us as long as you like – we have a guest wing. I'll be seeing you soon, I hope."

The conversation came to an end. Kaitrin sat at the port, feeling shaky. She had really done it – initiated something. Where would it lead? Only half jokingly, Griffen had said, *You have to be careful with Rianna – she can make you feel like one of her patients.*

Well, it was done now. Kaitrin turned to the port again and began to check out flight reservations to the Precinct of Sidny in the Union of Ostrailia.

Chapter 9

When I was one-and-twenty
I heard him say again,
"The heart out of the bosom
Was never given in vain;
'Tis paid with sighs a-plenty
And sold for endless rue."
And I am two-and-twenty,
And oh, 'tis true, 'tis true.
– from A. E. Housman, *When I Was*
One-and-Twenty

The new Professor could afford to take an ionojumper and a four-hour flight found Kaitrin swooping in above Sidny Harbor, with its fantastic rail bridge and its big domed hockey arena that was home to the Sidny Dingoes. To the west, the city sprawled away toward where the Blue Mountains beckoned from their eucalyptic haze. *Griff and I were going to come here together and tour the continent. Someday I want to do that, maybe with Mamá or with a friend, or both. Maybe with Luku – she'd love to see all the exotic wildlife. But that's far in the future.*

It was 1300h and it was a workday. In the Sidny Space Port Kaitrin checked out schedules and accommodations, then registered in a large, impersonal hotel as K. L. Olive in hopes of defeating snooping events people. She went to bed until 1800h, then got up and dared the hotel dining room, indulging her palate with

428

barbecued camel.

Back in her room she paced around, working up her nerve. She had not contacted Felisha Elswerth before she left Okloh because she feared a rebuff or even a disappearing act. Now she sat down at the relay port and entered the ID.

On the screen appeared a woman with hair bleached a silvery yellow, mascaraed dark brown eyes, and a face groomed to minimize the effect of its forty-eight years. "Felisha Elswerth," she said, then, with a puzzled expression, "I think you entered a wrong code."

"No, I have the right code," said Kaitrin. "My name is Prf. Kaitrin Oliva. I ... "

"Professor? Say, are you one of JoiLene's teachers? She's all right, isn't she?"

"No, no, I'm not one of her teachers. Sorry to frighten you. I'm affiliated with the Northwest Quad Educational Consortium in Midammerik."

Ms. Elswerth appeared genuinely puzzled. "Why are you messaging me? You look sort of familiar ... "

Uh, oh, thought Kaitrin fatalistically, *she's seen the vid.*

"I'm Griffen Gwidian's wife. I would like to come see you."

Ms. Elswerth's jaw slacked and she turned white. "Oh, that's where ... That vid on the link ... Crimey, what a shock! Everybody was talking about it, and when I viewed it, there he was ... Crimey, what a shock ... But you ... What do you want?"

"I just want to talk to you for a little while. I know Griffen was the father of your daughter. I just want to talk awhile, to resolve some issues."

"Any issues were resolved a long time ago, sweetie!"

"I know they were, for you. But he died in my arms, Ms. Elswerth, and left me with many unanswered questions. I'm on a quest, trying to find some answers. Won't you let me meet with you somewhere and talk for a few minutes? Then I'll be gone and you'll never hear from me again."

Felisha Elswerth rubbed the back of her neck. "My daughter doesn't know who her father was and I've brought her up not to care. I'm not crazy about men, Prf. – Leaver, was it?"

"Oliva. Your daughter is in university at the moment?"

"Yes, down in Cambera at the Ostrailien Consortium."

"Then there's no reason for her to know anything about our meeting."

"There's really nothing I can tell you."

Kaitrin sighed. "Please, Ms. Elswerth. Just a few minutes of your time. I'll buy you lunch tomorrow."

After a moment of annoyed silence, the woman said, "Oh, all right. Where do you want us to meet?"

"I'm staying at the Sea View Hotel near the Space Port. We could meet in the dining room."

"I work about ten minutes from there. I'll take a long lunch hour tomorrow."

"All right. I really appreciate this, Ms. Elswerth. I'll see you tomorrow – about 1230h?"

The woman nodded abruptly and cut off the feed. Kaitrin sat thinking, unsure whether it was wise to rake up the past like this, but it was too late to back out.

After a while she went back to bed and tried to sleep really late to cut down on the waiting time. She had brought Griffen's book with her on her quest; she put it on the bedside table to console her in the impersonal hotel room and set about adjusting to the time differential. As she was falling asleep, she thought, *Griff, would it distress you if you knew what I'm doing? But I can't believe you were really as indifferent toward this woman and this child as you maintained. I have to know what it was like, from her point of view. It's a place to start.*

*   *   *

The next day Kaitrin waited uneasily in the dining room. Felisha Elswerth was late. Kaitrin had ordered some of the wine that Ostrailia was famous for – in fact, it was from the same vineyard as the bottle Griffen had given her, but she had not yet become sufficiently accustomed to her new affluence to order such a top-of-the-line vintage. She sat sipping frugally and trying to keep her emotions under control. *Maybe she won't come ... If she doesn't, I'll take this bottle up to the room with me and drink myself to sleep ...*

But Felisha did come, about 1250h. "Sorry to be late," she said. "I got tied up with a vendor."

"Quite all right. Sit down. I haven't ordered yet, except this

... " Kaitrin indicated the wine.

"If you don't mind, I'd like a scrapper."

"Uh ... "

Ms. Elswerth grinned. "In this part of the world, that's a pint of beer."

"Oh, certainly." Kaitrin was annoyed with herself. *I've got to review Ostrailien slang.*

They made small talk while they ordered lunch. "Call me Felisha," said Ms. Elswerth with a hard geniality. She seemed to have regained her composure. "Just what do you think I can tell you about Griff Gwidian that you don't know? I might say this, though ... " she added while Kaitrin was taking a breath to speak, "I probably hadn't thought about him in years until one day in the office everybody was talking about these alien ten-meter termites that sing, and I said, 'That's a bit of a woof!' But when I looked at the links, I saw Griff's name and – well, that did pique my curiosity. Then when they published word of the accident or attack or whatever it was, and that he had been killed ... And then the wedding vid ... " Felisha regarded Kaitrin from under her eyebrows. "Having something that personal stolen and published – crimey!"

"It was unfortunate," said Kaitrin. "But – maybe not as bad as you might imagine."

"Undoubtedly it was pronked by a male."

"No, it was a woman. One of the ComTechs on our expeditionary ship."

"No! Don't tell me that!" Felisha dived into her salad. "You know, some cynics are saying that you probably engineered that pronking on purpose to milk sympathy and get yourself that promotion."

Kaitrin felt as if cold water had been dashed in her face. "They're saying what? That isn't true at all! To milk ... God! And that kind of behavior would never earn a person an academic promotion, I assure you!"

"Well, I didn't really believe it. Sorry I brought it up."

There was a brief silence while Kaitrin tried to settle her ruffled feathers and refocus on the information she was seeking. At length Felisha said, "So it took Griff – how many years? – to hook permanently with a woman. He must have been in his forties by now. You look a little young for him."

431

"He was forty-three. I'm twenty-six."

"You look younger. But I suspect he'd been contracted more than once before."

"No, he hadn't."

"Really? That's hard to believe, too. As charming and good-looking as he was at twenty-three – and he certainly aged well, from the pictures I saw."

"So you did find him attractive?"

"Yeah, as much as I ever did with any man. All the women in the office were twatty over him – this Brit with the classy accent – we don't get too many of those down here. And the beautiful manners – the dimply smile – and those eyes – really lookers, you know. It was right after I had started to work in the Entomology Office. He'd been on the fac about three or four months, I think, but he'd been up north diving on the reefs and had only just come back for the spring term. Didn't know a soul – first time away from familiar territory, you know? Here in Ostie the universities don't provide housing, so he was off on his own, staying in a hotel. He was a really shy young man in some ways. He'd come into the office and smile and seem to want to talk, but mostly he would ask you something and then let you talk. He was easy to be around – always seemed to be listening as if you were saying the most important thing in the world. A great come-to, I must say. What's the matter?"

"Nothing. He – he still knew how to do that."

"Too bad that sort of thing isn't genuine."

"Why do you say that?"

Felisha snorted. "All men want to put the hook on you – some are just more subtle about it than others. But I must say, Griff's act was top-flight! He'd taken out a couple of the other office drudges – I can't say what happened with those dates – and then I … " Felisha stopped. "I didn't mind his type. As I said, a cut above what I was used to. Most of those bug-men would come in all sweaty and prickly-bearded or smelling like a morgue. Griffen was always finical about his appearance – clean-shaven, and he always smelled good."

Kaitrin could not help giggling. "I never thought of that, Felisha, but you're right. Even in the field, there was never anything physically obnoxious about Griffen."

Felisha gave a hooting laugh, eyeing Kaitrin. "Are you an entomologist, too? I've forgotten what the link said."

"No, my specialty is anthropology and linguistics. This was a joint expedition."

"Huh. Pretty rarefied stuff, I must say. I'm not university myself. I went to a commercial tech school. Certed in managerials. I've done all right, though. The top thing is to be able to support yourself and not have to knuckle under to a male."

I wonder why she's so down on men, thought Kaitrin.

"Anyway, I asked him out myself," Felisha was continuing. "I had an ulterior motive. I was twenty-eight and I wanted to have a baby, but I couldn't afford AI – Ostrailia didn't have a program at that time. We're always about two steps behind the rest of Earth down here. So I thought I'd test out this cubbo. He was the right size, shape, and color, if you know what I'm trying to say, and he was intelligent ... " Again she regarded Kaitrin. "You look a little scandalized, sweetie."

"No, I knew ... but from the very beginning?"

"Believe me, I don't take on shacking up with a man for fun!"

Kaitrin just sat looking at Felisha.

"You look so clueless that I guess I'll have to tell you something," said the older woman. "When I was a kid, my father and my big brother both laid me – a lot. One of them would stand there watching and laughing while the other took his turn. And you wonder why I don't give a snake's snap about men?"

"Oh. Oh, my word. I'm sorry," said Kaitrin, feeling herself flush.

"That's all right. I don't tell most people about that. But I figure you want to know what made your late tick. The truth is, I don't know what made him tick. I only know what made me tick. I wanted a baby, but I'm telling you, if it had been a boy, I would have aborted. I wanted a daughter. I got lucky."

Kaitrin felt a little chilled.

"I asked Griffen out myself," Felisha said, "and pretty soon I asked him to my flat and we went to bed, and he moved in. Crummy flat, but better than a hotel, I guess. And ... I have to say, for somebody barely out of the pouch, he was awfully good in bed. He had quite the touch, even for somebody like me. He seemed to have an instinct about what would make a woman comfortable, you know? Seemed to enjoy doing whatever he could to give her pleasure … Now what?"

"Nothing. Something he said to me once."

"Huh," said Felisha again. "After a couple of weeks, I decided I could stand him around long enough to conceive. So I approached him with the idea. At first he seemed kind of shocked and I thought he was going to refuse. But … "

"Felisha, did you tell him about – what happened in your childhood?"

"Hell, no. You think I wanted him to know I was damaged goods?" Felisha hunched over her grilled fish. "He was obviously too high-brow not to be uppish about that sort of thing."

They both sat brooding for a moment. *You didn't know him at all,* Kaitrin thought. *He would have done anything he could to give you ease if you had let him know you had a need …* She considered this thought, startled by her own insight.

"So we set up the arrangement – he insisted on paying the apartment expenses, since he was living there – and we had at it. I never felt that he was completely comfortable with the situation, though. I suppose he talked to you about all this, since you knew about me. What did he really think?"

Griffen had said, *"I've never felt particularly clean about this whole affair."* But Kaitrin did not want to say that. "Oh, he did say it seemed wrong to get a child from a union that was so – clinical … "

Felisha snorted. "It was that, on my part at least. He tried make something warmer out of it, I think, but I resisted. And I was grateful to him, don't get me wrong. I even got a little fond of him. He was such a harmless sort – sort of colorless – almost too eager to please. Your mouth just fell open again, Kaitrin. I guess you didn't find him that way. Maybe he changed. I think he was bashful – feeling his way. Needed to grow up a little. Certainly he doesn't seem bashful in that vid."

Oh, Griffen. She really didn't understand you at all.

"But, you know, he was wrong – it wasn't wrong to get a child that way. If you saw my daughter, you'd understand. I got the child I wanted. I was so thrilled with the results that I broke my own resolution and messaged him once, when JoiLene was about a month old."

"He said that was the last time he ever heard from you. He didn't even know his daughter's name."

"You sound a little reproachful there. But I thought I told him the name. Maybe not. Frankly I've forgotten what I told him. I think I'll have a drop of that wine, after all. Pour it right in here. Do you get Ostrailien wine in Midammerik?"

"It's considered among the best there is."

"Good!" Then Felisha added unexpectedly, "JoiLene's majoring in drama."

"Drama! Really?"

"That's a funny reaction."

"Griffen was quite interested in the theater."

"He did take me to a few plays. I hadn't thought of that. Maybe it's the genes talking! Anyway, she's not doing too shabby. Had a couple of small parts in commercial vidnovels last summer. One was a mystery where she played the murder victim. Had about five lines before they killed her – had to lie around on the floor for hours wearing nothing but a bathing suit and fake blood and not blink. If she can get some bigger parts and make a following for herself on the pop links, she'll be able to demand a chunky rate for her services."

"Felisha, does she look like Griffen at all?"

"Not a lot. Her hair is naturally sort of middling brown, like mine – we both bleach – and she has brown eyes. Nice dark eyelashes and eyebrows – doesn't need much mascara. Griff did have spectacular lashes – his eyes were lookers. She has a good nose – that's like his. She's taller than I am – kind of statuesque. I think she's pretty good-looking, but I'm only her mother – what do I know?" Felisha's maternal pride peeked out in an unexpectedly girlish grin. "Here, I've got a stillvid. Mammas always carry around stillvids of their joeys."

Kaitrin wistfully studied the youthful, vivacious countenance. "And she doesn't know who her father is?"

The guardedness returned. "No! And I plan to keep it that way!"

"There's no shame in what you did. When she gets older ... "

"You stay out of my life on this! I'm talking to you out of the goodness of my heart because I felt sorry for you, but I won't have anybody interfering with the way I raise my daughter. I can't control what JoiLene does when she gets older, but as sure as hell I mean to keep her out of male clutches as long as I can! She's got some lesbian friends and I'm encouraging her in that direction."

The silence tingled between the two women. Felisha drained off her wine.

Kaitrin bent her head. "I apologize," she said quietly. "I have no intention of interfering or trying to change the status quo. I'm glad Griffen gave you what you needed. He did want to please the women he – associated with. I loved him very much – I didn't find him colorless or … And I've lost him. And I did find him puzzling. I only wanted to see if I could learn anything – anything that could help me to recover."

Felisha had simmered down. "That must have been pretty hard," she said, "to have somebody you care about die in your arms like that."

"Yes." Kaitrin was afraid to say more. She was getting wrung out. *I can't learn any more here. This woman didn't have the slightest insight into Griffen, and what's more, it doesn't matter to her.*

Kaitrin said, "I'll watch for your daughter's name on the vids. But I don't follow the pop links much."

"She's taken a professional name. She's using Joi Worth."

Kaitrin smiled and nodded. *At least the daughter has a better instinct for names.*

When they were leaving the restaurant and getting ready to go their separate ways, Felisha said, "I've probably given a bad impression. Griff was one of the least objectionable men I ever met, and I actually missed him for a while after he left. He almost made me believe that there are some men – only a very elite few, mind you – who can be called good guys."

"Well, I'm glad," said Kaitrin. "He *was* one of the good guys, I assure you."

"I think you're a snarking brave woman to come all the way down here not knowing what kind of reception you'd get. I suppose you'll be looking for a new bed partner soon."

"No," said Kaitrin. "I'm finished with men, too, Felisha, but not for any reason as unfortunate as yours."

Chapter 10

Out through the fields and the woods
And over the walls I have wended;
I have climbed the hills of view
And looked at the world, and descended;
I have come by the highway home,
And lo, it is ended. ...

– from Robert Frost, *Reluctance*

Kaitrin gave herself some recovery time, messaging her mother and even engaging in a little halfhearted sightseeing. Then she set about booking a flight to Jonnsberg. She found a regular weekly ionojump to Southern Afrik and she made a reservation. Then she messaged Rianna. At last the time was at hand.

It was 1600h in Jonnsberg, and she caught Griffen's sister just as she was getting home from work. "Kaitrin!" said Rianna. "I see you're in Sidny. Did you accomplish what you went for?"

"Yes. I'm ready to come visit you, if it's convenient."

"I told you, you're welcome any time. When will you be arriving?"

"In four days – the 16th of April. Let's see – the arrival will be about 1100h your time at the Mendala Space Port."

"Would you mind taking the Exurban Rail out to the Holdings? It runs in our direction every two hours – takes about an hour and a half. There's one at noon, I believe. Tell them you

The Termite Queen

want the Rusberg Line. Mention the Bock Holdings – most people know the place because of the dairy. I'll meet you at Far Point Road Station with transport."

"I'll do that. Thanks so much for smoothing the way."

And that was the total of their conversation. Kaitrin sat thinking, *I'm so nervous about this. Why am I so nervous? Because their lifestyle is so different from what I'm used to?* ¡Cielos! *I've slept in a Morlasapa hut and crawled around in a termite fortress!* And she thought, *I can imagine how Griff must have felt when he arrived in the middle of the veldt from the coasts of the Bristel Channel.*

But she knew that the real problem was not the geographical differences. It was what she was going to learn there. And it was the place of Griffen Gwidian's grave.

*   *   *

Kaitrin leaned against the window glass of the Exurban Rail car, taking in as much as she could of the places where the young Griffen had walked. She saw the tight cluster of featureless buildings that was the Southern Afrik Consortium and wondered why the architecture of large universities seemed to be equally drab the world over. Except Oxkam, of course … She remembered Oxkam as atavistic – carved wooden portals with vaulted lintels, lots of mullioned windows, broad green lawns graced with giant oak trees. She watched the gray urban vista of the Consortium sally past and tried to guess which buildings housed the Vitsrant Environmental University and its Department of Entomology.

Soon the train, an old-fashioned hydrogen propulsion model, moved into the countryside, past ancient undulations of rehabilitated mine tailings and the semi-camouflaged structures that covered the entrances to modern, robotized mineral workings. Then the industrialization gave way to a landscape full of wind towers, distributed across fields of maize, peanuts, and cotton. It was a pleasant autumn day, about 23°, with a clean blue sky.

Presently both cultivation and power generation ended and they were passing through the thorn scrub and rugged pastureland of the high veldt. Kaitrin stared in fascination at the herds of large herbivores – cattle, goats, semi-wild buffalo, flocks of ostriches, even horses. She saw little roads running off through the fields, some paved, but many only dirt tracks. One of the paved roads had an archway across it between two posts, apparently marking access through an invisible electromagnetic fence. One post bore a scanning port, and upon the archway a sign read "C, S, & G Bock Holdings. Access Restricted."

She gazed openmouthed. This was nothing like the Afrik far to the north where Jaq Mokiba had grown up and she had visited frequently. There, the Great Preserves dominated and, except for the residents of Niroba and a few other cities, everybody lived in walled enclaves where personal gardens were the only agriculture allowed and necessities were flown in. The enormous Serenghi Preserve arced from Lac Victoire to encompass Mounts Kimajaro, Kinya, and Elgon. The enclave called Nouvelle Victoire lay on the eastern shore of the eponymous lake and the people who lived there were among the dedicated guardians of a large percentage of Earth's last remaining wild megafauna.

At length the train reached Far Point Road Station outside the small precinct of Rusberg. Kaitrin descended, looking around for baggage claim. Several people were speaking a mélange of Inj and some ancient tongue. Fascinated, she strained her ears and decided the base tongue was a dialect of Tswana, as she might have expected. Very few vestiges of such archaic languages persisted, leaving the rich linguistic heritage of Afrik enshrined with minimal corruption only in Swahil.

"You must be Kaitrin."

She swung around to see Rianna Gwidian, a tall woman in tan pants, a blue-and-white-striped shirt, and soft leather boots. Her hair was pulled back into a bun; it was redder than it had appeared on the relay and showed no hint of gray. Kaitrin fleetingly recollected that Griffen had said his people did not gray early. The sunlight accented Rianna's strong cheekbones and pale skin. Her presence was imposing. And she had her brother's smile.

"Don't look so intimidated," she said softly, her accent more Afriken than British. "Come on, baggage claim is this way. I brought the electro-transport – it's a two-seater. It's about a twenty minute drive."

"Griffen told me they allow personal transport vehicles down here, but it still amazes me," said Kaitrin as they retrieved her luggage.

"In this vast land rail lines can't go everywhere," said Rianna. "You have to have some way to get around besides riding horseback."

"What a change that must have been from Britan!" said Kaitrin.

"You're not joking. When I first came down here, I thought I'd gone to hell. Now I wouldn't live anywhere else."

As they loaded the bags into the back of the hopper, Kaitrin noticed Rianna's gaze resting on her wedding ring, but she said nothing. They settled themselves in the car. Rianna turned into a paved lane marked "Far Point Road" while Kaitrin gawked at the surroundings. In about five minutes they came to one of the archways and Rianna got out and applied her eye to a scanning port in order to open the EM gate.

"This land all belongs to the Bock family. 'C' and 'S' are Gerit's two older brothers, Charles and Stefen. Their compounds are south and west of here. I named my son after Charles Bock. It's traditional – the first son gets the name of the eldest uncle, if there is one."

"I noticed his middle name is 'Griffen.'"

"Oh, yes. Had to be. Let's see, Kaitrin, your body thinks it is – what? Sometime in the evening?"

"I'm not sure. My body is very confused," said Kaitrin with a laugh.

"It's two hours after noon here. Do you feel like … ?" Rianna fell silent, slowing the vehicle in an intersection with a well-tended gravel road. "The Bock family cemetery grounds are down that way. But I don't know if you want to … "

"Oh, god," said Kaitrin, her stomach turning over.

Rianna glanced at her. "Not yet. Not today. Why don't you settle in a bit? I want you to stay as long as you need to. Not rush things." The hopper whined softly as she accelerated. "Kaitrin, I've already had a memorial stone set on the grave. I hope you'll approve of it. I realize you should have had his body. But when I got the word from Prf. Lindeman, I just couldn't … I'm sorry."

Kaitrin regarded her, her hand covering her mouth. "It's all right. This was Griffen's place. I … didn't have him long enough to make my places his … "

"My attorneys were sure you'd file a counterclaim, but you

didn't and you can't think how grateful I am. It made a very difficult situation just a wee bit easier. I want you to know you're welcome to come here any time you like."

"You're being awfully decent about all this, Rianna, considering you don't know me at all."

"Oh, I know you well enough. Griffen told me a lot. I'm positive you would have been his savior. But it wasn't to be."

Distressed, Kaitrin stared at her companion's profile, at the long straight Gwidian nose.

"That's the compound up ahead," said Rianna.

The courtyard was surrounded by a stuccoed wall that encompassed several structures, including a rambling one-story stone dwelling with a tiled roof. A wind tower and a water recycler stood amid agricultural buildings and workshops. Several smallish trees that Kaitrin could not identify were scattered across the courtyard. Rianna saw her looking at them and said, "Those are orange trees and those over there are lemons and limes. Can you believe that PDA this area was a center for citrus production? The pollution caused by all the mining ruined a lot of the local agriculture. Nowadays we mainly raise livestock."

"I love this place," Kaitrin said. "In Midammerik most of us den up in multistoried, windowless caves with synthetic atmospheres. And even away from the cities, the ag and tech centers are quite urbanized."

Rianna nodded. "Whenever I went to visit Griff, I got claustrophobia. I feel hemmed in even in Rusberg."

Inside the compound gate a human aide drove the car away while another carried in the baggage. Rianna conducted Kaitrin through a common room dominated by a stone fireplace that seemed fitted out to burn real wood. The walls and floors were all of natural stone, the ceilings plastered, the commodious furniture upholstered in buffalo hide. In the guest wing, Kaitrin's room was spacious, with a big, wood-framed bed, chests with mirrors, and an armchair. The large windows stood open, allowing a natural breeze to blow through.

"We have enviros," said Rianna, indicating a vent in the ceiling, "but in the autumn we don't use them much. The bathroom is in there – it has a tub and a shower – and through that door is a little room with a port station. You can use it for a sitting room or a study."

"This is bigger than my apartment at the Consortium," said Kaitrin.

"Why don't you freshen up or whatever?" said Rianna. "Come out when you're ready and we'll have something to eat."

A short time later Kaitrin was sitting at a table in a breakfast alcove off the kitchen, eating roasted ostrich meat on a roll and an orange-coconut salad, and drinking iced red-bush tea. Rianna sipped a glass of the tea, having had lunch a short time before. "You may not feel like dinner," she said. "We eat about 1930h, after Gerit and Charles get home. If you like, you can go to bed early and meet them tomorrow."

"That might be a good idea," said Kaitrin, who was beginning to flag. "But I already met Charles, on the relay."

Rianna grinned. "Yes, my loud-mouth son. Gerit will be around for a few days and then he's taking a class into the field. By the way, I recommend caution if you walk out alone. You don't want to step on one of his venomous associates."

"I know all about that. I've spent a lot of time in the field in Eastern Afrik."

"I remember. Griff said – your father, was it? – was from one of the Serenghi enclaves."

"My contract-father. Nouvelle Victoire."

"Griff said that was one of the first things that intrigued him about you – your Afriken connection – but it took persistence on his part to find out what it was."

Kaitrin dipped her head. "That's right. Rianna … " She looked up. "Do you have his thought recorder? From the expedition?"

"I do. The law requires that those things be placed in the estate."

"Yes, I know that. I just wondered … "

"What might be on it? It was only a week ago that the lawyers obtained the permit for decoding. I went through it. There's almost nothing but field notes. That's characteristic of Griff. He didn't trust encryptions or the integrity of humans and he would go back and edit heavily – delete any private ruminations that had crept in. I used to try to get him to work out his problems on a neural recorder, but he never would."

He trusted encryptions too much where his house ports were concerned, Kaitrin thought, but she said nothing.

"I'm going to give you the recorder to take back to his department when you go," said Rianna. "You can review it whenever you feel like it. In fact, it's sitting in the port room in your quarters right now."

"I hadn't gone in there yet! Thanks so much! Any of his thoughts – even just the ones about insects – are precious to me."

Rianna smiled tightly; she seemed to be holding herself on a short leash. Kaitrin saw her glance again at the ring, but she said only, "Would you like some ice cream?"

"Oh, do you have ice cream?"

"The Bock Dairy's best. Chocolate."

"My favorite! Rianna, did Griff like ice cream?"

Rianna laughed. "A lot. Why? Did you never eat ice cream with him?"

"Never. There were so many little things like that that I never had time to learn. So was chocolate his favorite flavor?"

"Actually, no. He liked fruit flavors the best – peach, particularly."

"Is that right?" said Kaitrin. "We would have had to buy two flavors then, because I don't like peach much. That is, I like fresh peaches and peach jam and tarts and such, but not peach ice cream."

The two women laughed emotionally together.

"I never ate chocolate with him, either," said Kaitrin. "He sent me chocolates once. Did he like it?"

"He had no aversion to it, but again he preferred candy like almond paste or fruit gels. But I know why he sent you the chocolates – what the occasion was." Rianna grinned wickedly at Kaitrin.

"So you know what happened on our dinner date?"

"Oh, yes!"

"And he made me swear never to tell anybody! I didn't even tell my mother!"

"Well, it was pretty safe to tell me. I was quite a ways from Okloh."

The two of them continued looking at each other, sizing each other up.

"Kaitrin." Rianna's voice turned serious. "I wonder if you went to Sidny for the reason I suspect."

"I looked up Felisha Elswerth," said Kaitrin quietly.

"Well! Then you know some things that I don't. May I ask you ... ?"

"I didn't know if she would talk to me, but she did. Griff told me about what happened with her. She has a beautiful daughter named JoiLene ... "

"That is her name?"

"Did you both really not know her name? I asked Felisha and she couldn't remember whether she had told Griff or not. He seemed rather – wistful – when he told me he didn't know the name, but I thought maybe ... "

"That he was lying? I doubt if Griff lied to you much at all. There are certain things he might have lied about if you had asked him point blank, especially early on, but generally he prevaricated only by omission or deflection or by talking all around the point."

Kaitrin nodded. "Anyway, I didn't meet her, but her name is JoiLene and she wants to be an actress."

"Is that right?"

"Yes. Felisha said she was grateful to Griffen for helping her out. She has a pretty jaundiced opinion of men ... " Kaitrin had resolved not to speak of Felisha's childhood secret, or of her determination to abort if the child had been a boy. " ... but she said she got fond of Griffen. She thought he was lonely and charming and physically attractive, and she thought he was harmless and – and colorless. Isn't that a strange thing to say about Griffen?"

"Mmm. Maybe that's what she wanted him to be."

Does she mean that Griffen could be whatever a woman wanted him to be? thought Kaitrin. *But I think that might be true.* Aloud, she said, "I don't believe she had the slightest insight into him. But she did say that there are only a few good men in the world and Griffen was one of them."

Rianna laughed. "You and I agree with that, don't we?"

Kaitrin said, "I know about Emmi Shermayne, too, and their son. He told me about both women before he proposed that we get married."

"I'm not surprised he told you, but I *am* a little surprised he told you the names."

"He didn't." Kaitrin decided she had to be honest before everything got twisted up. "Rianna, Prf. Lindeman pronked the files in his home port before you could lock them down. That was before I got back."

"Ha!" Rianna's laugh exploded. "Damn, my attorney was right! She said there were recent access markers in those files – looked like some markers had been deleted but a few got overlooked. Huh! Well, I guess Griff was right never to trust his private thoughts to any encryption." She was looking very annoyed.

"I'm sorry. I haven't looked at the financial stuff – just at the address bank. I shouldn't have even done that, I know."

"I don't care what you see. It's other people."

"Prf. Lindeman assured me she didn't look at any of it – I suppose she was telling the truth. Anyway, I brought the scarps with me – I'll give them to you."

"I would have given you those names. I've stayed in touch with Emmi. She lives in Jonnsberg."

"I know. I looked her up. I mean to go see her, too, Rianna."

"I think you should. You'll find an entirely different situation from the one with Felisha." Rianna gave a short, half-rueful, half-affectionate laugh. "'Griffen's women.' That's what I always called them in my head."

"Rianna, why did he live like that? – with so many loves that were not really loves, the way he said in the wedding. He told me I was the first woman he ever loved. He told me that what he needed was real love – and forgiveness. Always forgiveness. But he never told me what he needed to be forgiven for."

Suddenly Rianna said in a shaking voice, "God, he did love you, Kaitrin. I ... When I saw that vid – his face – your face ... " She bent her head, pulled out a handkerchief, and buried her face in it briefly. "I never knew if the day would come that I would hear him say words like that. I had always hoped it would, but I'd about given up hope. Do you have any idea what that ceremony meant for him?'

"I know that things changed after that," said Kaitrin. "I know that on our wedding night he – he cried, Rianna. He seemed truly frightened. He said, he had searched for me so long and now I was all he had. He begged me to keep him safe. But I didn't. I promised and I didn't. Rianna, I have to know – what did he mean?

What did he need? Do you know? That's why I'm here – why I'm on this quest. If I can learn the answers to these things that I don't understand, then maybe I can find some acceptance – some peace for myself."

Rianna's eyes were bright with tears. "Yes, I know what he meant, Kaitrin. I'm the only one who does. What you are asking me for is the whole story of his life. And I'm going to give you what you need. But not all at once. You're looking pretty dragged out and I'm not feeling so chipper myself. Why don't you go to bed – catch up on that time lag? Tomorrow – tomorrow, Kaitrin – we'll begin."

They rose, but at the door Kaitrin turned and said, "I have to tell you one other thing right now, Rianna. When he was dying in my arms – did you know he died in my arms? – he said several things and one of them was, 'Tell Rianna that I've always cherished her.'"

"Oh, dear god. Thank you." Rianna embraced Kaitrin swiftly, sobbing once against her shoulder, then turned and fled down the hall.

Chapter 11

The mother whose child was buried to-day
Turns her face to the window; her face is grey;
And all her body is cold with the coldness of rain.
He would have grown as easily as a tree,
He would have spread a pleasure of shade
    above her,
He would have been his father again.
His growth was ended by a freezing invisible
    shadow.
She lies, and does not move, and is stabbed by the
    rain.
    – *from* Conrad Aiken, *The Divine Pilgrim, III,*
        The House of Dust

Exhausted, Kaitrin fell asleep almost instantly and heard nothing of the return of the men or of their evening meal. Then at 0300h she was wide-awake, so she got up and peered out the window into the rustic darkness, listening to the cries of night birds, to the eerie, elemental cackling of hyenas and the squeal of their prey. That at least told her she was in Afrik.

She went into the port room and reviewed the contents of Griffen's neural recorder, using visual display because she could not bear hearing Griffen's thoughts uttered in a monotonous robotic voice. Rianna was right – there was nothing personal there. But there were some allusions to their joint fieldwork and to their adventure with the ten-legged saurian; she was surprised and touched to learn that he proposed to name the species for "Kaitrin Oliva, the member of the expedition who flushed the holotype from cover." What was at least a new reptilian order, and possibly a new vertebrate class, he was tentatively calling "Multipoda," and this species was to be *Rutidermasaur olivai* – Oliva's red-skinned lizard.

She lingered awhile over the first entries recorded after the Warriors' assault on the field party. The attack was not mentioned, but there were obvious lacunae – places where sentences were truncated at one end or the other as if deletions had been performed hastily. Later in the expedition, several entries displaying an unusually ebullient and optimistic tone – a sketchy but enthusiastic outline for a monograph on the findings of the expedition, as well as notes for future study projects. These entries coincided with the week following Griffen's dream of their eternal union. But at the day when Kaitrin announced her intention of entering the fortress, the entries once again became choppy and grimly terse, and then less and less frequent. The last – some curt data concerning the weather conditions and the hatching of a pupa case – occurred during the time when Kaitrin had been inside the fortress for her first meeting with the Queen.

Knowing the context, Kaitrin was able to draw more than Rianna could from this guarded record. At the very least, it gave her an image of her name in Griffen's thought patterns. And the phrasing, the British twists of diction, the organizational quirks and the kinds of facts that his mind found significant – those were all Griffen. Grateful to have one more keepsake, she copied the contents of the recorder to a scarp so that she could turn the original over to Jana Lindeman.

As she was dressing, she heard voices and a door shutting, and the whine of an electric car. Peeking out the window, she saw a dark, stocky man getting into a transport, which was being driven by one of the aides. *Gerit*, she thought, *going early to university ... He's quite bald! Strange the Bocks haven't had that gene altered ...*

Presently she ventured out cautiously into the common room. From the alcove where they had lunched the day before, Rianna spotted her. "Kaitrin!" she called. "You're up early! Come on in here!"

Kaitrin did so. Charles was sitting at the table bolting his breakfast. He looked at her with a good-natured grin that was nothing like the Gwidians'. "You remember Charly," said Rianna. "He overslept – has a quiz today."

"I was studying late," the young man said in his almost comically deep voice. "History of extraterrestrial exploration. It's a late morning class, though, so I'm all right."

"I know more than you'll ever want to about test panic," said Kaitrin, sitting down at the table.

"I'll get you some breakfast." Rianna stepped into the kitchen, where Kaitrin could see a human form moving about. *They have so many people working for them. Live people instead of servobots – that's so quaint ...*

"Where do you go to school?" Kaitrin asked Charles.

"Rusberg Prep," he said. "I'm about to pass to university – Closing Ceremony is in August. Everybody in the family has gone there – for centuries, I guess. Uncle Griff, too."

"Oh, did he!"

"Prf. Oliva," said Charles, "I just want to say – I'm blinking sorry about Uncle Griff. I didn't get to see him often, but I always looked forward to his visits. He'd take me out in the field. I mean, so does Dad, but with him it's all reptiles. With Uncle Griff it was insects, but he knew my big interest was birds and he liked them, too, so he was always happy to focus on birds – and he never got distracted or took messages on his MP, and he was more conversational than Dad. Dad just sort of feeds you what you need to know and that's it. Uncle Griff always made me feel like my opinion mattered, even when I was just a little nick." Charles was blushing to the roots of his hair.

Rianna came to the table with a plate of scrambled eggs, maize-meal muffins, and a glass of some tropical fruit juice. "Charles," she said softly.

"That's all right," said Kaitrin. "I like to talk about Griff. You got him right, Charly. And you can call me 'Kaitrin.'"

"'Aunt Kaitrin,'" said Charles, flushing even brighter, if that was possible.

Rianna laughed and Kaitrin tittered, slightly startled. "I never

449

thought of myself as an aunt," she said.

"My daughter Gwinneth was born when Griff was fourteen, so she was like a little sister to him," said Rianna. "But I was thirty-eight when Charly was born and Griff was twenty-six, so they developed a really warm uncle-nephew relationship. We usually drink tea, Kaitrin. Would you prefer coffee? I brewed some."

"Well, yes, I think coffee would be good," said Kaitrin, attacking her eggs. "I plan to start drinking more tea – mainly because Griffen always ... But it's going to be an acquired taste."

"I've got to go," said Charles, taking a hasty final gulp from his own cup as he rose. "Have to do some last minute cramming."

"Be ready to go down with Dow as soon as the car gets back," said Rianna.

"Yeah, I will! See you at supper – Aunt Kaitrin!" said Charles, his eyes crinkling up. He was gone out the door.

"He's charming," said Kaitrin.

"Well! Thank you! Sometimes he's a handful." Rianna sat down with a cup of coffee. The two women looked at each other. "The whole day is ours."

Kaitrin took a quick breath, expelled it. "You're taking time off from work? What about your patients?"

"My colleagues are filling in for me, but there are a couple of children that I want to get back to in a week or so. I don't want my work with them to get off track."

There was a speculative silence, then Kaitrin spoke impulsively. "Rianna, I saw you looking at this yesterday – your mother's ring ... " She slipped it off and laid it on the table.

Rianna reached out tentatively, then picked it up. "Yes. Our mother's ring ... " She turned it over, warm from Kaitrin's finger, then quickly looked inside it. "Ah. I see Griff had the inscription removed. It used to say, 'Ysabell and Lew forever, 152.'"

"What does that signify – that he had the inscription removed?"

Rianna hesitated. "That he knew already – that he had found ... He would never have given this ring to a woman with that inscription in there. It had to be both a clean break and a symbolic gesture." Rianna saw Kaitrin's puzzled expression and she said, "All this will become clear, I promise you."

"Your mother's name was Ysabell? He never told me that."

"Spelled Y-s-a-b-e-l-l. And Lew."

"He told me his father's."

Rianna handed the ring back and Kaitrin slipped it on. "Kaitrin, before I begin what I want to say to you, can you tell me about how he died? I asked Prf. Lindeman for more details and she referred me to Prf. A'a'ma. He sent me a written description, but it was pretty terse. If it won't keep you from enjoying your breakfast ... "

"It's all right. I'll try." So Kaitrin recounted the tale of that sad last day, trying to speak as objectively as possible. Rianna listened with closed eyes, her forehead resting on her fist.

At last Kaitrin spoke the faltering conclusion, "So, you see, time ran out. He knew – the winged chariot – had come 'round ... " and Rianna raised her head, wiping her eyes with a handkerchief.

"There," she said softly, "I did ruin your breakfast. Let me warm up your coffee."

"No, thanks, I've had enough. I'll just finish this muffin – this is real creamery butter, isn't it? – and maybe have another half-glass of juice. My throat got a little dry."

They sat silent for a few moments while Kaitrin worked at eating. Then Rianna said, "That business with the honeydew and the request for you to speak the challenge – bloody bizarre. You actually allowed a giant insect to regurgitate its stomach contents into your mouth?"

"It seemed perfectly natural at the time and the idea of it still doesn't disturb me. I don't know why it doesn't." In genuine perplexity, Kaitrin shook her head. "Some of that doesn't seem real to me. But not the things Griffen said – the feel of him in my arms – his pain. The panic when it finally began to hit home that I was going to lose him. Those things are so vivid. I'll never get over it completely, Rianna."

"He did so much want to have an ordinary life," said Rianna. "And a child. That was something he had grown toward." Then, after an additional moment of introspection, she seemed to take a resolution. "Kaitrin, I've been thinking about how to begin explaining Griffen to you and I've decided to give you the answer first, and then the reasons for the answer. The answer is brief. The reasons – why this whole sad affair evolved as it did – that's pretty

451

lengthy. You know I'm a child psychologist. Griffen was actually my first patient and I never stopped regarding him as my patient as well as my brother and my son. I would never have told you these things when he was alive. Not only would it have been professionally unethical – it would have violated the personal trust between him and me. Besides, if he had been alive, it would have had to come from him for the revelation to have had any benefit. So you see, I couldn't have helped you to understand him whilst he was alive. Is that too terribly unclear?"

"I ... think I know what you're saying." Kaitrin sat back in her chair, twisting her hands together tightly in her lap.

Conversely, Rianna leaned forward and folded her hands on the table. In a quiet, tightly controlled voice, she said, "Griffen Gwidian spent his entire life convinced to the depths of his soul that he had murdered our mother."

Kaitrin stared at her, feeling her face blanch. "What? Murdered! But surely he didn't ..."

"Of course he didn't. But he was obsessively convinced that he did."

"But he told me she died of breast cancer! So he really must have ... "

"Lied? No, it's the truth. Our mother died of breast cancer and our father drowned."

"But then, how could he ... ? Why would he ... ? That explains ... But how ... ?"

Rianna raised a hand. "Now you're asking for the reasons. But first there is another part to the answer and it's a little more complex. He discovered that he could ease the crushing burden of this guilt if he could successfully give pleasure to the sex that he felt he had harmed in the person of the very female that a child is closest to. And for a long time this worked for him – at least it provided him with a way to cope. But in recent years this sexual crutch had begun to fail him. I knew he had to find some closure – some way to achieve a genuine conviction that he had atoned – or else he would ... but I was beginning to despair ... " Rianna fell silent, frowning absently down at restless fingers.

Kaitrin covered her face. "So that's – the wound ... Oh, Griffen. I loved you so much. Why didn't you talk to me?" She looked up. "Rianna, he had that fixation with forgiveness and I confess I wondered more than once – had he really done something – committed some kind of crime – maybe even served prison time or something … ? It didn't seem in character, but people do sometimes make mistakes in their youth that they regret terribly later or feel guilty about. But I never thought it could be – just a misconception … "

"It was a misconception, yes," said Rianna, "but not in his own eyes. To him it was the most significant, most authentic truth in his life."

Kaitrin sat wrestling with her new insight, then said, "On his last night, something was said – some talk of a myth about forgiveness and something about mothers being more forgiving than fathers. And he had a sort of breakdown and cried – just desperately … "

"Ah … "

"And I couldn't understand – it seemed to have something to do with his mother, but I asked him if he had lied to me about her death and he swore he hadn't, so I said, 'Then it can't have anything to do with that.' But our wonderful Pozú doctor Trea is an empath, and she said he had a wound in his soul but that the layers were coming away and that he was getting closer to being healed, no matter how he seemed to be suffering. She said I could heal him. And so the next morning I told him that I didn't need to know what he had done that required forgiveness – that I forgave him unconditionally for anything he might have done. It was only words, but words can be so important. Was that a good thing for me to do?"

"Oh, Kaitrin, did you really say that to him? Oh, yes, it must have been like balm poured into his soul! Kaitrin, now can you see why he couldn't let you die? When he married you, he gave up that coping mechanism I spoke of and put you in its place. You literally were all he had. It was better to lose his own life than to try to live on without you."

They sat in shaken silence for a time. Then Kaitrin said in a small voice, "That must have been what Trea meant when she told me, 'His soul was too much yours.' Rianna, Trea could see a lot but not the source … " Suddenly she rose and paced around the room. "This seems so simple now. Or at least it seems simple on one level. But I still don't have all the answers."

453

"Let's clear the table here and go sit somewhere comfortable, and I'll begin the story of Griffen Gwidian's life."

*   *   *

In the common room, they curled up in the big leather-covered chairs in front of the unlighted fireplace and Rianna began.

"Our mother and father were married when she was twenty-three and he was twenty-nine, but I wasn't born for seven years. They wanted to have children, but Dad had a low sperm count and it just didn't happen. And Mum – well, she had this dread of any kind of invasive medical procedure, so they just took what fate – or god – gave them."

"Griff said that was why she died – that she refused to have the cancer treated. It was a waste, he said."

"When did he tell you about our parents' deaths? Because that was one thing he would usually lie about, or evade somehow."

"It was in our – maybe our second or third casual conversation – I've forgotten exactly. He had been inquiring about my family, so I asked him about his."

"That's strange. Griff could be fairly open about our father's death – it was traumatic for him, but he never felt responsible for it. But Mum ... That he would even mention how she died only goes to show how easy he felt with you even early on."

"He told me about swimming – about being afraid of the water."

"He usually avoided that subject, too, but more because it was a sore point of masculine pride. He really despised his own weaknesses, and yet he fed on them as a part of his self-punishment. But I'm getting way ahead of things. Where was I? Oh, yes ..."

"For twelve years I was the only child. They wanted another; Dad particularly wanted a son who could take over the tour boat business that our family had owned for generations. Did Griff tell you about that? Dad owned several hovercraft and some smaller boats – sailboats. He leased them out, but he also gave sailing lessons and took trippers on tours along the coast – into Kardigen Bay and up the Sevren and across to Eira and south to Landsend. He made a decent living at it and he passionately loved sailing. I could have taken over the business, but it turned out the sea and I

don't get along. I get seasick. I get sick on flyers and in swings."
Rianna grimaced. "I'm perfectly happy to live landlocked in
Southern Afrik! Anyway, that made me a bit of a disappointment
to Dad. That's not to say I didn't have a happy childhood. But
Dad was a big, outdoorsy, physical man and he just always wished
he had a son to share that side of himself with.

"Then when Mum was forty-one years old, by god, she got
pregnant! It was pure chance – luck. But even with a high-risk
pregnancy like that, she refused to see any doctors. She really was
a standoffish, obsessively private sort of person – not a person who
made friends easily. Furthermore, she had gotten very religious –
Generalist stuff. Both Mum and Dad were raised with that faith,
but she had gone a little kotty over it – swore that her pregnancy
was the answer to her prayers – and she simply hardened in her
belief that God would take care of her until 'the natural span of a
human's life passed by,' as some of the Generalist texts put it. The
baby was delivered by a midwife; at least she allowed that much
help. And everything went fine and they had their son – a gift
from God, something really special."

"Griffen told me that his parents believed very seriously in a
personal god who would look after them and that he lost that faith
quickly after they died."

"He did? Amazing!" Rianna fell silent a moment, then continued, "But let me go on. I was a bit old to be jealous of a new
little brother – in fact, I thought it was pretty exciting at first. But I
got ignored a lot after that. I was just coming into adolescence; I
was tall and gangly and had crooked teeth – I've had them worked
on since – and I really could have used more parental support than
I was getting. Now, understand, Kaitrin, I'm not blaming my parents for anything. They never neglected or mistreated me, and I
never wanted for anything material. It was just little things. If
Griff had a featured part in a preschool pageant and if my choral
recital happened to be on the same evening, guess which event
they would attend. It was always, 'Oh, you're a grown girl, Ree –
you understand.'" Rianna laughed rather shamefacedly. "But I
didn't really. I quite resented it and I insisted on going off to university at the age of seventeen. Oxkam or even the Lunden Consortium was beyond the family's means, although if I had stayed in
prep another year, a scholarship might have been in the picture.

But I was itching to get away from home, so I went over to the Bristel Colleges.

"But at the same time, I could see why Griffen got so much attention. He was an adorable little chap, Kaitrin. Nobody – not even a jealous sister – could dislike him!"

Kaitrin laughed emotionally. "I've wondered what he looked like as a little boy."

"I dug out some pictures after he died." Rianna went to a chest and came back with some stills and a couple of holominiatures. Kaitrin examined them hungrily – the chubby two-year-old with the dimpling grin and the long-lashed blue eyes – the leaner six-year-old with a missing front tooth, in a seafarer's suit and cap – the seven-year-old dressed up as the Mythmaker clown Tiffis, with a red ruff and a pointed hat.

"And here is the family. Griff was three and I was fifteen." Rianna held up a large plastiprint framed for display. There were the four of them – a rangy Lew Gwidian, with a boyish grin and a shock of unruly black hair, looking too fit for the age of fifty-one … Rianna standing next to him, thin and tall, smiling a closed-mouth smile, with an immature bosom concealed under a frilly blouse … seated in front, Ysabell, a large-boned woman with red hair, looking down at the figure sitting on her lap – a small form clad in sandals, short pants and a knitted shirt printed with starfish and sailboats. Her hands, with the wedding ring visible, were clasping her son's waist as he tried to wriggle free; one arm was stretched out toward the cam while the other pushed back against his mother's body in an attempt to break her grasp. He was laughing; obviously the cam operator was doing something to hold his attention – something much more interesting than sitting still to have his picture made.

Kaitrin inspected the four of them. "You look like your mother," she said.

"Yes. I got her hair and lighter eyes and bone structure – and her freckles, unfortunately. Griff got the best of both our parents – Dad's hair and deep-blue eyes and the eyelashes, and Mum's nose – we both got that – and we both got Mum's mouth, but Griff got Dad's good teeth and dimples and more sun-resistant skin tone." Rianna was watching sideways as Kaitrin gazed at the small boy struggling against his mother's embrace.

"I have the original holoscarps on these – I'll make some du-
plicates for you if you promise not to display them," said Rianna.
"Griff never was much for this sentimental stuff – embarrassed
him. Typical man in that. But I'm sure he wouldn't mind if you
had them."

"Would you do that? Even the family one? I'd be so grateful," said Kaitrin.

Rianna put the pictures aside with a sigh. "Anyway, Griff
was quite as charming as he was adorable – smart, quick-witted –
talked at an early age. He had such a sunny temperament – related
so well to people. You look surprised. Remember this is the pre-
eight-year-old we're talking about. Dad used to take him out on
his boat tours – gave Mum fits. She always nagged about wearing
the life jacket. But Griff loved to swim; he would dive off the end
of the boat and retrieve things that the trippers threw overboard.
He had absolutely no fear of the water even at the age of three.
And by the age of five, he had the tour patter memorized and Dad
started letting him deliver it. I can tell you, that tripled the business! Griff did love showing off for an audience! He would im-
provise answers to questions – had such a way with words!"

"He still had that," said Kaitrin.

"But later it was calculated – agonizingly studied. When he
was a little nipper, it was spontaneous. I truly believe, Kaitrin, that
if his psychic growth had not been arrested and his self-confidence
eroded, he would have ended up becoming an actor. With that mature voice and his looks, and if he could have drawn on that capped
emotional reservoir for his characterizations – god, he could have
been a world idol!"

"He told me he did a little acting in university."

"Oh, nothing but a few bit parts or non-speaking walk-ons …
But we're getting ahead of things again.

"I went to Bristel at age seventeen and when I was nineteen, I
took a course with this twenty-four-year-old zoology Assistant
from Afrik and we started seeing each other. We fell in love –
Griff always insisted it was infatuation – and when Gerit was offered an Associateship at Jonnsberg, I begged him to take me with
him. Mum was furious – vehemently disapproved of the match
and of my going so far away. We had a really nasty quarrel and
parted without any reconciliation.

"When I got to Afrik, I thought I'd landed myself in hell! I was twenty years old and contracted to a man from what was to me a bizarre culture. When they take a permanent companion, all Bock children are given land and a compound, so here I was saddled with running a big house and a spread of ranchland. What did I know about this sort of baronial lifestyle?

"Then a week after I left, Dad drowned when his boat capsized in a squall.

"The situation between Mum and me hadn't even begun to heal, so I didn't go back for the funeral. Gerit said I ought to, but I wouldn't, and when I think about it now, I realize it was partly for spite and partly because I was afraid that if I jaunted off back to Britan a week after I had come, he, or more likely his rather intimidating family, might think I hadn't made a serious commitment – maybe they wouldn't even want me to come back! And I was stubborn – I was determined to make a go of this thing I had gotten myself into. But I was also very young and lacking in judgment, and pretty insecure myself."

Rianna pursed her lips ruefully and shook her head. "All my life I've regretted not going back. If I had gone, I might have realized how shattered Mum was – how unstable ... Anyway, some of Dad's assistants took over the sailing business with Mum as a silent partner. She received half the profits; furthermore Dad had left a good amount of life insurance, so money wasn't a problem. Our house was free-standing, built behind the property where the business had its offices, and it was surrounded by a high privacy wall. In the beginning the partners would come by and check on Ysabell, but things were always fine and then it got so they would just wave occasionally over the wall at Griffen or Mum in the yard. If they had to speak to her on a business matter, it was almost always done by link. It's easy to ignore other people when you're busy, especially when it's somebody you've never had a very comfortable relationship with in the first place. Mum stopped seeing what few friends she had had and soon she and Griff were living an isolated existence.

"Whenever I did communicate with Mum either orally or in writing, she would put on a great show – it seems Griff got his acting talent from her! Everything was fine. Everything was always fine. And Griff – 'Oh, he's such a comfort and such a help,' she would say. 'He's my mainstay, Ree. I don't know what I'd do without him!'

"So time passed and I got used to things here and started to like it, and then I returned to school. I had already decided on a psychology specialty before I left Bristel, and Jonnsberg has a fine program. Mum and I talked less and less frequently. When we did, everything was always fine. I never knew that on the night Dad's body was found – it was three days after he drowned – Mum went rushing down to the dock taking Griff with her and they pulled the bloated body out with a hand and a foot and part of the face missing. Griff saw all that. It was the beginning of the trauma. He was always terrified of the water after that and the nightmares started."

"That soon," said Kaitrin, hugging her ribs. She found herself dreading the next part of the narration.

"Oh, yes. And apparently Mum didn't help matters. She had begun to pray obsessively and she convinced Griff that if they prayed intensely enough, nothing else bad could ever happen to them. He told me – you see, all this comes from what Griff told me later – he told me she overwhelmed him with – the god thing. Remember, this was an impressionable and inwardly quite sensitive eight- and nine-year-old child. She almost convinced him that, if they prayed with enough faith, Dad would come back from the dead. And at the same time she clung to him for support and he didn't know how to support her. He needed support himself. She would tell him – just say this, don't tell anyone that. He got very confused about what was real and what wasn't. Oh, god, if only I had been there!" Rianna ran her fingers distractedly through her hair.

Then she continued, "As I said, communications between Mum and me became less and less frequent, and toward the end, they were always written, no vid. If I messaged her, nobody would answer, and then I'd get a return message, in writing, saying she had been out or busy and had missed my call. I did wonder why this inevitably happened, but I was too involved in my own life to pay proper attention. It was because she was sick and she didn't want anyone to know she was wasting away.

"And I ought to say that if Dad hadn't died, I don't think any of this would have happened. He subscribed to the idea of a

benevolent God, but he was also a practical man and no fanatic –
he didn't believe that you could expect God to work miracles for
you and he had no aversion to medical treatment. He would have
forced his Ysabell to get help – he would have never allowed her
to die needlessly like that, no matter how much she resisted.

"Anyway, she wouldn't let Griff say anything. He could
sense that something was seriously wrong, but she would tell him
everything was fine. He went to school, but when he came home,
he was with her constantly; she wouldn't let him out of the house.
If there was some after-school affair he was supposed to attend,
she would write a note or instruct him in some lie to get out of it.
And he did everything she said.

"And toward the end she kept him at home a lot on false sick
days. The last few weeks he was forced to do physical things for
her that no ten-year-old boy should have to do for his mother, like
cleaning up after her when she couldn't make it to the toilet. 'I
need you to help me,' she would say. 'You're all I have, Griffen.
Let's pray together – that's all I need. I'm not sick. I just need
you to help me and pray with me.' And then it was 'I forbid you to
ever tell anybody that I'm sick, because I'm not. God will keep
me whole. I forbid you to say a word. God forbids you.' And at
last it was 'Griffen, you're the only one whose prayers can save
me. You're my innocent and the prayers of the innocent are always answered.' And he didn't understand – he was having endless nightmares about drowning and he was terrified, and yet he
was the only one who could save her. Kaitrin … "

Kaitrin had hunched over, her face in her hands; now she
looked up with a gasp. "Oh, Rianna, I know you say you couldn't
have told me, but if I had only known all this."

"I'm convinced he would have told you everything sooner or
later," said Rianna gently. "But if he had known that you knew
from some other source, he would have panicked and pushed you
away and you would have been lost to each other forever. He had
to come to you of his own volition. I'm convinced he was coming.
There just wasn't – enough time."

"But he told all this to you. Why didn't that heal him?"

"I'm his sister. I'm his surrogate mother. I have guilt issues
of my own in this matter. I could hold him together, but I couldn't
heal him. But let me go on.

"The school did wonder what was going on – not only was Griffen frequently absent and not engaging in any activities, but the level of his academic achievement had fallen off. But everybody knew about Lew Gwidian's tragic death and they were willing to give the family a period of adjustment. Besides, the school was overcrowded and sometimes the problems of individuals got lost in the shuffle. And the excuses for his erratic attendance were never implausible.

"Then one night almost two years to the day after Dad drowned, I got a relay message. Mum had been found dead in her bed. Griff hadn't showed up for school that morning and, when no excuse came in and the relay went unanswered, a counselor went to the house to check on him. When nobody came to the door, she brought in the constabulary and they overrode the lock codes and found her, with Griffen curled up on the floor by the bed, almost totally unresponsive. She had died, the coroner said, about 2300h the evening before. He had lain there beside her body for twelve hours.

"They told me only that my brother appeared to be in a state of severe post-traumatic shock, and could I come see to things? And if not, what course of action should they take? They should have immediately placed Griff in a clinic for dysfunctional children – a controlled environment – but instead, whilst Gerit and I dithered, they sent him to a foster home. I believe he started to respond somewhat there – the woman was a loving enough person – but a terrible mistake was made. The coroner's report came in and while they were conversing about how Mum died, Griffen was around the corner and he heard everything. He heard them say, 'She died of breast cancer! That's a ridiculous waste! Nobody dies of breast cancer these days! Wasn't there anybody that could force her to get medical help? Allowing her to die like that is no different from committing murder!'"

"Dear god," whispered Kaitrin. "I understand now. I understand."

After a moment, Rianna said, "She had told him over and over, 'You are all I have. Only your prayers can save me.' So who else but Griffen Gwidian could have gotten help for her? Who else but Griffen Gwidian was deficient in the eyes of God? Who else could be responsible for the death of Griffen Gwidian's mother?"

"I understand, Rianna. Now I understand." Tears were streaming down Kaitrin's face and she made no effort to staunch them. *Oh, Griffen, my dearest love. I didn't know. I didn't help you. Now I am the one who needs to be forgiven. Who will forgive me?*

"Here, Kaitrin." Rianna was bending over her with a handkerchief. "I knew this would be hard for you. Imagine how wrenching it would have been for him to tell you these things. It would have been like signing his own death warrant. What woman could love the craven matricide that he conceived himself to be?"

"Couldn't you convince him, Rianna, that he wasn't responsible?"

"Oh, intellectually, he came to understand that. But the trauma remained, sinking deeper and deeper into his soul, and I suppose he died with that inexorable guilt still intact. But maybe – just maybe what you said about forgiving him unconditionally eased it enough that … Kaitrin, would you rather I not tell you anymore?"

Kaitrin was blowing her nose. "I wouldn't mind a little recovery time, but I want to know everything there is to know, Rianna. Will you tell me more?'

"I'll tell you more. Why don't you go and rest awhile? Then maybe after lunch we'll take a walk." And Rianna shepherded Kaitrin into the guest wing.

Chapter 12

As a naked man I go
  Through the desert sore afraid,
Holding up my head, although
  I'm as frightened as a maid.

The crouching lion there I saw
  From barren rocks lift up his eye;
He parts the cactus with his paw,
  He stares at me as I go by. ...

I am the lion in his lair;
  I am the fear that frightens me;
I am the desert of despair
  And the nights of agony.

Night or day, whate'er befall,
  I must walk that desert land,
Until I can dare to call
  The lion out to lick my hand.
    – *from* James Stephens, *In Waste Places*

They went for a hike across the veldt, carefully avoiding the topic of the morning's conversation. Kaitrin talked about Jaq and her own childhood experiences in Afrik. They passed termite mounds, but Kaitrin only glanced at them and turned her eyes elsewhere; the sight of them stirred a queasy uneasiness in the pit of her stomach.

After they returned to the compound, Kaitrin slept for a while, waking up to the sound of the electro-transport bringing Gerit and Charles home. She got up and hastily changed her clothes, donning a dress she had picked up in Pikes – blue surrolinen with matching shoes.

When she encountered Rianna, however, Griffen's sister was wearing black twill pants with a green shirt. "I thought maybe you made a formal event of dinner," Kaitrin said a bit apologetically.

"We're not that baronial," said Rianna with a laugh, "but we all have such sweaty days that we generally do clean up a bit."

Dinner was in the main dining room, at a table for eight below a chandelier of buffalo horns. Both men rose when Kaitrin and Rianna came in and Charles stepped around to help Kaitrin with her chair. *Maybe Griff's polished manners weren't just British after all*, she thought.

Gerit was a solidly built man with dark skin and a fringe of grizzled, tightly curled hair around his bald scalp. His eyes were a darker brown than his son's, but they both had the same round face and snub nose. Dinner was a roast of young buffalo and a medley of rice and yams, with a lemon-dressed salad of mixed greens and grape tomatoes. A bowl of diced melons and a large hot-pot of tea occupied the center of the table. They talked of Gerit's work to upgrade the IQDB's educational standards for herpetology and Charles enthusiastically related his plans for becoming an ornithologist.

"First birdman in the family," Rianna remarked.

"Uncle Griff was advising me on what university to attend," said Charles. "He told me all about Oxkam – it has a top knobby ornithology program."

"I want him to attend Jonnsberg," said Gerit with finality.

"But, Dad, Jonnsberg is so provincial," replied his son, with a weary air implying this was not the first time this topic had come up. "I want to study more than Afriken birds."

"Northwest Quad has superior programs in every biological field," offered Kaitrin. "And the Ammeriken preserves are teeming with birds – raptors, songbirds, hummers – seabirds along the coasts – and condors in the Big Koloredo Canyon, Charly!"

"Makes my mouth water," said Charles, popping a piece of melon into the designated orifice.

"He could always go to Yakuta," said Rianna mischievously, and Gerit snorted.

"Eagles. Cranes. Denaly. Kamchata," said Charles wistfully.

"One of my closest associates is a real Bird-man," said Kaitrin, and she told them about Tió'otu A'a'ma.

Charles was ecstatic. "I've studied about those Kris – Krisa – those off-worlders – and I've seen them around the campus, but I've never talked to one. I've heard their language is unpronounceable and the falconiforms sing!"

So Kaitrin tried to explain !Ka<tá and to speak some for them, with hilarious results, and they ended the evening with laughter.

But always haunting the back of Kaitrin's mind was what she had learned that day, and the dread of what might emerge in the next conversation. When she would glance at Rianna, she could sense that her thoughts were running in that same vein.

*　　*　　*

After breakfast the next morning, the two women settled once again in the common room and Rianna picked up the thread of her narrative.

"Gerit could see that I was having a crisis over what had happened and he told me there was nothing for it but to go to Kardif and do what had to be done, so off we went. The authorities had finally come to their senses and transferred Griff to a children's facility, but the damage had been done. When we arrived, the counselor asked us how it could have happened that this autistic child had never been treated and I laughed in her face. The last time I had seen Griff, he had been the most sociable, friendly, sharp-witted little chatterbox you could imagine." Rianna shifted in her chair, pain flitting through her eyes. "When he came in, I couldn't even tell if he recognized me. I knelt down and took him by the shoulders and he stood staring at the floor. I said, "Griffen, I'm Ree, your sister. You remember me, don't you?" And he didn't say anything. He didn't smile, he didn't look up – it was terrible. He had this dreadful, closed-down look in his face – just dead. His eyes were dead. It was terrible.

"So I hugged him and held him to me, and I knew I had to take him home with me. It was such a painful transformation. What had become of that responsive little brother of mine?"

Kaitrin waited, forcing herself to unclench her hands, while Rianna disengaged herself from the memory.

"We made quick work of the funeral and we arranged for the tour boat business to be sold to Dad's associates and for the contents of the family house to be boxed up and shipped to Jonnsberg. And we took Griffen to his new home. Then the hardest time started – the first six months were the hardest. He told me later that he recalled that time – the months before and after Mum's death – mostly as a dark, disoriented dream shot through with flashes of terrifying reality.

"We tried to put Griff in school, but he hid under a table and wouldn't come out. After half a day the school counselor told us we would have to get him some professional help. Gerit was all for that – he hadn't the faintest notion what to do with a child who had lost the ability to interact with others and who was afraid to go to sleep because of nightmares. Remember, at that point nobody knew what had occurred to trigger this change. And I was only twenty-two and still had some growing up of my own to do. I was studying psychotherapy, but I was just beginning postgrad work so I was hardly an expert.

"For a month we took him to the local IPD four times a week. They ran a lot of tests and found no psychogenetic conditions, but they did find neurochemical imbalances and brain wave patterns indicative of mental disruption different from what the loss of a mother would commonly induce in a child. They diagnosed his condition as PITA – post-infantile traumatic autism – jargon for any state in a child or adult where a bad experience has induced withdrawal and the inability to connect with reality. They put him on drug therapy – a disaster! The stimulant akaenin hyped him up, but he still wouldn't communicate, and as it wore off, he would hallucinate.

"So the doctors said, well, we'll try a different drug – we may have to try several before we find something effective – and he may have to be on medication for the rest of his life. Somebody suggested behavioral conditioning, and somebody else, that we ought to try nanobotic neurotherapy – reconfiguring the brain chemistry at the source. Well! I couldn't see all that – muck around in the brain and the mind of this innocent child when nobody understood why he was as he was? Gerit and I both found such trial-and-error or invasive therapies repellent and we pulled him out of the IPD program.

"One of my child psychology instructors was a proponent of the theories of Patrise Sheppard and Loodmilla Arkis, a system that has become my specialty. We're sometimes belittled as unscientific throwbacks, because we refuse to view the mind as primarily an evolutionary genetic product – a physical assemblage of neurons sending chemical messages around the body. We regard many mental and behavioral disturbances as diseases of the soul; in fact we like to call ourselves 'psychists' rather than 'psychologists.' Our most virulent critics call us 'those religious quacks,' but of course that isn't accurate at all. We postulate no god-centered dogmas nor claim any overarching knowledge of spiritual truths; we simply acknowledge the existence of an inherent volitional life-force that generates the things that set us apart from animals and constitutes what the Mythmakers say makes us human: the ability to look beyond the evolutionary need to perpetuate one's genes and preserve one's life; the sense of the value of the other; the ability to take responsibility, to control one's impulses and strive for moderation, to form a conception of good and evil, to need and confer compassion – to punish, and to forgive. Those are all products of what we choose to call 'soul.'

"And we get very good results and so can afford to ignore our critics. We do employ some behavioral conditioning, but we prefer to call it choice training, because we believe in free will. Our methodology derives from the Mythmakers and even some PDA practices – creating understanding through metaphor, generating empathic connections, analyzing dreams. We use psychotropics and techniques like neural reconfiguration only to treat definitive genetic and neurophysiological ailments such as schizophrenia, electroneural seizures, brain trauma ...

"Well! I hadn't intended to give a lecture! Where was I? Ah, yes ... I conferred with my teacher and she suggested that, since Griffen's behavior was not violent or destructive, we should leave him in peace for a while – simply support him with a stress-free environment, spend time with him, give him opportunities where he could choose to interact. Give him love – touch him, hug him – show him that he had a place to belong where nothing threatened. Respond at once to any overtures he might make, and talk to him even if he didn't respond. Treat him as much as possible like a normal member of the family. Keep records on any changes in his behavior. See if he could begin healing on his own and recover the ability to talk about whatever trauma it was that had so deeply disturbed his soul. I found that approach quite sensible.

"You see, it wasn't as if Griffen never talked or responded. If you said, 'Do you want to go out on the veranda?' he would say, 'Is that all right?' Or if you said, 'Griffen, eat your salad!' he would pick up his fork and eat a bite or two. He was pathetically compliant because he had lost the perception that he had any power over his own actions – he would hardly get up from a chair without someone's approval. And yet, if too many demands were put on him, he couldn't cope and would withdraw – hide under the table, figuratively, if not literally."

Kaitrin sighed. "I was a little that way after Griffen died. Maybe I had a form of PITA. I hardly talked, I did what I was told … Believe me, Rianna, that isn't me!"

Rianna smiled gravely. "But you have obviously come a long way pretty quickly, even without formal treatment. Griff's withdrawal was so extreme that I did despair at times."

"It's so hard for me to imagine Griffen like that – hiding under a table. He told me once that he was excessively shy as a child, but … "

"That's his euphemism for something much darker. Well, anyway … We set up a home schooling program for him. Gerit could easily handle the math and the science. I struggled along with history, as well as grammar and literature, which had been somewhat neglected in the mediocre public school that he had attended in Kardif. I introduced some art therapy – encouraged him to draw, to write verse. He had to re-learn how to make self-motivated decisions, even if it was only to choose what color to make a flower or pick the best word to rhyme with 'tree.' I insisted he select his own clothes on the shopping links, beginning with simple choices like whether to get a plain or a striped shirt. I remember as a tiny victory the first time he told me voluntarily that he had changed his mind about a jacket we had ordered and would prefer the dark blue rather than the gray.

"I got him a little dog – something that would give affection, that would run up and lick him and beg to be petted and that required care in return. He didn't respond at first, wouldn't name her. So I named ... "

"Cookie," said Kaitrin.

"Oh, he told you about Cookie?" Rianna gave a little laugh. "I came up with the name off the top of my head – we had to call her something. In time he did make some connections with that spaniel and he always took good care of her. I think it helped.

"And Gerit would take Griff out in the field. I believe that did more good than anything.

"Charly spoke truth the other day about his father. Gerit really is a rather taciturn man, a little abrupt – never wastes words. He's so different from Lew Gwidian, who was impetuous and ebullient and extroverted. But Gerit has a very kind heart and he became a lot fonder of Griffen than he likes to admit. He established a quiet relationship, which was quite what Griff needed. Gerit would teach him some simple field task, like collecting scat samples or shed snakeskins and identifying them – and then they wouldn't talk much at all, simply be together and work. It was structured and supported, yet Griff was somewhat on his own – had a responsibility. It was actually Gerit who prompted Griff's interest in insects – he encouraged him to start collecting beetles, which are relatively easy to locate, catch, identify, and mount. Griff was always good with data and liked projects that required organization and concentration. It focused his mind away from that pain that was still such a mystery to us. I'll never forget ... "

Rianna stopped, took a long breath. "I'll never forget the day when they got home and Griff came up to me and said, 'Ree, guess what! We saw a mob of meerkats today, with babies! They have sentinels that stand up on branches and watch for danger, and some of the grown ones take care of the babies whilst the others go off to forage! They were jolly cute, you know?' And he laughed. That was the first time he had laughed, or even smiled, and it was about eight months after he arrived."

"Oh, Rianna," said Kaitrin. "Do you know all this is breaking my heart?"

"It would break anybody's. Gerit also had a big smile on his face that day. He was well aware that it was a turning point.

"After a year my Professors thought we ought to try putting

Griff back in school. I told him he didn't have to go if he didn't want to – he was doing very well in the home program. In fact, when he did go back, he had exceeded his peer level in both math and grammar. His response was typical: 'Do you want me to go to school, Ree?' I told him that I wouldn't mind if he tried it, but if he was too unhappy, he could come back home for a while. It would be his decision.

"So he went, and it was difficult but he stuck it out – I think, to please me. He was put under the mentoring of a skilled, sensitive, older teacher who had taught the Bock boys when they were about that age. She never pushed or hounded him, but she didn't coddle him, either. He had to take his turn doing problems or speaking in front of the class like everyone else. That was so hard for him. It was as if he believed public scrutiny would destroy him – inquisitive eyes might somehow see into his soul and discover the dark secret that lurked there."

Kaitrin said, "But later he didn't have any problems giving lectures, that sort of thing. And everybody says he was a fine teacher."

"Well, ultimately the dark secret buried itself too deeply to threaten in that sort of impersonal situation. But he never could utter emotional words in front of a crowd – words that might betray his inner self. That's why acting was out of the question, although it fascinated him."

"He read poetry to me."

"You weren't a crowd. He could cope with one person – judge how much was at stake and how far he could safely go."

"Rianna, he was terrified before the wedding. I teased him a little bit – accused him of getting cold feet. And he said, 'It's just the old stage-fright.' But now I don't think that's the right word for what he was feeling."

Rianna was shaking her head. "Kaitrin, when I saw that vid … You have no idea what torment that must have been for him. To expose his soul in front of so many people … "

"And now it's in front of the whole world. But, Rianna, when he proposed that we stage a marriage ceremony, he said, 'I want to make a public affirmation. I want the world to know that Griffen Gwidian belongs only to Kaitrin Oliva.'" Kaitrin's voice quavered in spite of her best effort. "And so that's why I'm not as upset by the theft of that vid as you might think, because now the whole world does know. And for the most part the world's response has been positive – a little too maudlin, maybe, but showing a lot of love and good will."

"And 'Griffen's women' all know that he is lost to them for good," said Rianna with a tremulous smile.

Then she returned to her tale. "When he was not quite twelve, he asked me to sit by him awhile after one of his drowning nightmares and at last he began to open up a little. He told me about seeing Dad's mutilated body. It was the first I had known about that, and I thought, *Maybe I've got the answer here.* Of course, I had only a small piece of it. But after sharing that pain with me, he seemed easier for a while. The nightmares became less frequent and his sleep more restful.

"His peers at school found him a bit odd, naturally. He kept to himself – avoided the usual horseplay of immature males. He would socialize with a group, but he had no single 'best buddy.' He did befriend a couple of youngsters who had mild learning disabilities – one was dyslexic and the other had difficulty with spatial concepts. He liked trying to help them learn. What does that tell you about him?

"He tried playing football, unsuccessfully. He had trouble judging how he ought to react in fast-moving game situations; he would either commit impulsive mistakes or hang back fearful of making the wrong play. After he cost the team a match, he quit. I was glad; that kind of forced competitiveness only added unnecessary stress to his life. Then Gerit had the inspired idea of introducing him to jukara and weight training. This allowed him to work one-on-one with an instructor – always the best situation for him – and compete only against himself, and it gave him a physical outlet for his frustrations. He received his black belt when he was at Oxkam. You know all about that, what?"

Kaitrin grimaced. "So – you know about what happened the one time we sparred against each other?"

"I do. He was greatly troubled about that loss of control. But let's save that for later. I'm coming to one of the most painful episodes of his childhood.

"At thirteen, Griff was just beginning his adolescent growth spurt – he was to shoot up over twenty-five centimeters in the next three years – and the hormone storms were coming on. He was beginning to contemplate the future as an adult, with all the responsibilities and demands that go with it, and he was worrying about how he was going to cope with it all, although he kept those worries pent up inside.

"In school, they were starting to read Shaksper; they read *A Midsummer Night's Dream* and *Henry the Fifth* and they mounted some skits. He tried to read for a part, but he was completely tongue-tied – got dizzy and almost fell off the stage – so he settled for a crowd scene. The teachers were disappointed; his voice was expressive even whilst it was in the process of changing and I think they would have liked him to try out for the part of Henry.

"But the crux of this is, it got him interested in Shaksper, and he bobbed around in the DB and discovered *Hamlet* … You have some inkling of what I'm about to say?"

"Not really, but I know he larded his conversations with quotations from *Hamlet* and he said he acted in it at Oxkam."

Rianna laughed. "Yes, it was a tiny, tiny part, but it was the most words he ever spoke on a stage! Oh, my, what a Hamlet he would have made if only he could have become a professional actor! But, anyway, here was this adolescent boy eaten up with anxiety about his future, with a dark, consuming secret that he had to keep hidden at all costs – sitting in his room alone when I thought he was studying, reading *Hamlet* obsessively, over and over." Rianna reached for a reader on a table beside her. "That scene between Hamlet and his mother – 'You go not till I set you up a glass / Where you may see the inmost part of you …' And the Queen cries, 'What wilt thou do? Thou wilt not murder me?'"

"Oh, I see what you mean," said Kaitrin.

"'O heart, lose not thy nature, let not ever / The soul of Nero enter this firm bosom … / I will speak daggers to her, but use none.' If he didn't understand the allusion to Nero, he knew how to look up information on the DB, and I'm sure he made use of that skill.

"But more ominous – ' … and by a sleep to say we end / The heartache and the thousand natural shocks / That flesh is heir to. 'Tis a consummation / Devoutly to be wished …'"

"What are you trying to tell me?"

"'Or that the Everlasting had not fixed / His canon 'gainst

self-slaughter … '"

"Rianna!"

"And a few thousand other pregnant, intense words, all bombarding this fragile, impressionable boy with ideas that had never entered his mind before. Did he identify with the introspective, suicidal prince? You judge, Kaitrin.

"One morning he complained of an upset stomach, so I let him stay home from school. He spent most of the day tucked up in bed reading. The last time I checked on him, he seemed to be asleep, so I let him be. I got busy with some things and then Gerit came home and more than two hours passed. But then I went to see if he felt like dressing and coming to the table for dinner. He was lying on the bed half-unconscious, with blood smeared all over the place. He had cut his wrist with a field knife."

"Oh, Rianna!"

"Yes … He had proved he could now make decisions; unfortunately that's the one he made. Recently the news links had been carrying stories of an Assemblyman in New Pretor who had committed suicide by slashing his wrists – that's what suggested the method. But Griffen had been timid about it and inflicted only a shallow wound that missed the major vessels and tendons – a good thing because it had been over an hour since he did it. But it bled a good deal, and he was unconscious from psychological shock more than from physical trauma. But – god, what a crisis!"

"You know," whispered Kaitrin, "I once noticed a little scar on the inside of his left wrist. It looked old and really minor – seemed like just an everyday injury, so I didn't ask about it. It was nothing like the big scar on his back where he fell on the spike."

"If anyone commented on it, he would generally tell a half-truth and say that he had cut himself on a field knife when he was a youngster. He would never say that it had been deliberate – just let people assume it was an accident. Likely he would have said the same to you, at least in the early days of your relationship.

"Anyway, I screamed for Gerit and he came running. He has training in field medicine and he assured me the injury wasn't life-threatening, so we didn't call anybody, just bandaged up the wrist ourselves. By that time Griff was conscious, lying there shaking. And I spent that whole night sitting beside him on the bed, holding him and telling him that I loved and cherished him and would have been heart-broken if he had died, and trying to convince him that he should talk to me about what had driven him to such a despairing act … And then he cried, the first time he had cried since we brought him here. And then at long last he talked."

"Rianna, this is … I'm getting about ready to stop for a while."

"Let me quickly finish this part. He told me everything he could about that dreadful period between the two deaths. He told me all about Mum – how she depended on him, how she clung to him and overwhelmed him with her need, how he didn't know what to do to help her … You understand, this was not spoken as a coherent narrative, only in bits and snatches that I had to piece together. And at the end, I said, 'Did you know she was dead, Griff? Why didn't you try to get help?'

"And he said, 'Because the last thing she said was never to tell anyone – for me just to stay with her and pray and she would be all right.' And then he said, 'But she wasn't and it was my fault. I killed her.'

"I was pretty shocked. I said, 'Oh, no, Griff, you didn't kill her. Mum died of cancer.' And he said, 'I know, but I killed her. I'm a murderer.' It was chilling the way he said it, with such hopelessness.

"I said, 'No, Griff! Is that what you've been believing all this time?' And he said, 'I know it's true. Those people said it was.'

"Well, at last it came out – what he had overheard. And there was no reasoning him out of this delusion. 'I killed my mother,' he said. 'I have to be punished. But I'm too scared – I'm too scared and too ashamed to tell everybody the truth and be punished in the proper way. I thought I could do it myself with the knife and nobody would ever have to know that I'm a murderer.' And he would beg me in one breath to punish him, and in the next never to tell anyone because he was disobeying Mum by telling me, and in the next he was imploring me to find some way to take the guilt away because he was afraid to die … All right, Kaitrin. I'm stopping. We don't need to belabor the sad truth any longer.

"Suffice it to say that I never told anyone, not even Gerit. I only told Gerit that I had learned some things I felt were governed by ethical considerations and I would rather not speak of them. But after Griff died, when I was feeling terribly low, I finally did talk to Gerit about it, and he said he admired me for not speaking of it all those years, but knowing the truth did make it easier for him to understand what we had been up against.

"After that night, my relationship to Griffen changed a good deal. He began to freely share all kinds of things with me. But he never again brought up his conviction that he was a murderer, except on one occasion that I'll get to later. Does that surprise you? We would speak of it obliquely – we would think about it together, if that makes any sense – but we never discussed it. But he knew that I knew and it made our relationship special. I was the only one he consistently trusted and confided in over the years. I was about to lose that privilege to you. Maybe I was a little jealous of you, Kaitrin. But that's neither here nor there … Why don't we stop now and pick up again this afternoon or tomorrow, whenever you feel like it?"

Chapter 13

When he, who is the unforgiven,
Beheld her first, he found her fair:
No promise ever dreamt in heaven
Could then have lured him anywhere
That would have been away from there ...
– *from* Edwin Arlington Robinson, *The
Unforgiven*

Kaitrin was glad for the breaks; this experience was excruciating even while it was bringing a beginning of the long-desired clarity. In the early afternoon, she and Rianna toured the compound – the employees' commodious living quarters, the utility buildings where the equipment and controls for the EM fence and enviros and generators were located, Gerit's reptile laboratory where he and his associates extracted venom from vipers and elapids and worked on biosynthesizing more effective immunotoxins. Last of all, they visited the animal barns, with their horse stalls and tack rooms.

"I've never ridden horseback," said Kaitrin, then she laughed ruefully, "except once, in a dream Griffen had."

She related that moving experience to Rianna, who said, "I didn't know about that. It's true – I can remember only three or four times that Griff ever had a positive dream, and it would influence his view of life for several days, until something negative intervened to break the spell." After a moment, she added, "I'm glad he was granted a few days of happiness before the end. I've always been grateful whenever he got a little relief, no matter how transitory."

"But I ruined it," said Kaitrin. "I destroyed the illusion."

The slight bitterness that informed her tone caused Rianna to glance at her, but she made no comment. "We still keep a few horses for cattle work and sometimes Derek and Charly use them in their fieldwork. Glider died years ago. That was his stall over there, where Mustard is poking her head out. I really was upset the first time Griff rode that old racehorse. It was not very long before the suicide attempt. After that, I considered getting rid of the horse. I was afraid Griff might purposely ride him off a cliff or something. But instead – what courage we caregivers all have to have! – I told him that I trusted him and I was sure he would ride Glider safely and I was counting on him to do that. And he said, 'I promise I will, Ree.' It was one of those moments of tacit understanding that I mentioned earlier. He and I were like conspirators after the crime. And he did ride him safely. Griffen always kept his word. It's as if he knew he had to be more honest, more decent, more trustworthy – better in everything he did – because he had so much guilt to atone for. And yet he never believed in himself – never believed that he could succeed in anything." Rianna shook her head.

Kaitrin took her arm. "Come on. We were going to talk about something else. I finally saw some servobots in the barn. I was wondering if human beings did everything around here."

Rianna laughed. "We use NDRs for the tedious routine stuff, like scrubbing floors and cleaning stalls and patrolling the fence line for breaks. But it's a lot more pleasant to have people cook and service the vehicles and take care of the animals, and it provides extra employment for the local population. Come on, I'll show you where we keep the herding dogs."

"I heard hyenas the other night, but no lions. Are there ever any around here?"

"We're on the northeast side of the Bock Holdings and the Pilenberg Preserves are not far away. The holdings are fenced, but occasionally an emitter goes out or something tunnels beneath the magnetic line. So you might hear a lion or a leopard along with those hyenas and see jackals and warthogs and aardvarks. We have resident honey badgers and several caracals, along with a lot of the hares that they eat. Sometimes we get springbucks – the original pronkers! They've actually been known to jump the magnetic fence!"

"I love this," said Kaitrin. "I grew up in cities, but I'm a field person at heart!"

*　　*　　*

Later in the afternoon, over tea and jam tarts, they continued their talk.

"Before we begin again," said Rianna, "I'll show you two more pictures of Griff. In this one he was nearly twelve."

Kaitrin saw the face of an unsmiling child with inexpressive eyes hollowed by fatigue. She mentally compared it to the chubby, laughing preschooler of the earlier pictures.

Rianna guessed what she was thinking. "At that time he wasn't sleeping well," she said, "and he always looked tired. The quality of one's sleep can really influence psychic health."

The second picture was of a lean-visaged Griffen just before his fifteenth birthday. He displayed the same bland, unrevelatory smile that Kaitrin remembered from his official university image; the eyes were level and remote and everything was carefully orchestrated, down to the meticulously combed hair and rigidly symmetrical jacket collar.

Sighing, Rianna set the images aside and said with a half-amused, half-regretful grin, "Next chapter – Griffen Gwidian discovers girls."

"Yes," said Kaitrin, with a final wistful glance toward the pictures. "How did he get from that tormented little boy to the man with the reputation for being a – a rake, to use an archaic expression?"

"When he was about the age in this second picture, his schoolmates were getting involved with girls, but – Griff was too shy to go near them! And he was getting pretty good-looking, too, as you can see. Oh, he was still skinny and gangly – growing too fast and never eating enough for his weight to catch up – but he always had those eyes, the profile – and the exercise program was helping to develop his body. And another thing I should touch on here – he had begun swimming again."

"He told me about that early on. We'd been to a production of *The Tempest*. I could tell that the stuff about drowning bothered him and I ventured to say something. That's when he told me about his fear of the water, and how he swam for years to try to cure himself of it, but he never could, so he finally gave it up."

Rianna was nodding. "I was really surprised when he told me he wanted to resume swimming. Apparently, his social group included boys who were competitive swimmers and they had been taunting him about his fear of the water. You know how boys are. Of course, he didn't tell them why he was afraid. So I said it would be all right to try it, and the first day when he came back, he triumphantly announced that he had swum the length of the pool twice and even dived and touched the bottom.

"I said, 'So it wasn't as hard as you thought it would be!'

"And he said, 'Oh, it was every bit as hard. I was terrified. But I did it and I'm going to keep doing it. Isn't that what the psychologists tell you to do, Ree? Face down what you're afraid of and conquer it?'

"Well, I agreed, but I wasn't sure it was the answer for him, because the reasons why Griff Gwidian undertook anything were never that simple. I think there was a strong element of self-punishment there. Suffering through what terrified him was an act of atonement.

"After he had been swimming twice a week for a couple of months, I said, 'Is it working? How do you feel about swimming now?'

"His face got very tight, and he said, 'I'm still bloody afraid. But I'm going to keep doing it.'

"I said, 'You don't have to, Griff. There's nothing so terrible about having this phobia. There's no law that requires a human being to swim.'

"But he said, 'I'm going to conquer it, Ree. I have to conquer something. I just have to.' And he persisted with it for years. I'll get back to that later.

"In the meantime I had had a baby. I named her Gwinneth for our paternal grandmother, who died when I was ten. I tried very hard to keep Griffen from feeling slighted the way I had after he was born, and I think I succeeded. He accepted her as a little sister – he enjoyed playing with her and he loved to read to her. Of course, he left for Oxkam when she was only three.

"Anyway, the swimming was also helping his physical development and I'm sure girls were attracted to him long before he got up the nerve to respond. He was still fascinated by the stage. Every time the school did a play, he would try to read for a part, and every time he would fail and become even more discouraged. So I said to him, 'Griff, even if you never become an actor, you can still work in theatre. Why don't you go in for production – lighting – holoset design – sound effects – that sort of thing?'

"He had been so fixated on acting that he really hadn't thought of that. So he served on the stage crew when his school did a Mythmaker play and he really found a niche. He discovered he could even supervise other people if he was sure of what he was doing. And there was a particular girl on the crew with him and she became the first girl he ever dated. Not his first sex partner, mind you – he hadn't built quite enough walls yet for that. But his first date."

Rianna laughed at the memories. "He didn't even initiate it. I'll always remember – he came home a little late after a rehearsal and when he came into the nursery where I was rocking Gwin, he had this big adolescent grin on his face. He said, 'Do you know what happened? Meriam asked me to go with her for a snack after the rehearsal!' I'll never forget how amazed he sounded! Like, 'Can you believe any girl would want to spend time with me?'"

Kaitrin also laughed in a slightly uncontrolled way, trying to imagine the sophisticate of the early days of their acquaintance astonished to discover that he could be attractive to women.

"So he worked up the nerve to ask her out on a real date – tea and a holoshow – and when he came back from that, he said, 'It seems like Meriam enjoys being with me, Ree. Fancy that! Do you think she really could, or am I only imagining it?' I said, 'Silly, of course she could. You're a nice-looking young man with good manners who always works hard at pleasing people. Why wouldn't a girl enjoy your company?' And he said, 'It felt so good – making her happy. It made me feel free somehow – as if I could breathe easier.'

"Now that set off a dim alarm in me, but I didn't know what it was. He started asking both Gerit and me serious questions about sex. Of course, academically he knew as much as he needed to know, but these questions were more practical. I asked him if he was considering having a sexual encounter and he got embarrassed. 'I suppose someday I will,' he said. What is it, Kaitrin?"

"I recognize one of his little evasive maneuvers."

"Don't you just! The walls were beginning to build themselves.

"So he and Meriam dated for a while, but then with the normal fickleness of adolescence, she got interested in a football star and told Griff she was going to go out with him for a while. Griff was crushed. I told him that was the way it was. Not every relationship could be permanent and anyway it shouldn't be at his age – not quite sixteen – and he should look elsewhere, too. And he did.

"He was in prep school by this time and he was in the choral group ... "

"Oh, did he sing? That's another thing I never knew! And whistle! Could he whistle?"

Rianna chuckled. "He could, but he hardly ever did. And he had a nice singing voice – baritone, of course. By the time he was sixteen his voice had finished changing and he became a mainstay of the school chorus. He even managed to do a few in-group solos, things where he didn't have to come out and stand alone in front of everybody. It was rather like a stutterer who can sing his name but can't speak it. He was in a choral group at Oxkam, too, for his first two years."

"I never got to hear him sing," said Kaitrin wistfully.

"I may have a holoimage of one of his performances around here, if you have a studio available to run it ... But back to my narrative. There was a girl in the chorus who interested him. She was a First Former and Griff was a Second, so she was a year older. He asked her out and she accepted, and then they went out again, and then on their third date, by three in the morning, he hadn't come home.

"I was scared witless, but Gerit said, 'Ree, can't you read the signs? Your dependent little brother is growing up.'

"When he finally came home about 0500h, I really lit into him about how worried I'd been. And he was very chastened – felt very bad. 'I should have let you know,' he said. 'I don't ever want to worry you. I love you, Ree.'

"Of course, that disarmed me, and like an idiot I said, 'What in the world were you doing all night?' And he said with perfect candor, 'Having sex with Lorna.' And that was the first. Griffen's first woman.

"He said, 'It was wonderful, Ree. I hadn't understood that girls could enjoy sex so much. It felt so good to be able to give her all that pleasure. Will it always be like that? Will I always be able to make women happy?' It was a strange reaction, don't you agree? In a sixteen-year-old male after his first sexual adventure?"

"Yes, one might think he would have been strutting around boasting about what a great stud he was becoming," said Kaitrin thoughtfully.

"Exactly. After that, he started cultivating all sorts of things – social skills, his appearance ... He asked me to teach him how to dance, which was pretty funny since I have two left feet! I'd find him on the shopping links, studying the offerings of florists so he would know what kinds of flowers to buy for his dates. He started learning about culinary matters so he wouldn't look foolish ordering in a restaurant. His interest in clothes intensified – male fashions and female ones as well. Jewelry – different kinds of music – anything that he thought women might find appealing. Gerit thought it was hilarious and when I would get annoyed at that, he would say, 'Every boy gets to the point where he obsesses over his hair,' and then he would run his hand over his own balding pate and say, 'Of course, later on, some of us have nothing to obsess about.' ... Bock men have been bald for as far back as there's a record – it's become a matter of family honor not to get the gene altered," Rianna interjected, observing Kaitrin's grin.

"But Griffen's activities concerned me because I knew about his guilt fixation and this looked like some kind of compensation technique. And I was right, of course. But in effect it was his salvation. If he hadn't found that way of relieving the pressure ...

"So he dated Lorna for a while, and then she went off to university, and then there was another, and then one day he asked Gerit if he thought it was unwise to be having sex with two girls at the same time.

"Gerit was a bit nonplussed and turned the whole thing over to me, and I came down on Griffen much harder than I usually did. I told him I thought it was very unwise; it wasn't fair to either of them. If one found out about the other, there was the jealousy factor; both girls would feel betrayed and be hurt, and he himself would be hurt as well. I asked him what he was thinking. I told him promiscuity was bad and he needed to take a long, hard look at what he was getting into. What if he got a girl pregnant and she had to go through an abortion? How would he feel about that?

"He listened intensely the way he always did and then he said, 'I don't ever want to hurt any girl, Ree. I don't know much, do I?'

"I said that certainly he needed experience, but this wasn't the way to go about it. 'Why do you have to jump into bed so soon with these girls?' I asked him. 'Why don't you simply date them and get to know them and let something more genuine develop?'

"He said, 'But it is genuine. Sex is the best way I've found to please them. And I never force anyone into it. They usually suggest it themselves. They seem to like being with me, Ree. I don't know why. And I do so much want to give them pleasure.'

"We had a variant of this conversation many times. I gave up trying to talk him out of this new obsession; instead, I tried to give him a proper set of behavioral ethics to bring to it. I think I at least succeeded in that. He limited himself to one woman at a time and always took suitable precautions – got the necessary immunizations and contraceptive shots, used condoms, never patronized street women ... He never had relations with a contracted woman, either – never broke up a marriage. A couple of times the woman lied to him about her status, and both times he immediately terminated the relationship when he found out. For a – a rake ... " Rianna's voice shook. " ... he was the most responsible and honorable rake anybody could ever want ... I see you nodding."

Kaitrin said, "What you say was true. I doubt he ever hurt a woman in his life, unless it was – by leaving them ... "

"Griffen's obsession – this new dependency – could easily have taken a more sinister turn, you know. He might have reacted with a desire to punish instead of please – to project his guilt onto females and make them a symbol of his suffering instead of seeking to atone for the crime he believed he had committed against them. He could have become a serial rapist or gynocide. His sense of right and wrong never became warped. I've always been grateful for that."

Kaitrin shuddered. "Yes, I see what you're saying. What a

scary … Rianna, I had a hard time reconciling his – what seemed like philandering – with what I observed of him. It's why I took such a long time to come around. Now I wish I'd come around the first moment I met him!"

"But then it wouldn't have matured as it did for the two of you, Kaitrin. You made him work for what he had to have." Rianna sighed. "At any rate, when he was between seventeen and eighteen years old, he went off to Oxkam. I was quite surprised that he wanted to go so far away and Gerit had a worse fit than he's having over Charles. But Griff said, 'I have to see if I can do this. It really scares me, but if I stay here in this refuge for my whole life, I'll only get more scared. I'll get too old to change.' This from a boy Charles's age.

"So we let him go. At first he wasn't at all … "

"Rianna, may I ask something? He told me you gave him this ring when he went away to Oxkam. Why did you do that?"

"Oh, that." Rianna regarded the hand that Kaitrin held up. "He asked me if he could have it. I was surprised and a bit uneasy, so I asked him why he wanted it. He said, 'I don't have anything of hers.' I suggested maybe he would prefer to have a picture, but he said quickly, 'No! I don't want a picture! But Dad's ring is lost, you see, and I would very much like to have her ring.' And he seemed satisfied that this was an adequate explanation for his request. So I didn't push him – I just let him take it. But I think … " Rianna paused and pondered a moment. "I think he was already considering that if he made a permanent liaison one day, he could use the ring as a wedding token, in order to make a substitution – satisfy some other woman as a means of atoning for his failure with the first woman in his life … "

Kaitrin sat frowning, spinning the ring with her left thumb. "So I'm a substitute for his mother? I'm not quite comfortable with that, but I think I understand in a murky sort of way."

"Believe me, your understanding is no less murky that his was. Actually, 'substitution' may not be the right word – 'symbol' is better. He could make the woman a symbol of his mother – or of the whole female sex, as it were – through conferring the ring on her. He could never acknowledge someone else his mother, because to do so would put her in dreadful danger. It would be horrendous to curse another woman with a matricide son."

"Oh, Rianna, I understand something else now. I once told him something that my mother had said – that she was looking forward to having him as her son. And he ... "

"Oh, yes, he would have found that alarming."

"He did. I was really puzzled by his reaction to such an innocent remark. I remember what he said – that it would be unwise for anyone else to play that part."

"He really feared he might endanger her – somehow commit murder again."

Kaitrin shuddered. "And to think all that twisted stuff was going on in his mind and I didn't know. He quickly pulled himself together and said you were his surrogate mother and that was all a man needed, and that he would rather consider my mother to be a friend."

"That's also how I would have expected him to react. A surrogate mother was acceptable. It was like surrosilk or surromarble – everybody knows it isn't the real thing."

"That night was the first time he had the drowning nightmare while we were together."

"Ah, yes, he told me something of that but not what triggered it. You see, that exchange stirred up the old obsession. He was having those nightmares all the while Mum was dying, and the sleeping and the waking nightmares became inextricably interwoven in his psyche."

"But then on the planet later – well, one time I asked him if he would like to send a message to my mother and he got very nervous and said he wouldn't know what to write and that he had never met the mother of any of the women he had been with."

"That's not quite true. We're friends with the families of some of his prep school romances. But I really don't know what went on after he left home. That's new to me, too."

"Then later he got that kind of absent-minded demeanor that he would get when he was waiting for an opportunity to say something ... "

"How well I know that demeanor!"

"And he said – and he stumbled over the words as if they were hard for him to speak – he said he wondered if my mother still would be willing to accept him as her son. He said he thought he would like that after all. And I told him, of course she would!"

"Did he say that? Oh, my god, Kaitrin, he really was making progress! If only, if only he could have lived!"

"I destroyed everything," said Kaitrin gloomily. Again Rianna glanced sharply at her before picking up her narrative.

"So Griffen went to Oxkam and I lose a lot of the day-to-day things after that. He was miserable at first – messaged me every night. Almost came home two or three times. But he stuck it out and he gradually got used to the people, the instructional system, the climate, the food ... They drink more coffee than tea in Britan – that was an adjustment! He wasn't sure what he wanted to specialize in; he liked field science, but he remained strongly attracted to drama and literature. But after a few courses – including, incidentally, a survey of love poetry – he decided literature was too emotionally draining, better taken in small, private doses. So he turned to zoology and ended up with insects. Gerit was pleased, of course.

"He continued to be active in theatre, though. He became quite a skilled holoscene technician – even took a couple of design courses – and occasionally he would act in crowd scenes or play bit parts with a few neutral words, like a waiter or a delivery person, and he had that one little part in *Hamlet*. I remember when he got it, he said to me rather sheepishly, 'Big victory, Ree! A speaking part with eight whole lines. Well, one is a double line.' I asked him what play, and he said, '*Hamlet*. I can't play the lead. I've already played that, what?' I only laughed a little bit – I was afraid to say anything more.

"Every time he would come home for a visit, he would have changed – acquired more sophistication, more confidence. Gerit thought he was improving markedly, but I wasn't so sure. He was developing those verbal compensation techniques that we spoke of earlier and he was much more poised and at ease in social situations – it was a superficial improvement, certainly. But I had some insight beneath that facade and I couldn't see any genuine healing taking place there. He was transferring that innate acting ability into real life – into concealing his self-perceived flaws.

"Then one time he said to me, 'Things are going pretty well, Ree. I've left rooms and I'm living with Ilsa' – his latest girl friend, somebody he met on a study project.

"I was a little surprised – he was just nineteen at the time. I said, 'That must be turning into a serious relationship.'

"He said, 'They're all serious.'

"I said, 'You should have brought her home with you.'

"'Brought her home?' he said, as if I were speaking in an alien tongue. 'Why would I do that?'

"I said, 'Are you going to contract with her?'

"And then he said, 'What? Flaming no! That would cut off everything I need.'

"I said, 'What do you need, Griff? What are you looking for?'

"And he dithered and huffed and got very distressed, and finally he said, 'I can't commit to anything – what if it didn't last? That's terrifying! I can't commit to anything.'

"I said, 'Do you love this girl?'

"And he said, again as if the word was a mystery to him, 'Love? Why – I daresay I do. I always love the girls I'm involved with.'"

Kaitrin sat hearing once again in her mind ... *that I renounce all other so-called loves, that never were loves – that I renounce all other women from this moment of time to the conclusion of eternity. There can never be another love for me but you, Kaitrin, my Kait ...*

Rianna was saying, "I could see that he was coping, but he had not healed. After he went back to Britan, he broke up with Ilsa and in a month he had found someone else to receive the pleasure that he yearned to give and was learning to give so well.

"Then he finished his pregrad work and fulfilled the requisite postgrad apprenticeship in quite short order, and then accepted the Assistantship in Ostrailia. He turned twenty-three right after he got down there. He hated every minute of it. That is, he liked the country and the fieldwork, but he was really lonely. I think the position was more than a means of advancement for him. I think he wanted to demonstrate to himself that he could survive on his own in an alien milieu. It's another example of his insatiable need to overcome his self-perceived weaknesses – and to punish himself. I think that's why he volunteered for that comparative arthopod project that required him to dive with a breather tank in an area full of box jellies and sea snakes. He really hated that, but he did it. Then he fell out of that tree and nearly killed himself –

you know about that. And he met Felisha. You know about that, too.

"He was extremely relieved to return to Oxkam for another year of Assistantship. And then, when he got a chance at an Associateship at the Jonnsberg Consortium, he jumped at it. He was ready to come home."

Rianna hesitated, shifted uneasily. "But he didn't live at home. He had more income than most Associates do; Gerit arranged for him to receive a Bock trust settlement at the age of twenty, and then Gerit made sure it was wisely invested. So Griffen found a flat in Jonnsberg and continued to live the lifestyle that he had developed during the years he was away. I wasn't sure how to feel. Kaitrin, I ... There's another reason why he didn't live at home, and I ... But I think I should tell you. You may have had intimations."

"What?"

"Kaitrin, I'm Griffen's sister and I'm his surrogate mother, and in each of those roles I love him dearly. But I'm also a woman, and I'm only twelve years older than he was ... "

"Oh!"

"Can you see where I'm headed? There's a large difference between the ages of ten years and twenty-two and even between fifteen and twenty-seven, but the line blurs between a mature man of twenty-five and a woman of thirty-seven. I hadn't spent a lot of time with Griff since he was seventeen. He had changed so much! He had become so physical – had such a presence about him! He came back planning to stay for an extended period of time and I found myself being sexually attracted to him. Now, Kaitrin, are you really as stunned as you look? You aren't so naive."

"Gwydion and Arianrhod."

"Who?"

"Nothing! Only an old Welsh tale, about a god-magician named Gwydion ... The spelling has varied, but 'Gwidian' is a really ancient West British name, you know. But, Rianna, I can hardly believe ... "

"No, don't believe it! Nothing happened, I swear that to you. I'm not that unprincipled. Griff was my brother and my patient – incest was absolutely out of the question! I mean, what would that have done to him?

"But there was a moment, when we were alone in the house and he was standing with me in the kitchen, when I started to give him one of my surrogate-motherly hugs and ended up kissing him on the lips. And he responded to the kiss. I'm not sure if it was the element of surprise, or if he ever felt that kind of attraction for me. But I do know he realized what was happening. He wasn't the sexual novice that he had been when he went off to Oxkam.

"He packed up and left. I was very upset. I had to hide what I was feeling because if Gerit had realized ... It was very painful.

"Then in a couple of days, Griff appeared back on the doorstep and said, 'I'm sorry I left so suddenly, Ree. I don't know why I left. I've taken a flat in campus housing until I can find something better. But I'd really like to stay a few more days here in the old place.'

"I told him, 'You know you're always welcome here. This is your home.' And I wondered if he really didn't understand why he had left.

"But as he headed for his room, he turned around and said, 'Ree, I want everything to be as it has always been. I cherish that – all you've done for me. I need for that refuge to always be there. Can everything be the same?'

"And I said, 'Oh, yes, Griff, I understand, and everything can be the same.'" Rianna took a long breath and expelled it, looking furtively at Kaitrin. "I swear to you, that's all that ever happened. But Griffen Gwidian had an attraction for all women – I would even say it was fated, if I believed in fate – and even I was not exempt."

"It wasn't so long after that that Charles was born, was it?" said Kaitrin.

"See, I knew you were perceptive! I turned to Gerit for sexual release. He never knew why. He was a bit surprised because we had been settling into a kind of long-haul complacency – I had even stopped using contraceptives. He jokingly remarked that West British women aged remarkably well." Rianna laughed without much mirth. "Anyway, I had Charles when I was thirty-eight. And he was not Griff's child, Kaitrin. I think I still see skepticism in your eye."

"Don't be so defensive, Rianna," said Kaitrin. "Charles has brown eyes. If he were Griffen's son, he would have to have blue eyes unless some kind of rare genetic anomaly occurred. Besides, except for the lighter coloring and the freckles, he looks exactly like Gerit."

The moment was rescued by Charles's return from school. "Heavens," said Rianna, rising, "is it that late? Here we sit with the cold tea still on the table! Kaitrin, we'll continue our conversation tomorrow."

Chapter 14

And the Lord spake unto Moses, saying,
If a soul sin, and commit a trespass against the Lord,
... he shall bring his trespass offering unto the Lord,
... and the priest shall make an atonement for him
    before the Lord:
and it shall be forgiven him for any thing of all that
    he hath done in trespassing therein.
– from Leviticus 6:1-2, 6-7

The next morning Rianna drove Kaitrin on a tour of the Bock Holdings. "Gerit's father – Papa Bock, I called him – died about five years ago," Rianna said, "and his mother several years before that. Papa Bock was an only child and ended up inheriting everything from several relatives, so at present the Holdings are divided solely amongst his three sons. I know all this seems novel to you, what with Midammerik's Government-administered agriculture."

"Yes," Kaitrin acknowledged, "in Midammerik private land ownership is usually restricted to a small plot with a house or commercial building on it, or you can just own the building without owning the land. But that's not always the case, of course. There are private ranches that raise specialty livestock like bison, and small farms that grow unusual vegetables or fruit or even flowers. But I must say, I'm no expert when it comes to the World Economic System."

Rianna laughed. "Neither am I! We need Gwinneth for that – she's a specialist in WES theory, mainly distribution systems. She works for the Commodities Distribution Board of the Afriken Continental Union – moves little numbered blips around on a port screen without ever seeing an actual steel bar or case of lemons." She waved a greeting at some workers who were chasing ostrich chicks around an enclosure. "This is Stefen's spread. He and his son and granddaughter raise ostriches and turkeys, like the one we had for dinner last night."

"Turkeys are native to my Quadrisphere, actually," said Kaitrin.

"Right! But they adapt well to our ecosystem and Stefen produces them by the thousands! Charles the Uncle raises buffalo for meat and manages the dairy operation. Several generations ago the Bocks were involved in bioengineering the Hemmias dairy cow. It's a hybrid of several British and Uropian breeds toughened up with the addition of Cape buffalo genes. The Bocks also operate a biogas plant – makes enough methane to run the Holdings' generators when solar and wind power slacks off and still trade a good quantity to Rusberg for extra water credits.

"Charles has a daughter and a son who work with him and will share his part of the spread someday. Our part will probably go whole to my young Charly. Gwinneth's only interest in practical matters like the control of bovine disease is how it affects the quality and availability of bioproducts. Takes after Gerit, I suppose. He can get all worked up over the biochemistry of snake venom, but the care and feeding of turkeys doesn't inspire him. So he plays no part in the ranching operation. He just lives here and rides herd on the local ophidians." Rianna laughed mischievously. "Charles runs his livestock on both his and Gerit's land and gives Gerit a cut of the profits – quite the ideal arrangement, what? The worldwide market for animal products – foodstuffs, leather, industrial bioproducts like boneblack and gelatin – is very lucrative."

"Anyone who's ever purchased top-grade beef in Okloh knows just how lucrative it is!"

As they continued to drive the roads that webbed the Holdings, Kaitrin gaped at the hundreds of herd animals, some placidly grazing, some being driven into portable corrals by dogs and horse-mounted chasers and by robotic hoverframes. She stared at the brown-feathered turkeys in their pens, eating, gobbling, and growing fat so that somebody in Midammerik could expend 40 regs for a frozen hen carcass. She found that she was not too sorry that vegetarianism was promoted in Midammerik, although she did hope that protein crackers and soy cheese would never completely replace meat and real dairy fare.

"I'm not introducing you to any of the family," Rianna was saying. "Uncle Charles offered to host a gathering of the clan while you were here – an outdoor roaster with a buffalo haunch cooked on a spit over a coal-pit. But I told him, not this time. I wasn't sure you'd be up to all that socializing."

"Thanks," said Kaitrin. "Normally, I'd love something like that, but – I came for a rather difficult purpose and ... Maybe next time, as you say."

Rianna smiled, turning into a main road that would take them back to Gerit's compound. "I'm glad you can foresee a next time, Kaitrin."

"Oh, I know I'll come again, if you'll have me!"

"I'm a wee bit embarrassed about what we were discussing at the end yesterday."

"I was thinking about it last night. I understand it, Rianna. I agree that there was something special about Griffen – something irresistibly appealing to women. Shall we put that behind us and go on? You do have more to tell me, don't you?"

"Yes, it seems there's always more."

*   *   *

The day was pleasant so they settled on the veranda, which ran the length of the south side of the house and was shaded by a large jacaranda tree. The slope of the terrain enabled them to see over the compound wall, across the acacia-dotted veldt where humped hybrid buffalo with stubby horns grazed. In the near distance a ravine cut between upthrusts of Southern Afrik's ancient bedrock while above it all spread the dome of a cloudless, intensely blue sky. Kaitrin had a fleeting sense that the sky was opaque – or perhaps it was a one-way viewing globe, allowing something to watch from the other side – some hulking, pulsating entity pointing curious antennae at her insignificant creation within.

Rianna brought out a tray with a selection of the Bock Dairy's premium cheeses, crackers, and pomegranate lemonade. "Let's see – where were we?" she said, seating herself opposite Kaitrin. "Oh, yes. Griff had just started his Associateship at Jonnsberg. He adapted really well; his teaching skills had developed and he could lecture and handle the Q and As masterfully. I went to hear him and I was so proud of him. When I spoke to him about it, he said, 'This pedestrian stuff is nothing like dramatic acting. This is something to hide behind.'

"He was searching for a research topic that would earn him a Professorship. He did an incredible amount of fieldwork and kept submitting his research to the World Board, and they kept rejecting his work – the topic was superficial, or it was too broad or too narrow, or it was poorly reasoned – that last one really galled him. He got deep into the phylogeny of dung beetles; he was sure he was on to something original. Then the Board discovered a monograph that he had overlooked that almost exactly mirrored his own conclusions. 'If this is not plagiarism, then it is shoddy and incomplete scholarship,' they said. That was just the last straw."

Kaitrin made a regretful noise. "It's awfully hard to please those old wheezers, as my Prf. A'a'ma calls them. He used to serve on the Board. In fact, he may have been on it when Griff was doing his work, but he would have had no input in the Terrestrial Sciences."

"You didn't seem to have too much trouble earning your Professorship."

Kaitrin dipped her head. "Oh, xenolinguistics has a surplus of unexplored topics. Most terrestrial fields have been seriously over-researched."

"That's true, but Griff was always easily discouraged, anyway. If he was rebuffed, it was because he deserved it, you know. And then he would go out and ease his soul with the pleasuring of a new woman and that kept him going. But no relationship ever lasted; sometimes the woman broke it off, maybe sensing that there was no future with him or that he had a dangerous need that made her uneasy. But he would break it off himself if it threatened to go on longer than two or three months.

"Once I said to him, 'Griff, haven't you ever found a woman that you want to stay with? Wouldn't that be more satisfying?'

"He looked at me with that vulnerable expression that he

could get sometimes – I see you know it, Kaitrin – and said, 'You know, Ree, I'm beginning to wish I could. But I'm so afraid of it. I'm so afraid that I'll fail if I try to hold a woman with something besides sex. I've never failed at what I've been doing all these years, and if I try for something deeper and do fail, then I'll have nothing. It will all be over.' But that was the first time I ever heard him acknowledge that his lifestyle wasn't the complete solution to his problem.

"He was thirty-one or thirty-two when his dung beetle project was so cavalierly dismissed and he didn't know what to do next. He had had affairs with two women in quick succession and neither had given him the kind of soul-ease that he needed. He showed up out here one day and the first thing he told me was that he had quit swimming. I asked him why, although I was sure I knew. He said that it was hopeless – he would never conquer the fear and having to perform a meaningless act of torture two or three times a week was exhausting him. 'It's time to give up,' he said. 'Sooner or later, we have to admit defeat, don't we?'

"Then he fell back on *Hamlet* – 'Thou wouldst not think how ill all's here about my heart' – and said that it was time to give up on a lot of things and that maybe it was time to play that quotation to the end that the poet had written, as he put it. That really scared me. But I figured that if he came and said such things to me, it was because he didn't really want that sword in the heart – he wanted somebody to convince him that conclusion was wrong. And that was the only other time when we spoke openly about Mum's death.

"He said, 'Remember when I was thirteen and cut my wrist? Everything we talked about then is still inside me and it's just as true as ever, you know. I'm not a child any longer and I know I didn't kill her – I mean, it's quite obvious that I didn't take a knife or a club – with my own hands ... But I did kill her, just the same. It was a sin of omission. I could have saved her and I didn't. It's the same thing. It's murder.'

"I told him, 'No, it isn't the same. You were a little boy and Mum was mentally disturbed. She laid all her terrors upon you and you put all your faith in her, the way a child naturally would, and she confused and misled you – made you believe things that weren't true. That is not your fault.'

"But he said, 'That isn't it at all. If I had been stronger – strong enough to disobey her – I could have gone to the clinic at the school, say, and told them she was sick. Maybe they would have forced her to go to a hospital whether she wanted to or not and maybe it wouldn't have been too late. Genetic therapy – immunotherapy – nanotechnology ... they do wonders with those things even when cancer is in its late stages. Maybe I could have saved her. At least I could feel that I had tried. But, you see, I wasn't strong enough and I wasn't good enough. I was weak – I was a coward ... I couldn't fight against her – I couldn't go against her will.' He was getting very agitated.

"I told him, 'Griffen, you were only a little boy and she twisted your perceptions. You couldn't be expected to be able to make those subtle kinds of judgments or to act that independently – you didn't have the experience or the mental maturity. You have let this eat away your soul for too long. You have got to find a way to let go of it.'

"But all he could say was, 'I don't deserve to have anything good happen to me. Maybe I'm finally getting the punishment I want – my career is ruined and I can't find a woman who eases me. What am I going to do, Ree? Can't you help me?'

"I said, 'Griffen, you have to help yourself. You have to let go of this baseless guilt! You have to break this unnatural bond Mum forged with you. None of that is real – none of that exists! It is all in your misguided perception.'

"He was casting about the room and pacing; the situation was escalating. He said, 'Will you stop tormenting me? You want me to expunge what happened from my soul, but I know what the truth is! I don't need to forget or deny – I need to be forgiven!'

"I can still see him with his back to me, leaning over a table, trembling and taut as a guitar string. I said, 'Griffen, I forgive you.'

"But he turned around and said, 'You can't forgive me, Ree, because you don't believe there is anything to forgive me for!' And I had no answer for that.

"I really was afraid for him. He stayed here a few days and I kept an eye on him constantly. He made some humorless jokes about my attentiveness. But then Gerit – my good Gerit – found an answer to at least part of his problem. He suggested that Griff switch to xenoentomology, where, as you said, the field is wide open and every newly discovered planet produces thousands of research topics. Griff was intrigued and distracted from his torment. Jonnsberg's xenology department is pretty basic and never mounts off-world expeditions, but he consulted their faculty and they advised him to go to Shiras-Peders. He put in some inquiries.

"But another affair turned sterile for him and he was soon back in my examining chair, as it were, and the topic was his 'women.' 'I can't keep doing this,' he said. 'In the beginning, it was all new and fresh and beautiful. Every time was different – like sunrise – a new day! I took so much joy from seeing their faces – the satisfaction I could give them. Now it's all old – the freshness, the joy – it's all exhausted. I'm exhausted. I'm so lonely, Ree. And I don't know what to do.'

"And again I said, 'Can't you find a woman you want to stay with? Where the relationship is more than sexual? You know it can be. Look at me and Gerit.'

"He said, 'You think it's that simple? I'm supposed to wave a wand and the perfect innocent bride will appear?'"

Kaitrin, listening to all of this with much torment of spirit, thought, *Blodeuwedd* ...

"'I've come to realize that in all these years I've never really loved anybody. And nobody has ever loved me for what I really am.'

"I said, 'Griffen, you don't let them see what you really are.'

"'I can't, Ree – because the real Griffen isn't lovable! If I show them the real Griffen Gwidian, they'll reject me and then I'll have nothing – nothing. If they ever learned about the thing I'm guilty of, every woman on Earth would loathe and despise me.'

"I said, 'That isn't true. The right woman will not reject you or despise you.'

"And he cried out of his despair, 'Then where is she? Will I ever find her? I don't think I'll ever find her!' Now, Kaitrin, I'm sorry ... "

"It's all right," said Kaitrin, mopping her eyes. "You're tearing me up again."

"Well ... He said then, 'Besides, I don't have only my guilt to fight in this. It's my whole life – the way I've lived. What decent, sensitive, principled woman would want me as a permanent

497

partner after the way I've lived? It seemed right when I started it and it's kept me alive, but now I have to pay a price for that, too.'

"And then, Kaitrin, then he met Emmi Shermayne.

"He was involved in the production of a musical drama – live musicians, all the bells and whistles. She was playing flute in the acoustic orchestra and they hit it off right away. They lived together for about eight months. I really think that was the longest he ever stayed with the same woman. He even brought her home here a couple of times so I could meet her, something he had never done before.

"On one occasion I said to him, 'I really like Emmi. She's warm and sociable and bright and she seems to adore you. Maybe she's the one you can be happy with, Griff.'

"He sat and looked at his hands and took a hard breath. 'I don't know,' he said. 'I think I'm fonder of her than I've ever been of anyone. Do you suppose it could be?'

"And I said, 'I can't tell you that. But I wish it could be. Can you envision living the rest of your life with her?'

"At that, he sort of shuddered. 'I don't know. It terrifies me to think about it. Oh, Ree, I want to have a home – maybe even a family ... do you know, I've been thinking about what it would be like to have children? But then I try to look ahead and nothing seems real. I can't really picture what it would be like. I think I'm too afraid – to have to keep hiding from the same person for so long.'

"'The idea is not to hide from her.'

"'I know, but that's the worst of all. I'm such a moral coward. I don't think I can do it.'

"And when his acceptance at Shiras-Peders came through, he left. He didn't tell me when he left – I think he was ashamed to face me. Emmi messaged me and she was crying. 'I'd have gone with him, Rianna, if he had asked me. But he never asked me. He just told me the acceptance came through and he supposed this was the time to say goodbye. Why did he do that? I really am in love with him, Rianna.'

"Of course I couldn't tell her. And I was very disappointed. But when Griff finally got in touch with me from Okloh, he was obviously so miserable that I couldn't reproach him. I just said, 'There'll be someone else, Griff.'

And he said, 'I don't think so. But at least I've got some meaningful work here to occupy me – and a whole new gaggle of females for the old rotter to wallow in.'

"I had never before heard him speak so bitterly about his relations with women. It made me very sad.

"Then Emmi messaged me and told me she was pregnant.

"'God, how did that happen?' I said. She said she didn't really know, but it was true and did I think she ought to tell Griff about it? And I said, 'Yes, definitely.' I thought maybe he would finally come to his senses and send for her. After all, he had said he wanted a family.

"But he didn't. When I talked to him, he said, 'I can't give a family what it needs, Ree. I've given up on myself. Too many years have gone by. I'm beyond redemption.'

"I said, 'You can at least see the child – be a presence in its life.'

"And he said, 'Give a pittance – a few scraps? That won't do at all! A child and a – a mother need all the attention the father has to give. And I can't do that. There are some things little Griff Gwidian never could do, you know.'

"I said, 'Griff, I think you're just seeking to punish yourself again.'

"'So what if I am?' he said. 'I deserve it, don't I?'

Rianna sighed and looked at Kaitrin. "You look pretty drained. I feel pretty drained. Do you want to stop?"

Kaitrin swallowed. "No. It's just – everything he went through in his life – all that emotional pain … How could he have been so good at hiding everything?"

"Oh, that was the one thing he could do better than anything in the world. So – he plunged himself into his work. He spent at least two of the next five years off-world and then he earned his Professorship and the respect of the academic world as a xenocoleopterist, and that at least was something. He settled in at Northwest Quad in Okloh and we saw him only once or twice a year. He never told me a lot about the women he was involved with during that time. I think he knew I really couldn't help him any longer. But then … "

"We're almost up to the present, aren't we?" said Kaitrin.

"Yes, and I think we really should stop. It's time for lunch.

This afternoon I want to start something new. I'm going to show you recordings of some of the conversations I had with Griffen around the time he met you."

Chapter 15

Suppose for once I set my doors wide open
And bid you in . . . Suppose I try to tell you
The secrets of this house, and how I live here;
Suppose I tell you who I am, in fact.
Deceiving you – as far as I may know it –
Only so much as I deceive myself.
– from Conrad Aiken, *The Divine Pilgrim, III,*
The House of Dust

So, after a lunch of maize and vegetable soup that Kaitrin could hardly swallow, they sat down at the port wall in Rianna's office while she searched a file of old messages, looking for a conversation that took place not long before Griffen left on the first Giotta expedition.

Kaitrin waited tensely for his face to come up on the screen. "Rianna, he told me he was thinking of suicide at that time."

Rianna stopped scrolling. "Did he! What did he tell you?"

"He had dropped hints earlier – about how empty his life had been, about being at a low emotional ebb – but I didn't pick up on them. It's not something I ever think of. I've always been such an optimistic, forward-looking person, at least up to the time I lost Griffen … It never occurs to me to want to escape from life. But on that same night when he said he might like to be accepted as a member of my family, one thing led to another and he told me that everything I had seen in him when we first met – the arrogance, the cocksureness – had been false, a mask to hide behind – that he had been thinking then of taking his own life, but he had put that behind him and now he wanted to live – more than any man – who had ever existed ... " Kaitrin's head drooped.

Rianna hugged her. "I understand. He didn't have all that much longer, did he?" She turned back to the port wall, looking a little grim.

And there was Griffen's lean, handsome face, dominated by the deep-set eyes and the striking nose. The expression was gloomy. Kaitrin sat blinking, her hands pressed to her mouth. Behind him, she glimpsed the interior of his office in the house that was to have been theirs.

"Hello, Ree," he said, and Rianna's voice could be heard responding.

"I'm so glad to talk to you, Griffen. How's everything going?"

"Well, the funding came through. I'm not particularly looking forward to this expedition – it's nothing but a baseline biological survey – but it beats sitting around this rubbishy campus all summer, I suppose. A xenoanthropologist has signed on as a consultant. He's an off-worlder – a Krisadia – Krisi-aida – I can't pronounce that, dammit! – one of the falconiforms. I already knew him slightly – he translated some Krisaidian research material for me awhile back."

"That ought to be interesting!"

"'I'm not looking for interesting. This Bird character makes me nervous. His name is A'a'ma – at least that's pronounceable. He's a bona fide Professor – the only off-worlder ever to hold a regular Professorship at a terrestrial university. He's led a lot of his own expeditions and he has a good many years' seniority on me. The ship that's been assigned to us is also Krisiaid, with a Krisiaid Captain and a mostly alien crew. I imagine there'll be some friction there."

"There doesn't have to be."

"I simply want to be left alone on this voyage – it's basically of no consequence and – I'm in the mood to be left alone."

"Griff, you don't sound good."

"I'm not. I'm really down, Ree. I've hit another wall. My

life is as empty as it's ever been."

"Are you still seeing Doriann?"

"Off and on. She's pretty good in bed. She says I am. The same old stuff. We go to the theater. I take her to dinner. Same old sterile stuff."

"Griff, maybe you should have come home and spent the summer here instead of ... "

"You know that wouldn't do any good. I'd better close off – I can see I'm getting you upset. I love you, Ree. Don't worry about me. Good night."

Rianna scrolled once more. "Now here he is, after the expedition returned."

Griffen's face again, tanned from the fieldwork. "We got back day before yesterday – really hustled," he said. "That giant specimen we brought back is dying – getting it to Earth probably won't save it."

"Oh, that's too bad," said Rianna's voice.

"Prf. A'a'ma is driving me insane," said Griffen savagely. "He's become fixated on the notion that this giant insect is an intelligent lifeform. This is the last time I ever go off-world with an XA! Their attitude toward science is completely skewed – and these Birds are particularly barmy, you know?"

Through her emotion, Kaitrin giggled.

Griffen was saying, "He's been badgering me about bringing in some Associate Specialist – a young female xenolinguist, one of his protégés. She's supposed to be some kind of genius. A linguist, Ree! – to study an insect? Can things get any more absurd?"

Kaitrin listened in guilty fascination.

"It does sound a bit unusual," said Rianna's voice.

"I finally agreed to talk to her just to keep Prf. A'a'ma from pecking me to death. She's coming in today – she's been at a symposium in Yakuta. Apparently, she's quite ambitious – plans to earn her Professorship before the age of thirty." Griffen coughed a laugh. "You and I both know how likely that is!"

"Oh, Rianna," said Kaitrin. "That was the very day I first saw Griff. It was on the relay. He came off as so arrogant! I couldn't stand him!"

Rianna laughed tremulously.

On the screen, Rianna was saying, "How are you feeling,

Griff?"

"Like bloody hell. When I got back, there was a message from Doriann. She took a job in New Washinten. 'We can still get together, Griff. Maybe not as often. But do message me.'"

"I'm sorry," said Rianna's voice.

"I hardly ever have a reason to go to New Washinten and she isn't worth making a special effort, anyway. It isn't the end of another affair that upsets me. It's just – well, I thought I could at least come back to something familiar. Now I have to start again. Ree, I don't want to start again." Griffen was scowling, rubbing the back of his head. "I'm so tired of all this. I'm just – bloody knackered. That bodkin is looking better and better."

Rianna's voice rose in pitch. "Griffen, please don't talk like that. Do you want me to come there? I'll come if you want."

"Oh, no. Forget I said that." He reached out toward the image on his screen, forcing a smile. "Don't worry – I'm probably too craven to take that course, anyway. You know, bear the ills you have rather than fly to others ... I'm too much Hamlet. I had more resolve when I was thirteen."

Rianna froze the display, bowing her head. Kaitrin took a hard breath. Then Rianna reactivated, forwarded. "Here – a couple of days later."

"Well, the last day was diverting, at least," said Griffen's image. "You know that young Associate – and I do mean young, Ree. Oh, I suppose she's maybe twenty-five ... "

"Twenty-six!" Kaitrin said indignantly.

" ... but she looks about twenty. Anyway, my intent was to just go through the motions and get her out of my hair as quickly as I could. I figured, if she was as brilliant as A'a'ma said, she'd see there was no purpose in her participation. But she turned out to be quite a surprise."

"You liked her?"

"I don't know if 'liked' is quite on the mark, but she made an impression on me. I admit I patronized her pretty badly, but she isn't the sort to be easily intimidated."

"You patronized her?"

"Well, yes. And she told me so, in no uncertain terms."

Rianna suspended the feed and grinned at Kaitrin. "Did you?"

Kaitrin glared at Rianna defensively. "Well, he started defining words and explaining that insects have no bones as if I were a preschooler, and he implied that the gory holoimage of the attack on the geologist was going to make me sick. Things like that."

Rianna chuckled. "That's not like Griff. But you can see what frame of mind he was in." She reengaged the port.

Griffen was saying, "She has a really reckless enthusiasm. She insisted on entering the envirocube with the insect and she ended up sticking her bare hand into its mouth, of all idiotic things! This creature has sharp mandibles and the alien flora in its digestive tract ... well, I rushed in to extract her and of course I bungled it and startled the creature and her, too, and she cut her hand on the mandible. Then we had a shouting – and swearing – match about whether or not she'd been in danger. A bit childish, what?" He laughed ruefully.

"Rianna," said Kaitrin, "I'm just realizing that the very first thing Griffen did in our relationship grew out of a desire to save me from danger."

"But that wasn't the half of it," he was saying. "Whilst she was in Detox, she got this cockeyed idea about using a neural interface recorder to investigate whether this creature was trying to communicate. She convinced A'a'ma to spring her from Detox and they burst into my research suite, and then A'a'ma pulled his seniority in order to coerce me into cooperating – I hate it when another Professor does that. But it turned out – not so badly. The creature died with its head on the Associate's lap. Honestly, there was something pathetic about it. It really did appear to be seeking comfort from her – and she didn't seem to mind giving ... " Griffen's voice shook suddenly. "We'll see in the morning if her neural recorder picked up any of the creature's brain waves. If it did – well, I'll be surprised. But it was an ingenious idea – no harm in making the attempt ... "

Rianna's voice said, "What's this woman's name?"

"Oliva. Kaitrin Oliva. Strange first name. Spelled K-a-i-t-r-e-n, I believe."

"Griff!" said Kaitrin reproachfully.

"Does she interest you – you know?"

"I don't think so. She's pretty in a natural sort of way – no make-up, quantities of fair hair all done up in a no-nonsense braid.

Very nice eyes – green. She made a remark about having lived in Afrik that intrigued me. But I'm so disillusioned at the moment – I'm not thinking of any woman as a sex partner. God, no." Then he added, "But she was so direct, and so unaffected by – by me. And I did find her very easy to look at."

*　　*　　*

The following morning, as Rianna prepared to resume running her precious hoard of vids, Kaitrin said, "I'm so grateful to you. It's so good to hear Griff's voice and see his face. And his thoughts – I'm really surprised at what he was thinking about me. I have a few recordings of messages from him, but – would you be willing to give me copies of some of these?"

"Gladly. Just tell me which you want," Rianna replied gently. "Now this one – some days later … "

"Hello, Ree," said Griffen with an almost expansive smile.

"You look a little more cheerful, Griff!"

"Well, I've gotten a good bit intrigued with this Oliva woman. She happened to be lunching in the entomology dining hall and I sat down with her. She mentioned Afrik again just as she was leaving, and then I chanced to see her go into a juice bar when she was out running, so I followed her in. She was wearing running shorts – has a quite beguiling figure."

Rianna cocked an eyebrow at Kaitrin, who annoyed herself by blushing.

Griff was continuing, "Her hair was falling down. I told her it would be attractive worn loose and she – well, she's very cautious. I always have to fight this damned reputation of mine – she's certainly aware of it. A day or so later I casually asked her to join me for lunch. And she came. I was a little surprised."

"Why should you be? You're aware of how women respond to you."

"But not this one." He laughed in chagrin. "She's a bit – what's a good word? – perhaps 'bristly.' Won't let me call her by her first name. Won't call me by mine."

"Really? You call each other 'Associate' and 'Professor' whilst you're socializing? How funny!" Rianna's laughter could be heard.

"Isn't it just! But, I say, it's rather refreshing to find a woman who's not an easy mark. She truly is a linguistic genius – learns languages the way a sponge drinks water, it seems. The Consortium analyzed her brain when she was eighteen to see what makes it tick but couldn't solve the mystery. You'd be interested, I'm sure … "

"Remind me to tell you about that," interrupted Kaitrin. "It was quite an experience."

Gwidian was saying, "She's the offspring of an A Level AI – a successful one, I'd say. But her contract father was from Nouvelle Victoire and that's the Afriken connection – I finally got her to talk about it in the juice bar. And do you know, it turns out that I worked with him one summer up in the Serenghi! He was a volunteer ranger. Isn't that a strange coincidence?"

"Griff, you sound a lot livelier," said Rianna's voice, "as if you had found something to perk up your interest in life."

He hesitated, his brows bending together. "Well. Maybe. At least for a while – until something goes wrong. It's always just for a while, isn't it? But I suppose I should be grateful for whatever I can get. She's – rather feckless – young and inexperienced. But – it's quite refreshing. I think I'll try to see something of her, just on a social level, for a while. But I behaved so shabbily in the beginning … I don't know if she'll accept … Well, we'll see if all this leads to anything."

As the vid ended, Kaitrin said, "Feckless? Good grief, is that the way I seemed to him? But he … Later, he hinted he thought I was frigid. I guess we never know what impression we're giving."

"I would say you were making the perfect impression," said Rianna. "So many of the women that Griff consorted with in later years were older sophisticates – a bit jaded or easy. I think you were exactly what he needed."

"Somebody bristly who played hard to get," said Kaitrin.

"Here we are a little while later."

Griffen reappeared on the screen, looking distressed and disheartened. "Ree, I tell you, it's hopeless. Kaitrin's – no, I should say, Asc. Oliva's work was going well, so on impulse she asked me to accompany her to the Karlinius campus to view the faculty art show … "

"Oh, dear," said Kaitrin.

"We stopped at the Archaic Crafts Studio – wonderful place –

I had known nothing about it. Seems it's one of her favorite haunts. I bought her a painted miniature of a fantastic creature called a 'griffin.' It's a hybrid of eagle and lion – not much like me, what? But I had no idea I was named for a mythical animal, did you? Anyway, we had lunch in their little dining room and she started telling me about an interesting West British legend, and – things were going so very well ... Ree, I was really getting out of myself, having a good time, but – it's hopeless. Am I quite doomed to have everything fall apart?"

"What happened, Griff?"

"You remember that woman named Margit Terrie that I broke up with awhile back? She always was a rubbishy little bitch – one of my least felicitous liaisons. She of all people turned up and started in with the flirtatious innuendo. God, Ree. I was simply squirming inside. I knew it would wreck everything – Kaitrin is quite high-minded and ... god, it matters to me! I got rid of Terrie finally, but it ruined the day. I made some lame excuse and re-treated, after enduring a cutting remark. Asc. Oliva is very good with a cutting remark."

"Oh, dear," said Kaitrin again. "My mother says the same thing."

Rianna's voice was saying, "Can't you explain things to her, Griffen?"

"Explain! You can't explain something like that to a woman like Kaitrin! She has her standards! And I'm convinced sex is of no interest to her so there goes my best ammunition."

"You see?" said Kaitrin. "Frigid. He basically called me that in the North Star, only I was too naive to understand what he meant until I thought about it. But ... " She straightened up defiantly. " ... I certainly proved him wrong about that later!"

On the vid Rianna was saying, "You don't have to have a sexual relationship with every woman you meet."

"Of course I know that! It's only that ... Dammit!" Griffen ran a hand distractedly through his hair. "Maybe I'm a little insulted on top of it all!"

"That might be a healthy reaction, Griff!" said the unseen Rianna with a light laugh. "Why don't you be persistent? View her as a challenge."

"A challenge? You think I should – oh, ask her out formally, something like that?"

"Why not? Ratchet up that charm of yours, Griffen! You're so good at that sort of thing – you know you are. All she can do is refuse."

After a moment's hesitation, Griffen said, "If she refuses me … Why does that alarm me? Ree, for some reason this means more to me than anything I've done in years!"

Then came the serio-comic happenings in Okloh. "The Gwidian charm you're always talking about – this time it definitely earned a failing mark! The evening was a disaster – went from bad to worse! I don't know why she accepted my invitation – she started out angry and only got more so as the evening went on. It was such a strong emotion that I couldn't help tuning in on it – even managed to lose my own temper."

"You? You never lose your temper!"

"Well, I did this time, I fear! But there was a redemption … " He proceeded to narrate what had happened, with the same wry humor that he had displayed during the actual event. "That laughter of hers – it was every bit as contagious as her ill temper! I never realized how much power there can be in laughter – how much healing … And on the way home we talked – we really talked. I've never talked quite like that with any woman except you. Ree, I'm beginning to wonder. Could she be … ? But I'm afraid to try to put it into words."

Kaitrin said, "I went out with him because my mother wanted me to – I told him so during that trip home. He thought it was a hilarious reason. But it seems he asked me out because his own surrogate mother recommended it! And you know – that night in Okloh was the second time he tried to save me from harm. Maybe everything that happened really was fated."

And next, after the sparring bout in the gym, "Now I know it's finished. I can't understand why I reacted as I did. She's so competitive – she can't abide losing – and she taunted me with an accusation that I deliberately allowed her to win one of the matches. That made me angry and I just threw her with no warning – purely to demonstrate my superiority. That scares me, Rianna. I lost control. I don't like the feeling of losing control. I may have hurt her. I'm not superior to her. Oh, I'm physically stronger – I have more skill in martial arts – that sort of inconsequential rot –

but in any way that matters, I don't begin to measure up."

"Message her."

"I'm losing my nerve – I can't push this any farther. And – oh, god, Ree, I had really begun to hope again that I was still salvageable. I always muck up everything for myself. I think the time really has arrived to put an end to the struggle."

"Oh, Griff, there you go again. Don't do anything like that. Wait a little while. You know you'll see her again because you have to work with her. And she may not have been as put off as you think. Wait and see what happens. I beg you, don't do anything rash."

Kaitrin said softly, "It's true. I found I didn't want the relationship to end, so I took the initiative."

"Yes," said Rianna, "and I think there's a good chance you saved his life."

*　　*　　*

The communications that touched Kaitrin the most deeply came before and after the party.

"Ree, I have to say this to you – will it make you happy or sad? I think I'm falling in love with Kaitrin – with Kait. She's allowing me call her 'Kait' – no one else ever has, so that makes it very special. I think I'm falling in love, Ree." Griffen's face was trembling, open; he leaned toward the port, half laughing.

"Griffen, I … What does that signify?"

"I don't know myself. But I want to kiss her. I don't want to go to bed with her – not until she's ready. But if I can take her in my arms and kiss her, then I think I'll know if this is only an infatuation, or if it's something that I – that I can sustain – or try to sustain … She's giving a little party and I'm invited, and I'm going to linger afterwards. I know she'll try to prevent it. She's resisting me with all her soul. I've never had to really court a woman like this before – I've never wanted to. If I sensed resistance, I simply backed away. But with Kaitrin … I think – if I can see any hope – and I'm with her on that ship – outside of time … There is something about TQ travel that makes people vulnerable. Oh, Rianna, if we didn't know it was futile, I'd ask you to pray for me!"

And then after the party … "I did it, Ree. I kissed her – and it was incredible! It was as if I had never kissed a woman before.

I can't describe it. Like a presence around us. Like joy. I don't know much about how joy feels, but this must be it. I mustn't lose her, Rianna. I can't survive it."

"Griffen, don't be so extreme. You always take everything to extremes."

"Rianna, I think she's the one – the one who can save me – forgive me – help me find peace. I'm in love with Kait Oliva, Ree. There's no going back for me now."

*　　*　　*

They took a hiatus while Kaitrin pulled herself together. "I don't know why I do this," she told Rianna, blowing her nose, which was beginning to get sore. "I've never been one of those weepy females – I've always despised them. Right after Griffen died, I was too dead inside to cry. But my mother got the spigot turned on and now I can't seem to get it turned off."

"I've never been one of those weepers, either," said Rianna, "and I've gone through more boxes of handkerchiefs since he died than in my whole life before."

"Have you? It helps get the bitterness out, I guess. But I hope it ends soon. Surely I can grieve privately without flooding the whole world and boring everybody to death!"

"It will end," said Rianna. "But what I'm putting you through here is enough to wring tears out of a honey badger!"

Rianna next proposed to display the messages that Griffen had dispatched from the *Featherlight* and Kaitrin asked, "You don't think it would embarrass him or offend him if he knew that I'm seeing his most private words?"

"I think he would want it," said Rianna. "I know he tried desperately to open up his soul to you, but he didn't have enough time to reach critical mass, as it were. So now this is the only way he can."

The TTR messages had no voice, no face – only the characters of Griffen's composition running down the screen.

Dearest Ree: I'm living in a perpetual state of trepidation – the highs and lows are almost unbearable. I contrived to be alone with Kait at the moment when the ship passed out of time and it was wonderful – she actually gave me an impulsive kiss, the first time she has initiated anything. She wouldn't allow more than that, but she said things about maybe loving me one day that gave me a most ecstatic hope. I hardly slept at all that night. But then we had a quarrel – for the silliest, most childish reasons that you can imagine ...

"Griff never told me what the quarrel was about," said Rianna.

"Oh," Kaitrin responded reluctantly, "one of our Security officers was from Shan-hy and I was sitting with him at lunch talking about the Chiness language. I was laughing and having a good time – and it made Griffen jealous! Then I got annoyed because Griff happened to be standing with our female Security Officer at the Captain's party – they were both having a drink and laughing at some dirty joke she was telling. He was jealous of my love of language and I was jealous of – of nothing at all!"

Rianna was chuckling. "It sounds like you both did have a bad case of it."

... and all because I'm so strung out. We had a confrontation and she really dressed me down – said if I was going to behave like that, she could see no future for us. Oh, god, Rianna, I've never felt like that inside! Like something was crumbling, turning to quicksand. I think it was the first moment I truly acknowledged to myself how much hope I'm pinning on a positive conclusion to this thing. I apologized and I must have said something right because she apologized in turn, and the situation resolved itself. She said she thought she was a little afraid of what was happening, and I asked her, Did she think that I wasn't afraid? I daresay that was not the wisest thing to say, but it just came out.

She said she wanted to know more of "my soul," but all she really meant was something of my life, my history. But maybe that is my soul. She also said she wanted me to read poetry to her. That may or may not be difficult, but it isn't something I can't do. We've talked a couple of times since then and I've managed to open up a little. I can't open up completely – not yet. You'll know what I mean. But I've been trying – I will try, Ree, I swear to you that I will try.

We talked about her childhood – her Eirish grandmother – and her opinions on contracture and marriage. She laughs at the idea of marriage. But that's what is in my thoughts – it's been in my thoughts from the first time I kissed her. Are you surprised to hear that? Don't be angry with me, Ree, or feel I'm abandoning you. You know I love you – I always have and that won't change. Ever since you took me home from that clinic in Kardif, you've been my anchor and my beacon – without you my life would have ended before it even began. But you've told me yourself that I need ... I'm out of space. There will be more to report in ten or twelve days. If I'm still alive. If I lose this gamble, there are no guarantees. Griffen.

Rianna grabbed for a fresh handkerchief, laughing shakily. "You know, I worried myself sick throughout this whole expedition. I was really afraid that he couldn't handle it all – directing the expedition and at the same time trying to cope with the unfamiliar experience of being in love and courting a reluctant woman. Thank goodness he was only co-leader and had Prf. A'a'ma to relieve some of the pressure."

"He did a good job with the expedition," said Kaitrin. "At least until ... But we had such a fine team. We all worked together so smoothly and enjoyed one another's company. It made the end that much harder to bear. But, Rianna, I'd recommend that you off-load these messages and then scour your port. If pronkers got their hands on this stuff, it would end up on the links alongside the wedding vid. This whole affair has become such a flash item."

"You know, you're right. I'll do that. The Vedders firm was already hit. They got the request for Griff's body."

"I saw it. If even attorneys' encryptions aren't foolproof, what can the rest of us expect?"

Rianna bent her head a little. "That did hurt. Gerit was really irate – he wanted to prosecute somebody, but I didn't feel up to it. But to be demonized in the record – even in a sensationalized pop link – when I was in so much pain ... "

Kaitrin touched Rianna's hand. "Let me assure you again – I never blamed you for claiming his body. And now that I've met you and seen this place, I don't think I would have wanted him to be buried anywhere else. He's at home here."

When Rianna was ready to continue, Kaitrin said, "Let's see – had we planned the wedding yet?"

"No. This one was sent right after he had that nightmare."

"I remember! I sneaked out and let him sleep, and left him a message that the TTR communications were due. At that time we hadn't even talked about his children."

"Some of that I didn't learn much about. But let me run this one."

Dearest Ree: Kait has come to me at last – we're in the same quarters, sharing a bed!   Sharing a bed!   It's all new again – as sweet as if I had never known a woman before!   She asked me to read love poetry to her and I almost bungled it – couldn't keep a steady voice.   Then she just about killed me – asked how many other women I had read to – said she feared I would get tired of her and throw her away as I must have done with so many others.   She said she couldn't bear the thought of that.   Frankly, I can't remember how I answered her – I was dreadfully torn up.   I know I told her she was the only woman I had ever loved, and that isn't a lie.   Even Emmi ...   I felt a huge fondness for her, but it was never like this – and she was one that I did throw away.   And then Kait told me she loved me – the first time she ever said that to me.   Oh, Ree!   I can't describe ...   But the days that followed – she wants to live with me, loved what I told her about the house.   She makes me laugh – her own laughter is so irresistible – so healing.   I laugh with her more than I ever have with anyone.   She has such lovely hair and I can finally caress it – I can't tell you how intensely I've wanted to do that.   I was feeling as if maybe I had been fully cleansed, restored, and without any struggle – a genuine miracle!

But yesterday something happened.   Some words were spoken – a totally innocent set of remarks – and it was all back.   It can't be that effortless, can it? – after thirty-five years.   Kait was startled – didn't understand.   Of course she didn't.   I owed her an explanation, but that was simply out of the question – I can't break the barriers, not yet.   Then I did something perilous – I promised her that one day all of me would be open to her.   Now, that took a modicum of audacity – perhaps you'll find that a good sign!   But I begged her to give me a little time, some space to rest and get my breath.

And then last night came the old nightmare – first time with her.   But she can be so consoling.   She's really very sensual – why did I ever think she wouldn't be?   And I confessed to her that I feared the same things she did – that she would get disillusioned with me and throw me away – and she said that she had taken me for all of what I am, not just for what she could see – that if she

*hadn't been able to do that, she wouldn't have taken me at all.
I've never had a woman say anything like that to me. It reassured
me and terrified me at the same time. Ree, how can I ever do what
I know I must? What I promised her?*

*I do need some rest, but I can't rest, really. I have to tell her
about the children I've fathered – I owe her that – and I'm going
to beg her to marry me. I know she'll laugh, but maybe she'll do it
for me. I want to do something right here on the ship – I don't
want to wait. I have this feeling we shouldn't wait. I brought the
ring along.*

*I'm out of space. We'll be at our destination by the time you
hear from me again. Send your love through space to help me, my
dear Ree. I still need it so much. Griffen.*

The next message was sent from the TTR set up at the planet.

*Dear Rianna: It's done! Kait and I are married! I dredged
up more nerve than I ever thought was in me and I made a public
vow to her, speaking in full sight and hearing of the whole crew.
Yes, this really is your timorous little brother writing here! I don't
know how I managed to get through it. If she hadn't been beside
me ... Honestly, a couple of times I thought I would pass out and
make a total laughingstock of myself.*

*Kait did laugh at first when I suggested a wedding, but she
has such irrepressible enthusiasm – she got into the spirit of it and
organized a service ... well, it was incredibly moving. The ship's
Captain, who happens to be a ciconiiform – a stork! – led the service. To top it off, he speaks Inj with a highly comical accent! It
was surreal, actually. The prayer was written by the expeditionary
doctor, Trea Dol Amarezka, who is a Pozú – a people of a spiritu-
ality more genuine than Earth has ever been able to generate. A
recording of the ceremony exists; Kait has a copy of it, although I
haven't found the fortitude to look at it yet – don't relish seeing
what a fool I made of myself. One day I'll play it for you.*

*Ree, I'm trying to put on a brave show here, but in fact I'm
very frightened. Right before the ceremony, the enormity of what I
was doing suddenly came home to me. I swore to give up all other
women – what else is marriage? I wanted Kait to be absolutely
convinced I will never be faithless to her. But now I have nothing
except her. It's like being on a cliff with proper climbing gear and
then suddenly realizing that the gear is gone and you're clinging*

to the cliff with only your fingers and feet a hundred meters above the crashing ocean. Kait is my cliff now. What if I lose her? God, Ree, you would have to reserve that room in the PD Clinic, because there would be nothing but my body left to take care of.

But this is going to alarm you and I don't want to do that. I love Kait so much and I know she loves me. And I have a great incentive to stay positive and make things work. I told her about the children and she accepted it with amazing composure and matter-of-factness. She says she would like to have a child with me. She even said she thought I would make a good father! Can you imagine me a father – a family man like Gerit? I can't wait for this new life of ours to begin – on Earth, I mean. I want it so badly, I ache.

We go planetside for the first time tomorrow. When I write again, we'll have met these intelligent insects, I suppose. I fear I haven't been thinking much about all that – I must try to refocus my mind. Till next time, I love you, Ree. Griffen.

"There it is again, you see," said Kaitrin. "He wanted to go home. Why couldn't I have understood before it was too late how much he needed that?"

Rianna regarded her for a moment but said only, "Here is his first communication from the planet. His mood had deflated a little, I'm afraid."

Dear Ree: So much has happened that I don't know where to begin. We made a brief exploratory landing and discovered that these creatures had constructed what appeared to be a small memorial to their fellows that we had killed. Eerie to contemplate. Then we settled in at our permanent location on the planet and waited for something to happen. And something did – the Shshi (I must call them that now instead of "Xenotermes") sent out their entire army and surrounded us! A bit alarming, I can tell you! But Kaitrin insisted on going outside the flyer to try to contact them and I hadn't the slightest control over her, either as her expedition leader or as her husband. She's willing to risk anything – absolutely dauntless. How could a timid man like me have fallen in love with a woman like that? But the ironic part of it is that she was right. She played that recording of our dying specimen's thought signals – and the Shshi understood it and withdrew their soldiers! She made her contact; her informant, as the XA people call it, is a winged creature who apparently is a shaman or priest of some kind.

But I don't know about myself – I'm not reacting very positively to all of this. This really isn't my expedition, it's hers. A'a'ma supports her in everything, of course; I think he involved himself in this for her sake – to help her fulfill her ambition of becoming the youngest person ever to earn a Professorship. She will earn it for this, no doubt; it's a unique undertaking. She's creating an entire language as she goes! But I'm not getting to do anything. I need a chance to examine these creatures firsthand, but of course one can't go around cavalierly poking scanners into the body openings of a priest.

And Kaitrin is so absorbed in her work. Damn it, she has no time for me! I realize that sounds petty, childish. I acknowledge it is that. But I don't really want to be where I am! It seems such an anticlimax after those exquisite days on the Featherlight. *I'm no novice when it comes to off-world situations – I'm accustomed to alien environments – but there is something disturbing about this place. You'll say it's only my old inadequacies thrusting up their heads and goodness knows I've never been prescient, but I'm very uneasy here. I believe Kait loves her work more than she does me, when all is said and done. Ree, I'm jealous.*

Now, don't get heated up about this. I'll be all right. Nothing has really gone awry – the problem is all in me. There was one particular night when we had the most exquisite sex I've ever experienced and that's saying a lot. I was trying to lure her away from her work. She's too tired for sex a lot of the time. Then afterwards she got into a strange mood and started asking me a lot of questions about the women in my past. It's not that I mind her knowing anything; I just ... well, I can't adequately explain how I'm feeling and the space is used up again. More another time. Griffen.

"It's true, you know," whispered Kaitrin. "I was neglecting him. When I'm working, I get compulsive about it. Near the time he was writing that, there was a little confrontation. He spoke of how he had never before tried to hold a woman except by the flesh. He said when he looked down the years, he could see me everywhere, but he couldn't see himself. Was that prescient? He scared me. He was always scaring me. But I just blundered along on my heedless way – I mean, maybe not always … but I continued to put my own preoccupations over his needs right to the bitter end."

"Kaitrin," said Rianna, "I see you accusing yourself too much and too often."

"Never mind!" said Kaitrin. "What had been happening when he wrote next?"

"He seemed a lot less stressed by that time."

Dear Rianna: Kait and I resolved our differences; I'm chagrined that I sounded like such a petulant brat in that last message. She is such a strong woman, Ree. Is that what I need? Sometimes I think so, but at other times she just exhausts me. I'm so afraid of losing her, you see. That induces a lack of balance at times.

Part of the problem is that all the other alien planets I've visited either lacked ILFs or were populated by well-studied, friendly species like the Te Quornaz. This is the only time I've ever been involved in a first contact – in the study of an undocumented intelligence. It's not something I ever thought about doing. I've found my minuscule beetles and the beauty of an unusual butterfly to be sufficiently satisfying. But I think I'm coming to terms with the situation.

I've had an opportunity to perform physical examinations on some of the Shshi. The alates are unique among insectiforms for their bioluminescent wings and remarkable eyes, and then there is this especially enormous warrior, which is of a different species. I confess it's fascinating stuff. Apparently, the shaman had a vision of the flyer – her description was an exact fit – and she also had been warned by her "spirit" that she would receive the "speaking of the dead." And what better way to describe the recording of the specimen's words that Kait played for them? Do you believe there could be any validity in all that? Are there alien beings whose connection with omnipotent powers is more intimate than that of us materialistic ILFs of planet Earth?

I've also been able to get out in the field – into the orchard and once into the outlying plain. I was a little wary at first because Kait's informant implied there might be some kind of danger, but so far everything has been routine. I'm acquiring quantities of data and some terrific specimens, so I have plenty of

*my own work to engage me right now. It helps to keep busy. I'll
be fine. Don't worry so much about me, Ree. Lovingly, Griffen.*
"Then the surprises started coming," said Kaitrin.

"Indeed," said Rianna, deactivating the port. "You're going
to be very surprised at what Griffen said in his last message to me.
Why don't we continue this after lunch?"

Chapter 16

Grant Anup's children this:
To howl with you, Queen Isis,
Over the scattered limbs of wronged Osiris.
What harder fate than to be woman?
She makes and she unmakes her man.
– from Robert Graves, *The Jackals' Address to Isis*

With her curiosity thus piqued, Kaitrin could hardly wait until lunch was finished. As she and Rianna resumed their places at the port wall, she said, "This must be after the attack and after we were visited by that scoundrel Mo'gri'ta'tu – the Shi who incited the rebellion in the fortress – and before the business of the dream about riding horses."

Rianna had a strange smile on her face. "You'll be very surprised," she said again.

Dearest Ree: This will be a long message because I'm using a double allotment of units. You won't hear from me again until we leave this planet, and the sooner that day comes, the happier I'll be. You'll recall things were going pretty well the last time. But then my field team (three of us) were assaulted by five of these big Warriors. Now, Ree, I can see your reaction in my mind. None of us was injured, but it was a thoroughly harrowing experience. Our sensors picked up their pursuit, but we couldn't evade them and they caught up with us and cornered us against some rocks. They made such alarming threat postures that I was convinced they were going to attack and kill us all. Then the Nasutes (another species of giant isopteroid who has some kind of obscure, almost feudal connection with this fortress) appeared, engaged them, and drew them off. We had been forced to fire laser pistols to keep them at bay, but fortunately we avoided hitting any of them. I shudder to imagine what kind of response there would have been if we had killed one of them! But now some foolery has developed concerning curiosity about our weapons. I thought anthros were supposed to distance themselves from the cultures they study, but I must say A'a'ma and Kait haven't conformed very successfully to that standard.

Anyway, we made it back safely, then of course the reaction set in. I got sick to my stomach – barely made it to the head, but I did make it, thank god! Throwing up in front of the others would have been more humiliation than I needed! Our good little doctor, Trea, used some of her off-world techniques on me – she's quite wonderful. You might like to look into Pozú medical practices.

"Actually, I've done some reading on that," Rianna said. "I'd like a chance to confer with one of their doctors some time."

That whole episode brought on the grandfather of all nightmares – no surprise there. One of these creatures had hold of me and pulled me down under the water. But my Kait was there when I came out of it. We lay in each other's arms and just talked – one of those sweet, soothing, steadying conversations that we have sometimes. She helps me so much and I love her so much.

Rianna, I want to come home so badly. This planet merits lengthy study, but I still can't shed my feeling of apprehension about it. Kaitrin hinted that she might go into that hellhole of a fortress across the way. It was only a hint, but I can't bear to even think about it. Why must she be so foolhardy – so optimistic and sure of herself and so relentless about having things her way? I can't bear to see her go in there, and yet I know, if she sets her mind ... And then this Shi that Kait doesn't trust – the one she calls the Chamberlain – turned up outside the flyer this evening. Rushed up and mouthed me all over, apparently searching for my pistol. That was unnerving in itself! And the Seer has been having visions again. Apparently it's some kind of Great Goddess that speaks to her – that sounds so absurd that it embarrasses me

521

to write about it. But she knew that the name of the flyer was a name given to a terrestrial manifestation of the Goddess, and she said her spirit told her, "Are you not all my Star-Children?" All this unsettles me greatly. I'm not sure what the proper reaction ought to be, but I can't help feeling threatened. There is something otherworldly about this place on more than one level.

Anyway, the upshot is, I have a request to make of you. The oaths that Kaitrin and I swore to each other at the wedding are binding to our souls, but they mean nothing to the powers-that-be on our legalistic Earth. You have my power of attorney when I'm off-planet, but if there should be a problem, you have my permission to consult Petra Vedders or one of her associates. I would ask you to contact Lars Beniten for me and buy an emergency insurance policy on my life. Name as beneficiary: Kaitrin Lise Oliva, Dept. of Xenoanthropology, S-P U, NWQC, etc. The amount is to be 200,000 regs and I want the shortest ...

Rianna laughed and cut off the feed because Kaitrin was sitting with her fists pressed to her cheeks, gibbering.

"Rianna, you didn't! *Two hundred* ... Rianna!"

"It took awhile to push through the application, but it was completed in time. When you get back to Okloh, you're going to find the Bank holding 200,000 regs ... Kaitrin?"

Kaitrin had slumped back in her chair, her eyes glazed. "Two hundred ... Rianna, I don't want his money – I want *him*! That's all I'll ever want! I would gladly eat bread and water and scrub toilets for a living – for the rest of my life – if it could only – bring him back ..."

"Kaitrin." Rianna bent to the sobbing Kaitrin and held her against her heart. "I want him back, too, my dear, but it can't be. And he did this for you. Don't reject it. You know he would be hurt if you did. Here, wipe your eyes and read the rest of what he said."

So Kaitrin did that, blinking and gulping breath.

I want the shortest waiting period you can get – I think it's five days – even though that may double or triple the first year of premiums. I want it to include a clause that if my death were ruled a suicide, the policy would be nullified. This is mostly to reassure you that I'm not contemplating the Hamlet thing again. Believe me, I want to live, Ree, more than I ever have since their deaths. I really believe at times that I can see some light – some hope for myself. And don't be overly concerned that I'm doing this. There are always risks whenever one visits an alien world, but after this attack, I've concluded that the risk here is greater than usual.

This doesn't change my will, or the insurance for Charly and Gwin. The trust for Emmi's son is inalterable. You get everything else, except I have one request, Rianna. It isn't legally binding, but I trust you to honor my wishes in this. I want Kaitrin to have the house on the Consortium campus, and everything ...

"What?" Kaitrin whispered.

"Read the rest of it," said Rianna gently.

... everything that is in it. If I never get to live there with her, I flatter myself she might sense something of me there – that our spirits might come together somehow, by some miracle. I know it's only a foolish, romantic thought, bred out of my yearning ...

"Oh, Griffen," Kaitrin whispered. "Rianna, I can't take this away from you."

"Read, Kaitrin."

... and she will probably want to sell the house because it's a bit far from where she works, but if she does, that's all right. I don't believe that you, Ree, really want the place. If I were gone, there would be no need for you to ever come to Okloh, and as far as the contents, Kaitrin is a very generous, giving person with a strong sense of fairness. I know that whatever you might want out of my possessions, she would give you, or share with you. There isn't much of any real interest – a hologram of Dad and me on the boat when I was seven and some pictures of Dad when he was boy and of you and Gerit and whatnot. Otherwise, just the material stuff every man accumulates.

Will you do all this for me, Rianna? I would be grateful beyond eternity. I love Kaitrin Oliva more than any man should ever love a woman and I owe her some recompense for accepting me with all my failings, even if it is paltry and inadequate. I want to come home, and I'm planning on coming home, and I'm hoping to be healed and have a child and a normal life. But you never know. I may be past healing. But if anyone can do it, it is my Kait, my best beloved, and I'll never let harm come to her, even if I have to return from beyond the grave. Fondly, your indebted brother, Griffen Gwidian.

When both women had pulled themselves together, Kaitrin said, "Rianna, I can pay you for the house out of the insurance money. And his personal things – I'll store them till you get a chance to look. I don't want to deprive you of anything. But are you really willing to do this? To give up ... "

"He's right that I have no use for the house. I would certainly sell it. But his things – that's a little harder for me. Could we look through them together? I'll be glad to share copies of the pictures with you. And I wouldn't mind having one or two pieces out of his folk art collection – and maybe a gold chain that was our father's, and the chronometer from our father's sailboat ... "

"Of course, of course! Oh, Rianna, I can't believe this! I was going to have to look for a new apartment. I'm living in this tiny postgrad flat – it's been a joke for years."

"Can you bear to live in his house?"

"I've never been in it," said Kaitrin, "but I think he's right, Rianna. I'll find a piece of him there that will be comforting, not painful. Wait – I want to show you something." And Kaitrin ran to get the book that Griffen had commissioned for her.

They sat on a sofa and looked at it together. "There are so many strange parallels in this story," said Kaitrin, "that I never realized. Nothing exact, of course, but the mythical Gwydion loved his sister and created the illusive ideal woman for his son. And the invocation at the end addressing 'Gwydion the Golden-tongued' ... When I found out about this book, I was at a low point just as Griff was when he met me, except suicide would be out of the question for me. But when I got this, it was as if his spirit were in it – it came and lay beside me in my mind and spoke to me and comforted me. I realized that I had been pushing his spirit away because of all the pain his physical absence caused me. After that, I was able to make the decision to begin this quest – to seek for what I didn't understand. So maybe it will be the same with the house. I'll find something of his spirit there and it will comfort me and make me stronger. But I can pay you ... "

"No pay," said Rianna. "Griff would never forgive me if I did that. Why don't we work out the legal issues before you go home? Then you can take the lock-down codes back with you. I'll come visit in a month or so and look at his things. In the meantime, we can stay in touch."

"Oh, Rianna, you have no idea how happy all this makes me! Do you know, in the beginning I didn't think I even wanted to see you? I think I was afraid you would hate me for getting him killed."

"Do you know," said Rianna, hugging Kaitrin with a little laugh, "that in the beginning I wasn't too keen on meeting you, either? I wondered if you could possibly understand how much I loved him."

Then she said, "There is really only one more thing we have to do."

"I know," said Kaitrin. "We have to visit Griffen's grave."

* * *

The two women were exhausted and decided it would be better to wait until morning for the ultimate, most draining ritual. Gerit had left on his field trip, Charles was at school, and Kaitrin and Griffen's sister tried to rest in the cool, silent house.

But Kaitrin asked Rianna, "Is there something on the grave to hold flowers?"

"I had a small holder set into the stone. It isn't for large bouquets."

"That's perfect. Is there a florist in Rusberg who could deliver something yet today?"

"Hartmen's. They'll do same day delivery for a small extra fee. Any time we need flowers, we use them."

So Kaitrin ordered an offering, along with a large arrangement of autumn flowers to present to Rianna as a token of gratitude. Charles came home from school and they had a relaxed dinner, laughing over his tribulations with language study, which was not his strong suit. They carefully avoided the topic that had occupied them so intensely earlier in the day.

Kaitrin went to bed, but slumber eluded her. Her mind ran endlessly over the words from Griffen's communications, particularly at the end – *If anyone can heal me, it is my Kait, my best beloved ... I'll never let harm come to her, even if I have to return from beyond the grave ...* And when she finally fell asleep, she slipped not into a dream but into nightmare.

She stood on a strand in the starlight and something was coming up out of the sea toward her – washing up a little farther with each surge of the tide. As it came nearer, she wanted to run away, but she was paralyzed with dread and could not move. Then she saw that the thing was a man – the body of a man – and as she watched in fascinated horror, it sat up and she saw that it was her love, bloated and swollen like a drowned man, with a hole in his side, and a hand and part of his face torn away. She tried to cry out but no sound would come, and then she was holding him against her breast in the cyst once again, but his body remained defaced by its sojourn in the sea.

And she saw his lips move and heard his voice, but the two were not synchronized. *Kait, I would never have let* you *die ... I thought you could heal me. You knew I was afraid of drowning. You promised to keep me safe. Why did you let me die?*

She clutched him, trying to groan his name, and pieces of his flesh came away in her hands.

Kaitrin woke with a loud shriek, jerking upright in the bed. In a moment a nightgowned form appeared in the doorway. "Kaitrin? I heard you screaming all the way in the other wing! Were you having bad dream?"

The light level brightened. Rianna came and sat down on the bed and took Kaitrin in her arms. "Kaitrin, not you – not you, too ... Can you tell me?"

So Kaitrin told Griffen's sister what she had dreamed. "I never have that kind of dream, Rianna. What's happening to me? I told him I never had that kind of dream. What's happening?"

"Oh, Kaitrin, I've seen too many hints and I so dread this for you. Why do you cling to so much guilt about his death?"

Kaitrin clutched at Rianna's arms, gasping. "Because I could have saved him, you know. The Seer Kwi'ga'ga'tei kept having visions – her Goddess was demanding that I enter the Shshi fortress. And I said I would, and that ended Griffen's joy from the horse-dream – he just couldn't accept that I would be all right in there. And the more he protested, the more stubborn I got. Oh, he was so right about me, Rianna! I was so stubborn – so arrogant – so sure of my course ... On our wedding night I promised to keep him from harm, without ever thinking that promises aren't just words, or easy – they have to be worked at to be kept, and maybe even sacrificed for.

"So I should have stopped then – not gone in – told the Shshi we had to leave. But I didn't, and twice I went into the fortress and he seemed to be enduring it. But I could sense it was the old protective facade, and even so, I took advantage of his love and his forbearance in order to get what I wanted. It was *I* – *I* – *I* ... it was always what *I* wanted – *I* couldn't give up my work ... And he was suffering a crisis and *I* wasn't willing to acknowledge it!

"Rianna, I could have stopped it at any time, but no, even after I realized – after Trea made me realize – that I had to choose between my work and my love – even then I told him, 'Two more times. I'll go in two more times and then we'll go back to Earth.' I could have stopped it then. And after I went in and saw the Queen and promised her I'd come back, and then Griffen had that breakdown about forgiveness, when he cried and I got sharp with him because I was so tired, and Trea came in and helped – even then, I could have stopped it! But still I had to go back one more time. Oh, Rianna, surely you can understand why I feel guilty!"

Rianna silently held Kaitrin against her shoulder, caressing her shorn hair.

"Trea said his breakdown wasn't such a bad thing ... the layers were coming off ... he would find the light soon ... the infection would cleanse itself ... "

"Did your Pozú doctor really say those things?"

"Yes, those were her words! And maybe if we could only have come home and lived a life without so many distractions ... but we were thrown against that mythic, elemental culture and everything just interacted – escalated ...

"But I could have changed everything, even to the very end. And I didn't. I always felt something was unfinished – something in my relationship with the Shshi. I still get inklings of that – uneasy feelings ... But it would have been better to leave everything unfinished on that planet and bring Griffen home to heal than to do what I did. He loved me and he seemed to think that I was his savior – the perfect woman – I don't know why ... and I loved him – I still love him, Rianna – and I don't know why. And I let the one I loved the most in the world be destroyed. And that's why I hold so much guilt about his death – because I *am* guilty!"

In a moment Rianna said, "Kaitrin, Griffen mentioned a couple of times how much he loved your hair. I saw it in the wedding vid. Why did you cut it?"

Kaitrin struggled away from Rianna, hunching over cross-legged on the bed. "Because it smelled of – oh, hell! That isn't the reason! I cut it off to punish myself – because I couldn't stand the thought that because of my own failure, I would never feel his touch on my hair again."

"I thought perhaps something like that. Kaitrin, can't you see what you're doing?"

Kaitrin, snuffling against her hand, stared blearily at Rianna. "What?"

"You are taking his guilt into your soul."

"His guilt? But ... "

"And that frightens me a lot, Kaitrin. You're making yourself responsible for his death the same way he made himself responsible for our mother's death. But you are no more guilty in his death than he was in hers."

"But ... "

"You could not possibly comprehend the depth of his need because he had never been able to express it to you. And, knowing my brother as well as I think I did, I believe he would have told you to keep your promise and go back into the fortress that final time. You had assured him it would be the last. He would have understood that it wasn't unreasonable and I know he understood how much it meant to you. So even if you had tried to change things ... "

Kaitrin hit the bed with her fists. "But if I had been insightful enough – strong enough – less self-centered – I would have seen what was needed! I could have controlled things – made everybody do what was best ... What? Oh!" Flinging her head up, she glared at Rianna's reproachful little smile. "Oh, I see ... That's something like what Griffen said about the last days with his mother, isn't it?"

Rianna nodded and they sat briefly without speaking.

"But I'm not a scared, compliant little child," said Kaitrin. "I'm an adult. I should have known what was happening, and what to do, and how to get it done."

"Being an adult doesn't ensure that we'll never fall short or make mistakes – far from it!" said Rianna. "Didn't the Mythmakers say something like, humans can only strive for but will never attain perfection?"

In a moment she continued, "Kaitrin, learning to acknowledge that you have flaws can be a positive thing. But the wisest of us can't see the future – at least not on this planet! – and there was no real indication that you were in danger. You had returned safely from your earlier visits – why should the final one have been any different? It was much more irrational for Griffen to be so convinced that there was peril – more irrational for him to cling so obsessively to you.

"We make choices all the time and we can't tell from one moment to the next what will happen, no matter how carefully we try to discern all the alternatives. I could slip on that throw rug on my way back to my room and hit my head on the table corner and die of a brain injury. Would you be guilty of my death because it was your nightmare that caused me to be walking down the hall? Griffen had to try to save you because the extremity of his guilt demanded a sacrifice. If he had restrained himself and not run out and you had died, it would have redoubled that guilt and utterly destroyed him. In a way what he did was a victory. He died like the hero that he never saw himself to be.

"And if you perpetuate this cycle of meaningless guilt – the plea for forgiveness, the need for reparation – then his guilt and his nightmare will never end. Break the cycle and then his guilt will be expunged and so will yours, and his spirit will stay whole and healed in your heart's memory forever, just like the Gwydion in your book said in that quotation you showed me."

Kaitrin had been listening carefully with her head bowed. "When Griff was dying," she said in a small voice, "I told him what he had done was heroic and he seemed to like that."

Rianna smiled tremulously. "Kaitrin, when Griffen was dying, did he say anything about forgiveness?"

"Once, when I begged him not to leave me. He said, 'Forgive me, I couldn't let you die.' Several times he said that last – 'I couldn't let you die.'"

Rianna pondered for a while. "I think in that instance he was asking forgiveness for being forced to leave you, not for his crime … " Again she sat silent.

At length she said, "You know, Kaitrin, I'm really beginning to believe that he was healed, or at least that the healing had begun, as your doctor said. It happened when you gave him the unconditional forgiveness. He was still raw and vulnerable and unaware, but if the guilt had been as heavy in him as it had been all his life, he would have been much less at peace whilst he was dying."

"Oh, Rianna, that reminds me of something else Trea said, when I talked to her before I left Okloh. She said she could see part of an answer in Griffen's soul, and that there was more peace in him when he was dying that one might have expected, and that there was also gratitude. That puzzled me."

"Gratitude ... I think, Kaitrin, for that absolution that you had given him."

"Oh ... yes ... that may be what it was ... So ... "

"The woman who wore the symbol of his mother's ring had forgiven him for his sin against her sex and he had atoned by saving the life of that same woman. Peace really had come within his reach. It's – rather a wondrous thing ... " Rianna took a deep breath. "Kaitrin, think carefully – which reflects the real spirit of Griffen Gwidian? The thing of joy that came to you from the book he left for you, or the grotesque, accusatory apparition that your guilt conjured up in your nightmare? There – of course you know the answer. Don't hold on to the guilt, Kaitrin, I implore you, or you will forever be distorting his spirit into a travesty."

In a moment, Kaitrin whispered, "So I took his guilt into myself."

"Symbolically, yes."

"And how do I let go of it, Rianna? Of this nightmare that I just had for the first time?"

"Try to look into your soul."

"I tried that when I wanted to pray while he was dying. All I saw were questions."

"Find the guilt amongst the questions. Think of it as a dark bird caught in a net of questions. Then reach in and tear the net with your hands, and let the dark bird fly away."

Kaitrin sat with her eyes closed, trying to see into her own soul. Then she looked up. "That's a splendid metaphor, Rianna. I'll try to do that. I'm not sure I can accomplish what you say in a minute or two or even by any act of will, but I understand what you've said to me."

Rianna took a long breath. "I think you'll be successful,

Kaitrin. You are adult, just as you said – an intelligent, mature woman grounded in a love for life, with a lot of common sense. Griffen was a frightened, impressionable, confused child when he took on his guilt, and in a sense he remained that his whole life. I think you will succeed where he could not."

In a moment, Kaitrin said, "Where does the guilt go, Rianna? When you let go of it? When the dark bird flies away, where does it go?"

Rianna laughed, a little startled. "Oh, I don't know. Into the air ... " And she added a little whimsically, "Into space, perhaps. Maybe it goes onto some scapegoat somewhere, in another reality or on another world."

Kaitrin sat dumb, then she frowned. The words stirred something in her, something half-forgotten, something that remained unfinished. Then the feeling faded, but it left an impression in her mind that kept returning to her.

Chapter 17

Fear no more the heat o' the sun,
    Nor the furious winter's rages;
Thou thy worldly task hast done,
    Home art gone, and ta'en thy wages.
Golden lads and girls all must
As chimney sweepers, come to dust. ...

No exorciser harm thee!
    Nor no witchcraft charm thee!
Ghost unlaid forbear thee!
    Nothing ill come near thee!
Quiet consummation have;
And renownèd be thy grave!
      – from William Shakespeare, *Cymbeline*

The following morning, Rianna and Kaitrin set out for the cemetery as soon as the hopper returned from taking Charles to school. Kaitrin carried a small packet carefully done up in plastifilm.

Rianna asked, "How did you sleep after I left?"

"All right, after a while," said Kaitrin. "I didn't have any more nightmares. How did you sleep, Rianna?"

Griffen's sister smiled ruefully. "Not too well. I lay there wondering if I could take my own advice about the dark bird."

"I think we always keep some regret when we've made

532

mistakes," said Kaitrin. "Perhaps we should. The alternative is indifference."

"Regret and guilt don't need to be the same thing. The goal is not to let these things consume us and destroy our lives."

Kaitrin stared out over the muted colors of the veldt as they bounced along. "I'm going to have to be leaving."

"This afternoon I'll copy those pictures and messages for you and we'll spend some time conferring with the lawyers about the house. It'll take a couple of weeks for the deeds to transfer, but I can request an immediate exchange of the lock-down codes."

"That's no problem. I mean to be in Afrik at least another week."

"You're going to see Emmi? Do you want me to message her for you?"

"No, I'll do it myself, if you don't mind. I guess I rather like to take people by surprise."

"I did tell her you were coming to visit me. But she doesn't know that you're actually here. I'm sorry."

"Oh, that's all right. At least this way she won't faint when I appear on the port screen. Rianna, have you talked to Emmi like this about Griffen?"

"No. I couldn't talk to her whilst he was alive for the same reasons I couldn't talk to you. And so much time had elapsed and he no longer had any part in her life, so I thought it best not to stir things up. You don't plan ... ?"

"Oh, no. But I thought I should understand how much she knew, so I wouldn't put my foot in my mouth."

"I think you'll like Emmi, Kaitrin. She's a very warm and caring and vital person. But that visit won't take a week."

"I'm going up to Nouvelle Victoire and spend some time with my contract father's family. I thought I should do that while I was over here. I may even make a little safari into the Preserves, for old time's sake."

Rianna nodded. "Get in touch with me when you get back to Okloh."

"Rianna, I hope we stay friends for a long, long time."

"Oh, I'm planning on it! Here's the gate. The cemetery is enclosed within a physical fence as an additional protection – to make sure animals don't tear up the graves."

They drove along a narrow track that led slightly uphill. At either side, scattered among acacia scrub, were widely spaced graves with memorial stones of varying ages, colors, and styles. Kaitrin's heart was in her throat.

They parked and got out to walk the rest of the way, toward an area where no graves were visible. Rianna said, "Gerit's parents are over that way. This section was set aside for their children. So far we've been lucky – nobody to bury. Gerit's section won't be crowded. Only Griffen, and most likely Gerit and me. And you, if you want it. Gwinneth is on the brink of contracting with a fellow economist who's from Ind, so I don't know where she'll end up. And god knows I hope Charly won't need a grave for another eighty years. Here we are."

They were approaching a large, flat stone at the top of a little swell of treeless ground. It was a natural oval of dark granite about forty centimeters high that covered the whole grave; it had been left natively rough and sloping on the sides but was cut smooth and polished on the top. The women stood looking down on it.

At the top end of the oval, inside a border curved to parallel the natural edge, were engraved several images – a sailing ship slanting its bow upward toward a star, a pair of masks such as were sometimes worn in the production of ancient dramas, a woman's hand reaching toward a butterfly that hovered just out of reach.

In the center of the oval were the words:

Griffen Gwidian
Born May 15, 171
In Kardif, Islands of Britan
Died February 5, 215
On the planet 2 Giotta 17A

We are such stuff as dreams are made on
And our little life is rounded with a sleep.

With a whispered sigh, Kaitrin knelt beside the stone and ran her hands over it, tracing the letters, the images, with her finger. *Griffen. This is where you are – part of you ...*

"*The Tempest*," she said. "Rianna, it's perfect."

"I thought so," said Rianna gruffly.

"And the symbols – so right ... " But Kaitrin was frowning,

534

touching the blank lower third of the polished surface. "But this is empty. Maybe you should have spread the symbols around."

Rianna had knelt across the stone from her. "That's for you."

"What? For my name?"

"No! For you to add whatever you would like. This memorial is for your love even more than mine."

"Oh! I see. I can put – my own … "

"Think about what you'd like to put there and I'll have the engraver come out and add it."

Kaitrin knelt in silence, tracing Griffen's name over and over. Then she looked up at Rianna's face. "I already know what I want. Two figures of Pegassus – do you know … ?"

"Yes. The winged horse."

"I want two beautiful figures of Pegassus flying side by side, with a man riding on one and a woman on the other. I want stars around them. And underneath, I want what I said at the wedding – that Griffen learned how to say to me – *dwi'n dy garu, 'nghariad.*" Kaitrin's voice trembled and a tear trickled silently down her cheek and fell on the stone.

"That's the ancient language of West Britan, isn't it? It means, *I love you, my dear*? Like the other things you said?"

"Yes."

"Did Griffen really learn to say it?"

"Oh, yes. His voice … The way he said it, you'd never know the language isn't spoken anymore."

The two women knelt silent by the grave for a while. Then Rianna said hoarsely, "Be sure to leave a transcription of that so we'll get the spelling right."

"I will. Oh, what's become of the flower? Here, I dropped it." Kaitrin found the packet, fumbled with the wrap.

"The container is at the top there. It's small," said Rianna.

"So is my flower." Kaitrin held up one Crystal rose, the stem sealed in a vial of water. "I wasn't sure you'd have these here."

"Oh, yes, they're very popular."

"Griffen sent me some before the dinner date in Okloh."

Kaitrin inserted the flower in the container and it stood up bravely, glimmering amber and silver against the dark granite.

"Rianna, I'd like to do something trite and romantic. Would it be all right with you if I arranged for the florist to deliver one of these every week and put it here? I know it's silly ... "

"I don't think it is," said Rianna softly. "I probably won't bring flowers very often – not that I won't be thinking about him ... But the family usually puts something on all the graves for Remembrance Day or for birth and death days, and then it's a large bouquet in its own container – rather impersonal."

"If you ever want to bring some little thing of your own, stick it in with my rose."

"I will. Hartmen's always has at least one deliveryman with security clearance for the gates. I'll arrange for them to have direct entry to the cemetery."

Thus speaking of the mundane artifices of grief, Griffen Gwidian's two best loves knelt beside his grave.

Then Rianna stood up. "Take all the time you want," she said. "I'll be in the hopper."

Kaitrin knelt alone with the dry breeze of the veldt blowing astringently on her wet face. From a distance came the coughing of baboons, while nearer at hand birds twittered in the thorn brush. Against the domed gazing-globe of the sky an eagle circled, casting a moving shadow. She continued to run her finger over the stone.

Love, this is as close to you as I'll ever be able to come. It breaks my heart that I never really knew you until after you were gone. But that isn't true – I did know you ... every inch of you in the darkness – every fold of your ear and pulse of your throat ... and your spirit will live on in me so that we will forever be close to each other. And I gave you my blood, so some of my body is lying here in the earth mingled with yours.

On our wedding night I held your soul in my hands and didn't know what a precious thing I had. Perhaps it's a good thing I didn't know. No woman should have as much power over a man as I had over you, Griffen Gwidian. Forgive me for not understanding that power or using it wisely. Forgive me as I forgave you on the night before you died – without qualification – without conditions. I forgive you now for leaving me. Goodbye for this time, 'nghariad. Wait for me. To you it won't seem long.

Kaitrin fleetingly touched the smooth spot where soon the horses would fly. Then she bent and kissed Griffen's name, rose to her feet, and left his grave to the sky.

Chapter 18

The snare of desire that bound us in is broken;
Softly, in sorrow, we draw apart, and see,
Far off, the beauty we thought our flesh had
    captured, –
The star we longed to be but could not be.
    – from Conrad Aiken, *The Divine Pilgrim, IV,*
    Senlin: A Biography

The events people had not foreseen Kaitrin's odyssey and she had managed to negotiate the early part of her itinerary undetected. But to be safe, she wore her hat and dark glasses and a cape against the cooling weather as she emerged from the Exurban Rail in Jonnsberg two mornings after the visit to Griffen Gwidian's grave. She checked in at a hotel and sat in front of the room's relay port trying to summon up nerve for a final act.

At length she spoke an ID and got a recorded reply, print only. *The persons who receive messages at this ID are unavailable. You are welcome to leave word.*

Of course. Emmi would be teaching at her school at this time of day. Kaitrin left no word. She had a long lunch and then spent some time wandering around the Consortium campus. In the evening she tried again.

A face appeared on the screen – a woman with plump, rosy cheeks; a small, full-lipped mouth; large dark eyes; winged eyebrows. Her hair was luxuriant, a lovely shade of dark auburn. She had exquisite skin. "Shermayne here," she said.

Oh, dear, she's a lot better looking than I am, thought Kaitrin, and she began, "I'm Prf. ... "

But Emmi interrupted her. "Oh, I know who you are. Rianna told me you were coming to visit. You're the woman Griffen Gwidian finally married."

Kaitrin felt a little chastened. "That's right. My name is Kaitrin Oliva. You're Emmi Shermayne. I was wondering if I might meet you somewhere for a talk – get to know you a little bit. I'm on a sort of a quest, you see."

Emmi was silent, one eyebrow bending. "Rianna said she imagined you would want to meet me. I, uh ... I suppose ... "

"If you'd rather not ... " Kaitrin began quickly.

"No, I ... It's just that this is all quite painful. I had gotten pretty well adjusted to what happened ten years ago, but his death ... "

A voice sounded in the background, a childish voice. Kaitrin felt a thrill of fear. Emmi turned and called over her shoulder, "No, it's not for you. Keep on practicing – I'll be in soon." Lowering her voice, she said, "Why don't you come here to my apartment tomorrow afternoon? I teach only in the mornings – I can afford to do that because of the stipend I get from ... But I don't know, he gets home from school about 1500h."

Kaitrin could hear muffled flute music, a complex exercise phrase repeated in a series of variations. "Ms. Shermayne, I would love to meet your son."

"Well ... I don't know. I don't especially want him to know who you are."

A million questions were flying through Kaitrin's mind, but she thought it prudent to stifle them. Emmi was saying, "Come about 1330h and we'll see. And you can call me Emmi."

Kaitrin smiled, took a deep breath. "And I'm Kaitrin. I have your address – 3002D Cape Court? I'll see you then."

*   *   *

The apartment was in an edifice called a cube building, where each unit had two floors and shared no contiguous wall with any other unit, like a chaotic pile of cubes joined only at the corners and edges. Most of the utility and enviro conduits were carried in an exposed decorative framework. Kaitrin had heard of these structures but had never seen one; Southern Afrik was noted for being on the cutting edge of innovative residential architecture.

Emmi opened the door. "Hello," she said. "Come in."

Kaitrin did so. "Thanks. I was admiring your building. We don't have these in Okloh yet. I think some have been built in New Washinten."

Inside, the rooms were small but convenient, with a lot of built-in furniture. Each level had two windows that overlooked an inner courtyard full of container plantings, espaliered fruit trees, and bright-colored playground equipment. The kitchen was visible through a glass wall at the rear of the living room and a little office with a port wall occupied a corner alcove. A narrow stairway with an ornate balustrade ascended through the ceiling in one corner.

"We just moved in last year," Emmi was saying, busying herself with a teapot at the dining table. "Actually, it's smaller than where we were before, but it's much newer and closer to the school and it's so architecturally interesting. They're building more and more houses with windows these days. Please sit down. Do you drink tea?"

Kaitrin seated herself at the table. She was beginning to doubt she would ever become a votary of the beverage, but she said, "Yes, please."

"I made shortbread."

"Oh, you didn't have to go to any trouble."

"I didn't. I made these yesterday afternoon before I even knew you were coming. Lew loves them."

"Lew ... "

Emmi seated herself. "My son. Griffen's son."

"Yes ... You named him ... "

"For Griffen's father. Yes."

"Do you know, in all the conversations – with Griff or with Rianna – your son's name was never mentioned?" *My word, another parallel. Gwydion ... Arianrhod ... Llew Llaw Gyffes ...*

"Well, it just seemed right. Here, have some shortbread." Emmi looked up again and then said almost defiantly, "I guess I thought maybe if I named him after Griff's father, it might encourage Griff to come back to me."

Kaitrin ducked her head. *This is going to be a lot harder than meeting Felisha ...*

Grasping at something to say, Kaitrin said, "Your surname ... does your son use that name?"

"Yes. It wouldn't have been appropriate to use 'Gwidian.'"

"No, of course not. What kind of name is 'Shermayne'? It's an unusual spelling. Was it originally 'Sherman' or maybe 'Jermane'?"

Emmi laughed. "I get asked that a lot. Our family has French ancestors way back and I've been told this is some kind of anglified French. The 'mayne' part comes from the word for 'hand.' I don't know what the 'Sher' is."

Kaitrin absently sifted the French compartments of her mind for cognates. *Sher-main. La main sher. La main chère ... la main serrée ... la main sûre ...*

La main sûre! Kaitrin sat up straight, her eyes widening. It could not be! That kind of coincidence – it was simply incredible! There had to be an intentional will at work – but that was preposterous!

"Arianrhod laughed aloud and clapped her hands. 'That was a good shot!' she cried. 'By the gods, it is with a steady hand that the lleu *hit the bird.'"*

And Gwydion had answered, "'... *now he is named; and good enough is his name. From this day men shall call him Llew Llaw Gyffes.'*

Llaw Gyffes means 'Sure Hand.' But the use of lleu *is a mystery today ...*"

Emmi was staring at Kaitrin a little defensively. "Is something the matter?"

"No, no. But I just thought of the strangest coincidence ... " *What are the odds that the sons of my Gwidian and of the mythical Gwydion should both receive the surname "Sure Hand" from their mothers?* "It's nothing, Emmi. What were we talking about?"

"My surname. You know, Kaitrin, I wish I could have called my son 'Lew Gwidian,' but Griffen refused to have any part in our lives and it would have seemed strange and required constant explanation. What did you do to hold him? Weren't you afraid he would leave you? Didn't you know about his reputation for – for never staying long with any woman?"

"Oh, Emmi, I ... Yes, I did know, and at first ... But who is to account for why men, or women either, fall in love? Griffen fell in love with me and that was the way it was. I didn't try to hold him. At first I tried to do everything I could to reject him. But I ended up loving him so much – so much … "

"Well … like you say – no accounting … I saw the vid of the wedding – in fact, I bought an offload of it … " Emmi looked a little sheepish. " … and the way he spoke – he never said anything that passionate to me. Isn't it embarrassing, to have that splashed all over the pop links? Everybody at school was talking about it. The people there don't know I was involved with him – I was still in university when I knew him, so I have a different set of acquaintances now. That's another reason I'm glad Lew doesn't use his name."

Emmi seemed to be getting a bit wound up. She stopped to take a drink of tea. "But, Kaitrin, Rianna tells me that you made Griff happier than she had ever seen him, and I can't be anything but glad for that. Years ago I gave up thinking that he might ever come back to me and I'm not sorry that he finally found happiness – someone he could love. I feel he needed that. He always seemed so fragile somehow, underneath all that controlled exterior. But I wish it could have been me."

"You've never contracted or married, Emmi?" asked Kaitrin softly.

"Oh, no. It would never be the same as with Griff."

"I'm sure of that," said Kaitrin. "I feel quite the same way."

The two women smiled tentatively at each other. Then Emmi said, "I couldn't help seeing your ring. Those plain bands are so uncommon – very elegant, I think. I believe I saw that ring once. It belonged to Griffen, didn't it?"

Surprised, Kaitrin twisted the ring on her finger. "It was his mother's wedding ring. You saw it in the vid." She pulled it off and handed it to Emmi.

Emmi inspected it curiously. "No, I don't mean there. One time I came into the bedroom unexpectedly and Griffen was standing at the chest looking at that ring. I don't know where he kept it – I never saw it in a drawer or anything. He was very private with his things. Anyway, I came in and I said, 'What's that?' And he looked startled and started to put it away as if I'd caught him doing something he shouldn't, but then he stopped – I guess he knew that would strike me as odd – and he just said, 'Oh, only a family heirloom.' I came up and tried to look at it, but he wouldn't let go of it and I could feel him pushing me away. So I only said, 'Very pretty,' or some such, and went and did something else. I never saw the ring again." Emmi handed the object back to Kaitrin. "I guess he finally found somebody that he didn't want to push away."

Kaitrin bent over her teacup. There was a pause. Finally Kaitrin broke the awkward silence. "Where are you from originally, Emmi?"

"I was born here in Jonnsberg. My dad is a Professor of mathematics at the Consortium."

"Is that right?"

"In me it came out as music. I got a recorder when I was three and I've been playing woodwinds and flutes ever since. I thought about a concert career, but Lew changed all that. And I don't know that I'm good enough, anyway. So I've never been anywhere much. I was only twenty-two when I met Griff. I thought it was so romantic that he was British and had lived by the sea and at Oxkam and in Ostrailia. I thought everything he did was romantic. Wasn't he the most romantic man you ever knew?"

Kaitrin nodded, smiling mistily, thinking of how he had sobbed in her arms on their wedding night – of his words when he was dying, *It does make me a bit of a hero, doesn't it?*

"Where are you from?" Emmi was asking.

"I was born in Pikes Precinct in Midammerik. My mother works for the IQDB ... " And Kaitrin launched into her usual bio.

"Oh, well, you're a lot more Griff's intellectual equal than I was," Emmi said.

"Oh, I doubt that. Besides, what Griff needed was ... "

"Was what? What did you have that could hold him?"

"Oh, Emmi, I don't know. He just needed love, as you said. Real love."

Dissatisfied, Emmi said, "My love was real. Why was your love better than mine?" But Kaitrin had no answer for her.

Then Emmi said, "I'm going to tell you something that even Rianna doesn't know. I'm don't know why I'm telling you. Maybe because Griff is dead now and you loved him, too. But the reason Lew was born is that I purposely stopped using contraceptives. I began to realize that Griffen was going to leave and not ask me to go with him. I would say things like, 'I'd really like to live in Okloh. I'd love to have a new experience.' Or I would say, 'I've heard the Northwest Consortium has a great music program.' And he would shut down – he wouldn't talk about anything that involved my going to Okloh.

"So I thought, surely, if I have his child, he'll take me with him. First, I sort of delicately broached the subject – would he ever like to have children? – et cetera, et cetera. And he would talk all around the subject and I'd never get a real answer. But he was such a self-effacing, considerate, gentle man in his heart – I couldn't believe that he would be cruel enough to turn his back on his own child. So when it was time for the annual contraceptive injection, I only pretended I'd gotten it, hoping I'd know I was pregnant before he had to leave. But his acceptance came through earlier than he had expected and he just left, abruptly. I guess he got tired of me. But yet, the night before he told me he was leaving, we had the most wonderful sex we'd ever had. I shouldn't talk about that sort of thing with you ... "

"I understand," said Kaitrin softly. "Don't be embarrassed. And I don't believe he got tired of you."

"Then I thought surely he would send for me when he found out. Rianna thought there was hope that he would. But he didn't. I only got this formal communication from him saying that he was very sorry he hadn't been more careful and, if I didn't want to abort – as if I would ever have aborted a child of his! – he would see to it that I had plenty of support. And he has, always. He paid the rest of my living expenses for university and he kept me solvent for two years after Lew was born so I could stay home with him and he has always paid a good portion of Lew's expenses since then. But he refused to see his son. Can you comprehend that, Kaitrin? Even if he didn't want to live with me, I would have liked for Lew to know his father. Why didn't Griffen want to know his son? Was he that ashamed of me?"

"No! Definitely it wasn't that! I think it was just ... he simply felt he had to give all or nothing. And at that time, he couldn't give all."

"I still don't understand."

"I really don't either, Emmi," said Kaitrin. "Griffen will always remain – a bit of an enigma."

Then she asked, "So Lew doesn't know who his father is?"

To Kaitrin's surprise, Emmi replied, "Oh, yes, he knows. Griff might have been ashamed of me, but I was never ashamed of him or of my liaison with him. Lew knows his father was a xenoentomologist who was an expert on alien beetles – we've read some of his treatises together. He knows he came from Britan. He knows what he looked like. He has lots of friends who have only one parent for all kinds of reasons, so it seems normal to him to have nothing but a mother. I simply told him that his father is a very busy man and lives too far away to see us."

"That may not be enough as he gets older."

"I know. I kind of dread the future."

"Does Lew know his father is dead?"

Again to Kaitrin's surprise, Emmi said, "Yes, I told him. I told him he died a hero, saving a member of his expedition from the attack of a savage alien. He was a little thoughtful for a while and then he said, 'I'm glad my father was a brave man. I wish I could have known him, though.' And that's about all he said … Now, I'm sorry."

Kaitrin had pressed her napkin against her mouth. "No, it's all right. I'm through with this weepy stuff, Emmi, at least in public. Does Lew know who Rianna is?"

"He has met her, but only as Rianna Bock, a friend of mine."

"Ah, I see. And he doesn't know about me. What if he sees that vid? And all that garbage on the pop links?"

"I keep pretty strict filters on what he sees. But he's likely to learn everything before too long. I guess I'll face it when it happens. And, no, he doesn't know that his father was married. I would just as soon keep it that way, but as I said, I probably can't forever."

Again Kaitrin said, "I would love to meet Lew, Emmi. Does he look like Griffen?"

"Not exactly, but there's something about him … Actually, it's uncanny how much he reminds me of him."

"Oh, god," breathed Kaitrin, bowing her head.

Emmi regarded her compassionately. "Were you and he planning to have children?"

"Yes. We … Yes."

"He took a long time to want them."

"I think he wanted them when he was with you. It's only ... Emmi, he couldn't face – he wasn't ready to face – a lifetime commitment ... " It was not totally accurate, but it was the closest Kaitrin could come to what Griffen had told Rianna – *I think I'm too afraid, to have to keep hiding from the same person for so long* ...

Emmi seemed to take a decision. "All right. If you stay another thirty minutes, Lew will come home from school. I have a lot of friends – teachers, musicians, actors – so he's used to meeting new people. He'll just accept you as one of my academic colleagues."

"Oh, Emmi, I would so like that. You know, I'm really glad Griffen had a son by somebody else, if it couldn't be with me. The primal urge to perpetuate the genes, you know? By the way, I picked up a little scarp at a literary shop on campus yesterday. It's a tale that's a favorite of mine and this shop has produced a nicely illustrated version. Do you mind if I give it to Lew? I assure you, it's perfectly respectable!"

Emmi laughed. "I don't doubt it. What is it?"

"It's a wry little piece from one of the Great Fantasists of the 20th century – a man named Tolkien. If I remember rightly, he was from Southern Afrik originally, although he lived in Britan most of his life. The tale is called *Farmer Giles of Ham.*"

Emmi was shaking her head. "I don't know it, but if you say it's good, I'm sure it is."

Then Kaitrin asked about the theater work that Griffen and Emmi had done together and they whiled away the moments over that, while Kaitrin's heart beat faster and her mouth dried. *"It's uncanny how much he reminds me of him,"* Emmi had said.

The door banged. "Hey, Mum! I'm home!"

"Over here, Lew. I've got company."

Her heart jumping, Kaitrin turned around to see Lew Shermayne striding toward them with an exuberantly bouncy step. He was carrying a school bag and an amorphous case that probably held a technoplayer of some kind. He came to stand by the table.

The ten-year-old was tall for his age, sturdy and solid-looking. Griffen's blue eyes, deep-set, with long, dark lashes, stared at Kaitrin. The mouth, wider than his mother's but with lips fuller than his father's, was flanked by the dimples that time had converted into lines in Griffen's face. The nose was on course to develop into the classic Gwidian configuration. Only Emmi's full, rosy cheeks and the auburn tint of the hair and brows showed that this was not Griffen Gwidian at the age of ten, but the hair was dark enough not to distract from the impression. Kaitrin noted that his hair was a bit untidy, with a cowlick standing straight up from the crown. She could hear echoes of Griffen's voice in her mind *… If I don't keep my hair short, it gets a bit unruly, like my father's …*

Emmi reached out to smooth down the errant lock, saying, "Kaitrin, meet my son Lew Shermayne. Lew, this is Prf. Oliva from Midammerik. She's visiting Jonnsberg for a few days."

Lew ducked slightly to evade his mother's hand, giving Kaitrin a grin that said, *You know how mothers are! Come on, stand up for me!* But all he said was "Happy to meet you, Prf. Oliva. What instrument do you play?"

"None. I'm an anthropologist," said Kaitrin, trying to keep her voice steady.

"Oh. Sorry, I just supposed. A lot of Mum's friends are musicians. Uh … " Lew was eyeing the plate. "Mum, is it all right if I have … ?"

Emmi laughed. "Go ahead. Sit down. Not the tea. It's cold as stone."

Lew dropped his bags on the floor, sat down, and lit into the shortbread.

"Are you a musician?" asked Kaitrin.

"Trying to be." Lew pointed to the case. "E-strings right now. I'm learning keyboard, too. And Mum started teaching me the acoustic flute before I was even in school."

"He's really very good," said Emmi. "Tell Prf. Oliva about *Midsummer.*"

"Oh, that. Last year Mum's school did a play by that old boy named Shaksper," said Lew through a mouthful of cookies, "and they thought it would be a good idea if some of us younger cubbos played the fairies. I was Puck. I had to wear this ridiculous costume – tights like a dancer and a hat with flowers – and glittery wings! That's the only thing I didn't like about it."

"I thought he looked kind of cute," said Emmi with a giggle.

Lew grimaced in disgust. "We had live music – Mum

composed some of it. You know where Puck first comes in and the other fairy sings, 'Thorough bush, thorough briar ...' – they talked blinking odd in those days, didn't they? Anyway, I played the flute while he sang that."

"Can you remember any lines from the play?" asked Emmi.

"Uh ... the first speech ... let me see ... 'I am that merry wanderer of the night. / I jest to Oberon, and make him smile, / When I a fat and bean-fed horse beguile,' – ha, ha, 'bean-fed horse!' – 'Neighing in likeness of a filly foal. / And sometimes lurk I in a gossip's bowl, / In ...' uh ... 'In ... ' I forget." Lew suddenly turned self-conscious. "Anyway, I remembered it when I had to. We got good reviews. My name was on the drama links! Score!"

"So you like to act," said Kaitrin, laughing and at the same time wondering how much longer she could hold herself together. *This would have been Griffen when he was ten, if those terrible things hadn't happened to him ...*

"I think it's a lot of fun," said Lew. "Mum says I'm a terrible showoff." The boyish grin that Kaitrin had seen on rare occasions flashed at her.

"He is. The more attention he gets, the better he likes it," said Emmi.

"What do you want to do when you grow up?" asked Kaitrin.

"Being an actor wouldn't be half bad," said Lew, critically examining another cookie. "But I'll probably be a musician, or maybe a mathematician like Granddad. I'm good at math."

"Do you like languages?" said Kaitrin.

"I don't know any except Inj. I read a lot."

"Here, speaking of reading, I brought you a little present."

"Oh, you did? Thanks!" Lew examined the portscarp as critically as he had the shortbread, then hauled out his reader and inserted it. "*Farmer Giles of Ham*," he read. "I say, what's all that gibberish?"

"Letin," said Kaitrin, suppressing hysteria. "It's translated right below. You don't have to know Letin to read the story. It's a kind of a mock-heroic tale about slaying dragons, with lots of satiric humor in it. And no, you're not too old for it! It's something people of all ages can enjoy, like *A Midsummer Night's Dream*. Actually, you might find it a bit challenging – you might even learn some new things. But maybe knowing that will spoil the story for you."

"Nah, I like learning new things – I don't understand why some cubbos think that makes you a sissy. And Granddad is always saying, all students should be challenged." Lew was scanning the beginning of the piece, one eyebrow bending more than the other, like his mother's.

"Lew, wait to read it until you're alone," admonished Emmi.

Griffen's eyes looked up one more time at Kaitrin. "Thanks again," he said. "This is really nice of you."

"You'd better go get ready for swimming practice," said Emmi.

"Yeah, I'd better," said Lew, consulting his watch. "I have to be there in an hour. We've got a meet next week." He jumped up and started to snatch another cookie, then grunted and said, "Huh. Better not eat too much. Meeting you was smashing, Prf. Oliva! I'm going to start the story tonight before I go to bed." He grabbed his bags and headed for the stairs, then turned back. "I'll be sure to write you a thank-you message, Professor. Oh, Mum's going to faint! She didn't have to remind me! Bye!" And with a final flash of that grin, he vanished up the stairs.

Kaitrin sat with her hand over her mouth, then she pressed it over her eyes. She heard Emmi say softly, "Kaitrin … "

Kaitrin gasped, lowering her hand. "So he swims?"

"Like a fish. He's very good. He's very good at a lot of things – really precocious. I know what you're thinking. Griffen was afraid of the water. Because his father drowned. I was always sorry about that, because I think it scarred him somehow. He'd have nightmares where he was drowning."

So he did give her that much insight at least, Kaitrin thought. "You're right – he still did. But, Emmi – oh, Emmi, I wish … Do you know I really wish Griffen had stayed with you? So he could have known his son. He would have been so proud of him. Lew would have made him so happy."

Emmi reached and touched Kaitrin's hand. "Now I know you must have really loved him, Kaitrin, if you can say you would have given him up so he could be happy."

Kaitrin pressed Emmi's hand in response. "You said you were glad he had finally found someone he could love, so I guess that tells me you really loved him, too."

They continued their brief moments of conversation together, the woman who could not hold Griffen Gwidian and the woman who had held him too well.

Chapter 19

It is morning, Senlin says, I ascend from darkness
And depart on the winds of space for I know
    not where;
My watch is wound, my key is in my pocket,
And the sky is darkened as I descend the stair.
There are shadows across the windows, clouds
    in heaven,
And a god among the stars; and I will go
Thinking of him as I might of daybreak
And humming a tune I know. . . .
    – *from* Conrad Aiken, *The Divine Pilgrim, IV,*
        Senlin: A Biography

In Pikes Precinct Brigit Oliva had just stepped out of the shower when the relay summoned her. Throwing on a robe, she leaped for the port and saw what she had hoped to see – her daughter's face.

"Kaiti, I haven't heard from you since you landed in Jonnsberg." said Brigit. "I was getting a little worried."

"What did I catch you doing? What time is it there?"

"Oh, it's 2130h and I just had a shower. Let me run get a towel for my hair – I'm dripping on the console. Don't go away, *hijacita.*"

When she returned, Kaitrin said, "It's the next morning here – 0630h. I would have messaged you yesterday evening but I didn't

550

want to bother you at work."

"Are you all right? What have you been doing?"

"I spent the whole week at the Bock compound with Rianna. And yesterday I visited Emmi Shermayne – and I met Griffen's son, Mamá."

Brigit paused with the towel half wrapped around her head. "Did you really, Kaiti? What was he like?"

"He's a normal, vibrant, little ten-year-old. Really bright. A wonderful boy."

"Are you all right, *querida*?"

"Yes. I'm not just saying that, either. This has been a harrowing week, but I got most of what I needed. And I've made a friend for life. Griffen's sister will be my friend for life."

"You got some answers? The answers you were seeking?"

"A lot of them. Griffen's life was darkened by a tragic experience he never shared with anyone except his sister. His son is such a justification for his life. And Emmi is a fine person. If it couldn't be me who gave birth to his son, I'm glad it was someone like her."

Brigit took a long breath. "Are you coming home?"

"Not quite yet. And when I do, I'm coming directly to Castle Bluff to stay with you for a couple of days. I want to tell you everything. I owe you that much for seeing me through my initial funk!"

"Oh, I'm so glad! But only a couple of days?"

"Well, I can't waste time. I've got a tremendous amount of work to do – and it's more significant than just keeping Prf. J. from taking over the department while Tió'otu is gone!"

Brigit laughed. "Now I'm sure you're back to normal. I'll be having to settle for pittances again!"

"Probably! But, Mamá, yes, I think I'm pretty well recovered. But I've changed, too. I feel as if my whole soul has been rearranged – my self-perception … I think I've always subconsciously considered myself to be invincible. Now I know I'm not. I know I don't have all the answers and probably never will."

Brigit gazed tenderly at her daughter. The crooked grin was there, but there was a somberness about the eyes, a new maturity, with all the gain and the loss that that implied. "Well, Kaiti, I can understand that. But this was a hard way to learn that lesson."

"There's one more thing I have to do before I come home."

"I think I can guess! You want to visit Henri and Suzane in Nouvelle Victoire."

"Partly."

"I was hoping you'd do that. Neither of us has seen them since Jaq's memorial service."

"Yes, I can't pass up the opportunity. And I mean to make a short safari into the Preserves. I want to visit a place where Jaq took me when I was a child."

"You do? Does that fit somehow into this quest you've been on?"

"I'm not sure. Maybe it doesn't. But there are so many coincidences in this whole affair – so many uncanny mysteries. There's something I have to try. I know I sound obscure, but I can't help it. I don't know myself exactly what I'm looking for. But I'll tell you all about it when I see you."

"Yes, we'd better close down. This is costing too much."

"Mamá, I don't have to worry about expenses any longer."

"Oh, right, Professor!"

"Not only that. Griffen had Rianna take out an insurance policy for me – I didn't know about it. 200,000 regs."

"*¡Ay caramba!* 200,000!"

"I'm going to invest most of it – I could live handily off the income even without my pay. And something else – he instructed Rianna to give – give! – me his townhouse on the campus. I'll be living there, Mamá. We'll still have the butterfly garden. I'll arrange for the Horticulture School to continue the maintenance."

"Oh, Kaiti!"

"Yes, it's … " Kaitrin's grin trembled, faded to wistfulness. "Of course, there's no need to say what I'd rather have."

"But still … Oh, Kaiti, come home soon so we can talk."

"I will, Mamá. Goodbye for now. *Te quiero*, Mamacita. Thanks for all you've done for me through my whole life. Everything is going to be all right."

When she was alone again, Brigit Oliva went back into the bathroom and stood in front of the mirror drying her hair, her soul far away on the Afriken veldt, cradling the life of her child within the protection of her maternal love.

*   *   *

The atmospheric flyer circled around to give its passengers a spectacular view of Kimajaro Mountain before landing at Niroba's Asante Kibwana Space Port. There, a red-cloaked Henri Mokiba and his blue-eyed spouse Suzane met Kaitrin with many hugs and pecks on the cheek. Trains were not permitted within the Preserves, but each inhabited Enclave was allowed two shuttle flyers in addition to its resupply transports. Because Nouvelle Victoire was one of the largest, it was allowed four flyers, one of which they now boarded for the quick hop to the edge of Lac Victoire. Kaitrin kept her nose pressed to the window; the rainy season was underway and the lush plains below her were filled with herds of wildabeasts and zebra, impala and gazelles. She watched the ungainly grace of galloping giraffes and was thrilled to spot a herd of elephants near a water hole.

Jaq Mokiba's brother was a retired supervisor of rangers in the Serenghi Preserve and his spouse was a pharmacist at Nouvelle Victoire's medical clinic. They lived comfortably in a seven-room bungalow near the outer ramparts of the enclave, along with their son Piere-Jaq and his wife and their two teenage daughters. They had arranged a welcoming feast for their Midammeriken kinswoman. The talkfest, conducted in a mix of Inj, French, and Swahil, appeared destined to last far into the night.

At length, however, Kaitrin said to Henri, "I want to go on a little safari before I leave. Can you arrange it?"

"Ah, *oui*. It will be muddy, though. Is there a particular place you want to go?"

"Down toward Lake Natren, near the Dono Lenghi Volcano."

"Oh, you want to see the white lava?"

"No, I've seen that. Where I want to go is this side of the volcano. There used to be a field of particularly huge termite mounds. Jaq took me there once when I was a little girl."

"I know the place you mean. Why would you want to go down there? I would think you had had enough of *mchwa* for a while."

"That's where Jaq and I ate live *mchwa* once."

Henri scratched his head, puzzled, and Suzane tittered. "You have a taste for those crawly things, Kaiti? We can get you some fried ones."

"I don't want to eat them. I just need to go down there.

Maybe camp overnight."

Henri said, "There are many *vichuguu* much closer."

"Call it a weird whim from somebody who has just come back from hell. Please?"

So, although he did not understand, Henri arranged it. Piere-Jaq and his wife Damisi, who were ecologists, accompanied Kaitrin, along with the safari flyer's pilot and the usual comple-ment of guards. Three days after her arrival in Nouvelle Victoire, Kaitrin found herself walking in the rapidly falling twilight among dozens of widely scattered termitaria that ranged between two and four meters in height. The ground was damp, the humidity high.

"When do the *kumbikumbi* leave these mounds?" Kaitrin asked Piere-Jaq.

"They may have already emerged," he said. "Alates like to disperse when the earth is moist."

Disappointed, Kaitrin went to bed in the no-frills flyer, crack-ing open a window port to admit the night sounds. She fell asleep to the yips of jackals, the hyena laughter, the plaintive huffing of a lioness searching for lost cubs. In the morning, she woke just be-fore dawn and peered through the port. The turreted mounds beckoned to her, standing up like sentries in the gathering light.

Donning heavy pants, jacket, and field boots, she went out alone in the dawn, oblivious to predators. She walked toward a particularly tall and broad castle that loomed like an overlord in the midst of the others. It seemed to shrink as she approached it until she stood beside it feeling like a giant. The last termite fortress she had stood beside had overshadowed her with its might.

But this was large enough. It had three grotesque chimneys and many ventilation ribs. At the bottom an aardvark had ripped a hole and even now in the early morning workers were industrious-ly applying the millions of minuscule dabs of mud and dung that would rebuild the wall. Kaitrin smiled, bending over to watch the tiny No'kris and Ti'shras laboring busily. The hole was probably three-fourths plugged. "Work harder," she said to them. "Your *na'ta'zei|* – your *ma'na'ta|* – is in there. She must be protected at all costs. She gives you your life."

Kaitrin reached down, allowing the workers to run up onto her fingers. Straightening up, she inspected them. They ran to and fro in their blindness, waving their antennae, dropping from her hands to the ground. "*¡daio|! wei| || sho'u'tailo| wei| ↳ shbei'a| ||* Don't be afraid! I'm not going to eat you."

Among the builders, soldiers stood vigilant guard, identified by their outsized heads and mandibles. One of them had run onto Kaitrin's hand along with the workers, and as she scrutinized it, it lifted its eyeless head into the air in a threat posture, then plunged it downward and stabbed Kaitrin's finger. "Ouch!" she exclaimed as a tiny drop of blood oozed. "*no'no| um'zi|*, why don't you pick on somebody your own size?" she challenged it good-humoredly.

She stood looking thoughtfully at the posturing soldier and at the blood drop, then lifted her eyes upward to the sky. In the east, some clouds, some fog, had smothered the sunrise, but now the rays shone through in a kind of whitish haze, suffusing an aura that sank with oppressive weight upon the world. She gazed into it open-mouthed.

Then she sensed a sound – a rustling – an almost unheard motile whisper. She looked again at the mound and saw that openings on the sides were seething with movement – a dull, immaterial shimmer of motion.

Kaitrin took a quick breath. Alates. The *kumbikumbi* were coming out. Piere-Jaq had said it had already happened, but here were alates coming out.

She peered toward some of the other mounds, but nothing was happening there. Emergences were usually coordinated to minimize inbreeding, but at the moment only this one termitarium was producing anything.

The alates began to take flight, rising up, fluttering diaphanous wings that were too weak to make them good flyers or bear them far from their parent Queen. There were thousands and thousands of them – rising, falling, riding imperceptible currents in the dawn air. They began to pelt against Kaitrin, bombarding her arms, her legs, her body, her face. They brushed softly against her hair, eyes, cheeks, lips, like fragmented leaves or petals. She stood motionless, letting the winged creatures tingle against her skin.

Then the sun burst through the haze and the cascade of leaves or petals became a rain of glittering stars as the iridescent gauze wings snared the new light. Kaitrin caught her breath, lifting her arms and hands to meet the spectral entreaty of the Star-Winged Ones – the Star-Winged Alates who sacrificed themselves by the thousands and tens of thousands, so that one or two pairs could slough their wings and dig into the ground, copulate and establish a new generation of life.

With tears on her face, Kaitrin looked toward the newly risen sun and saw from beyond the mound a raven fly up, beat its way against the sunrise on dark wings, and disappear into the heavens.

Laughing and weeping, Kaitrin Oliva held up her arms into the clouds of Star-Winged Alates that swirled around her. She knew where the dark bird had gone, she knew what was unfinished, and she knew what she had to do.

Chapter 20

Extracts from
Final Proposal for the
Second Shiras-Peders Joint Exploratory Expedition
to Planet 2 Giotta 17A
Submitted by Prf. Kaitrin Oliva
5.21.15 (2970 old cal.)

The initial Joint Exploratory Expedition to Planet 2 Giotta 17A, lead by Prf. Tió'otu A'a'ma of the Department of Xenoanthropology and Prf. Griffen Gwidian of the Department of Xenoentomology, was forced to depart the planet with its work unfinished because of the unforeseen demise of Prf. Gwidian. Certain insights have led us to propose mounting a second expedition on an urgent schedule. We believe that the welfare of the indigenous ILF called the Shshi may have been compromised when the first team abandoned its work so precipitously. ...

The KrˌƖisí'i'aid research vessel designated NT-219 is presently completing a refit on Luna Base and will be available to serve as the expeditionary ship for our new venture. Capt. Skrei Af'fork of our earlier ship NT-195, informally known as the *Featherlight*, will continue in command for the proposed mission, exchanging assignments with the current Captain of the NT-219, who will fly the *Featherlight* home. The *Silver Eye*, as Capt. Skrei has surnamed the new ship, is equipped with appropriate support flyers, specifically, a rescue vessel, a standard supply flyer, and a terrestrial SuperClass Expeditionary Lander called the *Arrow*. Several other participants in the previous mission are still on scene and have agreed to sign on. Capt. Zin !eye Taeva will command the rescue vessel and Capt. Willem Ayland will once again pilot the lander. Prf. Kaitrin Oliva (Prof. Spec. Xenoanthropology/ Linguistics) will serve as academic Chair for the mission and lead the planetside team. Senior ComTech Luku !eya Kash has been appointed Chief of Technical Support. Trea Dol Amarezka and Sev Dol Parozka of Pozúa have postponed their leave time and will again fill the role of Medical Officers; Trea Dol Amarezka will also function as medical xenoanthropologist.

New members of the current expedition include Prf. Jana Lindeman (Prof. Spec. Xenoentomology), a social-insect Specialist from Shiras-Peders, who will serve as Coordinator of Scientific Studies; Prf. Yanosh Dmitru (Prof. Spec. Xenopaleontology), from the Consolidated Colleges of Griece; Asc. Paulina Chow (Asc. Spec. Xenoherpetology) of the Southern Afrik Consortium, Jonnsberg; and Asc. Mery Keriya (Asc. Spec. Xenobotany) from Shiras-Peders.

We are also fortunate to have Freinok Sa<tákát (Med. Spec.), *Vo'anát/Enemát* (i.e., Doctor/Professor) in the Xenomedical Division of the University of <O'e^trát on Krisí'i'aid. This distinguished !Ka<tí scientist happened to be on Earth participating in a six-month exchange-of-information program at the East Uropian Educational Consortium in Moska. Prf. Sa<tákát is a Medical Specialist in Xenoepidemiology and the Confederation's leading expert in the field of xenotoxic infection syndrome (XTIS).

Support staff will include one Junior ComTech for the sciences, two Assistants for the sciences (a Field Assistant and a Biotech), and one aide from Xenoanthropology. ...

The expedition proposes to depart on or about July 14, 215, and arrive on or about August 1, 215, after a voyage of approximately 17 days at a speed of 1.91 TQU. We cannot emphasize strongly enough the urgency of returning to 2 Giotta 17A as promptly as possible. ...

The first expedition to 2 Giotta 17A generated much interest outside academic circles, eliciting an outpouring of monetary support from both governmental and private sectors. A second expedition at such an early date can only enhance the prestige and recognition of the academic endeavors to which we at Northwest Quad Consortium are committed. However, as we have detailed earlier in this presentation, the expedition's primary goal must be to rectify any adverse consequences created by the first team's lapses in ethical judgment. Only then can we of Shiras-Peders University be seen to honorably promote the goal expressed in our motto, *Humanity seeking a universe of knowledge.*

Chapter 21

Then ever with Him went
Of all His wanderings
Comrade, with ragged coat,
Gaunt ribs – poor innocent –
Bleeding foot, burning throat,
The guileless young scapegoat …
 – *from* Robert Graves, *In the Wilderness*

[The Council Chamber. Creatures in the darkness. The bio-luminescence of shimmering wings glitters from eye facets.]

The Council of Lo'ro'ra has been summoned. Let us name the names so that all may know who are present. I am No'kri, of the Worker Caste, Chief.

I am Gwo'no, of the Worker Caste, of the Growers, Chief.

I am Wi'tai, of the Worker Caste, of the Builders, Chief.

I am Ar'mu, of the Worker Caste, of the Feeders, Chief.

Now let the Warriors name the names.

I am A'gwa'ji, of the Warrior Caste, Commander.

I am Ni'shto'pri surnamed Loyal One, of the Warrior Caste, Cohort Chief.

I am Ki'shto'ba Huge-Head of To'wak, Champion of the for-

tress of Lo'ro'ra.

Now let the Holy Alates name the names.

I am Gri'a'vu'tei, of the Alates, Priest and Seer.

I am Zin'kwai'mo'mi, of the Alates, Keeper of the Holy Chamber.

I am Vei'a'wei'li, of the Alates, Chief Healer.

I am Di'fa'kro'mi, of the Alates. I am the Remembrancer.

[No'kri]: All are accounted for. You have been summoned to receive the word of the Holy Seer Gri'a'vu'tei, who has slept in the *bir'zha|* chamber and taken a significant vision. Let the Holy Seer give us his words.

[Gri'a'vu'tei]: The time of ending of our travail is at hand.

[Great motions of excitement, casting about, touching of bodies and antennae. The glow in the chamber waxes as Alates fan their Star-Wings]

[Vei'a'wei'li, the Healer Chief]: Does this mean the fortress of Lo'ro'ra will be healed?

[Zin'kwai'mo'mi, the Chamberlain]: Does this mean we will begin to renew again?

[Ki'shto'ba]: Does this mean that you have seen the return of Ru'a'ma'na'ta? I would very much like to speak with her again before I go away.

[Gri'a'vu'tei]: I have seen it! I saw a light in the sky falling toward the ground, brighter than any star that has ever been seen falling. And the Highest-Mother-Who-Has-No-Name pressed upon me and spoke the words I uttered even now: *The time of ending of your travail is at hand.* Then she said, *The new time begins before the falling of the strong flowers ends.*

[No'kri]: So soon! Highest Mother, let us pay the greatest honor to you!

[Ki'shto'ba]: Holy Seer, has Kwi'ga'ga'tei been told of this?

[Gri'a'vu'tei]: I have spoken to I'mei'o'nu, who will inform

Kwi'ga'ga'tei when she feels the former Seer can understand. She was not in a state earlier this day to take meanings.

[Ki'shto'ba]: Do you think there is hope now that she will recover?

[Vei'a'wei'li]: If you mean the healing of her body, I do not see it, unless the coming of the Comforter portends a miracle.

[Gri'a'vu'tei]: The coming of the Comforter is her hope, but the way of healing is not of the body for Kwi'ga'ga'tei.

*   *   *

[The courtyard of Lo'ro'ra. The *tho'sei|* orchards on the perimeter are in full bloom and a breeze carries their fragrance across the compound. A diminished number of Shshi scurry about excitedly. Outside the entranceway to the main tower huddle No'kri, Ki'shto'ba, Gri'a'vu'tei, Di'fa'kro'mi, A'gwa'ji, Zin'kwai'mo'mi. The Alates regard the flying dwelling that crouches on the opposite side of the compound. It returns their stares through a double row of eyes]

[Di'fa'kro'mi]: It is larger than the last one.

[Ki'shto'ba]: Respectfully, Holy Seer, does this flying shelter also bear a name of the Nameless One?

[Gri'a'vu'tei]: I was not told its name, if it has one.

[A'gwa'ji, nervously]: Should we approach it?

[Ki'shto'ba]: Let us wait briefly. I have no doubt someone will come out soon.

[The Shshi wait in the shade of the fortress. To their right the Warrior's Quarters squat. No citizen in the courtyard approaches this edifice. Stones have fallen from its walls, which are shaggy with vines and plants, and all entrances but one are stopped with mortared rocks. Outside the open entrance are many pails of honeydew and wheeled boxes full of fungus pieces. A few Workers emerge from the quarters and begin to convey these items inside. A Warrior in the compound who happens to have strayed near the entrance when the Workers emerge jumps when they appear and scuttles away in alarm. The Shshi before the main tower continue to wait]

[Di'fa'kro'mi]: The side is opening! Someone is coming out! Let us move forward!

[Zin'kwai'mo'mi]: Is that Ru'a'ma'na'ta? I was never privileged to speak with her.

[Ki'shto'ba]: It is Ru'a'ma'na'ta – I know her smell! And the large and the small female ones – the fuzz-covered one who was the Star-Beings' healer – are with her!

[Quickly the Shshi approach the returning aliens. The Alates Gri'a'vu'tei and Zin'kwai'mo'mi hang back behind the others. As the groups meet halfway across the compound, Ru'a'ma'na'ta kneels and stretches out her arms to them]

[Ru'a'ma'na'ta]: I greet you, beloved Shshi of Lo'ro'ra. I have come back. Am I welcome, or is my coming a thing that you regret?

[No'kri]: You are most welcome! It gives us joy to see you! There are many words for us to share.

[Ru'a'ma'na'ta]: I fear to ask this question. I do not see Kwi'ga'ga'tei among you. Is she alive?

[Di'fa'kro'mi]: She is alive. Your coming will mean everything to her. All is not well.

[Ru'a'ma'na'ta]: I am relieved to learn that she is alive, but your final words give me much uneasiness. Will all of you come and speak with us under the wing of our dwelling, as we did in the past season-cycle?"

[No'kri]: We would be honored.

[The Star-Beings and the Shshi rest beneath the wing and speak of the time that has passed]

[Ki'shto'ba]: Ru'a'ma'na'ta, you did not witness the combat. I killed Hi'ta'fu, a regrettable but necessary act. It was not I who was the true cause of the destruction of the Commander. It was not guilty enough in its soul to merit death.

[Ru'a'ma'na'ta]: There are many such among the stars,

Huge-Head. But before I left, when I myself was too wounded to be caring, I saw that Kwi'ga'ga'tei had herself been wounded. How can that have happened?"

[Di'fa'kro'mi]: The villain – the Unnatural Alate, whose name I will no longer speak! – leaped into the wind and flew above the Champion, beyond its reach, and came down upon the Holy Kwi'ga'ga'tei and sank his jaws into her side.

[Ki'shto'ba, posturing in futile wrath]: I killed him then, too! And I would kill him over and over if I could! I ripped his wings from him – I quelled his speech. I wish I could follow his soul into the World Beyond so that I might rip it to shreds! It was all his doing – all the pain, the deaths – the death of your *na'sha'ma|*. But twice I was surprised and twice I was too late.

[Di'fa'kro'mi]: Already, there is a tale of this creature and how he wreaked destruction on the mighty fortress of Lo'ro'ra. I have sought not to tell this tale, but the citizens clamor for the story, and if I do not tell it, my apprentices will. So, circumstances become legends in a time as quick as one season-cycle.

[Ki'shto'ba, gloomily]: Thus that villain has the last word. Before I ripped his antennae from him, he said, *They will speak of my exploits long after yours are forgotten! Did you not know that villainy always makes a better tale than the maunderings of virtue?*

[Ru'a'ma'na'ta]: But Kwi'ga'ga'tei lived.

[Gri'a'vu'tei]: But she has not been healed. There was a price to be paid.

[Ru'a'ma'na'ta]: I do not know who you are, my friend, nor your companion, either.

[The two unfamiliar Alates come forward and abase their heads]

[Zin'kwai'mo'mi]: I am Zin'kwai'mo'mi, who succeeded the villain Mo'gri'ta'tu as Keeper of the Holy Chamber.

[Gri'a'vu'tei]: And I am Gri'a'vu'tei, the Holy Seer.

[Ru'a'ma'na'ta]: The Holy Seer! But you said that Kwi'ga'ga'tei was still alive!

[Gri'a'vu'tei]: She is alive, but she is no longer Seer. The Highest-Mother-Who-Is-Nameless no longer comes to her either to comfort or afflict. We all wait. We have entered a Time of Waste.

[Ru'a'ma'na'ta is silent, reflecting on the Seer's words]

[Gri'a'vu'tei]: I was one of the lesser Alates. When the Nameless One withdrew the gift of Seeing from Kwi'ga'ga'tei, it passed to me. I was of no importance – merely a Light Maker for the Holy One, not even a priestly assistant – and I do not know why I was chosen. One does not question her reasons when the Highest Mother gives you a gift.

[Ru'a'ma'na'ta]: You say it is a Time of Waste. What does that mean?

[A'gwa'ji]: The Time of Perpetual Mourning. You have sight. How many Shshi do you see in the compound? How many crumbling gaps do you see in our walls? Our fortress has half the citizens it once had. Those Warriors who went mad and tried to destroy your dwelling took the contagion from it of which you warned Kwi'ga'ga'tei.

[No'kri]: They all died and they spread the sickness to the Charnel Workers and the Feeders and the Groomers, and to the Healers who tried in vain to cure them. Our medicinal compounds are effective on many of our common sicknesses, but not on this one.

[Ru'a'ma'na'ta]: I began to suspect that I might find such a situation when I returned. But I am ashamed. These great evils arose from our ill-fated visit.

[Gri'a'vu'tei]: You did not cause them. They were part of the price. The Nameless One told me so.

[No'kri]: Many fortresses in the history of the Shshi have been decimated by plagues like this one, but in later, more enlightened times some fortresses have adopted the ideas of a great Healer Alate named Fi'zu'ko'ti who lived many years ago in some forgotten place.

[Di'fa'kro'mi]: Her rule was that whenever a fortress is attacked by a spreading plague, all who fall sick are to be put together in one place and left to feed and care for one another until they all die. And the bodies of those who die of illnesses before their time are never to be consumed. That last has been much debated and is often considered sacrilege, although to me it seems to make good sense.

Lo'ro'ra has long subscribed to these practices, which seem cruel but are effective for the survival of the fortress. So, since this unfamiliar plague attacked us, we have been putting all the sick together in the Warriors' Quarters and we let them feed each other until they die. Then the bodies are dragged with hooked poles to a place far away from the fortress and left to the reptiles. I do not know if the reptiles take the sickness from eating the bodies, but the number of those falling ill in Lo'ro'ra has begun to wane.

[Ru'a'ma'na'ta confers with the small furred one beside her, then speaks]: We want to help you, to atone for bringing this plague to you. You must allow our small Healer who sits here next to me to examine you and take tiny bits of your bodies and samples of your hemolymph and your excrement to put in the learning boxes. And another Healer has come with us – one of the Bird-people – who understands much about the ailments that can spread among the peoples of the Star-Worlds. And if you will permit it, we will go into the marches and make sure that other creatures of your world are not suffering because of this star plague.

[The Chamberlain Zin'kwai'mo'mi]: Even if you can rid us of this sickness, we do not replenish. The Holy One herself languishes and produces few eggs, and many of those that she does lay do not hatch. Our nurseries are nearly empty. The Regeneration Rituals can have no effect when the *ma'na'ta|* herself begins to fail.

[Ru'a'ma'na'ta]: Oh, my friends, did A'kha'ma'na'ta take the plague from me as she and I comforted each other on that last day?

[Di'fa'kro'mi]: No, the Holy One is not sick and our new Chamberlain is careful that those who might endanger her have no contact with her Tenders. She is only old and lonely – the natural order brings her death closer every day.

[Ru'a'ma'na'ta]: All of this saddens me greatly. Do you have answers, Holy Seer?

[Gri'a'vu'tei]: We could only wait. Wait until the Nameless One is satisfied. But I no longer believe that this Time of Waste portends the End of Time. I believe now that the waiting is coming to its end.

[Ru'a'ma'na'ta]: You think my return is the answer?

[Gri'a'vu'tei]: Your return is the answer. I have seen it.

*　　*　　*

[Even as the Star-Beings' Healers perform physical procedures on the Shshi who are present, the conversation continues]

[Ru'a'ma'na'ta]: Ki'shto'ba, I am surprised to find that you are still here.

[Ki'shto'ba]: I stayed at the request of Kwi'ga'ga'tei and of Commander A'gwa'ji, to assist in organizing the remnants of the Cohorts into a single force and to help train Chief Ni'shto'pri surnamed Loyal One. The fortress is in a weakened state – vulnerable to any aggressor who might choose this time to attack it.

[Ru'a'ma'na'ta]: Where are Sa'ti'a'i'a and its Cohort?

[A'gwa'ji]: One of Kwi'ga'ga'tei's last acts as Priest was to release the Nasutes from their liege oath. Nearly half of them died defending the Star-Beings. She felt that they had more than fulfilled their obligation and they have returned to their own land.

[Ru'a'ma'na'ta]: Perhaps one day I can pay a visit to the forests of the Nasutes.

[Ki'shto'ba]: You would be welcome there, Ru'a'ma'na'ta, although I am not sure you would be able to pass through their small tunnels! I mean to leave Lo'ro'ra soon myself. I will return to my home fortress of To'wak to assess the situation there. But unless I find a reason, I do not intend to stay in To'wak.

[Ru'a'ma'na'ta]: Indeed? You mean to come back to Lo'ro'ra?

[Ki'shto'ba, dancing ponderously and waving its antennae]:

No, not to here! I caught something from you, Ru'a'ma'na'ta, and I do not mean a plague!

[Di'fa'kro'mi]: And I caught it as well!

[Ki'shto'ba]: I have decided that I want to wander! I would like to go to other lands – visit that Huge Water that you tell us is real, that you spoke of in your tale of Ul'i'seit.

[Di'fa'kro'mi]: And I mean to accompany the Huge-Head! If an eyeless one wanders alone, it is in peril no matter how great its strength.

[Ki'shto'ba]: I will offer my services as Champion to fortresses along the way, should they have need of them.

[Di'fa'kro'mi]: And I can render services as well, as a Remembrancer, a Teller of Tales. Perhaps I will speak the Tale of the Unnatural Alate and of the near downfall of the Fortress of the Strong Flowers. Even in that way, I can warn against the disasters that can happen when self-interest and hatred overpower the more natural emotions of giving and caring for the whole.

[Ki'shto'ba, bouncing with enthusiasm]: We will offer these services in return for food and hospitality. We will carry food with us so we will not die in the wilderness. Di'fa'kro'mi is willing to feed me, even though he is an Alate.

[Di'fa'kro'mi]: I have plenty of apprentices who can serve as Lo'ro'ra's Remembrancer until I return.

[Ki'shto'ba]: Di'fa'kro'mi and I will experience the greatest adventures ever known among the Shshi!

[Di'fa'kro'mi]: And from this questing will arise the greatest tales ever told among the Shshi! As great as the tales that you Star-Beings tell, of the Wanderer Ul'i'seit!

[Ki'shto'ba takes a few steps forward, thrusting antennae toward Ru'a'ma'na'ta and touching her body delicately]: I detect vibrations from you, Ru'a'ma'na'ta, that I believe you make when something is humorous. Have we said something humorous?

[Ru'a'ma'na'ta]: A Champion and a Remembrancer adventuring together! It is wonderful to contemplate! *no'no| um'zi|*, it is only that I see your culture embarking on a path similar to what mine once took, although I may not be able to explain it in your language.

[Gri'a'vu'tei]: The time is new. Kwi'ga'ga'tei proclaimed it at the beginning of these trials and it has been affirmed to me in the *bir'zha*| chamber.

[Ru'a'ma'na'ta]: I think I should not delay longer in visiting Kwi'ga'ga'tei, my friends. And perhaps I will be permitted to enter the presence of the Holy One.

[Gri'a'vu'tei]: Those very events have been foretold.

* * *

[The outer chamber of the apartments of Kwi'ga'ga'tei. Ru'a'ma'na'ta, Gri'a'vu'tei, and the Remembrancer Di'fa'kro'mi confront the Steward I'mei'o'nu]

[I'mei'o'nu]: She is the same. She waits. She declines. I do not think she can decline much further and still have life.

[Gri'a'vu'tei]: She will not need to. Does she know that Ru'a'ma'na'ta has returned?

[I'mei'o'nu]: I spoke of it to her, but I do not believe she understood.

[Ru'a'ma'na'ta]: This distresses me deeply, my friends.

[I'mei'o'nu]: Seeing Kwi'ga'ga'tei will distress you even more.

[Gri'a'vu'tei]: But remember that your coming will bring her peace.

[In her inner chamber, the former Holy Seer Kwi'ga'ga'tei languishes. She lies splayed on a bed of fresh *tho'sei*| blossoms, but even their intense fragrance cannot mask the odor of putrefaction. She twists against the pain of her wound, which has become a gaping ulcer through which the gut is visible. The ulcer oozes fluid, and violet and red streaks ray out from it like a star across the rotting chitin. She has sloughed her left wings; the right sag limp and lightless on the floor at her side.

[A Healer Alate hovers attentively with poultices, trying to cleanse the wound and damp its pain, but no aid avails. The head of Kwi'ga'ga'tei is supported on a larger pile of *tho'sei*| leaves and blossoms. Her eyes are dull, her antennae droop.

[But then her antennae lift slightly. Someone is coming. What was it that they told her? Something that gave her a dim hope, but it was so much easier to pay no heed ...]

[Ru'a'ma'na'ta]: Kwi'ga'ga'tei, I have come. So much was left unfinished and it took me too long to understand. I am sorry. I was in pain – the pain that turns the soul to dust.

[Kwi'ga'ga'tei]: Who is it? Ru'a'ma'na'ta? Is it really you, or do I have the fit?

[Ru'a'ma'na'ta]: It is really I. Forgive me for breaking my promise and leaving you to suffer for so long.

[Kwi'ga'ga'tei]: You are healed? The wound that went to you when your *na'sha'ma*| died? It has been healed?

[Ru'a'ma'na'ta]: It has been healed. I understand that you took the guilt. I wish I could have recognized it sooner.

[Kwi'ga'ga'tei]: It was not to be. The Nameless One told me that if the Wounded One were not healed, I would have to pay the guilt-price. Now I have paid it. Now I can die.

[Ru'a'ma'na'ta]: Perhaps you do not have to die. Let me bring our Healers to you. Let them try to save you – cure your wound.

[Kwi'ga'ga'tei]: It cannot be. It is the Wound-That-Has-No-Healing.

[Ru'a'ma'na'ta]: It may not be that, Kwi'ga'ga'tei. Let our Healers try. I do not want you to die because the Star-Beings came to you.

[Kwi'ga'ga'tei, trying to raise her head]: I do not die because you came. We are all creatures of the Nameless One's will. There were evils eating at all our souls that we could not find a way to cleanse with the wills she gave to us. If you had not come here, the Nameless One would have found another way ... But I have one request to make of you, Ru'a'ma'na'ta.

[Ru'a'ma'na'ta]: Anything.

[Kwi'ga'ga'tei]: Comfort A'kha'ma'na'ta once more. She is dying.

[Ru'a'ma'na'ta]: The new Seer spoke of that.

[Kwi'ga'ga'tei]: She was betrayed by those of her children whom she loved most, except for me, and I can no longer help her. She is old and sad and has lost the will to carry out her task. The King is afraid. He accepts that his own death must come when his Holy One dies, but he is not yet old and he is afraid. Talk to A'kha'ma'na'ta and Sei'o'na'sha'ma. Tell them tales. Ease their passing with the speech that I taught to you.

[Ru'a'ma'na'ta]: I came prepared to tell tales, but I did not know the circumstances would be so sorrowful.

[Kwi'ga'ga'tei struggles, writhes futilely]: *ru'a'ma'na'ta| ... sho'laio| ⤶ zifo| Ϛ bei'a| ||*

[Ru'a'ma'na'ta]: Let me take your head in my lap, Kwi'ga'ga'tei, as I did with Ti'shra.

[Kwi'ga'ga'tei]: *¡yino|! o| sho'a| || ... sho'laio| wei| ⤶ weio| kwi'il| ||*

[Ru'a'ma'na'ta]: I understand Ti'shra's words even as you taught me. I will stay with you. I will not let you die alone.

[Kwi'ga'ga'tei's faceted eyes see the Comforter who holds and grooms her head and drops moisture like balm on the roots of her antennae, while the simple eyes see through the Comforter and beyond her]

Highest Mother, it is you! You have come back to me!

It would have been too cruel if you had had to bear the Seeing during your travail.

Does Ru'a'ma'na'ta see you? Do you show yourself to her?

The creatures of her world do not know what they should believe. Ru'a'ma'na'ta believes in me but does not know it, so I show myself to her only in signs. The Shshi remain still among my innocents and so are fit to bear burdens for the weaker ones.

You show me your face … I have never seen your face before, *wei'loi'zei|* …

[The monumental visage looms against the belly's eternal procreative pulse – the enormous and destructive jaws that consumed the First King, the infinite antennae that web the universe and speak to all the worlds, the four eyes – two eyes of Seeing above, the cold white moons – two eyes of Love below, faceted with stars]

It is finished, my daughter. The atonement is complete. At last I can grant you rest.

Epilogue

Notation
in the Annals of the
Board of Astral Nomenclature
Dated 2.3.216 (2971 old cal.)

In response to a request submitted by Prf. Kaitrin Oliva (Prof. Spec. Xenoanthropology/Linguistics, Northwest Quad Educational Consortium, Planet Earth), the Board on Astral Nomenclature of the Confederation of Four Planets had agreed to confirm a change of name for certain galactic bodies. All star charts are to be immediately emended to reflect these changes, as set forth in the following extract from Prf. Oliva's communiqué:

The First Shiras-Peders Joint Exploratory Expedition to Planet 2 Giotta 17A chanced to engage the Shshi, an ILF evolved from isopteroids, at a critical moment of civil conflict. Caught in the crossfire, as it were, two innocent individuals perished – the human co-leader of the expedition, Prf. Griffen Gwidian (Prof. Spec. Xenoentolomogy, Northwest Quad Consortium), and the Priest/Seer of the Shshi, whose name was Kwi'ga'ga'tei. The undersigned members of the Shiras-Peders community and of the wider universe, who were friends of both these persons, would like to request that the star Giotta 17A and the planet 2 Giotta l7A be renamed as follows:

1) That the star henceforth be called *Kwi'ga'ga'tei*, in honor of the Shshi mystic who accepted suffering and death so that others

might find peace, and whose physical form is that of an alate termite with uniquely bioluminescent wings, the light of which is, according to the indigenous mythology, derived from the overabundance of stars at the time of creation;

2) That the planet henceforth be called *G. Gwidian*, in honor of the expedition's co-leader, who courageously sacrificed his own life to save that of a young and heedless member of his team. It is only fitting that his heroism be memorialized among the worlds of the universe where his soul now makes its home.

About the Author

A former catalogue librarian, Lorinda J. Taylor was born in Colorado Springs, Colorado, and worked in several different academic libraries before returning to the place of her birth, where she now lives. She has written fantasy and science fiction for years but has only recently begun to publish. Her goal is to write compelling fiction that delivers an emotional impact and leaves her readers with something to think about at the end of each story.

The reader can learn more about her writings and her ideas at the following websites:

http://termitewriter.blogspot.com

http://termitespeaker.blogspot.com

Information about the constructed languages used in *The Termite Queen* is available at http://remembrancer.conlang.org.

Made in the USA
Lexington, KY
16 November 2013